Mark of the Fool: Book One

Mark of the Fool: Book Two

Mark of the Fool: Book Three

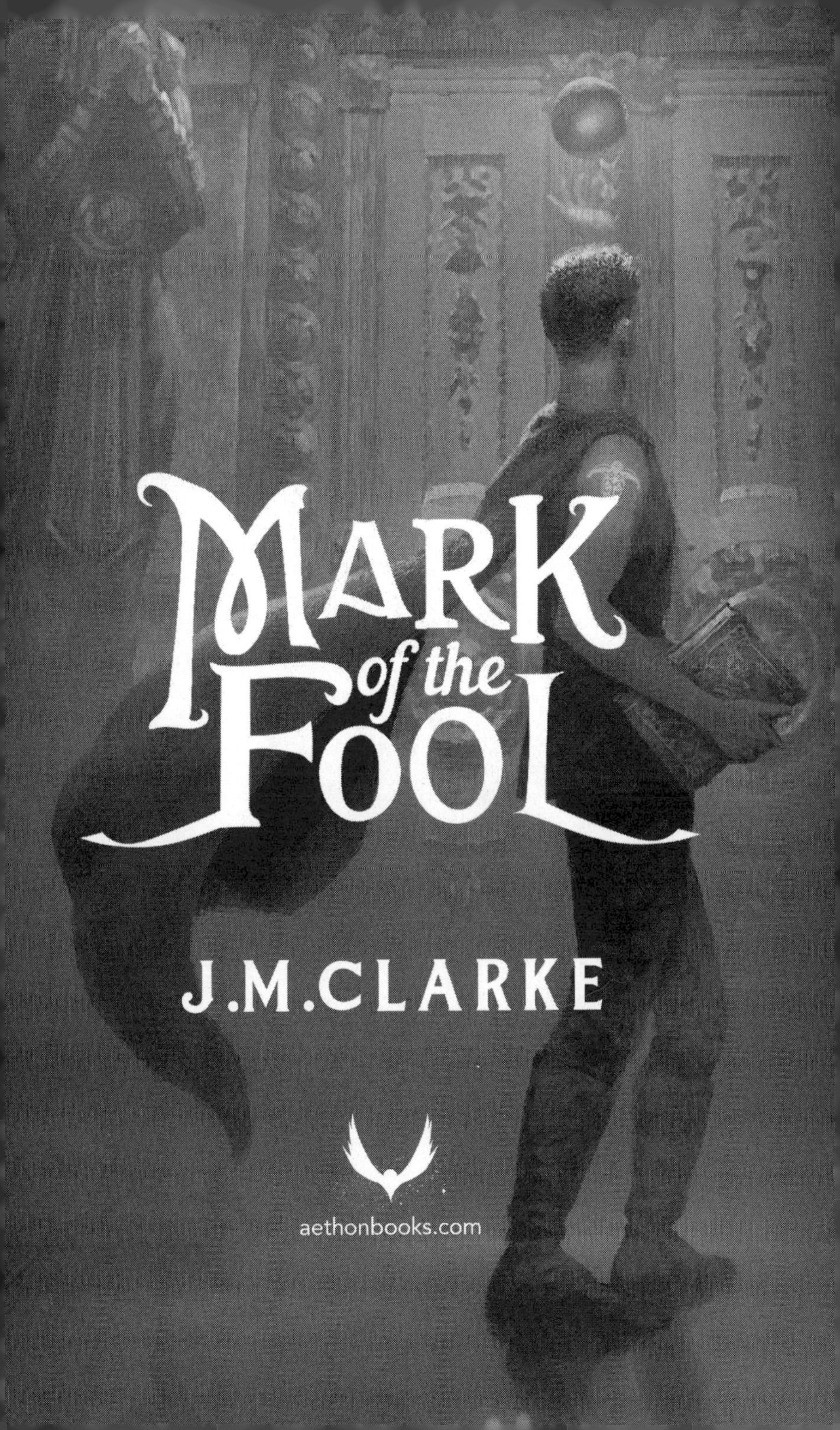
MARK of the FOOL
J.M.CLARKE
aethonbooks.com

MARK OF THE FOOL
©2022 J.M. CLARKE

Aethon Books
www.aethonbooks.com

Print and eBook formatting by Josh Hayes. Artwork provided by Shen Fei.

Published by Aethon Books LLC.

Dedicated to my mother, who told me all the stories of the world,
and to Ms. Sutton, who taught me how to tell them.

Chapter 1

Fools and Inheritance

The worst days tended to start with good mornings.

"You're fired. *Fired*! Get all of your things and get out of my shop! If I *ever* catch you here again, I swear on Uldar's beard, you'll *wish* I called the guards for you," Master McHarris roared, his face turning beet-red.

As mornings went, this one was shaping up to be *great*.

Alex Roth froze in the middle of a disaster: collapsed shelving, shattered eggs and flour dust falling like snow in the middle of the bakery. The young man gave an awkward cough and wiped the white powder out of his chestnut brown hair. "Does this mean you won't be giving me this week's pay?"

McHarris reddened further.

"I mean, not for today, obviously, but there was yesterday and Firstday, so that's two silver pieces—"

The baker made a choking noise before stomping across the disaster zone, jabbing his key into his strong box, ripping it open and whipping two dull coins into Alex's chest. They bounced from his chest before he could catch them, landing on the floor with a white puff of flour.

"*There*! And you only get that so folk know McHarris is no

cheat! Now *get* out—" The baker snatched up a rolling pin. "—or you'll need to put those silvers where your teeth used to be!"

Alex had seen enough of McHarris' rages to know he meant it. The young man tore off his apron and scrambled to grab his pay. He sniffed the air near the eggs as he bent; a nasty stench confirmed his suspicions from early this morning. Keeping his face neutral, he jumped up and scuttled for the exit to the front room of the shop.

"Boy..." McHarris said, scratching his head. "What happened to you? You were quickest-witted out of any assistant I've ever had, but today you act like a bull with half its brains slammed out of its skull. That sister of yours won't grow up proper if her older brother pulls things like this."

Alex paused just as he was about to pull open the kitchen door. That was all news to him. McHarris paid well enough, but he terrorized his assistants. Welts still marked the young man's arms from when he'd been too slow whipping the custard a couple of days ago.

"I dunno, sir." He gave a shrug and hid the grin threatening to spring up. "Maybe it's a special day?"

He was gone before McHarris could say anything else.

The town of Alric was shrugging off sleep when Alex emerged from the bakery for the last time. Sunlight filtered through a haze of clouds and townsfolk trudged past the square's fountain with their days' tools and lunches in hand. The scent of baking bread and boiling porridge drifted from windows nearby. A carriage—pulled by a set of proud horses—approached from down the road, their hooves clattering on the cobblestone. On the side of the carriage door was emblazoned the symbol of a lantern: the Sigil of the Traveller, the town's patron saint.

As it passed, Alex spied two guardsmen sitting on the side

of the fountain. They were bleary-eyed from the night watch, and squinted at Alex as he strolled up as light-footed as a pleased cat.

"Morning, Peter. Morning, Paul." Alex made sure to use their names. Remembering details about people made them friendlier to your cause. Just one of the tricks he'd picked up in the last four years of hustling together every coin he could. "I got something to report."

Peter groaned, scratching at his stubble-marked chin and craning his neck to look up at Alex. The young man was lean and gangly, and quite a bit taller than most.

"You caught in a snowstorm, boy? It's mid-summer."

"Naw, that's flour, idiot; you don't recognize one of McHarris' assistants? By the Heroes' good graces, I've been on night watch with a blind man." Paul shook his head and peered closer at the flour-encased youth. "Alexander… right? The Roths' boy? What's it you have to report?"

A dull ache touched Alex's heart at the mention of his parents, but he kept his face neutral. Even the largest wounds grew dimmer with time. He jerked a thumb backward toward the bakery. "McHarris is putting rotten eggs into his cakes and covering it with sugar. He could poison somebody."

Peter raised an eyebrow, reaching beside him and picking up his helmet, clapping it on his head. "That sounds like a guild violation, not a crime."

"I don't think the merchants or nobles that shop there would see it that way, and I don't have time to run to the guild before he cleans up the evidence."

Alex held up two flour-dusted silver coins. "This is *not* a bribe. I'm just saying that if you go over and take a quick look around, you might do the public some good *while* pocketing a silver coin each." He gave a winning smile and rolled the coins across his knuckles. "I know, you're tired and want to go home, but that's a third of a day's wages for you, all for walking fifty steps and having a sniff around his kitchen. If you find nothing, you keep the coin. Sound fair?"

Peter and Paul looked at each other.

"Boy." Peter shook his head. "You're *bad* at bribing people."

His winning smile shrank. "N-no, it's not a bribe, I'm—"

"You're trying to pay us to get a service done for you. It's a bribe. One where you might not get what you want, so it's a *stupid* bribe."

"The worst attempt I've ever seen," Paul groaned as he lifted himself from the fountain. "But, if he's willing to try something that stupid, maybe we should take a look. Last thing we need is for some bigwig to turn all green in the face and keel over. Come on, Peter."

Alex could hardly contain his excitement as the guards made their way toward McHarris' shop, though he made sure to hide his smile when Paul turned around.

"Oh, and don't try that again. Stupid or not, bribery of a guard'll get you ten lashes. Understand?"

Alex nodded vigorously and gave him a thumbs-up. "I'll be a good boy from now on, sir!"

Paul shook his head. "The hell's wrong with you?" He pointed up at one of the fountain's statues rising over their heads. "Act the fool long enough and you'll get the Fool's Mark. That little sister of yours needs a brother she can rely on."

"I have a plan for that, Paul, don't you worry," Alex said. "But thanks for asking. You're good people."

"Guardsmen have to make sure the youth are on the right path, don't we?" Paul rose to his full height, puffing out his chest unconsciously. "Anyway, off you go now. If you're right, this'll probably get ugly. Oh, and happy birthday, Alexander. Eighteen's a big number. Keep those coins and try to treat yourself."

Alex blinked. Well, he had been right. Remembering details about people *did* make them friendlier. He certainly felt a bit more friendly toward Paul. He'd have to do something nice for him later.

He grinned.

Once he became a full-fledged wizard.

Sliding back behind the fountain, he watched the guards enter the shop and chuckled as McHarris' cries of dismay echoed through the windows. When the crashing began, he outright cackled. Of all the food he'd ever had from McHarris', *revenge* definitely tasted the best.

"Serves you right, you old bully. That's for browbeating every helper who's ever worked for you." He smirked, tossing his last pay into the fountain. As of sunrise this morning, he no longer needed McHarris' coin. Alex said a silent prayer of thanks to the Heroes' Fountain—one of many that had been raised in the Kingdom of Thameland.

To the hulking figure of the Champion, Alex thanked him for bravery. To the bespectacled, stern Sage, he thanked her for the wits he had shown. To the kind figure of the Saint, he thanked her for the generosity he'd received. And lastly, to the handsome form of the Chosen, he gave him appreciation for luck and blessings.

Beside the four grand figures—who watched the square with benevolent granite eyes—crouched a caricature. It was an ugly sculpting of a man with a chin too curved, eyes too bulging, and a nose like a pumpkin's stem. A jaunty jester's hat sat on his head and his statue was the only one stained by bird droppings.

The Fool.

The last of the Heroes and the least of them. None who had borne the Fool's Mark left much of an impression in legend. Many had died. Others disappeared. Some even betrayed the very party they were chosen for.

The Fool—according to all of Alex's teachers—had nothing to offer anyone, save for a nominal but necessary service to the

Heroes. Uldar's Prophecies called those bearing the mantle necessary, though history suggested otherwise.

And so, to the Fool, Alex simply offered his empathy. He knew well how it was to struggle. Thankfully, those days were at an end.

Whistling a jaunty tune as the guards grappled with McHarris somewhere in the bakeshop, he strolled down the street with spirits higher than they'd been since before he and his sister were orphaned.

He didn't catch the slight itching on his right shoulder, nor the way the bulging eyes of the Fool seemed to watch him walk away.

Nine pounds measured out by the magistrate down to the ounce.

Exactly four hundred and fifty gold coins; the entire wealth of the Roth family after the fire reduced their alehouse to rubble. The parents' estate had been liquidated, placed into the town trust, and held until their firstborn child reached adulthood and could claim it under common law.

Now, Alex was eighteen, and it all belonged to him and his sister. A fortune that would have taken him more than twelve years to earn working for McHarris. And that was if he'd never missed a day. With how he had to split his time between the bakery and helping out at the Lu Family Inn, it probably would have been at least thirty. Decades' worth of his labour—and his mother and father's entire legacy—was all stuffed into a heavy burlap sack slung over one of his gangly shoulders. It was hard to believe his parents had been gone for four years.

With each step toward the inn, the weight of losing his parents and the heaviness of the sack weighed him down; a mix of guilt, excitement, regret and relief came. He wished to Uldar that he had his family rather than a cold sack of gold, but that coin would bring a much better life for him and his sister.

He rounded the corner onto the street he lived on and his eyes narrowed. The sun was setting. His whole day spent at the magistrate's office, wading through more paper than he'd ever seen at the church's school. Then he'd gone to spend time at his parents' graveside. Now, he was on his way home, planning to break the news of his future plans to the Lu family.

Their inn sat at the end of the street—a busy place near the centre of town—and it had been home for Alex and his sister ever since they had been orphaned. Master and Mrs. Lu were kind folks, and most of his childhood revolved around being friends with their daughter, Theresa.

Life normally quieted pretty early in Alric with the arrival of sunset. After darkness fell, burning wood and candles for light was too expensive, so it was avoided, leaving the evenings gloomy around town. But it seemed things were even quieter than they had been when he was in the graveyard.

This street was usually one of the last to go dark. The Bear's Bowl tavern should've been spitting out drunken, brawling farmhands by now. As Alex passed by, the entire building was already dark and silent. The Lu Family Inn would have firelight and laughter booming as the last diners finished up for the night, yet now there was only a small light burning through the shuttered windows. No guests could be heard.

Swallowing, Alex quickened his pace, making for the entrance at a half-run. His feet echoed on the cobblestones. The coins jingled in the sack. Moonlight poured over him and the night suddenly seemed colder. He reached the door, pulling firmly on the iron ring.

The door wouldn't open; it had already been barred.

"Hello?" he called out, feeling the hairs on the back of his neck rise. The street behind him seemed longer, unfamiliar and unfriendly. He switched his grip on the family inheritance so it was clutched to his chest.

Bang! Bang, bang!

He pounded on the door.

"Master Lu? Theresa? Selina?"

Rapid footfalls approached from inside. The bar slid away. A thin hand tugged the door open.

"Alex!" Mrs. Lu cried. The middle-aged woman, looking as though she was about to break into tears of relief, grabbed him tightly against her lean form in a hug. "Get inside, quickly!"

"What? What's going on?"

Instead of answering, she pulled him in with surprising strength and slammed the door. She quickly replaced the bar and dragged him into the hall.

Alex looked around in confusion as she led him toward the common room where he could hear banging and frantic movement.

Chapter 2

Uldar's Legacy

"What the—?" he gasped.

The common room was chaos. Dozens of sacks and chests were piled against the wall. Many were half-filled with clothes, tools, ornaments—anything portable. Most of the Lu family rushed back and forth, stuffing the bags with more supplies. Only Master Lu and Theresa were missing from the scene.

It was clear they were going on a trip.

A long one.

As he stepped into the room, the family froze mid-step, casting fearful and worried looks his way. Like he would turn into smoke and blow away at any moment.

"Alex," Mrs. Lu began, examining him. "Did you—"

"Alex!" a tiny voice cried.

A rapidly sprinting bundle of long chestnut hair and chubby cheeks slammed into his waist, nearly driving the breath from him. "Selina? What's wrong?" he asked.

His ten-year-old sister looked up with large green eyes shining. "Master Lu heard that th-the Chosen got found. S-so did the Saint."

His heart nearly stopped.

"*What*?" He dropped the sack of gold on the floor. It landed with an ugly clink. "When!"

"Today," came the deep voice of Master Lu. The family patriarch was taking the stairs down two at a time as though he were a man half his age. In his hands, he clutched the old Lu family ancestry book and the swords once wielded by his own grandfather.

The scabbards of the curved blades bounced in his grip.

Alex grew even more nervous. Those never left the master bedroom. Not ever.

He looked to the mural on the inn's wall. It was an amateur piece of art, painted through many hours of labour and love by himself, Mrs. Lu, and Theresa. On the left was the ancient form of Uldar, the prophet-god that guided the people of Thameland. He was the first to face their eternal enemy.

On the right floated a blot of darkness being cut through by the Chosen's sword.

The Ravener.

It was their eternal enemy who always arose—seeking to consume the Kingdom of Thameland as it had for generations—starting slow, taking its time and crafting armies of monsters from its inner core. Then it would bud, sending out scores of smaller pieces of itself to burrow deep into the land and sprout, creating nests and dungeons that spawned monsters.

After Uldar had defeated it in his age, he ascended to the heavens. Yet he had not destroyed it. He knew the Ravener would reform in time, for darkness always returns, as sure as the days grow long. So, he cast a part of his own power down onto the people, and foretold that five Heroes would rise in his place and defeat the Ravener once more. It had been his final declaration while he'd remained in the material world.

A century after Uldar's ascension, five young folk gained a shining Mark on their bodies: The Chosen. The Champion.

The Sage. The Saint. The Fool. Together, they defeated the Ravener again. A century after that, it returned.

Five more arose to triumph over it.

And so it was again.

And again.

A cycle of victory and horror. The pride of the Kingdom of Thameland.

And Alex cared absolutely nothing for any of that bullshit.

In the painting set between Uldar and the Ravener stood the five heroes from three generations ago. The Saint of that party had come from this very town of Alric. Well, sort of. The young woman claimed to have come from somewhere incredibly far away, but was settled comfortably in Alric when she'd been marked on her eighteenth birthday.

She had died in the next generation, though, when she—ancient and long retired—set off to defend Alric from a dungeon that sprang up in the caves just north of town. She had defeated the core and—in death—left her magic infusing the entire underground complex.

The Cave of the Traveller.

People who entered it emerged in all sorts of places. It was a portal that shot people out at random: the next town, the capital, somewhere in the wilderness to the north, or even in some cave on the continent. There were even stories of it flinging people into other planes entirely or places of unimaginable wonder. Or horror.

Now, it might hold something far more sinister.

Once the Ravener used a place as a dungeon, chances were high it would use it again. No wonder the town had been so quiet. How many others were frantically packing up their worldly possessions into as many bags as they could?

"We're going to stay with my brother in the Rhinean Empire." Master Lu placed the swords in a chest, then closed and locked it. "Until the Heroes can clear out the land." He paused, giving Alex an odd look. "You... you haven't felt anything strange today, have you?"

Alex knew why he'd asked. The Heroes all had their marks appear on the same day, when they hit adulthood. And he'd turned eighteen today. That wasn't ominous at all.

"Nothing, Master Lu." He shook his head.

"Good." The older man sighed in relief. "I didn't want you dragged into this, even if there was only the slightest chance. Especially not with the future you have ahead."

He gave a thin smile and tossed something across the room to Alex. The young man caught it: a scroll case, with a broken wax seal depicting the symbol of four towers flanking a taller fifth in the centre.

"I found that when I was packing your things. That's the seal of the Genesari University, isn't it?" His grin widened. "I've seen it on some of the embassies in the capital. Never went inside any of them, though. Biggest, fanciest wizard school in the world, right?"

"Yeah." Alex chuckled as some of the tension left the air.

"An acceptance letter. You little rascal, when were you going to tell us?"

Alex's chuckle became a full laugh. "Tonight. I had this whole thing planned. I was gonna brag and you would cheer, and I'd show you the spell I'd shown the examiner who came through the magistrate's office last year. Then we'd have a big party and I'd ask for Theresa's hand in marriage, then dodge you and Mrs. Lu as you tried to choke the life out of me."

Thankfully, that got a chuckle out of them.

He sighed at the bad timing. "But then the world had to go and end on me. At least, this part of the world." He grew more serious. "What's the plan?"

Master and Mrs. Lu looked at each other, then at him.

"You're going to school, Alex," Mrs. Lu said firmly, like a lord giving an order to one of their retainers. One that was used to having their word followed to the letter. "Your mother... she had a hard time bringing you into the world, and I'm not going to see her baby caught up in all this, or waste his opportunities."

Alex choked back emotion. He glanced down to Selina, falling to one knee in front of his sister. "You still ready to go, little goblin? Things have changed now, but... I still want you to come with me. We'd have a place together, just the two of us. That sound good?"

Excitement shone in Selina's eyes, but with it was a mix of worry and guilt. She slowly looked to Master and Mrs. Lu. "Are-are you going to be okay?"

Alex grimaced. She had been young when the fire took their own mother and father, but old enough. He sometimes still woke up drenched in cold sweat with her scream from that night echoing in his head. Ever since, she had been *strongly* protective of Alex and the entire Lu family.

Master Lu put an arm around his wife's shoulders and smiled gently at her. "We'll be alright, Selina. Go with your brother, and we'll come visit you."

The little girl watched them for a bit, trying to see if they were telling her a lie to spare her feelings. "I want to go with you, Alex," she finally said.

"Good!" He stood, patting her on the head. He looked at the Lu family. "Where's Theresa?"

One of her older brothers pointed toward the back of the inn. "Getting the mules ready. She's cleaning out the stables, getting the wagons ready, and feeding Brutus."

Alex winced. Brutus had never liked him much. He'd need to make sure to stay on whatever wagon he *wasn't* in.

"I'll... catch her when she's done." He coughed awkwardly and took Selina by the hand. "Come on, little goblin, let's get you packed and in bed. We've a long way to go tomorrow."

As he led her up the stairs, he idly scratched his shoulder.

A glowing red ball of force floated above Alex's finger, and on top of that, he'd balanced a small clay cup of honeyed milk. Four years working for a baker either gave one a sweet tooth or made it so one would never, ever want to eat sweets again.

In Alex's case, it was the former. Luckily, it hadn't gone far enough to double or triple his waistline, like it had for some of his coworkers.

He grabbed the cup and took a sip, enjoying the flavour while he let his mana dissipate from the spell.

"One... two... three..." he counted. "Fo—"

The room went dark as the spell winked out.

"Nearly four heartbeats," he noted. "New record."

Concentrating again, he spoke the words of power under his breath while constructing the spell array in his core. A sudden shift of energy flared within him as the words and array connected, forming a magical circuit into which his mana poured. The circuit sprang to life.

Energy coursed through it at rising speed.

"One... tw—"

Before two heartbeats passed, it formed the shape he desired. Red light flooded the room as another force ball formed. Smiling, he rushed to the open notebook on his tiny desk.

Across the pages were tables, lists, and even small charts that recorded his daily practice: numbers indicating how long it took for the spell to form, how long it took for his mana to dissipate when he stopped feeding the circuit, and how many times he could construct the ball before his inner mana ran dangerously low and the circuit reached for his life force to power itself.

He'd scribbled enough entries to fill half of the large book. A mark of how he'd never missed a day of practice, even if it was for only a few minutes at the end of the night after a long shift at the bakery. It'd been worth it. He flipped back to the front page and shook his head at the numbers.

Spell Formation: *Thirty-four heartbeats.*
Dissipation: *Half a heartbeat*
Number of times creating Orb of Force: *One.*

He flipped back to tonight's entry.

Spell Formation: *Oneish heartbeats.*
Dissipation: *Three and a half heartbeats.*
Number of times creating Orb of Force:

"Four and counting." He smiled and twirled the orb around his finger.

He might have been self-taught, and he'd only ever found one spell to practice, but he was sure as hell going to have it *mastered* by the time he got to Generasi. All in all, not that bad a day considering it started with intentionally getting himself fired and ended with the return of the land's ancient evil.

Scratching his shoulder again, he was starting to wonder if a biting fly had crawled into his sleeve sometime during the day, when he noticed the ball's red light shudder. He glanced at it.

His hand trembled.

The little ball tethered to his finger shook with it.

As much as he acted like all was well, the news about the Ravener *had* scared him. He, his sister and the Lu family—and judging by the dead silence outside his window, half the town—would be packed up and heading for port by morning. But there would be a lot of people that wouldn't be able to make a ship before things turned grim.

With the Cave of the Traveller so close, there was even a chance he and those he cared about wouldn't get out in time. Not if it became a dungeon again. A small chance, but still a chance. He would've been crazy if he wasn't a little scared. Alex took a breath and steadied himself. If he'd given in to all his heavy emotions over the last four years, he would've been a wreck. And with his little sister depending on him, he couldn't afford to be a wreck.

"Let it pass," he told himself. "It's going to be what it's going to be. You're one person. All that matters is what you can do for you and your own. If it's clear to the coast, then good. If it's not, then you *think*. *Adapt*. Survive, like you always have. Worrying about it now's not gonna help anybody."

Repeating that mantra had gotten him through the last four years alive and sane. He'd keep it up until it no longer helped him. Outside, the bell at the church of Uldar rang, dragging him from his thoughts. Eleven chimes. His birthday was nearly done.

Time to finish practice, then finish packing and try to find Theresa.

He killed the mana flow to the spell and counted.

"One... Two..."

Then came the agony.

He doubled over, his scream choking as his body locked up with white-hot pain. His teeth clenched, grinding together, and his vision wavered. Alex Roth hit the ground with a heavy thump, and he could not even writhe as his muscles tensed all at once. Skin burned like his clothes were made of sandpaper and needles. The taste of rust filled his nose and mouth.

His shoulder burned worst of all, paining as if ants chewed their way through his flesh. Ants that were on fire. His forceball winked out, but the light didn't fade. It changed.

A golden glow shone through the shoulder of his white shirt and filled the air. Through the radiance, *something* poured into him. Something that slipped into his body, his mind, his mana and somewhere deeper. His entire being wrenched as if a giant hand was puppeteering it.

Flashes of memory burst into his mind.

Chapter 3

The Mark's Mocking Grin

Memories whirled in his head.

Half-formed images of forests he'd never seen. Towering old men standing on altars. Landscapes blasted by war and teeming with monsters. A floating mass of dark.

Scents came next. Scorched meat. The rusty, sour stench of blood and ash. Others he could not decipher. Then completely alien sounds bombarded his ears; cries from beings that were neither mortal nor animal.

Time held no meaning.

His mind spun faster and faster, teetering on the edge.

And then, it was over.

The pain disappeared, leaving him gasping for breath as the golden glow dimmed, wavering like a candle in the dark. His lungs burned and his ears rang. As soon as he could think again, his mind began to race. Confusion and fear threatened to overtake him, but he pushed it down.

"*Think*," he gasped. "*Adapt*."

He had a sinking feeling.

Your mother... she had a hard time bringing you into the world.

That was what Mrs. Lu had said. Maybe that meant his mother had taken a *long* time in labour birthing him. If so, then by law, he might have been eighteen by sunrise, but he wouldn't have lived a full eighteen years until sometime late in the day.

Or, late at night.

And if he *had* really just passed into manhood, then logic dictated only one thing could have happened. Dread filled him. He didn't want to look, but he had to. With a trembling hand, he reached up on his desk and fumbled for his knife.

It clattered to the floor.

Shaking, he picked it up and slowly hacked at the shoulder of his shirt.

"Please be nothing, but if it has to be something, please be the Sage, please be the Sage," he muttered.

With one eye closed and one eye squinted open, he held the knife up to catch the reflection of his shoulder in the steel.

"*No*!" Both eyes flew wide open.

Reflected back was a glowing mark. A Hero's Mark. And not the staff of the Sage, nor the horned helmet of the Champion. What stared back at him was a mocking grin from the twisted face of a jester with bulging eyes and a belled cap on its head.

He could almost hear it laughing at him.

The blade fell from his fingers.

The Fool.

He'd worked so hard. He'd pushed himself to get into the greatest school of wizardry in the entire world. He'd lost his parents. Taken care of his sister. Endured a bully of a boss for more than a quarter of his life.

And for what?

Uldar had reached down from his 'oh-so-mighty' place above and *branded* him as the Fool?

"Oh, go to hell," Alex growled.

The rage hit him with its full force. He stopped thinking.

Think. Adapt.

Think. Adapt.

Think. Adapt.

His mantra brought him back. Alex had no idea how long he'd lain on the ground, throwing every curse word he'd ever heard at Uldar. But, it was pointless. It wasn't like the god was around to hear him. Only he heard his own protests.

And maybe that was a damn good thing.

"Okay." He clutched the desk and dragged himself back to his feet. It took him some time to catch his breath; his body felt like he'd sprinted for miles. "Okay. Let's think about this. Let's think about what we know."

His heart was thudding as he threw himself down in his chair. He wiped the cold sweat from his forehead.

"Okay. So. You got the Mark of the Fool. Worst Mark you could get."

He talked to himself, grounding his mind to focus.

"That means some church officials are gonna drag me to the capital and make me fight monsters with a bunch of strangers. Each of them are gonna be hand-picked by Uldar and have damn crazy powers. So, where does that leave me?"

He needed to write this down. The glow of the Mark had faded until it was only a dull outline on his skin. He needed some light. Concentrating, he began constructing another spell array in his core to conjure a forceball.

Then his brain exploded.

Memories *flooded* him, cramming their way into his mind like wild dogs on a piece of meat. Every mistake he ever made while practicing magic came back along with every single setback and moment of frustration. Past near-disasters and close calls surged through his thoughts. They destroyed his concentration and the array twisted.

"Ah *shit*!" He grabbed his head. The spell array warped. Panic surged through him. If the array formed with its shape so twisted, then the mana feedback might blast him unconscious. Even worse, the circuit might form *wrong* and make some wild magic erupt out of him. The image of blowing up the Lu's inn and watching a second home burn down nearly made him pass out from panic. He abruptly shattered the array before it could do any damage.

As soon as he let go of his mana, it all stopped.

Alex puzzled at the sudden silence.

"What the hell?" He slowly brought his hands down. "What was that?"

Frowning, he tried to speak words of power.

The flood returned.

Every mispronunciation. Every wrong word and stupid mistake he'd ever made shoved their way into his mind until his words were a stream of useless gibberish.

Grimacing, he stopped speaking. The flood ceased, leaving his mind calm. It took him a few moments to organize his thoughts. Then a terrifying possibility hit him. "Oh no... No, no, no."

Quickly, he dug out one of his candles and lit it. When the tiny flame caught on the wick, he dragged a book from his bag and slammed it down on the desk. The thump of it hitting the wood was deafening in his quiet room.

A History of Our Heroes and their Opposition of the Ravener, by Finnius Galloway.

Alex flipped to the second appendix. Each generation of heroes was listed with their originating towns, where they'd died, and their most important deeds. At the back of that was a definitive statement on what each Mark *did*, compiled from the descriptions of multiple heroes of previous generations.

Alex flipped to the Mark of the Fool's entry and began to read out loud:

> "*The Mark of the Fool is a useful, but pitiful Mark. While the Champion is granted incredible strength, speed and the martial skill of all his predecessors, the Sage's mana pool expands many times, and the Saint gains a divine connection to Uldar himself, the Fool gains no great gifts. In some ways, it is the opposite of the greatest Mark, the Chosen. The mighty Chosen gains lesser versions of the three preceding marks and the ability to synergize them all, but the Fool gains nothing. In fact, the Mark of the Fool actively interferes with any action related to Combat, Divinity—*"

"No, no, no." Alex's blood turned to ice.

"*or Spellcraft...*"

His words trailed off. *Interferes with spellcraft!* He was going to Uldar-damned *wizard university*! He glared at the *thing* on his shoulder. The thin, glowing jester's face seemed to cackle at him while it *utterly destroyed his life.*

Trembling, he forced himself to finish reading. If he didn't, he might've lost his mind right there and then:

> "*In return, the Fool gains vastly accelerated learning of any skill unrelated to these areas. Thus, the Fool can become the Heroes' guide through the wilderness, learn to operate watercraft, scout enemies, repair equipment (though they cannot craft great weapons), and take care of horses. Such things are needed on every adventure. Previous Fools have also become fine painters, jugglers, musicians and mastered other such skills. And yet many parties have defeated the Ravener even after their Fool has been killed, betrayed them, or is otherwise absent.*

"Uldar, however, is infinite in his wisdom. Fools serve as the heart of the Heroes' Party, which is perhaps why such marks find their way to young folk of good nature and good humour. Perhaps that is also why the deaths of previous Fools have motivated Heroes' Parties like the deaths of no other members have. Thusly, even absent, a Fool can bring a Heroes' Party to greater heights. If a Fool is reading this now, I encourage you not to despair, for though you might not be greatly rewarded by history, fulfilling one's duty is a reward on its own."

"Yeah, that's easy for you to say. I wonder how many of the Fools thought that Uldar's wisdom was 'infinite,' Mr. Galloway." Alex slammed the book shut and shoved it away in disgust. A part of him wanted to hold it to the candle's flame and set it alight.

That was it? Alex Roth: big brother, revenge enthusiast and future wizard forced into the role of nanny, clown and sacrificial lamb? No matter what he wanted to be before he got some Mark he didn't ask for?

"Oh sure," he muttered bitterly. "I'll just give up my whole life so writers can pity me. I might die, and in the end, they'll just build a statue of me that makes me look like the guy parents think about when they tell their children not to talk to strangers.

"And while I'm off risking my life, I'm abandoning Selina and giving up all hope of attending Uldar-damn *wizard university*! Wait, speaking of risk... Let me check something."

He dragged the book back toward him, flipping through the records of previous Fools and counting the number of entries that read 'disappeared' or 'tragically killed while—'

He shuddered when he'd gotten to the end.

Half of them didn't make it out of the final fight with the Ravener, and the survivors didn't do much better. Some were maimed, some made a fortune in the arts, or became good merchants, but their reputations chased them for the rest of their lives. It was like that for all the Heroes, but having the reputation of 'epic Champion' was a lot better than being the guy named 'The Fool' and being known as useless. Most of them left for other lands, it looked like.

This just got better and better.

For one crazy moment, he considered trying to cut the Mark off with his knife. Alex shook off the thought for what it was: irrational. The last thing he needed was *more* 'irrational' right now; it was like the market was having a two-for-one bargain sale on 'irrational.'

Right. So: 'accelerated learning of any skill unrelated to these areas.'

No Divinity, Magic or Combat. What did that mean? He snatched up his pen and flipped to a new page in his record book. The handwriting on all the charts was messy. He might have been a quick study with a pen, but his letters didn't *look* pretty, no matter how much his teachers tried to correct that.

He wrote a sentence: 'I, Alex Roth, am the unluckiest person in the entire Kingdom of Thameland,' and it came out like a chicken scratching across a page after sticking its feet in ink. Narrowing his eyes, he started writing again below the chicken scratch. This time, he focused on trying to do better.

If he was right—

The flood of memories came back, but in an entirely different way. Every single lesson he had been taught on writing. Every moment when he had written something in a slightly neater way. Every triumph came back in great detail, laying out how he'd achieved each previous success at bettering his writing. While the memories of his magic failures had been chaotic and ruined his concentration, these memories neatly organized themselves, as though *guiding* his hand as he wrote. It was like he was standing in a well-organized library, and the books he needed were floating right into his hands.

By the time his pen dotted the period, he was staring at the best-looking writing he'd ever produced. It looked like someone else grabbed his book and wrote the second sentence for him. Carefully, he tried it again. The memories returned. This time, they were joined by images of him writing this very sentence. Everything he'd done *right* just now floated up in his mind, guiding him to do even better.

The third sentence was a bit neater than the second.

He repeated the experiment a few more times, each time improving his handwriting in slight increments. The neater letters also grew easier for him to reproduce without thinking so hard.

"So, *that's* how you work," he noted and started neatly writing down his findings:

1. *The Mark uses memory.*
2. *The Mark will bombard and distract you whenever you do anything related to what the other heroes are supposed to do: fighting, magic and working holy acts. It does this by using every* ***failure*** *or mistake you've ever made and flooding you with it until you can't concentrate.*
3. *The Mark* ***helps*** *you when you're trying to learn something outside of those. It gives you everything you've ever done or heard of that's right and presents it in a neat little package. This lets you build easily on every success you've had and avoid things that made you fail in the past.*

He tapped his pen on the page, thinking back on what had just happened. He wrote down something else:

Question: *Does it make it* ***impossible*** *to use magic?*

Alex sat up in his chair and closed the book. The wood creaked beneath him. He blew out the candle, dropping the room into darkness. Last thing he needed was more distractions.

He took a deep breath and steadied himself.

Concentrating, he began to construct the array again. Slower this time. The flood came back, attacking him with every single one of his failures. It pushed its way into his mind, but instead of pushing back, he let it come while holding the partially complete array inside himself.

Think. Adapt.

Think. Adapt.

Think. Adapt.

He repeated his mantra, letting the distracting memories roll off, just like he had done with all the grief of the past four years.

Let it pass, he thought. *Just try to let it go.*

Patience guided him as he monitored the stream. As each memory forced its way into his head, he let them pass and built the array a little more in the brief instants between. Slowly, it neared completion.

Then he started to speak the words.

The flood flowed faster, interfering with his speech.

He shut everything out. Noise. Distractions, both in and outside of his head, just as he had when he was first learning the spell. The flood was just like McHarris' bakery or the inn on a busy night: it was *loud,* but if you went slowly and carefully...

... you could get past it.

Then he had a thought that was so significant, it burst through the flood:

What if it wasn't *just* about getting *past* the noise?

As he finished the array, he started to pay careful attention to every failure the Mark spit at him. He examined each memory, trying to analyze them through the chaos. Some came too quick to pick up on. They were just noise, but others let him clearly see his failures.

Let him see *how* he failed. These memories he didn't let pass; he focused on them.

For the few failures he figured out, he did the *opposite* of what he had in those memories.

The array came out different from his earlier ones, and when he grounded it and completed the circuit, an *immense* rush of mana swirled within him.

Voom.

He opened his eyes to find a bright red glow illuminating the room. Another ball of force floated at the tip of his finger, and he nearly screamed in triumph.

It was bigger than any he'd made in the past. About one and half times the size with a much brighter and steadier glow emanating from it. Creating it was slower. It had been more difficult. But it had been *better.*

He shook with excitement. One could learn from failure too.

What was that old expression? Failure was the mother of success? Road to success? Something like that. Alex opened the book and wrote an answer beneath his question:

***Not** impossible.*

It could be done. Just harder to accomplish. He could work with hard. Working for McHarris was hard, but he'd done it. Learning the beginning magic from rotted books in the church library was hard, but he'd done it. Helping his sister and the Lu family was hard while studying and acing every evaluation at the church school was hard. But he'd done it.

And what was the common thread with all those? He'd done it all for him and those he loved. He threw a dirty look at the history book. It wasn't for some god that tried to tell him what to do, Heroes that didn't need him, or a populace that would think of him as a joke. His sister needed him. He needed himself.

He could still use magic. It was just slow and difficult right now, and would've been impossible without the powers of concentration he'd developed by learning how to deal with his grief. He'd need time to truly learn how the Mark worked.

Explore it. Develop it and himself, and *use* it to learn something helpful.

He wouldn't get that time if he was off playing servant to a bunch of 'Heroes.'

Which left one option.

"Looks like you'll need to write 'disappeared' under the entry for another 'Fool,' Galloway." He stood and clenched his fist. "Because I'm getting the hell outta here."

There was something important Galloway mentioned about seeking out Uldar's priests. If *he* had to seek them out, then that meant they didn't know where he was.

But they'd likely start searching soon, and he doubted they'd accept 'no thanks, I don't really feel like fighting the Ravener' from him.

He needed to get out of Thameland as quickly as possible. He'd need to cover up his Mark, wake Selina and get—

"A... lex?"

He froze.

His head turned as though his neck were attached to a rusty lever. A young woman stood in the doorway, her long, black hair tied back. She gripped a key ring in calloused fingers.

Theresa Lu.

His oldest friend was gaping at him, with eyes darting between the red ball above his finger, and the jester's face on his shoulder.

"I..." she said. "I was coming to talk to you, but I heard you saying all these weird words through the door, then I saw a red light. I asked if you were okay, but you wouldn't answer me—"

Oh shit, he'd tuned out *everything*.

"—and I got the spare keys and let myself in... and..."

She trailed off.

He took a deep breath. Alright. Time for Plan A.

Lying.

"Okay, so." He straightened himself up. "This is *not* what it looks like."

"It looks like you got the Mark of the Fool."

"Okay, so it's *exactly* what it looks like."

Well, *Plan A* was dead. Oh well, Plan A sucked. It was thought of by a guy named the Fool. Of *course* it sucked. Time for Plan B, then.

...Too bad Plan B didn't exist.

"So, uh." His mouth went renegade while his mind raced. "Thing is, uh... You know, this... this is the worst birthday I've ever had."

"If you're leaving." She stepped into the room. The door creaked as she shut it behind her. "Then I want to come with you."

Alex blinked. "What?"

Chapter 4

Departure and Dogs

Theresa Lu was a force to be reckoned with.

One of six siblings, she learned to take initiative if she wanted to stand out. When the Lu family needed meat for the kitchen, it somehow ended up being her who had grabbed a bow and learned how to hunt with her father.

She'd taken to it like a fish to water.

Theresa had become one of the best hunters in Alric and—through hunting—learned patience, silence and determination. All traits needed to stalk prey. As she'd once told Alex, many people thought hunting was about taking a perfect shot. Piercing one's target through the eye or heart and dragging the carcass back to the dinner table. At times, it was like that, but for most hunts, it was about puncturing a blood vessel and watching the prey as it took off into the woods.

Then the hunter would follow. They'd track by prints, by drops of blood or scent if they had a dog. If they kept the trail, they'd eventually run their prey down. Humans were endurance killers, and Theresa embodied this.

Now her sharp eyes watched him with the same predatory look she got when she was on a hunt. She'd asked him to let her come with him. That was her arrow striking him. Any excuses he'd make? That was the trail of blood. All she had to do now was follow while he talked with that quiet patience until he finally grew too tired to argue and she at last caught him.

"I want to come with you," she said again, locking the door and advancing on him. Her steps made no sound across the floorboards. "I know what you're going to say—"

"*Yes*," he said quickly. "Please come with me. I sure as hell could use the help."

He decided to skip all the build-up and just jump into the trap himself.

He was rewarded by her pausing mid-step and blinking in surprise. He always found her cute when she didn't have her 'deathstalker face' on.

And when she did, as a matter-of-fact.

He did *not* have issues, he assured himself.

Her face went deathstalker again when she regained composure. "Good. I was already mad at you for not telling me about *that*." She pointed to the bright forceball floating above his finger. "So I'm glad you didn't make me chase you."

He shrugged. "We both know how it would've ended. When I'm not worrying that a bunch of priests are going to burst down the door at any second, I'll ask you why—"

Boom! Boom! Boom!

A heavy knock slammed against his bedroom door.

Alex and Theresa froze, looking at the doorway like it was some portal to hell. His stomach sank. They couldn't have found him already, could they?

"Theresa!" a familiar voice boomed through the door. "Are you in there?"

Alex sighed in relief. He was safe. It was just Theresa's father.

The door rattled in the frame.

"Why is the door locked? What's going on under my roof?"

His voice cracked like a whip. "What're you two doing in there? Alone?"

Never mind, this was *much* worse.

Theresa went as white as a sheet. "Father? Were you listening at the door?"

"I followed you!" He laughed in triumph. A harsh, barking laugh that promised death. "I was young once too. I know how it is. The young man you've grown up with is going to be leaving on a loooong journey. You might not see him again!"

"*Father*!"

"And who knows *who* he might meet in that big city, yes? So, you go and speak to each other, talk about your feelings, one thing leads to the other and then, *I'm a grandfather before any of my children are married*!"

Theresa turned bright red and buried her face in her hands.

"Wait, Mr. Lu!" Alex cried. "It's not what it sounds like—"

Click.

A key turned in the lock.

Theresa and Alex gasped in unison, looking at each other in horror.

"If there's nothing wrong, then I guess there's no reason why I can't just come in, is there?" Mr. Lu announced darkly from the hall.

"No, Father!" Theresa cried, starting for the door. "Don't come in—"

"Ahaaaaa!" The middle-aged man burst into the room. "I've got you-you... you..."

Mr. Lu stared at the glowing Mark on Alex's shoulder, his mouth hanging open.

Alex's tongue went renegade again. "This isn't what it looks —You know what? Never mind. It is what it looks like."

The older man's face went grim. "Downstairs. Both of you, now."

"It might not be all bad," Alex finished explaining, tapping the jester's face.

Theresa, Master and Mrs. Lu huddled in the kitchen, listening as he went through what he'd learned about the Mark. "It helps you learn, and it doesn't seem *too* specific on what it lets you pick up. *And* I can still work magic. That means there's holes in the way it interferes with you. If I can figure them out, it might even help me. But I need time to do that, and I'm not going to have it by going around and being the servant to four 'Heroes.'"

He looked up at them seriously. "And that's that. I'm going to the Generasi and I'm taking Selina."

"Good." Mrs. Lu clutched his hand. "We'll help you." She turned to her husband. "Right, darling?"

Master Lu was gripping the counter so hard, his knuckles were white. "Life stole your parents' lives, and it wants *your* future too? Well, it can't *have* it." He placed a hand on Alex's shoulder. "It's dangerous to go alone. You'll take the Lu family's most deadly weapons."

Theresa looked at her father sharply. "Great-grandfather's swords?"

"No, you and Brutus. Ouch!"

She'd slapped her father lightly on the shoulder. "Father! I'm *not* a weapon!"

But Alex was already nodding. "Yes. Thank you, Mr. Lu. With this human annihilator at my side—Ouch!"

"*Alex*!" she pouted, crossing her arms. "I'm leaving my family behind to try and save you. Why're you making fun of me?"

"One, because it's fun—"

Her parents nodded in agreement.

"—and two, because if I don't keep making jokes right now,

I might have to admit how *absolutely terrified* I am." He laughed nervously. "So, what now?"

Mrs. Lu gave her daughter a meaningful look. "Go and pack whatever you need, Alex, then get some sleep."

"Sleep? I'm not going to be able to sleep, Mrs. Lu."

"You'll need your strength," the middle-aged woman insisted. "I'll brew you a tonic if I have to. It'll put you out in no time, worries or not."

He bit back a reply, realizing she was right. Leaving half-cocked would only make it more likely that he'd be caught. Even if he somehow woke Selina and got her moving, he'd have to try and slip out of the kingdom with a sleepy ten-year old. It wouldn't work.

"I'll wake you all just before first light," Mrs. Lu promised. "Now, go."

"Alright," he agreed, looking at Theresa. "We'll leave at first light."

Alex Roth encountered a monster just outside the inn after he woke the next morning.

The enormous head of a beast emerged from the dark, snarling and baring gleaming fangs. Its eyes blazed with violence, and its canine snout was long and brimmed with sharp teeth. An identical head emerged on the left, and a third on the right. The faces of three savage hounds growled at the young man, as though warning they were readying to tear him apart.

Apprehensive and still shaking off the last of his night's sleep, he gingerly offered the three monsters a leftover piece of roasted pork from last evening's supper.

"Peace, Brutus," he said. "Come on, I've got some food here. That's a good boy."

Sniffing the air, the canine heads calmed, their eyes fixed on the meat. All three licked their chops and came out of a massive doghouse. The trio of heads were attached to one body the size of a small horse.

A cerberus.

Not every monster in the Kingdom of Thameland was spawned by the Ravener. Many were creatures naturally occurring in the wilderness, with some being deadly in their own right. Cerberi were some of the most dangerous among them, but also the most trainable if one got them young and knew how to handle them.

When Theresa had first brought home the orphaned pup after finding it in the woods three years ago, her parents lost their minds. But the young huntress was patient and stubborn, and gradually won them over, explaining how helpful having such a ferocious guard dog might be. What helped too was that Brutus —she had already named him before bringing him home—was as gentle as a lamb in her hands.

Truthfully, he was gentle with almost everyone... except for Alex.

Snap!

"Oh shit!" Alex jerked back as Brutus lunged, his teeth nearly snatching the young man's hand off along with the pork. As he stumbled away, the cerberus dove into breakfast with two of his heads. The third stared at him with a self-satisfied look and sniff of satisfaction. Alex shook his head. Failed again. Maybe most people would have hated the mutt, except... it was a freaking cerberus. How could he hate something so cool?

"I'll win you over one day, just you wait," he plotted quietly. He glanced to his shoulder, where a heavy, dark tunic and thick woolen cloak covered the Mark. Maybe he'd use it to learn about dog training...

"We're ready," someone called.

He shook off fantasies of training Brutus to fetch, beg and roll over.

He did *not* have issues, he assured himself.

Theresa was coming from the house hand in hand with Selina. The little girl was wiping her eyes and yawning, but she was all smiles. "How far away is the wizard city, big brother? Will we get there soon? Is there a lot of magic there?"

Alex returned her smile. He hadn't told her anything about what happened last night. When it was safe, *then* he could tell her. "It's reeeeaaally far." He spread his hands wide. "It'll take us a long time to get there. And from what I've heard, there's more magic there than any other place in the world."

She yawned again. "Okay."

Theresa smiled down at her before looking to the horizon over the surrounding rooftops.

"We've got a bit before light." She tapped a composite bow she'd slung over her shoulder. Black feathered arrows rose from her quiver, and a massive hunting knife shone from a belt-loop on her hip. Her calf-high boots made no sound as she walked. "We should get moving before the rest of the town starts to wake up."

Her parents emerged from the inn as Alex took his sister's hand and Theresa untied Brutus from his shelter. Master and Mrs. Lu looked over the group and the latter made a disappointed noise.

"You both really *are* all grown up, aren't you? Too fast. Too fast," she sighed, gripping her husband's arm. "You be *careful* out there, both of you." She looked pointedly at her daughter and then to the small, yawning Selina. "Stay on the roads and be careful of who you meet. Desperate times makes for desperate people, and they can do terrible things."

"Yes, someone like Scar the Bandit King would have a field day in these times. Thank Uldar Grandfather got him. You write to us as *soon* as you get the chance; when you're out of the kingdom," Master Lu added, his brow furrowed in worry. "Now, come here."

Theresa's parents caught their daughter, Alex and Selina in a tight embrace, dropping low so the small girl could be included. As their warmth spread through Alex, a tightness crept in his throat. Tears formed in his eyes. It might be the last time he would ever feel that warmth. He tightened his hug.

When they broke apart, Mrs. Lu and Master Lu's eyes were shining as well.

"Go," Mrs. Lu's voice trembled. "Before your brothers wake up, Theresa, or you'll never leave."

Selina sniffled loudly and Theresa kept her eyes low. "Goodbye, Mother and Father," she said quietly. "Come on, Brutus."

Crack.

The cerberus snapped the bone in two with one set of jaws while another picked up the pieces. His third head licked out the marrow as he bounded after his master.

"Goodbye, Master Lu, goodbye Mrs. Lu. Thank you for everything. You be safe on your journey too," Alex said. His hand tightened around Selina's. "I promise... I'll get there. We'll all get there."

With that, he turned and followed after Theresa, hoisting his heavy rucksack over his shoulder. He hoped what he'd said to her parents would end up being true.

Chapter 5

The Coins and the Priests

The town of Alric stirred with tension.

It seemed like half of the townspeople were out on the streets as Alex, Theresa, Selina and Brutus passed by. Wagons filled the sides of the roads while people rushed back and forth between townhomes and businesses, stacking their possessions into the wagons and tying them down. Torches flickered on poles or in tightly gripped hands, and weapons that hadn't seen the outdoors in years hung from the hips of many of the townsfolk.

There was no scent of baking bread or boiling porridge this morning.

Alex could *feel* the panic building.

"Make sure the silver's close at hand," a heavy-set woman told her husband as she finished hitching the horses to a cart. "With this many going to the continent, the shipmasters'll charge whatever they feel to take folks across the channel."

"It's already in the front; just don't let it out of your sight," an older man grunted as he placed a heavy chest into the cart. He glanced around, scanning the other wagons and carts. His hand remained close to his club. Alex recognized the man. They had always nodded politely to each other and exchanged smiles in the mornings. Now when he spotted Alex, his lips rose in the same wide smile, but his eyes were anxious and agitated.

"We should hurry." Theresa nodded to Alex. "Something ugly's brewing." She eyed their neighbours and her body tensed as though she was in the woods hunting on a moonless night. "Desperate people do desperate things. Let's get to the gate quickly."

Selina looked up to them. "Is there something wrong?"

Alex gave her another weak smile. "Everything's alright, Selina," he lied. "Everything's fine."

The southwestern gate was *not* fine.

Despite there still being some time before sunrise, a large crowd had already gathered, forming a line that stretched from the wall and down several blocks. Many had the same idea as Alex: come early in order to beat the crowd. Now, they were all made to wait as the guards stopped each solitary traveller and family, recording the names of every person leaving. Likely, they were keeping an accounting of who would be staying in town and needing protection during these dark times.

"That's it! That's it! Order now!" he heard the guard, Paul, shout from ahead. "Keep order and we'll have you on the road before sunrise."

Normally, none of the gates opened until daylight, but Alex took one look at the large crowd and recognized how ugly things might turn if they were not allowed to pass through now. People were fidgeting in agitation. Some watched the skies or the top of the walls as though monsters might come flying over at any heartbeat. Alex threw an uncomfortable glance to the sky too.

No monsters up there. None yet, at least.

Most folk clutched their possessions, and a great many were counting the coins in their purses; having enough for the ship's passage seemed to be on the minds of most. Alex stealthily patted the inheritance buried at the bottom of his rucksack, as well as the small pouch of coins on his belt, and he gave quiet thanks for his parents' hard work. The four of them wouldn't have to worry about passage.

As they stepped into the back of the line, folk took one look at the massive form of Brutus and gave them space. The cerberus seemed proud of himself as he flopped down onto his haunches and tossed the broken pieces of bone onto the side of the road. His three tongues lolled from his mouths and he panted in the mild air of the summer morning.

"Good boy." Theresa smiled and scratched behind one of his ears. He whined for more attention and pressed his other two heads into her waiting hands.

"Yeah, very good boy." Selina copied the young woman by rubbing his haunches.

"Yeah, super good boy." Alex reached out to pat his back.

Brutus gave a low growl.

Alex stopped reaching.

Instead, he chose to let his eyes wander over the buildings spread before the gate. He noted the stables and stalls usually staffed to serve travellers entering town. He noted the guardhouse, and the highchairs where ambitious town boys would shine shoes of any who could pay.

"I'm going to miss this place." He sighed fondly.

"Already?" Theresa gave him a look. "We're not even gone yet. Sure you don't want to stay?"

He shrugged helplessly. "What would be the point? I wouldn't get to stay *here* anyway."

"Well." She took a long look around. "Let's hope that it's still here when we get back."

Alex gently rubbed her shoulder. "I'm sure it will be."

"Next!" Paul shouted from ahead.

The line began moving.

"I hope so, Alex," Theresa said in a small voice.

They moved toward the gate at a steady pace, and Alex took

the time to consider their plan. It was about ten days on foot to the closest town on the sea, and it would be longer having Selina with them. She'd need to be carried part of the way, perhaps by Brutus if Theresa could convince him. They would have to be careful on the road too. The priests would be searching for the Heroes, and the Ravener's coming meant monsters would soon start to roam the land. Then there would be the bandits. All these folks on the road would make tempting targets. Anyone fleeing would have to move quickly and preferably in numbers.

There's safety in numbers, Alex thought. *Or at least more bodies between you and... whatever horrors are out there.*

"Theresa, you've got better eyesight than I do. Maybe look around and see if there's anyone close by that we know well. Someone we could join up with for at least *part* of the journey. For safety."

She glanced at him. "I was just about to suggest that."

With predatory focus, she scanned the crowd, letting her eyes drink in every detail. She was turning to look over those that joined the line behind them when she froze.

"Alex..."

"What is it?"

"I want you to turn around nice and slow, and casually, okay? Don't panic."

He nodded, feeling a knot tightening in his belly. He turned to follow her gaze... and his whole body became rigid. At the end of the street, three white robed figures passed through the crowds, pausing to help and comfort those who were readying to leave. Though they were still distant, they were clearly headed for the line.

"Oh *no*," Alex said under his breath.

Priests.

The priests of Uldar were coming right toward them.

They were making their way down the road, their snow-white robes standing out in contrast to the colourful garb of the townsfolk. None of them looked in his direction, but he had a sinking feeling it would only be a matter of time.

He was fairly certain some of the Heroes from past generations—especially the Fool—would have tried to run off, but there wasn't any record of the kingdom failing to find one, only that some disappeared partway through the journey. His eyes narrowed.

They had *some* way of detecting the Marks, he was sure of it, and he had no idea *how* or at *what* range. That put him at a disadvantage. His mind continued to work. The fact that they weren't rushing right for him meant he had not been found out yet.

But that could change at any moment—

"Alex!" Theresa hissed. "You're *staring*."

"Shi—" He paused, remembering his little sister was right there. "I mean, *crap*." He casually faced the gate.

The line before them had shrunk considerably. Only fifteen people stood between them and freedom, and the guardsmen were moving folks through as fast as they were able. His back tingled, and he imagined the priests' eyes focusing on it and calling out to him. Maybe if the guards worked quickly enough and the priests lingered, they might be alright.

"What're the priests doing?" he whispered to Theresa.

She threw another glance over her shoulder nonchalantly. "They're getting close." Her lips barely moved.

He grimaced. It would take too long to get through the line.

What could he do? If they cut in line, that would bring focus onto them and create a commotion. It would also bring attention they didn't want. He frowned. Alex had heard of some powerful wizards being able to disappear and appear wherever they wanted. He wished he had *that* spell.

His eyes narrowed in thought.

Wishing wouldn't get him anywhere. He could only use what he had.

Think. Adapt.

His eyes caught something curious happening up ahead. Six places ahead in the line, a skinny man in a rich doublet was turned on his horse and facing a couple behind him.

"Oi, watch yourself," he said loudly to the woman, his face tense with agitation. His horse snorted and pawed the earth, and he tugged roughly on the reins to still the scared animal. "Don't get too close."

He patted something on his belt; a bulging coin purse.

"Don't get too close, yourself," the woman snapped back. "I don't like the way you're looking at me."

"Doesn't much matter what you like or don't like. Stay back and keep your hands to yourself."

The woman's husband—a big bruiser of a man—stepped forward. "Are you calling my wife a thief?"

"I'm calling her *nothing*, but I want my proper space and you're both too close."

"Your horse is taking up half the line and folk are pushing from the back, what do you expect us to do?"

"I expect you to *keep* back. I am assistant to the mayor himself!"

"Then why are you running?"

The mayor's assistant sputtered like an angry teapot. "Say something like that again and I'll see to it that you and your wife spend the next *week* in the town dungeon. You'll be right here to receive the Ravener's monsters!" He drew a breath as though he were about to shout for the guards.

The bruiser turned red but said nothing else, and the folk behind him gracefully stepped back so he and his wife could give the pompous ass his space.

An idea formed in Alex's mind.

"Theresa, I need you to stand behind me," he whispered. "Block the view of me from the back and tell me if anyone's watching."

She shot a look toward the priests. "If you're going to do something, do it fast."

Theresa casually slid between him and the back of the line, making it look as though she were merely shifting in place. Alex stealthily reached into his pouch, drawing out a handful of gold coins. His eyes focused on the back of the bruiser. Everyone was desperate for enough coin to get on the ships. If he slipped up to him, pressed a couple into his hand and asked him to throw a punch at the jackass on the horse then—

No, that would make him stand out. Anyone would remember someone who paid them to start a fight. His eyes shifted to the rich man's back. Plan B, then. Alex slipped the coins to his other hand and wedged one between his thumb and index finger. He focused his mind on how he'd made coin tosses in the past, on the best ones he'd ever made.

Memories flooded in. Images of him flipping coins into the fountain yesterday, the feeling of rolling them back and forth across his fingers, other coin tosses he'd made; flipping and catching coins in the air when he was younger.

Each memory organized into a guide that pointed out what he had done *right* each time. Which movements of the body had generated distance, how he'd held his hand to determine direction, how much force he'd applied during his best shots.

All coalesced into a careful instruction that guided his hand.

He watched the people in line between him and his target.

When he was sure none were paying attention to him...

Ting.

He flipped the gold coin forward.

Chapter 6

Coin Tricks and Fire Light

The coin shot over the heads of the people in front of Alex, drawing a graceful arc through the air.

He winced as it missed his target: the back of the mayor's assistant's neck, but it *did* collide with his skinny back. The lean man flinched at the impact as the coin fell to the stones with a clink. The couple behind him did not miss it fall, and the wife was darting for it just as he turned around.

"What the—!" He grabbed his purse protectively, his face turning purple. "Thief! Robber! *Cutpurse*!"

"Hey, you dropped this!" she snapped. "I was going to give it back to you!"

Alex didn't know if she was telling the truth, but it didn't matter. The rich man didn't believe her.

"Guards! Guards!" he cried, drawing a sap from his belt.

"Hey!" the bruiser stepped forward, his hands balling into fists. They were the size of hams. "You touch my wife with that and you'll have my fist where your teeth used to be!"

All eyes turned to the commotion, including the guards.

Alex discreetly started flipping more coins toward the front of the line. The Mark improved his aim with each toss, using each previous one as a reference. The gold coins came rolling to a halt at people's feet. Eyes dipped, briefly glancing up to see if it was raining coins, and—desperate as they were to secure a ship's passage—many darted for them without questioning where they were coming from. Some muttered about Uldar's blessings.

"Hey! Get your hands off that one! That's mine!" a man cried.

"I saw it first!" a woman shouted back.

"Thieves! Those are mine! You're all thieves!" the mayor's assistant shouted and swept out with his sap, striking at someone who darted for a coin near his horse.

That turned out to be a mistake, for the person who was stuck by the sap had cried out in pain.

And that person was the bruiser's wife.

"That does it!" the huge man roared, cocking back a giant fist.

Bang!

The mayor's assistant flew off his horse in a limp heap. He splayed out on the ground like a dead frog, twitching slightly.

The brawl was on after that. Curses and punches filled the air as the front of the line disintegrated.

"Alex!" Selina cried out and as he scooped her up in his arms.

"It'll be okay," he said, resisting the urge to look back. "Theresa, where're the priests?"

"They're looking *this* way," she hissed.

"Crap. Come on, stay behind me and act like everything's okay." He stepped out of line, trying to look as casual as he could.

The Mark helpfully flooded him with images of himself walking naturally and calmly. He allowed it to guide his steps, letting guards pass as they sought to break up the brawl, and then stepped up to those who were left at the gate. Peter and Paul stood on either side of the town entrance, shaking their heads at the scrum.

"It's too bad about people." Alex sighed as he reached them. "Neighbours all their lives, and at the first sign of trouble, they eat each other."

"Eat each other? Bah, this is no worse than a festival night at the Bear's Bowl. They'll have a few bumps, lose a few teeth, and be fine afterward." Peter nodded as though he were doling out ancient wisdom.

"If *any* of us are fine," Paul muttered. "Evil times ahead."

There was a pause.

"So, do you mind if we cut in line?" Alex asked, trusting in the Mark as it reminded him what his face looked like when it was calm. His fear that the priests would notice him was mounting.

"There *is* no more line now." Peter brought up his list. "Or at least, whatever line is left, you're at the front of it. You had the good sense not to start any of this. Come on then, we'll get you on your way."

If Alex didn't have his arms full of little sister, he might have hugged Peter right then and there.

"Right, you three..." Peter continued. "Names?"

By the time the brawl had been cleared, Alex and his companions were long past the gate and onto the road. A nervous energy filled him and he hurried along, passing the folk streaming from the town of Alric.

"Are they following us?" he asked Theresa for the thirtieth time.

"No." She threw a quick look over her shoulder. "Stop asking."

"What are you looking at?" Selina tried to follow Theresa's gaze.

"Just making sure that fight's behind us," Alex said, throwing silent gratitude toward his parents and the two guards. When he made full wizard, he really *was* going to give those two beautiful guardsmen the biggest reward they'd ever seen. He didn't care if they saw it as a bribe. He'd happily force it into their hands if it came to that.

"Well, that's step one," he said to Theresa when they were out of earshot of the gate. With a grunt, he set Selina back on her feet.

"Are those people going to be okay, Alex?" Selina looked back worriedly.

"Didn't you hear those kind, honourable, brave guardsmen?" He chuckled. "They'll be fine."

Theresa looked at him with suspicion. "How did you do that? Some kind of magic?"

He couldn't resist shrugging his marked shoulder meaningfully.

"Yeah, let's call it a kind of magic."

He had a feeling he was going to *like* this Mark.

"Yessss!" Alex cheered.

He had struck the flint, sparking the tinder to crackle with a small flame. Carefully, he leaned down and blew on the little fire as the Mark guided him, providing memories of others starting campfires, showing him how to feed it with air to give it more life. Just like pouring mana into a spell array, the flame grew and caught the dried branches he and Theresa had gathered earlier.

At last, the wood popped and crackled as he tossed another branch onto the pile. The pleasant scent of wood smoke drifted into the air. Pleased with his accomplishment, he sighed happily, sat back, and began massaging his aching feet. It had been a long day of walking, but they'd made good time. The gloom from surrounding trees receded as their fire grew, matching the host of campfires stoked by other travellers dotting the fields beyond the southern reaches of Coille forest.

"Are you okay, little goblin?" Alex turned to Selina, who was sitting on her sleeping roll a good distance from the flame.

"M-mhm," she murmured. "Good job, Alex."

Selina would not look toward him, as that would mean looking at the fire. She did *not* like fire, and for good reason. Alex had needed two years of self-talk before he was able to work with it without hyperventilating. She was young and could take as long as she needed. Mr. and Mrs. Lu had given *him* the time he needed, and that had done him a world of good.

Forcing himself to stand, he walked over—his feet complaining with every step—and flopped down beside her at an angle where she wouldn't have to look at the flame.

Her gaze rose. "You... you didn't have to do that. If you want to, you could stay by the fire." Taking a deep breath, she glanced toward the flame and—to his surprise—managed to look at it for a few heartbeats before turning away. "I want to be like you one day... and be able to look at it." A steely note entered her voice. "I don't want to be afraid of fire anymore."

With a smile, he patted her head. "Were you practicing?"

She closed her eyes, taking another deep breath, and nodded.

"Well, I'm proud of you, but you don't need to rush yourself. Take as much time as you want, and it's okay if it gets too scary."

He leaned back and undid his cloak, taking in the air of the warm summer night. During the day, it had grown *very* hot, but fear of the Mark glowing like when it first appeared made him want as many layers over his shoulder as possible. He'd drawn some odd looks, but since he was naturally taller than most folk —and his group included a cerberus—he'd draw *some* attention no matter what. He figured he could live with the looks.

Shaking off his contemplation, he looked to the 'project' Selina was working on.

In her small hands was a strange figure of dried twigs in the shape of a person, held together by tied lengths of long grass.

Even as she watched her brother, her clever little fingers busied themselves attaching another twig to a wooden 'arm' to represent a tiny sword.

Alex smiled warmly. "What's your new friend's name?"

"Forrest," she said as though it were the most logical thing in the world. "He'll be finished soon, then I'll put him with his friends."

Alex glanced over his shoulder. A line of three dolls stood beside Selina's sleeping roll with their feet stuck into the earth, posed in a rough diorama that reminded him of...something. She had more materials set aside to make another one.

Throughout the day, she'd been making them with surprising rapidity during the walk. He supposed he shouldn't have been all that surprised at the speed. Her room at the inn was filled with constructed miniature fortresses, houses, and castles of wooden bricks carved for her by Mr. Lu. Tiny people made of clay filled the constructions with a reflection of daily life as seen through her eyes.

"And who are his friends?" He grinned at her.

She grinned back. "They're the Heroes!"

Alex laughed ruefully. That was what the diorama reminded him of, the fountain back in Alric. Of course she would make the Heroes. "And which ones have you made so far?"

She pointed excitedly to the large one that had twigs extending from his 'head' like horns on a helmet. "That's the Champion," she said proudly. "That's the Sage." She pointed to one with a long twig-like a staff. "That's the Saint." She pointed to another holding a construction of grass twisted together in the shape of a raised hand: the symbol of Uldar.

"And this," she held up the figure in her hands, "is the Chosen!"

"Well, that explains the sword and the Mark." He eyed her handiwork. She had used a stick to scrape a rough, tiny Mark of the Chosen into the doll's chest. A set of scales—like those a merchant would use to weigh coins and goods—representing the balance of combat, divinity, and spellcraft, as well as the balance in Thameland they were meant to restore.

He idly wondered what would have happened if a glowing golden set of scales appeared on his shoulder instead of the grinning face of a jester. He'd likely be running nowhere, and instead would be on his way to the capital to lead the march against the Ravener. He probably wouldn't be happy about being the Chosen, though he wouldn't have a choice but to do his duty if he wanted a home to return to. After all, the Heroes could lose a Fool. A Chosen? Not so much.

"Are you going to carve the Fool next?"

"Mhm." She nodded as she finished tying the sword to her little Chosen's hand. "I'm going to make him funny and have him stand on one leg or something. Maybe I'll give him a frying pan or something for a weapon."

"Well, he'd definitely bring *pan*demonium to his enemies that way."

"Uuugh." She glanced up at him and made a face. "Your jokes are gross."

"Not as gross as your face, little goblin."

Frowning, she stuck her tongue out at him. He responded by pulling up the tip of his nose and snorting like a pig. "This is youuuu." He pointed to his own face.

"That is *not* a good look for you," Theresa's voice said from behind.

"Holy sh—!" He jumped, catching himself at the last moment.

The young huntress was silently stepping into the firelight with her bow tucked over her shoulder and the massive Brutus padding loyally at her side. She had an amused smile as she hoisted up two pairs of rabbits. The cerberus licked his chops. All three sets.

"Supper's here," she said proudly. "And you have Brutus to thank. You really should be nicer to him, Alex."

"What!" he protested. "He wants to *eat my face*, and I'm *trying* to be nice to him."

"No, you're trying to win him over, and he knows that. He can smell the bad intentions coming off of you." She crouched by the fire and drew her knife.

"I *have* no bad intentions. I've never had a bad intention in my life!"

"Aren't you going to try and domesticate him? Make him play fetch and beg?"

He did his best not to fidget. "N-no, I'd never."

"Riiight. Come help me skin these."

"Coming, Grandmother."

She paused, looking over her shoulder. "What was that, Mr. I-Don't-Want-To-Have-Meat-Tonight?"

"I said I'm coming, oh beautiful and mighty huntress."

She stared at him for a moment before turning away. "Damn right."

Between Theresa, himself, and the Mark of the Fool guiding him, the skinning and cleaning of the rabbits went quickly. When it was time to cook them, he shooed Theresa away from the fire. After four years helping McHarris and Mrs. Lu in their respective kitchens, food had become *his* domain.

Calling upon the Mark of the Fool to guide him through his greatest successes over stove and oven, he spitted the rabbits and glazed them with an apple-honey sauce he'd recreated from one of McHarris' recipes. Next, he crushed a light sprinkling of salt, rosemary, and thyme, and rubbed them into the meat. Normally, he would have let it sit and marinate for a time, but he could already hear Selina's belly rumbling. And his wasn't exactly silent either.

Hsssss.

Fat dripped into the fire, popping and steaming as he turned the rabbits, filling the air with the inviting aroma of roasting meat. The skin sizzled as turned it a beautiful golden brown. He smiled as the Mark methodically brought up memories of his best meals, highlighting all the times he roasted meats to perfection. And judging by the way Theresa and Selina tore into the finished product, and how a drooling Brutus stared with envy, it seemed he had outdone himself.

"Alex, this is *so* good!" Selina said, juices dripping down her chin.

"It's even better than usual," Theresa agreed while wiping Selina's face.

Brutus licked his chops.

Alex grinned as he bit into his own. It *was* delicious.

By now, Brutus was whining pitifully, and before Theresa could move to feed him, Alex snatched up the fourth rabbit and tossed it in front of the cerberus' faces. "Good eating," he said to him cheerfully.

Three pairs of eyes looked at him suspiciously, but the heads they belonged to soon dipped and tucked into his meal.

Alex smiled behind his food.

Just as planned.

A red forceball winked into life above his hand after his third try at the spell. Shuddering from the effort, the bombardment of his previous failures receded into the back of his mind, and he set the glowing orb to float a few feet above his head.

He sat at the edge of their clearing, facing the southern fields, watching the other fires wink out as the night deepened. Behind him, Selina's soft snoring and Brutus' grumble as he rolled over in his sleep accompanied the quiet night.

"Here," Theresa whispered, handing him a cup of steaming

pine needle tea. The woodsy scent filled Alex's nose as he took the small tin cup, blew on the liquid, and drew a long sip.

"Thanks," he said, looking at her as she slipped down to sit close to him. "You can get some sleep now if you want. I've got first watch."

Sipping from her own cup, she leaned against the trunk of an oak. "I won't be able to sleep yet." She sighed in contentment.

For a time, the two friends sat together at the edge of the forest, watching the lights in the field below and the stars in the night sky above. The wind was low and warm, and the trees rustled peacefully. From somewhere in the field, someone produced a set of pipes and was playing them by their campfire. Crickets chirped through the night.

Alex took a deep breath, drinking in the peace of the moment. He idly wondered if such sights existed within the land of Generasi. But, knowing that in two months or slightly more he would be finding out for himself, the thrill of anticipation bloomed.

If it weren't for the nagging reminder lurking in the back of his mind that ancient evil was descending on the land, he could have easily thought that the folks in the field bedding down were simply camping in wait for a festival, instead of fleeing the near end of all things.

It was strange how people could find the calmest comfort in the most trying times.

Then again, that was something he'd had to learn how to do. And learn it well.

"Did it ever cross your mind to stay? All jokes aside?" Theresa asked from the dark. The red light of Alex's spell brought out the sculpted beauty of her face in new ways. He had to catch himself, otherwise he'd be staring at her for half the night.

He wasn't so stupid to not realize he'd developed a strong

crush on his oldest friend, but he had never had time to examine it. Maybe he would on this journey.

"Honestly, I thought about it earlier, if I'd gotten a different Mark," he admitted, settling further back against the tree. He felt the gentle course of mana through the forceball's magic circuit. "I'd have no choice then, but I don't know if that would have been good or bad. But I meant what I said back at the gate. I'm going to miss Alric and I'm going to miss Thameland." He sighed. "A lot."

He glanced over to Theresa and his breath caught to find her sharp brown eyes staring right at him.

"What about you?" he managed to ask. "You asked me if you could come with me, but you didn't have to. What made you decide to come?"

A part of him dearly hoped she would say "for you."

Chapter 7

Good Dreams and Bad Luck

Theresa continued to watch him for a moment, before sighing and turning away.

"I have dreams too, you know?" Something passed through her expression, too quick for Alex to catch.

"Yeah, I mean, that's what makes people wake up in the morning, right? Well, that and work. You never told me about your dreams before, though. What are they?"

The young huntress' gaze drifted fondly over the fields, before rising up to the southern horizon. Copses of trees, meadows, and farmer's fields spread out, illuminated by campfires until they disappeared into the gloom of night. "Well... Alric's my home, and I love it, but it's not where a smart person would have big dreams, is it?"

"What do you mean?"

"Well, it's... comfortable." She frowned as she searched for the right word. "It's safe. Most people have enough to eat and neighbours treat each other well. You can grow up there, work there, have a family and be happy there."

"I feel a 'but' coming," Alex said.

"*But* there's not much to it, is there?" She looked at him

sharply. "I've explored most of the Coille Woods—at least as deep as I want to go—raised Brutus and walked about as far south, east and west as I could while still making it back home before dark. And then... that's it." She shrugged. "There's nothing new anymore. Nothing exciting or dangerous or—"

"Dangerous?" Alex raised an eyebrow. "It's pretty dangerous *right now.*"

"That's *too* dangerous. You remember when Grandfather used to tell stories about my great-grandfather?"

"Oh yeah, 'Twinblade Lu: most feared man to sail under the Tarim-Lung Navy.'" Alex chuckled, fondly remembering how he'd crowded into the Lus' inn with his own father and mother —who was pregnant with Selina at the time—and watched the old Lu patriarch weave stories in front of the hearth. It was back when fire held a different meaning to him.

"He sailed with the ambassador's own crew," he recalled. "And fought off a hundred pirate ships before he retired. Fell in love with Thameland on a journey here, and ended up bringing his family."

Theresa smiled. "I *loved* those stories."

"I know, you—"

"No, I mean I wanted to be *in them.*" She spread her hands. "Adventure, seeing different lands, battles, fear... I wanted all that. Why do you think I dodged knitting lessons and kept going into the woods? I was *so* glad my brothers were shit with a bow."

"I... I don't think those adventures were so happy for him at the time," he said. "Exciting, maybe."

"I *know,*" she growled in frustration. "When others weren't around, Grandfather would tell us about some of the bad parts his father told him. That's what made me think twice about running off. Great-grandfather buried too many of his friends at sea. Sometimes I'd still think about leaving, though—and I still might have—but then... your parents." She sighed. "I'm sorry, Alex."

He grimaced. "Thanks. It put things in perspective, didn't it? There was Selina to think about. The future..." He trailed off.

She gave him another long look. "Right. The future. That's what I thought about too. What would Mother, Father, my brothers... you. What would any of you think if something happened to me? So, I thought I'd better just grow up. There's a lot in Alric to be thankful for: my family, my friends..."

"But then, you heard the Ravener was coming, and you thought, 'why not'?"

"Yeah." She ran her hand through her midnight-black hair. "Mostly I found out that you were preparing to run off to *wizard land* for Uldar knows how long, and didn't tell *anybody.*"

"Yeah..." He awkwardly scratched the back of his head. "Sorry, I thought it wasn't *that* likely I'd get in, and I would've gotten everyone's hopes up for nothing." He shrugged. "I only got the acceptance letter the day before yesterday, and I was going to tell you all last night. Like a little birthday announcement."

"*I* wouldn't have been disappointed," she muttered. "And maybe knowing would have made me think about my own path earlier. Here *I* was staying to be the responsible one, while you were looking to take Selina and go off to a wonder of the world. So, when I heard everyone was leaving Thameland, I thought... why not? I can see this wizard city for myself. And..."

She shifted in place. "We'd be together. You, me, Brutus, and Selina." Her eyes watched him closely.

His heartbeat started to quicken. There was a hint there. It might have been hope making him see it, but he was *sure* it was there. "I—"

"Shhh!" She raised her hand suddenly.

He startled, his head turning every which way. "What is it?"

"Shhh!" Theresa was on her feet in an instant, her sharp eyes scanning the dark. "*Listen.*"

Alex shut his mouth and held his breath.

And he heard... nothing.

The wind had stopped.

Crickets had fallen silent, and he could only hear the pipes playing in the south. Alone, they went from 'cheery' to 'eerie.'

"I can't hear anything," he whispered.

"Exactly. The forest is *never* this quiet." Theresa slipped back into the circle of firelight with Alex following close behind.

She crept to her sleeping roll and rummaged through it. When she rose, she had tied her quiver to her belt and had her bow in hand. On her opposite hip gleamed two blades: her massive hunting knife and—to his surprise—one of her great-grandfather's swords. As she silently went to wake Brutus, Alex moved near his sleeping sister and turned to peer into the trees opposite Theresa. This way, they'd be covering most directions. Or so he hoped.

He willed his forceball to drift a few feet ahead of him. It illuminated the foliage beyond the reach of the fire with its red light. He injected a bit more mana into the circuit and the glow brightened. A low, ominous hum groaned from the orb. It seemed deafening in the silence.

There was a scrambling as Brutus woke and rose to his feet, growling from all three heads. Selina groaned in her sleep.

"Do you see anything?" Theresa asked.

"No," he said, willing the forceball to rise higher. The humming spell drifted until it was just below the branches of the forest canopy. Its light bathed the undergrowth ahead and branches above, but he could see no movement or shape up ahead.

He swallowed saliva and fear.

"You?"

Brutus growled, rustling the grasses underfoot as he turned in place.

"No," Theresa admitted. "But *something's* wrong."

Alex believed her. It was like ice crawling over his spine. Only, no matter how long he looked, he couldn't see anything in the trees. He decided to risk a glance backward.

"Theresa, what do you—"

He stopped dead.

She couldn't see it from her position. Brutus couldn't smell it either.

But *he* could see it.

The red glow of his orb outlined shadows in the trees above. There—sliding along the bark of an oak near Theresa's side—was the shadow of a blade, long and wickedly curved. His gaze drifted higher until he was looking into the tree directly above him.

Something was nestled among the branches, illuminated by the fire and the red light of the forceball.

It looked like a cross between a spider and a giant crayfish. Its long, armoured tail wrapped around the tree trunk and each of its eight legs ended in long, scythe-like blades, which bit into the bark. Its front claws were pointed shears, long enough to cut Alex in half with one snip.

Its jaws were wolf-like and devoid of lips to hide massive fangs. Despite its densely armoured exoskeleton, it crept down the side of the tree in an eerie silence. It paused, meeting his horrified eyes with eight dead, black orbs. Jaws were parting, and saliva shone in the crimson light.

Alex screamed.

It tensed.

He grabbed his shocked little sister just before it lunged.

Thump.

He hit the ground hard, rolling away just as it crashed into the earth with all eight sword-like legs. They dug deep where he and Selina had been. Still, the thing landed in complete silence. Only the crunch of Selina's Hero dolls shattering could be heard.

"Aleeex!" the little girl screamed.

The monster reared up on its back legs, its jaws parting as if screeching, but no sound came out.

"Here! Over here!" Theresa cried.

Crack.

An arrow glanced uselessly off the spider's armour as it rushed for the prone forms of Alex and his sister. The blades on its back legs silently churned the earth. Its claws clacked together in rapid succession; the only sound as it rushed forward. Gritting his teeth, Alex mentally grasped the forceball and drove it toward the monster's head.

The Mark flooded him as soon as he aimed at the monster.

Every failure of throwing coins, rocks, sticks or anything else blasted into his mind, shaking his concentration. Through the mental noise, there was one thought: protect Selina. Through brute force of will, he blasted the spell at the creature's head, but his aim was shaky.

Crack.

The red forceball missed the head, but drove into the creature's large body with terrible force, sending it stumbling sideways.

Bang.

Three sets of fangs were on it.

With the creature off balance, Brutus had barrelled into it with all heads snarling, knocking it onto its side. He jumped on its underbelly as it rolled onto its back. He was too close for it to bend its bladed legs and strike.

Crunch.

Powerful jaws bit down, crushing chitin and pulping the meat beneath.

It writhed beneath the cerberus, trying to buck him off.

Theresa loosed two more arrows, cursing as they bounced off its flailing legs. She spotted a large rock and hefted it over her head, jumping onto the spider's tail. Forcing her full weight down, she pressed the creature in place, then crashed the stone into the joints of the chitin.

Holding tightly to his screaming sister, Alex mentally grasped the forceball as it flickered, poured more mana into it to re-energize the spell, then tried to direct it into the beast's soft underbelly. Again, the Mark flooded him with a stream of failures, sapping his concentration. The orb crashed to the earth.

Cursing, he poured more mana to reactivate it, conscious that his reserves were running low. Brutus yelped as a blade scraped his side. His tough hide narrowly saved him from being split open.

"Shit!" Alex cursed again.

He had to do something different. Brutus couldn't fend off those blades forever, Theresa was only *starting* to crack the shell, and the Mark wasn't letting him direct his spell properly. And, if he shot at it like he did the first time, he might hit one of his companions.

Think. Adapt.

Think. Adapt.

A thought occurred to him: The Mark flooded him with failures, but *not* those related to spellcraft.

These had to do with combat.

Think. Adapt.

His eyes narrowed, fixing on the beast's open maw.

What if he didn't *try* to hurt it?

He called the orb from where it rested on the earth, willing it to gently drift around the creature. No flood came. Concentrating, he gradually pushed it closer to the beast's snapping jaws. On reflex, it bit the orb, but its teeth slid off. Alex focused, pushing the ball further into the beast's open mouth.

The clearing darkened as the forceball's red glow slipped into the spider's throat and down its windpipe. No flood came. It began to panic and thrash, silently choking. Alex continued to will the orb deeper until the spell would go no further. Something had stopped the forceball.

Gritting his teeth, he grasped the spell.

The Mark flooded him again, but now, it made no difference.

The orb was inside the monster.

Distractions or not, he couldn't miss.

He drove the forceball into the side of the monster's core, forcing it to ricochet as hard as he could around its insides. He felt the spell slam into organs.

Crunch.

The orb crashed into something that burst.

"*Screeeeeeeee*!" the spider shrieked.

Suddenly, its muffled screams could be heard. Its claws snipped uselessly in the air. Alex smashed his spell until whitish-grey blood poured from its jaws. *Crunch.* Theresa cracked the shell on its tail. She dropped the rock and stabbed her hunting knife into the gap, twisting the blade. Insectile blood sprayed her face and hands.

Its leg movements weakened and Brutus lunged.

Two of his heads seized the beast's armoured shoulders. His middle jaws bit deep into its neck, cutting off its air.

Then he twisted and pulled.

Rrrrrp!

Its throat tore out.

The monster choked and shuddered.

It fell limp beneath the cerberus, in a spreading pool of monstrous blood.

The sound of panting filled the clearing and Alex's heartbeat quieted in his ears. Shouts and cries arose from the fields.

A man's voice yelled from the forest. "Hello! Are you okay? Stay there, I'm comin' for yous!"

"There's monsters in the woods!" someone cried. "Break camp, break camp!"

Groaning, Alex pulled the flickering forceball from the dead creature as Brutus rolled off of it.

"What was that? *What was that*!" Selina sobbed into his shirt.

"I don't know," he wheezed out. "Are you hurt?"

Whimpering, she shook her head into his clothes.

"Were you scared?"

She nodded into his clothes.

"So was I." He stroked her back, looking worriedly toward Theresa. "Are you and Brutus okay?"

She was rushing toward them, pale with worry. "I'm fine!" She knelt beside them. "Are you both alright?"

"Yeah..."

Nodding, she ran over to Brutus and gasped. "It hurt you!"

Theresa cursed and dug into her bag.

As she did, a group crashed into the clearing from behind Alex. Men and women armed with torches and assorted weapons.

"We heard a devil-like racket," a bearded man said cautiously. "Is everyone oka—Uldar's beard!" he gasped, along with several others. "What in all heavens is *that* thing!"

Alex opened his mouth to answer.

"It's a silence-spider," a strong voice named it from the other side of the clearing. "One o' the Ravener's spawn."

All turned to follow the sound.

The brush crashed.

A young man stepped through the undergrowth into the light of fire and the forceball's red glow.

Alex's breath stopped.

The newcomer was about his age and nearly as tall as he was, but corded with the powerful muscles of a warrior. Red hair fell to his shoulders and he gripped a strange spear of shining white metal. Alex's eyes widened. The stranger's other hand held the head of a silence-spider. It looked like it had come from one at least twice the size of the creature that nearly killed them.

He was shirtless, and his chest and arms were covered in blue woad tattoos of knots and spirals. The scent of ancient pines drifted from him.

What drew Alex's horrified eyes, though, was the tattoo on the young man's chest.

It glowed gold: a shining set of scales just above his heart.

The Mark of the Chosen.

The Heroes' leader had walked right into their camp.

He looked directly at Alex and smiled as though he had run into a long-lost brother.

"You got a great gift, friend," he said. "Glad I found you."

Chapter 8

The Chosen

Alex's mind raced, trying to think of a thousand lies while feeling his hopes crumble. Why? How had the Chosen found him? He'd been on the road for *one* day! What were the odds?

Theresa had stilled by her pack, and everything seemed to move at a crawl.

The Chosen stepped toward him, glancing to the red orb floating near Alex.

"Spellcraft's a mighty gift, friend. Something I've laid eyes on only once or twice in all my years. Glad you was here to help these folk out. Silence-spiders're no bloody joke. You some sort of magician?"

"It's the Chosen! We're safe!" someone in the gathering crowd cried before he could respond. Many tried to shuffle forward, shouldering their fellows out of the way to get a better look.

The rest began to murmur.

The stranger smiled again and—now that he was closer to the light—Alex could see that one of his teeth was made of gold.

"Aye, I's the Chosen, that's so." He dropped the spider head with a heavy thump and jerked his head toward Alex. "But it's this friend right here who've you got to thank for all your lives."

He offered him a big, calloused hand. "Little help up, eh?"

Alex hesitated. It seemed he wasn't suspected, but who could know what would happen if they touched. There was no way out of it. Holding his breath and praying for luck, he grasped the other Hero's hand and was hoisted to his feet by a strength that should've belonged to a bull.

A big one.

Thankfully, the Chosen gave no sign he recognized his fellow Hero.

"There ya go, there ya go." He dusted off Alex's dark shirt. "That's the way. Man o' the hour has no business being all mussed up with dirt." He glanced at Selina. "You alright there, wee one?"

The tiny girl was looking up at the red-haired Hero with eyes the size of plates.

"Aaaah, you're fine." He turned and took a step toward Brutus. "But this beastie here's hurt, isn't he?"

"What're you doing?" Theresa shot to her feet.

"Just taking care o' this brave boy." He held up his hands.

The crowd gasped as his shining spear shimmered like quicksilver. It warped, collapsing on itself, and poured over the young man's arm until the limb was sheathed in a metallic sleeve.

The uncovered hand began to shed a blueish-white light. "Thaaat's it, brave boy, I ain't going to hurt you."

He crouched before the growling Brutus and began to pray. "*Oh, Mighty Uldar, I ask you hear the call of your servant and share your divinity with the stout-hearted soul before me. Mend wound and balm suffering, so that this soul might live in health for further days.*"

The light around his hand swelled to a bright incandescence and—when it touched Brutus' wound—the cerberus' flesh began to shine in the same way. It healed over in mere heartbeats.

"Thaaat's it, as good as when you were a pup." The Chosen stood with his hands on his hips as the light faded. Brutus gave him a long look, followed by a dismissive snort before he padded back to Theresa's side.

Alex felt just a *little* smug about that.

"Thank you." Theresa nodded as she checked the cerberus' side.

"Oh bah, no thanks needed. I'd be a pretty shit Chosen if I didn't do this much of my duty. Now's all he needs is a good night's rest and it'll be like the fight never happened. And speaking of rest..."

The tattooed man turned and spread his hands to the crowd. "Right, that's enough of the gawking." He kicked the dead silence-spider. "I just wiped out a swarm o' the beasties coming south from the caves up there. The dungeon's active again."

The crowd gasped.

"Yeah, that's right, but I cut up the first wave all nice n' neat, and it'll take a while for it to make more of the crawlies. I'm thinkin' you leave these poor folk be and get some sleep. You'll want to be off quick. If the priests' talk of how dungeon cores work holds up, you should have a couple days before it gets enough juice to make more. I'd use 'em to get far from here."

Silence fell on the clearing.

"Well, what're you waiting for?" He frowned, waving them off with a silver-sheathed hand. "Winter festival? Go, go, off you go!"

Startling, the travellers thanked the young man and shuffled out of the clearing, throwing nervous glances at the trees. After the last of them left, he looked to Alex's group, raising an eyebrow. "And you lot?"

"You said you wiped out the spiders?" Theresa stepped over to the corpse of the creature, peering at it clinically.

"Aye, though this bugger got away. They've got..." He

scratched his hair. "Ach, the priests I'm with called 'em something."

Alex's ears perked up at the word 'priests.'

"Ah, they've got a kinda organ in them... don't remember the exact name they said, but it makes it so they don't give off either sound or smell. Right creepy, these ones. When they get up in the trees, it makes them devilishly hard to track. That said, this one here's the last. Why d'you ask?"

"Then we should stay in the trees," Theresa said. "I know Coille forest, and if you cleansed it, then we *know* there's no monsters here anymore. We *don't* know that about the fields. Here is safer than whatever might be lurking out there."

"Hah!" The Chosen threw his head back and laughed. "Well, there's a smart and brave one. S'too bad they already found the Champion and Sage." He peered hard at Alex and Theresa. "You two're about the right age and I *know* you've got good heads an' hearts."

Theresa and Alex exchanged a quick glance.

Alex's mind raced. Every instinct was screaming at him to try and get away from this man, but another part of his mind clamped down on his emotions. If he could keep a straight face, this would be a *rare* opportunity to gain information.

"Likewise." Alex rose, hoisting Selina up with him. He focused on keeping his face straight and avoiding using the Mark. He had no idea if *using* it around another Hero would call their attention.

"Say, where—"

"Ach, before we go on, I must've left my manners behind in my village. My mum would have my hide. My name's Cedric of Clan Duncan. What about you, my friends?"

Alex paused. Should he lie? ...No. If it were just Theresa and him maybe, but Selina would get confused. If she asked him why he was lying, it'd all go to hell.

Nothing for it. He didn't want to give his name, but he had

no choice. To get evasive now would just make him look suspicious.

"Alex Roth," he said, projecting every single bit of cheer he did not feel. "And this is my sister, Selina."

"Theresa Lu," the huntress introduced herself cautiously.

"Aye." Cedric grinned, his golden tooth shining. "Fine to meet you all. Now, you was saying, Alex?"

"Where *are* the priests?" Alex asked, fighting the urge to check the trees and hoping they weren't about to come crashing into the clearing.

Cedric paused, then coughed awkwardly. "I, ah, sorta ditched 'em for a time. Fine men and women, all of 'em, but they wanted to drag me to the capital straightaway, even though the Cave of the Traveller is so close to the folk in Alric. It was near our route anyway, so I thought I'd slip away for a bit, hunt anything that already jumped outta the cave, and be back with 'em by sunrise."

Alex frowned. "I thought the whole point of the Heroes *was* to fight monsters. Why didn't they want to let you go?"

"'Cause of weak spines, most like." Cedric rolled his eyes. "Said something about 'a Ravener dungeon being too dangerous for *one* Hero,' but we got a duty, don't we? Least I could do is take a night to clear the forest, then we could come back and finish the dungeon off. Besides, they're taking forever with all that searching under every rock in every town."

"Searching? For the Heroes?" Alex asked carefully.

"Ah, yeah, but don't you worry." Cedric threw himself down on the corpse and picked his teeth. "They got most of us now. Only one left to find's the Fool."

Alex fought to keep his expression neutral. Theresa's face stiffened—might not have noticed it if they didn't know her well—but luckily, Cedric wasn't facing her.

"Well, at least it's *just* the Fool." Alex shrugged. "I mean, the legends say the Heroes don't really even *need* one, right?"

The Chosen's eyes narrowed. "Oi, no matter the Mark, a Hero's a Hero. Whether it's Champion or Fool, each has got a role, duty and purpose. I say we find 'em all. I know the Fool's Mark hasn't got the best history, but I'd protect 'em. Hope to Uldar they're not hiding."

"I'm sure the priests would find them easily enough," Alex probed a little. "Wouldn't they?"

Cedric snorted. "I wish. I was nearly on top of them myself before their holy symbols started singing."

Alex couldn't help his scrunched expression in response. "Singing?"

"Oh, yeah!" The Chosen's laugh rumbled through the clearing. His voice was like warm thunder. "*Actual* singing, if you'd believe it. The damn things sounded like half a choir shoved down their bloody shirts! But they don't work so well unless you're *close*. The Saint's different, they can pick us out from a lot farther off than the priests can, so they said. Anyway, we'll be nipping over to the capital to do all the ceremonies and such, and then—if we don't have all of us by then—we'll need to find wherever the Fool got scared off to and bring 'em with us. All the priesthood's out in force searching. Same with *my* priests... half-escorts, half-hunters."

Alex's heart pounded so loudly, he was certain it echoed through the clearing, yet he still kept his face and voice neutral.

"That's too bad," he said. "You'd be better off getting the Saint into the hunt as fast as you can. If it were me, I'd just bring whatever Heroes together that I'd found and send them hunting with the Saint for any that were missing," Alex pushed a little further. "Meantime, I'd leave the priests at all the ports. Since we're an island, if you cover most of the docks, you'd probably get the Fool easy enough."

"That's what I said!" Cedric slammed his armoured hand onto the silence-spider's corpse. The creature's exoskeleton cracked a little under his strength. "Ah, friend, good to meet someone with sense. But, at least they thought of that last part. They've got priests at outposts all over the coasts. They'll form a ring of Divinity to link aaaaall their holy symbols to make a kinda circle." He formed a circle with his large hands. "It keeps the Ravener's beasts from flying over the waters *and* picks up if any of the Heroes cross the circle."

Alex's blood ran cold, but he managed to keep the smile fixed on his face. "Well, at least you'll find them eventually. They can't sneak away from that."

He definitely couldn't, he added bitterly in his head.

"Well, there's that, yeah. Better to have all of us together earlier than later, I say." Cedric perked up a bit. "You want me to put a word in with my escort? Could see if they'd spare one or two to help your party to a ship. Might get 'em to pay for your passage too. Killing a monster with your wee sister at your side's a deed that deserves reward, I say."

"No, no." Alex held up a hand. "I can't ask that. Duty comes first, right?" He used Cedric's own words. People tended to listen more when one used their own words. "You need all your priests if you have *any* hope of finding the Fool."

Cedric looked a little wounded at the refusal.

"Ach, you're right. Still, feels a little poor to leave you off with nothing, though. But you probably want to be on your way. Your wee sister's been through a lot."

With a grunt, Cedric rose to his feet and grabbed the severed head of the massive silence-spider. "Right, friends! I'd better go find those priests before they think of burning down the forest to search me out. You all sure you'll be fine here?"

"There's no need to worry yourself," Theresa said.

"Right..." Cedric gave them a long look. "Night then, and safe journey."

With a long, languid stretch, the Chosen swept from the clearing and disappeared into the trees. Soon, even the shine of his strange, morphic weapon faded into the night.

They immediately moved camp to another part of the forest. It took a long time and a *lot* of comfort to get Selina to go back to sleep. Alex, meanwhile, was exhausted. The fight had drained him, the forceball sapped most of his mana, and the encounter with the Chosen frayed his nerves.

He and Theresa crouched in front of each other in the dark of the new clearing. The trees ringing seemed to loom over them in the night, and their rustling sounded like beasts in the shadows. Brutus was on his haunches, watching the trunks with six eyes, while Selina snored only a few paces away.

"We're in trouble, Alex," Theresa whispered. "A lot of trouble."

"I know." Alex glanced around. After the night's work and the mana drain, he could barely keep his eyes open.

"What do you think we should do?" Theresa asked.

"Well, I know what I want *you* to do: take Selina and go to the ships."

"What? Why? They'll catch us."

"No, they'd catch *me*." He tapped his shoulder. "*This* is what their circle searched for, not anyone else. You and Selina would just be two more people from Alric getting on a ship."

"Wait, so you're going to stay?" Theresa stiffened. "Alex, if it weren't for Brutus holding that thing down, it would have *killed* us. Did you hear what Cedric said? He fought a *swarm* of those things, and that's what *you'll* be expected to do with the rest of them." Her lips trembled. "You'll *die*."

"Whoa, whoa, whoa." He held up a hand. "Nobody's staying here to go fight swarms of blade-monsters with Cedric or anyone else. At least, *I'm* not."

"Then... you plan on hiding all alone in some wilderness?"

"Not a chance." He looked at her seriously. "I need a way to get to the continent that doesn't cross their circle, right?"

"Right."

"And Cedric said he cleared the forest of that swarm and that it'd take a while for the dungeon to spit out new monsters?"

"Ri—" Her eyes went wide. "Alex, *no.*"

"Alex, yes," he said. "I've thought about it, Theresa. The only way I'm getting out of Thameland is if I head north—" He clenched his fist. "—and find a way through the Cave of the Traveller."

Chapter 9

Telling the Truth

"No, that's *suicide.*" Theresa grabbed his hand.

"Not if our Chosen friend cleared the forest as well as he said he did," Alex insisted. "Think about it. *You* take Selina the safe way, while I slip in there before the core can make more monsters. I don't need to fight anything, I just need to sneak through until I come out somewhere. The Mark can help me sneak; at least it can do that. And if I come out somewhere on the continent, I can make my way to Generasi over land."

"Somewhere?" Theresa shook her head. Her grip tightened. "That's your plan. *Somewhere*? Alex, that could be on the continent, or somewhere in the northern seas, or in a cave to the west, or another dungeon, or the capital, or *right* in front of *the* Ravener for all you know. Besides, one of those spiders would kill you if you're alone."

"I've got no choice and I'm *not* taking Selina in there. That's why you need to take her, Theresa. *Please.*"

"Alex." She shook her head. "You're not thinking this through. What do you think she's going to say when you wake up tomorrow morning and run into the cave with all the horrible monsters?"

"I'll leave tonight."

"You can barely stand." Her grip on his hand was so tight, it hurt. "Your eyes are closing as I'm talking to you. I can't find my way through the forest in the dark even when I'm fresh. You wouldn't stand a chance. And besides, Selina'll wake up and find her brother missing. What am I supposed to tell her?"

His jaw hardened. "That you'll meet me in Generasi City."

"You're the only family she has left. She'll try and follow you. She'll kick and scream. She'll try to sneak away. I know *I* would if I was her."

The young man frowned as Theresa's merciless reasoning piled on.

"*And*," she pushed. "Suppose I get to port without you and run into someone from Alric, maybe even my family. People know you and they're going to wonder what happened to you. They'll talk and then it'll spread around that someone who turned eighteen the day the Heroes were revealed just *disappeared*. You'll put them on your scent."

He grimaced. She was right. Leaving his sister behind didn't mean keeping her safe. That monster had taken Theresa, Brutus' strength *and* his magic to defeat it. If another one came along, he needed to be sure Selina had every bit of protection, including from himself.

"What do you suggest?" he asked.

She glanced down to the sleeping girl. "We make for the cave together. *All* of us. I'll search for some herbs in the morning. I might be able to come up with something for those spiders."

His lips tightened. "Bringing Selina there... If something were to happen to her—"

Her other hand clasped around his. "I won't let it happen, Alex, I swear. She's the closest I've ever had to a sister, and together, we *won't* let anything happen to her."

He stared into her eyes. "...alright. We'll all go to the cave together and check it out. If it seems dangerous, then we'll think of something else. Even if that means I have to make some hard decisions." He drew a deep breath. "Now let's try and get some sleep. I'm dead, and it'll be a long day tomorrow."

Coille Woods gave no sign there was anything amiss.

Sunlight fell between lush tree branches and onto a healthy undergrowth of ferns and wild herbs. Birds trilled above, and a cicada let off a loud, grinding call in the distance. The air was fresh and clean... though Alex thought he detected the scent of blood beneath the forest smells. He wasn't sure if he was imagining it or not.

Brutus padded ahead of him, swiveling his three heads and sniffing the air. He seemed determined to make up for his failure to detect the enemy the night before. Selina was quiet, her tiny hand gripping his tightly.

"Are you sure it's safe this way?" she asked for the tenth time.

"Of course," he told her. "The Chosen made all the monsters go away, so it should be safer this way."

"But... wouldn't going by the road be faster?" Her head whipped back and forth almost as constantly as Brutus'. She drifted closer to her brother's side.

"Maybe, but we don't know if there're more monsters coming out on the road. We'll just go through the forest and come out farther down. Okay?"

She gave him a long look, then nodded. In truth, she probably suspected *something* was wrong, but he'd deal with that later. For now, he just needed to keep her safe. Theresa scouted ahead with an arrow nocked on her bowstring. Sometimes she'd stoop and cut some sort of herb from the undergrowth. Her movements were so practiced that even these pauses took only moments.

As the day wore on, the undergrowth thinned and she took no more plants. Rocks began to dot the forest floor, and the ground started to slope upward. Over time, something began to burn his nostrils.

"Ugh, what's that stink?" Selina asked. "It's like rotting frogs."

"I get the feeling we'll find out soon enough." Through the trees, he spied a massive hill rising from the earth and reasoned they might be getting close.

Theresa raised a hand, signalling them to a halt. She crouched in the undergrowth and crawled forward, peering up the hill. Eventually, she waved them toward her.

"We're here," she said as they drew up beside her.

Alex peered through the trees.

'Here,' as it turned out, was the bottom of a lonely hill in the middle of the woods. It was ancient—like most hills were—and covered in sparse patches of undergrowth like a balding man's last few hairs. From its centre, a massive cave mouth yawned wide.

Both Roth siblings gasped.

This had been a place of recent violence.

Animal bones were scattered across the sandy rise just below the cave. The bones had been picked clean. Even from their distance, he could see the impressions of massive tooth marks etched into many.

The owners of those teeth were shattered all over the sand.

Cedric had obviously passed through here on his rampage. Silence-spiders lay everywhere. Some had carapaces crushed by massive blows, others had heads pierced through by stabbing weapons. More had been blackened by massive fire-blasts, the earth scorched with them. The scent of ash, rotting meat and something else filled the air.

"Look at the *size* of that one." He pointed to a massive beast. The headless corpse dwarfed the others, and he doubted his own head would even have reached its shoulder. Its claws looked able to snip a small tree trunk in half.

"At least they're all dead." Theresa squinted at the cavern.

It was difficult to believe this place had become a spawning ground for the Ravener. Without the bodies, it looked to be no more than a common forest cave.

"There's lots of tracks all over the place," she continued. "But... it doesn't look like there's fresh ones. Look at the blood and ash, there's no prints in them. Nothing's walked there that I can see. Brutus?"

The cerberus sniffed the air, pointing his three snouts in different directions. He gave no sign that he smelled anything out of place. Then again, what had dwelled here were creatures that gave no sound or scent while they lived, so one couldn't be sure. Not completely.

"W-why are we here?" Selina had pressed herself so tightly to her brother's side it was like she was trying to hide beneath his cloak. "I don't like this place. Where are we?"

Her wide green eyes searched his for answers. He considered what he should do. On the one hand, he wasn't sure how she would react if he told her now. Not only did he have the *worst* of the Heroes' Marks, but he was also *fleeing* the kingdom. Some would charitably call it 'deserting his duty.' Would she think that? Would she grab his hand so that he could join the other Heroes, excited that her big brother was one of the people she made figures of?

Or would she be disappointed that he ended up with the Fool? Would she sulk?

He steeled himself. It was time to tell her, no way around it. Before, when it looked like they could slip quietly onto a ship, it would have been fine to wait until they were out of Thameland altogether. Even though she might still have reacted badly, at least they would have already been in the clear.

Now, on the doorstep of an active dungeon, it would be too

dangerous and unfair to keep her in the dark. Growing suspicions had a habit of making people act in unpredictable ways, and she needed to be close and safe.

"Selina," he began, dropping down to one knee and facing her at eye level.

"Y-yes, Alex?" Her grip tightened on his cloak.

He hesitated. This time, he tried to focus the Mark on 'telling little girls bad news.' Unfortunately, nothing came back. Even if that was a skill, he had no successful memories to draw from. Typical.

"You know my birthday was yesterday, right?"

"Yeah..."

"Well." He took a deep breath. "You know how we left early, before the rest of Theresa's family?"

"Yeah."

"It's because." He searched for the right words. "Well, it's because your big brother discovered something on the night before last that's dangerous."

"Dangerous?" Her lips quivered. "You're not going away, are you?"

"No, but some people might want me to go away from you. And I'd be going somewhere dangerous..." His words trailed off.

Selina's head lowered more and more and her entire body trembled. Though her mop of brown hair had fallen to hide her chubby face, he knew she was fighting back tears.

"Y-You," she stammered. "Did you get the Fool's Mark?"

He bit the inside of his cheek. "Yeah, that's right."

They fell silent, though he could hear Theresa's breathing and Brutus' panting behind him.

"I thought something was funny," Selina said. "You were acting weird when we were walking on the road. And... when you were talking to Cedric, your hands started shaking."

Alex blinked in surprise. He hadn't even noticed.

"And then you and Theresa were whispering last night."

His eyebrows rose. "You were awake?"

She nodded. "But... how can you be the Fool?" Her face shot up. Her chubby cheeks had washed red while tears and snot ran from her eyes and nose. "You can use magic! I saw it! You *can't* be the Fool!" She started to sob. "M-my teacher said the Fool can't use magic. S-she said the Fool dies most of the time!"

"Hey, hey." Theresa scooted up beside Alex. "Remember what Mr. Cedric said? Did *he* think the Fool was useless?"

"N-no," Selina sniffed. "But he said he has to protect the Fool or he'll get hurt. Alex, don't go!" She jumped into his chest, clinging to his shirt. "Don't go, don't go away, please. It... I don't want it to be like Mum and Dad."

Alex grimaced. *That* stung.

"I'm not leaving you, Selina." He wrapped her in a tight hug. "We're going to the big wizard city together, and I'm going to buy us someplace to live, and you're going to go to the *best* school, and see all the sights there, and *nobody* is dying. Okay?"

She sniffed. "Promise?"

"I promise."

Selina sobbed quietly against his chest.

"Good. Now, if we're going to go together, you have to be very brave, okay?" He pointed to the cave. "Do you remember the 'Cave of the Traveller' from school?"

She nodded. "P-people go in and then come out in different places. My teacher said we should never go there, or even play near it."

"That's right. She's right, and you shouldn't go into the forest by yourself." He patted her back. "But we're going to use that to get out of the kingdom, and we're only going because Mr. Cedric got rid of all the monsters that were in the forest. But, we'll only go in if you want to. If you can't, or if you don't want to, then we'll turn right around and find another way. How's that?"

Selina swallowed, pulling away from Alex and giving the cave a long, fearful look. "L-let's go."

Theresa smiled at her and her entire face softened. "That's a brave, brave, brave girl." She reached past Alex's shoulder to pat Selina on the head. "Don't worry, I'll protect us. And Brutus will too."

The cerberus looked over with one of his heads. Theresa smiled and scratched him behind an ear. Alex chuckled. She was taming both beasts and children at once.

"And I can pull my own weight." He flexed his skinny muscles and posed in front of Selina. "I'm a mighty magic-user, after all!"

Despite herself, a small smile started to form on the little girl's lips.

"Alright, here's the plan." Theresa opened her sack of herbs and drew out a strange plant with leaves that were silvery underneath. "Wormwood."

"Bug repellant?" Alex raised an eyebrow. "You think it'll work on those monsters?"

She shrugged. "They *looked* like bugs... I think it's worth a try, and they're going to smell us anyway. We might as well use what we can."

"Wait, isn't that also called stinkweed?"

"Yeah."

"Isn't it called stinkweed for a reason? Y'know... because it stinks?"

Theresa gave him a look. "How much do you think the inside of those spiders' bellies stink?"

"Well, Cedric said they had an organ that made it so you couldn't smell them, so maybe—"

Her eyes grew icier with every word.

He winced. "Yeah, okay, bring on the stinkweed."

She drew out a mortar and pestle. "I'll crush the leaves and add water to make a juice we can rub over our skin and clothes."

She drew an empty waterskin from her pack. "We'll put the rest in here and we'll need to reapply it every hour or so." Her eyes flicked back toward the cave mouth.

The opening was quiet and unassuming, but the darkness ran deep.

"Hopefully, we won't be in there very long."

Alex gave the cave a long look. "With the Traveller's magic in it? Who knows. I just hope that it's *empty*."

They stood in silence for a few breaths.

"Right, let's get started. I'll help grind the herbs. We'll need all the juice we can get." He stood up. "After that, let's hope our luck holds out."

Wormwood stank, Alex confirmed. A *lot*. 'Stinkwood' was a perfect name.

As he wrinkled his nose, he wondered if that was the reason insects stayed away from it. Brutus had sneezed from all three snouts too many times to count as Theresa had coated him in it, while Selina's face scrunched up like a tiny, miserable dried cranberry.

Even his forceball seemed to be shying away from him, though he was sure *that* impression was all in his imagination.

Probably.

"Done," Theresa said as she finished rubbing the smelly stuff over herself. She put the rest of the juice into a small spouted pot and poured it into the empty waterskin. Alex had used the forceball and memories from the Mark's guidance to help crush the plants into a juicy paste before they'd combined it with water.

Theresa checked herself over, making sure her arrows were straight and her great-grandfather's sword was loose in its sheath. Its steel gleamed as she drew it partway, then slid it back.

"Your parents aren't going to like that you took that," Alex noted.

"If it keeps me alive, and I tell them that's what Great-grandfather would have wanted, I'm sure they'll let me live. If it doesn't keep me alive, then I won't care either way. You ready?"

He adjusted his pack and checked over the magic circuit one final time. It was strong and stable. It had only taken him a couple of tries to form the circuit this time. Good. He was starting to get used to the Mark's interference. *Starting* to. Hopefully, he would get even better with time.

"Ready." He glanced down to Selina. "And you, little goblin?"

Selina raised her scrunched-up little face and eyed the cave ahead as though it were a live beast ready to gobble her up. "I-I'm ready."

Wow. He doubted he'd been half as brave at that age.

He took her hand in his own. "Then, no sense giving the core more time. Let's see what we'll see."

Together, with Brutus taking the lead, they stepped toward the darkness awaiting inside the Cave of the Traveller.

Chapter 10

Red Eyes in the Dark

The hair on the back of Alex's neck rose, and his heartbeat pounded like a blacksmith's hammer in his chest.

Darkness filled the tunnel. Only the red glow of his forceball lit the way. Brutus padded in front, sniffing and scanning the dark with all six eyes. One of his heads turned back, making sure his companions were close and safe. His canine eyes flashed, and Alex was reminded of the old folk stories of cerberi being born from the netherworld long ago. He was glad Brutus was on their side.

The stench of the slaughter outside faded the farther they slipped into the tunnel, replaced by the rich scent of wet earth. From somewhere ahead, water dripped onto stone.

Alex and Selina marched in the middle of their little formation, while Theresa took up the rear with a small lantern burning at her belt. It cast less light than his forceball, but if anything 'popped' the magical sphere, at least they wouldn't be left blind and without a back-up. Alex swept his spell through the cave. Its crimson light shone over the walls, ceiling and sloping, rocky floor. After their encounter with that silent monster, he wanted there to be no risk of them walking below one while it clung to the stone above their heads.

Each of the group crept as quietly as they could, with the Mark feeding him a constant stream of memories. To his dismay, it kept focusing on two memories from when he was little: one where he'd covertly searched for his father's paring knife and another where he'd tried to find a batch of cookies his mother had hidden from her 'greedy son.'

The Mark made both memories crystal clear. It had been a long time since he'd seen his parents so distinctly. Forcing himself away from those thoughts, his legs matched the same stealthy movements he'd made then. Theresa and Brutus stalked with the grace of predators while Selina tried her best. She was so small that the only sound from her was her frightened breath. His sister's hand gripped his, and he made sure to keep her close. If they were attacked, then he'd do everything to protect her.

He just hoped it wouldn't come down to a fight.

If silence-spiders were anything like ants—and they seemed to move in a group like ants, judging by the small army outside—then workers should have already cleaned up their dead swarm-mates from last night. That meant Cedric likely had guessed right, and the dungeon's core would need time to replenish its fighters.

If it were *him*, though, he would have held some fighters in reserve, waiting quietly for the attack to pass while also guarding the core. Then—when the threat seemed to have passed—he'd release them into the tunnel. Alex shuddered at the thought, forcing away images of wolf-toothed spiders with reaching claws waiting in the dark. Hopefully, they'd find whatever magic transported people out of the cave quickly, and never have to find out.

"Wait," he whispered to Theresa, pointing up.

She followed his gaze and frowned.

His forceball was illuminating a tunnel in the ceiling about ten or twelve feet above their heads. It was nearly hidden in the natural bends and formations of the rock, but the bright light from his spell revealed it.

Theresa stepped up beside him, drew back her bowstring, and pointed an arrow at the tunnel overhead. Alex floated the forceball up higher, illuminating the darkness. Crimson light receded into the passage, shining on fang and sword-like marks where the spiders had cut through the stone. None of the creatures lay in wait, but he noticed the ceiling-tunnel turned in a different direction.

They watched for a few moments—in case one suddenly appeared and attacked the forceball from the side—but nothing emerged. Theresa and Alex exchanged a look, and sighed with relief.

"Let's hope it stays this way," she whispered, relaxing her bowstring. "Maybe we can—wait, Brutus. What do you have there? *Drop it.*"

The cerberus had dipped one of his heads and chomped on something from the cave floor, but obeyed and dropped it.

Clatter.

It made a noise like a bundle of cracking sticks. While Alex watched both ends of the passage, Theresa bent down to pick it up.

"Uldar's *beard*," she swore, drawing back as if a snake had bitten her.

"What? What is it? Is it—" Selina whimpered.

"Shhhh, it's okay, it's okay, stay over there, Selina." Theresa moved beside the small girl. "Close your eyes for a little bit, okay?"

"Okay..." Selina shut her eyes tight.

Theresa looked to Alex. "Go take a look."

Steeling himself, he bent over what she had been looking at and gasped; the stench of rotten meat hit his nostrils.

It was a hand.

Brutus found a human hand on the cave floor. Most of the

flesh had been stripped away, leaving mainly bone behind. Enwrapping the tattered remains of the index finger was a plain iron ring with a symbol of two crossed pick-axes.

"Delvers' Guild. Ugh, poor bugger." Alex shook his head. "Right below that ceiling-tunnel." He brought his forceball lower to shine across the rough floor. It illuminated a large, dark stain. "I think it got him from above."

"*What* got what?" Selina whispered.

"Brutus found something, but it's nothing for you to worry about, little goblin," he reassured her, shining the light closer to the finger bones. He noted tiny chips gouged from their surface. "Theresa, look at this. What do you think of these marks?"

The huntress covered Selina's ears then peered over Alex's shoulder. "Teeth. Small ones. They were probably fairly sharp and strong, almost like needles. Hmmm, then again, none of the bones are broken... Maybe the jaws might not be *too* strong."

They looked at each other. Alex knew the same thought was passing between them: whatever stripped the flesh from this hand was too small to have been one of the silence-spiders.

There must have been some other creatures lurking in the dungeon.

He thought back on ants, remembering seeing two different sizes of them when he'd watched an ant hill as a child. Workers and soldiers, his teacher had called them. Mr. Lu just called them pests. Maybe the big spiders that swarmed outside were soldiers, while the workers stayed behind in the cave somewhere. Still, judging from the tiny tooth marks, whatever left them was dangerous enough even if they were just workers.

Either way, 'here, there be monsters,' and that was not good. Alex shared his theory with Theresa.

"We go a little bit farther," he proposed. "If we see *anything*, we leave."

She glanced down to Selina, removing her hands from the little girl's ears, and nodded. "You can open your eyes now."

Moving along, the group ranged farther into the dark.

The minutes passed as they trekked deeper beneath the earth, and—though they found more tunnels in the ceiling and walls—they saw no more body parts nor signs of any potential workers. All began to fall quiet.

Then the temperature began to shift. Some parts would be cool, then warm, then cool again. A little farther in, it started to swing wildly.

Near some of the side tunnels, it would be as hot as a peak summer's day at noon. From another tunnel, a wind blew as cold as mid-winter. Sometimes the air smelled stale. Other times, clean and fresh, or there'd be a tang of salt to it.

Sounds echoed through the walls. High wind. Bird song. The deep rumble of water moving in a tide. He and Theresa exchanged a glance. Selina grasped his hand tighter.

And then Brutus stopped.

The cerberus bent two heads toward the ground, sniffing, while the third eyed the tunnel ahead.

"What th—" Alex brought his forceball down toward the floor.

Just ahead of Brutus' feet, the rough cave floor abruptly ended. Instead, chipped and worn marble tile reached as far as his light extended and beyond.

"Alex, there's another light up there," Theresa said.

He glanced up. In the distance, some of the stone was more visible. It was dim, but there was definitely a light source ahead. He tried to quiet his pounding heart.

"Right," he said, sounding calmer than he actually felt. "I'll send the forceball up. If it pops, then we get the hell out of here, alright?"

"Sounds good to me," Theresa agreed, scanning the tunnel behind them with her lantern.

Willing his spell forward, the crimson light glided down the tunnel until it reached the brighter area. It bumped into a corner then headed toward a slight bend to the left in the passage. It glided along for a count of ten, with its magic circuit still firing within him.

"Nothing's happened to it." He started calling it back.

"Forward march." Theresa swept her lantern up toward the ceiling, just in case. In the flickering light, she still wore her deathstalker face, but fear was buried in her eyes. At least he wasn't the only one. He remembered Cedric and wondered how the Chosen seemed so calm knowing he'd be doing things like this every day. Even this short time in the cave made him want to sprint for his life back into Coille forest.

He looked down to Selina, who was trembling next to him. Well, if little girls were brave enough to keep going, then he supposed he could manage too. Even *if* there might be a big, horrible spider waiting for them with some sort of tricky magic light.

Of all the things he'd expected, a *temple* wasn't one of them.

The passage walls turned smooth as they rounded the bend, and the floor changed from rough and chipped smaller tiles, to far larger, unmarred ones. Some twenty paces around the corner, the tunnel opened into a massive chamber.

They stopped at the entrance and stared inside, awestruck.

Large tiles spread across the entire floor of the temple like a colossal chessboard, with each broad enough for Brutus to stand on comfortably. They extended to the opposite end of the chamber where two statues rose, maybe twenty feet high. Each was carved in the likeness of some sort of snarling goddess, their mouths bristling with pointed teeth. Or perhaps they were demons. They looked an awful lot like demons.

The statues' eyes were red rubies that glowed with an inner light, sending a chill down Alex's spine. He could swear before

Uldar himself they were watching him. Strange writing marked the statues' bases, but Alex had no clue as to what it might say.

A pair of massive doors stood between the goddesses on the far wall, stretching up to a soaring ceiling. An equally massive lock sealed them shut.

His eyes were drawn to the light source they had seen from the tunnel. About twenty feet in the air, a doorway floated in the middle of the room. Through it, the sun shone bright, surrounded by blue and nothing else. A cool breeze blew from it, filling the room with fresh air.

The sky. It was a portal to the sky, and the first true sign of the Traveller's magic they'd found. For a brief time, his earlier fears lessened, replaced by complete awe. This was magic, true, ancient magic. And he fell a little in love with it.

"Awesome," he couldn't help but murmur. "So that explains why we kept hearing wind, and why it kept getting hot and cold. You see that, Selina, Theresa?" He scanned the temple one more time. "Maybe that's how this whole temple got here. Maybe it came from somewhere far away and melded into the dungeon. I doubt the *spiders* built it."

"Wooow," his little sister muttered, her eyes growing in wonder at the portal. "It's so pretty."

"It is..." Theresa agreed, but the little smile touching her lips faded when her eyes flicked to the side. "Look at that." She pointed to the walls.

Puncturing and chipping marred the stone, as though blades had bitten into it. It must've been from the spiders' bladed legs, coming out from multiple tunnels lining the ceiling and walls. Alex grimaced. There were so many passages, it felt like an insectile town square. He shuddered at how many monsters must have regularly passed through this place. Just the thought of a mass of silence-spiders crawling over each other across the ceiling and walls made his skin creep.

His eyes narrowed.

"Wait a minute." He looked at the tracks above, then glanced to the floor tiles. Some near the portal looked stained, like from rain drops.

"What's wrong?" Theresa asked, while Selina stiffened with a quiet whimper.

He brought his forceball out to the tunnel, noting that the spider's tracks extended behind them into the passage. When he brought it down to the floor, he noticed more of the bladed prints marked *those* floor tiles. They were chipped. Yet, when he looked back into the temple chamber…

"Look at the floor in there." He pointed. "It doesn't look like the spiders walk across it. There're tracks all through the walls and ceiling, but I don't see any sign of them touching the floor tiles. There's no chipping from their blade-legs on the stone."

Theresa's eyes narrowed. "Why wouldn't they walk on that floor?"

He studied the temple tiles. The ones just comfortably large enough for two or so people to stand on. He glanced back up to the goddess' ruby eyes. That spine-tingling feeling swept through him again.

A thought began to form in his mind, and he closely scrutinized each tile. Each one was nearly perfectly square and symmetrical. Some appeared faded from the passage of time. They were a whitish-grey, varying in shade.

Others, though…

He leaned forward, *very* careful not to step into the room, and peered at one with a faded black mark staining it, lightened enough to almost blend with the stone's colour. His teeth ground. He knew the sight well from the wreckage of his parents' alehouse.

The stone had been burned.

Alex called his forceball forward. "Selina, Theresa, Brutus. C'mon, there's something I need to try."

Chapter 11

The Goddesses' Wrath

Alex, Selina, and Theresa crouched in the tunnel some ten paces back from the entrance to the temple. Brutus sat on his haunches beside them; two of his heads pointed toward either end of the passage.

"I think it's some sort of trap," Alex said. "I don't know if it came from the dungeon or from wherever the temple was—"

"Wherever the temple was?" Selina asked.

"Yeah." Her brother pointed to the statues. "They don't look like they're from Thameland to me—not with that writing on the bases—and we've heard of people walking into the Cave of the Traveller and coming out other places, right? Well, what if that worked both ways? What if it pulled things *in* as well? This temple *could* be something made by the dungeon core, or something that got pulled in and integrated into the rest of the cave. I don't know. Either way, I think *something* happens if you walk on those tiles."

"Something like what?" Theresa peered ahead, thumbing the pommel of her great-grandfather's sword.

"I'm not sure, but we're about to find out. Let's just say that there's probably a *very* good reason the spiders avoid walking on those tiles." Alex willed the forceball to float through the air and hover above the burn-stained tile in the temple. "Get ready to run if... well, if we're about to get blasted into teeny, tiny pieces."

"*Alex*," Theresa whispered harshly, slapping his shoulder. "That's not funny."

"I know." He slapped her shoulder back. "That's why we'll be *running*."

"It's still not funny. You're scaring your sister." She slapped his shoulder again.

"It's a little hilarious, and *you're* scaring *me*." He slapped her shoulder once more.

"If you keep doing that, those big spiders will come." Selina stared at them.

Alex and Theresa immediately shut up.

Concentrating, the young mage glanced from the burnt tile and up to the statues' eyes. He had a bad feeling he knew what might be coming. "Alright, get ready."

Both Theresa and Selina tensed.

His will grasped the forceball and drove it into the tile below.

Bang.

They yelped, expecting the world to explode. The sound echoed through the tunnel, blending with the other strange sounds coming from the distance.

Nothing happened.

"Let me try again." Concentrating, he raised the forceball into the air until it was halfway to the temple's ceiling, and held it there for a breath. Then, he accelerated it toward the floor, crashing it against the tile like a stomping footfall.

BANG!

The tile echoed from impact.

WhooooOOOOM.

The goddess' eyes flared bright red.

"Oh shit! Ru—"

Before he could finish, they fired.

Red beams blasted from the rubies and struck the floor near the base of each statue.

Where each ray touched the temple tile, a massive column of flame crackled into the air. The beams traced across the floor, leaving massive lines of fire as they went, and blasted into the forceball.

It snuffed out.

Selina screamed, pushing her face into Alex's side. He felt like there was a brick of ice in his chest as he watched the flame. When the beams died, fire crackled before winking out and lines of sorcerous smoke rose in their wake.

Soon the smoke dissipated from the portal's breeze; silence filled the passage.

"If... we had stepped out there..." Alex murmured.

"Teeny, tiny pieces," Theresa gulped, her face very pale.

"I-is it gone?" Selina peeked from behind her brother's cloak.

"Yeah, it's gone." He stroked her back, looking at the goddess' eyes while his mind worked. Crossing the floor would mean instant death... or would it? Noting that some of the stones had fewer dark marks than others, he started to recast his forceball.

Theresa began to creep forward. "That made a *lot* of noise. I'll go check and see if anything comes out of those wall tunnels to investigate."

He grew nervous. "Maybe going over there alone isn't a good idea."

"It's only ten paces, Alex." She gave him a reassuring look. "If I see anything, I'll be back before they know I was ever there."

He winced. In every story he'd ever heard travelling bards tell, anyone who said something like that was soon torn to shreds and in some monster's stomach.

He shook the thought away as Theresa told Brutus to stay,

and moved to the opening of the temple. She crouched down, scanning the walls.

All he could do was finish his experiment. His mind had already started conjuring sounds of spider legs creeping up behind them. Of course, the terrifying part was that, if they came, they wouldn't make a single noise. He shuddered and looked back to Theresa at the mouth of the passage by herself.

He needed to get on with it.

Unfortunately, the Mark had other ideas.

It ruined his first casting by bringing up a memory of misaligning a magic circuit a few years earlier, nearly causing the mana to reverse. The backward flow could have made him explode, had he not cut the circuit. His second try fell apart at an image of practicing in the woods, when he'd poured in too much mana. The forceball *had* exploded—nearly ripping his face off—while the magic circuit overloaded and sent mana rampaging through his body. It'd left him on the ground covered in his own tears and bruises, with the scent of his own singed hair stinging his nose. He'd explained it away to Mrs. Lu by telling her he'd taken a bad fall while running through the woods. It had taken a lot of washing in a pond to get the burnt hair stink off of him.

He grimaced, fighting panic as mana surged up in the same way now, and he cut the flow in time. He was panting as it dissipated, while Selina watched him with eyes as wide as saucers.

"Alex? A-are you okay?"

"Yeah..." He tried to catch his breath and ignore the cold sweat covering his skin. "Yeah, I'm okay. Just... give me a second."

His mind began to work.

He was scared. The sensation was firm in his chest, and that made *anything* harder, let alone spellcasting. Understandable, since he *was* in a monster den trying to work magic. But when nerves combined with the Mark's interference... well, shit, it was lucky he hadn't blown his own head off.

Closing his eyes, he slowed his thoughts.

Taking a deep breath, he endured his nerves but disengaged from them, letting go of any images of danger.

Slow and steady. Slow and steady. Slow and Steady.

The best he could do for Theresa was do this properly, and he and Selina had Brutus for protection. Fear finally released his mind and he began to recast the spell. As expected, the Mark shoved the memory of the forceball exploding into his mind again, and this time, he noted the exact details of that particular failure and avoided them.

A new forceball winked into life.

"Yay, you did it," Selina whispered.

"I did." He smiled, wiping the sweat from his brow. He maybe had two more forceballs in him for the day before his mana would drain and his lifeforce would start to weaken.

He'd best make this one count.

Sending the crimson orb forward, he gently tapped Theresa on the back with it to get her attention.

"Are you ready?" she whispered across the passage, taking care not to shift her eyes from the wall tunnels.

"Yeah, come back."

She rose and backed her way to the safe spot through the tunnel. As she crouched close again, relief washed over him. Alex aimed his forceball at one of the first temple tiles at the mouth of the temple—it didn't bear any burn marks.

Bang!

Bang!

BANG!

The sphere wouldn't trigger the stone goddess' wrath no matter how hard he drove it into the floor. He shifted the spell deeper into the room, holding it above the tile in front of the first he'd tested. It didn't have that slightly burnt, discoloured look from what he could see.

BANG!

No death-beams.

He shifted the spell again until it hovered above the tile he'd struck earlier. The one that triggered the trap.

"What're you doing?" Theresa asked.

"I'm going to test if the beams aim at the tiles, or at whatever triggered them. If we're going to cross that floor, we'd better know *every*thing we can. We're only going to get one try at this."

"Alright..." Theresa continued to thumb the pommel of her great-grandfather's sword. "Do what you need to, but do it fast. I didn't see anything come out of those tunnels in the temple, so either everything in here's dead, busy or..." She glanced nervously back along the passage. "Flanking us like wolves."

Alex imagined hundreds of little spiders silently creeping up behind them on tiny dagger-legs. He tried to remain calm, pushing away the thought of hundreds of needle-like teeth. "Okay, I'll hurry."

He raised the forceball above the trap-tile, this time measuring the distance between it and the portal hovering in the centre of the room. He slammed the spell into the floor—

BANG!

WhooooOOOOM.

—and immediately shot the ball behind the portal.

Fire-beams lanced from the goddesses' ruby eyes, directly toward the forceball. Their rays dove into the portal and disappeared, leaving the hidden sphere unharmed. For a count of ten, they poured through the portal in the spell's direction until they flickered and faded to a silent glow. For a few heartbeats, the portal's breeze turned hot before cooling once more.

Alex hoped there weren't any birds flying on the other side of the portal.

"Okay, here's the plan." Theresa and Selina tore their eyes away from the statues. "I'll use the forceball to feel out a safe path across the tiles. Once we have one, we can cross—"

Clack.

Tile struck stone just behind them.

Everyone whirled.

A fox-sized silence-spider had partially emerged from a tunnel hidden *beneath* one of the passage tiles. It was just behind Alex, and out of Brutus' line of sight.

Its dagger-like claws were poised to hamstring him, but the monster recoiled as it got close. Maybe the stink of wormwood repelled it. The tile it crawled from had fallen over, clattering to the floor as it jerked back.

Alex scrambled away. The spider recovered and struck out, drawing a gash through the side of his calf.

"Argh!" he cried, hot pain lancing through his leg.

Theresa sprang at the monster, slamming the pommel of her great-grandfather's sword into its back. *Crack.* Its shell crunched like a boiled crayfish, spilling insect innards over the floor. A raw stench escaped its body. She shifted her attention, focusing on its head, and repeatedly smashed the sword's pommel into its skull. The spider collapsed, twitching.

It spasmed, screeching on the floor.

Clack-clack-clack-clack-clack-clack-clack.

Dozens of small spiders surfaced, scrambling from beneath tiles around them like they were heeding a call.

"Shit!" Theresa swore. "Run! Back down the tunnel!"

Alex looked as a horde of spiders emerged from the tiles down the passage, blocking their escape. The creatures slid their largest blades along each other, like they were sharpening them.

"No! Into the temple!" He scrambled up, ignoring the pain in his calf and the wetness against his pant leg. "Maybe they won't chance the floor there!"

With a thunderous bark, Brutus charged ahead. The worker spiders' legs flailed silently as he shoved them aside, but their glancing cuts couldn't pierce the cerberus's tough hide. Theresa swept with her sword, knocking them away, and Alex scooped up the screaming Selina.

They rushed through the spider swarm, running to the temple as more emerged.

"Brutus! Go to the second tile the red ball hit and stay! *Stay there*!" Theresa shouted, pointing.

The cerberus barked and bounded onto the first tile, then over to the second, waiting for them and growling as they leapt after him. Alex landed, struggling to regain his footing as he clung to Selina. Theresa followed and both of them tried to balance on the first tile.

"They'll follow us!" Theresa shouted, whirling toward the passage. "They'll see this one is safe!"

Alex's blood ran cold.

The swarm poured down the tunnel in eerie silence, their claws and teeth gleaming.

She was right. He glanced into the rest of the temple, but there would be no way to figure out what tiles were safe before they were overrun. Then there was the locked door at the back of the temple...

He forced his panic down. He couldn't afford it now.

Think. Adapt. Think. Adapt.

He glanced to the forceball.

Think. Adapt.

He looked at the goddess' glowing eyes.

"Theresa, Brutus!" he shouted, moving his spell over the trap-tile. "Get down!"

"What're you—"

He pulled her down and held Selina close.

He drove the forceball downward.

BANG!

The spiders scuttled toward the end of the passage, prepared to leap on the intruders.

WhooooOOOOM.

The goddess' eyes flared.

Chapter 12

The Traveller's Magic

Alex shot his forceball back—willing it to stop just before the spider swarm—then commanded it to rapidly circle the end of the passage just above the walls, ceiling and floor. He didn't hit any of the spiders, but he wasn't *aiming* for them. The Mark didn't interfere, not registering what he was doing as combat.

The spiders also ignored the spell and tensed to leap on their prey.

The goddesses fired.

Four beams shot across the temple, spitting heat, and slammed into the walls of the passage. All four chased after the ball as it rapidly circled, lancing into the stone of the tunnel.

Boom.

The passage filled with columns of flame.

Alex, Theresa and Selina screamed as they flattened themselves into the tile while a wall of heat whipped around.

Then came the pops.

The worker spiders screeched as their insides fried, exploding inside the tunnel like boiling eggs bursting in a pot. Heat built as the beams chased the forceball, racing along the sides of the tunnel. Alex's eyes stung from it.

His mind flashed back to watching his home burn. Heat stinging his eyes as he fought to slip through Mr. Lu's grasp and reach his parents. And the smell. The odour of burning silence-spiders mixed with that scent from his memories. The scent of... of... He shoved it from his mind, forcing his concentration into the spell until, at last, the goddess' eyes ceased.

After that, their own quiet breaths filled the temple, and the only heat was the warmth of his trembling sister between him and Theresa. His arms were around them both, while Theresa clutched him and Selina so tightly, they could barely breathe.

The passage had burned black and many of the tiles crumbled into the hidden spider tunnels from the blasts of flame-magic. The stone of the walls had cracked. Sizzling ash—all that remained of the swarm—coated the floor, and pieces of bladed legs folded over themselves in death. The stench of seared arachnids filled the air.

Cool air from the portal began dissipating the odour and smoke.

Aside from the twitch of burnt claw and the whine of steam escaping from burst shells, no sign of movement came from the passage. Alex drew his forceball back over the trap-tile, ready to blast again if anything moved. Heartbeats passed with no sign of any creatures emerging. Either they were all dead or the blast had scared them off. He hoped for the former, but he'd take anything that wasn't swarming them en masse to open their insides.

"I think..." He slowly raised himself up. "I think they're gone."

Despite him rising to his knees, Selina was still pressed against him like a baby bird to its mother. Theresa rose with him too, their arms clutching each other harder than before. All three trembled.

A low whine made him turn. Brutus was shaking, pressed to the tile and burying all three of his heads beneath his paws. Not for the first time, Alex was glad the big dog was so smart.

'I guess it helps to have three heads and three brains. Three really smart dog brains.'

"It's okay, boy," Theresa said quietly, turning her face from being buried in Alex's side. "You're okay. We're okay."

She almost seemed to be telling herself that as she disentangled from Alex and Selina, reaching out to the cerberus. Brutus crawled to their tile on his belly and stuck his leftmost head beneath his mistress' hand. She sighed as she petted him, and Alex felt Selina shift, peeking at Brutus. She crawled to the edge of the tile and reached her little hand out to pet his rightmost head.

"Good boy, Brutus." She stroked him.

Alex, without thinking, put his palm on Brutus' middle head, then froze as he thought the dog would snap at him. The cerberus remained quiet and even pressed his head into Alex's palm. Eager to act before Brutus remembered he didn't like him, he petted him while focusing on getting as much as he could.

The Mark flooded his mind with all the times he'd pet his neighbours' animals, reminding him of which movements made them happiest and which spots made their eyes close in delight.

Guided by the Mark, he found scritches on a particular spot behind the ears the best, and he gave the cerberus the best damn scritches he could, smiling as his head pushed and rubbed against his hand.

He supposed that was *another* advantage to three heads. Three sets of head-pats at the same time. Cerberi really had it all figured out, hadn't they? At least this one did.

"Good boy, Brutus," Alex echoed his sister and best friend. "Goood boy. Best boy, even. Better than all the other boys."

Theresa burst into low laughter that turned into a snort. "You're such a dork, Alex."

"Says the one who just snorted."

"No I didn't."

"Yes you did."

"You're both dorks," Selina said without pausing petting Brutus.

"Yeah... yeah, you're probably right. Agh!" Alex grunted.

Theresa looked to him sharply. "What's wrong?"

The adrenaline draining from his body made the searing pain rise up in his leg. "One of them got me." He grimaced.

The colour drained from her face.

"Alex!" Selina started to spin around, but Theresa caught her arm. The huntress pointed to the trap tiles around them.

"Stay still, Selina; we don't want to set off the statues," she said, patting the girl's shoulder. "Where is it?"

"My right leg."

Careful not to touch the surrounding tiles, Theresa peered at the cut on his leg. He winced as she gently examined the wound.

She let out a sigh of relief. "It's shallow. No worse than that shaving cut you gave yourself last Sigmus Eve. I'm gonna have to ruin your pants."

"Better ruined pants than a ruined leg." He hoisted himself to his feet, flinching as he did, and called the forceball back. "Do what you need to do."

Carefully heading back into the tunnel, the group paused while Theresa cut off the lower part of his pant leg and tied a dressing to the wound. He bit back a flinch when she used a small bottle of spirits to clean it. Things could have been worse.

He glanced at the arachnid corpses scattered around.

A *lot* worse.

He and Theresa carefully checked each floor-tunnel to make sure they were empty. For now, at least, they found no silence-spiders lurking.

"Ummm," Selina said. "I can see light through these cracks."

The small girl was peering into a crack in the blackened wall.

"Light? Are you sure?" Alex and Theresa glanced at each other. The huntress crouched beside the young girl.

"She's right." Theresa scraped away some of the ash, peering through the crevice. "There's some sort of light, like a—oh!"

Crumble.

They jumped back as the wall crumbled into thin fragments, revealing a wide tunnel. It appeared to be some sort of natural crossroads with branching passages connecting to it. In the depths of each passage, dim lights shone, shifting in colour and shade.

"Look." Theresa pointed to the floor with the tip of her sword, indicating a few chips and holes in the rough ground. "There're some tracks in the floor that look like those spiders' tracks, but there's a lot less than back in the temple."

Alex glanced between the floor of this new passage and the walls and ceiling of the temple. "You're right. Maybe they don't come in here often."

"Do you think it's safer in there?" Selina asked hopefully.

Alex shone his forceball down into the tunnel, looking for any threats.

"Maybe. If this place was hidden, especially if the spiders don't come in here often, we should find out why. I definitely want to go in the direction of less spiders."

The little group stepped through the rubble and into the hidden passage. Alex drew on the Mark to guide his steps stealthily. Memories of him sneaking into the cave entrance rose up. He adjusted his movements, picking the best ones from how he'd moved then, and proceeded cautiously.

It was getting a little easier, he noticed.

Brutus sniffed the air, looking at the side tunnels. Alex moved his spell's light all around. No spiders were hidden. The passage was wide, but completely empty.

As they walked deeper, he could feel something *different* in the air. An abundance of mana, he realized. There was so much of it, that even he—a self-taught mage—felt its edges.

A powerful magic surrounded them, distant and cold.

"There's a lot of mana around," he said, thinking back to the tales of the cave. "It might be the Traveller's."

He glanced at the changing lights shining from the surrounding tunnels. "Maybe her portals are close. We could have just found our way out of here."

He stepped toward the nearest.

"Wait." Theresa put a hand on his chest. "Look up there."

Another tunnel had been carved into the ceiling, with the spiders' blade marks apparent in the rock.

Brutus and Theresa took up flanking positions on either side, ready to strike anything that dropped down, while Alex shone his forceball toward the dark.

The spell illuminated what was within.

A dead end appeared after a mere ten feet.

He frowned. "Why would they start digging a tunnel here, just to give up after ten feet?"

Theresa's eyes narrowed. "I wonder..." She glanced back to the remnants of the thin wall with the opening they stepped through. "The thin stone back there looks similar to the dead end up top."

"What're you thinking?" Alex asked.

"I don't know yet." Her eyes turned to one of the closest tunnels where the multi-coloured lights shone from. "Let's check there."

Creeping forward, they slipped into that tunnel, eyes searching in case *anything* was another deathtrap. Coming closer to the light source, they started to feel the same shifts in temperature they'd felt when they first entered the Cave of the Traveller. Brutus sniffed, and all three heads growled. Scents shifted constantly and sounds crashed over each other.

They came to a bend in the passage. The light was close.

"Selina, stay back with Brutus." Alex put a hand on her shoulder. "Just in case, okay?"

Selina nodded and held on to the cerberus, while he and Theresa glanced at each other before peering around the corner.

Alex gasped.

A portal floated in the middle of the tunnel, knee height from the ground.

It shook and shimmered in the air, and the images that appeared through it melted over each other in chaos. One moment, it was filled with huge swaths of the ocean, and the salty tang of the sea filled the tunnel. In another, it was deserts of white sand, carrying a dry dustiness underlaid by a subtle herbal scent. Another showed a darkness so deep, Alex had no idea what he was looking at. There was a tugging on the inside of his nose, like if something was trying to steal the air from his nostrils.

In that instant, the air turned very cold before the portal shifted again.

It paused. For several breaths, it held the image of another cave opening up to a meadow dotted with fireflies at night. The scent of wildflowers drifted through the tunnel. Alex frowned. It had been morning when they'd entered and they hadn't been in here for that long.

"Did it just stabilize?" he asked. "Maybe we shou—"

Voom!

The portal slammed shut.

Alex and Theresa recoiled.

"What happened?" Selina gasped.

He blinked. "I don't kno—"

BOOM.

They all screamed and Brutus yelped.

With a boom like thunder, the portal reopened farther down the tunnel, and the image within was of a rocky shore overlooking a lake.

Voom.

It disappeared again.

BOOM.

It reopened far closer to them.

The images swirled too quick to track.

"Get back!" Theresa cried.

Alex ran, grabbing Selina's hand and rushing toward the main tunnel. He kept looking back, imagining the unstable portal reappearing close by, or worse, on top of them.

Reaching the crossroads and skidding to a stop, they stood panting in a mixture of relief and fear. Alex looked back to the tunnel where he could still hear the booms of the portal appearing and reappearing. It stayed around the bend, never opening where they'd stopped.

I wonder if that's what happened to people who entered the cave, he thought. *One minute, they're walking along minding their own business. Next, they find one of the portals that suddenly vanishes, then it opens up right on top of them and they're plunging into the middle of the ocean, or falling from the sky, or appearing in some other deadly place.* He shuddered at the thought. *Or maybe, if they were lucky, in a nice meadow with fireflies.*

"What *was* that?" Selina gasped.

"I think... that's the Traveller's magic."

There was no way they were going through that.

"We should check those other lights." She glanced to the ceiling-tunnel before leading the way down the next passage.

Each passage held much the same as the first. Portals chaotically popping in and out of existence, leading mostly to certain death. Some had items strewn beneath them. Pine cones. Fallen leaves. Stones. Shells of strange animals.

Alex wondered if they'd been pulled in from other places.

The last tunnel they explored revealed a far more gruesome sight.

Soldier spiders lay beneath a portal, and they looked even more devastated than those Cedric had destroyed. One was cleanly split in half. Another looked like it had been turned inside out. The others were in various states of 'ripped apart with extreme prejudice.'

Their stench filled the air, mixing with the changing scents drifting from the ever-changing portal.

"Hah, I guess the magic of Alric's patron saint doesn't play well with the Ravener's monsters," he said with some satisfaction. "The Traveller's fighting the fight even in death."

"Good for her," Theresa said. "And if I'm right, let's look at the tunnel that had no light."

The final tunnel held no portal, abruptly stopping at a blank wall of stone.

"Dead end," Alex grunted. "That's strange."

"Maybe not." Theresa stepped up to the wall, pressed her ear against it and knocked.

Thump. Thump.

Her eyebrows rose. "Come listen to this."

After Alex pressed an ear to the wall, she knocked on it again.

Thump. Thump.

The tap seemed to echo, as though—

"It's hollow!" He stepped back. "Another secret chamber, you think?"

"No, I don't think so." She tapped her chin in thought. "When we first reached the Traveller's Cave, we went straight into the hill. Then turned left at the temple, left again at the secret passage here, then left *again* to reach this dead end. If I'm guessing the distance right, I think this leads back to the tunnel we came through on our way in."

"So... this 'portal crossroads' has two ways in." He added it up. "Each blocked by thin stone and a ceiling-tunnel, also blocked by stone. It's like..."

She nodded. "It's like the spiders got in here, found out what the portals could do to them, then closed it off with those thin walls. Alex, do you think something in here can build walls? Or maybe shape stone?"

Chapter 13

Walls and Keys

"I ... I don't know if there's anything that can build walls," Alex said. "Dungeon cores are supposed to make nests for their monsters, right? Maybe it's the dungeon core here making and moving walls for its spiders."

He thought back on all the stories he'd heard about the cave.

"I don't remember anything about the Cave of the Traveller having a temple in it," he said. "Or *anything* about horrible, fiery death-beams."

"Yes, I think that's something the whole town would have remembered." Theresa shuddered. "You know, I once thought about exploring this place when I was younger... By myself. Can you imagine?"

He grimaced. "At least there weren't any silence-spiders then."

"Just statues that burn you to ash!"

"Hrm." He looked to the hollow wall. "I'm not sure you would have found the temple back then."

"What do you mean?"

"Do you think you can find where this wall is in the front passage?"

She glanced at it. "I think so. Come on."

They looped out of the portal crossroads and back into the entrance tunnel, watching closely for more silence-spiders. None came.

Thump. Thump.

Thump. Thump.

Thump. Thump.

After a time, Theresa started pausing and rapping on the stone on the side of the passage every few steps until—

Thump. Thump.

"Found it." She tapped the wall again. "It's hollow, and it's about the right distance."

"Okay." He peered at the tunnel's walls. "Let's look around the stone here and see if we find anything strange."

The three of them examined the walls while Brutus stood guard and Alex activated the Mark, focusing on thoughts of *finding*. Memories of the stone arose as he studied it, detailing its contours, bumps and grooves. As he inspected the passage, more memories were added with even more details emphasized. He was *learning* the exact shape and structure of this one passage with every pass of his eyes until...

He noticed it.

"Something's messed with the tunnel. Look." He pointed to the wall just near the hollow section. "It looks natural, but the stone's a *bit* smoother from here—" He traced his finger from the hollow section along to where the tiles began in the passage. "—all the way to *here*. I think the pathway to the temple used to be hidden. The stone seems to have been moved out of the way by whatever raised the walls. Or maybe the worker spiders chiseled this tunnel and the wall... mover... thing, smoothed the stone back."

Theresa followed his gaze. "The portals we've seen so far look a lot more like what the tales say about the cave leading to all kinds of random places. Maybe they sealed off what the cave led to before."

"Yeah, but then they opened the temple instead, *and* gave themselves a straight path in and out of the dungeon... and a path right to Cedric. Too bad for them." He looked back down the passage. "The legends didn't say anything about any temple, so I thought it probably got pulled in from a portal, but now I'm wondering if I was just plain wrong there."

"But you said the scary statues didn't look like they were from here." Selina looked up, trying to follow along.

"They still might not be. The Traveller was supposed to have come from somewhere really far away. Before she settled in Alric. What if those statues and that writing are from wherever she came from? Maybe the temple was the hidden part of the cave—*her* hidden part—until the spiders opened it up."

"Um, is that why the portal back in the temple didn't look like the ones that were all weird and moving?" Selina asked.

Alex and Theresa held each other's gazes.

He slowly turned toward his little sister like a door on rusty hinges. "Selina, you're a genius."

She blinked. "I am?"

"Yeah! Come on!" He waved them back to the temple.

When they got to the entrance, he took a long look at the portal in the middle of the room. It was stable. It didn't flicker. It didn't change or pop in and out of existence.

It was silent, peaceful, and simply fixed open onto that endless blue sky. There was almost something... welcoming about it.

The Traveller's magic was different here.

"Hey..." Theresa looked over the room again. "This is a deathtrap."

"I know." He considered the sky-portal. "No way we're going in there, even if we *could* reach—"

"No, I mean this room."

He blinked, confused. "I uh, know that too..."

"No, *listen*, I mean it's a deathtrap created by the spiders." She pointed to the floor-tunnels. "Think about it. Someone is walking along, when the little ones come up behind them from under the floor like they did with us. Then they herd their prey into the temple. If the prey runs onto the trap tiles, they burn to ash. If the prey knows the right tiles to step on, then the spiders can just follow and their victims are trapped." She pointed at the large wall tunnels. "And those big spiders can just come out of the walls and ceiling and surround anyone that survives."

Alex imagined it. Running from the passage while being chased by silence-spiders. One step onto the floor while panicking and then being obliterated. If they'd forced them onto the safe tiles where they'd be trapped, little silence-spiders would fill the tunnel and big ones on the ceilings and walls.

He shuddered. "That's a nasty way to go."

"That's an understatement. You'd die terrified." Theresa gave the tunnels a disgusted look. "It's lucky Cedric killed the swarm of big ones when he did."

"And that we managed to get rid of the little ones," Alex added. None had come for them since that ambush. He wondered if the dungeon core was nearly out of forces now.

He looked to the keyhole in the massive doors.

"Let's have a look at what's on the other side of those doors. If the Traveller's magic *here* is stable, then what's behind them might hold the answer to what we're looking for. I think we need to get across that floor."

Backing into the tunnel, Alex began testing the tiles again with the forceball, using any burn marks on the stone as a guide. He made a few mistakes. The statues' eyes drew lines of fire along the floor on the way to the targeted tiles, leaving many of them scorched. It became a practice of trial and error. Trying one with the forceball, then shooting it back behind the sky-portal to protect it in case the fire-beams activated.

He discovered some of the tiles in the back of the room were trapped, and that the goddesses *pivoted* on their pedestals to blast at his fleeing forceball.

There were several paths across the temple floor that weren't trapped, but most led to dead ends against the walls. He kept experimenting and was able to pick out a safe path leading directly to the doorway. He wasn't about to take any chances, so he kept checking the floor tiles until he'd tested every last one in the temple.

"There, that's all of them," he said.

"We still have a problem." Theresa pointed to the lock on the massive door in the temple's far wall. "I don't see any place to find a key around here, and it doesn't look like the spiders use the doors."

"Give me a second." He scanned the room. "Stay here, I think I might be able to find it."

The Mark of the Fool focused on memory and its details, and he had just used it to learn the cave wall. It had focused on the successes in his searching to reveal differences in the structure. The same principle might apply here.

Concentrating on his Mark, he cautiously stepped onto the safe paths, taking in every detail of the room, focusing on thoughts of searching and memorization.

The Mark responded as it had in the front passage. Raising memories of every detail his eyes caught and comparing them as he searched for anything that stood out. He paced the paths, repeatedly looking over the same tiles and stone. The memories piled up with sharper details being added with each repetition.

Then he stopped.

The Mark focused on an image within a section of one of the temple walls. Every time he'd looked at it, the Mark sharpened the details. He'd learned every contour just as he had in the cave.

He also learned the average shade of the stone in this chamber.

In the daylight shining through the sky-portal, the section of stone was lighter in the image. He carefully crossed the room along one of the safe paths. Kneeling beside the slightly discoloured area, he looked through the sea of blade marks carved by silence-spider tracks.

There. A slight indentation, nearly hidden by claw marks.

Warily, he pressed his finger into it.

Click.

The indentation sank further—and a hidden panel in the stone swung open with the creak of ancient hinges. Within lay a single wooden box.

His smile of triumph quickly faded.

"Oh no." He slid the box out of the compartment, grunting at its weight.

Its entire surface was gouged and shredded by the silence-spiders' blades.

He gingerly pushed aside the remnants of the lid and cursed.

What was left of a massive key lay within—large enough for the temple doors. It had been destroyed. Silence-spider's claws had clipped and bent the metal until it was nothing but useless junk.

"They wrecked the key." He pushed the ruined box back in disgust.

He was really starting to *hate* these knife-legged bastards.

Theresa's lips pressed together.

Selina looked between them. "What do we do now?"

"Let me try something." He went to the temple doors across one of the safe pathways and concentrated on the lock, activating the Mark.

He focused on lockpicking.

No images arose.

It made sense. The only experience he had with locks was

turning a key and opening them. And even then, they weren't exactly common back in Alric. Locks were expensive, and many of the townsfolk just relied on a metal latch or wooden bar across their doors. All in all, no memories for the Mark to draw on, not even related ones.

"It means..." He sighed, turning to give them the bad news. As he turned, his eyes caught the statues in front of him.

He stopped.

He looked at the wall destroyed by the flame-magic in the passage, and then toward the temple doors. And again at the statues.

A wicked grin spread across his face.

"It means, my dear little sister," he gave an evil chuckle, "that we have *four* spares."

He rose and strode toward his companions, already moving his forceball above one of the trap tiles.

"Alex? What do you—"

"Selina, Brutus, back into the tunnel!" Theresa pulled them back as she saw what he was about to do. She held Selina, telling her to close her eyes.

Once Alex reached a safe distance from the temple chamber, he drove the forceball into the trap-tile.

BANG!

As soon as the trap triggered, he shot the forceball in front of the locked doors so that it hovered before the lock.

WhooooOOOOM.

The goddesses turned on their pedestals.

And fired.

He shot the forceball all around the doors, forcing the flame-magic to chase the glowing orb. The beams blasted the lock apart in their attempts to hit the spell.

Crck.

Cracks spiraled through the blackening doors until both

doors blew apart. Popping and screeching rose from behind them, followed by a whoosh of smoke.

A mass of worker silence-spiders had been huddled behind the doors. Alex hadn't expected them, but *they* hadn't expected fire-beams.

"Well, so much for *that* trap." He smiled in satisfaction as they blazed in the inferno.

As the fire cleared, a massive passage loomed through the doorway, with a stairway leading farther into the dark. Grand columns framed the passage running into the distance until the stairs curved out of view.

"By Uldar," Theresa murmured. "That was clever." Alex saw that some of her fear was starting to give way to excitement. "Shall we go, Mr. Wizard?"

"Hey, *you* were the one that figured out the walls moving," Alex said lightly. "And we're nooot going yet." Alex brought his forceball above a trap-tile again. "We just went through hell in that room. We should get *something* for our trouble."

Bang!

As soon as the forceball sprang the trap, he moved it between the statues, hovering it at face-level between their heads.

WhooooOOOOM.

The statues pivoted, facing each other. Their eyes flared, firing just as he drove the spell downward. Fire-beams blasted the faces and necks of the sculptures, heating the stone, and cracks spiraled through their surfaces. The two fractured statues tremored on their pedestals until they shattered into hundreds of tiny shards. Shining among the rubble, four magical rubies had clattered—unharmed—to the floor.

"Hahah, *victory*!" He pumped his fists.

Gaping, Theresa, Brutus and Selina followed as Alex ran across the now useless trap floor, and began digging through the rubble to scoop up the fist-sized fire-gems, laughing madly to himself. He could *feel* the mana coursing through the jewels' magic circuits. They were quite complex. Four individual circuits joined together. From the magic theory he'd learned, that made the gems' flame-magic the equivalent of a fourth-tier spell.

A full three tiers higher than his humble forceball.

"Do you have *any* idea how much these are worth?" He grinned.

"Do you?" Theresa asked.

"Nope." He shrugged. "But it sure as hell won't be nothing. The gems alone are bigger than any I've seen nobles wearing, and there's *powerful* magic in all of them."

"Can... can you make them shoot the nasty spiders?" Selina asked hopefully.

His little sister stood beside a very excited Brutus. She was smiling and, in that moment, seemed not to be afraid.

He looked at the gems, feeling their pleasant warmth in his fingers.

It shouldn't be impossible, he thought.

From what he'd learned in his books, there were three major kinds of magical items. Some were enchanted or naturally magical: anyone who picked them up could use them. The second kind were a bit more complex. Each held their own mana, which could connect directly with the mana of its wielder. Then—just like how he controlled his forceball through pure mana and will after it had been cast—the wielder could utilize it without any spellcraft. Items like those tended to be rare and needed a *lot* of skill, time and practice to use.

The third kind were what these gems seemed to be. Items built from spell arrays.

A wizard's staff or wand contained its own mana and magic circuitry that its master could connect to. By pushing their own mana in, a wizard could use the items as though they were their *own* magic in a form of spellcraft. Judging by the magic circuitry, it seemed these gems functioned similarly, and likely followed commands set into them when they were built into the statues.

But such items were for experienced wizards with magic items they knew well.

Alex, self-taught and inexperienced, didn't trust himself to *not* do something catastrophic by trying to interfere with strange, complex gems that spat fire and death. Especially when the Mark would, no doubt, interfere with the spellcraft required.

If his humble forceball exploding had nearly ripped his own face off...

"If I did it wrong, I might blow us up," he said, stowing the gems in his pack. "Come on, we'd better get moving. Who knows if there's more spiders around."

Having Selina stay back with Brutus, Alex and Theresa crept to the ruined temple doors and peered through to the other side. Only burnt spiders greeted them. He took Selina back by his side and the little party crept deeper into the dungeon, with Brutus taking the lead.

As their footsteps echoed lightly on the stairs, Alex began to feel the same cold and distant mana as he had in the portal crossroads. It seemed like they were getting closer to another place thick with the Traveller's mana.

And it was growing stronger with each step.

Chapter 14

The Sanctum of Doors

"I think we're getting close to something," Alex whispered, shining the forceball across the ceiling and walls. Murals had been etched into the stone, but many were now ruined by the silence-spiders' claws.

It was a shame. Even through the cuts, it was clear someone had poured a lot of skill and effort into this place.

"Look." Selina pointed to one they were passing on their left. "Don't they look like those scary statues?"

Barely visible through the blade marks were the snarling faces of the goddesses from the temple above, though all else in the mural had been obliterated. Luckily, these images had no fire-gems for eyes.

"I can't believe this was so close to our little town." Theresa gazed at the architecture in awe. "It's like something out of a fairy tale... or it *was*. Those spiders are awful."

Brutus growled as he padded down the stairs, as though agreeing with his master.

"At least there don't seem to be any more of them. For now," Theresa said.

There had been holes in the ceiling and walls here and there, but not a single sign of any worker or soldier silence-spider. With so much destruction to its swarm so soon after awaking, it seemed the dungeon core might have run out of things to throw at them.

Alex held on to a cautious optimism. 'Two days to regenerate its forces,' Cedric had said. Hopefully, that meant a straight, safe run to whatever was under the temple. With the way the stairs turned, it looked like where they would be directly below it.

"Wait, listen." Theresa held up a gloved hand for them to stop. "Do you hear that?"

Alex strained his ears and everyone held their breaths.

From somewhere ahead came a low roar, like a rainstorm or river, echo from somewhere in the deep.

"An underground river, you think?" Alex asked.

They continued forward and lights came next. A glow in multiple colours radiated from down the passage. They were like the lights they'd seen in the portal crossroads, but these didn't move and change nearly as much.

There also seemed to be more of them.

"Maybe more portals," Alex commented.

The Traveller's magic had increased in the air. Now even stronger than it had been in the portal crossroads. Moving quietly, they crept closer to the lights, coming to the end of the stairs. A stone doorway framed the exit.

The light was stronger, nearly as bright as full daylight. Etched into the stone above, spoiled by the spiders' claws, was the symbol of a lantern.

The Sigil of the Traveller, Alric's patron saint.

They looked up, amazed they were standing in a place she had passed through long ago.

"Are we ready?" Theresa asked.

Alex looked to his little sister.

"Yeah..." She clutched on to his cloak.

Brutus nuzzled his master with one head while the other two pointed forward, ready for what lay ahead. He constantly sniffed the air.

"I'm ready," Alex said last, calling his forceball close. "If we see anything bad, we run, okay?"

As one, they nodded to each other and stepped out of the stairway, blinking as their eyes adjusted to the unexpected brightness of the light.

"Oh, Uldar's beard," Alex swore.

A hive.

An empty hive.

It was like stepping into the heart of a giant wasp nest.

The stairs opened onto a massive, circular chasm—closed up at the top by stone—that reached down into the depths of the earth. A rock pathway spiraled down the sides of the open shaft, passing cells upon cells cut into the wall like the honeycomb pattern in a wasps' nest. Broken egg sacs were stuck to the stone beside cocoons with deer-antlers, hooves and other parts of snared animals sticking out.

Cocoons that likely held captives for future meals.

A thick liquid dripped onto the stones below. Some of the eggs had been recently torn open, and a mass of spiders—dead and half-formed—lay in front of the dripping sacs. Maybe the dungeon core had tried to replenish its forces from these egg sacs, but they weren't ready to hatch and died. Either that, or something else was down there that had torn them open. Whatever the case, Alex hoped they wouldn't run into anything and find out.

He kept an eye on the half-formed spiders in case any were still alive, but his attention was more focused on the portals.

Dozens of them floated through the chasm. Some moving and some flickering in and out of different places, spreading a mix of sun and moonlight. The scents and sounds of a hundred realms filled the chamber, and Alex's skin goose-pimpled from dozens of temperature fluctuations. Each portal was like the one in the temple. They were stable, but what lay inside them was far more than just empty sky.

The four companions gaped, awestruck at the sight. The true remnants of the Traveller's's magic was here, bringing scenes from all over the world into this one cave outside of their hometown.

One portal roared as water poured from a river it had opened into and fell through another portal that opened far below. The second showed a scene of snowy plains from hundreds of feet above with water pouring down and building an ever-spreading hill of ice. Another spread open to a scene of hot fire mountains burnt by their own eruptions, with a river of lava flowing just beneath the doorway on the other side. Alex noticed the air shimmering around it. He was amazed at how much heat must have been coming from the thing.

Another portal opened to a forest very different from Coille. The trees were larger and covered with vines, while the forest floor was a steaming marsh where something massive and slithery swam along the surface.

They'd be avoiding going near *that* place.

Some places the portals opened to were completely strange. One revealed a desert of blue sand under a blue sun. Another opened over a range of crimson mountains and above, a flock of bat-winged creatures flew.

While many of the portals hovered in the middle of the chasm, some were close to the pathway. Around them, there wasn't a single sign of spider eggs or spiders. It seemed the portals here didn't play well with them either.

Broken items lay all along the path. Shattered statues, columns and other sculptures that looked like they would have suited the temple and staircase. The damaged objects all bore the spider-claw marks. Yet, despite the scarring and empty nests, this place was amazing, and the best part was, there wasn't a single spider crawling around.

They weren't safe yet, but Alex could almost *taste* freedom.

"It's so beautiful..." Selina gasped at the portals. "It's like a big wonderful tower underground with doors that go wherever you want."

"All over the world..." Theresa added in a dreamy voice.

Even Brutus seemed excited, with his heads swiveling in every direction.

Alex admired the majesty around them. "That's the legacy of our Saint. Remember her sigil on the way in? Maybe this was her sanctum all along, before it became a dungeon. She mustn't have been too pleased that monsters got in here." He looked around at the portals and sighed in growing relief. "It looks like we have our way out."

"We did it!" Selina laughed. "I wish we could take all these pretty doors with us."

"Yeah, me too, Selina, me too," her brother agreed.

"Maybe... maybe if I get some clay I can build a littler copy of this place..." Her eyes narrowed in thought. "After we find where we're supposed to go."

"Yeah, we're going to have a hard time figuring out which portal to choose."

"Maybe not the one with all the volcanoes?" Theresa suggested.

"Oh, come on, where's your sense of adventure?" He chuckled.

Marveling at the portals, the little party crept down the ramp while looking for their door out of Thameland and toward Generasi. They fell quiet as they went deeper into the cave, eyeing the walls for any signs of threat.

As they went lower, the Saint's magic filled the air so thickly that Alex wouldn't have been surprised if it suddenly became visible.

Theresa gasped. "Look. Someone's lying on the ramp down there. By Uldar's beard… is it *her*?"

Alex and Selina turned to the spot where she was looking and gasped in shock.

A few floors below them on the opposite side of the chasm, a body lay. It was small and thin, and dressed in a plain brown robe. Its hands were cupped upon its midriff. A blue light covered it, shimmering and brightening the surrounding stone like the sunrise. Across the chest, a symbol of a lantern glowed a deeper blue, and wherever the blue light touched, the spiders' presence was absent, like they never existed.

"I think you're right. It's wearing the lantern symbol," Alex said in awe, a small part of him hoping the Saint wouldn't be too angry at him for using her power to escape. Hopefully not… He was only a 'Fool' after all.

"Thank you, Ms. Traveller," Selina said, bowing her head toward the body. "Thank you for fighting the monsters, and thank you for helping me, my brother, Theresa and Brutus go to the big wizard city."

Alex smiled warmly. "I hope she hears you."

Theresa bowed her head. "Thank you, Traveller, for your magic that stopped the monsters from leaving this place."

Alex looked between them. He might as well pay his respects too.

He bowed his head and closed his eyes. "Thank you for your sacrifice, our patron saint. May you rest well. And… for what it's worth, I hope the spiders we killed in your home made you a little happier."

When he opened his eyes, he was gazing directly toward the chasm's bottom.

The hair rose on the back of his neck.

The portals ended at a point below, and their light failed to pierce the dark at the bottom.

Shuddering, he stepped away from the edge. "Let's get going and take a look at the portals."

The problem was that there were a *lot* of portals, and many led to certain death.

"I'm pretty sure that's something's stomach." Theresa winced at one opening into a fleshy cavern. It was filled with green liquid and dissolving meat.

"Gross." Selina gagged, looking away.

Brutus snorted and turned all three of his heads.

Theresa scanned more of the portals that were in reach of the stone pathway. "We could step through one that looks safe, look around and step back if it isn't some place we want to go?"

Alex thought about that, glancing at some of the doorways. "Problem is, we don't know if they'll close on us on the other side, since we don't know how they work."

"Um, maybe... maybe we could look and see if there's any with mountains or rivers you know from one of your books?" Selina asked. "Since you read so much. Then we can go there if it's safe?"

Both Alex and Theresa paused, looking down at the little girl.

"Like I said before, *you're a genius*, little goblin." Alex grinned.

"I am?" Selina blinked.

"Yes, you are!" Theresa mussed the young girl's hair. "You think you can do that, Alex?"

He rotated his marked shoulder. "Watch me."

He'd already used it to search out details in the caves above. So, why not landmarks?

Taking in the portals, he concentrated on the idea of *navigation*. In his book, Galloway said that previous Fools had guided their companions through the wilderness, hadn't he?

The Mark responded.

Images of books burst into his mind. Old geography books,

poems and histories that mentioned landmarks. Some he'd only flipped through in passing, but they rose up now as clear as a sunny day. What surprised him, though, were the conversations that appeared. Every relevant half-snippet of geographical knowledge he'd ever heard, even if he hadn't been focusing on it at the time, neatly organized itself in solid detail.

His eyes flicked from portal to portal and the Mark compared the sights to the landmarks he'd heard of. Many he didn't recognize, but soon, a grin spread across his face.

The views were from far, far above, but he was finding distinct landmarks.

There was Mount Tai, looming from the eastern peaks in the Tarim-Lung Empire, just as Theresa's grandfather had described it. An ornate gate sat above the stone staircase that led up its forested slope. Alex could see the mountain as clear as crystal.

The Tree of Knowledge of New Alfheim rose from a green valley in the middle of a snowy wilderness. He'd heard of it in passing from a travelling skald visiting Alric; the only elf he had ever seen.

From far above, there was the Lighthouse of Indlu-Yesibani, far south of Generasi, home to one of the greatest libraries in the world. It had been told of by a griot—a southern storyteller—who described it in tales while he was in Alric on the way to the capital.

And there...

"Yes!" Alex cried.

A secluded bend in a river, and beyond that in the distance, four mountains: one that burned, one lined by hundreds of waterfalls, and one that towered above the others, formed of earth, solid rock and sparkling with gemstones the size of villages. The fourth mountain didn't touch the ground at all. It floated in the air, high above the others, held up by a constant wind.

He'd found the Peaks of the Elements. The holiest place in

all the Rhinean Empire, and one of its most southern landmarks. A short journey would take them from the mountains to Port Mausarr on the River Austrus. From there, it would be a couple days' voyage to Generasi's outer islands.

Alex pointed down to the Rhinean portal, which hung near the ramp several floors below where they stood. "That's where we need to go. Right to the southern part of the Rhinean Empire." He couldn't help but smile at the irony. "We're going to get there before your parents."

He glanced down. "We should be able—"

Something *moved* in the dark below.

"Oh shit! Get back!"

They sprang away from the edge.

Whoosh!

A line of webbing shot from the darkness, hitting the ceiling and whipping dust from the cave walls. The sound of rock crumbling announced something rising from the depths. The web above flexed like a sail, but made no sound.

From the size of the web and the loud crunching of stone, Alex's blood chilled.

If they were in a hive...

...then, the hive would have a *queen.*

Chapter 15

The Hive-Queen

"Something's coming! We have to get to the portal! *Now*!" Alex screamed.

Theresa tensed. "We won't make it down there in time!" She scanned closer doorways, but all led to inhospitable lands or death traps. The huntress pointed toward the archway to the stairs. "Let's go back! We can—"

Crunch.

Her words died.

A massive, scythe-like blade had bitten into the stone wall below. It was large enough to cut any two of their group in half with one slice, including Brutus. Before they could decide where to run, the creature partially rose into view.

All three screamed and Brutus barked frantically.

Alex expected to see a spider.

But the emerging monster's—the hive-queen's—upper half had little resemblance to her soldiers and workers.

A chitinous, humanlike torso rose, covered in carapace like knight's armour. Five sets of dead, black orbs filled its armoured forehead above a long jaw packed with needle-like fangs. Four plated arms had humanlike hands, the fingers of each ending in claws that curved like daggers. In one, it gripped the end of the webline. In another, it held an orb the size of Alex's head.

He, Theresa and Selina were terrified.

The orb was grey, but its tone flickered and changed, sporadically plunging into complete darkness. It looked like the black sphere painted in the mural across the Lu's common room wall.

Alex began to tremble. Was this the same thing?

It came closer, soaking the air with a new mana, one that clashed with the Traveller's mana.

Hers was peaceful and cool, but this was *alive.* It pulsated, sticking to his senses and leaving a feeling of pure dread behind. The orb *had* to be from the Ravener's spawn, the maker of the monsters in this dungeon.

The dungeon core.

The queen's maw opened wide, her cry silent. Something in the dark orb shifted. Alex could *feel* the pulsating mana twist with the mana of the Traveller, and the two struggled in the air.

The hive-queen emerged, revealing her full form.

Her human-mimicry ended at the waist.

Instead of two legs, her lower body was that of an enormous centipede—with each of her hundred legs ending in a sharp knife edge. Protruding from chitinous plates below her torso were two colossal arms with massive blades. She ascended like a snake, her sinewy body weaving between the portals to avoid the Traveller's power.

Alex's eyes focused on the portals.

"Alex! Aleeex!" Selina wailed, grabbing on to him and crying in terror.

As she sobbed, the darkness in the dungeon core began to deepen.

Theresa was scrambling to draw her bow while trying to shove the Roth siblings toward the stairs. Her face was stark white. "We... w-we-we—"

His own terror threatened to overwhelm him, but he

clamped down on it. If they ran to the staircase, she would chase them, and he doubted they could outrun her with all those legs. With thoughts racing, he shot a look down the path toward the portal to the Rhinean Empire.

Portals hung throughout the air in the chasm. Some were near the path or even hovered over the path itself.

Then he remembered the portals hurt the monsters.

That was the key.

"She can't touch the portals!" Alex shouted, taking hold of Selina's hand and Theresa's arm. He pulled them down the path. "Run! We can use the portals as cover!"

Theresa shook away her fright. "Take my hand!" She grabbed the little girl's other hand.

The three of them tore down the path, avoiding the rubble and debris, while Brutus followed, barking and snarling at the queen, trying to make her back off.

The monster kept coming. "*Hu... mansss.*" She broke her silence, hissing words in the common tongue. *Scrrrrp.* She accentuated her words by scraping one scythe-blade across the other. "*Humansss... must... feaaaar...*"

Alex's mind worked to smother his terror.

His heart slammed in his chest, speeding up with their footsteps on the stone. The hive-queen silently chased them.

Whoosh.

She shot another webline into the ceiling and pulled herself toward her prey, weaving between the portals with grace. Her body slipped by a portal that led to the middle of the ocean. No seawater poured through it. She ducked through the stream of water pouring from the river portal above and weaved below a portal leading to a secluded mountain crevice.

Whoosh. Crack!

Another webline drove into the ceiling above.

Selina sobbed as Theresa and Alex pulled her as fast as she

could manage. A portal lay in the middle of the path ahead, leading to a lake that boiled and smelled of sulfur.

The hive-queen silently opened her jaw and lowered her arm toward them. Alex saw her aiming through a small gap in the chasm's floating doorways.

"Stop! Back here," Alex cried. They abruptly ducked behind the portal.

Whoosh.

The webline struck where they would have been, slamming into the stone and spreading a line across the path.

"Stay here!" he shouted. "She won't be able to hold it tight if she chases us."

Alex peered from behind the portal with Selina hiding behind him. Theresa peered out too and Brutus snarled.

The hive-queen didn't give chase. She waited, watching the grey orb in her hand. It was flickering more now. Growing darker. He didn't like the look of that.

"We have to move; the core's doing something!"

Theresa's eyes hardened. She started running.

Back *up* the path.

"Theresa! What're you doi—"

The hive-queen's head swivelled after her. The monster only had one free arm. Two held tensed weblines while the last palmed the dungeon core. The fourth aimed at Theresa.

Whoosh.

She fired.

As she did, Theresa dove down to the stone.

Crunch.

The webline struck the wall above her, and she jumped to her feet then ran back down the path.

"Go! Below her line!" Theresa shouted. "She's out of hands!"

"Selina, c'mon!" Alex pushed his sister beneath the webline blocking the pathway down. He rolled under it, and Brutus leapt over. Theresa sprinted to them and ducked under, joining them on the other side.

The hive-queen silently screeched and tore the webs away as she began to weave between the portals in pursuit.

The distance between them and her was growing.

Hope rose in Alex's chest. They were close to the Rhinean gateway, and shortly beyond that lay the Traveller's body, shining with its blue light. They were close. So close.

Yet not close enough.

The hive-queen let out an audible screech that shook the cavern and nearly sent Selina into fits of screaming. The little girl struggled to keep her legs moving as fast as she could, while Alex and Theresa pulled her along.

As Selina screamed, the darkness in the dungeon core deepened.

The hive-queen raised it high.

Something shifted in the darkness and the orb's mana pulsed.

Krooom!

A rock wall erupted in the path in front of them, stopping them dead.

"No!" Alex cried.

The hive-queen's jaw clicked in something that might have been laughter.

"Back up the path!" Theresa shouted. "If we can—"

Something shifted in the orb again.

His Mark shuddered and he could *feel* that pulsating mana flow from the core and toward the path leading back up.

Krooom!

Another wall of stone arose, blocking the only other avenue of escape.

The darkness in the orb faded to a lighter grey as it used its power.

The hive-queen's clicking jaw quickened. It almost sounded

like laughter. Leisurely, she weaved between the portals toward them.

Selina sobbed.

Theresa screamed and loosed an arrow at the monster, but it bounced uselessly off her armoured body. In response, the hive-queen bared her fangs, looking like she was hissing, but her voice had creepily returned to silence.

She continued to close on them, her sinewy body snaking between the portals. The spot they were trapped in only had a few of the Traveller's doorways nearby, with more than enough room for the monster to maneuver if she got close.

They were going to die. When she reached them, they were going to die.

Alex's mind raced and he shot his forceball at one of her hands.

Right at the dungeon core.

The Mark blocked combat when attacking creatures, but it hadn't interfered when he'd struck objects with his spell. If he could knock the dungeon core from her grip, then maybe—

Memories poured into his head.

Fire. Fear. Spiders. Death.

His aim spoiled, and his forceball ineffectively slammed into the queen's armoured body. A swipe from one of her claws shattered it.

His only weapon was gone.

No! His mind screamed. *Don't give up! We are not going to die down here! Think! Adapt!*

The hive-queen snaked above a portal where stones floated in a grey sky. She was getting closer. She raised the dungeon core. "*Humansss... feaaaar... Ravener.*"

Once more, the dark faded toward grey.

The closest of the walls she'd made shimmered.

Egg sacs formed on its surface, swelling rapidly until they burst apart one by one, unleashing worker silence-spiders onto the path. They started to skitter forward, and Brutus snarled and lunged at them with his fangs ready.

Crunch!

His jaws shattered their chitin, ripping into the little beasts. Their knife-like legs scratched at his snouts and he yelped, but he didn't stop.

"Die! Die!" Theresa fired arrow after arrow toward the queen, aiming for joints, eyes and anything else vulnerable. They bounced off the chitin as she closed. Selina's screams heightened in pitch and—for a moment—the fear was just as raw as it had been four years ago.

When the Roths' lives burned.

The queen let out a satisfied clicking sound. The dungeon core's mana began to grow thicker in the air. The orb's darkness deepened. Alex noticed the change. Each time the core used its power, the dark lessened.

Each time their fear surged or his sister screamed, the darkness grew deeper.

A memory from when they were in the temple returned to him.

"*You'd die terrified*," Theresa had said about the deathtrap the spiders had created.

The temple chamber had been right over the dungeon core's lair. Its victims would be terrorized to the height of fear just as the hive-queen was doing to them now.

And as their terror grew, so did the dungeon core's mana.

Fear.

The core must have been *feeding* on it.

And now the queen could take her time weaving between the portals, letting the core recharge as she came close enough to pluck her harvest.

Think! Adapt! his mind pushed. *Think! Adapt! Think! Adapt!*

Theresa's arrows hadn't worked. With no effort, the monster

had ended his forceball. He wouldn't be able to channel another one in time—not with the Mark interfering—and even if he could, it would do *nothing* against the queen's armour.

The hive-queen was close now. She drove a final webline into the stone and swung around another portal. Now only two more lay between them: one near the pathway that led to an endless night sky, and one farther into the chasm that led to the fire mountains and the river of lava beneath.

Twang.

Another of Theresa's arrows flew straight, shooting right for one of the hive-queen's insectile eyes.

Clack.

The monster raised her hand and the arrow bounced uselessly off her armour.

They couldn't hurt her. And she knew it. Lazily, she ducked beneath the portal to the fire mountains—giving it lots of room—and began drifting her torso toward them.

Only the night sky-portal lay between them and her claws.

"Alex!" Theresa was shoving a waterskin at him. It was partially slit.

The stench of wormwood drifted out.

Theresa nocked a broad-headed arrow onto her bowstring.

"Throw the bag at her when I tell you!" she screamed.

Alex drew himself out of his thoughts.

With a final crunch of Brutus' jaws, he killed the last of the workers. This was it. There would be no more hesitation from the queen now.

"Wait," Theresa said.

The monster drew closer.

He focused on the bag using the Mark. He'd only get one chance at this.

Memories of tossing coins flowed into him. Images of tossing empty flour sacks away at McHarris' bakery. Memories of tossing dough to make flatbread.

Mundane times coming to help him in crisis.

Then a final memory.

Him knocking down the old, shaky shelf the baker had been too cheap to have repaired. Watching the flour bags burst open, covering everything in a powdery mess. The stale eggs rolling off and bursting, exposing his employer's rotten secret.

Strange. That last memory hadn't been called up by the Mark. He'd remembered it on his own.

Still, it made sense that it would come back now. That moment had changed his life.

This would too.

Trusting his own experience, Alex Roth hoisted the bag of wormwood, letting the Mark of the Fool guide his aim. Not *at* the monster. Just in front of her.

The hive-queen weaved her body around the left of the night sky-portal. Her centipede half drifted back as her sword-legs poised, ready to strike.

The portal was almost behind her.

"Now!" Theresa roared.

He threw the waterskin.

It whirled toward the queen, trailing stinkweed.

The monster casually raised an arm to bat it aside.

Twang.

Theresa's broad arrow shot forward.

Riiiip.

It struck the skin mid-flight, piercing it and slamming it into the hive-queen's arm.

Splash!

The bag tore open, splashing the thick juice over her forearm and monstrous, surprised face. She let out a silent chitter and recoiled.

Part of her body brushed against the portal.

BOOM!

In a flash of blue light, a section of her body—all that

touched the Traveller's power—simply vanished. The creature screeched out loud as insectile blood poured from her wound and she clawed at the mess in her eyes.

"She'll bleed now!" Theresa snarled in triumph. "We can esc... a..."

She gasped.

Even as the monster scraped wormwood from her face with one hand, another claw raised the dungeon core. Its darkness shifted. Mana poured into her, and her wound began to rapidly close. The bleeding slowed. The orb was losing its darkness, but the wound had almost entirely healed.

"No! No!" Theresa fired again, aiming for her open mouth.

The arrow glanced off an armoured hand.

A grim look entered the young woman's eyes.

She took Alex's hand and started to pull him toward the wall between them and the Rhinean Empire's portal. "Get to the wall up there!" Resolve burned in her voice. "I'll boost you and Selina over, then go! Brutus and I will hold her off!"

"No!" Selina screamed. "Theresa, no! You can't!"

Alex was nearly sick with horror.

Was this it? Was he supposed to leave his best friend and poor Brutus to die in the dark?

"No!" he snapped at her. "*No one* is dying!"

The flames of the Roth alehouse roared in his mind.

Think! Adapt!

What did he have? His spells were useless. Their weapons were useless.

Think! Adapt!

The queen kept swiping away the insect repellant. The wound continued to heal, even as the core faded to grey.

He glanced past her and the portal to the fire mountains behind her, and saw the staircase leading up to the temple.

The fire-gems.

No, they wouldn't work. The beams were *powerful* magic

and he didn't know how to use them. If he messed up—if the Mark interfered—he might break them or cause a mana reversal, which would... which would...

Think! ***Adapt!***

He hardened his resolve. It was either this or die.

Ripping open his pack, he dumped the contents on the floor and grabbed the first gem that rolled out.

Its magic circuitry touched his mana.

The Mark flooded him with failures in spellcraft, but he had counted on this.

He only needed to see two memories in detail. The image of him nearly blowing off his own face in the woods, and the time he'd nearly caused a mana reversal in himself. He followed every foolish error, reversing the mana and pouring in too much to overload the circuit.

He felt something crack in the gem.

Its warmth built to such a searing heat that he needed to clench his teeth to continue to hold it.

The image of the forceball in the woods overlapped the gem in his mind.

How it had *shaken*.

How it had *exploded*.

Chapter 16

The Core

"Theresa!" Alex raised the gem.

Crimson light swelled within and cracks split its surface as the mana reversal tore apart its magic circuitry. Flame-magic began to run rampant.

Theresa's eyes went wide.

"What's happening!" Selina jumped away from the gem.

"Throw it at that piece of shit!" He pointed at the hive-queen. "It's going to explode!"

His best friend looked at the fire-gem. Then at the bleeding queen, confusion and fear flowing out of her expression.

It was with her deathstalker face that Theresa took the stone in her gloved hand. "Get down!" she shouted.

She drew her arm back.

Selina dove behind the night sky portal and Alex threw himself over her like a shield.

Theresa's eyes briefly locked on the hive-queen's face, then quickly shifted.

In a blur of motion, she whipped the jewel through the air.

The fire-gem burned like a miniature sun. Alex could feel its heat swell as it flew past the hive-queen... and through the portal hovering behind her.

"No!" Alex screamed.

"Stay down!" Theresa dove by his side.

Her hand grasped his, squeezing it as Brutus threw himself against the stairs, pressing into his master's side.

Alex looked up as the queen reared in rage, letting her voice fill the cavern with a sharp screech. How had Theresa missed?

She couldn't have, not from this distan—

The answer hit him as he realized what was happening behind the monster. The gem's light burned from the portal to the fire mountains. The flame-magic struck the river of lava just inside the doorway.

It flashed once.

The hive-queen paused as red light poured into the cavern and she half-turned.

CRACK!

The gem shattered.

"Holy shi—" Alex murmured.

BOOM!

A blast of flame-magic rocked the other side of the portal, filling the doorway with leaping fire. The explosion ripped over the lava field, blasting into the bubbling pool.

It erupted in a geyser, and boiling rock poured through the portal in a wave, right onto the hive-queen's face and body.

Screeching echoed through the chasm as a whirling mix of inferno and lava slammed into her, blasting her forward.

Crash!

Her long body writhed in the air, then dropped, narrowly missing the sky-portal and slamming into the pathway, cracking it. Her screeches went silent as she convulsed. Tremors shook the cave. Flame-magic and molten rock burned the humanoid torso and twisting, centipede lower body. Her armoured chitin fractured.

The creature tried to raise the greying dungeon core. Mana trickled into her as the wounds tried to close, but the orb's power was too low to heal her. The queen's weakening hand slipped from the dungeon core.

Its darkness faded to sickly grey. Alex could hardly feel its mana.

The healing had snuffed some of the flame, but she remained a smouldering, writhing wreck.

He shivered, realizing he'd underestimated the sheer amount of mana in one of those gems. Even hiding behind the portal, they would've been blown to bits if the gem had exploded in the cave instead of inside the fire mountain portal. Most of the force was directed to wherever the portal came out.

If Theresa had listened to him and thrown it at the queen...

Bang!

The hive-queen continued to spasm. She was weakening, but still wouldn't die. The lava was beginning to cool on her.

Theresa was on her feet, drawing her great-grandfather's sword and charging at the smouldering monster.

"Theresa! *No*!" he shouted.

But she didn't stop.

She reached the hive-queen as the creature raised one of her twitching foreclaws. She dove, sliding under the upraised pincer just before the queen slammed the claw down, impaling it deep in the stone.

"Theresa! Theresaaaa!" Selina screamed, trying to get up, but Alex gripped her tightly, just as Mr. Lu had gripped him in front of his parents' burning alehouse. The little girl could not turn her eyes away.

The hive-queen's movements slowed.

Flinching against the heat, Theresa shot up to the monster's head and drove the sword down.

Clack!

The blade bounced off the chitin.

"Damn!" She dropped her sword and bent to grab something unseen. She hefted it.

The huntress' deathstalker face met the queen's half-melted gaze.

"Humans fear?"

Theresa raised the dungeon core above her head. "Fear *this*."

Bang! Crunch!

Theresa drove it into the queen's lava damaged skull, bursting it with a single strike.

The creature stiffened, her hundred sword-legs twitching and slashing the air. Then, the massive body slumped, collapsing to the stone.

The giant foreclaw ripped from her ravaged torso as she began to slide from the ramp. The webline burnt, and what was left of the hive-queen slipped from the pathway and plunged toward one of the Traveller's portals.

BOOM!

Another flash of light. The insectile monster was pulled into the portal, its chitin crunching as it was contorted and forced to fit through the door. Light flashed. The hive-queen's remains blasted back through the door, returning in dozens of pieces. They tumbled, falling toward the bottom of the deep, dark chasm, crashing into the rock far below.

Theresa rose up, ripping off her steaming glove and panting in the multi-hued light from the portals. Her lean, strong form heaved with each breath, and sweat poured over her brow as she basked in their survival.

She stood triumphant like a warrior from a lost age, and Alex couldn't tear his eyes off of her.

In the back of his mind, a small voice assured him: he did *not* have issues.

"Theresaaaaa!" Selina escaped Alex and rushed at their friend, throwing her arms around her waist. "You're alright! You're alright!"

With three loud barks, Brutus tackled them both.

"Ah, Brutus! Brutus, no!" Theresa laughed as he licked her face with all three tongues. His tail wagged so fast, it looked like it was about to shoot off. Alex stumbled over and flopped down cross-legged on the stone close by.

"You know," he said. "That was the most amazing thi —Agh!"

Her ungloved hand grabbed him, dragging him down beside her, Selina and Brutus.

"Alex! We did it! We *did* it!" Theresa's eyes were filled with tears of joy. She pulled him close, weeping softly into his shoulder.

"Yeah..." He sniffled, relief washing through him. "Yeah, we're alive. Can't believe it, but we're *alive*."

For a time, the little group just lay on the stones and held each other in a mixture of ugly-crying, laughter and relief.

"That... that was smart, Alex. That thing you did with the stone." Theresa turned to him.

"Yeah... but what *you* did was *genius*, throwing it in the lava portal like that. You saved us." He smiled at her.

"Yeah... you did too." The grin she returned was brilliant. "For a second there, you looked a bit like a Hero of Thameland."

Alex felt his face grow hot, and could imagine the blush spreading across his cheeks.

A tiny hand grabbed his shirt. Selina was looking up at him. "A-are you okay, Alex?"

He laughed and patted her shoulder. "Of course I'm okay, I'm your big brother, aren't I? Are *you* okay? The fire—"

"I'm okay," she said quickly and looked away. "...I'm okay."

The beginning of a frown touched Alex's forehead. They would need to talk about this later. He glanced toward the portal to the Rhinean Empire, past the wall the hive-queen had raised.

"We're going to have to get over the wall," Alex groaned. "But maybe after we lie here for, y'know... a few days? Maybe weeks? Maybe forget Generasi altogether," he joked wearily. "We'll just hide here fore—"

His eyes fell on the grey orb.

The dungeon core lay on the stones just past them, still covered in hive-queen brains. Even though it was weak, its pulsating mana was active.

"Hey, where are you going?" Theresa asked as he got to his feet. She watched him approach the sphere. "Ugh, don't touch that. It's covered in bug juice."

"Theresa... you just used it to cave a giant monster's head in. What do you mean don't touch it?"

"Yeah, but it didn't have bug on it then."

"And whose fault is that?"

She looked at him sidelong. "Never mind. Is that what I think it is?"

"I'm pretty sure it's the dungeon core."

She sat bolt upright.

Selina gasped, scrambling back. "Is... is that the thing that makes a dungeon spit out monsters?"

The darkness deepened as they shrank back.

"Don't be afraid of it," he said. "I know, that's hard to do because it's terrifying, but I think it gets stronger when you're afraid."

Theresa's jaw hardened and she glared at the sphere, taking Selina's hand. The little girl took a deep breath, and tried to match the young woman's glare. The dungeon core's darkness lessened. He wasn't sure if it was the 'just survived certain death' speaking to him, but he was reminded of just how much he loved the two of them.

His attention went back to the core.

And this thing had nearly killed all of them.

Alex Roth protected his own, repaid debts and tried to treat others how they treated him. He had no interest in nearly dying in battle alongside the Heroes, but he wasn't about to just walk off and let this thing regenerate to make more monsters.

He was also a revenge enthusiast... As McHarris had found out.

"I'm gonna break the hell out of this thing!" His hands balled into fists.

Theresa climbed to her feet. "It deserves it, but how? The Traveller did it with her magic, didn't she?"

"It's too bad she's not around to tell us what she did."

"Maybe... maybe your Mark will tell you?" Selina offered.

"Hmmm, it *is* still a Hero's Mark." He rolled the core on the ground to try to clean it off, then grunted as he took it up in both hands. He concentrated on the Mark.

He waited.

No helpful images arose. No rush of power or divine revelation.

He sighed.

Fine, hard way it was then.

What did he have available? He looked to the portals. The Traveller's magic had destroyed the spiders. It might do the same with the dungeon core itself. Should he toss it through a portal? He dismissed that idea pretty quick. If it landed somewhere and started spawning monsters...

Maybe it was time to go to the expert.

He looked toward the Traveller's body and the blue light shining around her. If the magic in her *portals* worked on the monsters, then what about the magic still in her body?

"Theresa, could I get that boost over the wall now? I think it's time we introduced this thing to Alric's patron saint. Properly."

The group gathered up their supplies, with Alex collecting the three remaining fire-gems. It was a shame he'd had to destroy one, but their lives were *definitely* more valuable. To them, at least.

They took some of the rubble created by the hive-queen's convulsions and built a mound against the wall. Brutus used it as a boost to bound over the top, and avoiding the wreckage of the eggs, the rest followed, with Theresa lifting Selina up to Alex, then scaling the wall last.

On the other side, the portal to freedom and the Traveller's body lay.

With quiet reverence, they approached the body of their patron saint.

Her form was mummified, and her features were preserved. In death, the Traveller looked timeworn, like an ancient village elder ready to tell stories at the harvest festival. Her hands lay against her belly with palms raised. In one hand was a faded golden glow in the shape of Uldar's hand: the Mark of the Saint. Beside her lay a thick book bound with iron.

Her mana was so strong, it felt like it was physically touching Alex. The remaining darkness in the core shuddered, and drew away from her light.

Alex bowed his head to her. "Thank you. If it weren't for your power, we'd all be dead. I know you probably wouldn't like what I'm trying to do—running away from the fight and all—but... I hope you'd at least approve of this."

Crouching beside her, he placed the dungeon core in her hands.

The sphere shuddered, and the darkness shot to the top of the orb, away from the Traveller's hands.

"Oh, you really want to slither around, don't you?" He glared at the thing.

He remembered when the hive-queen had used the core. Its mana shifted in the air at the same time as the darkness shifted within.

Hopefully, it worked by way of mana and will. If it did, since it was so weak now, even he might be able to force the dungeon core's mana to touch the Traveller's. His mind went to his Mark.

This would be a task that wouldn't involve spellcraft, unless he'd really misread what the hive-queen had done. It wasn't combat, and he hoped it wouldn't count as divinity.

If he focused on the task of breaking the dungeon core, then memories *should* build up that would eventually let him get there. Taking a deep breath, he focused his mana and placed his palms on the sphere, pushing into the core. It was a bit similar to how he used will and mana to control his forceball after it had been cast.

His mana bounced off as though slapped away. Alright, one failure.

Now for the moment of truth.

He concentrated on the Mark.

A single image rose in his head. It was of himself pushing his mana toward the core, trying to break it. It pointed out what he had done right. He grinned. Now it would be a matter of repeating the task.

"This could take a while," he warned his companions. "You might want to have a seat."

Again and again he threw his mana at the core, at first to no effect. With each try, though, he attempted something different with his mana. Minor successes built up and—guided by the Mark—he began to make some headway.

The dungeon core fought for its existence, trying to push him away. Sweat poured from his brow. If it still had even a little more of its strength, he doubted he could have done this much. He didn't know how long they battled—minutes or hours—but he was able to get a little deeper into the core each time.

His mana weaved through the maze of its defences.

The weakened darkness began to slide lower in the sphere, approaching contact with the Traveller.

Soon.

He drew on his mana harder to push deep this time and keep building on his successes. His mana chased the core, ready for the next failure or success to guide him. But the attempt did something he didn't expect.

Click.

Something slid into place, like a key sliding into a lock within the soul.

The pulsating mana shuddered.

In an instant, his senses stopped being lucid. He was everywhere in the cave at once. The pulsating mana overlapped with his mind, fighting him viciously. Images poured into his thoughts. Dark spheres. Blasted landscapes. Monsters in the dark.

He screamed and thought only about escape.

Just before he was pushed out by the core, his mana moved with the thought of escaping.

The dark in the sphere moved with it.

The key slid out of the lock.

Kroom.

A small wall rose in front of the portal to the Rhinean Empire, high enough to serve as a stepping stone to the door.

High enough to help them *escape*.

Then he was back in his body, and the last of the dungeon core's power faded.

Left defenceless, the Traveller's magic poured in eagerly. It flooded the sphere with blue light and rushed in so strongly, it flashed through Alex as well.

For an instant, her mana touched his.

Then it was gone.

With a scream like scraping glass, the dungeon core crumbled into shining sand.

Selina clutched her brother's clothes. "Are you okay? You were screaming!"

"Alex?" Theresa grabbed his shoulder. "Alex, did the core do something? That wall appeared!"

He stared at them, uncomprehending. The magnitude of

what he'd just done melted every thought from his head, except for one.

It was only for a moment, and only because it was so weak, but he had controlled one of the Ravener's copies and built a wall. It was impossible. It had to be. Dungeon cores were for the Ravener's monsters, humans couldn't manipulate them. Could they?

Then something occurred to him.

He concentrated on the Mark again, focusing on the idea of control, and what happened turned his blood cold.

The Mark of the Fool brought up the proper memories, neatly organized, pointing out everything he had done right. Like if it was just another skill to be learned. A skill that let one *control* one of the enemy's most precious resources.

No legend mentioned this, nor had it been written in Galloway's book.

Yet, he'd done it. The core had been weak, but he'd controlled it.

He thought back on all the cases where Fools had disappeared or betrayed the Heroes. If it was something to never be done, there should have been a warning to future Fools or to anyone. Why wasn't something about this written anywhere. Was it a secret? And... and if a Fool could learn to control the enemy's greatest weapons, then *how* was that useless? And, if humans—or maybe other races—could take control of the enemy's cores... what did that mean about the Ravener itself?

He shook his head. Either he was the first to figure this out, and the most clever Fool to ever bear the Mark—which he sincerely doubted—or...

"Theresa, Selina," he finally said. "Our legends... what's recorded... there's something wrong with them. Something. Is. *Wrong*."

Chapter 17

Out into the Light

"What..." Theresa stared at Alex. "What do you mean? What's wrong?"

"Listen." He pointed to the wall in front of the gate. "I'm—" He paused, trying to figure out how to explain without sounding like he'd lost his mind. "I... I controlled the core."

In the silence that followed, Alex noticed the scratches on Brutus' noses had a salve on them.

"What're you talking about?" His best friend looked at him like he *had* lost his mind. "You were holding that thing for a long time. Do you need to lie down?"

"Alex...?" A worried Selina shuffled from foot to foot. Her little hands clutched his clothes.

"I was trying to break the core. Trying to bring its mana together with the Traveller's..." He slowly tried to get his bearings back. "Next thing I know, I was sharing its... senses."

Growing confusion crowded Theresa's face. Brutus cocked all three of his heads.

"Are... are you okay?" Selina asked.

"Yeah, yeah, I'm fine. But... listen. The Mark was just showing me how to do it again."

"*What*?" Theresa asked incredulously.

He shrugged helplessly. "It's... a skill, and it's not spellcraft, divinity or combat."

"No." She shook her head. "That... if that's true this... this changes the war."

His hands gripped his head. "Our history should mention this! I mean... look at all the Fools from the past! All the ones that were *supposed* to have disappeared?"

"D-did that thing tell you to do bad things?" Selina stared at the remains of the orb in fright.

"No," Alex said. "It fought me, but ran out of energy. The Traveller did the rest."

"Should we tell somebody?" the young girl asked. "If it's so important, I mean."

"I think what your brother just did is something like, highest blasphemy," Theresa said gently.

"What do we do?" the girl asked.

Theresa drew a long breath. "Alex, I know you might say that you—"

"Need to figure this out?"

"—don't want anything to do with this, but—wait, what? I thought you just wanted to get your own life back?"

"That was *before* I found out that huge parts of our history might be *secrets and lies*." He chewed his lip. "Theresa, *humans* can use the Ravener's dungeon cores. What does that mean? Can other races? Why is this a secret? Why is this hidden? Who's hiding it? *How* are they hiding it? There's something rotten in the Kingdom of Thameland." He looked to his companions seriously. "And the thing with rot is that it *spreads*. When we get to Generasi, we'll have access to one of the greatest libraries in the world and some of the greatest minds to have ever lived. We can look into this discreetly, then figure out who we can trust and maybe give them whatever we find."

The image of a smiling young man with a golden tooth came to his mind.

"Maybe Cedric. Maybe. I don't know if we can trust him, but—" He gestured to the broken core. "—either way, *someone* has to look into this. And right now, it seems we're the only people who know. And besides..."

He gave a tired smile.

"We're still going to go to a city of wizards. We're going to *have* lives; we'll just be doing a little service to our country too. On the side."

"I, I think that's a good thing to do," Selina said. "If it's something dangerous, then we should do something."

"I agree, but..." Theresa gave a grim look and gestured to the chasm. "That thing nearly killed us. If Cedric hadn't destroyed all of her soldiers, if you didn't think of using the temple eye gems, and if we didn't have the Traveller's portals here, then we'd all be dead. Three times over."

She looked down at her great-grandfather's sword. "If what you say is right, then something has gone through a *lot* of trouble to keep this a secret. I don't imagine the lives of three people and a dog would be spared. This is going to be dangerous. We *can't* meet such a challenge as we are now, and just hoping nothing bad happens would be fatally stupid."

"There you go, talking sense again." He smiled weakly. "I agree. We don't need to be Cedric, but we *do* need to at least be able to protect ourselves. Generasi is called the City at the Center of Creation for a reason. It has knowledge from all over the world. We can learn what we can, get some more money together and buy what we need. I can use the Mark to learn *every* skill I'm able to, and try to exploit it and learn to be a Proper Wizard."

Theresa frowned. "I don't know anything about magic. I

won't have much of a way to grow in a city of wizards... unless." She looked up to the portal with Mount Tai. "When you say all over the world... does that mean knowledge from the Tarim-Lung Empire?"

"Where your great-grandfather was from? I'm sure. Why?"

Her eyes glinted. "I'll explain later, but there's a reason why Twinblade Lu was so feared. And it wasn't *just* for his swords."

Brutus barked with all three heads and brushed against his master, who smiled at him. "And you too, Brutus. We'll grow together."

She was giving off that 'warrior from a lost time' vibe again, and Alex fought to tear his gaze away. His eyes landed on Selina, who was balling her little hands into fists.

"I-I'll grow too," she said with determination.

He smiled warmly and patted her head. "The only growing kids have to do is growing up."

"Your brother's right, let him and me handle this," Theresa said gently. "You just need to focus on going to school."

Selina looked between her brother and friend. Her chubby little face fell. "Okay." She briefly looked toward the portal with the fire mountains. "Okay."

Something lay in her eyes, but it faded.

"Right, then that's the plan." Alex rose to his feet. "Now, who's tired of this horrible death hive?" He glanced at the Traveller's body. "Uh, no offence."

"I am." Selina raised her hand.

"Absolutely," Theresa agreed.

Brutus barked once.

"Alright." Alex took a deep breath, looking at their portal to freedom. "Then let's get out of here."

He approached the Traveller one more time.

"Listen," he said quietly, crouching beside the body and touching one of her hands. Her mana brushed against his skin. It was calming, almost like a grandmother's hug. Though it was cool, it had its own kind of warmth. "I wish I could repay you for everything you've done for us, even in death. I owe you everything, but all I can say is that I'll honour you, in my own way. Oh, and uh, sorry about breaking your statues...

"I ask that you continue to watch over us. And the Lu family. And Peter and Paul; they're guards in Alric. Maybe not McHarris. Oh, and if you feel like expanding from Alric, Cedric of Clan Duncan. I think he'll need it."

He named others he wished her to protect, then scraped up a good portion of the dungeon core's remains and tied it into a pouch. Hopefully, he could learn something by examining it at the university.

Just as he was about to get up, he stopped. Didn't Cedric say something about priests' holy symbols singing when a Hero was close? Wasn't the Saint's supposed to from even farther away? Judging by the glow of her Mark, it still held some power.

He noticed a chain around her neck hanging to the side. Gingerly, he brought it up into the light.

He burst out laughing.

No hand of Uldar hung from it. Her holy symbol was that of two faces. Red-eyed goddesses with snarling mouths and sharp teeth.

"I guess you had your secrets too." He laid her symbol back down. "Well, I won't tell if you won't."

He looked closer at the book lying beside her. Across the spine was writing in the same language that had been etched into the statues' bases. Opening it revealed more writing in that language. He closed his eyes for a moment, then took the book and carefully laid it in his pack.

Maybe more of her story was within. Maybe it would be something else. Either way, he wanted to know more about her. He could borrow it and put it back someday.

When he stood, Theresa and Selina came forward and said final thank you's to the Traveller. Brutus whimpered. One by one, they stepped up onto the little wall in front of the portal to the Rhinean Empire.

Alex eyed the magical doorway and took a deep breath, holding out his hands.

Selina nodded nervously and took his left.

Theresa drew a deep breath and took his right. Her hand shook in his. He was fairly sure his hand was shaking too. Brutus simply barked, nuzzling up to his master to calm her.

She gave him a weak smile and put a hand on his leftmost head. "I'm okay, boy. I'm okay."

Together, linked tightly to each other, they stepped through the portal.

As they disappeared, the only motion left in the chasm was the shimmering of the Traveller's light.

In that radiance, she almost seemed to be smiling.

Vertigo hit Alex as a whirlwind of scenery flashed before his eyes. A castle that looked to be underwater. A city of silver, steel and glass. A silver chariot that roared past stars.

Then he was stumbling into tall, warm, grass, and falling to his knees with his head spinning. Selina tumbled past on his left, groaning and splaying flat on her back. Brutus landed in a heap of legs and heads.

Only Theresa managed to keep her feet. She gracefully stepped into the grass and held her hands out to keep her balance. She steadied and proudly rose to her full height.

Then her face turned green.

"*Bleeeergh*!" She threw up in the grass.

Slowly rising to his feet, Alex stretched and took a long look around.

The grass was different, and so was the light.

It was late afternoon in the Rhinean Empire, judging by the

position of the sun, which might have explained the pale shades of the grasses. Or they just might be different kinds of grasses. Alex had no idea, and this delighted him. So many new things to learn! The air was warmer and a soft breeze carried the hint of fresh water. The trees were shorter and less ominous than the tall trunks of Coille.

To the north were the Peaks of the Elements: one burning, one stony and studded in gem deposits, one covered in waterfalls, and the last floating above the earth. What a sight!

A weight lifted from his shoulders. One he had carried since being branded two nights before. Joy swelled in his chest so fast, he had to choke back tears. Tough times would likely be coming, but he couldn't ignore life's joys purely to focus on its worries. As someone who'd met grief at a young age, he knew that path wasn't the best one to stay on.

With a huge smile, he crouched beside his sister and his best friend, who had finally finished throwing up. He made sure to place himself between Selina and the fire mountain to the north.

"Are you okay, little goblin?" He patted her tummy.

She groaned. "I don't ever want to do that again."

His joy made him absolutely giddy, and he giggled. "I don't think we'll be doing that too much. Here." He helped Selina stand.

He glanced back to the portal and noticed it had faded to just a barely noticeable shimmer in the air. He brushed his hand through it. Nothing happened. It looked like this one was one-way only.

Brutus dragged himself up and shook, his jowls flapping on his faces. The cerberus perked up his ears excitedly, all three of his noses sniffing all the new scents of this strange land, as his huge body bounded through the tall grass.

Alex chuckled to himself as he rubbed Theresa's back. "He's having fun."

"I'm not," she groaned, holding her head. "It feels like my head was spun around, put on backward *and* upside down."

"Well." He clasped her shoulder. "I just wanted to say, you've started your dream. Look. Strange lands, like your great-grandfather saw."

She looked up, giving a little gasp of amazement. Her eyes swept around in wonder, taking in the new sights. From the Peaks of the Elements, to her own Brutus frolicking in the grass, barking and chasing bird-sized dragonflies.

"Oh, *Alex*," she sighed. "If I didn't stink of puke, I'd hug you right now."

"I'll ask for it later." He chuckled, glancing up to the sun's position. "Well, let's get out of sight of all that fire." He jerked his head to the mountain. "See if we can find a town. If not, we can camp. You have relatives in the Rhinean Empire, do you have any idea if this place is safe?"

She shrugged. "I don't know much about it. My uncle lives on the northern coast, and my parents say he doesn't really travel more than a day's walk from his smithy, except for when he comes to visit us. And when he visits, he talks about the town where he lives and that's about it."

"Well, I guess we'll find out together. Besides, I'd say we're safe. We just killed a giant monster! What can threaten us now?"

She gave him a withering look. "What did we *just* talk about, Alex?"

He sighed, and gave the withering look right back. "I *know*, Theresa, I was *trying* to bask in victory. Why're you ruining the mood by being sensible?"

While they weren't fortunate enough to find a town by sunset, the walk was pleasant. Following the River Austrus, it wasn't long until they found the closest bridge and the highway it belonged to. The road itself was broad and well-travelled, and they passed several farmers—some humans and some beastfolk—carrying livestock to market by cart.

It was such a strange, peaceful contrast to the tension they'd experienced during the mass exodus from Alric. None of the farmers travelled with any weapons, and they waved with broad smiles and greetings in the Rhinean tongue. Theresa responded haltingly with the same words, drawing on parts of the language she'd picked up from her uncle's visits.

Alex noted to himself to use the Mark to practice the language when they stopped for the evening. It was time to start finding useful skills wherever he could.

Just before dark, they found a small copse of trees close to the roadside, and with Brutus sniffing for, and not finding, any beasts-of-prey or other threats, they made camp.

Brutus *had* found some wild hares, though, so he and Theresa went rabbit hunting for their supper. To Alex's delight—after he'd cooked up another minor feast—the cerberus actually came to *him*, looking for his food for the evening. Progress!

His mind sparked at all the new-trained cerberus-related possibilities, and he picked up a stick.

"Don't even *think* about it," Theresa said from across the fire. She had her full deathstalker face on. "You *just* started to earn his respect. Don't ruin it now."

He held up his hands in mock innocence. "It's not what it looks li—"

"You're going to try to make him play fetch."

"Okay, so it's *exactly* what it looks like."

He looked to Brutus, and saw that one of his heads stared directly at him. The big dog did not look impressed.

Alex laid the stick down.

She smiled, letting deathstalker face slip. "Remember, it's all about patience, whether it's hunting or befriending an animal.

Don't act too quickly just because you *think* you have the advantage."

Something passed through her eyes. "When you *know* the time is right, *then* you strike."

"Right, I think I follow."

"Good," she said before taking Selina's dinner scraps to dispose of.

Glancing at Brutus, he smiled wickedly to himself. First, trust and respect. Then, when the time was right...

...fetch time.

The night passed far less eventfully than their previous night, and Alex had time to use the Mark to go over his few memories of the Rhinean tongue while on watch. As soon as it was Theresa's turn, he slept the sleep of the dead. All the previous days' excitement had completely exhausted him.

When he woke up in the morning, his muscles felt like McHarris had beaten them for hours.

He forced himself to move through the pain while promising to start strength training soon. He'd need to be physically ready for trouble in the future.

But trouble didn't come that morning, and they made good time during the rest of the day, especially once Theresa convinced Brutus to carry Selina on his back. By noon, the road had filled with other travellers, and soon, they began to hear a roar in the distance.

They looked at one another and took off, racing up a hill toward the distant roar. Surprised travellers watched them go. When they reached the summit, they could only stare.

Before them rose the walls of a city—the largest they had ever seen—and beyond, spread the beautiful blue waters of the Prinean Sea. Port Mausarr. They had come to the last leg of their journey. Now, finding a ship was all that stood between them and Generasi.

As they stared in contentment, Alex's eyes drifted to Theresa's beautiful, excited face. Her dream was coming. His dream was coming. He looked to Selina, ready to begin a new life. He looked at Brutus, happily frolicking through the grass.

He could almost taste the new life ahead of them.

But, whatever was wrong in Thameland could ruin that.

There on the hill in the morning sun, he made a promise.

He'd learn to use the Mark of the Fool's potential as best he could. He'd gather skills that could help him understand what was happening in Thameland, skills he could exploit to help his magic, and even any other skills he wanted.

He'd think. He'd adapt.

Then, with any hope, he'd be ready for whatever was coming.

Chapter 18

Using What You Have

"Well, this here's a mighty fine mess we gots." Cedric of Clan Duncan stepped through the fire-blackened tunnel, over the bodies of burnt spiders. "Damn little buggers're all over the place, and here I was thinkin' I'd killed the whole lot. Well, it don't matter now. Place's emptier than an ale barrel after a clan chief's weddin'."

He looked through the hole broken in the tunnel wall.

"Oi, Hart, you see any more of them beasties over there?"

"Just dead ones," a deep voice rumbled back.

"Oh, an' don't get too close to them portals. Remember what them guards back in Alric told us about the whole business of portals poppin' folks around the continent or into the bloody sky and such."

"Only place they threw the spiders is in the grave," the voice came back. "Almost done."

"Chosen, I really should insist we continue on to the capital," murmured one of the two priests that had accompanied them into the cave. The other simply bowed his head before his hands, praying constantly into his holy symbol of Uldar.

"Oh bah, put your spine back in, friend!" Cedric clapped the first priest on the back with a grin. "We gots three Heroes here, an' Alric's right on this bloody place's doorstep. This dungeon needs puttin' down, and there ain't no way around it. I think we can handle one that I already mostly cleared out. Then we can pop off to the capital to do bloody ceremonies and all that sort o' thing, don't ya think? Am I not right, Drestra?"

He glanced back to the Sage.

A lean woman stayed at the back of the group with her hands buried within her earth-toned cloak. On the side of her neck glowed a symbol resembling a staff. The Mark of the Sage. A veil hid her face from the nose down, and her eyes...

They were golden in colour, and their pupils were slitted like a snake's.

"We are enough," Drestra of Crymlyn Swamp said. Her voice was low and crackled like fire. Golden eyes slid over to one of the priests, who shuddered under her inhuman gaze. "Even these ones are enough. I sense none of the Ravener's mana. Only that colder mana we sensed in Coille. It is strong in this room. Stronger below."

"Aye, I sense that too." Cedric looked back to the temple chamber ahead, noting the sheer destruction that had occurred. "But the core might still be as weak as freshly hatched hens. With its mana so low, so we might not be pickin' it up from far off. Oi, Hart, you alright in there?"

A giant of a man stooped through the tunnel, the top of his helmet nearly scraping the stone. From beneath the steel, Hart Redfletcher looked back at Cedric with large, dark eyes. He bristled with weapons over his breastplate and chain armour, and a massive bow was strapped to his back.

A quiver of arrows with red fletching bobbed at his waist and he gripped an inhumanly large warhammer in both hands.

The symbol of the Champion lay on his bicep beneath his armour, as he told Cedric when they'd met on the road the night before.

"I only saw strange portals, which I stayed away from. Like a smart person." His voice was deep and would have suited a far older man. "The portals looked like they killed those spiders you talked about. No sign of a fight there."

"Then just here, eh?" Cedric put his hands on his hips, looking between the shattered statues and the burnt spider horde. "An' what do you suppose happened in here? Maybe somethin' with them statues? Almost feel bad when rock's doin' my damn duty for me."

"My father used to say that the best battles are ones won before they are fought," Drestra said.

"Used to say?" Hart glanced at her with interest. Cedric had noticed the big man's gaze lingering on the witch's eyes. With curiosity, not distaste. "Where is he now?"

"He died in battle."

"Ah, pity. Happens to the best."

Drestra raised an eyebrow. "I understood that it is victory that belongs to the best in battle."

Hart shrugged, and the wooden mercenary-badge of the Ash Crows bounced on his tabard. "Sometimes it does. If they're lucky."

"And speakin' of victory, if'n there's nothin' to worry about, then I says we finish clearin' out the place." Cedric jerked his head toward the fragments of doors on the opposite end of the temple that had been blasted "C'mon, 'brave Heroes,' let's go."

"Well, if that ain't the most amazin' sight you've ever seen in your life." Cedric gawked at the floating portals as the Heroes and priests trudged down the path into the chasm. His eyes lingered on a portal that led to the sky where sinewy, reptilian forms flew on bat-like wings. Figures rode on their backs, though none seemed to notice the portal.

"Real bloody story by the bonfire stuff. Did any o' yous priests know anythin' about this?"

"I... I... No, Chosen, we have no details of this place." The first priest gaped. "The Cave of the Traveller should... this is an incredible discovery!"

"It is." Drestra stared at the portals. "A unique magic. The Witches of Crymlyn would give much to study this place."

Hart scanned the portals and darkness below for any sign of threats, with his giant bow readied. "Do you feel any of the dungeon core's mana?" he asked the two spellcasters.

"Not a bit." Cedric shrugged as Drestra shook her head. "Either the bloody thing went an' hid on us, or it's dead."

"Perhaps the Traveller intervened," Drestra offered.

Cedric glanced to the body far below in its shimmering blue light. "Let's check that theory, shall we?"

They passed through the dead hive, stepping over egg sacs and fallen weblines connected to the wall. They took care to avoid stepping into any portals close by.

When they approached two walls raised in their path to the Traveller's body, Hart drew his hammer with one meaty hand. He limbered up his shoulders and cracked his neck.

"Stand back." He swung at the wall.

Crash!

A single blow shattered a giant hole in it.

Crash!

Another smashed it entirely.

As he crossed the rubble, he looked down. "All clear here. But, the stone's blackened. Some sort of fire happened here."

Drestra looked at a nearby portal. "Fire Mountains are through there. Perhaps an eruption?"

Hart looked from Drestra to the fire mountains. His eyes narrowed, not trusting the stability of the volcanoes.

"Well, that's bloody terrific, even faraway mountains're killin' our enemies for us." Cedric threw up his hands in pretend frustration. "Guess we might be out of a job, eh, friends? Maybe we'll all go after the next core an' find a big old tree's taken it out, or some titan of a mole's dug it up and moved in with her kin."

Hart knocked a gauntleted fist against a giant claw half-buried in the earth. "Hm, good, strong material. Can we use materials from monsters? Or do they get all corrupt?"

He glanced at the priests.

"Er, previous Heroes have." The first cleared his throat, while the second continued to pray. "Though it is not proper. Our enemies' materials should be destroyed, but there is no law stopping others from using what they find."

"I'll be not 'proper' then. Looting is half a mercenary's pay. Maybe more." Hart tapped it one more time. "Claw's bit right into the rock without bending. One would make for a hell of a blade."

With a grunt, the Champion took hold of the monster's claw and tore it from the stone with ease, sending up a shower of rock. The priests jumped back from the flying dust and pebbles.

Hart tested the edge that had been buried in the stone. "Cut rock and not even dulled." He set the claws on the ground. "I'll be taking those."

His hammer swung at the opposite wall.

Crash! Crash!

"If it's all this easy, we'll have the Ravener dead by Sigmus." He stepped back over the rubble. "Fire Mountains or not, something's done our work for us."

"Ahhh, or maybe *someone*." Cedric bounded past the Champion and peered at the body of the Traveller, giving her a short bow of respect. "Ahhh, would ya look at that?" He gestured to the shining sand in her hands with his spear. "If I were a bettin' man—which I am, we'll get the cards out later—I'd say our old predecessor here did the work. Oi, holy ones, would yous say that this stuff here's what's left o' the dungeon core? Or did some beastie happen to drop a bunch o' glass into the Traveller's hands?"

One of the priests drew a small, leatherbound book from his robes and flipped through the pages, peering at little descriptions, illustrations and diagrams within.

"According to *The Bestiary of the Ravener and its Foul Spawn*, a dungeon core shall crumble into fine glass-like dust after destruction."

"Does this here look like that stuff?"

As the priest approached the Traveller, his holy symbol began to sing like a heavenly choir had been tied to his neck. He looked between an illustration in the book and the sand. "It matches."

"It would appear her magic destroyed the core," Drestra said. "But after some sort of battle, perhaps?"

"Maybe something came out of one of those portals." Hart shrugged. "Could be anything. More magic in here than I've ever seen, and that's not nothing. The Ash Crows have killed a fair share of wizards."

"Charming." Drestra gave him a look.

"What? We were paid for it. Nothing personal."

"It was no doubt personal to the wizards."

"Yeah, and that boar you put away three steaks from last night?" Hart grinned. "It was pretty personal to him when I shot him, but I didn't hear you complaining about that while you were stuffing your cheeks like a baby squirrel."

There was a light playfulness to his tone, but the only reaction he received from Drestra was an unreadable stare.

"Now, now, let's set aside matters of wizards and piggies." Cedric chuckled, raising his hands. He'd been measuring both of his new companions, and so far, he'd been pleased. Both clearly knew their jobs well, though he did wonder how they'd get along.

A hermit witch from the western swamps and a hardened

warrior who'd grown up among mercenaries didn't exactly speak of fellowship, teamwork and sociable nature. Well, maybe they'd warm up in time.

"Praise be to Uldar and to his Saint, the Traveller, for she is the first to defeat a core during this cycle," the second priest said into his symbol. "Praise be to you, oh past Saint."

Cedric nodded, looking down at the particles of the core with regret.

In truth, he was a bit disappointed in not having a nice little scrap ready and waiting in the dungeon. The fight against the spiders outside had made the old blood of Clan Duncan sing in him, even if the battle had been a little easy.

He kept his disappointment to himself.

Probably wouldn't do for the Chosen to complain the fight against the land's ancient evil wasn't hard enough.

"Can material from the core itself be used?" Drestra's reptilian eyes were fixed on the shining sand.

"Er, yes," the priest said. "It is a strong mana conduit. If the proper apparatuses are used, there is a history of crafting powerful potions or pressing them into weapons."

"We take that too, then." Hart rubbed his hands together. "Loot and no fighting. Best job I've ever had."

"Aye, agreed. No sense in leavin' resources lyin' about to gather dust." Cedric bowed his head to the Traveller. "Thank you kindly, Saint o' times past, you did the people about the land near a fine service."

A thought occurred to him, and he turned to the portals appraisingly.

"Say... spekin' o' using things. Ya think we could get some wizards down here to take a look at this place?" Cedric willed his spear to melt down and pour over his arm. No need for it, most likely. "I'm thinkin', if we can put sense to how this place and all its fancy doors work, then we gots ourselves a way to get all the folks that need out of Thameland away real fast. Lot less death and a lot less not affordin' a bloody boat."

He smiled in anticipation.

"Aaaand, if we see any portals that lead to places here on the island, then we gots ourselves a way to pop around quick and stomp out a bunch o' dungeons before they get too fighty."

Well, hopefully, they'd be a *little* fighty. His da didn't raise a warrior that knocked around opponents who couldn't fight back.

"As you say, Chosen." The first priest bowed. "We will send for wizards and inform the priesthood and nobility about this find. Once your support team is ready and you have been joined by the Saint in the capital, you may use this place as you wish when its safety is confirmed. I will have the local garrison fortify this location in the meanwhile."

"Good, good stuff. Fine, then, let's get to the capital and get things truly started. Hopefully, we'll have the Fool by then." He looked to the Traveller. "We can't have the dead doin' *all* the work."

"Meh, the Fool's not with us and we've already got a dead dungeon," Hart said. "Let them hide if they're hiding. Either way, we'll have this all fixed by Sigmus."

"Aye." Cedric glanced one more time to the dungeon core's remains. "Let's hope that's so."

A titanic orb of darkness floated somewhere deep beneath the earth.

The cavern surrounding it was large enough to fit an entire castle, and it *teemed* with monsters. Hive-Queens of Silence. Hulking scaled behemoths that breathed brimstone and poison. Humanoid giants with no skin.

Other monsters crawled and flew through the cavern—the

Ravener's direct spawn. The dark swarmed with their cries and their eyes were filled with death.

The Ravener floated above them all, over a pool of black, stagnant water. Shadows stirred in its depths. Something had destroyed one of its cores. No, more than that.

Something else happened. Something which had not occurred in many cycles of its reincarnation. Something that could not be tolerated.

An ancient commandment was renewed within.

The darkness of its surface swam, and its monsters went silent, bowing toward it. Its darkness swirled faster until it finally spit out five creatures into the black pool below.

They were humanlike in shape, though covered in skin that was like thousands of scabs joined together. Their eyes had no pupils and their humanoid skulls had no nose or lips, revealing teeth like scorpions' stingers. Claws the size of short swords dripped poison and the webbing between their fingers and toes let them bob in the dark waters with ease.

They listened closely as the Ravener instructed them.

Seek.

One of the creatures swam to shore and stepped onto land. The other monsters, its older siblings, parted to let it pass as it stepped into a passageway that would lead it to the surface. Thameland would be its area of search.

The other four creatures dove into the dark water.

Swimming deep into the earth, they followed underwater tunnels deep beneath Thameland. Eventually, the water changed from fresh to salt, and they emerged into the ocean far below where light touched, and far beneath where the priests had erected their barrier.

Only they, of all the Ravener's children, could survive the horrible pressures of this deep. Only they, its assassins, could seek what it told them to find.

They broke apart, each swimming in different directions.

They let out long-range pulses of mana, which echoed back to them like a bat guiding itself in the dark. Each would pass through the world, until one of their pings found a marked one.

One who had usurped a core.

One who needed to die.

Chapter 19

The Red Siren

Port Mausarr was overwhelming.

The sights. The smells. The energy.

Alex once read that the city was the largest port in the south of the Rhinean Empire. And it showed. Seagulls trumpeted at each other above marketplaces bursting with activity.

Farmers, fishermen and vendors called to travellers throughout the cobblestone streets, all working for an early sale. Tempting scents rising from the many food stalls made Alex's belly rumble, even though they'd recently had breakfast. Half a dozen languages swarmed around them and he listened to them all.

Then there were the people.

Alex had seen an elf in Alric once, as well as one of the beastfolk—a pinkish merchant with the head of a pig. They were surrounded by a multitude of peoples now, including the oceanic folk—or selachar, as they called themselves—and several races of beastfolk.

Most of the beastfolk around the markets shared the traits of human and pig, but there were also some that were dog-people, cat-people and even hulking minotaurs. Brutus tilted his heads as he sniffed and eyed the dog-people. Theresa had to keep him from chasing after the cat-people.

The selachar were similar to humans, except for the silver-grey cast to their skin, solid-black eyes, and the gill-slits framing their necks. When one laughed nearby, Alex noticed their mouths were full of sharp, jagged teeth. Selina quietly asked him if they also lived in the water, but he had no idea. That was something for them to learn about in Generasi's library.

And by talking with people, he guessed.

"This is what Great-grandfather saw most of his life," Theresa murmured. Her voice held a dreamy quality, and she tried to hold her gaze straight so they wouldn't look like gaping bumpkins. "So many things. So many people. So many ports."

"It's all sooo cool." Selina held her brother's hand, her eyes shining at the stone architecture. Of particular interest to her was a cathedral they passed in midtown, one dedicated to the four elements. The symbols of fire, water, stone and air chased each other in the stained glass of its largest window. It felt a little strange to him, seeing a temple without Uldar's hand raised over its front.

Luckily, it didn't look like Uldar had any presence here.

Which meant none of his priests.

"Yeah," Alex agreed. "It's pretty cool, isn't it? And you notice the stares *we're* getting? I guess cerberi are as rare in the Rhinean Empire as they are back home."

When they'd first arrived at the city-gates, and before the guards would even consider letting them through, they'd been questioned about Brutus' temperament. They kept making comments about his size, the fact that he had three large heads, and that he *looked* dangerous. For his part, Brutus ignored them, staying by Theresa's side as two of his heads swivelled every which way, while one would dip to investigate new scents.

"I hear it's even wilder in Generasi," Alex continued.

"Tamed monsters, wizards everywhere, people that can fly… It's going to be great."

"I can't wait to see it." Theresa drew a long breath, her imagination taking over. A thoughtful look crossed her face. "It's funny. Great-grandfather used to see all of this for most of his life. Then one day he thought, 'that's enough' and left to settle down in quiet Alric." She chuckled. "And here I am, one of his descendants, who just kept wishing I could get away from there."

"People are just different, I guess." Alex shrugged. "Maybe we always want what we don't have."

He thought back on Cedric, and how *completely ready* the young Hero had been to go do his duty. It wasn't just that he was brave or tough, it was that he was ready to jump into his destiny with a smile. His Mark had… *chosen* well.

Alex snickered at his own pun.

He liked Cedric well enough from the short time they'd met, but they were different in a lot of ways. Alex definitely wouldn't have been happy about receiving the Mark of the Chosen, but he wondered what would have happened if he had gotten the Mark of the Sage.

It expanded a person's mana a hundredfold, if the legends were right.

That would have been incredible. Having a pool large enough to construct a slew of spell arrays at the same time, and keep a number of magic circuits running without draining reserves. As Alex practiced magic, his mana pool would expand naturally, which would both increase his reserves—allowing him to cast spells more often—*and* increase the number of magic circuits he could fit inside his pool at once. Eventually, he'd have enough room to link magic circuits and cast spells of higher tiers.

What could he have done with a mana pool a hundred times the size it was now, with room to grow even more?

He imagined standing on some battlefield, raining down

hundreds of glowing forceballs onto a horde of silence-spiders like a meteor shower. Or blasting apart the hive-queen. Despite himself, the fantasy brought a smile to his face. Maybe *that* scenario wouldn't have been so bad. Helping Cedric and the other Heroes by using the tools *he* knew how to use. Putting down the Ravener for another hundred years and going off to Generasi with experience, a colossal mana pool and the most amazing practice.

Then again, maybe none of that glory would have happened. Maybe he would have died in some dungeon.

He sighed, looking over the peaceful folk surrounding them in Mausarr, completely separated from the plight—or as the legends called it—pride of Thameland. How many people here yearned for more adventure? How many from home would have sold their left arm for this peace?

He brought himself back to reality. There was no use pining for things that hadn't happened. He'd gotten the Mark of the Fool, and learned of what was likely a deadly secret. His eyes hardened. Besides, if something *was* wrong with the legends, then he'd rather have the Mark of the Fool. Better to be a Fool who could figure out what was wrong and be ready for it, than a Sage who was completely blind.

He studied the people of Mausarr closer, noting once more how peaceful they were. Oblivious to the threat of the Ravener.

A thought occurred to him.

He only remembered ever hearing of Thameland's Heroes battling their ancient enemy. Had it never gone to other lands? Some tales spoke of Heroes whose origins were from far off places, but they were all Thameish when marked. The people fled to other lands while the enemy was being fought at home... Had the monsters never once escaped the priests' encirclement that Cedric had spoken of?

What of other realms? Were there other things like the Ravener *they* had to face?

His list of things to investigate once they reached Generasi was growing.

"Brother, look!" Selina pointed ahead.

He pulled himself from his thoughts. They had come to another hill. Past the bustling city, split by the River Austrus, were docks and shipyards, where dozens of high-masted vessels drifted in and out of port on the Prinean's gentle waters.

Once they reached one of those ships and departed, they'd soon be at the city of wizards.

"Passengers! Passengers to Generasi!" a huge selachar man called, revealing sharp teeth every time he shouted. A massive scar ran from his forehead, over the bump on his short nose, and ended just above the lip.

His words were followed in a stream of accented Rhinean—too quickly for Alex to begin to understand, even using the Mark. He was only able to pick out the words "full," "morning" and "drinks." The giant of a man looked around and made a strange clicking noise with the side of his jaw. He eyed the crowd, but received no takers.

"What about that one?" Alex nodded toward the giant. "What's he saying?"

The group had bought an early lunch of skewered fish balls seasoned with sea salt and shallots. It took some negotiating to get the seller to take Thameish coins, but Theresa had finally reached a sort of agreement while Alex watched closely, listening to the language.

The food had been worth it. The fish balls were delicious, and Selina tore through about six of them and showed no signs of stopping. Brutus was slobbering all over them too, which definitely meant he liked them, and—though the meal was saltier than Alric's cuisine—Alex and Theresa couldn't get enough.

Now the huntress peered at the sailor—probably the captain judging by his fine but patched clothes—while translating some of the Rhinean words. "Cargo's full... and something about passengers. They're leaving tomorrow morning. Meals... can't understand the rest."

"Finally, one that's leaving soon." Alex relaxed. For much of the morning, they'd combed the docks, but most of the ships that were taking on passengers either weren't bound for Generasi or weren't leaving for at least a week.

The sailor grinned wide when he saw the group approach, and said something in Rhinean. Theresa started to reply. "Passage... we want... ummm."

While she paused to think, the sharp-toothed man's grin widened.

"Are you all Thameish?" he asked in the common tongue.

Theresa startled. "Uh, yes."

"I *thought* that was the accent," he said proudly. "Looking for passage? Well, we're still taking passengers, but cargo's full, if you have cargo. Departing in the morning. Meals are on me, but drinks—if you take to drink—are on you!"

"No drinks, just passage," Theresa said. "How much?"

The man's jet-black eyes ran over them appraisingly. "Ten Thameish silvers each. Five for the child. Twenty-five to board your big three-headed friend." Those eyes lingered on Brutus. "Is he house-trained?"

All three of Brutus' faces managed to look offended.

"Since he was a pup," Theresa said. There was a note of defensiveness in her voice, and she reached out and patted him.

"Good, better that way. I do half upfront and half when we get safely to port. Fair deal?"

He held out a massive hand, and Alex noticed his fingers were webbed. Both he and Theresa shook the offered hand, and he passed the captain two gold coins and five silvers. The man studied them with an expert's gaze, testing the gold against his teeth.

"Real enough." He slipped them into one of the pouches on his belt, which didn't appear very full. "Welcome to the *Red Siren*, my passengers! I'm Captain Fan-Dor, and I'll have you in Generasi's harbour in two days. I've got three rules. One: You listen to what I say. Two: Treat my ship like you would your mother's marriage-pearl. No damaging it. No fooling around. Three: Treat me and my crew with respect. Got it?"

"I'm pretty sure the only people that wouldn't agree with those rules are massive idiots," Alex said lightly.

"Hah!" The captain gave a barking laugh. "I like that, boy, but you'd be surprised just how many idiots we get."

"Um." Selina was looking at the ship's rigging and sails with utter fascination. "Um, Captain Fan-Dor, is... is it okay to ask questions about the ship?"

The captain's smile turned warmer when he looked down at the small girl, though his sharp teeth still gave him a vicious look. "You like ships, little one?"

"It's... I've never seen anything so big float." Her eyes traced the sails. "And move with the wind. It's amazing that you can make it go where you want!"

The captain stared at her for a moment before digging into his pouch and handing five silvers back to Alex.

"The little one rides for free," he said seriously.

As they boarded the ship, Alex was nearly vibrating with excitement. The last potential obstacle between them and Generasi was falling away. More than that, he had never *actually* been on a ship before. The stories Theresa's grandfather told drifted back to his mind—no Mark of the Fool needed to call them—bringing images of high adventure and danger by sea.

The high adventure part awakened boyish dreams, though any adventures could do without the danger by sea part. Then he remembered his earlier fantasy about being the Sage and blowing up silence-spiders.

Well, *maybe* a little bit of danger. He'd likely have to deal with that anyway soon enough.

The crew inspected the ship around them, a little over a dozen sailors in all. Powerfully muscled humans from many lands worked alongside beastfolk that looked similar to frogs—speaking to each other in low, croaking voices—and black-eyed, grey-skinned selachar. Here were folk who'd seen more of the world in a single week than Alex had in all his life.

He had nothing but respect for that.

"Passengers?" a familiar voice said close by.

Alex turned toward it and stopped in surprise.

Rising up from inspecting a long crack in the deck was... Fan-Dor?

Well, not quite, he realized. The new man's face and build were identical, but he lacked the immense scar that marked the captain's face.

"Gel-Dor, First Mate," the large man introduced himself. "Twin hatchling to Captain Fan-Dor. If you're staying until we depart, passenger cabins are down the stairs—" He jerked a thumb toward the stern. "—and straight forward. Two of the cabins are occupied, but the third on the right's—"

He paused, giving them an appraising look.

"You know what? Take the third on the right and the one across the hall."

"Two rooms? What about more passengers?" Theresa gave a glance back to Captain Fan-Dor, who had returned to his calling to potential takers.

People avoided his gaze.

A strange look passed over Gel-Dor's face. "Yeah... others," he grunted. "Anyway, take the two rooms. You'll need the space."

Theresa and Alex exchanged a look.

Now that he looked around more carefully, he noticed a fair

number of patches in the first mate's clothes, and the other crew members' trousers and shirts were threadbare. Alex just assumed that one just wouldn't be able to keep clothes in good repair at sea. But now...

He thought back on how light the captain's coin pouches looked, and started to wonder if they might still be able to get their coins back. Then again, he *had* let Selina ride for free, and that was decent. Maybe being decent was the reason why they didn't have much coin. If that were the case, why weren't people boarding?

"Oh, and this evening." Gel-Dor pointed to a space cleared on the deck toward the bow. "We'll be holding the Ceremony of the Spear-and-Oar Dance to honour Ek-u-Dari, the Ocean Goddess, for safe travel."

"Spear-and-Oar Dance?" Theresa asked with sudden interest.

He nodded. "One of our people's sacred dances on land. A cousin of our fighting style. You're welcome to attend and watch, if you've got interest."

Theresa and Alex exchanged another look, this time in shared excitement.

Possibilities whirled in his mind.

The Mark of the Fool hindered combat, but would it do the same to a *dance* similar to combat?

He intended to find out.

Chapter 20

Cookies and Dances

The cabins were tight and cozy with low ceilings, which meant Alex had to stoop to enter. Each had a single bed with a grey blanket that looked like it had seen better days. At the foot of the bed, an old chest sat with an iron key in the lock, ready to be turned.

The air smelled of straw that had gotten wet too many times, the leftovers of too many fish dinners, and dried salt.

"Well, home sweet home for a couple of days," he said.

"It smells funny," Selina whispered, following after him as he set his rucksack on the bed. She padded over and pushed the bag aside to flop down on the bed. The straw pallet rustled as she wiggled on it.

"It's... it's softer than the ground?" she offered hopefully.

"Stinkier too," he added.

She snorted.

Across the way, he heard Brutus whining and Theresa's lowered voice trying to soothe him. Alex winced in empathy. If Selina and *he* could notice the scent, then what about poor Brutus with *three* sensitive noses?

"Well, we'll have to share the bed," he pointed out. "And we're going to have to deal with the smell."

"What? Noooo," she groaned, and her long, chestnut hair puffed a little as she rolled back her head. "You turn and kick too much when you sleep."

"I do not."

"You *do*." She frowned at him. "I've seen you and I don't want you to kick me on the floor. *And* you're too tall for both of us to fit."

He waved a hand dismissively. "Oh, c'mon, little goblin, you're the size of a squirrel."

"Yeah, but you're not!"

"We'll make it work."

"But—"

"I'm your big brother, and I say we're going to make it work."

She sighed like a prisoner who'd just found out they'd been sentenced to spend the rest of their life in a dungeon. A castle dungeon, not a monster-making dungeon.

Alex frowned.

Why *did* those things share the same name anyway? They were completely differe—

"Alex... can I ask you a question?"

Her voice had taken a very serious note, and he pulled himself from his idle thoughts.

"Anything, little goblin, you know that." He dropped onto the pallet beside her. "What's on your mind? Is it what happened in the cave?"

"Yeah, in the cave..." Selina's eyes met his; the Roth siblings' eyes were an identical shade of green. "...Why did you and Theresa keep making jokes?"

"Huh? We did?"

"You were slapping each other's arms, and you joked when

you were about to break the core and... I don't think it was very funny. It was really, *really* scary."

"It's true, it was scary."

"Then why were you making jokes?"

He gave her a long look. "It's not... It's not really making *jokes*."

"'Itty bitty pieces?'"

"Okay, to be fair, that actually could have happened, but I know what you mean." He spread his hands. "I mean, it's weird, right? We're in a cave full of monsters and it's scary, we don't know where we're going, and me and Theresa are slapping each other."

"Mhm!" She nodded. "That's right, why? It doesn't make sense."

He sighed. "Well... sometimes..." He scratched the back of his head, trying to find the right words. "Sometimes it helps to have a little bit of normal. Sometimes it helps to laugh when you're scared or sad."

He looked away, his eyes falling on the old chest, and he let out a bitter chuckle. The one that had sat at the foot of his parents' bed had looked similar.

"After Mum and Dad were gone... do you remember how I was?"

She went silent and shook her head. "No," she said in a small voice.

Alex gave a short, self-mocking laugh. "I'm kind of glad you don't. Do you remember when Thomas Gwent lost his cards last summer? Do you remember how sad he was?"

"Yeah. He kept crying and crying and crying all the time, and he kept hiding by himself under Mrs. Walder's apple tree."

"That was like me, except it went on for a lot longer, and I used to hide in that old house by the wall all alone. Then one day, Theresa and Brutus tracked me and found me there."

He thought back. It'd rained a lot that day. More than he remembered happening in Alric before or since.

"She brought cookies." He glanced at his sister, who watched him with full attention. "She and Mrs. Lu made them from a recipe they had from Mum. They thought they'd make me feel better. So, Theresa walked all the way in the rain over to the old house with these cookies, but I didn't want to talk to her or anybody. But, she wouldn't leave. She just pushed her way in and sat down beside me dripping wet and took out the soggiest cookie you've ever seen."

"Gross." Selina made a face.

He laughed. "It was super gross. I didn't want to eat it, but she wouldn't move until I tasted it. I mean, it tasted alright, but sitting in a wet bag with rain soaking through'll ruin any cookie. Anyway, I spat it out and told her to leave and she just started yelling at me. So, I got mad and yelled back, and we keep screaming at each other so loudly that the watchman came running to see if someone was getting murdered."

He shook his head, continuing to laugh. "And boy, did he *ever* scold us. And when he finally let us go, it was just so awkward. We didn't say a word to each other. Then partway back home, I start thinking, 'Gee, I'm hungry' and—not even thinking—I asked her for another cookie."

"Did she smack you?"

"No, but she gave me this look like, 'You made me go through all that just to ask for a cookie now?' And I saw that look and just started laughing and couldn't stop, and then she did too. And you know what?"

He looked back to the chest. "That day, it hurt a little less. I spent the rest of that summer baking her family cookies every week. I put some aside just for her out of every batch, and I wouldn't let anyone touch them but her."

"I remember that!" Selina perked up. "They were... okay."

"Hah, I was still learning." He hadn't combined his mother's cooking with all of McHarris' secrets back then. "The important thing is that it didn't make all the bad go away. It didn't make things better every day—some were still hard—but it did make things a little easier."

She frowned. "So… when it gets scary or sad, you laugh?"

"If you can, sometimes, as long as people are laughing *with* you." He tapped the side of his head. "When you think about a scary thing and think about how scary it is, sometimes that *makes* it scarier. If you think different, then maybe it's a little less scary."

He shrugged. "It works for Theresa and me. Maybe not for everybody. But sometimes when you're scared, doing something you normally do makes things seem a little more normal and a little less scary."

"Hrm," she grunted. "I still don't get it."

"That's okay. Maybe when you're older, or maybe our way isn't for you. But, I think you'll figure out what works for you as you get bigger."

"Okay…"

"Do you have another question?"

"Mhm." She gestured at his shoulder. "Can I… can I see it?"

Alex nodded. "Of course you can."

He glanced to the doorway. He didn't hear anyone close by, but went to the door and bolted it just in case.

When he carefully pulled the shirt off of his left shoulder, the grinning jester's face was revealed, seeming to watch Selina. The little girl gasped, her chubby hands going to her cheeks. "Does—" she whispered, looking around as though someone might be listening. She leaned forward. "Does it hurt?"

"It did, but not anymore," he whispered back, dropping down to one knee so the Mark was eye level with her. "It doesn't even feel different. You can touch it, if you want."

She poked it with one finger, watching the dim glow disappear beneath her finger. "It's… kind of cool, Alex."

"Hah, you have funny taste, little goblin." Frowning, he eyed his skinny arm, and when she finished poking the Fool, he pulled the shirt back up and looked at the floor. *Time to do something about these skinny arms,* he thought, and lay down with his palms pressed to the floor.

"Uh, what are you doing?" Selina asked.

"Push-ups." He squared his shoulders in the way Theresa's oldest brother had taught him long ago. "We don't have a lot to do, and I think your big brother could use a little more iron in his arms."

"Okay." She gave him a weird look before slipping from the bed and making for the door. "I'm going to see what Theresa's doing."

"Alright, have fun. Go straight to her room and nowhere else, okay?"

Selina paused at the door. "Hey, Alex?"

"Yeah?"

"I love you, okay?"

"Yeah, me too. Selina. I love you too."

She turned to the door, standing there for a long moment. Alex waited, wondering what she might say next. Was she going to bring up another memory? Was she—

"Alex."

"Yes?"

"Could you get the latch? I can't reach."

He barely resisted the urge to chuckle, stepping over quietly to unlatch the door for his little sister. Before he could say anything else, she slipped from the room and shut the door behind her.

Alex Roth watched the door for a long time after she'd left, and when he finally started his push-ups—concentrating on the Mark to guide him to the correct form—tears were in his eyes.

"Ek-u-Dari, we dedicate this clash to you!" Fan-Dor roared.

Thm. Thm. Thm.

He drummed the deck with the butt of his spear.

"Ek-u-Dari, we ask for protection from you!" Gel-Dor roared.

Thm. Thm. Thm.

He drummed the deck with the butt of his oar.

"Just as the rain dances to feed the sea, we dance a dance of arms and oar."

Thm! Thm!

They drummed the deck once more, then raised their spear and oar in perfect unison. The identical twins faced each other across the deck.

They touched the flats of spear and oar, then turned and faced those watching. The crew and few passengers were seated around them in a circle, eating a late supper of sausages and cabbage; a final hot meal of land-food before the short voyage began.

With a bow, the twins stepped into the dance.

They moved in a complex display of footwork, punctuated by rhythmic stomps and sweeping hand movements, keeping their bodies perfectly balanced. Their feet danced across the ship, in perfect time with a drumbeat kept by three sailors. The spear and oar spun and flashed in their hands, with the hafts spinning in their fingers. They made no strikes, but as the brothers' feet stomped the deck, their objects of devotion rose in flashy, defensive guards.

The spinning steel caught the moonlight like ocean waves on a windy sea, and the two men leapt like acrobats, jumping and spinning like whirlwinds in harmony. Then they changed. No longer mimicking each other's movements; instead, they complimented them. The spear would spin high while the oar would spin low, then they would switch. One would guard left and the other right.

As the dance continued, they seemed to transform from two warriors mirroring each other, to a single warrior inhabiting two bodies.

Alex couldn't look away, while Selina gaped beside him. Theresa was half-raised from her seat, her eyes sparkling in the moonlight. All the sailors watched with a deep respect, while the selachar had dipped their heads in prayer.

Two of the other passengers—a couple that looked only a little older than Theresa's parents—smiled and clapped along with the drumbeat. The last passenger—a man even skinnier than Alex—only paid attention to his meal, eating as though he'd never seen food before. Already, three empty plates were piled beside him.

With a final flourish, the captain and first mate softly landed on the deck in unison with the spear and oar pointed toward the sky. "And so, we have *become* the storm in place of any storms Ek-u-Dari might send to us! Goddess, we hope we have pleased you and ask for your kindness!"

The ship fell silent.

Theresa was suddenly on her feet, clapping as hard as she could. Alex joined her right after and a startled Selina followed.

"And thanks to all of you for attending our ceremony." Captain Fan-Dor held his spear up. "And by all of you, I mean our guests. My crew had better be here if they want their pay."

The crew gave the laugh of folk who had heard the same joke a thousand times.

"Storms are always witnessed, and the more eyes to witness the sacred dance, the more Ek-u-Dari will show us her kindness." He approached the passengers. "You enjoy yourselves?"

He glanced at the skinny man, who scraped the last scraps of food from his fourth plate. "Well look at you, been stuffing yourself like you've got hollow legs."

The passenger looked up and asked something in Rhinean,

to which the captain responded. With a weak smile, the man said something to the captain.

Fan-Dor chuckled. "'Just a hollow belly,' he says."

"Captain, that was one of the most beautiful things I've ever seen." Theresa had a dreamy expression.

"Then you should see someone who's actually good at it," Gel-Dor said dryly. "You've been getting lax on your practice, brother."

"Only so you can keep pace with me," Fan-Dor shot back.

"Does it take a lot of practice to learn?" Alex asked.

The captain frowned. "Any dance does, boy, and the Spear-and-Oar Dance is more complex than most. Why?"

"Well, I was just thinking I'd, well, I wouldn't mind learning something like that."

Theresa shot him a surprised look.

Fan-Dor's frown deepened. "Listen, if you're asking so you can get free passage like your sister—"

"No, no!" Alex raised his hands. "I was just thinking that it'd be just... just..."

A way to learn how to dodge horrible death-beasts in a way that wouldn't make an ancient, magical Fool-brand have a tantrum? How the hell was he supposed to put this?

Then Gel-Dor elbowed his brother, and threw a meaningful look between Alex and Theresa.

The captain stilled and a massive grin spread over his face. "Huh. What was your name?"

"Uh, Alex."

"Right, then. Alex. Come here and I'll tell you all about it."

The captain dragged Alex to the side then put an arm around his skinny shoulders. "I see what's happening here."

"Huh?" Alex cocked his head, trying not to pull away. Fan-Dor's breath stank. It smelled like a mix of smoked sardines and rotten eggs, and it was slamming right into his face.

"You're trying to swim up the river, aren't you?" The captain's grin widened.

"What?"

"Y'know? Swim up the river? Burrow in the seabed? Slither under the coral?"

"...Pardon?"

"You're trying to spawn, aren't you? With your friend there?" He glanced over his shoulder. "Nice choice by the way. A little short, but you humans tend to be, and she's broad-shouldered for a human female. You'd spawn strong hatchlings together. At least she'd make up for, uh..."

He looked over Alex's skinny frame. "Well, at least you got height."

All the colour drained from Alex's face as he glanced back to Theresa, noticing Gel-Dor had taken her aside and was whispering something to her as well. Even worse, the older couple were giggling to each other while the skinny man's eyes were darting between Theresa and Alex.

For a wild moment, he strongly considered breaking out of the captain's grip and throwing himself into the sea.

"Well, don't you worry." Fan-Dor laughed. "I had a good captain to teach me the basics and strut myself properly in front of my wife at the Tide Festival, and I'm not one to not pay it forward."

He looked him up and down.

"You ever dance, boy?"

"N-no."

"Can you?"

With the Mark's help, the answer to that was a very strong *maybe*.

"Probably," Alex half-lied.

"Right, well we'll know what that 'probably' means soon enough." The captain looked to the cathedral's tower in the city. "Meet me up here when the last bell chimes. Least I can do is teach you the first three steps. We won't have time for more than that, but it should give you a head start. You'll need to think about your own marriage-pearl, though."

While Alex Roth was glad he'd gotten this opportunity, a part of him just wished the hive-queen had killed him.

Chapter 21

The Spear-and-Oar Dance

"The Spear-and-Oar Dance always begins with one thing: the spear." Captain Fan-Dor lifted his spear, showing Alex its shine beneath the moonlight. "But that is not how *we'll* be beginning."

He tossed Alex a long object, which the young man barely caught.

An old mop.

"Why don't we start with the oar?" Alex asked.

"Because that's a lot harder. Safer, but harder." Fan-Dor lifted his spear, holding the haft up by the middle and balancing it on one finger. "Weapons are balanced for quick movement. Oars aren't. That makes it harder."

"That makes sense."

"Normally, that's why we're taught the Way of Weapons before the Dance."

The captain's footsteps thumped over the deck as he took up position in the cleared area across from Alex. Only a few of the crew still stirred, leaving them mostly alone. Oil lights blazed on Mausarr's docks as sailors worked through the evening to get cargo loaded onto their ships.

"But, from the way you walk, I'm thinking you've never held a weapon before." Fan-Dor thumped the butt of his spear into the deck and leaned over the hilt.

"Once." Alex remembered when he'd begged Mister Lu to hold one of Twinblade Lu's swords when he was a child. He'd gripped the hilt while Mr. Lu held the scabbard. It was a fond memory, but it'd never made him want to get his own sword, or run off to be a knight like in so many stories he'd heard with young, heroic children in them. He wondered how the Mark would react to him doing that now. Probably not well.

"So then, we don't want you fumbling around and stabbing yourself. Or worse, stabbing me. So, a mop it is. Tonight, I'm going to start teaching you the first stance, the first step, the second stance and the first guard of the dance."

"Out of how many?"

"Of the basics? Five stances, five positions of the feet, and five guards. There's also basic jumps and flourishes, but you won't have to worry about those until about two years of practice, and trust me, you'll only need a little to look impressive for your... purposes."

He grinned at Alex, who felt a hot blush creep over his cheeks.

"So! First position!"

Thm.

He drummed his spear on the deck.

Alex watched him closely, making sure to note as many details for repetition with the Mar—

"What're you waiting for? First position!"

The young mage startled and scrambled into first position, holding his mop by the top and pressing the bottom to the deck.

"Come on, you can do better than that." Fan-Dor shook his head as though Alex were a fish trying to hop around on land on its tail. "Think of your eggs! Let that motivate you!"

Alex's cheeks burned. "Listen, uh, humans don't actually lay eggs. We, uh—"

"Oh, I know." Fan-Dor grinned. "But you should see the look on your face right now."

Alex stopped, then burst out laughing as his blush faded. He'd get him back for that.

Shaking off fantasies of amusing, petty revenge, he straightened his back and tried to copy Fan-Dor's exact stance. He focused on the Mark, and it offered him the best points of his first attempt. He matched it.

Fan-Dor looked him over. "Passable, for a second attempt. Not good. But passable. Right, so next, you'll want the front-step—"

"Uh, Captain, is there a back step?" Alex asked. "Can we learn that instead?"

First thing he'd need to learn was how to open distance from an opponent, not approach one.

Fan-Dor raised an eyebrow. "Of course there's a back step; it's a dance based on spearmanship. What sort of fighting style doesn't allow for retreat? The 'Get-Dead-Quickly-Spear Technique'? But why would you want to learn to retreat first? The approach step is more impressive."

"Because, uh..." Alex's thoughts whirled for an excuse. "Oh, because, when a noble bows to their partner in my country, they step back."

To demonstrate, he copied the bow he'd seen some of the richer townsfolk use to bow to each other, stepping backward with one foot and clumsily bringing his hand across his chest as he bowed. "I thought if I could combine that with your backward step in the dance, then it'd uh... look more impressive."

"I like it! Creative thinking there, boy, and using what you've already got. Fine then, back step it is. So, from first position, take your left foot and step back."

The captain demonstrated, and Alex followed his

movement.

"Not like that; you have no balance that way. Point your back foot out a bit to your side."

Alex shifted his foot.

"More."

Alex shifted his foot.

"Little more... There!"

Alex stopped, knowing the Mark would be noting this position for later.

"Is this good?" he asked.

"Not yet, now bend your knees. That's it. Lower... lower... there it is!"

Alex held his position, keeping his knees slightly bent. It was an odd feeling, but he felt like he had more control over his balance. Not complete control—he fought to keep his back straight.

"Better and better. Now use your hips, and make sure you're lining your spine upright. Like it's the mast of the ship. How's it feel?"

"Strange." Alex told the truth. Using his hips to keep himself in position felt odd and used muscles he didn't know he had. His chest and arms were already sore from the push-ups he'd put his body through. Embarrassingly, he'd only been able to do nine before flopping down on the floor like a gasping fish. Hadn't Theresa's brothers done about fifty? Had he remembered that right? He hoped not.

He didn't want to even imagine how many Cedric could pull off.

"Right. Not bad, boy. You're now in second stance. That's a fighting stance, by the way: on land, it keeps your weight on both feet."

"Right... and that's important because you don't want to lose balance?"

"Losing balance is bad. It makes for all kinds of possibilities for falling over and being murdered."

Alex thought back to the silence-spider that Brutus—who had been sleeping in Theresa's room since late afternoon—had thrown over. Once it was off its feet, even they—as inexperienced as they were—were able to kill it.

Balance. Keeping balance then. Dodging around only to land on your ass would be a disaster.

"And, for a dance, losing balance means looking stupid and defenceless. And speaking of defences: first guard."

Alex gulped. Things were sliding closer and closer to combat.

"So, first guard's simple." Fan-Dor brought up his spear in both hands on a diagonal. "You just do this."

Alex looked at his mop.

He was just holding up a mop. He was just holding up a mop. Hear that, Fool? He was just holding up a mop as a part of a dance. Nothing else.

Slowly, he copied Fan-Dor's motion.

And breathed a sigh of relief when the Mark didn't react.

"A little clumsy-looking, but not the worst." Fan-Dor wiggled his spear a little bit. "Bring up the butt of the mop just a liiittle more... That's the way." The captain grinned.

Alex grinned back. *Alright, so it doesn't seem to mind me holding up a mop, even if it's similar to a guard with a weapon.*

There were lots of actions with different objects that might appear similar to combat, such as swinging an axe to chop wood, or cutting meat with a knife. Or lifting up a mop in front of yourself. If the Fool blocked every action similar to fighting, then he'd *never* be able to live life.

Maybe that was the reason why he could use his forceball to slam into objects and walls, but it interfered when he aimed at living creatures or the things they held. Would it only interfere if the situation he was in was direct combat? Later, he would need to try and test its limits.

"Why frowning so hard, boy?" The captain cocked his head. "No need to push yourself; you're doing well for a first attempt. Right, let's go again."

Time after time, the captain guided him from the first position, through to the first step, the second position and then the first guard. Using the Fool, Alex kept part of his attention on the captain, while noting the detailed memories of what he'd done right in each attempt and letting them guide him.

It was as though he had two teachers with him the entire way. With each repetition, he improved slightly. Only slightly. Alex Roth was known for many things, but his dance prowess was not one of them. He had little previous experience to draw from and his height made it more difficult for him to keep proper balance.

Still, Fan-Dor grew more impressed as the early night wore on. "Well, now I think that's enough for both of us. And I have to say, you're a quick study. I wouldn't say you're a natural, but you're a lot better than you were when we started."

"I guess it's thanks to all your great teaching, Captain."

"Oh, save it for your lady friend. You're not going to get free passage from me no matter what you say."

Alex shrugged lightly. "Ah, well, there goes my clever plan. Is it too late to warn you that I'm out of money?"

"Better now than tomorrow night. Now I can drop you back on the dock. Tomorrow, I'd be tossing you overboard halfway to Generasi."

Alex paused. "You wouldn't really do that, would you?"

"Hey, half the pay means half the trip." The captain grinned wickedly. "Am I joking? Am I not? Count yourself lucky you don't have to find out. Now, come on. We both need to catch our rest. Oh, and keep the mop with you. I won't be able to teach you again, but feel free to come out here and practice tomorrow night."

As Captain Fan-Dor and Alex trudged back toward the stairs below deck, Alex looked over the ship one more time.

An odd feeling crawled over his skin, and for a moment, he was sure he was being watched. He shook away the feeling. Port was close by and any number of folk could have been looking at the ship. He'd be spending the next part of his foreseeable future investigating possible ancient conspiracies and studying remains of a dungeon core.

Plenty of real monsters to worry about.

No need to conjure imagined ones.

It was with this thought that he made his way below deck, ready to sleep and trying to push that creepy feeling from his mind.

Alex was awakened later in the dead of night by Selina pounding on him with her little fists, complaining that he'd pushed her off the bed in his sleep.

He wasn't sure if the Spear-and-Oar Dance had pleased Ek-u-Dari, but the sea goddess seemed to have smiled upon them the next day. The sun was high, the air pleasant, and a gentle wind filled the sails to push them south toward Generasi.

The Prinean sea was calm and seemed to glow a beautiful greenish-blue in the sunlight. The air was warmer than most summer days in Alric, and the scent of sea salt gave the air an inviting odour.

The only thundercloud on the horizon was Selina herself, who woke up cranky and refused to talk to him. Fortunately, depositing her beside Captain Fan-Dor seemed to clear up her mood, and soon the hulking selachar was eagerly answering the little girl's endless questions as he stood at the wheel, guiding the *Red Siren*.

Brutus lazily dozed on the deck, letting the sun warm his body.

Alex leaned against the rail at the bow, watching the waters ahead while keeping his ears open to the many languages spoken by the crew. He was also trying desperately to ignore the muscles screaming all over his body. Maybe forcing himself through another set of push-ups that morning hadn't been the smartest thing to do.

Theresa leaned over the rail beside him, sighing contentedly as the sea breeze rustled her ponytail.

"Enjoying yourself?" he asked.

"Like you wouldn't believe." She idly traced a finger on the rail while peering into the horizon. "It's like finding something you never knew you *needed*. It's wonderful. Just all this water and the wide world around you."

"Yeah, it's pretty great, isn't it?"

They fell into a contented silence, though he did notice Theresa give him a strange, sidelong look. She had been for much of the morning.

Then, that odd feeling from the night before crawled over his skin.

It felt like they were being watched.

Turning, he saw the skinny Rhinean man seated on a barrel behind them, stuffing himself with salt pork and biscuits. It was his second meal and it wasn't even noon yet. The lean man watched the two young people with intensity, but quickly looked away as Alex met his gaze.

Was he looking at Theresa?

An odd rush of jealousy sprang up in Alex. He shook it away.

Turning back to the sea, he hoped the man would stop staring at them. He wouldn't want that to continue for the rest of their trip.

Chapter 22

Tests by Moonlight

Footsteps creaked across the deck.

"Good morn—Afternoon, I suppose."

The middle-aged woman from the couple that attended the ceremony the night before drew up beside Alex and Theresa, and leaned against the rail, yawning. "Late evenings get harder as you get older, just to warn you two. Of course, I never seem to learn." She laughed. "Are you vacationing in Generasi?"

"Uh, studying, actually," Alex said, throwing another glance over his shoulder. The skinny man's eyes burned into Theresa then flicked to Alex and the newcomer. Sliding off the barrel, he gave a quick nod and made for the stairs leading below deck.

Another small wave of jealousy stirred in Alex, but now it was joined by a feeling of creepiness.

"Ooooh, you got into the university?" The woman brightened, all traces of tiredness disappearing. "You're both very, very fortunate. Both my husband and I were born in Generasi, but we've only ever toured the university."

"Oh, are you both wizards?" Alex asked.

"Oh my, no." She chuckled. "Could never wrap my head around all that spell array and circuitry stuff, and my husband has enough mana to maybe fill a shot glass. We work as administrators for the ruling wizard council. We're not very high in the office, but high enough to be worked to the bone!"

"Sounds impressive," Theresa said.

Alex tried to force the image of Alric's mayor's assistant being punched in the face from his mind.

"It's mostly pens, ink and candlelit nights—not the fun sort either. Oh, and not enough vacation time of course. Still, it's nice seeing all those young wizards in the city, walking toward bright futures. Together."

She gave them a meaningful look, and Alex couldn't help but blush. He made sure his face was turned from Theresa.

"What's it like? The city?" she asked, giving no hint of embarrassment.

"Oh, if you've never been, I shan't say." The older woman giggled. "Telling now would be like telling you the ending of a book before you get there yourself. It's something my husband and I are used to now, so I shouldn't rob travellers of the magic of seeing it for the first time. Trust me, though, you'll love it. Just take my advice: book a sky-gondola when you arrive. Will you be staying on the campus?"

Alex looked over his shoulder to his sister beside the captain. The wind carried her voice over, and he could hear her asking exactly how sails worked. He smiled. "Maybe for a bit. After that, we'll be buying a place for my sister, myself, and... Theresa."

"Don't forget Brutus." She tapped him on the arm.

"Oh, I could never forget Brutus. I don't think anyone could. Could you?" he asked the older woman lightly.

She didn't laugh. An odd look lay on her face. "Buying... property, you say? Young man, you wouldn't happen to be a noble, would you?"

"No, why?"

"It's just... Hmmm, do you have coin?"

Alex's cheeks flushed. He felt a little insulted.

"Not to assume anything," the woman said quickly. "But it's just that... you're so young."

"Oh, we have coin." His voice had a little more heat than he'd intended. His parents had ensured they'd be well off, and it hurt a little to have that questioned.

"Ah." The older woman's hand flew to her mouth. "I apologize, that must have sounded positively dreadful. It's just... my husband and I are near retirement now, and we've been blessed with fine careers. It's allowed us to vacation from Generasi many times. See our children. See many sights."

Her gaze drifted over the rolling waters. "We've seen many, many young folk climb aboard a ship for Generasi looking to begin a life. Some come to study. Some come for the Games of Roal and simply fall in love with the city and wish to stay. I can't blame them, but a comfortable life is a difficult thing to achieve there. At least financially. You're a student at the university, so that would exempt you from some of the bureaucratic process, but property is very expensive in the city. I've seen just as many disappointed faces on the return journey, or worse, cramming themselves into tenements and just scraping by. I'm sorry, but I'm only trying to spare you from disappointment."

Alex bit down on his anger. Likely, she meant well, but her assumption that his fortune—the material sum of his parents' lives—wouldn't be enough, made his teeth grind nearly as hard as they had in front of the dungeon core. He pulled himself away from the emotion, acknowledging it and trying to let it pass.

Feeling his anger couldn't be helped, but acting on it and making an enemy before he'd even set foot in the city, could be avoided.

"We'll have enough," he said through a forced smile, calling upon his Mark to guide him and make it look genuine.

She searched his face, and he could tell by her blush that she was a little embarrassed. "Well, you know your business. Again, I apologize. I should go and drag my husband out of bed before he sleeps the whole day away. Enjoy the morning air, both of you. I'll see you at lunch and, if not, hopefully during dinner this evening."

The woman made her way to the back of the ship.

Theresa watched her go. "Awkward," she muttered.

"Yeah," he agreed, turning back to the sea. "Actually, she reminded me of something I wanted to ask you about this evening. Can you meet me on deck tonight? And bring your great-grandfather's sword? And your knife?"

Her eyes searched him. "I can, but why?"

"I want to try some things with..." He let the statement hang in the air.

She nodded, seemingly knowing he'd referred to the Mark. "We'll meet after the others have gone to bed. We can leave Selina with Brutus."

Twinblade Lu's sword gleamed in the moonlight as Theresa drew it from its sheath. Now that he had time to look at it closely for the first time in years, Alex couldn't help but be amazed at how beautiful its steel was.

Like polished silver.

"Actually..." Theresa slid the blade back into its sheath. "It's probably safer if we do it this way."

"Yeah, good point." Alex imagined the Mark spoiling his concentration while he held a sharp blade. He shook away images of severed fingers flying overboard.

"Before I give you this." She looked at him seriously. "I want you to understand something: this isn't a stick. This isn't a knife. This isn't a toy."

"Yeah, it's your great-grandfather's sword," he said respectfully. "I'll treat it with respect, Theresa."

"That's not the only reason to treat it with respect." Her eyes were as grim as grave stones. "This is a weapon. Pure and simple. A bow is for hunting, targets, fishing and war. A spear is a hunter's weapon, and a knife is used in most parts of our lives. But I'll tell you something my grandfather told me: a sword is different."

She raised up the blade until it was level with his eyes. "A sword has one purpose, Alex: killing. It's a tool of battle. It's not the *first* tool of battle. That's usually a bow or a spear because even though a sword has bite, it doesn't have reach. People use them as a decoration, but that isn't its purpose. Its true purpose is for killing monsters and people. Treat it with the same respect you would one of your spells."

Alex nodded.

Theresa studied him, then handed him the sheathed sword.

Gingerly, he wrapped his fingers around the hilt.

Nothing happened. No interference from the Mark. So that meant he could handle weapons. Or swords at least. What were its limits, then? Would it only react if he attacked someone with it?

"Theresa, how do you strike with a sword?"

"That's... that's like asking how do you use a knife. There're lots of different strikes."

"What's an easy one?"

"Hmmm, I'll teach you a push cut. First, make sure both feet are planted on the—"

He dropped into second position from the Spear-and-Oar Dance, only wavering a little bit on his bent knees. "Does this work?"

Something passed through her eyes. "Yes..." Her voice warbled a little in what sounded like a suppressed laugh. "That works. Now bring your sword up." She drew her knife and held it in position before her. "Into this guard. This lets you strike and defend against strikes coming from above."

He watched her form then carefully raised the sword into guard.

The Mark did not like that one bit.

It flooded him with memories of the absolute clumsiest moments in his life. Tripping over his own feet during the harvest festival dances. Nearly falling down the stairs when he'd been running out the door as a young boy. Leaning too far over the railing of a bridge while he was fishing and plunging into the stream below.

The images slammed into his mind so hard, he didn't have any idea where he was or what he was doing. He tried to get past them like he had when casting his forceball, but he couldn't. He'd had lots of experience and practice casting the forceball, and that helped him improve or avoid failures, but he'd had zero experience with swordplay, so there was nothing for him to draw from. All he had was the Mark's flood of wrong things to do.

He stumbled backward—his hands flailing as the sword went flying—and tripped on a heavy rope on the deck, flipped over a nearby barrel, and landed flat on his face on the other side.

Groaning, he curled up and nursed his aching nose and pride.

"Alex?" Theresa's feet approached him. Her boots were in front of his face. His teacher crouched, holding the sword. "Are..." She was desperately holding back laughter. "Are you oka..."

A low chuckle burst from her mouth.

He groaned feebly in response.

From across the deck, he could hear soft snickering coming from the few night crew sailors nearby, concealing their laughter. Trying, at least.

"I guess that's a failure?" she asked when she'd finally gained control of herself and held out a hand to him.

"Well..." he grunted as he got to his feet. "I guess the sword's not a good idea. But we're not done yet."

A pure weapon was out of the question. But what about something with a more general use? He looked at her hunting knife. "How about we try your knife?"

They took up position on the cleared area of the deck again, this time with Alex gripping Theresa's sheathed knife. She stayed very close to him, with her hands spread out to catch him if he toppled.

"Alright, now bring it up like I showed you."

Grimacing, Alex brought the knife into guard position.

Nothing happened.

"Okay, were getting somewhere." He sighed with relief. Slowly turning toward Theresa, he kept the position of his body and hands as close to how she'd showed him as he could. "We're getting somewhere."

Again, it occurred to him that he should hold the knife in similar positions to how he would if he was using it for everyday tasks. A person couldn't very well cut a rope or skin a carcass hanging from a rack without holding a knife in front of themselves, could they?

"Hrm." Theresa stepped back and raised her sword into guard position. "Strike at my blade."

Carefully, he tapped her sheathed sword with the knife.

"Alright, now do it faster."

Another tap. No complaint from the Mark.

"Hmmm, unsheathe the knife," Theresa said, drawing her sword.

He startled. "Uh, are you sure about that?" Again, images of severed fingers drifted through his mind.

"If anything goes wrong, I'll knock it out of your hand, okay?"

Alex didn't like the idea of waving any sort of weapon toward Theresa, but better to know the Mark's limits now, rather than later during some nasty situation.

"Okay… just, be careful." Steadying himself, he slid the knife from the sheathe.

Her eyes hardened. "Now strike my blade hard."

Taking a deep breath, he stabbed toward her sword.

The Mark flooded him.

Images of failures rose; the strongest was him tripping over the barrel minutes before. His concentration and balance were ruined, and he wavered on his feet. Though, the memories weren't as aggressive as when he'd used the sword. He felt the position of his body, his feet stumbling around over the deck, and suddenly, Theresa was there, catching him.

The images cleared shortly, leaving Alex in her grip. Her knife lay on the deck.

"That…" he panted. "Hold on."

She let go and he bent down, taking up his notebook that he'd laid on the deck nearby, and flipped it open. He wrote a new entry:

Strong interference with direct combat. The more focused the action on direct combat, the stronger the interference. Full weapons cause the strongest reactions. More general use items grant more freedom.

Sword: full weapon

Knife: weapon, tool, kitchen implement.

He thought about what this might mean for other areas.

Forceball is a utility spell. Can use for multiple actions once spell is cast. Only problem is when used on direct combat against another.

Direct combat spells out of the question? Maybe. Maybe not. ***Test later***.

If combat spells not an option, focus on utility spells used for indirect combat? Defensive spells? More research needed.

He closed the book.

When they get to Generasi, he'd need to experiment with

different sorts of spells and skills. For now, the dance seemed like a good option. The Mark didn't seem to mind when he was using the mop. Hopefully, the dance would give him a way to be evasive in combat, but using a weapon with it would probably be a bad idea.

"Well, maybe the mop is your weapon of choice. It seems like you're best with it," Theresa offered with barely concealed laughter.

"Yeah, it wasn't all that ba—Wait... mop?" He hadn't told her a word about the dance practice the night before.

"Did... Were you spying last night?"

He thought back to that feeling of being watched.

"N-No," she lied badly.

"Liar. Where... where were you?" he choked. Images of himself dancing around with a mop came to mind.

Her eyes flicked guiltily to the staircase. "Gel-Dor told me about the dance and uh... suggested I watch the deck when the others went to bed."

Alex stared at her in horror. "You... you... you..."

"I wanted to tell you earlier, but there were so many people around and I didn't want others to hear of your..." She shuddered. "Glorious... mop slinging."

She broke down in helpless laughter.

"I'm going to kill you!" he promised.

"Not unless you're using that mop!"

In a fake rage, Alex chased Theresa around the deck until they were scolded by the nightwatch.

It was a familiar feeling to both of them.

Chapter 23

The Nightwatch

"Looks like rain's coming in after all." Gel-Dor eyed the clouds to the western horizon.

"Damn," Fan-Dor cursed beneath his breath. "Well, at least it doesn't look like a bad storm. Clouds are too light and the wind's too low. Ek-u-Dari must have liked our dance well enough."

The crew and passengers had gathered on the starboard side of the *Red Siren* to see what was happening when they'd heard a storm might be brewing.

"He's right," Theresa said, petting Brutus as two of his heads chewed a bone while the third lapped from a water dish. She squinted at the sky. "If the clouds over the sea look like they do above land, then it shouldn't be a heavy rain. They aren't that big or dark."

"That's good." Alex yawned into his hand, sitting on a barrel behind the crowd. He watched Selina looking at the clouds, her hands gripping the rail.

Her energy amazed him. Between everything they'd faced getting out of Thameland—his nightly exercise routine, learning the dance and testing the Mark's limits—he was exhausted.

He rubbed his aching arms and chest. Two days of push-ups hadn't increased how many he could do yet, but his technique was getting better. It was getting easier to hold himself in a position that let him feel controlled and strong.

Hopefully, he'd start to see some results soon.

He yawned again.

But for now, he felt like he could sleep for a year.

"Wind... direction..." one of the frog-folk said nearby in his croaking language, along with some other words Alex couldn't make out. Using the Fool to help him understand languages he heard in passing was starting to show results. He was beginning to pick out the odd words in other languages if he heard them often enough.

The skinny Rhinean man approached Captain Fan-Dor and said something very quickly. Too quick for Alex to get any of what was said. The man had a piece of salt pork clutched in his fist and was chewing it even as he talked. It was his second snack since lunch.

The captain said something back to him, then raised his voice. "Before I get this question a hundred times, no, the rain won't delay us. It'll probably hit us around midnight, but we'll still reach port in Generasi by the morning. No need to panic. No need to worry."

He gave the skinny man a look.

The Rhinean stepped back, glancing over to Theresa, his eyes lingering, then to Alex. He shuffled to the stairs, no doubt to find more food.

Alex worked hard to keep his face neutral. With how much of the ship's food he was going through, it really seemed he should be charged extra.

"Hey." Alex elbowed Theresa and nodded toward the man disappearing down the steps. "What do you think of that guy?"

"That he eats more than Brutus?" Theresa whispered.

"Yeah," he said. "But more than that. What do you think of him?"

She shrugged. "He eats a lot, I guess? That's it."

"That's all? You don't find him creepy?"

"Not really. Well, maybe a little. After the, you know..." She made a wriggly, crawly motion with her hand, copying the silent-spiders' movements. "My standards for what's creepy have gone up."

"Yeah, good point. But you never noticed him watching us? Watching you?"

"A bit? Why?"

"I don't know. I suppose it's nothing." Alex really didn't want to say it was because he felt the man was staring at her and it was making him jealous. She'd never let him hear the end of it.

Another yawn hit him. He winced as his chest muscles ached. He really needed a nap.

"Are you gonna make it?" Theresa asked.

"Maybe. Too many late nights, and I've been doing these push-ups."

She nodded in approval. "Good. A strong body helps. Is today your rest day?"

"Rest day?"

"You rest between days you do hard exercise."

"I thought your brothers did them every day?"

"Yes, but they've been training for years. Have you ever done push-ups before?"

"Not really."

"Then I think you need a break. Usually when you're starting, you do it every other day. Even every two days."

"Well, that's a relief," he said, yawning again. "Gives me an excuse for a nap." He dragged himself to his feet. "I'll grab a quick one then come up for supper."

She smiled. "We'll watch for the rain while you do."

He chuckled. "Make sure it doesn't sneak up on us."

As soon as he opened his eyes, Alex realized his nap had turned into a 'sleep for half the day.'

The cabin was dark and the ship quiet, except for the creaking of wood and the splash of waves against the hull. Beside him, Selina snored lightly.

He got up, careful not to disturb her, and slipped on his boots. For a moment, he considered doing his push-up routine but remembered Theresa's advice: rest.

Well, sleep wouldn't be coming to him for a while.

He crept from the room—quiet enough not to wake Selina—and slipped into the hall. From Theresa's room, he could hear Brutus snoring, and no sounds came from the other passengers' cabins.

Most of the crew, including the captain and first mate, were asleep in the ship's common area. Their ranks and status allowed them to avoid all night duty.

Heading up the stairs, he used the Mark to continue improving his stealth as he stepped onto deck. It was dark, though he could see the low glow of the moon through the clouds. Rain hadn't come yet, but the pressure was changing in the air.

The nightwatch—only a few of the crew—busied themselves toward the stern of the ship with a game of dice. They exchanged nods with him and he briefly considered joining them. It might have been good practice for his languages at least. Maybe not so good for his purse. Gambling with people he barely understood was probably a really bad idea. Instead, he walked to the bow and leaned against the railing, watching the dark ocean. In the far distance, he could have sworn he saw a glowing blue light above the water. Maybe it was a trick of the moon.

He listened to the gentle waves against the ship as he took in the salty air and the sound of the wind. He could barely make out the surface of the sea under the dark clouds.

It was time for a little light. He concentrated, slowly muttering the incantation for his forceball. It was still slower than before he got marked, but he was starting to get better at shutting out the mental interference from the Fool.

The forceball's red light winked into life.

He smiled at the familiar spell. It had gotten them through a lot lately.

He willed the spell to float above his head and illuminate the sea and deck nearby. He thought about the spell and how his practice with it helped him use it since he'd been marked. It might be worthwhile to experiment with spells similar in structure to the forceball. Learning new spells was going to be hard, so it'd be smart to start with ones that were at least somewhat familiar.

As the wind rustled the sails, he yawned again.

Suddenly, sleepiness came over him in a wave, but he shook it away. His mind was racing with ideas of what spells might be good ones for him to experiment with first, and he wanted to consider that some more before going back to bed.

Again, sleepiness hit him with an abruptness and an insistence.

What was happening?

The sudden tiredness didn't feel natural. It felt draining. Different. Almost like it was coming from outside of himself. Because of the way the Mark worked—entering his mind from the outside to influence him—he recognized this sudden overwhelming wave of exhaustion was definitely coming at him from outside.

He fought it away.

Creak.

Something quietly stepped on a board behind him. He couldn't hear any sounds from the nightwatch anymore.

Again, he had the feeling something was watching him, and he doubted it was Theresa. He didn't move. Didn't give any sign that he suspected something was wrong.

No. He could do even better.

Faking another yawn, he let his head hang a little, as though he were about to fall asleep.

Whispering picked up behind him in Rhinean. A familiar voice.

The skinny man. What did he want? Had he been looking at him *and* Theresa? Or had he only been interested in *him*? What was his plan? To rob him?

He activated the Mark, listening to the man's whispering.

The Rhinean words were coming quickly, but Alex was able to pick out one he kept repeating: Hollow. Hollow.

Alex held the forceball tightly in his will and mana, keeping it ready above him. Direct combat wouldn't work. His experiments had shown he could move items into positions like into guard, as he had with Theresa's knife. What if...

Yawning again, he let his head drop.

Feet rushed up behind him.

He willed the forceball to move behind him and down, like he was trying to light that area of the deck. It shot down and stopped right in front of the sound of running feet until—

Bang!

The man ran headfirst into the forceball, smashing his face and collapsing. Alex grinned. No reaction from the Mark. He added 'studying traps' to the list of research he needed to do. The skinny man was flat on the deck, groaning at his feet and holding his face.

Alex drifted the forceball down to shine on the attacker and hovered it over his head in a threat. Of course, trying to hit him wouldn't do much good, but his attacker didn't need to know that.

"Don't move," Alex said in Common. He didn't know if the man would understand him, but he let his threat be clear in his tone.

The man obliged.

"Crew, Fan-Dor!" Alex shouted, edging around the fallen figure to make sure he wasn't between him and the stairs. Even if the man was down, he didn't want to be trapped. He listened carefully for any sounds of his attacker muttering incantations. From the overwhelming sleepiness earlier, it seemed he was some kind of spellcaster. Alex had the advantage now, but he'd feel a lot better with reinforcements.

The Rhinean's hands shot up.

Not toward Alex; toward his forceball.

They grabbed the spell.

An awful sensation slammed into the young mage.

Schlrp.

The man's hands warped. Fingernails disappeared and his fingers lengthened and sprouted suckers like a squid's tentacles. They wrapped around the spell and Alex felt something flowing out of him.

His mana.

The man—or whatever he was—was sucking his mana through his spell.

Alex abruptly killed the flow to the magic circuit and the spell winked out. He backed away as the thing jumped to its feet, its flesh shifting before his shocked eyes.

Its skin merged into blue-grey flesh and its facial features sank into the meat like a rock disappearing into water. Its eyelids tore away and its eyes swelled until they bulged from a deformed head. It spit its teeth out, and they melted and steamed when they touched the deck. Its mouth twisted sideways.

A long grey tongue covered in suckers emerged, and the creature let out a sucking noise like quicksand swallowing an unsuspecting traveler. Its frame shrank even further until it was as thin as a rotting corpse.

"Oh, shit!" Alex shouted. He glanced at the nightwatch. They were fast asleep against the deck.

When he whirled back to the creature, it tensed and sprang at him.

Chapter 24

Other Dangers

The creature leapt with unnatural speed. Alex stumbled away as it crashed into the rail he'd just been in front of. It shook its head, seeming to clear its senses.

Dazed, Alex thought. *Still dazed from when it ran into the forceball.*

His mind worked. He sprinted toward the stairs leading below deck. He hated the idea of bringing it close to where his sister slept, but if he could wake the crew, and Theresa and Brutus, then it'd be the best hope for stopping it.

If it killed him there on the deck, then it could roam free on the ship. She'd be in danger anyway.

"Monster! Fire!" he yelled. If it had the power to put the whole ship to sleep, everyone would be in trouble. Since he'd managed to resist it, that might mean it wasn't likely. He hoped.

His feet pounded over the deck, purposely stomping hard into the wood. Hopefully, the racket would wake the crew and make the thing back off and rethink—

Feet pounded over the deck, racing after him. Alex swerved as though he was running for the stairs, then rushed forward instead, trying to fake the thing out. The sound of feet chasing him abruptly ended.

Crash.

The creature landed in front of the stairs where he would have been.

Alex turned, backing to the cleared area of the deck. It rose, tearing the cloak from its body. Its breaths came in gasps as though it had been running for miles. Its eyes moved frantically, like it was desperate. It grasped for him.

Seeking his mana.

And it wouldn't stop until it got it.

Alex glanced at the nightwatch. They were still fast asleep and showed no sign of waking.

"Shit," he cursed, turning back to the monster.

The nightwatch couldn't help him, and he heard no shouts or stirring from below deck. If help was coming, he needed to survive until it came. He couldn't be sure that help was going to come soon enough. Alex had to try to find a way to take the creature down himself. But he couldn't use a weapon thanks to the Fool, even if he did have one. His forceball couldn't help him; it would just drain his mana through it. What did that leave?

He cautiously stepped around the deck, putting the mast between him and the monster. He searched for anything to use close by.

He spotted a familiar object.

The mop.

Better than nothing.

Quickly taking it up, he called on the Mark to drop into second position of the Spear-and-Oar Dance, keeping his balance on both feet. He raised the mop into guard, pointing the head toward the monster. He tried to clamp down on the terror running through him.

The creature stilled, unsure of what he was doing.

He used that moment to scream at the top of his lungs.

The monster rushed him.

His scream turned into a shout of surprise and he used the dance's back step to retreat, increasing the distance between him and the creature. He put the mast between him and the creature's mana draining hands. It made another gulping sound and jumped to the right, while he wheeled to the left, still keeping the mast between them.

The creature panted and gurgled in frustration. Its movements seemed weak. Alex remembered all the food it had been shoveling while in human form. Starving, maybe? Whatever it was, the thing was struggling.

While its attempts to catch him grew more desperate, the Mark continued to add successes in the dance to his mind. Bit by bit, he was improving. But he couldn't keep it up forever. One slip and he'd be done.

His eyes flicked around. Looking for anything to use. Ropes? No. Barrels? No.

Then he saw the mop bucket, filled with water.

He edged to the bucket, creeping out from behind the mast. If it was desperate, it would—

It rushed him at full speed and Alex kicked over the bucket.

Salt water poured across the deck. The creature, in its rush, slipped and crashed into a set of barrels.

Thm. Thm.

Alex stomped the deck and slammed the end of the mop against the boards. "Monster! Fire!" he shouted again. "Mon—"

The creature began to climb out from beneath the barrels.

Alex ran, sprinting for the stairs. He heard it jump out from under the barrels and its footsteps echoed his own.

Terror screamed in him, making him faster, but the creature was gaining. He wouldn't make the steps in time. Spinning, he got into second position just in time with the Mark's guidance. He swept the mop head back and forth.

He remembered tapping Theresa's sword with a knife didn't

trigger the Mark's interference, so swishing the mop around at the creature should also not cause it to react.

The mop head whipped around its face like Alex was wiping the deck, slowing it down. The strings annoyed it, but didn't harm it. No interference came from the Mark, allowing him to back closer and closer to the stairs, screaming hard. His heart hammered in his chest, but the Mark guided his backward steps until he stepped onto nothing.

With a cry, Alex fell, rolling down the stairs, the mop flying from his hands. He grunted, trying to grab at the railings to slow his fall. It seemed like he was falling forever as the breath was knocked out of him and he finally came to rest. He was flat on his back, groaning and trying to blink away stars swimming in front of his eyes.

The creature leapt from the top of the stairs.

Time seemed to slow as it dropped toward him with its grasping sucker-hands extended. Alex could hear the liquid noise its mouth made, as well as sounds of movement nearby.

Think! Adapt! his mind screamed.

The forceball. It had run into the forceball on its own. The Mark hadn't interfered.

Grimacing, he rolled and grabbed the mop, placing its head on the floor and holding it in place, with the handle pointed high, facing the creature. It was not a weapon, and the monster was falling with full momentum.

In midair, it couldn't stop itself.

Scrltch.

The Mark didn't react when the creature slammed itself, gut first, with all the force of its fall, into the mop stick. Alex let go and the stick snapped, with the splintered ends driving into the creature's stomach.

It landed on top of him with the broken mop half-buried in its stomach. A watery liquid splashed over his shirt as he pushed the flailing creature off and crawled to his feet.

A woman screamed behind him.

The bureaucrat from Generasi.

"Get back, it's a monster! Captain! Captain Fan-Dor!" Alex scrambled into the darkened common area as the creature got to its feet, lunging after him with a final, desperate surge of strength.

Then a spear shot out of the dark, passing Alex.

Shcnk.

It stabbed into the monster's chest, impaling it. The creature screeched.

Gel-Dor's rage-filled face emerged from the darkness, his snarling teeth shining in the low moonlight.

"Not this time, you chum-sucking piece of scum," the first mate growled.

Schnk.

Another spear shot from the dark and pierced the monster through the head.

The creature flew backward, shuddering. It sighed as the final blow ended its life. Its form crumpled in its clothes.

Hsssss.

White smoke began to pour from it as its body ran like hot wax.

It was like a snowman melting at winter's end, with water that boiled and steamed as soon as it touched the ship's floor. From within the steam, Alex felt the tang of mana—it was weak and originated from many different sources. With a final, shuddering sigh, the creature collapsed into a steaming puddle.

The steam drifted up the stairs and out into the ocean air. Alex's laboured breathing mixed with the clatter of weapons and running feet as the crew rushed about.

"Where? Where were you?" Alex panted to the first mate.

"Getting our weapons as soon as we heard you shouting," Gel-Dor said. "We were just heading to the stairs when you came flying down them."

Really? To Alex, it felt like they'd taken hours to come. Then again, as his mind slowed, he began to recognize how little time had actually passed.

Running across the deck must have taken only a few seconds or maybe a little longer. He'd backed away from the creature as it advanced on him. Then ducked around the mast a few times, kicked over the bucket of water, and ran for the stairs.

All while shouting at the top of his lungs.

It really must have been only a short time.

It'd only *felt* like he'd been fighting the thing for hours.

He leaned against the wall as Fan-Dor cursed and Gel-Dor looked grimly on the empty pile of clothes.

"What about the nightwatch?" Gel-Dor asked.

"Asleep. I think the monster put them to sleep."

The first mate ground his teeth. "I'm going to give them a good thumping for this. Nearly letting a passenger die and..." His teeth ground.

"What's happening?" He heard Theresa's voice coming from her cabin as Brutus barked frantically.

"What?" Alex tried to calm his racing heart. "What was that thing?"

"A mana vampire," a voice said from the cabins. The husband of the Generasian bureaucrat emerged into the hall, adjusting his spectacles.

He looked at Alex. "You, my young friend, are either very skilled or very, very lucky."

Both, Alex thought. *Definitely both.*

"It must have been starving for mana," the older man said as they watched the creature's clothes burn in a brazier. The flame reflected on his glasses. "They always avoid drawing attention to themselves and make it a point to blend in. That's one of the reasons they're so hard to detect. This one was different, though, and caught everyone's attention by eating so much. That makes me wonder if it had grown careless because it was desperate. It seemed to be trying anything to hold off starvation until it could get to Generasi and feed off all the mana in the wizard city." He looked at Alex. "Perhaps desperation is why it tried to attack you a mere evening before reaching Generasi. In a way, you were lucky. When they're well-fed, they're quick and incredibly strong. And their natural magics can put entire households to sleep."

Across the fire, both Gel-Dor and Fan-Dor were laying into the nightwatch. The poor buggers were on their knees before their commanders with heads bowed. The entire mood of the crew had dipped hard, and many glanced at Alex with something like fear.

He'd been offered rum rations at least half a dozen times in three different languages, but he'd politely refused them.

He stood beside Theresa before the fire consuming the clothes. She gripped his arm like he was about to disappear. Selina was back asleep in the cabin. It had taken a lot of hugs and reassurance to calm her after she'd heard her big brother screaming for help, but she was better now and safe with Brutus.

"Filthy murdering wretches." The older woman looked like she wanted to spit into the fire. "That was quick thinking, not using spells against it. They can absorb any magic their vile hands or tongue touch. Many young mages have met their end by just throwing spells at them."

"Are those things common?" Theresa demanded.

"Not common, no, but not rare enough," the older man said grimly. "Once in a while, one will try and slip aboard a ship and sneak into Generasi to feed. Since they're so hard to detect, sometimes they're successful and no one knows they've entered the city until the attacks start. That's when the authorities have to send out trackers to hunt them down. Finding one isn't an easy task unless the tracker is fortunate enough to find it soon after a recent feeding. You see, while they're digesting new mana, it tends to leak for a period of time, but if they're hiding, they're nearly impossible to detect." He sighed. "Which I think is little compensation to Captain Fan-Dor. Ugh, perhaps his goddess hasn't smiled upon him after all."

"What do you mean?" Alex asked.

"Generasi does not put blame onto ships or captains that transport mana vampires unintentionally. Remember, they're nearly impossible to detect for wizards, let alone those with no skill in magic. But, sometimes the families of victims do. Some time ago, a mana vampire killed the son of a successful merchant of magical items. Captain Fan-Dor took responsibility and paid a *hefty* compensation out of honour. That took a lot out of the ship's coffers, and left him with the reputation of transporting one of the creatures. The unfortunate incident left many leery of boarding the *Red Siren*. Foolish, of course, since mana vampires have no interest in those without mana."

"What happens to their victims?" Theresa looked on at the fire as the last of the creature's clothes burned to ash.

"First, their mana is drained, then their lifeforce is sucked out until a shrivelled husk is all that's left of them."

Alex's blood chilled. Theresa's grip tightened on his arm.

For the first time, Alex was very, very thankful for the Mark. If it weren't for its interference, he would likely have tried to use his forceball on the thing again.

But since he'd learned the dance to see if he could get around the Fool, using its movements had given him the time he needed to save his life. There was also his experience escaping Thameland. What if he hadn't been forced to find creative solutions and try different things to fight for their lives?

He shuddered to think what the outcome would have been.

No wonder the Heroes had to protect the Fool. Anyone who got his Mark was like the sitting duck among the Heroes.

Hsssssss.

The fire steamed as rain began to fall.

"We'll talk in the morning." The older man winced, wiping his glasses against the rain. "Try to get some sleep if you can. There'll be things to discuss when we're fresh. Mana vampires have a standing bounty in Generasi, both for their discovery and destruction."

"We'll see that you get it," his wife finished. "But try to get some sleep. It'll be a long day tomorrow."

Alex and Theresa stood as the older couple left, and Alex began to tremble. There were more dangers in the wide world than the Ravener it seemed, and he was glad he'd started preparing for them. Next time, he'd be even more ready.

"Theresa?"

"Yes?" She looked up at him.

"Remember that hug you offered me? Right after you puked?"

Her face softened. "Yes."

"I... I think I'd like it now."

Their arms wrapped around each other as the rain began to pour.

Chapter 25

The City at the Center of Creation

When Alex Roth imagined his arrival at the city of wizards, he'd always imagined the sun being high, and his mood being high too. That morning, as the *Red Siren* passed among the outer islands, the sky was grey and the rain poured.

He'd hardly slept, and he was still thinking about the fight from last night. His entire body ached from his fall down the stairs. He'd been lucky it hadn't been worse. His hands shook against the rail. At least they were shaking less. He hadn't had any nightmares, which had been a pleasant surprise. Maybe he was getting a little more used to danger, and maybe that was something to take comfort in.

Even considering last night and the rain now pouring around him as they stood on the ship's deck looking out, this moment was incredible.

"I can't believe it," Theresa gasped beside him as Brutus stared at the city ahead.

Selina gaped under her hood, the rain dripping off her cloak.

In the distance, the City of Generasi rose high upon a massive hill, stretching as far as the eye could see. Seeming to rise from the mist and rain like a titan. The city's walls were of white stone and at least fifty feet high. Massive gates to a broad road lay open, with carved statues standing guard beside each. On the left was the towering figure of a djinni and on the right, a horned demoness.

Deep behind the city walls, a tower that very well could have touched the clouds, defying the winds, rose high above all the other tall towers.

Above even that, floated wonders.

Objects flew through the rain.

Most were too far away to make out from the deck of the *Red Siren*. But a couple were enormous. Entire flying ships cut their way through the downpour above the peaks of the towers. In some spots, the clouds swirled, revealing holes leading to clear blue, sky-like tunnels.

Before the city walls—closer to the shore—was a port station the size of a small town, and its docks were bursting with ships. A lighthouse rose from the centre of the station, lighting the way with a shining blue magic. Alex realized that must've been what he'd seen the night before the mana vampire attack.

Mana blazed from the city, almost as strong as it had been in the Cave of the Traveller.

Truly, this was the city of wizards. The City at the Center of Creation.

They'd finally reached it.

Sure, it was a place where mana vampires might lurk, and where Alex would need to research a doom conspiracy, but he didn't let those things ruin the moment.

Clnk.

The sound of metal sliding on metal came from his side.

Captain Fan-Dor had approached him with his brother, holding out the coins paid for the passage to Generasi. The selachar men had grim looks. "Here. The first half of the fee. I don't intend to charge the second."

"What, why?"

"What do you mean *why*? You nearly got killed by a chum-sucking mana vampire while under my watch on my ship. I'd be a real barracuda's son if after something like that I just went, 'Oh yeah, that's full services rendered, pay up.'"

Alex looked from the captain's face to the coins.

Fan-Dor *did* have a point. He *had* almost died while on the *Red Siren*. But he didn't really see how that was the fault of the captain or crew. Everyone believed the mana vampire was just some greedy man with odd habits until last night.

If anything, *he* might have seemed more suspicious and strange playing around with swords and all. And when he'd called for help, Gel-Dor and Fan-Dor came as quickly as they could. They'd finished the monster off, and the only reason the nightwatch hadn't helped was because they'd been affected by the creature's magic.

The more he thought about it, the more he came to the conclusion that there wasn't really much anyone could have done. Fan-Dor teaching him the first few steps of the Spear-and-Oar Dance was what helped save his life.

If anything, the situation might actually help him in the long run. If anyone ever came looking for an eighteen-year-old from Thameland that could be an escaped Fool, they probably wouldn't consider a young magic wielder who nearly killed a mana vampire with a broken mop as their first candidate.

Still, Fan-Dor was a fair and emotional man who was trying to make amends. Refusing the gesture would probably insult him.

Alex had an idea.

"Tell you what, if that's what you feel you need to do, then fine. I accept." He took the coins from Fan-Dor. "But, hold on for a second." He turned toward where the tired-eyed Generasian administrators were leaning against the rail.

"Excuse me," he said to them. "What's the reward for finding and destroying a mana vampire?"

The older woman looked between Alex and Fan-Dor. "Why, twenty-five golden marks for discovery, and another seventy-five for slaying. All in all, an even hundred."

"Well, isn't that a nice number." He turned back to the captain and first mate. "Twenty-five for me, because I discovered the thing, then another twenty-five for each of us since we each stuck the monster once. That splits seventy-five three ways."

Gel-Dor's black eyes searched Alex's. "Are... are you sure? You fought the monster longest, you brought it right onto our spears, and that wound you gave it would have seen it bleed out eventually."

"Oh, I'm sure." Alex clapped the big men on the arm like he'd imagine Cedric would have done.

A gesture like this would both reward the captain for the lesson that helped save his life, and likely win the two men's gratitude and respect. Nothing wrong in building a relationship with an honest ship that regularly came and went from Generasi.

And, if he were honest, he liked Fan-Dor.

"I nearly died, so you gave me my coin back for passage," Alex explained lightly. "You also helped save me from the monster, so you get rewarded for that. Perfect sense."

A smile slowly broke over the captain's face and Alex could see the relief in it. Being boarded by a mana vampire a second time, especially when the ship's coffers were already low, would see business suffer even further. No matter what Fan-Dor said, the reward would probably go a long way to helping the *Red Siren* survive.

"I don't know what to say," Fan-Dor said.

"Then how about this. Next time we meet, you teach me more steps of the dance. Sound fair?"

The selachar twins glanced at each other then broke out into identical grins. "Boy, we'll teach you the *entire* dance next time we meet. Whenever you get settled in the city, come over to the docks and leave where you're staying with the mail office. We'll come see you when we can."

"I look forward to it."

"Oh and, um," Selina moved up beside Alex. "Thank you for teaching me about ships, and thank you, thank you, *thank you* for helping my brother."

Brutus, who had slept for most of the trip, gave a contented yawn.

"You've been wonderful hosts." Theresa bowed her head to the twins. "I'm not sure if this is the right thing to say, but may Ek-u-Dari keep the storms away from you."

"Hah, that's close enough," Gel-Dor said in appreciation. "And may whatever deities and spirits that watch over you always provide their protection."

Oddly enough, when Gel-Dor said that, it wasn't Uldar that came to Alex's mind, despite worshipping the prophet-god for years.

It was the Traveller.

Then a wicked thought occurred to him.

"Actually, we worship a spider god." He thought back to the soldier silence-spider they had fought on the outskirts of Coille. "He hangs above us all in the night while we worship him, waiting to spring down and eat our souls so we can fill his spirit-y stomach."

The twins' smiles dropped.

Fan-Dor coughed awkwardly. "Well, that's... I don't suppose to judge, I mean if—" He looked at Selina as she frowned at her brother in confusion. "Wait... is that true?"

"Not a word." Alex chuckled. "But you should see the look on your face right now."

Fan-Dor's eyes widened as his own words were thrown back at him and the captain burst out laughing.

His laughter echoed over the waters until the *Red Siren* docked at Generasi.

"Ugh, guard reports are so tedious," the older Generasian woman groaned as she, her husband and Alex's group emerged from the guardhouse by the wharf. "I work with paperwork for most of my day and even I find it taxing."

Her husband looked tired too, and both Captain Fan-Dor and Gel-Dor had departed as soon as their part was finished. Selina and Brutus had quickly gotten bored, while even the patient Theresa stopped herself from fidgeting in the chair as they'd been buried in questions.

Only Alex hadn't minded all that much. His supply of gold had gotten fifty coins heavier. He wasn't going to complain.

"What now?" he asked the middle-aged couple. "Going to walk to the city with us?"

"I'm afraid not," the husband yawned. "Unfortunately, our luggage is still on the *Red Siren*. We'll be parting ways here."

"But don't be strangers, please!" The woman dug out a small sheet of paper from her carry bag and scrawled something down before handing it to Alex. "Since it's never too late for introductions, my name is Anna Escofier and this is my husband, Vincenzo."

Alex, Theresa and Selina introduced themselves and Brutus as the young man took the piece of paper. He found the couple's names had been written on it.

"If you should ever like to know anything about the city, do not hesitate to go to the Wizard's Forum. That's where the ruling council and all the administrators work. Leave a message for us, along with where you are staying, and we shall get in contact."

"We might take you up on that," Theresa said. "Thanks for

taking the time to help us with all…" She gestured to the guard building.

"Think nothing of it," Anna said. "Until we meet again."

With final goodbyes, the groups parted.

As they approached the city, Alex and his companions fell into a shocked silence. Mausarr was big, but Generasi made it seem like a lonely hut in the woods. More people pressed around them on the road to the city than they'd seen in Mausarr's main squares.

Humans from all over the world walked alongside beastfolk, the occasional elf and selachar, and other races of humanoids Alex had never seen or heard of. Some were shorter than Selina, despite their adult appearance. Others towered far above Alex, and would have been taller than Fan-Dor and his brother, or even the minotaurs they'd seen in Mausarr.

People walked with, or rode on the backs of many kinds of beasts. Giant birds taller than horses, massive red-scaled lizards, and even beetles almost as large as Brutus. The smells were wild. Foods and spices from all over the world drifted through Generasi's open gates.

And, above all, mana.

The mana hit him in waves. He'd only felt it stronger in the Traveller's sanctum.

Surprisingly, no guards stood at the gates, though Alex did notice glowing lines of magical writing surrounding the entranceway to the city. Was it to find mana vampires that had recently fed? Maybe something else? After being attacked on the ship, he was pretty sure there'd be more dangers lurking inside this magical metropolis.

A strange feeling came over him as he realized just how distant this city was from the problems of Thameland. He wondered if most here had even heard of their home country.

"Thameland!" a voice shouted over the crowd as the group entered the gates. "Alms for Thameland! Donations to Uldar's faith so that his people might be supported while his Heroes destroy the evil menace of the Ravener!"

The group slowly turned their heads to the central square in front of the gate's entrance.

On a tall podium stood a figure dressed in the familiar robes of a priest of Uldar, with other priests on their knees praying beside her. In front of them hung buckets—collecting coins for the cause.

Alex sighed, thankful the crowd between them was thick.

Of course... City at the Center of Creation, where *all* the world's cultures came together. Including Thameland. Of course Uldar's priests would be here.

They'd have to watch out for them.

"This way," he whispered to Theresa, and the group pushed through the crowd and down the street.

The priest's calls faded.

Chapter 26

Wonders in the Sky

"The good news is Uldar's priests aren't common here." Theresa rejoined Alex and Selina in the crowd. Brutus padded behind her, his heads moving every which way, following all of the new sights and smells.

The amount of people on the streets—even in the rain—was overwhelming. Despite Alex wanting to move quicker, there was no way he could without forcing through the press of hooded figures. He held tightly to Selina's hand.

His eyes kept darting around, looking for the robes of Uldar's priests.

"I asked a few people," Theresa continued. "They said that Uldar has a church in one of the districts where most of the other temples in Generasi are. I got good directions to both the church and the university, It's almost on the opposite end of the city from the school."

"That's good news, at least." Alex cocked his head at Theresa. She was frowning. "What's wrong?"

"I don't know what I said, but when I asked if there were any churches close to the school, I just got the strangest looks."

"Did they say anything?"

"No, it was just the looks. They did say Uldar's priests have been out in the streets trying to collect for the war effort." Theresa watched the passing crowd closely. Discomfort passed over her face.

"And we wouldn't see them coming in this crowd," Alex finished for her.

"It's too thick. I think I've seen more people in the last hour than I have in my whole life."

Alex understood. While he'd spent more time in town and less in the forest than Theresa had, Alric wasn't large. They might've been able to fit fifty Alrics here. All the sounds, sights, the sheer amount of magic...

"Look at that! Look at that!" Selina pointed up.

A group of people were having tea where she pointed. Only, they were all sitting on a carpet.

A flying carpet.

It passed overhead, the rain bouncing off some sort of invisible shield above its passengers, and vanished around the nearest street corner.

Alex and Theresa gawked at it like country bumpkins.

All of this would take time to get used to. If they ever did.

"You know, it's weird," Theresa said. "Everyone I talked to knew about *something* happening in Thameland, but the way they talked about it was like how we'd talk about a neighbour's cow getting sick. It was so..."

"Matter-of-fact?"

"Yeah," she said. "Looking at all this, I can kind of see why our troubles would look so..." Her eyes hardened. "Quaint."

"I was thinking the same thing in Mausarr..." Alex's eyes followed a woman in fine purple robes walking on the opposite end of the street. Behind her like a trained hound was a figure that must have been eight feet tall. It looked like it was made from clay, and aside from its thick fingers, it didn't have much in the way of features. Just a pair of glass eyes and a closed mouth.

It carried a crate above its head that must've weighed at least a thousand pounds. Its heavy footsteps could have shaken the cobblestones.

"Alex?" Theresa poked him.

"Oh, yeah, um." He pulled his attention back. "People in Mausarr were just going on with their lives. Like the world's this enormous, unconnected place."

Even here, where the priesthood had been spreading word about the Ravener, it didn't seem that somewhere else in the world, a century-cycled apocalypse was happening. In a way, seeing his people's pride and their greatest enemy reduced to some minor, distant issue people could ignore while sipping tea on a flying carpet, kind of stung.

Then again, he'd lived his whole life in peace in Alric while people here were trying to find ways to keep out mana vampires. The world *was* a big place.

"I wanna see the school," Selina said. "Are we going soon?"

He looked down at her, a bit envious of how comfortable she seemed with all the new sights and sounds.

"Well, that *is* what we're here for, so I gueeeeess we can."

Theresa nodded toward a few streets ahead. "One of the people I talked to said we should take a sky-gondola, like Mrs. Escofier suggested. There's supposed to be a dock for them a few streets ahead."

"A dock?" Alex cocked his head.

It turned out there *was* a dock a few streets ahead.

One leading to the sky.

Vertically built, multiple short piers extended off its 'trunk' like branches. At the end of most of those piers, a long, lean boat floated in midair. People crowded around, lining up to book passage to other parts of the city on the waiting boats.

"Uldar's beard," Theresa gasped.

"I wanna ride on one!" Selina eyed the stairs excitedly.

Brutus stared up at the boats with a look of distrust.

Alex was already rushing into the line for one.

"Welcome to Generasi Sky-Gondolas, I'm Lucia, your gondolier," a woman said from the back of the boat as Alex's group carefully approached along the pier. The boards beneath them were stable enough, but it was still a good thirty-foot drop. Alex kept a firm grip on Selina's hand and the railing.

"Please show me your booking tokens and place them in the box at the end of the sky-pier."

She indicated a box with a single slot in its front.

Alex showed her the four wooden tokens they'd received after paying the first part of the fee to a dock-head below. She nodded and Alex placed them in the box.

"Enter the gondola one at a time, please remain seated and don't push on the wind-and-rain shield." She seemed to be fighting a yawn. "Where're you headed?"

"To the big school!" Selina said, jumping into the boat before Alex could stop her.

The sky-gondola bobbed slightly but didn't collapse. Slowly, the rest of them stepped onboard, with Theresa having to coax Brutus before the cerberus finally followed.

The boat was long, but things got crowded once Brutus lay down at their feet. As soon as they got in, they stopped feeling the rain as it winked off an invisible shield above their heads.

With a single tap of Lucia's pole against the hull, the sky-gondola shook and lifted from the pier, rising into the sky.

Alex's stomach flip-flopped, and Theresa grabbed the seat while Brutus buried his heads into the bottom of the boat.

Selina nearly vibrated in excitement, bouncing up and down in her seat.

"Ek-u-Dari, we ask for protection from you," Alex muttered beneath his breath.

"What was that?" Theresa asked, though her face was turned to their surroundings as they gently soared over the rooftops.

"Never mind."

Generasi shrank beneath them as they drifted between its tallest towers. Throughout the city stood massive castles, buildings of different architectural styles, and titanic statues of people and monsters. Once they were high enough, Alex could see beyond the walls of the city.

Inland was a pleasant countryside of grass and small forests, dotted by estates and vineyards. Beyond them was another wall, and beyond that made Alex blink in surprise. A wasteland. Nothing but blasted rock. Almost like what he saw through the Traveller's portal to the fire mountains. Strange chasms ran throughout, glowing with different coloured lights.

"How does the boat work?" Selina asked the gondolier.

For a moment, Lucia cringed before she put on a forced smile. "Wizards made it to rise on Generasi's natural mana-currents. It's simple enough so that anyone can use it. I just turn the pole to make it go where I direct it."

"Are these everywhere in the world?" The little girl was examining everything about the boat. "I didn't see any in the big port on the way here, and the other boat we were on had to float on water. Captain Fan-Dor said the water lifts up the wood in the boat."

Lucia's eyes seemed to grow a little more dead, a stark contrast to the captain's enthusiasm in explaining the ship. Alex wondered how many times she'd gotten the same questions.

"You won't see these outside of this city. They're a cheap design, which means a lot of them can be made. But they can't fly outside Generasi because they have to use the mana that's in the air here."

"So, they *can't* make one that goes outside?"

"Some wizards have, but they take a lot more magic and expensive materials to make, and you'd need your own mana to drive it. If they made one that could fly outside of Generasi, *and* that anyone could use, you're looking at 'treasure of a lost empire' kind of coin." She sighed. "So please don't go to Generasi Sky-Gondolas to negotiate an order for your city, town, merchant organization, or village elder."

That last sentence sounded like she'd repeated it so many times, she could have said it in her sleep.

Alex wondered just how many of the other magic items in the city would only work here. Would the carpet still have carried its tea-drinking passengers over Coille forest? He glanced at the sky-ship floating above their heads, imagining some clever thieves commandeering it and cheering as they got past the city's limits...

...Only to scream as the entire ship plunged hundreds of feet to the water or ground. He looked at the wasteland beyond the wall in the distance. Maybe they'd fall into one of those glowing chasms.

"What is that place?" Theresa pointed to the wasteland.

"The Barrens of Kravernus." Lucia steered them past a neighbourhood of massive estates surrounded by gated walls. A couple had curved roofs, like the gate on top of Mount Tai. "The game preserve of the university and where students go to be trained in combat magic." She gave a bitter chuckle. "The mighty chancellor's monster park."

Silence followed.

"What is—" Selina started.

"We're almost there," Lucia cut her off, pointing ahead.

The massive campus sat on a hill above the rest of Generasi. Greenspace surrounded what was a small city unto itself. Its own rivers flowed along uninterrupted, and its own roads ran through the campus. The central building was an imposing castle of white stone with golden rooftops. It must be incredible in the sunlight.

Five towers rose from the castle, and the central one was by far the tallest in the entire city. In its courtyard stood two huge statues. One of an elderly human woman with plaits running down past her shoulders, and another of a tall and stately elven man. There was a third massive platform lying close to them, but it was empty.

As they passed over the outer walls of the campus, several figures—mounted on circular stone discs that floated in the air—watched them pass. Staffs were in their hands, and swords were belted at their waists.

Their faces were hard.

"Who're they?" Theresa asked.

"The Watchers of Roal, campus' guardians," the gondolier said dryly. "Keeping the university safe from the city, and the city safe from the university."

Alex frowned at the strange response as they drew closer to the courtyard.

"You seem to know a lot about this place." Alex looked closely at their gondolier.

"I should. I was a student here for six months."

"What? What happened?"

"I dropped out," she said with no hint of embarrassment.

He stiffened. "Why? This is the greatest school of wizardry in the world!"

Anger rose in him. He'd nearly died twice to get here, and this person had attended for half a year before dropping out to drive a boat?

An odd look entered her eyes.

"It is, isn't it?" Life entered her voice for the first time. She pointed to a building to the south. It was squat and had windows with metal shutters, most of which were closed. Some of the white stone was blackened. "You see that place? That's—"

BOOM!

"Oh, shit!" Alex swore, recoiling from the sound.

Selina screamed, Brutus yelped and Theresa started jumping

to her feet before her head slammed into the wind-and-rain shield. Alex caught her as she fell back into the seat.

From the building, a massive blue fireball exploded, ripping two of the metal windows out. Shouts echoed from the distance as several of the Watchers shot toward the building on their floating platforms.

"Perfect timing." Lucia grimaced as she set the sky-gondola down in front of the main castle. "It helps make my point. The University of Generasi is the greatest school of wizardry in the world, but..." She leaned forward. The neckline of her shirt shifted, revealing a tremendous burn-scar reaching up to the top of her chest. "Wizardry is dangerous. Ask one day how many students' acceptances are cancelled due to incapacitation. Or don't. Maybe you won't have to worry about it. Anyway," She held out her hand. "I'll be taking the rest of my fee now."

Chapter 27

Negotiations in the Hall of Magic

"Was that a potion detonation?" A tiny, white-haired woman sprinted through the courtyard with a staff in hand. "Please tell me that was a potion detonation. If it was another bad summoning circle—"

"There's no demonology scheduled in the Cells today," said a sharply dressed man in spectacles. "If that *is* a summoning circle, that student better *hope* all they get is expelled!"

"Um, excuse me?" Alex got their attention. "Which way do we go to register?"

The man hurriedly jerked a thumb over his shoulder toward a set of open doors at the top of a flight of stairs. They were at the opposite end of the courtyard.

"That way! Welcome to Generasi!" he barked as he and the other wizard rushed out of the courtyard. As they exited, Alex saw them wave their hands. From out of view, two of the same stone platforms used by the Watchers of Roal appeared, and the two wizards jumped aboard and shot away in the direction of the explosion.

Alex's group was speechless, eyeing each other nervously while approaching the doors.

They kept glancing around, only relaxing a little when they made it to the doors without hearing anymore blasts.

Just inside, there was another large, marble staircase with railings carved into dragon heads. They climbed the steps in awe, with Brutus' nails clicking on the rough stone and breaking the silence. At the top, they emerged into an antechamber so large, the entire church of Alric—bell tower and all—could have fit inside.

Two statues—one of a dragon and one of a kraken—framed a desk set into one of the walls where a blue-skinned man with horns read a book. A massive monocle sat on his face, reminding Alex of a one-eyed owl.

"I think this is the right place," Alex whispered.

"We'll..." Theresa's eyes traced a mural on the ceiling where wizards battled strange, demonic creatures. "We'll, uh, go have a seat while you do that." She indicated a bench beside a wall.

The bench had clawed feet. As they sat down, Alex could have sworn it moved its stone toes.

He approached the desk. "I, uh." He glanced back in the direction of the explosion.

The man looked up at him. "Yes? Here for a tour?"

"No, uh, to register, actually."

Though he managed to keep his tone even, inside he was screaming, his elation was running so hot.

Wizard Time. Wizard Time. Wizard Time, one part of his mind screamed.

You're going to explode. Some horrible demon is going to eat you. You could have stayed in Thamelan—

The first part of his mind stamped down the second part with prejudice.

Now was a time of joy.

"I was accepted for the upcoming year, to begin my studies."

The blue-skinned man closed his book. "Well, well. Aren't

you keen. Classes for first years don't start for at least another month and a half."

"It was uh... a long trip from where I'm from," Alex said, not mentioning the part about using an ancient saint's power to cross over a month's journey in a matter of days. "Thought I should get here early in case anything went wrong. Is that a problem?"

"The opposite, really. If we had more come in early like you, then orientation week wouldn't be such an animal house. Well, my name is Hobb and I'm the registrar here at Generasi. Allow me to welcome..."

He stopped and the leather on his chair squeaked as he peered around Alex. On the opposite end of the hall, Selina sat on the bench looking at the hall's lights—blue forceballs floating on top of columns—while Theresa examined a hole in her sleeve. Brutus was panting and sniffing everything.

"Would that be your wife and..." He looked at Alex, squinting. "Chiiild?"

Alex's face flushed. "No, just a friend."

"So, your friend and your chiiild?"

"No, no! That's my sister," Alex said.

Hobb looked at him for a long time. "I see," was all he said. "Well, if they're friend and family, will you be registering them as well?"

"Oh, they're, uh, not spellcasters."

"Not even for the auditing program?"

"The what program?"

Hobb adjusted his monocle. "Hmmm, might I see your acceptance letter? Mr...."

"Alex Roth, and one second."

He reached into his rucksack, feeling around for the paper.

Panic started. He couldn't find it. Did he leave it in his room back in the Lu family's inn? No, no, he remembered taking it.

Maybe he left it in the Cave of the Traveller after dumping everything to get the ruby.

A horrifying nightmare of a long side journey back to the cave started taking over his mind until his fingers touched paper.

"Here it is." He relaxed and handed the letter to Hobb, who examined it with his monocled eye.

"Aaaaah, recruited from Thameland. You were right; that *is* far." He glanced up at Alex. "Sorry to hear about all that Ravager business."

"Oh, uh, it's called the Ravener actually."

Hobb paled to a lighter blue. "Oh, sorry! How ignorant of me, I meant that I hope you and your family are safe."

Alex thought of Mr. and Mrs. Lu, and Theresa's brothers. He hoped they'd gotten onto a ship safely. "They should be alright."

"Good. Good. Dreadful business that. Though I suppose all the world has its own troubles. Anyway, back to the business at hand. I see you were accepted based on aptitude. With one spell, even. You must have practiced to the bone. *Very* well done, young man!" Hobb said enthusiastically. "That's the sort of ethic that'll have you flying through the spell-tiers in no time. Hmm, I can see the issue, though. That far out, you likely didn't get much of an explanation as to *why* we're considered the greatest institution of magic in all the world. After all, there really are no competitors in your realm as far as I know."

"Er, I thought you were called the greatest because you have so much of the world's knowledge."

"Oh, we do. We do. But we also take *care* of our wizards."

A scream tore through the large room.

He whirled to see Selina and Theresa jumping off the bench as it began to scuttle sideways like an angry crab. Brutus was barking at it.

"*Don't like dogs*," the bench ground out in a voice that was rock on rock.

"Stop that! Stop that at once!" Hobb half-rose from his chair. "You blasted, rebellious piece of furniture! I swear, one of these days I *will* send a request to have you carved into a chamberpot. Back to your post!"

Grumbling, the bench scuttled back to its original place.

"You can sit back down now," Hobb said pleasantly.

Selina and Theresa edged away from the bench.

"Ah, pity. It always does that." Hobb made a face. "So, as I said, we take care of our wizards."

He reached beneath his desk and produced a massive, leatherbound book. "Proper wizards always have an entourage. These could be summoned demons. They could be golems. They could be trained magical beasts like your handsome furry friend. They could be a party of delvers. And in some cases, they're hirelings, apprentices, or even family. And on that note, Generasi takes people from all corners of the earth. Many, like you, come with friends, parents, children and..."

He squinted at Selina. "*Liiitle* sisters?"

"Yes."

"Good, good. Children most certainly need to be educated, and entourage members or apprentices often need to be trained so they might support a wizard. As such, Generasi has a program where up to four members of your immediate group may audit certain courses—no direct spellcasting or for credit courses, of course—so they might better aid you when you go off to set up your own tower and *bend the forces of the cosmos to your unbreakable will.*"

His eyes flashed with intensity, and Alex thought he was going to leap out of his chair and start calling unearthly hordes.

Instead, he just smiled. "We also have a junior school where children may be educated in general subjects, and should they show aptitude, the preparatory courses for their own practice in wizardry. Of course, the auditing program and the junior school add additional nominal fees to your tuition... Though there would be a significant discount for you as I see you are a partial scholarship student. Considering where you are from, and the aptitude you demonstrated with limited resources, Generasi would not see a bright young mind crushed by a lack of coin."

Hobb smiled knowingly. "Now, avoiding being crushed by a miscast meteor spell is unfortunately entirely your own responsibility!"

He laughed as though it were the most natural thing in the world to say.

Alex did not join him.

"Ah, excuse me, excuse me, just some wizard humour. You'll get it in time. Now, since you'll be staying with... friend and sister, and large cerberus, I take it you'll wish for apartment accommodation?"

"For now," Alex said. It would give him time to search for a place of their own.

"Very well." Hobb picked up and flipped through another book, sliding his finger along a series of tables and names on a page. "Ah, this one is free. Are you and your entourage used to living in one room?"

Alex thought back to the ship and how Selina hammered on him for kicking her off the bed. He imagined what would've happened if they'd been living in the same space for months...

"Separate," he said.

"Hmmmm." Hobb flipped through the book until his eyes lit up. "Ah, the southern insula would be perfect. Two rooms off of a central living area complete with a writing desk, balcony overlooking the building's central courtyard, fireplace—though I don't suspect you shall use that often; Generasi's weather is *much* milder than in your homeland—and immediate access to the common cooking facility and baths located at the bottom of the building. Would this suit your needs?"

"Uh, hold on," Alex said, calling Theresa and Selina over and introducing them to Hobb.

He explained what sort of room would be available.

Theresa frowned. "How much would all that be? A suite like that would cost a lot of gold in a good inn."

"Aaaaaah, pleasure to meet you, Ms. Lu, and I can assure you our rates for our students ensure they are able to stay in comfort for the duration of their stay in Generasi. After all, we aren't exactly hurting for money. Twenty gold pieces per month."

Alex balked inwardly. This was a good rate? The reward for the mana vampire would pay for two and a half months. His inheritance would be enough to pay for two years. He began to think about what Mrs. Escofier said about Generasi being expensive...

"What do you think?" he asked Theresa, who'd paled considerably at the sum mentioned. Selina was simply still eyeing the architecture. A part of him yearned to be the age where he didn't know the value of coin. "Two of us would have to share a room so—"

Selina startled. "Theresa, can I share your room? Please, please, please, please." She grabbed the young woman's cloak.

"Uh, sure?" Theresa said. "I don't mind bunking with you, Selina."

"Yay!" the little girl sighed in relief.

Alex couldn't help but feel a little insulted. "Are you sure you'd be okay sharing for a bit?"

"Selina's small." Theresa smiled at the girl. "And it'd be fun. Like a sleepover until we get a place of our own."

"Alright, we'll take it," Alex said.

"Delightful." Hobb wrote into the chart. "Alex Roth... Theresa Lu... Selina Roth... Perfect." He dotted the final period. "And, Ms. Lu, would you be interested in auditing courses as part of Mr. Roth's entourage?"

Theresa frowned. "Auditing?"

"It means you get to take a few courses. No credit or anything, but you'd get to learn the subject."

"Oh, I, uh, I'm no wizard," Theresa said.

"That is of no matter; we have a number of diverse courses here in addition to wizardry." Hobb glanced at the sword at her hip. "We are by no means an academy of martial arts, but the Watchers of Roal do host classes on weaponry and hand-to-hand combat to train more for their number. Many who have taken their courses have successfully entered their number, or have gone onto other paths. Even some of the Rhinean Empire's elemental knights have taken the courses."

Growing interest sparked in her eyes.

Hobb smiled in the same way that cattle salespeople did. "We also have a number of courses on tactics, general combat, general knowledge in mathematics, lore on beasts, several forms of arts such as sculpting or painting—though those are not our specialties—I assure you, your education would not be lacking here."

Theresa was struck by a sudden thought. "Mr. Hobb—"

"Oh, just Hobb, please."

"Hobb, on the way here, we saw some buildings that looked a lot like how my grandfather used to describe the ones in Tarim-Lung."

"Here in Generasi, we are influenced by most of the world's cultures and have had many make their home here. Those of Tarim-Lung are no exception."

"Then, does the university have any courses on... qigong?"

Hobb's eyes flashed as though he had just clinched a sale. "Ahhhh, the art of life-energy cultivation. By no means is it a comprehensive subject of study here, but blood magic—which *is* a comprehensive subject here—draws from lifeforce instead of mana. Techniques that fortify one's lifeforce are useful in such a branch of magic, and so we have adapted a short set of courses to teach the basics of the subject. It is the only course categorized under Divinity offered at Generasi. If you look at the course guide—available in the library—you will find a course called

LIFE-1075: Lifeforce Enforcement I. I do believe that if you are interested in exploring the subject, it should be a suitable beginning. I do warn you however, there is a test of affinity before one can gain entry into the course, as it is a dangerous subject."

A wide smile bloomed on Theresa's face.

Alex watched her smile. "How much is it for auditing and junior school?"

Hobb's eyes were triumphant. "Ten gold coins per month."

"We'll take them both."

Chapter 28

Welcome Home

Thump. Thump. Thump.

Three bags landed on the floor.

Creeeeeak.

The door to the apartment closed and locked.

"We're finally here!" Alex pumped his fists. "We did it!"

The apartment was a fine place, just as Hobb had described it. The central area was narrow but long, leaving enough room for a circular dining table, desk, small bookshelf, and small pantry. The hardwood floors had been freshly polished and the doors to two bedrooms lay open. Through the curtains on the balcony doors, Alex could see the rain had finally stopped.

Groaning, Theresa slumped toward one of the chairs at the dining table and suddenly stopped. She cautiously bent down, examining it from every angle—including poking at the chair's legs with suspicion—before collapsing into it and letting her head loll back. Her eyes stared at the ceiling. "Yeah, we're here." She pulled off her boots and massaged her feet. "And I guess we're *all* students now?"

"Yep, all in a big fancy school at the centre of the world."

Alex smiled contentedly, watching Brutus sprawl on the floor near the balcony. Selina sprinted to the pantry and tore it open.

"Empty." She made a face before going to explore more of their new home.

"It won't be for long," Alex promised.

"So..." Theresa continued to stare at the ceiling. "The *benches* move."

"Yeah, what *was* that?" he said.

"I don't know. The bench just shook when Brutus lay down beside it, then started crawling away... and then it talked and..." She shook her head like she was in a daze. "And boats fly, and carpets fly, and stones fly..." She trailed off again. "I don't know. In the last two days, we've seen monsters and—" She looked around before mouthing the word 'dungeon core' to him. "I dunno, right now, my head is *pounding*. Did you know the benches move? Does everything move?"

Alex shrugged. "Probably not? Lucia said magic items can be expensive, right? That's why the gondolas have to be made cheap."

"Yeah, those flying boats." She pinched the bridge of her nose.

Alex took her waterskin from beside her bag, dug through the cupboards, and poured water into a copper cup. He slid it over to her across the table.

"Thanks." She gave him a pained smile and drained the cup, before glancing at Selina, who had stepped onto the balcony with a tired Brutus. Theresa leaned closer.

"Are... are we going to be okay?" she whispered, making a motion like she was rubbing two coins between her fingers.

He sat down beside her. "For a while," he whispered. "About two years, maybe. The program is four, though. At minimum, we should have our own place long before that."

A part of him felt sick at the idea that the entire material wealth of his parents' lives would barely amount to two years at the university, and even then, they only had the two years on account of his partial scholarship. If he had to pay the full amount, they'd be out in the street in about a year. He pushed that thought from his mind.

The larger issue was if the university was this expensive, then what would *buying* a place in the city be like?

They'd need more coin. What options did that leave? Selling the fire-gems?

No. Not unless they got desperate. Each one was so powerful, giving them up would be a big mistake, one they should try to avoid if they could. He wouldn't want to run into something as deadly as the hive-queen without them.

"There might be opportunities here," he suggested. "We just need to keep our eyes open and look around."

"Alex! Theresa! Come out here!" Selina called.

They looked at each other and—groaning like they were five times their age—stepped through the curtains onto the balcony.

The southern insula, the complex of student apartments, was somewhat empty. A few pieces of clothing hanging over balcony rails revealed that some students were in residence, while other balconies had one or two students seated on the same chairs as their dining chairs, bent over books.

Except for one. One was studying while seated cross-legged.

In midair.

Theresa groaned beside him. Selina laughed.

The courtyard below had multiple benches, stone tables and chairs for dining and socializing. A few more students were gathered below—eating from a variety of colourful and interesting-looking dishes. A pair of older students with books piled high on a table, had young children playing with blocks beside them. A warm breeze floated into the windows and balcony door.

Alex sighed in contentment, though a hint of nervousness remained as he remembered the Mark's presence and the secret of the Ravener. He wondered how differently he'd be feeling if he'd never been branded and had simply arrived with Selina and nothing hanging over him.

A beat of wings startled him from his thoughts.

From the sky swooped a huge bird with a black-feathered body and white-speckled wings. Its wingspan must have been at least ten feet across and it carried a dead rabbit in its claws. Fluttering, it landed on a balcony on the opposite side of the courtyard on the top floor—same level as their room—and let out a fierce, triumphant cry.

"Look at *that*!" Selina pointed. "What a big, pretty bird!"

Pretty? More like terrifying.

Brutus was watching it with all three heads and his ears perked up.

The curtain on the balcony parted and a muscular young man almost as tall as Alex stepped through. He was dark-skinned, similar in complexion to the griot that had passed through Alric, and his long hair was plaited and fell to mid-back. A sculpted, imposing beard covered his chin, and he was built more like a metalsmith than a wizard.

The giant eagle cooed as its master approached, then stepped onto the young man's outstretched leather gauntlet. He took the rabbit from the bird, petting the raptor with his free hand and stroking its head toward the beak. He said something loudly in a language Alex had never heard, then looked up, seeing them across the way.

He watched them for a moment before giving a polite nod.

Selina waved as Alex and Theresa returned his nod, and the young man stepped back through the curtain.

Alex briefly wondered if the young man was a first-year student who arrived for school even earlier than him, or an upper-year summer student.

"Okay. I think it's time to get some stuff done," he said, thinking out a plan and stepping back into the room. The others followed.

Theresa slipped back into the chair.

"Anyone want to come to the library?" he asked.

She groaned.

Brutus grunted.

Selina had already jumped into one of the beds.

In the bigger room, he noticed. That little goblin.

"Alright, I'll be back in time for lunch."

Theresa groaned again as he headed to the door.

"See you later, and look out for angry benches," Theresa said.

He heard Selina laughing from the bedroom.

Walking to the library was pleasant. The southern insula was close to the library building, and the path leading there passed through sculpted parklands and past great, old buildings of white and grey stone. Gargoyles and other winged figures holding staves and books stood in silent vigil at the top of the buildings. Students walking by spoke in multiple languages, and Alex paid close attention to their words.

Using the Mark, Rhinean had started to become more familiar. He was picking out at least one word every few sentences now. Not bad for a couple of days' practice. By the time he was ready to graduate, he planned on being able to speak as many languages as possible.

Maybe one of them would help him translate the Traveller's book, and perhaps the library would have something on that too. He was getting more and more excited as he made his way there.

Several of the conversations were in the Common tongue, though, and most were about the explosion earlier.

"I heard it was some sort of transmutation gone wrong," a squat young man in spectacles was saying, walking along with two others. "Someone tried to transform into a fire elemental, misaligned the spell array, and just turned into a fireball."

"That's not what I heard. I heard it was a magic item that

someone caused a mana reversal with," one of his companions said; a lanky, redheaded girl clutching a long glass flask. Inside the flask was a glowing ball of light, which flitted about like an insect. "The whole thing blew up in their face, literally."

"That doesn't seem right to me. It's gremlins," said their third, his frizzy brown hair bouncing as he walked. He had at least five books in his hands. "Gremlins sabotaging a potion."

"Well, whatever it was, whoever did it is completely done for," the first young man said. "Definitely expelled."

Alex glanced at them as they passed.

Raised voices burst from a garden on his right. He jumped as two students—maybe only a little older than him—emerged from the hedges.

"Isolde, will you stop!" A man chased after a woman in a mix of anger and desperation. His long red hair was disheveled and his face flushed. "You're not listening to me!"

An unusually tall woman—maybe only a few inches shorter than Alex—walked away from the man as though he wasn't even there. Her long black hair billowed behind her. "I don't listen to trash rolling along the ground."

"That's not fair!" he snapped, running in front of her. "It was a onetime thing!"

"No, it was not." She stepped around him without even giving him a second glance. "We're done. Keep it civil. I walk my path and you walk yours. Separately."

"But you're not giving me another chance!" he shouted.

Heads whirled from all around the greenspace and path.

"Derek..." Isolde's blue eyes hardened. "You need to quiet down, now."

"And *you* need to listen to m—"

"*No*." Her voice boomed. "You want to do this, then fine. We're done, Derek. Finished."

"But why—"

"Because you're a cheater, and I don't mean just on me—

which you have, as I've found out—several times. You're a cheater in everything." She began listing things off with her fingers. "You cheated on me. You cheat in dice and cards—"

"That's not a—"

"You cheat on your exams."

The colour drained from his face.

"What?" She glared at him. "You didn't think I'd find out? Professor Jules posted the announcement in the potions department this morning that someone cheated, which you would have known if you didn't skip class. Again."

"Wha-wha..." Derek stuttered, backing away from her.

"Of course, I knew earlier than that, when she called me into her office because our *potion analysis write-ups* were *word-for-word* the same. I had to spend an hour showing her my rough notes and analysis logs to prove *I* wasn't the one who copied. You would have been at the meeting if you didn't skip class. Again."

"Why... but..."

"I wanted this quiet, but *you* wanted to make a scene. There. Scene made. Now you'd better stop wasting time with me and go explain to her why you should remain a student here."

With a low cry, Derek sprinted away toward the main castle.

Isolde watched him go, then drew a long, steadying breath. Her teeth were grinding as she turned. Everyone looked anywhere but in her direction, including Alex.

In a dignified but angry silence, she walked away.

Alex let out a sigh when she'd passed. The problems of young love—apparently maniacal levels of cheating—was downright pleasant compared to nests of silent death bugs.

He continued toward the library.

His eyes rose to find the squat, windowless structure just ahead. Hobb had said the building had no windows so the temperature would be more even, and the books would be protected from sunlight. He hoped that wouldn't mean it'd be dark like a cave. He'd had enough of caves to last him a lifetime. In front of the library stood a fountain with a hooded figure holding two books and stone scrolls hanging from its robes. Water poured from the space in its hood where its head should have been.

Curious, he glanced over to see if any coins had been tossed into it.

A few.

He might add some later.

The doors to the library's welcome area were open, but on the other side, the room was sealed shut. Alex could see green, glowing writing surrounding the doorway.

He took a deep breath.

Ahead of him lay the accumulated knowledge of the greatest institution of wizardry in the world.

It was almost intimidating.

Chapter 29

Selecting One's Path

"Can I help you, young man?" a woman, whose complexion seemed to shift from orange to brown, asked from behind another desk set into the wall. Her ears were long and pointy like the witches in Alric's fairy tales. But unlike Alric's witches, hers were covered in feathers.

"Um, yes, it's my first day, and I'm looking to use the library."

"I see, well, welcome to Generasi. Might I see your student's plate?"

With pride, Alex dug out the round wooden card Hobb had given him after his registration was completed. It had a blue stamp on it, followed by the number one under his name.

"Hmmm, first year, and capable of first-tier magic. That will give you access to the first three floors of the library."

The woman spoke an incantation and traced a spell array over the card. A green, glowing symbol appeared beside the one.

"Please do not approach anything beneath floor three, as the wards will stop you from entering."

Alex's cheer dimmed. "I can't go to the other floors?"

"It's for your own safety, you understand," she said pointedly. "In times past, the university would have its knowledge freely available to all students, but some decided to sprint before they could crawl and took out spell-guides to magics far too advanced for their experience. You do not want to see what happens when a neophyte dabbles in demonology or advanced explosion magic."

Alex remembered the blue fireball that had burst from the Cells—whatever they were—earlier.

'Wizardry is dangerous,' Lucia's words echoed in his head.

"Right, that makes sense," he said.

"What languages can you read?"

"Just the Common tongue," he said, somewhat embarrassed. *For now,* he mentally added.

"Very well, many of the books are not written in that tongue, but you can make a translation request from the service desk on the first floor. The books are organized by a filing system that you can read about from the master tome on each floor. Have you chosen courses yet?"

Alex winced. Was he supposed to do that? Hobb hadn't mentioned anything about that. "N-no. Hobb said I could use the guides here."

"Not a problem, then. Normally, we send out a letter with a list of courses for students to select from before arrival. However, letters become lost, ships sink, caravans get diverted. To the farther realms, even acceptance letters can and have arrived late, leaving no time for course selection before the journey to Generasi must begin. It's why we hold a second round of selections on campus beginning approximately three weeks before classes begin."

She smiled warmly. "No need to worry; the course guides are set on the first floor on your right. When you've chosen your courses, you simply submit the form to the registrar's office."

"Um, do you have any books on the Ravener? Ones I can access?"

Her eyes flickered as though they were quickly turning pages he couldn't see. "Third floor, fourth shelf on your left on the upper balcony. Third book from the rightmost end. There *are* others, but they are within the deeper levels."

Alex groaned internally. He wouldn't be able to do any in-depth research on the dungeon core until he became more advanced in his studies. He really hoped the first book would be enough for now.

"Thanks, you've been very helpful," he said and stepped toward the door.

The green writing around the steps brightened as he approached, flashing in time with the symbol on his card.

There was a click as the doors silently parted in front of him.

"Best of luck with your studies," the librarian said.

The doors silently shut behind him.

Each floor of the library had two levels and the bookcases rose to the top of each, about ten feet tall. The second floor had a balcony circling the main room, while the middle of the chamber was filled with long tables and desks that were largely empty, except for a couple of robed figures who glanced up before returning to their studies. Green glowing forceballs illuminated the library, and Alex could see a sign close by that had a drawing of a lit candle with a giant 'X' through it.

He shook his head, wondering if anyone in their right mind would actually bring open flame near so many precious, and *flammable* books. Especially when there were spells that provided plenty of light.

He glanced to one of the closest shelves, grabbed a course guide, then made for the stairs. As it turned out, the second and third floors didn't lead up, but down into the earth. He was uncomfortably reminded of the dark descent into the hive.

Finding where he was going was easy enough, luckily. The librarian obviously had an unnaturally good memory. As he mounted the stairs toward the bookcase in question, he took a deep breath. Here it was. The moment he would begin his research on the Ravener.

His eyes skimmed the titles, looking for the one she indicated.

His heartbeat quickened.

Soon he'd have a book in his hands that could give him some answers. A book he'd been waiting to search since leaving Thameland.

Then his eyes stopped. So did his heart.

"It... it can't be." He stumbled back. Disbelief raced through him. His mind couldn't believe what he was seeing. It was impossible.

Impossible.

There, in the middle of two books that were written in languages he couldn't understand, was the name of a single title and its author printed on the spine of a volume:

A History of Our Heroes and their Opposition of the Ravener, by Finnius Galloway.

Alex Roth barely resisted screaming and finding himself being thrown out of the library on his first day.

Sighing, Alex sat at a table surrounded by books and paper.

On one side was his course guide, and in front of him were multiple first-tier spell-guides, and a few books on general magical lore and Thameland's history. Some of the books were somewhat helpful. Going into more details on the Traveller's life and how she had used her unique abilities to aid the other Heroes of her time.

There was talk of how her portals had come from another power outside of the Mark of the Saint, and how she had directed that power against the Ravener and its spawn.

He'd spoken to the librarian, and a book called *The Bestiary of the Ravener and its Foul Spawn* was available in the first-floor area, dedicated to students who could cast second-tier spells, along with most books on monsters' physiology and lore, and the beginnings of demonology.

That sounded like it would be a good start.

But for that, he would need to advance his spellcasting and prove he was able to handle the knowledge on the next floors. That brought him to the courses he'd need to take, which was what he'd been looking over.

First thing he needed was to not be discovered. He'd need to find out why people found it so strange for priests to be near the campus.

He also needed to make sure that, oddly enough, he stood out.

The Fool was known to be a failure at spellcasting, which meant if he *excelled* in magic, he would actually draw less suspicion than if he failed or was average.

Second and relatedly, was that he would need to advance fast enough to start rising in the spell-tiers. Not only would that enhance his power to defend himself—

A deep cough sounded near him.

Alex looked up at one of the only other occupants on this floor of the library. He was a massive figure—a beastfolk that looked like a bipedal goat—with iron-grey fur and a long beard decorated with a number of golden clasps. His eyes were the strange eyes of a goat, and they leisurely scanned a book in front of him, until they looked up to Alex.

The goat man winced. "Apologies."

"No problem." Alex waved to him and went back to sketching out his plan.

Where was he? Yes, defending himself. Advancing in spell-tiers would make him better able to investigate the Ravener, help him succeed at Generasi, *and* let him defend himself from mana vampires, horrible silence bugs, and anything else the world throws at him.

The issue was the Mark.

It wasn't going to make that easy.

He'd started his course selection with that idea in the front of his mind.

MAGT-1020: Magic Lore I was his compulsory. He'd already studied a fair amount of it before coming to Generasi, and the Mark hadn't interfered with him recalling facts about how spellcraft worked. If he could figure things out, it might even help him excel at the course.

That left four others.

A huge number of courses were listed in the course guide, ranging from magical lore, to different traditions of magic from all over the world, to other traditions such as minor courses on history, arts, and philosophy.

Briefly, he considered trying *LIFE-1075: Lifeforce Enforcement I.* Considering he would be physically training anyway, empowering his life force might be useful. Then again, that course could be a problem. Hobb said it was dangerous, that one needed an affinity for it, *and* that it was a Divinity. The last thing he needed was for the Mark to interfere while he was trying to learn some dangerous new subject he had zero experience in.

He'd leave that to Theresa.

That left a bunch of others he'd skimmed.

BLOO-1000: *An Introduction to blood magic. Achieve new avenues of spellcraft such as healing, the creation of homunculi and sympathetic magic with this ancient discipline.*

ELEC-1400: *Lightning Magic I. Learn the elemental art of lightning to power apparatuses, stun foes and blast enemies with a thunderbolt. Starts with a study of electricity, air elementals and basic shock spells.*

SUMM-1020: *Summoning I. Call upon spirits of the ether* *to enact your will in the world. Begins with the binding of least elementals.*

Most of those looked interesting, and he put them in the 'later' pile. For now, he needed to focus on things he had experience with, or that he was sure the Mark wouldn't affect.

Going over the list again, something interesting caught his eye.

POTI-1000: *The Alchemy of Potions I. Learn to brew draughts from the ancient recipes of the masters. Requires direct mana manipulation.*

That really looked promising. If potion-craft was mostly mana manipulation and combining ingredients, then there might not be much in the way of actual spellcraft. Mana manipulation was hard, but using the forceball had trained him in it to some extent. Besides, he'd been a baker's assistant for years. He could learn recipes in his sleep.

He thought about the dungeon core.

The Mark had helped him use mana manipulation against the core. It would probably help him with this subject. And learning mana manipulation through potions might even help him fight a core again, if it came to that.

A thought occurred to him and he flipped through the guide.

He smiled when he found what he was looking for.

MANA-1900: *The Beginnings of Mana Manipulation. Learn this challenging, ancient art complimentary to spellcraft. Learn valuable mana regeneration techniques and how to operate certain spells and ancient magic items.*

Perfect.

He checked off another box.

His second to last course choice was easy.

FORC-1550: *Spells of Force I. This is a specialty course in the arts of force magic. From spells such as the humble forceball or magic missile, to shields, force bubbles and walls of force. Spells from this family are versatile and powerful.*

This main course in spellcraft would allow him to specialize in magic similar to the spell he was most familiar with. A good way to counter interference by the Mark.

That left one more.

Flipping back to the beginning, he started to turn the page when he noticed an entry he'd missed earlier.

COMB-1000: *The Art of the Wizard in Combat. There is more to using magic in battle than simply learning battle spells and sending them flying to explode at your enemies. A Proper Wizard knows how to conduct themselves in battle and use every resource available. Combat spells. Vast knowledge. Physicality. Allies. These are all tools, and battle will make students grow like no other.*

WARNING: *COMB-1000 is a danger-oriented course that does not pull its punches. Live combat against creatures of the Barrens of Kravernus is the preferred teaching method. Beware.*

Alex stared at the course for a long time.

A few days ago, he wouldn't have even given it a second look. Now?

'Every resource available.'

Something about that spoke to him on a fundamental level. There was a course for battle-magic, but it focused on spells that blew things up or enhanced the physical form. This, though?

This sounded like it could teach him the true nature of combat, resources, survival and adaptation.

This could teach him how to survive mana vampires and silence-spiders and whatever else was waiting for him.

He thought it over for a long time.

Another deep cough, from close by.

Alex startled. The goat-fellow had risen from his table and was making his way to the door, his cloven hooves emerging from beneath his robes and making a dull noise on the floorboards. Still, they were oddly quiet.

Alex hadn't even heard him approach.

"Apologies," the man said again as he stepped by.

His eyes fell on the course guide.

Slowly, he turned, and Alex was struck by just how *big* he was. Maybe a good foot taller than he was. Maybe more.

"Hmmm, forgive me for being nosey, but are you considering COMB-1000?" he asked, his beard clasps clinking.

"I, uh, I'm thinking about it," Alex said, wondering if he was a professor.

"Good. It's good to see even the consideration of it." The man's goat-like eyes twinkled. "If I might advise you, I would suggest taking the course, though I am a little biased. After all—" He leaned forward slightly, and his bulk seemed to fill the room. "—I teach it."

Chapter 30

The Means of Survival

"Oh!" Alex stood up quickly in respect. "Hello, Professor..."

The goat man waved him back into his seat. His fingers were almost as big as Selina's wrists. "Don't bother with all that. I'm not one for formality. And the name is Baelin."

"Alex Roth, First Year, and whatever you say, Professor, you're literally the boss here." Alex sat down. "So, you think I should take it, Professor Baelin?"

"If I had my way, it would be compulsory," Baelin said, and his voice was like quiet thunder. "Proper Wizards deal with forces that can, and have, annihilated entire civilizations. It's madness to not teach one to defend themselves."

"Um, forgive me if I sound like I just crawled in from the countryside, because I did, but I thought that's what the battle-magic course was for, Professor. Same with the course on weapons taught by the Watchers."

"Both fine courses that I highly recommend." Baelin pulled out the chair opposite the young spellcaster and sat down. He placed his book on the table, but Alex couldn't read the writing on its spine. His heavy robes rustled as he settled himself. "But what is a wizard to do when their mana runs dry? What is a wizard to do when their staff breaks? When a sword is dull or cannot pierce the enemy?"

Alex thought back to the recent fights he'd experienced.

Against the silence-spider in Coille, he'd used his forceball to destroy its insides, but Brutus and Theresa had done much of the work in pinning it down. It had been the cerberus who had torn its throat out. His magic was useless against the hive-queen; only the fire-gems' explosion and the Traveller's portals saved their lives. Then there was the mana vampire. A mop and two spears had brought it down, not a spell.

"Then you need to adapt," Alex found himself saying. "You have to think of what you have available and use that to defeat your enemy or survive."

Baelin sat a bit straighter, surprised. "Well said; not many students come with that attitude. Most trust in optimal magics too much. I suppose I can't blame them, though. Much of the world seems a little less dangerous when you can conjure storms with a few careful words of power. Of course, that belief is how the world kills so many who think themselves invincible."

There was a casualness in the way Baelin talked about death, like if he were discussing the market price of fish. "Hmmm... You're from Thameland, judging by your accent?"

"Yes." Alex nodded. "You've heard of the Ravener?"

"Oh yes, I know of the Ravener," Baelin said. "It is one of many great threats in the world, and threats must be fortified against. That's why I implore you to take my course. Wizardry is dangerous."

"Isn't the course dangerous, Professor?"

"It is, and that is the point." The hulking beastman spread his hands. "What is better? One can learn combat in a safe classroom or a gymnasium, flinging spells at targets or having nonlethal duels against fellow classmates—with all the rules and fairness of a chess tournament—only to be destroyed when true danger raises its ugly head. Bandits and mercenaries play by no rules. Monsters do not attack you in a classroom, and if they do, you would not expect it. Things that seek your life attack you from surprise, from the dark and in rough terrain. They do not seek fairness; they seek your life. I cannot count how many of those trained in 'fair conditions' have died to decidedly unfair circumstances they had not prepared for."

He pointed to the course entry. "So, one trains and fights in more dangerous scenarios under my careful supervision, against opponents who seek to maim or kill. You learn of yourself and your resources while under supervision. You face your fears. You strangle your hesitation. When you emerge, you know how to fight as only a Proper Wizard can fight: with everything you have."

Alex looked to the course entry again. He had misgivings about it. Lucia's injury was fresh in his mind. Then again, wouldn't gaining experience in defending himself be exactly what he'd need to avoid her fate? A lot of what the professor said made sense to him. The mana vampire had tried to ambush him, and the hive-queen terrorized them, trying to corral them into a deathtrap.

He looked to the hulking beastman whose eyes seemed to burrow through him, almost as if he was peering through his shirt and flesh. Unconsciously, Alex shifted his right shoulder away from his gaze.

"Professor, I'm honoured, but why me?" Alex asked. "I'm just a normal first year, and the only spell I know is forceball. Aren't there other more skilled students you'd want to recruit?"

Baelin snorted. "The course does not attract much interest, for reasons you can guess, which keeps the class size small, if one puts it charitably. To put it uncharitably, the course has very little enrollees. I cringe to see students walking from the doors of the university into a great, dangerous universe that has opened up to them thanks to our teachings, without the proper defences in place. So, if there is a student—even if that student wants to go off and brew toe-rot cures for villages—who shows any interest, then am I to let the opportunity pass? Am I to let them pass unprepared?"

Alex looked over the course again. There would be risk to this. A strong risk. Of course, judging by the explosion that just took place, this entire school presented risks. Magic always did. He thought back to his early experiments learning the forceball. Nearly blowing his face off in the forest. Nearly causing a mana reversal.

Better to be prepared now and alive later, than safe now and dead forever.

Decisively, Alex wrote in *COMB-1000* as his final course choice.

Baelin gave a low rumble of approval as he rose from his chair. "Welcome, to the Art of the Wizard in Combat, Mr. Roth. Along the way, you'll curse yourself and me for bringing you into the course. Later, I guarantee you'll think of it as one of the best decisions you've ever made."

He extended a hand toward Alex.

Without hesitation, Alex shook it.

Maybe he'd found his first ally at Generasi. Time would tell.

For now, he had a month and a half to prepare.

Training Day 1

Three Sets of Push-Ups: BEGAN. 9,8,7. DONE.
TOTAL=24
Spell-Testing: BEGAN.

Alex finished scrawling the note into his book—shining his forceball onto the page—and closed it. It was still dark. Brutus snored by the balcony while Theresa and Selina hadn't yet moved from their room.

Filled with anticipation and energy, he'd woken up just before sunrise, and decided to get things started. With only a limited amount of time before courses began, he needed to make as much progress as possible.

He stretched after the push-ups as Theresa had instructed him to do, then slid the borrowed spell-guides from the bookshelf and slipped them into his bag. He got dressed, cut the mana to the forceball, and quietly left the room, concentrating on the Mark to focus on his stealth.

He'd been doing a lot of sneaking lately, and memories for the Mark to draw on were a lot more numerous than when he'd started. He noticed his steps were making less noise than they had in the Cave of the Traveller, and the movement—placing his weight carefully with each step—was becoming more natural.

Good. Progress.

He silently entered the third floor lav for a quick wash, then headed out.

Across the grounds were clashes of light and sound. Other students diligently practicing utility spells for their summer courses. According to the course guide, the school had a stadium for combat practice, duels, and other games. It was only there—where they wouldn't blast or burn up parts of the campus' greenery—that students were allowed to practice combat spells.

Exploring it could wait until later.

This morning would be for preliminary baseline tests.

He laid out the five first-tier spell-guides he'd borrowed from the library, ordering them from left to right. Leftmost spells were those he thought would be easiest for him to work with. Rightmost were those he guessed would be more difficult.

On the left was forcedisk, a spell very similar to his forceball, which created a floating plate. Next was Wizard's Hand, a spell that created a floating hand of force that was weaker than his forceball, but had the advantage of dexterous fingers. It contained a more complex spell array.

The middle spell was outside of the school of force, Orb of Air, which created a sphere of compressed air that could be used underwater to surround one's head with a bubble of air, or to create a small, harmless blast of wind if one burst it.

The second to last was Lesser Heat, which simply heated an object, such as warming up a cold cup of tea, or one's hands on a winter day. It was a simple elemental spell, and it would be his first entry into fire-magic. If he learned more about the subject, then one day, he might be able to use the stone goddess' fire-gems properly. He smiled at the thought.

Finally, there was Summon Stone. One of the simplest summoning spells one could practice. It conjured a small rock from the elemental planes, holding little practical use. Unless one was at a lake and had no rocks to skip. It was good practice for aspiring summoners, according to the spell-guide. It was completely unrelated to anything he'd studied.

He cracked his knuckles and opened forcedisk.

Alex studied the spell, noting the similarities in its spell array, and the spell array of his forceball.

This would be a good starting point.

He'd need to warm up first, though, and take a careful account of how his forceball functioned. Concentrating, he began to cast a forceball, going through the familiar motions while the Mark bombarded him with failures. He diligently constructed the spell array, guiding his thoughts through the invasive images. He felt his heartbeats and counted them.

The forceball winked to life. He grimaced as he finished counting, then cut the flow to the magic circuit and waited, counting the beats until the forceball winked out.

His eyebrows rose as he recorded the results.

Spell Formation: *Ten heartbeats*

Dissipation: *Six heartbeats*

He flipped back to his last entry before he'd been branded with the Mark of the Fool.

Spell Formation: *Oneish heartbeats.*
Dissipation: *Three and a half heartbeats.*

Spell formation speed was a tenth of what it used to be. He could have conjured forceballs in his sleep before he'd received the Mark. Still, dissipation had nearly doubled, which meant the spell was packed far more efficiently with mana. The modification he'd done to the spell array when he'd been branded had continued to show results.

He looked at the spell-guide for the forcedisk, rethinking his plan.

If he was going to start learning spells similar to the one he already knew, wouldn't it make sense to truly explore what he already knew first? One didn't build the second floor of a house if the first floor didn't have all of its supporting walls. If the Fool was going to use his memories of failed spellcasting to hinder him, then better he observe those failures with a spell he knew well.

"I'll analyze the problems first," he noted, scrawling another note into his book.

Explore failures. Use every failure possible that is presented. Analyze them. Use that to generate improved forceball. Could impress professor for FORC-1550.

Use experience with tweaking spell array to serve as a basis for learning new magics.

Conclusion?

Explore forceball first.

What had the librarian said? Something about students getting into trouble because they tried to run before they could crawl? He wouldn't make the same mistake.

He closed the book on forcedisk after copying the incantation, spell array and diagram for the magic circuit into his book. He would compare the two spells and analyze their similarities.

Falling into himself, Alex began casting the forceball again, noting any failures the Fool showed him. His mind drank in their details like a mana vampire would drain a wizard, then he ended the spell before the magic circuit would complete.

He wrote down the details of those failures. The exact misalignment of mana circuitry, the exact orientation of the spell array and anything else that stood out. He recorded the results of those failures as well.

Over and over, he cast his forceball, observing the failures the Fool presented. Each time he took a note, he used the Mark to continue improving his handwriting, focusing on increasing both its neatness and speed.

Through repetition, his writing transformed, growing smaller and cleaner, allowing him to fill more notes into each page.

By the time the sun had fully risen, he'd stuffed three pages with tiny observations of his failures. It wasn't even a comprehensive list yet. The Mark seemed dead set on calling up every single mistake he'd made in spellcraft since he'd first *heard* the term forceball.

Well, that was alright by him.

Failure could be just as excellent a teacher as success. If not even better.

Chapter 31

The Chancellor

Training Day 3

Three Sets of Push-Ups: BEGAN. 10,9,8. DONE.
TOTAL=27
Spell-Testing: BEGAN.

Alex closed the book and slipped out of the room, stretching after his morning exercises. His footsteps were very quiet now, at least to him. He was nowhere near Theresa's natural silence, but he'd reached the level of someone who had been putting effort into the skill for a while.

The insula was almost devoid of life this early in the morning. Some students were speaking incantations in low voices as he left the lav and headed down the hallway past their apartments.

As he stepped into the courtyard, he hesitated, moving back inside to glance into the kitchen. It was fully equipped with a large stove and oven, a deep sink, countertops and a fireplace. There were logs nearby, but the stove, oven, and fireplace were etched with spell arrays that were similar to what was written in the spell-guide for Heat.

Fire-magic.

Clever. Wood for students who hadn't gained experience with the spell arrays of fire-magic, and arrays for those who had. He hoped in time he'd be able to use the spell arrays himself. For now, it would be good to gather ingredients and do some cooking or baking down here. The food at Generasi was incredible, but he was starting to miss Alric's home cooking.

Walking through the courtyard, he spied the massive eagle asleep with its head tucked beneath a wing on its master's balcony. No sign of its master, though. Leaving the insula, he reached the quiet spot he'd been using to practice in for the last couple of days—a group of trees about five minutes' walk from most of the school's buildings.

He set himself up and opened his notebook, wincing at what was inside.

Ten pages of failures and counting.

All of them with detailed notes, courtesy of the Fool, examining the precise details of said failures. Put nicely, it was an entire page listing all the ways he could improve his spellcraft. Put another way, it was a detailed record of every stupid or embarrassing action he'd done, including some where he'd nearly gotten injured, or ones that could have ended his career as a mage before it had really even begun.

The alarming thing was that there seemed to be no end.

At first, he'd thought there might have been a finite number of failures to record. After all, he hadn't been practicing magic for an infinite amount of time, so there had to be a limit to the failures it would throw at him.

He'd been right, but only to a certain extent.

Even on his successful castings of the forceball, it wasn't as though he cast the spell perfectly each time. It was like any other task. One could never repeat the same movements exactly every time they made them, even with something as common as walking. Little tiny inefficiencies, wasted motion, slip-ups when one wasn't fully paying attention, or mistakes caused by outside circumstances were constant in every task in life.

Most didn't notice these tiny deviations; they were just part of life. But the Mark of the Fool did, and it amplified them, screaming them into his mind to ruin anything it didn't want him to do.

Just by living life, he would generate an endless line of tiny failures for it to grind into his face.

He shuddered. This Mark could definitely give someone a complex.

Looking back to the book, he tapped his pen against the pages. He'd accounted for most of his largest mistakes at least. Getting those down was worth it, then would come the time to experiment.

Training Day 5

Three Sets of Push-Ups: BEGAN. 12,10,8. DONE. TOTAL=30
Forceball Failure Documentation: COMPLETE (enough).
Today: Begin experimentation

He started to slip his books into his rucksack.

Creak.

"Alex?"

"Uldar's beard!" he jumped, whirling around.

Brutus flew up, his paws scrabbling on the hardwood floor as he looked around with all three heads.

Theresa stood in the middle of the doorway to the larger

bedroom, rubbing her eyes. She had a clear case of bed-head. Her hair hung down, wild and messy from the night's sleep, and her long nightdress was crooked. Behind her, Selina was still asleep.

"You scared me." Alex let out a sigh of relief. "What're you doing up so early?"

"I think I've had enough sleeping in." She padded up to the pantry and took out a hunk of bread baked the day before and offered him a piece, which he took. Their pantry was starting to fill with breads, cheeses, butter, fresh vegetables and more.

The top section of the pantry was ringed with a spell array that kept things cold, while in the middle and bottom, food that could stay at room temperature like bags of flour and apples were arranged.

He wanted to treat Theresa and Selina to a pie soon.

"You should stay for a bit longer." Theresa leaned against the pantry. "Selina misses you at breakfast."

"It's just temporary," he said. "Besides, she's been missing you at supper."

Theresa threw a guilty look at her sword leaning against the wall in its scabbard. "Like you said, it's temporary."

"Then we both have the same excuse." He smiled. "How's it been, watching the Watchers?"

After they had explored the campus over the first few days, Theresa had taken to observing the evening practices held by the Watchers of Roal.

"Informative." She made a face. "I didn't know how little I knew about the sword. You should come with me one evening. It's something else."

"I might just do that. Actually sounds kind of fun."

"Good. Just do me one favour... don't bring a mop."

"Hey!"

She grinned at him. "I think I'm going to audit their weapons course. Even if I only watch, I'm learning a lot. If I put that together with Lifeforce Enforcement, that'll get me on a similar path to the one Great-grandfather walked."

Her eyes twinkled and Alex couldn't help but smile, unable to take his eyes off her, bed-head and all.

"That's really cool," he said. "I'm sure he'd be proud. You thinking of taking anything else?"

"Geography of the World's Realms."

"Really?" He raised an eyebrow. "I thought you more wanted to see the world, and less wanted to hear about it from dusty old books."

"If I'm going to see the world, then I should know something about it. Why waste time and knowledge? Besides, I'm just auditing the course. There's no credit; I don't have to worry about studying or writing exams. I just have to listen and read what I want to read about. So, why not?"

Alex chuckled. If only his situation were the same. Judging by the continuous practicing he'd seen summer students doing, the exams he'd have to face wouldn't be a joke.

"You'll have to tell me what you learn," he said. "It'll be a nice break from grinding magical knowledge into my head. Maybe—"

Creeaaak.

The floorboards whined under a sleepy-eyed Selina's foot as she padded into the common room—also with bed-head. "Mmm, you're still here, Alex? Are you going to stay for breakfast?"

He sighed, amused at himself. "I guess I am."

The announcement came the next morning.

"Attention, students!" a voice boomed in the insula's courtyard, startling Alex from sleep. He scrambled to his bedroom window and pulled aside the curtain to see a Watcher of Roal floating just above the insula's rooftop. A few other students tore open their bedroom curtains, and the young man who owned the eagle stumbled onto his balcony, his whole body tense.

"Please assemble at the stadium in one hour," the Watcher of Roal barked. "The investigation into the explosion at the Cell's has been completed, and Chancellor Baelin wishes to make an announcement regarding the findings."

Wait.

Chancellor Baelin?

Lucia's words returned.

'The Barrens of Kravernus,' the gondolier had said. 'The mighty chancellor's monster park.'

"Well, shit," Alex muttered as the Watcher flew off. Across the courtyard, he met the eyes of the eagle-wrangler.

Both of them exchanged shrugs.

The stadium was large enough to fit thousands of people, but only a few hundred students filed tiredly into the seats. Some came with their entourages. Some older students arrived with partners and children, while some of the younger ones—who were extremely well-dressed—were followed by attendants and bodyguards. Alex wondered just how many nobles were here from all the countries in the world.

Alex's entourage—his friend, his sister and a three-headed dog—had dragged themselves onto the stone benches beside him. Selina glared grumpily down at the stadium. "Why are they sooo earlyyyy?"

She clutched a little reed-doll she had been constructing for the past day.

Alex noticed it had a thick torso and a little stick that looked like an oar. She also held a little book of general studies

—one of the books she'd be learning from when the junior school started.

Alex stared at the field below in rapt attention at the line of administrators sitting by a podium. He noticed the white-haired woman and sharp-dressed man they'd seen on the day they arrived at Generasi sitting close to the podium, while a number of Watchers of Roal floated above, grim-faced as usual.

Hobb was there as well, minus the inquisitive cheer from when they'd met.

Then the air began to shimmer.

Like fish emerging from a pond, Profess—no, *Chancellor* Baelin stepped out of thin air, towering over the other administrators. Unlike when Alex had met him in the library, the wizard was grim in both facial expression and the stiffness of his body.

"I will now begin," he pronounced.

Mana shuddered in the air as his voice reached out across the entire stadium. It seemed as though he were speaking no louder than a regular conversation, only it was amplified, cutting through the surrounding noise as clearly as if he'd been shouting at the top of his lungs.

"Five days ago, an explosion took place in the Cells. The explosion was stronger than a third-tier fireball going off in a confined room. One experimental cell was destroyed, and—were it not for the reinforcements in the building—the damage would have been far more catastrophic than it was. As it is, one student lost an arm and suffered other devastating injuries, and a member of his entourage tragically lost their lives."

There was a collective gasp from Alex, Theresa, Selina and some of the other younger attendees.

He noticed others simply looked on as though the news was expected.

"This was tragic, but it was also avoidable." Iron anger crept into the beastman's voice. "We have used equipment from the potions department to examine the residue, and have also conducted interviews. And so, we have determined the cause. The explosion was the result of a first-year summer student attempting to create a potion of Wizard's Daylight. A potion *not* recommended for those who have not mastered appropriate mana manipulation techniques suited for *third*-tier magic. We determined the recipe was followed correctly, but the student could not manage the build-up of power caused by the reaction of sun-spore with the catalyst, which then caused a runaway mana build-up and consequently, a potion detonation."

He leaned onto the podium. "This student should not have had access to the potion manual that contained such a recipe. All students are repeatedly cautioned on the dangers. We have concluded that an upper-year student borrowed the recipe book from the library and unwisely shared it with the younger student in return for monetary gain."

Beard clasps clinked in the wind. "Both students have been expelled, and the upper-year student will be charged by the Wizard's Forum for negligence that resulted in bodily harm and destruction of property."

Alex's blood ran cold and he exchanged a look with Theresa and Selina.

He thought about the librarian's warning about how students were not allowed books from the lower levels. It made sense to him then, but he *really* understood why now. Anything down there would have to be treated with respect.

"I can't describe how much this disappoints me," Baelin said. "Magic is not a toy. It is not a pet to take running for fun and it is not a stallion you need to gallop." He snorted in disgust. "It is not most divinity, where gods hand out power like handing a child their favourite treat. If you have been accepted into Generasi, it *should* mean you have shown a recruiter knowledge, will, intelligence, drive and *common sense*. Learn from your fellow students' examples. Our instructors are here to walk you through a dangerous path. Let them guide you. Do not sprint before you can crawl. That is part of the path to being a Proper Wizard."

He sighed.

"That is all. You may go on about your day. I wish summer students luck in their upcoming examinations."

With that, the chancellor turned and walked back into empty space, disappearing through shimmering air. Whispers broke out among the students.

"That big explosion came from a potion?" Theresa leaned toward. "Like, 'drink from a bottle' potion, like 'the class you're about to take' potion?"

Alex chewed his lip. "Yeaaaah, that's the one."

He wondered if there were any summer classes in potions still being held.

If there was, he'd find out where one was and go see first-hand what the subject was about. If potions could explode like that...

He paused, remembering the dungeon core's remains.

They used some sort of equipment in the potions department to analyze residue, Chancellor Baelin had said. Maybe the same equipment could be used to examine the core's powder.

It was time to visit the department and see exactly what he'd gotten himself involved in.

Chapter 32

Responsibility and Paths Forward

"This is a dark day for the potions department, I want you *all* to know that," a voice cracked like a whip as Alex opened the door to the lecture hall.

The door emerged onto the back of the class, which was set up like a half-bowl with built-in long tables for students to sit at on each level, like how the stadium was built. At the bottom of the incline, a woman stood on a stage in front of a massive slab of obsidian, covered in half-erased diagrams and formulae.

Alex recognized her as the white-haired woman who had first run to investigate the explosion with the sharp-dressed man.

He also recognized two students, to his surprise.

One was Isolde, sitting at the front of the class, her eyes forward and back straight. She gave off a powerful aura—a towering confidence similar to the one coming off of Cedric.

This was in contrast to a person sitting in the upper rows of the back of the class.

Her ex-partner, Derek, had his face clutched in his hands, and his entire body shook. His skin was pale and sweaty. He looked like he hadn't slept in days. Alex quietly eased the door shut and slipped into the closest empty seat. A couple of the students and the professor glanced at him, but they didn't really seem to register him much.

Whatever was going on held all of the attention in the room.

"Brewing potions is not the same as making wine in the countryside." The professor shook her head, her expression of someone who'd just been told a family member had just suddenly dropped dead. "I said this repeatedly. And what do I see?"

Iron-grey eyes leveled on the class. "Irresponsibility. Childishness. *Fool*ishness."

Alex nearly startled at that last word.

"The university trusts that you are all adults—ones ready to wield forces few others in this world can fathom. Instead, days ago, one of our number decided to cast away that responsibility. They are now maimed and someone is dead. This would be bad enough, but on top of this—Mr. Warren!"

Derek jumped up from his seat. "Professor Jules!"

She gestured at him. "As we have discussed, you have something to tell the class, don't you?"

The redheaded man swallowed. "I uh... I'm sorry," he muttered. "I... on the project for the potion of flight, I copied another student's assignment. In, uh, in doing this, I have tarnished my record as a wizard of Generasi, I have harmed the department, the student I copied from, all of you and myself. I, um..." He began to shake. "I showed that I am not ready to advance to POTI-2000. I'll be withdrawing from the course and repeating in the fall semester. And I apologize to you all."

Isolde turned toward him, staring at him for a moment, before giving a short nod and returning her attention to the front of the room. Most of the other students turned away from him, while Alex's eyes lingered a little longer.

"You may sit now, Mr. Warren," Professor Jules said.

Derek collapsed into his chair, deflating.

"Cheating is a high-penalty offence at Generasi. Cheating in the mundane scholarly arts will lead to you not bearing the knowledge you should. Cheating in the Arts of Wizardry is putting your own life and the lives of others at risk." Her eyes swept the room. "As you heard from our Chancellor, were it not for Mr. Warren's public apology, he would be expelled even as we speak. I ask that all of *you* learn from these mistakes and conduct yourselves properly."

She folded her hands behind her back, chin raising. "I was a student once too. I know how it can be. The graduate programs require very high marks to enter, and some even examine your first-year performance. The pressure is strong. But remember, wizardry is a dangerous subject. Cutting corners will only increase this danger. High marks in an exam mean nothing if you lack the fundamentals that will *kill* you a year from now. That is all. I'll be ending class early today. Read chapter forty-five from *Dexter's General Alchemy of Potions.* Two more weeks until the final and then your break. Stay the course. We are almost there."

As students rose and began to file out of the room—Derek tore through the doors at a half-run—Alex took out a piece of paper and wrote down the name of the textbook. His course selection was still being processed, and he hadn't received his list of texts yet. Better to get a head start on study.

He glanced up as the towering Isolde glided up the stairs. She frowned and her eyes were down even though her head and back were straight. Another couple of students were talking with her, but the young woman hardly said a word as she pushed through the door.

When the room was empty, Alex got up from his seat and made his way to the stairs and down toward the stage at the front of the class. Professor Jules was quietly packing her own bag, though she looked up as he approached.

"Hello, is there something I can do..." Her eyes narrowed. "Are you in my class?"

"Not yet," he said. "I'm a new student here and I'll be starting in the fall."

"I see."

"We, uh, met once before."

"We have?" She squinted at him. "Were you in someone's entourage?"

"No, uh, in the courtyard when you were on the way to the explosion in the Cells?"

"Hrm... wait, were you the young man with the cerberus?"

"Uh, he's not my Cerberus, but I *technically* was with him. I'm surprised you remember, Professor; you were a little bit busy that day. I'm Alex, by the way."

"Professor Jules, though you already seem to know that. 'A little bit,' he says," she muttered. "I noticed the dog more than you, I have to admit. Either way, welcome to Generasi. Apologies that today's class was not more of a good impression."

"We all have our bad days. Even magic departments, I guess. Professor, I wanted to ask you a question."

"I have to supervise a practicum in the Cells shortly, so it will have to be quick. Follow me?"

"Sure."

They stepped out of the classroom together as the short woman hurried through the halls of the main castle. His longer strides easily kept up. "Professor, I was wondering, and I know maybe this isn't the thing to get out of the chancellor's speech this morning, but he said something about the potions department having something they analyzed the explosive residue with?"

"Yes, why do you ask?"

"Ah, I was just wondering how that worked?"

She chuckled. "'How it works' is about an entire month of the curriculum for POTI-1000. Much of the course involves the careful analysis of ingredients."

"I see..."

How was he to ask her: 'Hey, can I use it to analyze the remains of one of the horrible doom cores that have plagued my country for centuries? Oh, and it might be able to be controlled by humans? Okay if I just toss that into your magical analysis thingy?'

"Can..." He thought his way through the question. "Can we use the equipment to study things on our own? Like... herbs and monster parts and stuff like that?"

"Unfortunately not."

"O-oh. Because it's too dangerous?"

They had stepped into the courtyard of the main castle and she waved a hand at the air. One of those floating disks emerged from behind a rooftop and shot toward them.

"Exactly. This isn't a cooking class. You can't just dump a bunch of ingredients into a pot and hope it turns out for the best. If one makes a bad stew, that might cause indigestion. Here? The wrong sort of material used in the wrong apparatus could ruin the magic circuits, and our equipment is very expensive. At worst, you could cause an unseen reaction that would lead to catastrophic results."

He thought about the explosion. "Yeah, that makes sense, Professor... But what about projects we run ourselves? Is that something we can eventually do?"

"Of course, though that is not usually for first-years."

The disk floated down beside her. "I can see you are very keen." Her eyes both held sympathy and warning. "I was the same. My suggestion to you is that you focus on the curriculum. Depending on how quickly you advance, you are afforded more freedom. Fill the basics first, and maybe we can have a chat about personal projects in your second year. Now, if you'll excuse me, I don't want to be late."

She boarded the disk and shot off through the air toward the Cells.

Alex watched her go, thinking about what she just said.

'Though that is not usually for first-years.'

So, *not* impossible then.

Training Day 8

Push-ups: Rest Day
Experimentation Day 3: BEGIN
Skills: Writing (Other), Reading, Running

"You should stay here and study," Selina said as she finished chewing her last hunk of cheese. "Why do you need to go outside?"

He took her plate, piling it into the bucket to take down to the scullery by the baths. "Because you'd just be bored."

"No I wouldn't," she protested.

"I'm just going over books for my classes." He waved *Dexter's General Alchemy of Potions* at her before slipping it into his bag. "You're going to be bored and then you're going to want to come back home."

"I won't! I won't!"

He sighed, turning to Theresa. "You exercising Brutus this morning? Maybe she'd like to come with you?"

"I want to come with you," Selina insisted.

Theresa sipped from a cup of weak tea and made a face. "Food from all over the world here, and no pine needles to boil for a drink. I'm just taking him to the beastarium."

"The what now?" Alex asked.

"It's a place on the north side of the campus where students can let their beasts run and explore this wilderness area. Some of the Watchers of Roal were telling me about it last night."

"Oh? Making friends already?"

She shrugged. “They’re strange… They’re like two different people at once.”

“What do you mean?”

“Like…” She struggled for her words. “When they’re training, they never smile. Never laugh. When one of them falls or gets hit, they’re completely restrained and don’t make a sound. They hardly talk.”

“They sound like walking statues.”

“Yeah, but when their training ends, it’s like they become completely different people. It’s so weird. Suddenly, they’re smiling and joking and laughing—hammering each other on the shoulder—like they’d just come out of our inn after a few pints.”

She shook her head, wearing her deathstalker face.

Brutus whined and shoved one of his heads into her lap. Her face softened, and she smiled as she pet him. “It’s okay, boy, we’re going soon. Anyway, it’s strange, right? Watching someone change so fast?”

When she looked back up, she had her deathstalker face back on.

“Oh yeah, who would be like that?” His mouth began to go renegade. “There’s *no one* we know who would just go from terrifying killer to ordinary wom—” He coughed. “Person, in about a second.”

Silence followed.

Theresa’s eyes bore into him. “What do you mean by that, Alex?”

“Well, uhm… Not, uh… you. You see, the thing about that is… This—Selina, why don’t we *all* go to this beastarium? I could study and you could see the animals and stuff at the same time!”

“Can we? Yay!” Selina slid from the table to get her bag.

“Now, I know what you’re thinking.” He turned back to Theresa. “But if you murder me, I want you to know that you’re going to make Selina hate you for life.”

Silence.

"J-just a thought," he said.

Her chair scraped the floor as she stood. "Remember, it's all about patience when it comes to hunting, Alex. It's all about patience."

Ominously, she went to get ready with Brutus following after her.

Was it just him, or did Brutus give him a dirty look?

No, he probably just imagined it.

Maybe.

He went into his room, and—checking to see that no one was watching him—made a new entry in his notebook on a page he'd carefully folded in the back.

Project Fetch Progress.

Setback?

Chapter 33

The Beastarium

The beastarium had been a good idea.

It was a soaring, round complex of forest and field—that most of Alric could fit within—surrounded by circular stone walls capped by a massive dome of magically enhanced, supporting crossed brass bars.

To one side, there was a sitting area with tables and benches throughout for folk to sit, study or contemplate. They could also picnic in the field or treed area. The sheer number of unique animals and trained monsters were mind boggling.

Dog breeds of all sizes chased balls, sticks and each other across the grass, while ravens, owls—awake in the day, surprisingly—falcons and brightly coloured birds flew above, filling the air with both their songs and their cries.

Some didn't make typical bird sounds. Instead, they were communicating using what sounded like words strung together. At times, they roared with laughter like they were sharing a joke. Alex watched all of this dumbstruck, wondering if it was just his imagination running away with him. Then he recalled talking, moving benches—among other things—were normal here, so why not laughing, chatting birds?

Orthri—large, two-headed hounds—bounded around with other breeds with long black fur and puffs of smoke spouting from their nostrils. Massive wolves ran with them, and Brutus—frisky as a pup—joined in with the pack as they raced each other around the field and forest.

Here and there, long lizards or giant toads sunned themselves beside their masters.

Alex's group had finished an early picnic lunch. Selina had scooted off and was building a small model of the main castle—with all five towers—out of sticks dropped from above by well-tended trees.

Her brother looked at her while taking a short break from his forceball experiments. He'd have to see if he could get her some more bricks like Mr. Lu had carved for her, and clay for her to sculpt people with.

Well, that would be a later task.

Theresa scanned the reptiles as she shook her head. "You know, in all of this, I really thought *someone* would have a dragon."

"Yeah, you'd think," Alex said, his notebook on his lap.

"Hah! Forty before the end of the month!" someone shouted from nearby.

A bald man with tattoos covering his scalp pulled out a small scroll, unrolled it and drew a line across it with his index finger. "Bloody knew it."

"What's that?" Theresa called at him.

The man chuckled, golden buttons on his uniform shaking with his laughter. "The other warden and I have a running bet. How many times in a month will someone ask: 'Why isn't there a dragon?' Well, you're the fortieth and he owes me all the pitchers of stout I can drink!"

As the warden, still laughing, stepped away to continue his rounds, Alex and Theresa looked at each other.

"There really should be a dragon," he said.

"Yeah," she agreed.

Sighing, he returned to recording the latest results of his forceball experiments.

Spell Formation: *Nineish heartbeats*
Dissipation: *Six heartbeats*
Result of acting in opposition of 'flicker' failure:
No improvements.

This morning, he'd been focusing on a Mark-dredged-up memory of when he made a spell array incorrectly a year ago that resulted in magic circuitry that was too—for lack of a better way to put it—narrow. It was like having a pump well with too small a pipe. The mana had only trickled through, starving the forceball, and it flickered and wobbled like a candle flame in the wind.

He'd *thought* if he did the opposite of what he'd done during the mistake, he'd be able to make the magic circuitry more robust and better able to channel mana quicker, strengthening the spell. The theory seemed sound, but he couldn't be sure since the experiment didn't really work. He didn't have enough mana to make a difference. He compared it to a bucket of water being able to overflow a cup, but a cup of water wouldn't fill a bucket.

Still, continuing to practice the spell—sometimes to completion and sometimes only partway before killing the magic circuit—was helping him get used to steering his mind through the Mark's interference to focus on specific memories. He wasn't able to tune out the interference, but he was beginning to get faster.

He glanced over at the forcedisk spell-guide, tempted to try it instead.

No. Not ready, he thought, leaving the book alone as he remembered the explosion that ripped through the Cells.

He wondered what to do next. He could dive into the spell

again, but he'd already done it dozens of times that morning. His mind was starting to feel fried. Maybe it was time to switch to something else. He made a quick note before moving on to skills training.

Training Day 8

> ***Push-ups:*** *Rest Day*
> ***Experimentation Day 3:*** *BEGIN. FINISHED. Result:* ***Increasing speed. No improvement of forceball***
> ***Skills:*** *Writing (Other), Reading, Running*

Maybe it was time to switch to reading.

He pulled out *Dexter's General Alchemy of Potions*, flipping to the introduction, which he'd already read twice. His eyes focused on the familiar words while he concentrated on the Mark and focused on the skill of *reading*.

Memories of all the books he'd read appeared, showing him which words to focus on to understand a sentence's meaning fast. It pointed out which words could be skipped as "noise." Words such as the 'howevers,' 'therefores,' and definitely the 'insomuchs.' His speed had already begun improving, and with the Mark aiding him in picking up key details on the page, he was quickly gathering the most important content from each page.

This way of reading used the same skills as those he'd used when the Mark learned the surface of the walls in the Cave of the Traveller. Each time he read a page, he was gaining more and more subtle detail about the content. It meant the information he was able to recall improved each time he went over it.

But he wasn't only reading the same passage over and over. With each read, he'd go a little further in the book, adding more pages each time. After several passes, he started doing the little quizzes at the end of each section, testing how much of the new material he'd absorbed. The results were exciting. As the Mark improved his reading skills, he was beginning to pick out more details, even from new material, quicker and more comprehensively after just a single read-through.

He was also finding that he was learning some really interesting things. Potion-brewing and other forms of alchemy were based on combining unique magical and mundane substances in recipes. A wizard could then use a special apparatus—such as a magic cauldron or flask—to inject their own mana into the mixture to transform it and guide the reaction. This meant that a wizard could create substances with strong, specific magical effects without having to use spell arrays.

A problem, from what it said in *Dexter*, since mana manipulation was difficult and the substances needed for the process were often rare or expensive, potion-brewing and alchemy weren't nearly as wide-spread of a practice as simple spellcraft.

Reading that caught Alex's interest and led him to wonder if past Fools ever followed the path of potions. Since the Mark didn't seem to interfere with basic mana manipulation, it seemed like a perfect way for a Fool to prove useful by accessing magic. It wouldn't have been a simple thing to do, though. Mana manipulation wasn't an easy skill to train. Also, if someone didn't already have experience with it before getting marked, it would've taken a while to get the basics down. They definitely would have needed some level of experience, since the Fool worked faster with more successful memories to take from. Even then, trying to practice would've been really hard to do while constantly on the road with the other Heroes, dodging monsters and dungeon cores.

Alex thought about his situation and considered what the odds were that in all the centuries of Thameland facing the Ravener, he would be the only mage ever to have gotten the Mark of the Fool. Not for the first time, he wished he could have talked to some of his predecessors.

If some of them had escaped Thameland...

He shook off the thought. Later problems for later. Now problems for now.

Losing himself back in the book, he became so absorbed in it that Selina had time to switch to several different games, get bored, and repeatedly ask, "What are you reading about?" He teased her, reminding her that he'd predicted she'd be bored, and she stomped off back to the trees in annoyed silence.

Theresa watched Brutus run for a while, then got up and ran with him when he separated from the other canines. She'd clap and rush around with him, they'd chase each other, and she'd rub his belly when he rolled onto his back. No fetch, though. She really was wasting an opportunity.

Eventually, Alex finished and shut the book, preparing to note his progress as Theresa returned, leaving Brutus with his new canine friends.

"Najyah!" another voice shouted. "Najyah!"

After which came more words in another language Alex hadn't heard before, spoken rapidly in annoyed tones. Crossing the field was their neighbour, the young man from the southern insula who had the eagle.

The emphasis was on *had*.

His eyes scanned the skies above, and he looked worried. "Najyah!"

The man looked toward the trees and spied Alex's group. He remained firm to the spot for a moment, then started making his way over to them, waving slightly.

Alex and Theresa waved back, while Selina only glanced up, before double-taking and focusing on the newcomer.

"Eh, hello," the stranger said—his Common tongue thick with an accent. "Sorry to interrupt you."

"It's alright, neighbour." Alex shrugged, closing the notebook. "You need something...?"

"Khalik," their neighbour introduced himself with a dignified dip of his head.

"I'm Alex, this is Theresa, and that's my sister, Selina."

"Hello," the little girl said in a small voice and Khalik responded with another nod.

"Good meeting you," he said. "Erm, yes, you have seen my eagle, Najyah, yes?"

'I think you could see it from ten miles off,' was what Alex wanted to say, but responded instead with, "Not recently. What about you, Theresa and Selina?"

They both shook their heads and Theresa said, "Not since we got here. Did you lose it?"

Khalik sighed. "She is my familiar, but ehm, sometimes she can..." He searched for the word. "Go away? Mischievous thing. I feel she is somewhere close, but she is not letting me search her out. I had hoped someone had seen her."

He placed his large hands on his hips. "No help, I must search the woods. Er, thank you for your time."

"Hold on a second." Alex climbed to his feet. "Last time I checked, four eyes were better than two—just ask those two-headed dogs or Brutus over there, though he's got six—if you want some help? It's the neighbourly thing to do."

Besides, this would be a nice break before he did his notes.

"Very well, I accept your help." He waved Alex over. "Walk with me."

"I'll be right back. Keep the spot warm while I'm gone?" Alex asked Theresa.

"Already on it," she said lazily, stretching out on their blanket.

The two young men entered the well-kept forest side by side. Alex glanced at Khalik, noting the man's broad shoulders and barrel-like chest. He wondered how many push-ups he'd need to do to look like *that.* And how did Cedric look like Cedric? Was that all Mark of the Chosen or was he always like that?

"Najyah!" Khalik cupped his hands over his mouth. "Najyah! I hope she is alright. There are many beasts here, and I do not know if all are friendly. Do you know this place well? Are the creatures safe?"

Alex shrugged, scanning the trees for any sign of giant eagles. "We got to the university about a week ago. I think you might know more about this place than we do."

"I only arrived a week earlier." Khalik stepped beneath some branches and looked up, but only a pair of hawks and some of the colourful birds perched there, laughing. "I have not explored much."

"Then we both know nothing," Alex said. "I see you're in the apartments. Did you bring an entourage too? Will they be auditing courses?"

Khalik clearly fought to find the right words. "The... journey from my kingdom was difficult. There were dangers. Only Najyah and I made it."

Alex's almost missed a step. "Oh... I'm sorry."

"Hm, for what?"

"Well, uh, your friends and family. They... died."

'Oh wow, good job, Alex,' he chided himself.

"Hm? Oh, no! Excuse me, I did not use the words of the Common tongue correctly. My companions did not die. Some were injured and needed to rest. Others said we should turn back and return home." His eyes hardened. "That was not a choice for me. I continued alone with Najyah."

"Oh..." Alex winced, thinking of having left the Lu family behind to escape Thameland. He thought about what would have happened if Selina or Theresa had been hurt on the way to Generasi. What would he have done? Even with people to take care of them, could he have gone on by himself?

Would he have wanted to, even if the Heroes weren't after him? He was thankful he hadn't needed to answer those questions like this young man had to.

"It's hard to go on alone; can't imagine what it must have been like," he said.

Khalik glanced at him. "It took will," was all he said.

"No wonder you're so worried about her. Your Najyah." Alex turned in place, glancing up through the canopy. "She's the one that stuck with you."

"Hah, you sound—Wait."

Khalik squinted through the bushes only to suddenly cry out and start crashing through them. Alex followed and winced at what they found.

The magnificent eagle was collapsed on the ground, its wings splayed in the dirt and its neck at an unnatural angle. She didn't look like she was breathing.

Alex ran up beside Khalik as the man shouted something in his mother tongue. Tension rose in Alex. Had something killed her? Was there something dangerous loose in the beastarium? Was it another mana vampire? Did familiars have mana?

For a moment, he was sure some monster sent by the Ravener had—

A sudden screech split the air.

As the two young men reached the eagle and bent over her, she shot into the air and screeched at the top of her lungs, spreading her beak and wings wide. Khalik and Alex screamed, stumbling back and tripping over tree roots to land on the forest floor.

The pair groaned and looked up to find Najyah—very much alive and looking quite proud of herself—standing in front of them. A twinkle lay in her sharp eyes as she spread her wings and shot up through the trees, leaving a series of short cries behind.

They almost sounded like laughter.

Khalik shook his fist at her, yelling something in his mother tongue before grumbling and jumping to his feet. He held out a hand to Alex and dragged him up. "I am so sorry, Alex, as I said, she has a mischievous spirit, though *this* is too far even for her!"

"Well, I guess better mischievous than 'unbelievably evil and vicious.'" Alex groaned, rubbing his back. "Still... ow."

The other young man shook his head. "I shall need to scold her later." He glanced at Alex then helped brush dirt off of the young man's clothes.

Together, they started out of the forest.

Khalik said something under his breath. "And I must buy you a meal. For you and yours. I wasted your time."

"No, no, you're fine." Alex waved him off. "Now, your *bird* might have taken ten years off my life, but hey, what's life without a little terror, right?"

The beginnings of a smile formed through Khalik's beard. "Agreed, danger is to life as salt is to food. Too much ruins all. Too little makes meals bland and unpleasant. But just enough? Makes a feast."

"Well, I guess I like my food bland, usually," Alex said as the two young men made their way toward the edge of the forest. "I say that, but then I go and enroll in COMB-1000 like a genius."

Khalik raised an eyebrow in interest. "You too? How fortuitous! I had thought I wouldn't meet anyone taking that course until it started, I think—"

Another scream tore through the air ahead.

Alex's heart stopped.

He knew that scream well.

"Selina? Selina!" He sprinted through the trees.

Chapter 34

A Clash of Beasts

They ran out of the forest to see a reptilian monster rushing toward Selina from across the field.

It was huge—the size of a half-grown brown bear—and covered in white scales. All four claws churned the earth. Horns rose from its head and steam burst from between its jaws and nostrils. A massive tail whipped back and forth as it sped through the field.

At its back, Alex could see someone running after the beast—frantically calling and waving a hand—but the only thing he could hear was his sister screaming. She was near the picnic area, running as the monster rushed toward her. Theresa ran up beside her, drawing her hunting knife and facing the monster. Alex ran as hard as he could, his mind working to find a way to stop whatever was about to happen.

And then Brutus was there.

He jumped between Selina, his master and the beast, lowering his heads and growling at the monster. It skidded to an abrupt halt. The reptile shifted its gaze from Selina to Brutus, staring at him and arching its back like an enraged cat. The creature snarled and hissed, trying to intimidate him.

Two of the cerberus' heads growled back while his hackles rose. His third head barked, warning the monster to back away.

Neither budged.

Then they lunged at each other.

"Get away from him!" Theresa screamed as Alex pulled up beside Selina and her, wrapping his arms around the two of them.

"No!" his little sister cried. "Leave Brutus alone!"

The two beasts snapped and fought each other, sending most of the smaller beasts into a panic. The larger ones simply watched, while students stared in shock. The massive red-eyed reptile had the weight advantage, and kept snapping and trying to tackle Brutus. As it snapped, white smoke poured from its mouth and nostrils. The air began to grow cold.

Frost started to cake the grass beneath it and touch the cerberus' fur.

But Brutus wasn't backing down.

The big cerberus was faster than the reptile.

He darted, snapping with all three heads to make it retreat before jumping out of the way when it tried to bite back. His charges were driving the beast further into a frenzy, and the differences in their experience became clear. The beast was strong and obviously magical, but it fought with only instinct. Brutus was a trained hunting dog who had not only instinct, but experience in taking down large animals and—recently—silence-spiders.

The monster roared, then jerked its head forward. Brutus darted past its long neck. It swiped at him with its claws but he dodged, then leapt forward as its leg came down.

All three of his jaws closed on the reptile's hind leg as its master shouted in panic.

Though his teeth didn't pierce its scales, Brutus tugged while the monster struggled and lost balance, tipping onto its side. The cerberus jumped on it then, seizing its neck in his jaws. The reptile froze.

Brutus looked up at Theresa, waiting for her command.

She said not a word, glaring at the creature's owner. If looks could kill, the student would have been dead *and* buried.

"Get away! Get away from Glacius, you brute!" the beast's master rushed toward Brutus and his pet, reaching into one of his pouches and pulling out a dagger with a blue-glowing blade.

"Have you lost your Uldar-damned mind?" Alex roared. "Your piece of shit lizard was charging my little sister! It would have *crushed* her if it wasn't for Brutus! Step. Back!"

"If you *touch* a hair on my dog," Theresa snarled, "I am going to break your jaw so badly, you'll be eating broth for a year."

"Your monster is *killing* my Glacius!"

"He's *not*, you idiot!" The huntress took a step forward, pointing her knife at the reptile. "Brutus is *trained*, unlike your wild beast. He's not going to make a kill now that *your* pet's not trying to rip him open, unless I tell him to! Train your beast or keep him away from people!"

Khalik stood off to the side, folding his arms over his chest. A fierce cry signalled that Najyah circled overhead.

The reptile's owner was turning red in the face, but he took one look at the knife in Theresa's hand and didn't move any further. "It's *your* monster that overreacted! My Glacius wouldn't hurt a fly!"

"Then *why* was he charging my sister?" Alex ground his teeth.

His hands balled into fists and he shook with anger.

"I..." the other young man stammered. "I don't know! He's never done this before! He probably wanted to check her out, and then your savage monster—"

"And *that* is enough of *that*!" a new voice shouted.

There was a crack in the air.

Iron chains sprang up from the grass and shot over both Brutus and Glacius, wrapping around them both. The chains clinked as they flexed, pulling them away from each other and dragging them to the ground. The lizard screeched and Brutus growled.

"Who did that?" the reptile's owner screamed. "Unhand Glacius!"

"Get that off of him!" Theresa pulled away from Alex, starting toward Brutus.

The warden of the beastarium stalked toward them, his face like a thundercloud. "Stay where you are. I'll not have *violence* in my sanctuary. You put those weapons away *right now*, both of you, or I'm calling the Watchers."

The reptile's owner's mouth opened and closed like a gasping fish, but he reluctantly sheathed the glowing dagger. With a glare, Theresa put her knife away.

"That's better. Civil-like, even." The warden glowered at everyone involved. "Now, better someone explain to me what happened here."

"Their beast attacked my Glacius!" the reptile's owner said, stepping toward the warden. "He's a peaceful frostdrake, well-behaved and used to children! Their monster tried to kill him!"

"Our monster? *Your* monster charged my little sister! It would have killed her!" Alex took an aggressive step toward him, even though the Mark would have made such a threat pointless. He silently cursed it.

"Your filthy lizard tried to hurt Selina," Theresa growled, holding on to Selina tightly. "It attacked Brutus—"

"Glacius was defending himself!"

"—*after* he tried to attack a ten-year old girl?" Theresa snapped. "Are you *listening* to yourself?"

Brutus growled, struggling against his chains while Glacius remained still.

"Alright, that's enough. Enough!" The warden held up his

hands. "Everyone's saying their own story, and everyone that's talking is involved."

"Then what of my story?" Khalik's deep voice cut in. He stepped forward, eyeing both beasts. His arms remained crossed. "I saw the frostdrake's approach. I do not know if it was aggressive or not, but I can say it looked like the charge of a lion. The reptile might look docile now, but to me—and I think anyone with eyes—it looked like it was about to attack the child."

He looked around to the gathered students. "Did anyone else see? What did its intentions look like?"

Silence followed, and then someone raised a hand. "Um, it looked like it was about to attack the little girl."

A few other murmurs spread through the crowd.

The warden watched them all carefully, then looked down to Brutus' struggles and Glacius' quiet acceptance of its restraint. He looked to Alex's group. "Someone tell that cerberus to calm himself. I'm going to check for injuries and I don't want him taking my arms off."

Theresa looked at the warden for a long time before sighing. "Brutus, lie down. Stay."

One of his heads cocked at her, but the fight immediately went out of him. He lay down on the grass by his own will, no longer fighting against the chains.

"That man is going to look at you, okay?" Theresa's voice was gentle and soothing. "He's a friend. Friend," she repeated.

The warden watched as Brutus whined, then looked at him with caution but no threat in his eyes.

"Well-trained," the warden commented as he bent by Brutus' side.

The other young man looked like he wanted to say something, though decided against it.

The warden clucked his tongue while examining the cerberus, then shifted over to the frostdrake. "A little bit of frost on the cerberus' fur and a few scratches on the frostdrake's scales. No harm done."

Finally calming enough to think straight, Alex looked down to Selina. "Are you okay?"

"Yeah." She looked at the frostdrake with more curiosity than fear now, though her breath still shook.

Glacius was watching her very closely, studying her with his burning red eyes. The lizard sniffed the air in her direction, then turned its long neck back toward its master.

"Right, this could have been a lot worse," the warden said. "Cerberus teeth can tear through frostdrake scales if they get a good grip, and this frostdrake didn't use its ice breath at all. It seems neither was going for the kill in this little scrap. I'm going to let 'em up now. Call your pets when I release them."

The chains melted into a rusty powder that disappeared. The beasts' masters called their companions back to their sides. Brutus gave the frostdrake a final look before padding over to Theresa, while the reptile looked not at the cerberus, but at Selina, before rejoining his master.

Both creatures sat beside their owners, as calm as though the fight never happened. They seemed to have completely lost interest in each other. The warden watched them carefully.

"Alright. They both look quiet now." He glanced at Selina. "Are you alright, child?"

Selina nodded.

"Okay, then. The way I see it, the frostdrake went to the child out of curiosity, but came off a little aggressive. Frostdrakes aren't known for looking gentle and friendly. Cerberi are pack beasts. When a big predator is charging one of their own, of course they're going to protect. He made a threat, and the frostdrake responded. Fight got out of hand, but both beasts are trained enough to not have made it as bad as it could've been. No ice breath and no scales torn away to deal real damage. Since no damage was done, and the child wasn't hurt, I'll be lenient.

I'm going to ban both of your pets from the beastarium for a week. Any argument makes it two weeks. When they're back, I expect proper behaviour from both of 'em. Understood?"

Glacius' master eventually sighed. "As you say, Warden. Sorry for the trouble." He gave Alex's group a confused look. "I... as I said, Glacius never acts like this."

Tapping the reptile on its side, he led the frostdrake toward the gate to the beastarium.

Alex glanced from the monster to Selina, who was nearly calm now. He looked around the beastarium. It was full of beasts and people, but the monster had not bothered with any of them.

Why Selina? Was it because she was a child? He didn't see any other children around, so he couldn't come to any conclusions.

"Well." Khalik sauntered over to them. "That could have been a lot worse, and I'm glad you are unharmed, little Selina. And your beast also, Theresa. You have trained him well and he might have prevented a catastrophe."

"Thanks, he means a lot to me." She smiled, rubbing Brutus and making sure the warden hadn't missed any injuries.

Khalik smiled. "Maybe you can work your magic with my Najyah. She can be a little willful sometimes. But for now, who's hungry? I still owe you a meal. Walk with me. I'll show you somewhere a little better than the regular eatery; it even has a separate place for familiars and pets to have a meal too."

The food at Generasi was good, and most importantly, its cost was included with tuition. Raw ingredients and fine foods could be fetched from the central student market with a simple flash of Alex's student card. For those with a little extra coin, though, there were other options.

One was the Titan's Lens.

It was a restaurant located at the top of a tower deep within campus; high enough so there was a view of the sea over Generasi's walls. Its walls were mostly glass and its roof was left open to the sky, though the interior was protected by a massive wind-and-rain shield. The room slowly revolved atop the tower, allowing diners to have a panoramic view of campus, city, ocean and inland vineyards.

The food itself was incredible. The menu had maybe twenty times more items than McHarris could ever dream of making.

Alex, Theresa and Selina had stared at it in choice paralysis, until Khalik made some suggestions. Alex ended up with a spicy chicken dish on skewers, with pickles, turnips and a heavy helping of creamy garlic sauce. It was delicious, even if he wasn't sure he could handle such rich food every day.

Khalik watched them all tear into their food with an amused look as he bit into a spiced beef rib dish. Theresa had a venison steak in wild mushroom sauce with baby sweet potatoes, while Selina had a smokey bacon steak with glazed apples that was rapidly disappearing from her plate.

"I need to steal some recipes," Alex said in approval.

"Good luck with that." Khalik finished swallowing a chunk of meat. "I was told the chefs guard their recipes more carefully than the books are guarded in the library. I am glad it is to your liking, though."

"How couldn't it be?" Theresa cut another piece of steak. "Do kings eat like this? This is how I imagine kings eat."

Khalik merely smiled.

"But," she continued, "is this okay? I saw those prices. They're not cheap."

"Please, do not worry for that." The young man shrugged as though it were of no concern. "When we finish eating, we shall simply get up and run for the door. They cannot catch all of us."

The table went dead.

"I joke! I joke!" Khalik laughed. "I shall be paying, of course. It is a matter of recompense, fellowship and hospitality."

Suddenly, Najyah's sense of humour started to make sense.

Alex couldn't help but feel a little jealous, considering their own financial situation. He and Theresa had been thinking of ways to start generating an income, but nothing had come up yet.

"Alright, Khalik, this is worth way more than me walking a few minutes to help you find your bird." Alex spread more garlic sauce on his chicken. "I assisted a baker for years. Sometime soon, I'm going to bake a couple of pies in the insula's kitchen. You should come over for a slice or two."

"Or more," Theresa added. "Alex always bakes them too big."

"That's not what your brothers say."

"My brothers are at *least* half pig. But what was this about your bird?"

Alex and Khalik recounted the story about Najyah, and Theresa burst out laughing when they got to the part about them falling over in fear.

"When you come over, you should bring her; she sounds incredible," she said.

"I want to see her too, she's so pretty." Selina swallowed her last bite of bacon steak.

Khalik raised his hands as though in surrender. "Alright, it seems you have left me no choice. I shall attend your residence... with Najyah. Though I will make sure she is on her best behaviour. No frights. No playing dead."

"Right, I thought of something." Alex put his fork down. A clever thought had occurred to him earlier, one he hadn't needed the Mark to come up with. He was fairly proud of it too. "That act she put on? I know it scared us, but it's a great way for meeting people. Especially women. Imagine it: someone comes with you looking for her, she plays dead. You get scared, then

Najyah scares you both! You fall into each other's arms, laugh about it, exchange names and… uh… and…"

Khalik was listening with a look of curiosity.

Theresa was also listening. With her full deathstalker face on.

"How very *clever*," she said, with a politeness so sharp it could have cut steel. "Do you regularly think of things like that?"

"Well," he stammered. "Well, uh—"

"I am sure Alex was only giving advice to me, since he knows I am alone and have neither friends nor sisters to keep me company," Khalik cut in, as brave as one of Thameland's Heroes. He gave Alex a pointed look. "A simple suggestion to meet people, and not one for himself. I am surprised he even *had* time to think of it earlier, with how quickly he jumped to protect you and young Selina."

Theresa turned her eyes on their new friend.

Khalik continued. "Truly, I have seen few people move so quickly. In my homeland, our warriors wrestle crocodiles—after years of training—but your friend jumped to protect you both from that great reptile with the same ferocity. A fine companion you have. He gives friendly advice on meeting people—since he knows I came to Generasi alone—*and* he rushes to protect his friends and loved ones."

Deathstalker face shifted a little. "Yeah… he's a good friend." She gave both of them a sidelong look.

As she looked away and Selina watched her, Khalik threw Alex a quick wink.

Of all the people Alex had met in Generasi—including the chancellor that walked out of thin air—Khalik might have been the most deserving of the title *Wizard*.

He had a feeling they'd get along.

An idea occurred to him. "Say, Khalik, since we're both in that spicy COMB-1000 course, what do you say we do some training together before it starts?"

Chapter 35

The Beginning Fruits of Failure

Alex's breath came in gasps as he ran along the path.

With each dull thud of his feet hitting the ground, images of previous times he'd run or exerted himself flooded him from the Mark. Beside him floated his forceball. He'd hung a basket over it using a cross tie of ropes, filling the basket with just enough items to not exceed the spell's limit of weight it could support.

At twelve days into his training, the Mark had corrected his push-up form greatly, and now it was fixing how he ran. Spending most of his time in either McHarris' bakery or hitting the books hadn't exactly left him a lot of time to become a cross-country runner. Most of the images had been from play during childhood.

Lately, between running from monsters, and toward monsters or help, the Mark had gained plenty of material to choose from when it came to that skill.

Which meant even the running he'd started doing recently had also been fueling it with new memories.

One thing he hadn't anticipated learning in his experimentation with the Mark was just how *many* things were considered skills. Simple everyday actions, like running, walking, reading—the list seemed endless—could be skills to the Mark. For years, he'd just assumed that how fast someone ran was a simple matter of how fit they were. The Mark showed him there was more to it than that.

By drawing from previous examples of him running well, it pointed out when and how to place his feet to lessen impact on his legs and tire himself less quickly. It guided his muscles in how to propel him forward without wasting motion. It aided his posture, showing memories of him running upright and leaning slightly forward, and set him in that position. Even his arms were brought into the movement by the Mark, which showed him images of when he'd pumped them at his sides, guiding him toward more and more controlled movements.

There was far more to it than 'move your legs as fast as you can.'

Even his breathing had been corrected by the Mark, which showed him memories that gradually guided his breath into a steady rhythm.

Unfortunately, it couldn't do anything about how fit his body was.

Alex slowed down and came to a halt on the path, with hands on his knees and his breath nearly wheezing from his chest. His feet hurt, his thighs burned and he was light-headed from the strain. It was better than it had been when he started, especially once his technique really began to improve. In the end, though, he'd still been a bookworm for most of the eighteen years of his life.

It'd take more than several days of running and push-ups to change that.

At least he'd made it to his goal again today.

Panting, he looked up to the Cells.

The ominous building had been completely repaired since the potion detonation incident, with only a slight new blackening of the stone to indicate the catastrophe had happened. He'd picked this spot as the end of his running trail mostly to watch the speed at which it was being restored.

After the repairs were done, the spot was familiar and convenient, but also reminded him of one of his goals.

From what he'd learned, the equipment for analyzing substances for potion-craft lay within the Cells, along with other rooms reserved for Generasi's most dangerous arts.

He'd heard the summoning circles for demonology were only placed here, along with experimental cells for potion-craft and magic item forging, as well as rooms for summoning other dangerous spirits. It would likely be here that he would start to get answers about the dungeon core's remains.

At least, if he advanced in potion-craft enough.

A day ago, he'd thought of using the mana connection between himself and his forceball as a way to train his general mana manipulation using the Mark. Unfortunately, that hadn't yielded much in the way of results. Not because the Mark interfered, but because it really couldn't teach him much.

Years of using the same spell repeatedly made it almost as familiar to him as his own heartbeat. He really *couldn't* get much better at commanding this particular spell. Mana manipulation training would have to wait until he learned some other technique to practice.

Luckily, that should be coming soon. Students who'd arrived early would be getting their hands on their textbook lists soon.

Sitting down on a bench by the path near the Cells, he pulled *Dexter's General Alchemy of Potions* from the basket beneath his forceball. He also took a small bun from the basket and took a bite while cracking open the book. He started at the introduction once more, letting his eyes run through the familiar page, using the Mark as he did.

He'd essentially memorized the beginning, and rapidly flew through the next hundred pages. These were familiar to him as well, having gone over most several times. Even with the repetition, he quickly reached the chapter on how mana interacted with the four classical elements and different categories of magic, which he hadn't read before.

As spells can be categorized into schools, mana can have different inclinations. Though in most people, mana is so generalized that it does not overly favour any element or school of magic. This is not true for the alchemical substances used in potion-making. Firedrake's gallbladder, for instance, contains a strong affinity for magical applications involving flame. Sunspore is of strong light attribute, and Giant's Tongue Treebark bears strong earth affinity. Note, though, that different cultures have different naming schemes for mana-rich substances and not all might be obvious to you.

Take Burn-Moss. While the unstudied potion brewer might think to use such a substance to craft a draught of fire-breath, Burn-Moss actually has an affinity for cold. In the region where it is found, there are thirty words for different sorts of snow and frost. Burn-moss—so named due to a translation from the original tongue—references a type of ice so cold that it burns the hand in a form of frostbite.

Let this be a lesson to you: any substance needs to be analyzed if it is not comprehensively described in an ingredient encyclopedia or potion manual available to you. (Note again that the ingredient encyclopedia at the end of this book is not comprehensive). Even though a substance's name or appearance might make its function seem obvious, such assumptions can prove deadly.

Further, affinity can change depending on if a substance is from a living specimen or harvested from a corpse. Take Kraken Eyes—

Alex absorbed the conversational tones of Dexter far quicker than before and slowed only a little when the book began to range into the technical formulae of different affinities and how they interacted. His reading speed and comprehension were rising, all while absorbing the contents of the book.

Dexter's book was 1168 pages long, and he'd already gone through ten percent of it in detail. At this rate, he'd be finished before classes even started. His progress would have been even faster if he hadn't bothered with repetitions. Except there was no sense in speeding through if he didn't get the details right.

His plan was to walk into POTI-1000 with most of the book's knowledge well in hand. It would decrease his study time later, and hopefully start his task of impressing Professor Jules enough to let him use the apparatuses for his own private project. He could say he was doing something fairly safe, then smuggle the core's remains into the Cells and hopefully be able to analyze them.

He frowned, wondering if there were any records of previous analysis of the substance done at Generasi. If he were a wizard that bore the Mark of the Sage, he'd be showing up to the school with a bucketful of core dust as soon as he could. That was something else to look for in the library when he was able to access lower levels; something else to aim for when he reached the next tier of spellcraft.

His forceball's glow seemed cheery beside him, almost like a happy dog. One that liked him a lot more than Brutus did. He'd almost started to think of it more as a companion than a simple magic spell.

He did not have issues, he assured himself.

His previous four days in experimentation on the forceball had begun to yield results. By going through the catalogued failures, he started to make adjustments to the spell array that improved the forceball's mana efficiency.

He glanced at his notebook.

Number of times casting forceball: *Eight*

He glanced back to an earlier entry from three days ago:

Number of times casting forceball: *Six*

Even with his relatively small mana pool, the number of times he could cast the spell was rising quite nicely. It had been a good thing he was so familiar with it before he'd gotten the Mark. His experimentation was also leading him to a better and better handle on the spell's basic structure. He was starting to see *how* adjusting different parts of the array affected the magic circuit, much like learning the different parts of a machine and *why* they worked together.

After he finished reading through his daily chapter of Dexter's book, he took the basket off, killed his mana to the forceball and waited for it to wink out.

Spell Formation: *Nine heartbeats*
Dissipation: *Sixish to Six and a Half heartbeats*
Result of Acting in opposition to Combination of Flicker Failure and Forceball Explosion Failure: *Unknown.*

Today, he was going to try something a little dangerous.

Hopefully, being near the Cells where explosions seemed to regularly happen would mean he was close to people who dealt with disasters of spell and mana.

The time he nearly caused the forceball to explode had been the result of pouring too much mana into the magic circuit. Meanwhile, doing the opposite of what caused the flicker failure made the magic circuit strengthen and allowed more mana to flow safely within it. Unfortunately, he didn't have enough mana running through the circuit to really make many changes.

Then he thought of combining the two. Increasing the strength of his magic circuit *while* pouring in too much mana. A combination of one failure with the learning he'd gained from another.

In theory—if he got it right—the effect would be flooding the strengthened circuit with enough mana to actually make it work.

As to how that would affect the spell, it'd likely draw more of his mana so he'd be able to cast it less times in a day. Though the extra mana would likely strengthen it. He hoped.

Falling into the spell, he made both adjustments to the array—one that resulted in failure and one generated from failure—and fell deeper into the spell. Repetition had made the process grow easier, even in the face of the Mark's onslaught.

He made the necessary adjustments and completed the spell array, feeling the magic circuit form. The circuit shook, and for a moment, he was sure he'd need to cancel the spell.

Then, it completed, humming to life.

Voom.

This time, the forceball appeared with an audible noise.

"Oh, shit!" He recoiled in surprise.

Instead of exploding, the new magic circuit had taken in the overflow of mana and swelled the forceball.

The crimson orb floating in front of him was one and a half times its usual size. It took a lot more mana too. He almost felt like the mana vampire had jumped him again when his mana flowed into the circuit. But it didn't drain him.

His eyes sparked.

This he could experiment with. He might be able to use those two parts of the spell array to adjust the size and mana requirements for the spell as he needed. As his mana increased, he might be able to make the forceball pretty damn big.

He was one step closer to knowing the spell completely. This would make the learning of forcedisk easier.

With a shout of triumph, he jumped up from the bench and pumped his fists in the air. Experimentation was starting to bear fruit. He'd use the remaining failures he had and try different combinations in the future.

After he got his textbook for *FORC-1550: Spells of Force I*, he might be able to make even more progress. Things were looking up.

He recorded his training results, then stretched, preparing to head to the registrar's office.

Time to get in line and get his text lists and timetable, then practice with the time he had left before the start of classes. Just under forty days.

Plenty of time.

"Two weeks early?" Alex murmured, staring down at his timetable.

There, in bold black pen: ***"Initial session for this course begins two weeks before the start of the semester. Please prepare accordingly. When you arrive, you will know why we start early. –Baelin."***

The note was written below *COMB-1000: The Art of the Wizard in Combat*.

The 'just under forty days' was suddenly mid-twenty.

Less than a month until what might be his most difficult course began. One taught by the chancellor himself. Alex took a deep breath.

If there was anyone he should be impressing at the university, it should be *him*.

Chapter 36

Dummies and Forceballs

Training Day 21

Push-ups: *16, 15, 12 TOTAL=43*
Experimentation Day 3: *BEGIN. FINISHED. Result:*
Increasing speed. No improvement of forceball
Skills: *Running - COMPLETE, Reading - COMPLETE, Writing - COMPLETE, Spear-And-Oar Dance (8th day of practice)*

Alex let out a breath as he shifted from first position and back-stepped into the first step of the Spear-and-Oar Dance. He raised an old broomstick into first guard then proceeded to 'dance' his way between the second stance—which kept him balanced—and the first step. He used the Mark, letting it correct his form, while he willed the forceball to float around his body in a slow, steady figure eight.

He'd arrived a little early at the regular spot in order to go through this routine before Khalik arrived.

His main goal was to become used to controlling his spell with precision while doing a physical activity requiring concentration and focus. If he could master both at once, then he'd get to a point where he could control the forceball in dangerous or distracted situations.

And *now* was a perfect time for training against distraction.

In the past few days, campus had become *full*.

Students from all over the world were arriving in masses, streaming through the front gates of the university every day. He was glad he'd picked up his textbook list when he had. The line had been long then, but lately, he couldn't even *see* the registrar's office because of the crowds of students.

Even now, his favourite training ground in the copse of trees was surrounded by new students wandering around campus, looking for different buildings, going to the library, and for many, going into course selection. At the same time, exams for upper-year students had ended a week earlier and they'd turned to celebrating with a vengeance. They were having as much fun as they could before results came back to either make dreams or shatter them.

Recently, he'd had to clean up at least two or three empty wine bottles and beakers from his training spot each morning before he could start. The southern insula had gotten loud at night and was growing even louder as new students piled in.

Complicating things for him was information that some of the new students were from Thameland.

He, Theresa, Selina and Brutus had gone wandering around campus for a good half a day, searching out students from their homeland to get news of what was happening back home. They'd found a few who gave them some interesting and surprising information.

The Cave of the Traveller had been found by the Heroes and was being used to evacuate the people who were still in Thameland. Apparently, before the cave could be used to evacuate anyone, wizards had come from the capital to investigate the area. After the wizards were done, priests were called to do their own investigation, followed by a benediction. And after all that, *then* it had been about securing and fortifying the area. The humble Alric had suddenly become a major stopover for people using the cave to escape the Ravener.

Alex had wondered how Peter and Paul were dealing with everything that was going on now.

Doors to friendly countries had been chosen, then emissaries from Thameland had been sent through the portals to negotiate the migration. Once the ink had dried on agreements, the people flooded through the portals to safety.

Unfortunately, the students hadn't talked about much more than that. From their clothes covered in filigree, gold lining and silver buttons, they were from the wealthy class. Ones among the first through the portals and knew basically nothing of the common folks' situation. They did say the Heroes were together and taking the fight hard to the dungeon cores. But they didn't mention anything about the missing Fool. Alex didn't ask any questions, not wanting to draw attention to himself by showing interest in the subject. After talking with the Thameish students for a while, the four of them had gone off to have a little celebration, proud of their role in making it possible for the Cave of the Traveller to be used to get the people to safety.

As Alex shifted from second position to first step—a movement that was now starting to feel natural—and weaved the forceball between the gap in his legs, he wondered if any of those Thameish students would be in his classes.

Crash!

He jumped at something smashing through the canopy above. He quickly recovered and fell back into second position, not losing his balance. He looked up, raising his broom into guard and... saw Najyah perched there, with an amused twinkle in her eyes.

"Hello, Alex, you are early!" a familiar voice boomed from

outside the grove. Khalik stepped between the trunks, raising his hand in greeting. "I see that you are in fine form."

"I was." He shot the bird a look, making plans for revenge. "But we'll see when the course begins."

"That we will," Khalik agreed, stretching. "I wish more were said of what would happen. It would make it easier to prepare. But we will still try to prepare for whatever comes."

Alex tied the broom handle vertically to the bottom of the basket. "I suppose the point is that we're supposed to adapt to situations, right? So, I don't think Bae—the chancellor's going to give us a nice big warning as to what we're in for."

Khalik shrugged. "One can wish. Are you ready?"

Alex stretched beside his forceball. "Yep, let's go."

The two young men stepped out of the trees and back onto the path, then broke into a swift jog, leaving the path that was now crowded with students.

Najyah followed above.

Though Khalik was in far better condition, Alex kept pace with him. He was doing a lot better than when he'd started.

In addition to the near constant burn that had taken up residence in his muscles, he'd begun to notice positive results from his new routine. His skinny form was starting to harden, and his arms and shoulders had grown a bit thicker. There were hints of muscle definition all over his body, and he was less winded after his exercise routine.

The run to the stadium was less tiring than it had been in earlier days, and when the two young men reached the doors and slowed, Alex's breath was heavy, but he wasn't gasping for breath as they entered the arena like he used to.

Boom.

Flashes of light and power spread through the air as students practiced battle-magic against fortified targets. On their left, a line of students fired icicles, stones, arrows of acid, and glowing blue bolts of magical energy at a line of impenetrable targets.

At the far end of the stadium, a few students were launching explosive fireballs, beams of exploding light, and crackling lightning at large stone pillars. The explosions were loud even across the stadium's field. Though there wasn't an official practice or event going on, new students filled many of the seats above, looking down on the field at all the flashy battle-magic hitting targets.

Some were studiously taking notes, while others stared with more of an open-mouthed-gaping-like-it-was-the-end-of-the-world perspective. Some weren't watching much of what was happening on the field at all, though. One group of boys passed around a wineskin filled with something that made their faces red and happy as they watched a group of young women a few seats below them with interest.

If only they had a giant eagle that liked to play dead as a conversation starter.

Alex and Khalik dropped their gear in front of a couple of training dummies they'd booked for the morning and stretched again. Alex used the Mark to guide his stretching routine, letting it focus him on past positions that gave his muscles a good, long loosening.

Khalik looked at him curiously. "Have you been exercising for a while? Forgive me, but at first, I thought you were new to the physical arts, yet you seem to have a certain grasp of the fundamentals."

"Thanks." Alex leaned into a long stretch of his back and legs. "I'm just a quick study."

"Good, if you keep to proper eating habits then you will make gains quite quickly."

"...proper what now?"

Khalik regarded him with an odd stare. "You... The way one eats to build a larger, more powerful body?"

"I know how someone eats to build a larger, more powerful belly," Alex offered, but Khalik did not smile.

"This is no good, Alex. How one eats is just as important as how one moves when it comes to the body of an athlete or warrior. One must eat enough to fuel one's growth, but not too much at once. Meat, fish, fowl are important to fuel the muscles, and fresh fruit and vegetables are needed to balance the diet along with dense breads and grains. Did you not know this?"

"I never really considered the specifics," Alex admitted. In Alric, he'd seen strong-armed farmhands and smiths swallow ale, bread and meat by the plateful, but he'd never considered the specifics of it. Hard work made you hungrier, and that was that as far as most in Alric were concerned.

He concentrated on the Mark, focusing on the idea of eating for strength.

Images came back to him of plenty of previous meals, especially those rich with wild game from one of Theresa's hunts, or fish from the nearby river. He noticed only a small number of desert memories.

Eating's a skill too? he wondered. *What next? Is breathing a skill?*

On a hunch, he thought of improving his breathing.

Images came up of times he'd exerted himself, pointing out details on how his chest *and* belly rose with his deepest breaths.

"Well, I'll be damned," he muttered.

"What was that?" Khalik asked.

"Nothing." Alex waved his hand. "Just thinking about what you said about food."

"Haha, think about food *after* training, my friend."

The two young men faced off against their dummies, and then readied their spells. Alex called the forceball he'd already created, while Khalik summoned Najyah to land on his leather-gauntleted arm.

Alex willed the forceball forward, driving it into the dummy.

Crack!

The crimson orb slammed into the object with such

impact that several students looked over in surprise. Alex couldn't help but smile a little. He'd seen a few other students cast forceballs, but none of their spells moved as quickly and smoothly as his, none glowed with the same intensity, and none were as large. He smiled again when the Mark didn't protest. He'd calculated it wouldn't interfere and wouldn't find a difference between him slamming the forceball—a utility spell—into the dummy, and him slamming it into any other object. It was like when he'd slammed it into the tiles in the Cave of the Traveller. The Mark hadn't registered that action as combat.

Willing the forceball back, he slammed it into the dummy again and again, enjoying the sound of the heavy impact. His utility spell had really come a long way through years of practice, and had come even further in the last month of his experimenting.

It was hitting the dummy hard enough to shake it a little—like someone had thrown a ten-pound stone with good speed—and would have done a fair amount of damage if the dummy hadn't been reinforced by mana. Too bad targeting objects and enemies during actual combat would make the Mark attack him. Otherwise, the forceball would make a great weapon.

Instead, he concentrated on whipping the forceball around the dummy in complex patterns. Circles. Figure eights. Zig-zags. Anything that might surprise or confuse an enemy. Then he focused on stopping the forceball abruptly in midair. An enemy who ran into it at full speed like the mana vampire did, could do some serious damage to themselves.

As he continued to alternate between smashing the dummy with the spell and dancing the orb around it, he glanced over to Khalik's practice.

First, he would send Najyah flying toward the dummy, and her fierce talons—enhanced by his mana through their link—slashed at it before pulling up. He would then speak an incantation—something similar to the Summon Stone spell Alex had looked at—which conjured a swarm of rocks in front of him.

The stones flew forward as fast as arrows and struck the dummy. Again, Khalik cast the same spell, but this time, the summoned rocks were as sharp as stalactites and struck the dummy with a crack. On the third time he cast the spell, the rocks didn't appear in front of him; they appeared above, beside Najyah. As she banked past the dummy, the stones fired into the target from her like a rain of arrows from a horse-archer.

Finally, Khalik spoke another incantation then snapped his fingers.

Boom!

A loud blast of sound detonated by the dummy as though a fireball just ruptured. It wasn't loud enough to do damage to the dummy, but Alex imagined a living opponent would be pretty disoriented by the sound-burst.

Khalik had obviously been practicing magic for a long time too, and likely had access to more resources and teachings than Alex ever had in Alric. Even so, the other young man soon ended his strenuous spellcasting as his mana ran low, while Alex continued to practice with his steadily running forceball.

"Hoo, I need more building up." Khalik let out a breath. "You must have practiced with that for a *long* time."

"Years," Alex said. He bounced the forceball along the ground before ricocheting it into the dummy again. "I think I know it better than my own hand. You know I—"

"Attention, new students!" a voice called from the middle of the training field, where a group of three young men—pale and with harsh accents—stood. Each wore finely tailored, emerald-green shirts, with the silver symbol of a beast: a two-headed monster with the howling head of a wolf and the snarling head of a bear.

Beside the trio stood a line of young male students looking uncertain.

The speaker—wearing a glowing full-finger ring—jerked his thumb toward the line. "Today, we're taking any comers who think they have what it takes to enter the Ursa-Lupine Brotherhood of Generasi; one of the oldest fraternities of battle-mages in the history of our fine school. We don't have room for the gutless, so if you're tough enough to take our little test, come and see us."

The leader grinned widely and his eyes searched through the faces of the bewildered, and some annoyed, students.

Then they fell on Alex and Khalik.

"What about you two? You look fresh. Think you have what it takes to be one of us? Or are you two gonna coward it up?"

The two young men looked at each other.

Then they burst out laughing.

Chapter 37

The Spell-Joust and the Second Spell

The fraternity leader's smile faded as Alex and Khalik roared with laughter.

"Why-why are you laughing?" Alex wheezed.

Khalik was nearly coughing as he tried to catch his breath. "He does not know what he says! In… in my country, calling someone a coward is insult enough to trigger an honour duel. But look at him! He is no warrior! It is like a young child trying to give insult. Rarely, have I seen anything so ridiculous! Why do you laugh?"

Alex was laughing because of how ridiculously stupid trying to join a fraternity of battle-mages would have been for him. The Art of the Wizard in Combat was one thing—Baelin had said it was about using all of one's resources to conduct oneself in battle—but a fraternity *for* battle-magic?

The Mark would be screaming at him just for *thinking* of going down that path.

"I just wouldn't fit in!" was all he said. "Sorry, man, all respect to your brotherhood, but I don't think it's for us."

"You've got a funny way of showing respect," one of the

other boys said. "Last I checked, laughing at someone's brotherhood was an insult."

"It's fine," the leader said. "It's clear these two aren't warriors. Let them have their little laugh party."

"*We* are not warriors?" Khalik raised an eyebrow. "Look at the way you walk. I am no master of weapons, but you do not move with *any* grace of one used to the battlefield."

Alex studied the three young men closely. With a thought, he focused on standing in the way a warrior would. The Mark showed him enough details in his own movements and that from others to recognize what Khalik was talking about. Cedric had moved with an easy grace that hinted at explosive, deadly movement at any time. Captain Fan-Dor and his brother Gel-Dor maintained perfect balance on the rolling ship and were quick, despite their bulk.

Theresa moved with the graceful silence of a predator on the hunt.

These three were slouching and had a lack of balance in their posture. If it weren't for the Mark's memories and details on his own posture, he likely wouldn't have noticed.

The three boys looked at each other, and then they burst out laughing.

"You hear that, Gregori? He says we don't 'move' like warriors," the leader said to one of his 'brothers.'

Gregori stepped forward, his long blond hair blowing in the low wind. "In *my* country, that's a deadly insult."

Alex looked between the two long-haired men, feeling the tension rise.

"Well, I guess everyone's even?" He shrugged, trying to keep his voice light.

"Maybe." Gregori's eyes narrowed, then scanned the stadium. Many students had lost interest in the exchange, but others were still watching. Something changed in the young man's eyes. "Say, are you two the betting type?"

"Nooope," Alex said. The last thing he needed was to gamble away part of their savings on whatever *this* was going to be.

Gregori continued. "Well, a bet would have made it more interesting. Fact is, we both insulted each other. We could let bad feelings stand—"

"I literally have no bad feelings," Alex said a little loudly.

"—or we could have a little game to settle things. Like wizards."

Khalik cocked his head to the side. "What sort of game is this?"

"Spell-jousting," Gregori said. "We each pick spells we're good with. Same ones, if each of us know them, and we crash them together. Fire bolt against fire bolt. Frost spray against frost spray. Loser's the one whose spell gives out or gets crushed by the other. What tier of magic can you both cast?"

"Interesting." Khalik crossed his arms. "I have just reached the second-tier last month."

Alex barely kept himself from raising his brow at Khalik, and then crossed his arms too. "I'm almost at the second-tier myself."

That was probably true. Probably.

"Well then, I'm at the first, and my two friends are at the second. Let's settle this by way of competition. Come on, or was our coward comment from earlier less insult and more fact?"

Khalik's smile had faded. "I know *I'll* accept your challenge."

Alex looked at Gregori carefully. The young man had definitely been exercising, judging from his build, but that wouldn't matter in a contest of spells. As for if he could beat him...

Alex wasn't sure if that mattered either.

There was nothing on the line for him, except pride and showing he knew his way around spellcraft. Then again, this might be a way to test the limits of the Mark. How *would* it react if he targeted others' spells? Also, it'd be a chance to practice against someone else before he took whatever test the chancellor had waiting for them.

"Hey." He pointed at Gregori. "Can you cast forceball?"

"I can."

"Alright, I'm in. Let's do this."

The brotherhood had booked a large section of the stadium's training grounds for their welcoming tests. A section that was clear stone with no targets.

"Let me get this right." Alex called his forceball over. "We smash our forceballs together like two deer in mating season, and the first that goes *pop* loses."

"Y-yeah..." Gregori was eyeing Alex's forceball. "Say, uh, *that's* your forceball?"

"Uh-huh."

"The *first-tier* spell forceball?"

"Uh-huh."

"The spell that's supposed to be able to carry things, be a child's toy and shed light?"

"Uh-huh."

"It's bigger than your head."

"Yeah. Are you going to start casting now or what?"

Gregori's eyes narrowed. "How long have you been practicing with that spell?"

"Years?"

"I'm a battle-mage," Gregori said quickly. "We should be using battle-magic to battle with. This utility spell is not worthy of jousting. You should cast—"

"This is the only spell I know."

Gregori grimaced. "I see." He sighed. "Well, then—"

He spoke an incantation, and after three seconds, his own forceball winked into being. It was maybe half the size of Alex's and its blue glow was not nearly as bright. His own version of the spell had once looked like that. About a year ago.

Gregori's ball floated up beside him while Alex's zipped to float above his shoulder.

Alex tried to make that same easy grin as Cedric and Captain Fan-Dor. "Ready when you are."

"This is beneath me. Like fighting with a mop."

"Hey, don't knock it 'til you try it."

"What was that?"

"Nothing."

The battle-mage shot his spell forward.

Alex's eyes narrowed and he willed his forceball at Gregori's at full speed, tensing in case of—

The Mark began to flood his mind with failure.

Oh, shut up, he thought.

It was time for 'operation mana vampire smashes face.'

Anticipating the Mark's interference, he stopped the forceball dead in its tracks, letting its protests fade. Gregori's forceball slammed into his with a hollow thud.

His didn't budge.

Gregori's eyes narrowed.

Bang! Bang! Bang!

Again and again, Gregori smashed his forceball into Alex's spell and it vibrated from the sheer force. Alex simply waited, watching. Then he began to try different movements. While Gregori's forceball drifted through the air, Alex's shot around like an arrow, completely under his control.

He circled Gregori's, made figure eights, whirled around it, and then always stopped right in its path. The other mage was starting to grow redder in the face. "Why won't you attack?"

"I am. Very, very gently."

"You're not funny."

"I strongly disagree."

Bang!

After an agonizingly long time, Gregori's forceball took one too many impacts and popped out of existence. Alex's hadn't even flickered.

He shrugged. "Well, I guess that means I—"

Gregori spat out another incantation and raised his finger toward the forceball. A beam of blue light shot from his palm and blasted deep into the crimson orb. For a few seconds, Alex's spell held firm before he pulled it away. Any longer and it would have been extinguished.

"You were right." Gregori dusted himself off. "You are no battle-mage. If I'd known you would not be taking the challenge seriously, I never would have spoken about you coming to the brotherhood."

"Okay, look, I don't care about your brotherhood." Alex gave him a look. "I don't know what your problem is, but me and my only friend on campus were having a good time, practicing hard, when you all waltz up like you're some chosen heroes—"

Like me, he added dryly in his head.

"—acting like if anyone joins you it's some great honour. I was thinking that I was soooo unsuited, and had a gooood old laugh about that. But *you* all made assumptions and took my laughing as some personal insult, then you insulted *my* friend and it was all 'spell-jousting makes hard feelings go away,' and, well, *that* was a lie because I'm pretty sure you've *only* got hard feelings, and I'm getting them myself. Then you complain about the spell choice, and I dick around because I'm not a battle-mage and *I never said I was*, and now *you're* acting like your wounded pride is somehow *my* fault?"

"You were to take the spell-joust seriously! Not act like you were my superior just because you practiced one utility spell for a deranged amount of time!"

"Look, if practicing a utility spell for a deranged amount of time is good enough to get into the greatest university for wizards in the world, then I think it's good enough for anyone."

Gregori made an irritated noise. "Why are you even in the combat stadium? If you have no interest in battle-magic, why are you here?"

"Because I'm enrolled in COMB-1000. Are you?"

Gregori's next retort died in his mouth.

"Well," Alex pushed. "Are you?"

"Hm," was all Gregori said before turning and leaving the field.

Alex stepped over to where Khalik waited for his turn.

"Good job." Khalik laughed. "Do me a favour, though, please don't act as such a fool when the *actual* class starts?"

Still laughing, he stepped forward to begin his own battle.

Alex sighed as he watched him go.

He would have if he could have. Maybe through their class, he'd learn more about *how* to do that.

Training Day 31

Push-ups: *20, 19, 16 TOTAL=55*
Sit-ups: *25*
Spell Formation: *Seven Heartbeats*
Dissipation: *Seven Heartbeats*
Number of times casting forceball: *Ten*
Number of times casting super forceball (extra-large with a side of potatoes): *Five*
Skills: *Reading - COMPLETE, Writing - COMPLETE, Spear-and-Oar Dance (18th day of practice) - COMPLETE, Breathing (still can't believe this) - COMPLETE, Running*

Alex, Khalik and Theresa tore through the beastarium, running around the field while Brutus bounded along with them. Selina watched from one of the benches with her general studies book in front of her. She'd reached a chapter on Generasi, which had lots of pictures of its oldest buildings. The girl had been lost in the book ever since.

Alex's form had improved tremendously in the last month, and his stamina was starting to rise sharply since he'd altered his diet following Khalik's advice and the Mark's suggestions. Now, he could almost keep up with both his oldest friend and his newest through their daily running practices. His breath had become steadier since he'd started to use the Mark to practice controlled breathing, which increased his endurance even more.

His forceball was nearing as close to perfection as he'd likely get it before combat class started. He'd figured out how to make it smaller in addition to super-sizing it, though he hadn't found any practical applications for the smaller version yet. He'd gone through just about every string of failures the Mark generated, mixing and matching them. Some proved to be dead ends, others proved they might be promising when he had more mana.

The spell's efficiency going up had been a nice surprise, and it felt like his mana was increasing too. Very productive month. He was glad he'd actually had the downtime to *practice.* He laughed to himself as a thought occurred of trying to build up while racing from fight to fight and dungeon to dungeon.

That led him to think about Thameland and wonder what was going on there.

They hadn't heard anything on campus recently, and he was still too afraid to go into the city and ask around. Not with all the priests out there. Still, Alex knew he had to do it sooner or later. Theresa had sent a message to the Lus to let them know they'd arrived safely, and left a note at the docks for Captain Fan-Dor so he could find them.

There was still the matter of looking into more permanent housing and some sort of income to settle.

Maybe I could see if the sky-gondola company is hiring, he thought glumly as they finished their final lap and slowed to a stop.

"You're getting better." Theresa stretched, taking a deep breath as she grabbed the waterskin from their table and drank deeply.

"You are; it is impressive," Khalik watched him with curiosity. "Your technique especially."

"Thank... you..." Alex panted. "I still got a long way to go until I can compete with you two."

"I have been training for much of my life," Khalik said. "There is no shame a later start."

"There is if you lose the race. Or can't out-run horrible, hungry monsters. Speaking of that, you think I'm almost ready for the horrible death course?"

"Time will tell." Khalik shrugged, then looked to Theresa. "What of you? How goes your preparation?"

"Yeah," Alex jumped in. "You steal any secret techniques from the Watchers of Roal?"

The huntress held out a flattened hand and teetered it up and down. "I've been practicing what I see, but sword-arts aren't like what you do. I can't exactly read a book a bunch and pick it up... And I don't even know *how* to prepare for lifeforce. It's like... affinity test day one and if it doesn't work, that's it. I'm almost glad it starts early like your course does. I think I'd go crazy if I had to wait anymore."

"You'll be fine," Alex assured her. "I mean, I believe in you. Seriously. You got what it takes."

"How can you be so sure?"

"If it's something you're interested in, you've got what it takes," Alex said firmly.

"Thanks." She smiled at him. "I'll... I'll try to remember that."

Alex had to ignore Khalik giving him a thumbs-up from behind her.

Training Day 34

Forcedisk Experimentation Day.

Alex took a deep breath as he laid his book in front of him. Across two pages were multiple diagrams. Most of them were various alterations of his forceball's spell array with little—very bolded—notes on which parts were the same as those of forcedisk.

On the right was the spell array diagram for forcedisk.

Beside it was a long list of instructions; parts of the spell that were identical to forceball's casting. These he could concentrate on and trust his practice to see him through. Then there were the new parts.

He'd written up safety procedures. When to end the spell, how far to push it, and what dangers he might need to be careful of. He glanced down at his shoulder and then up to the Cells. He'd picked a secluded area near the back of the building for this.

Taking a deep breath, he started spellcasting.

The Mark came at him hard.

The trouble with doing so much experimentation lately was that he gave it even *more* failures to throw at him, and now he didn't even have the complete familiarity with the spell to guide him along. The parts he knew well were easy enough, but the new parts were dangerously hard.

Again and again, he had to stop the spell as the Mark broke

his concentration and threatened him with disaster. Each failure was written down, as well as what caused it. Things to avoid for next time.

Then he'd go at it again.

Hours passed. Then even more.

Training Day 35

Forcedisk Experimentation Day II.

He'd failed more than fifty times now.

And he'd also made progress.

Aspects of the spell array were starting to go more right than wrong. Its structure was becoming more familiar. Each failure generated a potential outcome for success and he recorded it and what to do differently.

He just needed to keep trying.

Training Day 36

Forcedisk Experimentation Day III.

Mental fatigue was setting in. Progress kept him pushing forward.

The last two nights, he'd dreamt continuously about forcedisks and spell arrays and failures. There were a lot of them now. But he was getting closer. The magic circuit was starting to form.

He was getting *closer.*

Training Day 37

Forcedisk Experimentation Day IV.

The last words of the incantation left Alex's lips. The spell array completed in the midst of the Fool's flood of failures. The magic circuit formed. Mana flowed.

A crimson glow winked into being, but not from Alex's forceball.

A new spell hovered in front of him. It flickered. It was unsteady. But his disbelieving eyes couldn't mistake it.

It was a flat, glowing crimson disk, about as wide as a dinner plate.

Alex was so elated, he could have cried.

Despite the Mark of the Fool and all of the barriers it put in front of him, he at last learned a second spell.

He was on his way to becoming a Proper Wizard.

Whether or not his new knowledge would help him in Baelin's class?

He'd know that in just a few short days.

Chapter 38

An Endless Forest

Something chimed from the top of the hill, carried to Theresa's ears by the late summer wind. The air was fresh and warm, but inside, she felt cold.

Theresa Lu, great-granddaughter of Twinblade Lu, was almost as scared as when that giant insect monster had come rising from the dark beneath the Traveller's sanctum. Taking a deep breath, she glanced at her little map of Generasi's campus, and found the spot on the green indicating where *LIFE-1075: Lifeforce Enforcement I* was supposed to be held if the day turned out to be sunny. She looked back up the hill.

A single immense tree rose from the hilltop and a number of students already gathered there, with even more climbing the slope. Steadying herself, she wished she'd brought her great-grandfather's sword along. Its solid hilt would have given her something to anchor herself.

She'd even left Brutus with Alex—who was back home watching both her dog and his sister before *his* class later in the morning—and hoped they were getting along. Brutus would have been a source of support, but today, she needed to do this alone. Theresa started up the slope.

Once at the top, she noted how some students looked around like they didn't know what to do. Others had already sat down on blankets or cushions they'd brought to class, looking expectantly at the instructor.

Professor Kabbot-Xin was seated cross-legged beneath the tree, and one look at her actually made Theresa gasp. She was old; something about her seemed ancient. It wasn't just her appearance—even though her face was crisscrossed by wrinkles and her hair was as white as a winter day after a snowstorm—it was something more. The way her breath seemed to be absent. The peace across her face.

Between her and the healthy tree above, Theresa would have guessed the woman was older. It didn't seem possible, but the last month had opened her eyes to all sorts of new possibilities.

She thought back to when she was a young girl, during those first few times she'd ventured beyond Alric's walls and the roads into the trees of Coille. It had been like the world exploded. Her whole life in town became tiny compared to the endless sea of trees and green fields surrounding it. As a child, she imagined those trees and meadows had spread forever, and she would never see another town again if she kept walking.

Of course, she knew even then that wasn't true. Her mother and father had told her about other towns, cities, roads and even the sea to the south—across which her uncle lived. Over time, the world had shrunk as her family took her farther from Alric and she continued to explore Coille.

She quickly learned that endless forest world had been just a small patch of wildland in a country that had mostly been tamed. Stories of her great-grandfather's adventures had promised a larger world.

A world she was now seeing with her own eyes.

Burning mountains.

Portals to other realms she couldn't imagine.

The sea.

Magic and monsters, and even moving benches.

The world was a vast place, and she was learning not to assume too much about it too quickly. Here, where birds talked and benches walked? It was easy to believe a woman could be older than a giant tree.

Finding a patch of grass on the edge of the hill, she sat down cross-legged like some of the others, wishing she had brought a blanket. A young woman seated in front of her turned around and paled.

Ah.

Theresa's face was doing that thing again which tended to creep people out.

She tried to soften it and gave the woman a nod of acknowledgement. She had similar features to hers and her family's, and she wondered if she too had Tarim-Lung ancestry.

She gave Theresa a little bow, and to her horror, started speaking in Tarimite, the language of her great-grandfather's country folk. "*Hello.*"

Theresa desperately scrambled internally to recall what she knew of the language. Only her grandfather had spoken it regularly in the house. "*Yes, uh... hello,*" she stammered back.

"*Ah, are you from Tarim-Lung?*"

"Uh, no, I'm from Thameland," she said in Common, then tried to add in Tarimite: "*I... don't speak... Tarimite... good.*"

The young woman smiled expectantly and began talking very, *very* fast. Theresa tried to follow, only catching the words 'day,' 'good,' 'Tarim-Lung,' and 'expect.' Inside, she was screaming.

"*Day... good...*" she tried to say.

The young woman continued to smile expectantly.

"*Don't... speak...*" Theresa muttered, then added in Common: "Oh, Uldar, help me."

"*Uldar? Who is Uldar?*" the young woman asked.

"*God... Thameland...*" She strongly considered burrowing into the earth like a mole.

A chime sounded, and the young woman turned toward the tree.

She thanked Uldar, the Traveller, Ek-u-Dari and any other deity that might have been listening.

Professor Kabbot-Xin slowly opened her eyes and took a breath that seemed to last a lifetime. "Good morning, class, and welcome to the first seminar of *LIFE-1075: Life Enforcement I.*" Her eyes scanned the students. "All forty of you have arrived. Good to see so much interest this year. It always warms the spirit when I see the young come for the teachings of my mother's homeland."

Her eyes glanced to the school. "In a few minutes, my teacher's assistants will bring the testing bowls and the medical supplies, and we can begin testing your affinity. Before we begin, though, can someone tell me what their understanding of Life-force Enforcement is?"

A short young man with long brown hair raised his hand.

"Yes, Mr...."

"Olaf!" the young man said brightly. "Life Enforcement is based off of qigong—the art of cultivating one's life-energy, which originated in Tarim-Lung—which practitioners use to advance themselves and grow closer to becoming immortals and gods. That's why it's a form of Divinity."

The professor waited a few long heartbeats, making sure he was finished before she answered. "I can see you have some familiarity, Mr. Olaf. Unfortunately, you are only partially correct."

She turned her attention back to the entire class. "Mr. Olaf said Lifeforce Enforcement is based on life-energy cultivation, which is true. It is also true that the art was created in Tarim-Lung as a form of health promotion. Unfortunately, life-energy cultivation is no path to immortality. If you have come here with thoughts of transcendence, godhood, immortality and splitting the heavens with a tempered fist, then I am afraid you will be sorely disappointed."

Theresa nearly gawked in surprise. Was *that* what people thought cultivation was supposed to do? Was that what they believed?

"Life-energy cultivation is the practice of empowering one's lifeforce through a careful regime of breathing, energy circulation, meditation and—most importantly—building a connection to the natural world and taking in its energy to build your own. The result is a greatly invigorated body. In addition to granting greater lifeforce to draw on for spellcasting, one will enjoy a healthy body, greatly enhanced strength, reflexes and speed, an energy pool that can be used to reinforce compatible physical objects and, indeed, an extended lifespan. But this does not mean living forever or splitting mountains in half or anything else that the imaginative writers and poets from Tarim-Lung or elsewhere come up with. If you have dreams that indulge those fantasies, then I would suggest using the next three hours to go and select another course."

Theresa thought about what the professor suggested. It all sounded incredible to her. She had no real mana and little interest in all of the spell-guides, and formulas, and complex this-and-that which fascinated her best friend. But this course seemed to promise its own wonders.

That was why she was confused when a full five students stood up, seemingly disappointed—including Olaf—and started back down the hill.

Aren't you being a bit too greedy? Theresa wondered. Then again, most of the folk here were wizards. Maybe the things offered were too mundane for them.

"Alright, to everyone still with us," the professor didn't give the retreating students a second glance, "we will now begin a ten-minute guided meditation. I will ask you to remain silent the entire time. Focus on the sound of my voice and let other thoughts pass. They are distractions. Now, please, close your eyes."

Theresa did as she was asked, opening her ears to the sound of the wind, the rustle of the tree branches and their professor's calm, ancient voice. The old woman guided them through their own thoughts and away from distractions, bringing their focus onto their own breathing. The huntress found the exercise soothing, pleasant and easy. She was used to walking through the woods, listening only to the sound of nature and not saying a word for hours at a time.

The ten minutes passed quickly, and she was surprised to find several students fidgeting as the professor told them to open their eyes.

"To those of you that found this uncomfortable, might I suggest bowing out of this course for the semester. There will be some classes where we will be engaged in breathing meditation and lifeforce circulation for an hour at a time and more. You will need to concentrate for all of it, so if you found these ten minutes difficult, then I would suggest joining a meditation club, practicing the skill and returning to this class next semester. Of course, the choice is up to you, but this is a dangerous art."

Professor Kabbot-Xin's eyes flashed. "You will need to decide carefully."

A few more students got up and filed down the hill. As they did, several higher year students climbed the slope, carrying large bowls of liquid balanced on wide glowing disks that hovered at shoulder-level.

"Ah, the testing bowls have arrived." The professor stood, almost like she was gliding to her feet. "Please form a line in front of me. We are going to begin testing your affinity. The bowls are half-filled with distilled water for pure conduction. You will place your hands in the water, and I will use my energy to examine your energy. Each of us has pathways in our body in which our lifeforce flows. Think of it like a magic circuit, but it powers *you* instead of a spell. I will be using my energy to stimulate those pathways. If you have an affinity, your channels will begin to open, which will make you ready for the art of Lifeforce Enforcement. If not... then unfortunately, you will not be able to partake in the course. Also, please keep absolutely calm during the process."

For the first time, she frowned. "Agitating your energy during the test could have *dire* consequences."

The young woman from Tarim-Lung looked at Theresa and gave her an encouraging smile before getting up. The students formed a line that extended down the hill, while the teacher's assistants set up the testing bowls.

Professor Kabbot-Xin sat, facing the front of the line, with the first bowl in front of her. "Step forward," she said.

She would ask each student's name and why they wished to learn the art. Then, she would give them reassurance and ask them to place their hands in the bowl, then raise her hands over the water.

She would let out a breath, close her eyes and press her palms to the water's surface.

Sometimes the water would remain still. To these students, she would lean in and quietly say something. They would rise, gather their things and start back down the hill with a dejected slump to their shoulders.

At other times, the water would churn and splash onto the grass. After whispering something to these students, they also gathered their things and took the long walk down the hill.

With some, the water would remain still and the Professor would hold her hands on the water's surface for a long time. Then there would be a cracking sound. The professor would move her hands away and just say, "Into the bowl."

The students would vomit black liquid into their bowl that smelled so awful, that even from where she was, it made Theresa's eyes water. At first, she thought something had gone wrong, but the professor only smiled at those students.

"Congratulations," she said gently. "You've just expelled some of the impurities in your body as my energy opened your channels. Some of my energy will stay in you now, to encourage your Lifeforce Enforcement. Rest by the tree for now, and I will teach you how to circulate it."

One by one, the line decreased, and Theresa's nerves doubled with each student that finished the test. Only about a quarter of the remaining students vomited black and took their place beneath the tree.

For one student, things went badly.

The young man screamed and fell back from the bowl, with every muscle tensed and every vein in his body standing out against his skin. His eyes had gone completely bloodshot and foam ran from his mouth. Bruises appeared rapidly as blotches formed on his skin.

"Hold him down!" The instructor shot up from beside the bowl and bent over the student. She placed her hands on his chest and pressed down once. His body flexed and then relaxed.

She pressed two fingers against his wrist and sighed in relief. "Lifeforce reversal, but not bad. He'll recover quickly." She glanced to her teacher's assistants. "Take him to the infirmary."

Two of them flanked the young man, cast a spell, and he rose in the air between them. Carefully and with haste, they ran down the hill toward the main castle in unison.

"And this is why I say to remain calm." The professor sighed. "If you do not have the affinity, the process will feel strange. If you do have it, there might be some discomfort. In either case, please remain calm. Too much turbulence in your mind and body can cause your energies to grow unbalanced. This is one of the results."

As she said this, two more of the students suddenly stood, holding their mouths, and ran down the hill. At last, it was

Theresa's turn. Trying to calm herself, she sat cross-legged in front of her bowl. It was only still water, but still water could hide dangers.

"And what is your name?" the professor asked her gently.

Theresa forced her gaze up to the instructor's eyes. "Theresa Lu."

"A pleasure to meet you, Theresa. Tell me, why do you want to learn Lifeforce Enforcement?"

The huntress took a deep breath. She had considered how to answer this question. There were many reasons. The mystery of the dungeon core promised dangers and she wanted to prepare for those. The hive-queen in the Traveller's sanctum had left her feeling unprepared and she wanted to correct that.

Yet, there were only two reasons she wished to say here.

"I want to protect my loved ones, and I want to follow my great-grandfather's path, to gain his strength and step into the world prepared for its dangers."

Kabbot-Xin regarded her. "Your great-grandfather was a cultivator? What was he called?"

"Twinblade Lu."

The professor's eyes widened. "You are the Twinblade's descendant?"

"Yes."

"Then I think you should be fine, child. If you inherited even a grain of his talent, then you will have the affinity. Now, place your hands in the water."

Inhaling, Theresa did as she was told and closed her eyes. The water was cold against her hands. She thought of calming memories: painting the mural on the side of their common room wall. Picnicking in the woods as she watched Brutus—still a puppy then—jumping around and snapping at the fall leaves. Playing with Selina just before her bedtime.

The summer that Alex had baked her cookies.

Her heartbeat slowed.

The water shifted as the professor's hands touched it, and her energy coursed through the water. The lifeforce conducted through the liquid and spread over Theresa's hands. She felt energy pour into her through her fingertips. Her breathing remained steady as she focused on letting the energy pass naturally. Pathways sprang to life in her body that she never felt before.

For an instant, her lifeforce touched her instructor's.

Something shifted.

There was a burning, wrenching feeling as she felt those channels stretch with the new energy. The energy coursed through her until it pooled in the pit of her abdomen. Something sprang to life. Her body shuddered. More wrenching as liquid shifted within.

Then her stomach was full.

Nauseated, she leaned forward and spewed a line of black filth into the bowl.

"Well done," the professor said. "Take your place by the tree and rest."

Stumbling like she was sleepwalking, Theresa Lu collapsed beside the tree, panting hard. The professor's energy coursed through her, continuing to open her channels. She felt as weak as a half-drowned kitten... but beneath that, she felt good.

Everything was a little sharper. Sound was fuller. Light was brighter. The taste of filth in her mouth... unfortunately, was a little stronger. As her head lolled to the side, her eyes fell on the young woman who had sat in front of her. She also panted against the tree, covered in a cold sweat.

The young woman looked at her weakly and slowly gave her a thumbs-up. "Good... job."

Theresa's eyebrows rose. "You... speak the Common tongue?"

The young woman teetered her hand. "Don't speak Common well. I am Zhao Shishi. And you?"

"Theresa. Theresa Lu."

"Theresa. Congratulations."

"Yeah," Theresa sighed. "Congratulations."

A memory came back to her. Of the first time she stood before Coille. She remembered very clearly the first step she had taken into the woods.

Today felt the same.

A first step into a wide forest, ready for exploration.

In a way, she wished this forest would be like those she imagined as a little girl.

Endless.

Chapter 39

The Beginning of Baelin's Test

"Do you think we are ready?" Khalik asked as the two young men walked toward the training grounds.

"Maybe?" Alex shrugged. "There's no way we're going to know until we actually get where we're going and find out what sort of evil's been planned for us."

"True enough." Khalik forced his eyes forward as the stadium loomed in front of them. "I wish we knew more."

"Yeah, so do I, man, so do I."

Alex had woken up before dawn that morning feeling like he'd swallowed a bucket of snow and ice. His nerves raced, getting the better of him, and he'd asked himself a half dozen times what madness made him take such a dangerous sounding course. Each time he'd answered in the same way: learn to deal with the dangers now, before they faced more serious ones later.

It had been a quiet morning, helping his sister do some preparatory homework for her classes beginning in two weeks. The morning passed slowly and he kept looking at the door, waiting for Theresa to arrive and signal his time to go.

When she finally did—dead-tired, stinking of something terrible but about as happy as he'd ever seen her—he'd fixed her something to eat, gathered his supplies and stepped out the door. Khalik had been waiting for him just outside the now very busy insula, and the two men started their long walk toward COMB-1000's meeting place.

There was no running today.

They both had a feeling they'd need their strength.

"Do you think we are ready?" Khalik asked again as they stepped into the stadium.

Alex sighed. "I hope so, Khalik, I hope so."

The stadium was empty except for a small gathering of students in the centre. Most of them tough-looking individuals, reminding Alex more of hard-bitten soldiers than wizard students. One was a hulking male minotaur and another was a selachar woman. Two others were beastmen that looked like Dobermans. All of them appeared versed in battle. There were some exceptions, though. Some of the younger-looking ones had a naive excitement in their eyes. Some of the more well-dressed looked confident, but soft.

One student wore a green shirt with the Ursa-Lupine Brotherhood's symbol on it. What he didn't expect were familiar faces. The tall, raven-haired Isolde stood on the opposite side of the crowd, her arms folded, and her brow furrowed in concentration. Her mouth moved constantly, muttering something under her breath.

On the other side stood—surprisingly—the familiar form of Derek. The young man looked nervous, but he was among the only students who had come equipped for battle. He wore a chainmail shirt that hung down to his knees and a longsword belted to his waist. He paced back and forth, glancing from time to time at Isolde across the crowd.

Khalik and Alex took up positions on the outer edge of the crowd. With a low cry, Najyah descended from the sky, landing beside her master and examining the students with her sharp eyes. There was no amusement coming from the familiar this morning. Only fierce caution.

Alex looked at Khalik. "Think this is all of us?" He counted maybe twenty students out of more than a thousand that arrived on campus a week before.

"Maybe," Khalik said. "A brave group, nonetheless."

"Yeah, brave." Alex glanced over at Derek again. What was he doing here? What was Isolde doing here? Weren't they second-years? And from what little he'd seen and heard of the red-haired young man, he didn't seem the type to be taking the most dangerous course on campus.

Alex's eyes narrowed.

A known cheater suddenly taking a course run by the chancellor himself.

He'd have to watch him.

Then the air began to shimmer and the entire class went silent.

Chancellor Baelin stepped out of thin air as he had when he made the announcement about the potion detonation. The towering, grey-furred goat man scanned the gathered students, his eyes lingering on each one. Again, Alex couldn't help but feel that gaze pierced right through him. He shifted his right shoulder away from the chancellor.

Baelin's beard clasps jingled. "That looks to be all of you. Welcome to *COMB-1000: The Art of the Wizard in Combat*. First, I'm going to tell you that I am proud of you. You have made a choice to start down an ancient path of wizardry. The *first* path of wizardry."

He rose to his full height and his eyes seemed to look not at them, but at something distant. Something long passed. "Before there was Generasi. Before there were *any* schools of wizardry, there was only the spellcaster, the power they wielded, and the world trying to wrench that away from them. Magic was a tradition written not in ink, but in blood. Spells were transferred not in books, but on stone tablets, on the skins of monsters, or by the sacred word of master to student. These were barbaric times... and the lie we tell ourselves is that they ever ended."

He gestured to the empty sky. "Dragons in the frozen wastes. The rune-marked to the north. The Ravener in Thameland. Leviathans in the western sea and zaratans in the east. The Metal gods to the south, and the demon rulers of the realms beyond the sky and earth. These threats are ancient. And they have *not* disappeared into history, like so many young and foolish wizards have."

Alex gulped. There was a gravity to the old wizard's words that set the hairs on the back of his neck rising. The old man didn't speak of things like he'd read about them; he spoke of them like he'd *seen* them.

"The wizard plays with powers. Great powers. The higher the wizard climbs in the spell-tiers, the more danger the wizard opens themselves up to. Assassins. Demons. Greedy rivals and more. One must defend oneself against all these threats, using *all* resources. Today, you are starting down that ancient path that ensured the first wizards survived long enough to build the school you attend today. Now, some might ask why we are beginning two weeks early. The answer is simple: today is a test."

He waved a hand through the air, and an illusion shimmered into being above him. Alex recognized the wasted landscape of the Barrens of Kravernus, which Lucia had pointed out when they'd arrived in Generasi.

"Today, we will be going into the Barrens," the chancellor said. "And we will measure how much you bring into this class. One must already have survival instinct and talent if one even hopes to take the first steps down this path. Today, I'll be randomly splitting you into groups of..." He mentally counted off the students. "Four."

He waved a hand at the illusion, which shifted until it pointed to a natural tower of stone rising from the blasted landscape. "You will use all of your magical skill, your ingenuity and your combat skill to reach the escarpment by the time class ends in three hours. If a group member, or if the group as a whole fails to reach it, then that individual or group will be required to visit the registrar's office and select another course."

Another wave of his hand created a series of shimmering symbols in the air. "I am marking you all with this spell." The symbols flashed, streaking forward like birds in flight, landing on the back of the students' hands and pressing themselves in like tattoos.

"I will monitor you through those. The area we're going to today is one of the safest in all the Barrens. The monsters there are some of the weakest, and those that are somewhat stronger can be avoided or even defeated with the correct application of power or wit. If you find yourself in danger or no longer wish to finish the test, call my name and say 'release me.' My spell will then summon you to my side and I will transport you back to the university, where you will need to select another course. If you are gravely injured during the test, the spell will automatically summon you to my side, and I shall transport you to the infirmary. If this occurs, you will need to choose another course, if you recover."

A grim silence had fallen among the students.

Baelin looked at them solemnly. "Do be aware that this course involves *real* dangers. I am with you as a safety net, but accidents have occurred. People have died during this course, though I have prevented many, many more from dying either during the course's run, or after they complete it. Nonetheless, if the only reason you are taking this course is to 'impress the chancellor,' then I warn you, you should leave now. That is not the only way."

Though the chancellor did not look at any one student, Alex caught Derek startling at his words. Some of the other students shifted uncomfortably as well, but none left.

Baelin nodded. "Very well. You are all adults. I trust you can make this decision with eyes open. Now, are there any questions?"

Isolde's hand immediately shot up. "Chancellor—"

"Call me Baelin. I'm not one for formality."

The tall woman winced. "I—Can you tell us what kind of monsters we'll encounter during the test?"

"Likely muupkaras—some troops of them make their homes in the area."

"What are those?" Alex whispered to Khalik.

"I have no idea," the young man whispered back.

"Shh!" a student near them hissed.

"And, though they are not common in the area, bonedrinkers have been known to hunt these grounds."

Someone gasped.

Alex did *not* like the sound of that.

"Are there any wild mana vents in the area?" Isolde asked.

"No, you will be safe from that threat. My expectation for you today is not to destroy every threat you meet," Baelin said. "It is to test your judgment and basic ability to adapt. Evaluate your obstacles. Cross difficult ground at speed using magic and wit. Defeat what you should. Avoid what you can. The challenge today is not easy, but not impossible. If you cannot overcome this, then there are other courses at the university I might recommend before trying your hand at COMB-1000 again. This course is rigorous. Its learning curve is steep. Finding that you are not ready today is better than discovering it three months from now when the challenges are far more perilous. Any other questions?"

Someone raised their hand. "Um, sir, couldn't you teach us some things before we go into the test?"

Baelin nodded. "I could. I could teach you the geography of the area. I could teach you the exact hunting grounds of the bloodthirsty creatures there and *how* to defeat them in the easiest way. I could teach you spells, weapon craft, the anatomy of your enemies. And at the end of it all, you would easily be able to destroy these enemies and reach the tower like you were just having a quick walk across campus. We could do this all semester, and you would be able to survive the Barrens of Kravernus quite well. And then, you would graduate and encounter a situation you had *no* preparation for, and you would likely die. At best."

He gave them all a grave look. "Today tests your ability to adapt with what you have. It is the basic requirement to take this course safely. After, we can grow your knowledge and give you more resources to use. Remember, if you are not ready, there is no shame in admitting that and using my spell to escape harm. Knowing your limits is also the mark of a Proper Wizard."

The chancellor's goat-like eyes scanned the students, but no one raised their hand. "I shall see you all on the other side. Be safe."

With that, he waved his hand forward and the air shimmered between his fingers. That shimmering spread out in front of him like he was throwing a net over the class.

Alex and Khalik nodded to each other.

"See you on the other side, if we are lucky," Khalik gave a nervous smile.

"You too," Alex said.

Baelin's teleportation magic washed over them.

Then the stadium was empty.

Chapter 40

The Plain of Dust

Baelin's spell was different from the Traveller's magic.

When he passed through the Saint of Alric's portal, Alex had seen scenes of many places. Almost like he was speeding through different realms and worlds with every blink. With this spell, he only saw swirls of light.

A rushing sensation filled his gut, and the magic felt somehow familiar.

With a pop, suddenly he stood alone in the Barrens of Kravernus.

Blasted rock crunched beneath his feet as his weight settled on the ground, and a strong, hot wind whirled dust into his face. He began to cough, shielding his eyes as he looked toward the sun through the churning dust. It was a lot hotter here than it had been at the university. The mana in the air was so thick, it felt like he was wading through a magical pea soup. The ambient mana could have been vibrating with its own energy.

Near to him was a large rise of rock, and beyond that, a slope that led down to a canyon. In the distance rose the escarpment that served as the goal of their test.

"Alex?" Khalik's voice asked behind him.

"Khalik!" He turned around, thankful to see his friend.

Two other figures appeared.

Khalik was closest, with Najyah perched on the leather gauntlet on his arm. She had tucked her head beneath her wing, shielding herself from the dust. Behind them were the last two members of their group.

The first was the massive minotaur he noticed standing with the class—a foot or more taller than Alex—now shielding his eyes with a thick arm holding an iron mace. Standing near him was the coughing form of a tall young woman.

Isolde.

"We have to get out of the dust," Khalik coughed. "Quick, behind that rock!"

The powerful young man, covering his eyes, leaned into the dust storm and strode toward the rise with the others following him with their eyes half-shut. Coughing and sputtering, the four students reached the stone and pressed against it.

"Holy shit, this is a hell of a test." Alex coughed, wiping dust from his hair and face.

"Well, we were warned." Khalik grimaced as Najyah shook herself, ruffling her feathers. "It was not a windy day at the school, so I hope this is just a short gust. For now, dampen whatever cloth you have and tie it around your nose and mouth. The wind is howling like a desert sandstorm. Try not to talk for now; it will just bring more dust into your chest."

The other three students quickly took their cloaks from their packs to tie around their faces. Alex was glad he'd packed his as he moistened a corner with his waterskin and wrapped it around his face and head. The wind couldn't have blown for more than a few minutes, but it felt like hours while they waited—pressed against the rise of rock as the dust hissed against it.

Eventually, the wind lessened, beginning to grow quiet, and the dust began to settle.

Soon, the four students were able to remove the cloaks from

their faces—or snout in the case of the minotaur—as the dusty air settled.

"Well, that was terrible," Alex said, wiping his hair. "Anyone having regrets yet? Maybe they still have openings in Summoning Fairies and Unicorns I."

That wasn't a real class, but it would have been amazing if it were.

Khalik's lips crooked up a bit, but the other two didn't laugh.

"If we're going to be working together as a team, then we should learn about each other and our capabilities before we start our journey," Isolde said, rising to her full height and shaking off her cloak. "I am Isolde Von Anmut, and I am in my second year. A pleasure to meet you all." She nodded to them but did not smile. Her eyes were already flicking toward their destination, as though she were trying to measure time and distance between them and the escarpment.

"Khalik, I am in my first year, and this is Najyah." Khalik wiped the dust out of his familiar's feathers.

"Alex, first year, first class, first time in a horrible dust storm. Lots of firsts." Alex conjured his forceball by the side of his head and peered around the rock-rise. The dry earth was flat as far as he could see, with the occasional stone-rise breaking up from the ground and canyon cutting through the stone. The stone-rises almost looked like crooked, branchless trees made of sunbaked rock.

"Thundar, first year," the minotaur's voice rumbled. His ears flicked off the excess dust.

"All first years?" Isolde said. A note of disappointment lay in her voice. "You're all brave. Most students who try this course wait until at least their second year."

"Perhaps we are brave. Or perhaps we are just fools," Khalik said, then looked at Alex, who was trying to control his laughter. "What is so funny?"

"It's a bit mad, isn't it? That we're actually here in a horrible wasteland? Ah well, we're already here, so we may as well see what we're made of. So, have any of you had experience in a fight before?" He raised his own hand. "I have."

As soon as he'd heard that disappointed note in Isolde's voice, he knew he'd likely be considered nothing more than deadweight once she and Thundar heard the only spells he knew were forceball and forcedisk. Better to control how and what information came out before they started asking questions and making a bunch of assumptions.

"I have been in combat as well," Khalik confirmed.

"I've brawled among my generation and undergone rites of passage in my clan." Thundar clapped his mace in his hand. Alex eyed the brutal-looking thing. Its head was bigger than his forceball, and its flanges ended in vicious-looking points. Thundar's arms were as big as Khalik's thighs. One swing from that weapon looked like it could cave in half of Alex's body.

And Thundar was going to be a *wizard*? He looked like he should've been pulling silence-spiders in half with his bare hands. Still, best not to judge, Alex thought. He himself was trying to be a wizard after all, and he had a magic Mark that actively tried to ensure he could never cast a spell. So, who was he to question anyone else being there?

"I have not seen real battle, though," the minotaur finished, looking to Isolde. "What about you?"

"I have partaken in a number of wizard duels... but have never engaged in a fight with monsters." Isolde grimaced. "I took the first year of battle-magic and learned lightning spells from ELEC-1400. Now, I can cast up to third-tier spells."

Her tone was quick and serious.

"I know a body-strengthening spell and an Illusory Duplicate spell," Thundar said. "Both are first-tier."

"I can cast second-tier spells," Khalik said. "And Najyah, my familiar, can scout, attack and serve as an origin point for my spells."

"I've killed monsters before," Alex said, partly to let them know of his competence, and partly to reassure himself. "I think we've got a good group here. Brains, magic, brawn, experience. We're bringing different things to the table. As long as we bring *cooperation* too, we'll have just about everything the chancellor wants. We can do this."

He emphasized the word cooperation, and saw the others nod in agreement. Good. The last thing they needed was an argument over who would be leader.

"What's our plan?" Alex continued, pointing toward the open wasteland. "That big canyon is between us and where we need to go. Can any of you fly? Like those floating disks at the school?"

"Najyah can."

"Thanks," Alex said dryly.

Isolde shook her head. "Flight is a third-tier spell, but I haven't learned it."

Khalik eyed the canyon. "I am serious, Alex. I will send up Najyah to survey what's around us. That could help us find a path. I cannot imagine the chancellor would place us somewhere where we cannot even *try* to pass the test."

He thrust his gauntleted arm into the air and sent Najyah flapping into the cloudless sky. "She will circle for a time, then tell me if there is any path ahead, and if there are any threats nearby."

They waited, watching Najyah soar as her massive wings caught a hot air current, sending her high into the blue sky. Alex noticed more specks in the distance. Tiny wisps of cloud shooting up into the sky. Farther still, a bat-winged shape flew up.

"Are those going to be problems?" He pointed to them.

Isolde peered toward where his finger indicated. "No. Those

are summoned air elementals, and the last looks like a summoned greater imp. Other parties must also be scouting by way of—Huh. Look at that."

A pair of figures—humanoid shaped—had risen into the air and floated toward the escarpment. They crossed the sky at speed for about thirty seconds, then flew back to where they had taken off from.

"Flight magic," Isolde said. "But it looks like they're not able to go all the way before their will mana runs out. Not good."

"What is it?" Thundar asked.

"Unless they were scouting, they played their hand too early. They probably thought they could cross the distance to the escarpment before their mana ran out, then realized just *how* far it was. Now, they're weakened and have to go back to whatever teammates they left behind. And that's a bad position to be in."

"That'll cost them trust," Khalik said. "An unwise strategy."

Isolde's eyes narrowed. "Trust doesn't matter to many at Generasi. Sometimes, it's all about who can get ahead the quickest... no matter what method they use."

Alex had a feeling he knew who she was referring to.

A cry signalled Najyah's return, and she landed on top of the stone-rise. She met Khalik's eyes and something passed between her and her master.

"Good news and bad news." Khalik turned to the rest of them and pointed along the canyon. "There's a path down to the canyon floor ahead and another that leads up and to the other side farther down. We can cross, but... The bad news is she saw tracks at the bottom of the canyon. Something moves through there a lot. She thinks it is small, though."

"Muupkaras," Isolde said. "Little monsters covered in fur who walk upright like us. About three feet tall. They are smart enough to use rocks as weapons, but they haven't learned the use of fire."

"Dangerous?" Thundar's grip tightened on his mace.

"Yes," Isolde said. "Monsters in the Barrens are aggressive, especially if there's a lot of them. Muupkaras are no exception. Though, four wizards of Generasi should be able to deal with them, and escape. They've got short legs and they're not that fast, but they have excellent endurance. We'll likely only have a problem if they're in a *very* large troop."

"How large can those groups be?"

"Most of the time? Between forty to fifty, but hunting groups are smaller, only about three to ten or so, according to *Mazlow's Hierarchy of Monsters Volume I.*"

"Ten would be trouble, but three to five we can handle," Khalik said. He looked to Najyah, who flew off the rock-rise. "She will scout ahead and tell me if the canyon is safe."

"We should get going. The dust has settled and we don't have all the time in the world," Thundar said.

Alex eyed the canyon, looking at the rough walls. "Just a second."

He willed the forceball up and slammed it full force into the stone-rise they were standing beside.

Crack!

Stone cracked from the impact, and a few more blows dislodged large chunks of rock, which landed heavily on the other side. Good, it looked like the stones in the Barrens weren't unbreakable, and his powered-up forceball could shatter them if they were hit enough or just right.

"What are you doing?" Isolde frowned.

"Testing how stable the rock is." He centred his pack on his back. "Shall we?"

The group moved from the rock-rise and began making their way toward the edge of the canyon. Najyah fluttered ahead of them, diving toward the canyon and swooping along its length. Alex peered over the side of the canyon wall. He was glad he wasn't afraid of heights. It was a long drop. At least a hundred feet. Maybe more.

He eyed the canyon's sides. The stone looked like limestone, the same as the rock-rise—layered and flaking, while the floor of the canyon was covered in dust. Two resources for him to use. More rock-rises seemed to grow out of the canyon floor like miniature trees, and many of them didn't look stable.

Isolde was muttering beneath her breath nearby, and now he heard what she was repeating: facts about the Barrens as well as spell formulae. Her back was straight and her arms stiff. Her eyes darted around constantly.

"You okay?" he asked.

"Yes. Yes I am," she said stiffly. "I should be asking you that, being your senior."

He shrugged. "Today, we're all on the same ship. The same rapidly sinking ship."

Again, not a laugh. Ah well, at least *he* thought he was funny, and humour was helping to keep him calm.

"I'd prefer if the ship were sound," Khalik said.

"I'd like not to be on a ship at all," Thundar added.

"I'd at least take a sky-gondola," Isolde said. "That would make this entire test elementary."

Alex snorted. "We should've brought one, if it'd work outside the city."

He glanced up ahead and saw a pathway leading down into the canyon.

There. That was step one done. Easy enough so far.

Thundar stopped, his nostrils flaring. "Wait..." He sniffed the air. "I smell blood. Blood and rot. Coming from close by."

Chapter 41

Predators

Thundar crept forward, and they followed cautiously as he led them away from the canyon.

The minotaur sniffed the air while pointing his snout down toward the earth. Alex kept his forceball close and had unslung a staff—it was just a broomstick with its head off; he was taking no chances with the Mark's interference—from the top of his pack. He held it in first guard and was ready to drop into second at any moment.

Both movements were feeling quite natural to him now.

Khalik had drawn a short sword from a sheath at his side and had called Najyah to circle low overhead, ready to swoop down on any attackers that might suddenly appear. He had one hand raised, prepared to direct a spell.

One of Isolde's hands was raised to cast spells while the other held a needle-pointed stiletto knife. From the comfortable way she gripped it, it looked like she'd been trained in its use.

Soon, a foul smell hit them. Alex couldn't recognize the smell of blood like Thundar could, but there was a familiarness to the bad odour. It reminded him of when McHarris left out ground meat for his pies for too long.

Thundar stopped, tilting his head so that one eye looked at a dust pile in front of him. It was so low, Alex hadn't noticed it in the distance. "Smell's coming from this pile."

They scraped the dust away and drew back from what they uncovered.

The corpse of some kind of animal was half-buried in a hole in the dry, blasted earth. Its flesh had been mostly stripped away, leaving sun-bleached bones connected to rotting tissue. It might have been some kind of big, two-legged lizard. Its face resembled the frostdrake from the beastarium, but the head was thinner, hornless and had less teeth.

It was also a lot smaller than the frostdrake, maybe the size of an average dog. Definitely a lot smaller than Brutus, but then, most dogs were.

"Ugh, this has been here awhile." Khalik held his nostrils shut. "It's hard to know how it died, but it doesn't look like it died well."

Alex followed Khalik's eyes and noticed several of the bones had been broken open. Rocks the size of fists lay nearby covered in the dark stain of dried blood. The bulk of the flesh around its head and long neck had been stripped off. Cleanly. Though there appeared to be tooth marks on the bones, it looked like the meat had been peeled.

It reminded Alex of how Theresa had shown him how to clean a rabbit by peeling the flesh and skin from the bones, like pulling off a pair of pants.

This kill looked a lot messier and more gruesome.

"I think it's a vent-drinker," Isolde said.

"A what?" Alex and Thundar asked at the same time.

"A vent-drinker. It's one of the few creatures that can process ambient mana in the air well enough to survive absorbing it from wild mana vents directly. They don't need anything more than mana and some water to survive. They're peaceful creatures. It's too bad they can't live outside of the Barrens. Even the city doesn't have enough mana in the air for them to survive for long."

"It seems this one had trouble surviving even *in* the Barrens." Thundar knelt down beside the corpse and eyed the broken bones. "More meat left. Either whatever got this is on a diet, or they left it behind to come back to later."

"Muupkaras, most like." Isolde held her nose. "Mazlow said their hunting parties will bury a kill if they plan to return to a region later." She pursed her lips. "Hmmm, I wanted to save mana, but I think we might need some protection. If you gather around me, I can cast Lesser Force Armour on all of us. It will blunt attacks and protect us from blows to the head. I have enough mana for it to last roughly five hours. More than enough time for us to complete the test."

From Alric and its peaceful nature, to having two spells cast on him in the space of what felt like minutes. Alex's life kept changing more and more.

Isolde spread her hands—reminding him of a sorceress that might lock a princess in a tower in one of his favourite childhood books—and spoke an incantation with her palms raised. Alex felt mana pour through a magic circuit that surrounded him, which weaved a latticework of white force magic over his head, chest, trunk and groin.

As the magic solidified, the glowing force disappeared, leaving only a slight distortion in the light to hint that it was there. In curiosity, he reached down and prodded at the distortion. It was solid; harder than his forceball.

"It's invisible?"

"Yes." Isolde tested the point of her stiletto against the invisible armour over her. "Some spells from the school of force are just an invisible magical force. Not all of them glow."

He glanced at his forceball. An *invisible* version might be useful. Through his experiments, he'd figured out what part of the spell array was responsible for how much light the spell shed.

If he could tweak that, it might cause the spell to basically disappear. His eyes narrowed in thought.

The hive-queen couldn't have struck his forceball down if she couldn't see it.

Something to work on later.

"Thank you, Isolde," Khalik said. "It will be much safer with these on us."

Isolde nodded. "It takes a fair portion of mana, though, so my casting endurance will suffer down the line."

"Well, that's why we're here," Alex said, tapping his forceball with his staff. "We'll pull our weight as you get tired."

He looked back down to the dead animal's corpse.

He wished Theresa was with them for a lot of reasons. For one, from her experience, she might have had a better idea of what a buried kill meant in terms of where the burying predators might have gone. He had a vague memory of her talking about bears burying their kills. He focused on the Mark, concentrating on predator's habits and avoiding predators.

An array of memories arose encompassing little snippets of conversation with Theresa or other hunters on what to do if you found bear droppings, or a kill left behind. Unfortunately, nothing specific and helpful came up. All of the advice just amounted to 'leave their territory quickly.'

'Leaving this place' was definitely on the urgent to-do list.

He thought of using his forceball to smash the bones and splatter the meat. That would kick up the smell in the air and maybe send these 'muupkaras' looking to see what happened to their food, instead of directly following the tracks the four of them were leaving in the dust. Glancing back, he took the forceball and tried wiping away their path, but that left long, curved edged trenches behind.

He considered pressing the forceball close to the ground and spinning it to spray dust over the path behind them, but that wouldn't mask their smell.

He looked at the corpse. It really didn't make sense to try anything that might make things worse. The last thing they needed was for him to draw the monsters closer because of the smell, and then have them ignore their kill and come after their trail.

"We should keep moving." Khalik squinted up at the sun. "Three hours to complete our task means we will likely not be able to stop for rest. In this heat, that will be difficult enough. So, now that we have seen where the smell is coming from and have protected ourselves, we should move."

"I'll take up the front," Thundar offered. "I can smell most things coming from up ahead and I have no magic that strikes from range."

"I shall hold the rear," Khalik said.

"You and I in the centre, then." Isolde nodded to Alex.

"Like the filling in a juicy pie for hungry monsters," he said.

"Why are you like this?" Khalik asked.

"I've been asking myself the same question for years."

The group fell back into silence as they made their way back to the canyon. Sunlight shone hard onto the Barrens, making the air shimmer in the distance. By the time they reached the edge, Alex was starting to sweat. He took a long drink from his water-skin and shook it. Still nearly full.

The path down into the canyon was narrow and covered in dust. The group slowed, carefully watching their footing, and Thundar stretched out his arms for balance.

Loose rocks crumbled away from the path beneath the minotaur's hooves. They froze. Thankfully, nothing gave way. Cautiously, they kept moving and finally reached the bottom, sighing with relief.

Thunder's nostrils flared. "There's a musk in the air from a beast I've never smelled before. It's old."

"Hopefully, that means it's long gone." Alex used the Mark to scan the ground in case there were any hidden tracks. Unfortunately, a few passes of his eyes didn't yield any information—the dust storm had likely covered any trails. "Khalik, how far ahead did Najyah see those tracks?"

"Some distance ahead." His gaze followed his familiar's flight-path over the canyon. "There. Do you see where she stops and flutters? That is where the tracks are. The path up to the other side of the canyon is farther ahead."

"Then we'd better keep moving."

They continued through the heat with boots, shoes and hooves scraping through the dust. Their footsteps echoed from the canyon walls, and their eyes scanned the path ahead and the stone to the sides. They circled the rocky formations rising from the canyon floor, making sure nothing was hiding around them.

As the silence grew—broken only by the odd, low gust of wind and their own footfalls—tension began to rise in Alex.

He glanced down at the symbol on his hand for reassurance.

If things became too rough, he could always leave. That was what the safety net was for, but leaving now wouldn't help him get experience for further dangers when it came to delving into magic or the mystery of the Ravener. And one day, there would be no safety net.

"Smell's getting stronger." Thundar sniffed the air. "Newer too, but whatever it was, wasn't just here."

"Najyah has not seen anything. But the tracks are close."

Passing another stone-rise, they saw footprints ahead. They were small, maybe the size of a young child's, and were human-shaped except for the toes, which were long like fingers. From the points in front of the tracks, they ended in claws like a bear's or wild cat.

"More blood and rot," Thundar said, his nostrils flaring. "Another buried kill is close."

"Then this is part of their hunting grounds too. Look there." Isolde pointed at a dark stain splattered on the canyon wall to their left. Beneath it, broken bones lay, half-buried by the dust.

"I read that muupkaras will chase prey—like vent-drinkers—across the Barrens. They surround them with numbers and herd them toward the edge of a canyon wall. Then, the prey falls to the ground and the muupkaras go down and feast."

"Well, I guess we're safer being at the bottom of the canyon," Alex said. "Unless they start throwing rocks from up above. At least since we're already down here, they can't herd us to fall to the bottom." A light wind blew toward them, not strong enough to kick up much dust.

Thundar went into a sneezing fit.

"You okay?" Alex asked.

"Yeah, fine, I just..." He trailed off, sniffing the wind. "New smell. The beast smell from before. But a lot newer. Close too."

The group looked toward the ramp that led up the other canyon wall. It was maybe one to two hundred yards ahead.

"How new is new?" Alex asked.

"Very new."

Isolde stiffened. "Could creatures be hiding somewhere ahead?"

"It's better if we find out now, than when they are close," Khalik said.

Alex's mind began to work. Where could they be? There was one of those little natural stone-rises in front of them, but there were no more ahead, only the dust-covered, flat canyon floor.

No cover to hide behind.

Then Alex remembered the silence-spiders.

The workers had hidden beneath the hallway floor. These muupkara things buried their prey. They were diggers.

His eyes narrowed.

"I think I'll use my forceball to see if anything's hiding over there."

"Good idea. I can check in my own way too." Khalik raised a hand and pressed his fingers together. "Ready."

"I'll guard the front," Thundar said, squaring his shoulders.

Isolde watched them, then moved to the side toward the closest stone tower for cover. As soon as they were tucked behind the stones, Alex willed his forceball over the dust ahead. Khalik watched carefully, with fingers ready to snap.

Then Alex willed the ball to spin.

Then he willed it down.

Bang.

It struck the earth.

Khalik snapped his fingers.

Crack!

Sound burst ahead like an explosion going off.

Screeching filled the air.

Monsters burst up from beneath the dust. More than a dozen.

Each was about three feet tall with short, stubby limbs. Grey fur covered their bodies and round faces, but their hands and feet were bare. Their fingers and toes ended in long, vicious-looking claws. They had enormous coal black eyes protruding from their heads, and their noses were small and black like a canine's. Massive, bat-like ears rose from their heads, and their little paws clutched them from the pain of Khalik's sound-clap.

They were...

They were...

Cute?

They almost looked like little upright fluffy shepherd dogs from Alric. *Look at their big, brown eyes!* Alex thought. *How could...*

Then they opened their mouths.

And he screamed.

Their jaws *unfolded*, spreading apart far wider than it seemed physically possible. He'd seen garden snakes unhinge their jaws to swallow a fat mouse. These creatures' jaws reminded him of that, but much, much worse.

Teeth unfolded from all sides of their mouths. Hundreds of

hooked, sharp fangs that jutted from the insides of their cheeks, the roofs of their mouths, their gums... Just teeth everywhere. They had no tongues and the back of their unnaturally wide mouths—big enough to swallow someone up to the shoulders—pulsated, making hideous sucking sounds.

Alex was suddenly reminded of Mr. Lu sucking meat off chicken bones.

“Oh, shit!” he screamed.

He commanded the spinning forceball to shoot forward.

Chapter 42

Ambushing the Ambushers

The spinning forceball shot over the ground, ploughing through the dust and kicking clouds of grit into the air. Alex guided the spell to shoot in front of each little monster, spraying the dust into their open mouths, eyes and large ears as he whirled it along the ground in between them.

The Mark didn't react to the indirect effect, much like how it didn't react to the statue's eye-beams chasing his forceball and striking the spiders in the Cave of the Traveller. The creatures began coughing and sputtering at the spray in their faces.

The young wizards didn't waste a moment.

Isolde spat an incantation.

Crackle.

Blue bolts of lightning danced between two of her raised fingers. She shot her hand forward, pointing toward the little monsters as they coughed and hacked on dust.

There was another crackle like snapping branches.

Then lightning shot forward.

Two thin rays of crackling electricity magic fired from her fingertips, hitting two of the little creatures in their chests. They stiffened, shuddering as her power surged through them, conducting into the ground. With raspy, gurgling sounds, they dropped in limp heaps, their monstrous jaws twitching.

The others screeched as their companions fell, and stumbled forward, picking up large rocks they'd hidden. Alex shot his forceball in front of them, keeping it skidding and spinning along the ground, whipping more dust into their faces.

Khalik spat another incantation.

Sharp rocks were conjured in front of his hand, and fired like crossbow bolts deep into the chests and frightful mouths of the monsters. As they dropped, a sharp cry signalled Najyah entering the battle.

She shot down on one—talons extended—and with weight and speed, drove it off its feet. Her razor-sharp beak finished it.

Almost half of the creatures went down in seconds. Those still alive screeched louder, throwing their rocks at the wizards, then dropping to all fours and sprinting toward the canyon wall. They moved surprisingly fast considering how stubby their legs were, and reached the wall as the wizards burst from cover.

"They were waiting in ambush!" Khalik shouted.

"We shouldn't let them get away!" Isolde raised fingers. "They might go for help, if their troop hasn't already heard them!"

Alex's eyes narrowed. The creatures *were* running away, but that didn't mean they were really giving up the fight. He thought back to the silence-spiders. How they hid, scurried and ambushed their prey. These muupkaras had just tried to ambush them. Letting them escape now to try again later would be foolish, and probably a good way to get killed.

"Don't waste your spells; I've got this." Thundar rushed toward the monsters with his giant mace ready. The minotaur's long strides saw him easily catch up to them, and with a single swing, one dropped to the ground.

The others had made it to the bottom of the canyon wall

and started climbing the rock face. Their sharp claws bit into the stone.

"I've got 'em," Alex yelled, eyeing the cliff face above.

He called his forceball up and began smashing it into the cliff face high above the fleeing creature's heads. Searching the stones for cracked areas and protrusions on the rock-rise above, he aimed at them, cleaving the forceball into each at different angles.

With a few precise blows, the rocks cracked, sending pebbles and larger stones raining down on the climbers. The muupkaras screeched as several of them were hammered by falling rock. One lost its grip and dropped to the canyon floor, where Thundar was waiting. Then another fell. Then another.

The last few clung to the cliff, but Najyah dove at them, striking from behind with her talons extended. Each time her claws connected, they screamed, letting go of the wall and plunging toward the canyon floor. Thundar's mace swung, finishing each one as they dropped howling and snarling to the ground. When the last one was dispatched, he rose to his full height and wiped his mace. When he turned, he was spattered in red.

"Done," was all he said.

"I... I thought you never saw battle before?" Alex stared at him.

Thundar shrugged. "Not true battle, but our brawls among the clan are... vigorous."

Alex looked down at the smashed monsters, noting to himself to never, ever piss him off.

"I am glad we did not walk into that unawares." Khalik stepped to one of the little creatures' bodies and knelt down beside it. The fangs in its mouth still twitched slightly. "If they had surprised us with a successful stone attack, we would have been unbalanced, and had they then jumped us with their numbers, things could have been grim."

"We *could* have survived with our skills and Isolde's armour spell in place. Most of us, at least." Thundar's hooves scuffed over the dust as he approached. "But there would have been wounded, which would slow us, or maybe the wounded would have been taken by the chancellor's spell."

"It is good we found them before they could attack us," Isolde agreed. "And I am well pleased with what each of us brings. That battle was solved with two spells, a bird and a mace. We are still left with plenty of mana resources." She looked to Alex. "Your forceball is *incredibly* versatile. I've never seen one that can crack stone and move so quickly."

"I had a lot of time to practice with it." Alex shrugged. "If I had a choice, I'd kinda like to *shoot freaking lightning* from my fingers."

Isolde's face softened a little. "ELEC-1400 is not an easy course, but it's fun if you can get through the initial unit on the history of electrical magic and the unit on conduction. Did you pick it?"

"No," Alex said. "Maybe later."

Khalik glanced to the sun. "Let's hope their troop was not close enough to hear their cries. Either way, we should be moving."

The four wizards took a final look at the fallen monsters then began climbing the ramp up to the other side. The sun's heat grew stronger as they reached the top of the canyon.

Boom!

They abruptly stopped, gaping at the horizon.

Light flashed in the distance followed by a roar, and a massive fireball soared into the air followed by clouds of smoke and dust. Moments later, a crack like stone tearing, and more dust shot up from the ground elsewhere in the distance.

"Looks like the other groups ran into their own troubles." Khalik sent Najyah into the sky, letting her lead and scout again. "Let's go. We have a long way yet."

The group pushed on through the wastelands, wrapping their cloaks around their heads for protection from the sun. There was no wind to blow dust into their faces at the moment, but an unexpected gust could stir it up and sweep away visibility. The cloaks would protect them against those two threats at least. As they continued toward the escarpment, the sun rose farther into the sky, closing in on noon.

The heat continued to climb.

Alex and Isolde were sweating profusely, and Thundar was starting to pant. Khalik was more used to the heat, but even his broad shoulders had started to sag. Alex took long sips from his waterskin as they trekked through the plain. On the horizon, another flash of light would suddenly appear from time to time, marking signs of more battle.

They watched their surroundings with sharp eyes, tensed for another ambush, but none came. For a long time, they were alone in the wastes, left only to the searing heat that cracked the dry earth, and the thick mana in the air.

Najyah circled above, watching for threats.

Soon she wasn't alone in the sky. Massive birds with black feathers began soaring above the plains. Many circled the canyon to their backs, just above the spot where they had killed the muupkaras. Others flew over areas ahead of where the battle had taken place. Their wingspan appeared to be about as wide as Najyah's, but they were thinner, at least from what Alex could see.

"Big crows," he said.

"Vultures," Khalik corrected him. "They are birds that feed on the dead."

"Well, I guess we left them a lot of food back there," Alex said.

"Hrm." Thundar watched the vultures behind them. "If the muupkaras' troop is around and looking for their hunting party, they might go check why vultures are flying over where their hunting party was. If they're smart enough."

The students quickened their pace.

As they continued through the wastes, they saw other signs of life.

Large insects burrowed from the earth to bask in the heat as the sun approached midday. Fist-sized beetles shook the dust from their shells then unfolded green, leaf-like wings.

Some flew from the earth, making a loud droning noise, and swooped to the top of rocky rises dotting the plain. There, they would look around and splay their wings wide to take in the sunlight. Despite the heat, Alex shuddered, remembering insectile eyes watching them in the Traveller's Cave. He pushed the memory of silence-spiders from his mind.

'They're just bugs,' he told himself. 'They're just bugs... Aren't they?'

He pointed to the large insects. "Know anything about those, Isolde?"

"Green Wings. They take their energy from the sun. They're harmless, unless you eat them."

"What happens if you eat them?" Thundar asked.

"It's a strong poison. Especially to those with a lot of mana in their bodies. That trait helps keep them safe from predation in the Barrens."

"Oh." Alex was glad eating bugs, or anything else they found out here, wasn't part of the test.

He took another long sip of water, mentally cursing the sun. Even the hottest summer days in Alric felt like a cool fall breeze compared to the merciless beating the sun was giving them here.

The heat was sapping his strength—all of their strengths. His feet were hot and felt like weights were tied to them. Isolde's straight-backed stride was starting to droop forward and Khalik's shoulders continued to sag. Thundar's panting filled the air. Alex was glad he'd trained for endurance over the past month. If he hadn't, he doubted he could have made it this far.

He looked up to the escarpment. It was getting closer, at least.

"Hold on." Khalik stopped them. He squinted up as Najyah flew down to land on his gauntlet. "Najyah has seen something."

He and his familiar locked eyes for a moment, and information passed between them. Khalik quickly looked back over his shoulder.

"Oh, damn everything," he swore. "The muupkara troop pursues us."

The group whirled around, squinting at the horizon. In the distance through shimmering waves of heat, *something* moved. It was far enough away that they couldn't make it out clearly.

"How many?" Alex asked.

"Najyah says many more than we killed. *Many* more."

"And we're on open ground," Thundar said. "They've got short legs; we should keep moving. Keep ahead of them. No need for a fight if we can avoid it. Especially against a lot of them, and in this heat."

Alex looked up to the escarpment. It seemed deceptively, tauntingly close. They pushed on through the sun, with each of them looking back over their shoulders to look for signs of movement.

Thundar sniffed. "New scents ahead, more of them. And something else. Something strange."

Cautiously, they removed the capes from their faces and moved on with hands raised for spellcasting. They were tensed, ready for an ambush.

They didn't encounter living muupkaras.

They encountered corpses.

On a patch of earth that had been torn up, half a dozen lay scattered on the plains ahead. Each of them was half-collapsed, like waterskins that had been punctured. Their flesh sagged, giving them a strange, soft, deformed look. Because they were so fuzzy, it took Alex a bit to figure out what was wrong.

Their claws were missing.

Their bones were gone.

Gone from each one of them.

Their faces looked like someone had half-flattened clay dolls and left them in the rain to melt. The plump features were sunken in and their limbs were crooked and displaced, like shrivelled sacks of flesh drying in the sun.

Large puncture wounds pierced each of them. Some to the chest, some to their arms, and some to the backs of their heads.

"Uldar's beard," Alex swore. "What the hell happened to them?" He remembered one of the monsters Baelin had warned them about. "Oh shit, did one of those bonedrinker things the chancellor mentioned do this?"

Paling, Isolde studied the bodies, then scanned the horizon. Still empty. "Yes. They have sharp tails they use to bore into their prey, then they release a substance that liquifies the skeleton. The skin and flesh is left behind, but the bones and marrow become like a thick soup for them to drink their fill of." She checked the horizon again, this time apprehensively. "From the way these muupkaras' bodies are punctured and how they look deflated, I think we can say that there was a bonedrinker here."

Khalik grimaced. "Dammit, the dust storm must have blown away any tracks. Can you smell where it might have gone, friend Thundar?"

The minotaur sniffed. "That way." He pointed south, away from the escarpment. "The scent is old, though. It might be anywhere."

Khalik frowned, lifting up the hand that had been spell-marked by Baelin. "Remember all, there is no shame if we need to retreat."

Alex looked at him sharply.

From the way Khalik had said that, he wondered if he meant

that for himself too, or if he just meant it for them. After all, he was the one who persevered in his journey to Generasi with only Najyah after the rest of his entourage couldn't continue.

"You're right," Alex said, his mind working. "But we're getting close. We should be able to get there before anything gets us. I hope."

"Yeah, if we keep moving," Thundar said.

They pushed onward, scanning every direction. They glanced back toward their pursuers far in the distance and scanned the horizon for any sign of bone-drinking monsters. The wind blew toward their backs, giving them an extra push forward, thankfully. Only a light spray of dust kicked up, not enough to hinder their progress.

The wind made their journey easier.

But it also turned out to be a curse.

With it blowing at their backs, Thundar couldn't smell what was ahead. They continued scanning the horizon for threats, but the dust obscured a lot of the terrain.

They never saw the second ambush until they walked right into it.

Chapter 43

The Escarpment

Dust exploded from the ground.

Muupkaras emerged from the earth around them, screeching, rocks raised above their heads. There were only eight this time, but now *they* had the element of surprise. They threw the stones with full force and surprising skill.

"Oof!" Alex groaned as one struck him in the chest and another cracked off his forehead. The Lesser Force Armour absorbed much of the impact, but the weight of the blows was enough to send him stumbling backward and drive a hot burst of pain through his body. The little creatures were surprisingly strong for their size.

Stones struck the others, glancing off their force armour or clipping Khalik's leather gauntlet. Thundar grunted as one struck him in his powerful thigh, but his tough hide and muscle made the impact little more than annoying.

Then the beasts rushed in, swarming and dodging past Khalik and Thundar to head for Isolde and Alex, the weakest-looking members of the group. Isolde stumbled back in surprise, but Thundar recovered quickly, spitting out a short incantation.

His form shimmered, and he suddenly split into a twin of

himself. He and his image went to Isolde, and he swung out with his mace, warding off some of the attackers. The muupakaras skidded to a halt in front of both massive weapons, trying to dart between them. Some stayed focused on Isolde and Thundar.

The others went for Alex, their jaws opening and splitting, ready to grab him and tear at his flesh. He quickly dropped into second stance and shot his forceball down in front of the closest one.

Bang!

The creature ran into it, falling backward in a heap.

The others swarmed forward as Alex backed away, sweeping the air in front of him with his broomstick. His heart pounded as wet sounds bubbled from their throats, while scores of pointy teeth twitched and throbbed as they advanced.

He called his forceball, dropping it in front of their faces and weaving it rapidly in circles and figure eights around them. The air whooshed around like a swarm of bees. He danced the forceball between them, guiding it close enough to make it look like he was aiming for their faces. They skidded to a halt, dodging out of the way of the spell.

"I have them!" Khalik shouted.

Najyah shrieked out a battle cry.

She swooped over the line of monsters with her master's spell shimmering beneath her. Sharp rocks rained down in a line behind her, bombing and striking the creatures through their fur. They howled and stumbled back. Now Alex swept his forceball forward in front of them, spinning grit into their large eyes and mouths. Wounded and now half blind, they screeched and scampered back.

Alex's eyes looked for anything he could use against them, anything indirect. But there were no mop buckets of water, no fire-gems in the eyes of goddesses, or rocks to rain down. All he had was dust and flat-earth.

Think. Adapt.

Gritting his teeth, he swept the forceball back and forth in front of them, inching it closer, driving them back on their heels. Suddenly, their screeching intensified. Khalik's sharpened stones were vanishing from their wounds, and blood began to pour over their fur as the deep cuts opened. Panicked from their injuries and fear of the forceball, they were forced into full retreat, leaving behind long trails of red on the dust.

Boom!

Isolde raised her hands. Sparks danced across her palms and burst into flame-blasts that reached out in a cone, sweeping the air fifteen feet in front of her. The scent of burning filled the air as some of the monsters' fur caught fire.

One of her attackers leapt around the flames and tried to duck toward her, but a swing from the closest Thundar's mace stopped it in its tracks. It froze in surprise as the minotaur's mace passed into the ground where it had just stood, disappearing like a rock dropping into water.

That Thundar had been the illusion.

The real one swung while it was distracted.

Splat.

The last of the attacking muupkaras was a crushed mess beneath his mace.

The others ran away, all badly bleeding. Theresa had told him about animals she'd hunted—bleeding from her broad-headed arrows—these creatures would not get far with that amount of blood loss.

The second Thundar shimmered out of existence and the four wizards panted in the heat. Despite catching them by surprise, their attackers lay dead, dying, or would be dead soon enough.

"Anyone hurt?" Khalik asked.

"Fine," Thundar grunted.

"Just my pride." Alex wiped the sweat from his brow.

"Filthy creatures." Isolde glared at the corpses. "Filthy, filthy creatures." She glanced to Thundar. "Thank you, if you were not so quick to act, that would have been much worse."

"Just doing my part for the herd," Thundar said.

"Khalik, you and Najyah saved me there too, thanks." Alex clapped him on the arm.

"Your distraction helped us," Khalik said. "If you had just started to attack one of them, then the rest would have swarmed you. Keeping them away was good thinking."

"Y-yeah," Alex said. "I'm just glad we all got out of that in one piece."

"Mhm, though my mana reserves are dented," Khalik said.

"Mine too," said Isolde.

Alex looked happily at his forceball. Practicing a sustained spell for so many years to up its mana efficiency was paying off quite well. "I still have more juice." He glanced over his shoulder. "We should get moving. These things had brown fur instead of grey. Maybe they're from a different troop. If we don't get going, we might have two groups after us. Oh, and, Isolde, your force armour saved my ass. Thanks."

She shrugged. "We're a good group so far. That's all there is to it."

They pushed on through the dust, squinting their eyes against the sun. Noon was nearly upon them. They still had time, but the test's end was getting closer.

It seemed like they'd been walking for days. The sun was high and the air seemed to burn. Earlier, Alex would have sworn the Barrens couldn't get any hotter, but the heat seemed to double with each passing moment.

Najyah had taken breaks from soaring above by flying down

and perching on Alex's forceball. He was glad he'd gotten it to the point where it could carry heavier weights. The group's steps had slowed as the sun continued to sap their strength, and the movement on the horizon behind had grown more distinct as time went on.

The muupkaras were gaining on them.

"Persistent little demons." Alex glanced back over his shoulder. He was sure he was imagining it, but he thought he could already hear their angry screeches carrying on the wind.

"They have a lot of endurance." Isolde poured sweat, and her raven hair was plastered to her shirt. "They... run prey down for miles."

"We can't slow down," Thundar panted. The minotaur wizard's breathing sounded as loud as the wind from earlier. His mace hung loosely in a loop on his belt. "If anything, we've got to speed up."

Khalik poured water over his plaits and face. It dripped from his beard. "We are close, but Najyah says there is some kind of change in the terrain ahead. With hope, it will not slow us down."

"Wish one of us knew ice or water spells," Alex groaned. "At least we're not one of those people that showed up wearing some kind of armour."

He thought of Derek, and noticed Isolde's jaw harden.

"If *someone* did, then they had better have taken it off," she said. "That metal will be as hot as the smithy it was made in by now."

"Don't I know it," Thundar groaned, looking painfully down to the metal mace by his side.

Even with all that shaggy fur covering him, the weapon must have been hot and burning his leg. Alex couldn't help but feel for him.

"We're almost there," he said, trying to keep his voice cheery. "Just a little more of a walk and we'll be there. We've got plenty of water left, or at least I do, and I'm willing to share. I swear I don't have pox or anything."

He laughed at his own bad joke, and was surprised to hear all three of his companions chuckle weakly too. The heat *must* have been getting to them. "Just a little longer. As long as we don't run into anything else."

They pushed harder, trying to open distance between them and their pursuers, all while keeping their eyes on the goal ahead. The heat had seeped into Alex to the very bone. If anything, that just spurred him harder. He'd done well so far in this test, and he'd already learned more about how to use his forceball in new ways just by wielding it in true combat. The class was already proving to have value.

Besides, after coming so far and training so hard for it, he couldn't help but have a little pride at the thought that he'd succeed. Alex Roth, the Fool of the Heroes of Thameland, was close to passing a test of ability given by Generasi's own chancellor. Proving himself here would strengthen his own confidence, open new opportunities, and help convince anyone who might suspect him of being the Fool that he likely wasn't.

The challenge was tough, but less dangerous than he'd feared.

He glanced ahead, peering into the horizon through the shimmering air, and took another long sip from his waterskin.

All he had to do was keep putting one foot in front of the other.

The ground ahead had broken.

At a point close to the base of the escarpment, the terrain shifted from flat, dust-covered wasteland, to cracked and broken rock that was crisscrossed by narrow canyons and crevices.

"Oh shit," he groaned, and the others groaned with him.

Some of the rocks were angled and would need to be maneuvered past with great care. Others had wide gaps between them that needed to be jumped. To make things worse, anything could be hiding in those crevices, waiting to attack.

And a lot of their party's strength had already been drained.

Alex glanced back over his shoulder. He was starting to be able to make out their pursuers as they were getting closer—their forms were becoming more apparent.

"This is going to be tough," Isolde said, eyeing a section of the ground that was angled up like a dagger sticking out of the earth.

"Yeah, and we're going to lose time and those little demons'll get closer." Alex jerked his thumb over his shoulder.

Khalik examined the crevices, then looked to Thundar. "How much strength do you have left, my friend?"

Thundar grunted. "More than I'd hoped, less than I'd like."

"Okay." Khalik stood in front of the first crevice, watching Najyah circle above the plain. "We are almost there. If you and I can help Alex and Isolde in making some of the jumps, then we should be able to cross quicker and with no issue."

"Khalik, if you try to bridal carry me over the canyons..." Alex looked at him.

"I would never." Khalik grinned. "Now, Thundar might."

The minotaur grunted at Isolde and Alex. "You're both getting thrown."

Najyah landed on a stone ahead as they began crossing the crevices. When the gaps were narrow, the entire group easily stepped over or made the short jumps needed to get from one massive stone to the next. As the gaps widened, the athletic Khalik would make the running jump to the other side and wait. Isolde would go next, starting a jog with Thundar behind her, his arms braced under her armpits, and then she'd jump with the minotaur's massive arms helping to propel her forward across the gap.

Khalik would catch her on the other side.

Alex felt a little pathetic needing to be half-tossed across the gaps like a sack of potatoes, but he consoled himself with the fact that he'd only really been training for a month now. None of the training had involved jumping. Something he would correct soon. That is, if he survived this place. For now, he'd swallow his pride, since missing one of the jumps and plunging fifty feet down one of those crevices was something he'd rather avoid.

Najyah circled around them, eyeing each crevice for any sign of muupkaras or any other hidden threats.

As they closed on the escarpment, their spirits began to rise, but so did their tension. Now they could hear their determined pursuers' cries and shrieks, and they were growing louder. The muupkaras could climb well, while they needed to pause at the crevices to cross safely.

"Oof," Alex groaned as he half-jumped, half-landed after being thrown into Khalik. "Isolde, what tier is a flight spell again?"

She grunted. "Third."

"First thing I'm learning when I hit third-tier is a flight spell, I swear to the Traveller—" He paused. "Oh hell, look at them!"

He pointed up to the south. Two figures were flying over the landscape—the students that had tried it before. They were at speed, though only about half as fast as Najyah, and kept looking back over their shoulders.

"They must have waited until they were close enough to make the whole journey with their mana," Thundar grunted in disapproval. "Left the rest of the group behind."

Khalik's eyes narrowed. "From their body language, they look... scared, don't they? Najyah!"

The eagle swooped to the south, passing the flying wizards. She halted, fluttering in the air, then swooped down and gave a loud cry.

Her master swore in his mother tongue. "We have to move! There's only one of their group left, and they are being chased."

Isolde looked at him sharply. "More muupkaras?"

Khalik's face turned grim. "She said it was much larger. That... it was white and had many spikes."

The young woman paled. "It's the bonedrinker! Hurry, we have to reach the escarpment!"

Chapter 44

The Bonedrinker

The group pushed as hard as they could, trying to scramble over broken rocks and ground. Dust scattered. Stones and pebbles shifted. The heat blazed mercilessly and their goal aggravatingly refused to get any closer.

The Barrens were starting to come alive with sound.

The flying students who had abandoned their companions reached the top of the escarpment and disappeared out of view.

Now that they were getting closer, Alex could see a narrow, circular flight of steps cut into the side of the escarpment leading up to the top. He swore. He'd hoped that reaching the foot of the escarpment would mean the test was over, but since there was no sign of the chancellor, he realized their ordeal wasn't over. It *did* make more sense for Baelin to be on top of the escarpment, using his magic to observe them during the test.

"Najyah has checked the escarpment! She says that the 'horned one' is at the top!" Khalik called as he scrambled to the next crevice over a massive stone. "The chancellor waits up there!"

Hope had entered his voice.

The noises around them continued to build.

Explosions sounded from the other side of the escarpment. More battle. Shouts were coming from the south, mixed with some sort of hideous clicking.

Like rheumatic bones rolling against each other.

Meanwhile, behind them, the muupkaras continued to gain. Alex glanced over his shoulder. He could see them clearly now, and there were a *lot* of them. Fifty, perhaps more. They loped along on all fours like a pack of feral dogs, crying and shrieking to each other. Alex remembered how easily their claws had sunk into the rock, allowing them to scale the canyon wall. If they reached the broken area, they would quickly overtake them.

Thundar grunted. "Dammit, I was saving this for a big fight!"

An incantation flew from his lips.

Silver-grey mana materialized around him, emerging from his mana pool and seeping into his physical form. For an instant, he was outlined in his mana before it completely vanished. His muscles tensed and swelled, and his fur bristled.

"Hang on to me!" He reached out and grabbed Alex and Isolde, tucking each beneath an arm, feet first. The smell wasn't pleasant, but Alex had no time to dwell on that.

Thundar's hooves slammed against the stone as he jumped effortlessly from the edge and over the nearby crevice, despite carrying two fully grown humans.

"This won't last forever," he grunted to Khalik. "Keep up."

"Yes!" Khalik cheered.

Alex hung on to Thundar and kept his eyes on the troop approaching the crevices.

As Thundar and Khalik jumped from stone to stone, Alex and Isolde bounced against the minotaur's sides. Alex kept his mouth shut to avoid biting his own tongue. More screeching and battle noises echoed from all around, sounding like the other groups had dragged a horde of enraged muupkaras with them.

Soon, only a handful of crevices lay between them and their goal.

Then, a human-sounding scream rang out from the south.

It seemed to last forever before abruptly disappearing and reappearing at the top of the escarpment. An instant later, it disappeared again. The bonedrinker's prey must have been teleported to Baelin, and then to Generasi.

"I can see other students now! And a lot of muupkaras," Thundar shouted.

Alex craned his neck but couldn't see much around the minotaur's bulk. He exchanged a look with Isolde, who appeared more tense than a cat around Brutus. She was muttering beneath her breath again.

He glanced up, noticing their little pursuers reaching the edge of the broken rock area. They streamed over the stones, climbing through the crevices like ants swarming a fallen piece of meat.

"Shit, guys, they're getting close!"

"So are we," Thundar grunted.

They landed hard after one last jump, and he set Alex and Isolde down. They'd finally reached the bottom of the escarpment. Now only the stairs lay between them and their goal.

Snorting, the minotaur glanced to the south. "We'd better keep moving."

Alex followed his gaze and gasped.

Approaching them at frightening speed, the bonedrinker crawled over the crevices. It was huge—at least as big as a carriage—and twisted. Its body was massive and ill-shapen, like a deformed, giant shelled creature. Spikes and calcified protrusions rose from its back and limbs. Its head was crowned in misshapen horns. A long tail that looked like vertebrae swung behind it, capped by a needle the size of a longsword. The creature was humanoid in shape, but it crawled, moving with the same sinuous movements as a lizard.

From what Alex could see of its head, its massive crowned skull was also humanoid, with endless rows of fangs and bony protrusions sticking from its cheeks. Its mouth gaped open, glistening with slimy, white, pulsating flesh. Its eyes sat on a pair of long tentacles like the eye-stalks of a snail. Bone shifted and shimmered along its form as it moved, and more protrusions appeared on its back.

"Oh *hell* no!" Alex shouted. "Run! Holy shit! Run!"

They didn't need to be told twice and everyone sprinted for the narrow staircase on the side of the escarpment. They climbed, running as fast as they could over the rough, rocky stairs. The steps were ancient but stable. As they rounded the side, they looked down and saw other students—a group of three—running from a troop of muupkaras toward the stairs.

The selachar woman and the two Doberman-like beastmen scrambled over the stones, firing behind them with bolts of blue and green light that tore rock apart or blasted muupkaras in their chests. The selachar student shimmered as though she were coated in armour made of liquid and shadow, and when she cast spells at their pursuers, blasts of water emerged, which froze on impact. Ice coated some of the muupkaras and the ground beneath their feet, sending them slipping and falling into the crevices.

Another exhausted-looking group of students appeared, tearing across the landscape. Nothing pursued the foursome. Behind, they had left a trail of blackened craters and the twitching bodies of burnt monsters.

"Get back!" one of the group of four shouted. As he roared an incantation, fire danced around his hands and then a glowing orange orb shot toward the back of the muupkaras chasing the other three students.

Boom!

Half the pursuing troop was swallowed by fire, reducing

them to burning corpses in an instant. The rest of the group shrieked and scattered.

"I'm out of mana!" the fireball slinger shouted, exchanging nods with the other group of students as they came together, and all seven raced up the stairs. The troop of muupkaras that followed Alex's group started to swarm toward the escarpment, then pulled back when they saw the bonedrinker. They didn't flee but watched from a distance.

The students were a quarter way up the escarpment when the massive bonedrinker reached the bottom of the rise. It was too large for the steps, so it let out a gurgle from deep within its chest like it was choking on liquid, then flexed its clawed hands.

It slammed the claws into the stone, biting deep into the rock, and started climbing up the escarpment walls after the fleeing students.

"Run!" Alex shouted. "It's coming!"

It climbed at a frightening rate, much faster than the running wizards scaling the ridge.

"Back, beast!" another of the group of four shouted.

He screamed another incantation and launched a glowing orange ball down. The bonedrinker gurgled again, withdrawing its slimy tentacles into its eye sockets and slamming its bony face into the stone for protection.

Only its bone carapace was exposed when the fireball went off.

Boom!

The spell tore along the side of the rocky elevation, bathing the creature in flame-magic. There was a hiss and whine as its flesh heated in its bony covering, and it let out a scream that was like the hiss of steam escaping a pot lid.

The monster raised its head and gurgled at them. Some of its bones were blackened, but it started to climb again, undeterred. The fireball wizards raced up the stairs, but the bonedrinker pulled itself up even faster.

One student was falling behind, winded by the sprint. The bonedrinker's tentacles flailed wildly and it surged toward him.

Its tail whipped back then lashed out.

Crnch!

"Aaaaaargh!"

Alex knew he'd never forget those sounds until the day he died.

The student wailed, falling backward, impaled through the arm as the bonedrinker's tail held steady. The young man's arm began to collapse as his bone liquified. His scream intensified.

Then he shimmered and was gone.

The creature paused, then bolted up the wall after the other students. Its carapace shifted and another protrusion formed on its back. It had absorbed the bone of the injured wizard.

Alex's stomach churned.

"Dammit!" Khalik swore. "We won't be able to outrun it!"

Isolde glared down at the creature. She trembled, but her eyes were set and dangerous. "Get back from me!"

She raised her hands and began to chant an incantation. Lightning shot between her fingers, then creeped down her hands and arms. Thunder rumbled as she shot her hands down.

Bang!

With a crack, a lightning bolt flew from between her arms.

The electricity magic crackled as it struck the bonedrinker—while it again pressed its head into the wall—and blue and white light flashed over the stone. The creature groaned, stiffening, then fell.

It hit the stone with a colossal impact, snapping many of the protrusions on its back. It lay still, and for a moment, Alex's heart jumped. The other students caught up with his group, and he grinned, happy to see them.

"You see that?" He laughed. "One boiled bonedrinker courtesy of our resident thunderstorm, Isolde Von Anmut! We... are... Oh shit!"

With a gurgle, the bonedrinker rolled off its back and climbed back to its hands and feet, shaking itself like a wet dog.

"Do you, uh..." He glanced at Isolde. "You got another one of those in you?"

"Not without drawing on my lifeforce. Not a spell that grand. I can cast one of the lesser electricity bolts, but then I'll be done." She gritted her teeth. "Infernal creature."

Alex grimaced, watching the monster shake itself. It definitely wasn't unharmed. It wasn't dead or badly wounded, but it definitely wasn't unharmed.

"Hey." He glanced at the other students on the steps. "That fall did *not* do that thing any favours, but it's gonna keep coming. If we can get higher and drive it off the wall again, it might not get back up."

"Good idea! Plan as we run!" Khalik shouted, and the other students tore up the stairs after him.

Alex kept glancing down to the bonedrinker as its tentacles emerged from its eye sockets. He watched them turn and twist in the air, then focus on the fleeing students above.

So, that was how it saw...

He called his forceball close to him.

They climbed as fast as they could, making it halfway up the escarpment before Thundar glanced down. "It's getting closer!" he warned.

Alex whirled. "I'll distract it! When it's distracted, everyone do whatever you can to get it off the wall!"

"Can you really divert its attention without getting killed?" the selachar woman asked from her armour of seawater.

"He can. You should've seen him do his tricks with the muupkaras!" Thundar said.

"I'll open up the road," Alex said. "All of you just have to run it!"

As the creature closed on them, he shot his forceball down.

The glowing crimson orb shot between the bonedrinker's

eye-tentacles. They twitched. The monster hesitated. He shot the forceball back at it, skimming around its tentacles to the right. Then he swung it back around, swinging to the left.

The monster was unsure about this new threat. That was when Alex started to get complex. As he'd done in training, he shot the forceball all around the creature's eyes, making it swirl in figure eights, zig-zags and other confusing patterns. The bonedrinker gurgled as its tentacles tried to follow the object that kept threatening to smash into them.

Crunch.

It tore a claw away from the wall and swung at the forceball with surprising speed. If his spell had been at the same level as when he and Theresa fought the hive-queen, then the bonedrinker could have easily crushed it. Now, though, he danced the orb rapidly around the creature.

Then the others acted.

With a screech, Najyah dove at the bonedrinker's left eye-tentacle. Distracted, it wasn't able to react in time.

Riiiiip!

Her talons tore away the bulbous eye at the end of the tentacle. As she swooped past the second, Khalik's magic shimmered around her, launching sharp rocks that drove into the creature's other eye-tentacle, wounding it.

It gurgled in agony, slamming its head into the wall to protect the soft eyeball.

Bolts of magic slammed into its bony hide, but it was too tough to crack.

"It will not drop!" Khalik snapped.

With a roar, Thundar pulled back his mace and threw it down toward the creature's head. It wasn't the most masterful throw in the history of battle, but the monster was large and not moving. It made for the perfect target.

Crack.

The mace's flanges smashed into the skull, cracking it.

The bonedrinker wrenched its face away from the rockface gurgling, half blind, and rushed along the wall toward them.

They screamed.

The selachar wizard shot a bolt of water into the creature's open mouth. The bolt froze solid. Isolde aimed her twinned rays of electricity into the ice and it conducted through the frozen water, into the creature's soft flesh. It stiffened and shuddered, its teeth clenching so hard, they cracked.

Then Alex moved his spell.

Slowly.

Slow enough not to trigger the Mark.

As the electricity passed, the monster opened its mouth.

Remembering the first silence-spider they'd fought outside Coille forest, he guided his spell gently into the creature's mouth. Then he sent it rampaging. The Mark threw every failure in combat at him and he let them come, confident he couldn't miss with his forceball solidly in the creature's maw.

He slammed it into the soft, wounded flesh, battering it further. The monster swiped at its mouth and lost balance.

Its claws ripped away from the rock.

Gurgling, it plummeted from the escarpment.

Crash!

It slammed into the stones. Bone exploded and flesh burst. The creature screeched and writhed, convulsing in the dirt. Then, the muupkaras attacked. They charged the now helpless predator and spread their monstrous jaws. Leaping *into* its cracked shell, they began sucking the soft flesh into their toothy mouths.

The bonedrinker writhed as more swarmed over it like ants on a fallen fly. They clawed at the soft nourishing body parts until the massive monster finally shuddered and went still.

Spellbound, the students looked down in silence at...

Victory.

They all drew a breath.

"Yeaaaaaah!" Khalik shouted, raising his fists like the victor in an arena challenge. He roared something in his mother tongue.

"Yaaaaaah!" Thundar raised his head and roared, punching the air.

Isolde smiled.

The canine beastmen howled.

"Ek-u-Dari be praised!" the selachar wizard cried.

Pride filled Alex's chest, and he mouthed off at the defeated bonedrinker. "That's what you get! That's what you *get*!"

On the ancient stairs overlooking the Barrens of Kravernus, the students of the University of Generasi roared out their victory like gladiators from a lost age.

"Are you finished with your celebration?" Baelin asked, his tone amused as—panting—they climbed up the rest of the way to meet him.

The chancellor was seated on a large boulder, and the two students who had flown to the top of the escarpment sat nearby. They didn't meet their classmate's eyes.

Baelin rose from his seat, his beard clasps swaying in the hot breeze. "Congratulations, you have passed the first test of the Art of the Wizard in Combat. Where twenty of you started, now there are twelve. An admirable performance."

He took a deep breath.

"I must say, I am pleased... But there are things for you to learn."

Chapter 45

Lessons and Gods

"Have a seat. We'll debrief on the test and talk about what you can learn from your experiences today." Baelin waved a hand over the flat top of the escarpment.

Stone benches with curved backs shimmered into being atop the stone. The students poured their tired bodies into the seats, some stretching over the backs of the benches. Now that they'd made it through the test and could finally savour a moment of calm, Alex realized Derek wasn't there. He wondered what happened to him.

He eyed the bench skeptically before dropping down between Khalik and Isolde. Despite her fatigue, the raven-haired young woman was sitting upright, posture perfect. To their immediate right, Thundar reclined on a bench, which he had all to himself.

The four of them gave each other tired, victorious smiles.

Alex swore he wouldn't just bake a pie for Khalik, Theresa and Selina. He decided he was going to feed his entire team so well, they wouldn't be able to move for days.

The chancellor began.

"First of all, you are all here because you defeated the dangers that were before you. Well done." Baelin nodded. "But the nature by which you achieved this varied. I believe that just as on a written test, it is important not only to see that you passed, but also to examine *what you did well* and *what you did poorly*. It is only through these examinations that we improve. It is only through improvement that we survive greater threats."

Alex found himself nodding at the words.

"First, let us get the painful parts out of the way. I find it better to deal with life's difficulties early in the day, and then consider its positives after." He looked to the two students who flew to the top of the escarpment. "Minervus and Rayne."

"Y-yes, Chancellor!" One of them jumped in their seat.

Baelin's lip twitched. "You were the first to reach the escarpment. And that is to be commended. You showed quick thinking in using your flight spells to arrive at the end goal without danger to yourselves. What do you think of your performance?"

"Uh, we got here safely and used our resources to do so," one said nervously. "We did well."

"You performed *adequately*," Baelin corrected him. "Your first attempt to fly to the goal did not take into account your immature mana pools. You are only second-year students, and flight is a taxing spell. It was obvious you would not be able to make the journey from the beginning. Yet, out of instinct and without proper consideration for your current abilities, you made a decision to try, only to discover partway into your first attempt that you could not succeed, and then, you were forced to return to your group. Not surprisingly, this destroyed any trust you might have built with them."

A heavy silence followed.

"I observed all of you throughout the test using the spell I laid upon you. Minervus. Rayne. Your group was then forced to make its way through the Barrens with the added burden of keeping an eye on one another as potential internal threats, while also watching the surroundings for external threats. With your attention split, your group could not defend against the first muupkara ambush you encountered and lost one of your number.

"Then, when you came upon the bonedrinker, you did not have the resources to face it. You two took to flight, leaving your last remaining member to deal with it alone. This allowed you to escape, and I am not one to argue about the morality of leaving companions behind. Some find it deplorable. Some find it a tool of survival. It is up to you which of these beliefs you choose to follow...

"From a practical standpoint, a Proper Wizard must ensure that any resources abandoned can no longer be useful to you. Otherwise, you will be wasting resources in the long run. So, in return for guaranteeing your own safety, you have now very likely made enemies. And the last thing a wizard needs is more enemies. Further, you will now have to go through the rest of the semester with a class that knows you abandoned your companions. Think about how this might affect your future performance or group work."

Rayne and Minervus fell into an uncomfortable silence as their classmates' gazes lingered on them. Baelin turned to the group of fireball wielders.

"Rhea, Malcolm, Shiani," Baelin said. "Your entire group consists of second-years who have all passed the first year of battle-magic. You are trained for combat. Many of you also have skills in the weapon arts, and you used these skills to overcome the threats you encountered through a direct approach. If we were grading you on confirmed kills, you would definitely score the highest. How would you say you did?"

The three battle-mages looked to each other, then leaned together, whispering. Finally, they nodded and one spoke up. "We relied too much on our mana, our experience and magic.

We faced every threat head on, using the magic we were trained in. In the end, we were all almost out of mana when we got to the escarpment. That's why one of our members failed..."

Baelin gave a gruff sound of approval. "That is my assessment as well. You made excellent use of your magic, but once your mana ran low, you became as helpless as any other ordinary mortal. Had you made use of less powerful spells earlier in the trial, had you made use of the weapon arts or even simply avoided threats, then you would have had plenty of mana in reserve for the final leg of the journey. Remember, wizards must use all resources, for mana is limited. We will go over more of this in time."

He turned to the next group. "Caramiyus, Angelar, Nua-Oge." He addressed the canine beastfolk and the selachar wizard. "Two first-years and two second-years with various skills. You performed well in using a combination of stealth, superior senses of smell, hearing, and tactical movement to avoid most threats. This left with you plenty of energy for the final rigours of your journey. You lost one of your number in an ambush, though you tried to protect each other. How did you perform?"

One of the canine folk growled. "We tried to protect the last member of our group. But he panicked during the second ambush and we couldn't save him."

"A fine assessment." Baelin nodded. "You were able to save as many as you could, but the last was unable to master their own fear. Despite him being the most powerful—in terms of magic—of your group, he was the first to fall. In future, focus on expanding your range of magic. At times, only power can solve a situation. The skill is to determine when. Still, you performed very well. I expect great things from you."

Baelin swept his knowing gaze over each of the students. "You will have already noticed that one group did not make the escarpment. I shall not reveal the mistakes of those not present, which leads me to the final group."

He looked to Alex's group, and all of them rose slightly on the seats.

"P—" Baelin paused. "Khalik, Isolde, Alex and Thundar. One second-year and three first-years. You showed cooperation from the very beginning, and used a multi-pronged strategy: spellcraft, falconry, melee combat and distraction. Oh, wait, before I forget."

He made a clutching gesture.

The air shimmered in front of Thundar, and his mace materialized before him. Its flanges were bent from the fall, but another twist of Baelin's hand straightened them in midair.

The overwhelmed minotaur gingerly took hold of the weapon. "Th-thanks, Baelin."

The chancellor smiled. "Think nothing of it. Now where was I? Ah, yes. You used a varied strategy to overcome the threats you faced and minimized them as much as possible. Khalik, your use of your familiar for scouting helped the party avoid most trouble. Isolde, your knowledge as a second-year gave the team the knowledge they needed to react properly. Thundar, your physical prowess and bravery in addition to your spellcraft helped protect more vulnerable members of your team. Alex—"

Alex tensed.

"—your use of a first-tier utility spell—practiced and modified—as a tool of distraction was able to help the rest of your team react to situations and put your enemies down. To the team, what do you think of your performance?"

The team looked at each other.

Isolde spoke up first. "We performed well. We defeated less enemies than other teams, but we were the second group to arrive at the tower. We took no injuries and defeated or drove off any enemy we came across."

"Well said," Baelin nodded. "I must particularly commend Alex. Though he did not defeat any enemy himself, he used a simple spell—a resource most wizards in the height of their power would disregard—to turn the tide of each fight you came into. That is the Art of the Wizard in Combat. To turn all resources into ways to achieve victory. My only critique for this team is that the second ambush you faced might have been avoided with more thorough attention to your surroundings. But, then again, perhaps not, considering the level of experience of most of you. Well done."

He rose from the boulder. "You all will be welcomed into class as the term begins. Remember, from next week on, if any of your entourage would be interested in auditing this course, please invite them. A wizard must learn to make use of all members of a group regardless of their varied tactical strengths. Next time, we will continue to break down how today went for each of you, and then we shall continue with a lecture on general tactics. The week after will be another practical class. Go home and rest. You deserve it."

"Thank you," the class responded, and Nua-Oge said, "Blessings to you, sir."

"I would say that I hope each of your deities bless you," Baelin said. "But... such a thing would not be appropriate for me to say. Come, let us return. If any of you have any questions, I shall wait for a time after class."

The world shimmered back into focus around them, and they reappeared in the stadium. The class of COMB-1000 was exhausted, yet their spirits were high.

Baelin stood at their centre, watching the groups come together for a time and then go their separate ways.

Before his group could say a word, Alex turned to them while the other groups were reorienting themselves from the teleportation spell.

"So! Who likes pie?" Alex grinned. "I'll be baking up a storm for my sister and friends this weekend. And, if none of you are busy, it'd be great if you all came by. We have a place at the southern insula. I'll be making meat pie, chicken pie and apple custard pie for dessert. Seriously, we were awesome today. You should come over."

"Free pie?" Thundar cocked his head. "Sounds like a great deal to me. It's good to celebrate after a hard victory."

"That's great! And you, Isolde? Come on, you've got to come."

The second-year shifted. "Well, I suppose it would be rude to refuse such an invitation, and I do enjoy apple cake." Her eyes bore into him for a moment. "Very well, I shall attend."

"Awesome!" He grinned. "This'll be great. You're all gonna love it, I swear."

He'd been cooking since they had gotten to Generasi off and on, and he'd been using the Mark each time. This would be the first time he'd have a chance to really push himself in the kitchen since he'd left Thameland.

"You promise much, Alex," Khalik said as Najyah fluttered to his arm. "I cannot wait to try your cooking. Today is a day to be celebrated."

Alex agreed and said goodbye to Khalik, Thundar and Isolde before turning to leave the stadium. Then he hesitated, looking at the chancellor. Others had asked him the questions they'd needed to, and the old wizard looked to be readying to depart.

One of his final comments had stayed with Alex. The one about the gods.

Baelin seemed like a potentially valuable resource for later when he began looking into the mysteries of Thameland... For now, he felt it would be premature to ask those sorts of questions. Anything that might be related to him, the Ravener, Thameland or the Fool could wait until trust was built. If it was built at all.

But there was one question he could ask now. One he'd been curious about for weeks.

He approached the chancellor. "Um, Cha—er, Baelin."

The chancellor looked down at him with those ancient, soul-piercing eyes. "Yes, Alex? Good job today, by the way."

"Um, thank you, sir. Uh... about what you said at the end. About deities... Why is there no divinity on campus? Why are the priests not allowed near Generasi?"

Baelin looked at Alex for a long moment, almost seeming to become a statue. Like an ancient gargoyle perched on one of the school's buildings. "Do you follow Uldar, Alex?"

"Er, yes," Alex said, though the Traveller came to his mind. She'd done a lot more for him, even passively, than Uldar had lately.

"Are you devout in your worship?"

Alex thought about that. "Not... not as much as others."

"Then I will speak candidly, since you asked." Baelin looked to the sky, and for a moment, a dark rage crossed his face with such intensity that Alex took a step back. "I have lived a long time." His voice sounded as old as the earth. "And have seen many things. Over time, I have come to certain conclusions. One... is that deities are *parasites*."

Alex gasped, less at the words and more at the sheer amount of venom in them.

"They are no more than overgrown mana vampires that suck faith and spirit." As Baelin spoke, each word seemed to echo from an impossible age. "Most sit on their thrones watching the world, its triumphs and troubles, from a distance. Some sleep and do nothing, and others just take, only visiting cruelty upon their followers. They are mighty, but how does that make them different from a sufficiently practiced user of magic or a ruler of spirits or demons? Or even a mortal tyrant?

"Yet, they claim rulership over the soul. It sits poorly with me. It was my decision to set the policy that bans priests from campus. Wizards are to master the strands of the cosmic tapestry even as a warrior masters a blade, or a painter their brush. There is no need to muddy up life's journey with beings that take, and then only give back irresponsibly."

His lips tightened. "They hand lumps of power to their priests like a father handing a child a sharpened sword. Some are good, but they still claim lordship over a universe that could continue spinning long after they have all died."

He glanced at Alex. "Cultivation is an example where mortals can access the power known as Divinity without the need of deities. They are simply gatekeepers to a power that can be open to all."

Alex swallowed. "I-I see."

The chancellor smiled. "Ah, hear me prattle on. Pay no heed to my words, and go have yourself a rest. You've got enough to worry about in the upcoming semester."

With that, the old wizard gave him a final nod, shimmered and stepped back into the air, vanishing from the stadium.

He left behind a young man who had gained an answer.

And many more questions.

Chapter 46

A Pie Party

At last, he had all the components needed for his greatest masterpiece yet. Grinning like an evil warlord in an old legend, Alex Roth gloated over the fruits of his labour.

From outside this place of incredible heat, he heard groans of misery. Students had dragged themselves from their beds at midday, most the worse for wear from partying the night before. Wine bottles filled the tables, benches and ground of the courtyard, where a muttering groundskeeper was cleaning up.

The hungover students wandered toward the eatery or other places, but most importantly, they avoided the insula's kitchen.

Good.

Alex would need it for his ultimate project.

His ingredients lay before him.

Finely ground flour. Fresh custard and apples. A large cut of mutton. Two whole chickens. Salt. Pepper. Vegetables. Condiments and spices both familiar and new. He was ready.

It was pie time.

The first thing he'd started was the gravy.

He'd placed meaty mutton bones in one large cauldron and

chicken bones in another, filled them with fresh water, and set them to simmer yesterday afternoon, until the two pots of broth were done. Now that the meat was falling off the bones, he'd restarted the pot and began adding herbs, spices and vegetables: garlic, onions, and other root vegetables.

In the meantime, he'd stacked wood under a grill in preparation to start a fire. He spooned flour into a large cast-iron pan and set it on the grill, then gathering flint and tinder, set the wood on fire. Soon, a roaring flame blazed beneath the grill and he began stirring the dry flour. He stirred slowly and carefully to avoid whipping the fine dust into the air. Flour was flammable, and if enough kicked up in an enclosed space, it would explode. Blowing up the insular kitchen probably wouldn't be very well received.

McHarris had driven the need for extra care into his head. He always remembered the baker's warnings whenever he was cooking. As he stirred the browning flour, he wondered if other students knew how important it was to be extra-careful in the kitchen. The last thing that needed to be mixed was airborne flour and the flame-magic in the ovens. An image of drunk students having a flour fight came to mind. Maybe he could ask the residential assistant about caution signs for the kitchen.

Using the Mark, he watched both dishes cooking while it fed him images of previous triumphs in the kitchen. It had *years* of memories to pick from. Alex reveled in his food preparation and seeing all of the successes he'd ever had cooking or baking—large and small—paraded in front of him.

This time around, the Mark's intrusions were only beneficial and would help him feed his guests with the best food he could create for them.

Watching the flour, he stirred it until it had toasted to a nice brown, dry roux, then he set it aside for later.

Next came the pie crust.

"Do you need me yet?"

"Aaaargh!" he screamed, shattering his absorption in his cooking.

He looked behind to see Theresa giving him an amused, crooked smile. He hadn't heard a hint of her entering the kitchen.

Was it his imagination or had she somehow gotten quieter?

He looked her over critically. "You're sure you're up to this?"

From the way Theresa blinked bleary-eyed, and the slight scent of soap from her hair, it looked like she had just woken up and bathed. It was becoming a pattern.

Ever since she had gone to Life Enforcement I, she had acted like a woman possessed. She'd taken her textbook and had been devouring the thing like a wolf over a fallen doe. All day she would hunch over it at the dining table and then wordlessly get up and go onto the balcony.

She would sit, cross-legged, with her eyes shut and stay that way with a bucket close by.

Her breathing would grow quiet—despite her breaths being slow and deep—and would stay that way for an hour at a time. Then, she would suddenly stand, looking exhausted even though she'd only been sitting, and start poring over the book again.

Some days she'd keep at it until she suddenly made a horrible sound, reached for the bucket and coughed up stuff that smelled absolutely nasty. It was only a little bit each time, but she'd always be exhausted afterward.

Yet, no matter how many times he asked if she was okay, she always said, "I'm fine. Better than fine. What do you need me to do?"

Sighing, he looked over to the kitchen supplies. Well, if she said she was fine, he'd just have to trust her. She had said the coughing and exhaustion was all part of the beginning processes —according to her book—so all he could do was believe her.

"If you could cube this mutton and rub some flour on it,

that'd be great. Oh, and debone the chicken. Oh, and cut the apples too if you get a chance."

"You got it." Theresa rolled up her sleeves.

The two of them stood beside each other in front of the counter top. Theresa cut meat, and peeled and chopped fruit, while Alex started to make two sets of dough for the pie crusts—buttery for the apple and custard, and a potato-wheat and herb crust for the mutton.

They stood in contented silence, listening to the sound of crackling fire and boiling broth.

"Is your friend from your class still coming tonight?" Alex asked.

Theresa nodded, her ponytail bouncing as she did. "She won't talk much... We're still figuring out the language thing, but she was excited. Are all yours?"

"I think Isolde—that second-year—might be the only one that might be a no-show. Thundar was really looking forward to it, and well... If Khalik doesn't show, I can just go bang on his door."

She chuckled. "It'll be a full house. Just like back home."

"Yeah." He smiled. "Have your parents written back yet?"

"Not yet." She finished cubing a chop of lamb. "But the post station said my letter might take time to get there. Then it might be longer to get a reply... I wish it were faster."

"Worried?"

"A little," she admitted. "And I miss them."

"Yeah, me too."

"What'd you think they'll say about me?" She looked at him. "You know, following Great-grandfather's path?"

"I have no idea. You think they'll be happy?"

She shrugged. "They were never really interested in that kind of stuff, even when Grandfather was alive and would tell the stories about *his* father. I have no idea *what* they'll say."

"How about... 'Oh, Theresa, please don't split the heavens?'"

She stifled a laugh. "I *told* you, Professor Kabbot-Xin said that *wasn't* true."

"Ugh, so what good is it then?"

"You have no idea," she said, a wistful look coming across her face. "It's like this this... warmth. Like... you know how good you feel when you *just* get over being sick? You spend a week not being able to breathe through your nose and then you can?"

"Yeah?"

"It's like that but better." Her eyes grew distant. "Each time I get a little further, it's like getting over a sickness you never knew you had. The book says I'm expelling years of built-up impurities, and starting to replace it with the lifeforce of the world itself. Can you imagine that?"

He chuckled. "You're really enjoying it, aren't you? Listen to you, quoting the book, Miss 'A lot of books are more boring than the trees they're made from.'"

She winced, recalling an incident at the church school a few years ago. "I still can't believe I said that to the teacher."

"I can. I just can't believe she let you live." He laughed. "Think about it, if you'd put this much effort into learning back in the church school, I think she would have liked you a lot more."

"Yes, but... Ugh, I wish I could have taken it all a bit more seriously, it's just... A lot of books made me want to sleep. It was fine when we were learning about other realms or more practical stuff, but 'the philosophe of Uldar's sects?' I just couldn't."

"Hey, you don't like cabbage, right? Well, to me, it was like eating the cabbage so you could have dessert."

"Maybe I just needed to find the right kind of cabbage, then," she said. "Like this course. It hasn't even really started yet and I already wish it would never end."

He smiled, watching her from the side. "I'm glad you're happy."

"I *am* happy. Very happy. And you?"

"Yeah," he said. "Yeah, I really am."

Another period of peaceful silence passed.

"Hey, could you pass me that cleaver?" Theresa asked. "Gotta split this bone before I can cut it out."

"On it."

Concentrating, he slowly built the spell array for forcedisk. Focusing on the parts of the array that were growing more familiar with practice, he completed the mana circuit in about twenty seconds.

The forcedisk came to life a lot more solid than it had been when he'd conjured it for the first time.

Willing the crimson glowing disk into the air, it floated across the kitchen, slid beneath a cleaver hanging from a hook high on the wall, and balanced the blade on top of itself. It floated over to Theresa, who took the cleaver and then—seemingly unsure—gave the disk a gentle pat like it was a small cat.

"Er, thanks," she said. "Hey, you're getting better with that. It's a lot faster than it was earlier in the week."

Chnk!

She split the bone.

"You noticed? Awesome." He felt a little flutter of pride. "I've been practicing a lot with it. It's pretty similar to my forceball spell. That's the thing with studying spells from the same school. Different parts of the spell arrays are the same, so if you—"

She nodded, listening intently despite the fact he'd excitedly told her that part a half a dozen times already. A little smile touched her lips.

"—Once I got the initial parts down, it's been pretty easy to figure out the rest." He kneaded the dough into a nice consistency, following and building on all the most successful little movements of his hands the Mark showed him. "Even with... distractions."

She nodded, understanding what he meant by 'distractions.'

"Has..." He changed topics. "Has Selina said anything to you that I should know?"

"No." She shook her head. "She's still into her book, still talking about how excited she is for school."

"She didn't say anything about the beastarium?"

Theresa shook her head. "She seems... fine."

"Yeah, that's all she said when I talked to her about it too."

"She's okay, Alex. She's tough."

"Yeah, I know, but I worry." He set aside one disk of dough to be kneaded later, and started on the next. "At least she seems happy."

Hopefully, things would stay that way. At least, for a while.

A very stiff knock sounded from the door, and Alex rushed to pull it open.

"Isolde! I didn't think you'd make it!"

The tall young woman shifted awkwardly. "As I said, it would have been rude to refuse. Here, I have brought this for your table." She held out a jar. "Strawberry marmalade, sent from the countryside near my home in the Rhinean Empire. Do enjoy it."

"Oooo, I think I will." He smiled excitedly at the stuff. "Now, come in! Come in! Everyone else is here!"

The fairly small apartment was bursting with life.

To make room for everyone, Alex and Khalik had hit upon the idea of bringing Khalik's chairs and dining table from his apartment and putting it together with Alex's to get more space. The muscular young man was seated across the table from

Thundar, and both were talking about combat festivals from their homelands.

Shishi had arrived first, and was sitting between Selina and Theresa. The two young women were having a conversation in a mix of slow Common and Tarimite. Each needed to concentrate and repeat themselves to make sure they were understood, but they looked relaxed in each other's company.

Selina's heart had been completely captured by Najyah, who rested on a tall perch Khalik brought over. The gigantic bird of prey preened herself and leaned into the young girl's caresses as she pet her feathers.

Brutus sat beside Theresa, letting one of his heads be pet, while the others looked at Selina and Najyah with something akin to jealousy.

"Everyone!" Alex got their attention. "This is Isolde Von Anmut, the mighty storm wielder who struck down a bonedrinker with a single spell!" Alex cheerily introduced her to his best friend, Selina and Shishi.

"I..." She stiffened. "I did not strike the creature down."

"You hit it with your lightning, right? Struck it, even?"

"Er, yes."

"And it fell down, didn't it?"

"I, technically yes, but—"

"Then you struck it down, congratulations! It getting up after that is no big deal." He waved off her objections. "Now have a seat, have a seeeeat."

He dragged out a chair beside Thundar and across from Theresa.

Isolde cleared her throat. "Erm, greetings, everyone. I am Isolde Von Anmut. A pleasure to meet you all." She stiffly sat in the chair and exchanged a nod with Thundar.

Theresa eyed Isolde's stiletto hanging from her belt. "That is a beautiful knife."

Isolde blinked in surprise. "Oh my, you mean this old thing?"

The tall woman drew the thin-bladed knife from her belt. "It is quite plain. My father wanted me to have one that is more ornamental. Jewels in the hilt and all. I decided for something more practical."

"Practical is beautiful." Theresa nodded. "And I can see its sturdy construction from here."

"How marvellous!" Isolde smiled. "I am no practitioner of the weapon arts, but a blade *is* a beautiful thing. Do you admire such things?"

Theresa got up and fetched both her hunting knife and her great-grandfather's sword. "This one my father made for me when I turned fifteen." She held up the massive hunting knife, which drew Isolde's widening eyes.

"How remarkable," Isolde said. "Very solid construction in that. It's almost a sword on its own... and the *sword*." She looked at it like a chef might look at the finest cut of meat.

"Yes, that is a beautiful blade, Theresa," Khalik agreed, and Thundar leaned forward, interested as well.

Shishi stared at the sword, and then started saying something to Theresa that Alex couldn't understand; for now. Another language he'd work on with the Mark.

But that was a later issue.

"Right! No more blades at the table," he said. "Unless they're table knives. The pies are ready. Today, we have chicken pie and mutton pie, followed by baked apple and custard pie for dessert. You shall all eat like royalty today!"

"Hoho, I cannot wait!" Khalik grinned.

Thundar licked his lips, his nostrils flaring at the scent coming from the balcony, which they'd been enjoying for a while now.

Alex grinned, fetching the cooling pies from the balcony, and prepared to serve everyone. His guests gasped at the dishes, while Theresa gave a knowing sigh.

The pies were monsters. As deep as he could make them and so wide, they could barely be simply called 'pies' anymore. Maybe mammoths might be a better name.

Alex had confirmed there was no limit on how much he could take from the student's market, then completely threw away all notions of restraint. He overstocked on ingredients, and the results were six massive pies—two of each kind—ready and waiting for devouring. The aromas from each had his guests' mouths watering, much to his delight.

He gave an evil laugh. "They're going to have to take you all home in wheelbarrows by the time you're done. Well, let's get you all sorted."

Masterfully cutting a thick slice of their preferred savoury pie, he served them each a still steaming piece. Once they had their first portions, he sat down at the end of the table and held up his cup.

"To all of us," he said cheerily. "We all went through hard times to get here. Study, practice, hard journeys. All of it tough. Theresa and Shishi passed the test for Life Enforcement and we passed the test for COMB-1000. Selina survived me kicking her off the bed on our journey here, Brutus survived me in general, Najyah survived Khalik not roasting her for scaring him, and I just want to toast all of that. Here's to a good year!"

"To a good year," the rest echoed.

After a few first bites of pie, everyone began oohing and ahhing, tearing into the meal with a vengeance. Even Theresa and Selina—who were accustomed to his cooking through years of experiencing it—completely lost themselves in the food.

Sounds of conversation mixed with scraping forks across plates filled the room.

Even Alex lost himself in the delectable flavours of the pies. It was true what cooks said: good ingredients made good food.

The Mark had improved his cooking quite a bit since they arrived in Generasi, and using high quality ingredients really made for a lot of the extra flavour in the meal.

They all found themselves going for seconds, and Theresa and Khalik each had a third, with Thundar eating five slices on his own.

Even Brutus and Najyah were taken care of. Alex had roasted some lamb for the cerberus and eagle to feast on while the others had supper and dessert.

Over the course of the evening, the conversation shifted to all sorts of topics.

"And then!" Khalik said. "Thundar cast a body-strengthening spell and just picked up Alex and Isolde like they were two babies!"

Alex and the guests laughed while Isolde turned red despite a small smile playing on her lips.

"I am glad not many were around to see that," Isolde said. "It was most unseemly... Though better to be unseemly than to be dead. Or worse, a failure."

"Speaking of failures. So." Thundar placed his cup on the table. "I asked around, and found out what happened to the last group who got eliminated."

Chapter 47

The Path of Potions

Alex nearly choked on his apple pie as Khalik worked to swallow his. Isolde looked at Thundar as she stopped eating.

"What happened to them?" Khalik asked. "For them to fail altogether. Did they run into another bonedrinker?"

"No... I talked to one of the group. She's going to be in first-year battle-magic class with me. It seems it went bad right from the beginning. One of their members came in wearing a full shirt of chainmail."

Isolde twitched.

"He kept it on for a while, trying to tough out the heat, and finally took it off when the thing was about to cook him," Thundar grunted. "He didn't have the best reputation, so people were already annoyed with him. They were splitting their attention between him and potential enemies. Got ambushed. He went down first, broke their formation, and the muupkaras swarmed. End of course for all."

"Oo," Khalik made a face. "I am glad none of us were in *that* group. Hm? Isolde, you alright?"

"Oh, yes, fine." She immediately went back to her pie.

Alex frowned. So *that* was what happened to Derek. He'd have to keep that information in mind. If this Derek was going to be retaking POTI-1000, they could end up in the same class, and he'd probably be looking for easy ways to pass. If he was inclined to cheat again, Alex would prefer to stay as far away from him as possible.

Alex stared up in shock, wondering if he had been truly cursed by Uldar.

The last week had passed quickly, almost in a blink, and he'd made advances with both his forceball and forcedisk spells. Learning the forceball so thoroughly was making mastering the forcedisk easier, and he was starting to consider moving to Wizard's Hand in the next week or so.

With repetitions, his reading comprehension and speed had increased sharply, and he'd completely finished *Dexter's General Alchemy of Potions.* Some parts toward the beginning of the book were in his memory so solidly, he might've been able to quote the first fifty pages on command.

Selina would be starting her first day of school the next day, Theresa was attending her geography class, and there hadn't been any news from Thameland.

He'd come to POTI-1000 with a spring in his step, first to arrive, and found a seat in the second row from the front, on the far end. He was ready for the semester and to begin his quest to advance enough to research the dungeon cores in earnest.

And then *he'd* walked in.

By some infernal luck, the newcomer kept walking past the other students filing into the class, passing row after row while Alex willed him to stop. He'd paused in front of the second row as an increasingly panicked Alex had switched from willing him to stop, to willing him to keep going to the first row.

And he had kept going.

Right into the second row.

All the way down.

The newcomer's eyes had lit up with recognition, to Alex's horror.

And then he'd dropped his bag on the long desk at the seat next to Alex.

"Hello, stranger," Derek Warren said with a thin smile. "I remember you from COMB-1000."

The second-year sank down into the seat beside him, while Alex wondered if Uldar was sending divine punishment after him, after all.

"It's nice to meet a familiar face." Derek smoothed his long, red hair and caught it up into a ponytail. "Thought I'd know no one in the first-year class."

'Still don't,' Alex nearly said before catching himself.

The last thing he needed was to get involved with this known cheater. He glanced up to the front of the class. Professor Jules was still setting up, drawing familiar formulae from Dexter's textbook. In front of her were a line of flasks filled with coloured liquids halfway to the top.

She had thrown a few curious glances at Alex as he'd filed into the room, and her expression had become a mask of neutrality when Derek entered. He'd seen that expression before on teachers when facing a student they quite *obviously* did not like.

Yeah, it would be bad news getting even remotely involved with this guy.

"Uh, you were in my class?" Alex asked. Remembering people's names often made them friendlier toward you and, by the same token, forgetting people often put them off.

Derek's cheer faded slightly. "Yes, I was, though I didn't make the cut. I heard you did, though. I heard the chancellor praised you, a first-year, specifically."

That caught Alex off guard. "People are talking about me?"

"Classmates talk to classmates, and those classmates talk to friends. Then those friends talk to *their* friends, and some of *their* friends happen to be *my* friends," Derek said. "Word gets around. It's like that in all institutions. When I was a page for the duke my father served, there were many other pages serving at the same time, and no one could *sneeze* without all the others knowing. Especially if you learned how to listen."

"Uh, I wouldn't know anything about that," Alex said.

"Ah, my manners are deserting me." The second-year extended a hand toward Alex. "Derek Warren, second son to Count Theodoric Warren of the Rhinean Empire. And you...?"

Alex's mind worked. The urge to tell him, 'My name is *Piss Off*, don't drag me into whatever *this* is,' was strong, but he suppressed the urge. If Derek heard what he'd done in COMB-1000, then what were the chances he didn't already know what his name was?

No, he didn't really need to find out what Alex's name was; he was opening the road to further connection. And that further connection would lead to something unpleasant, Alex could just *feel* it. Introductions were sometimes made to start bonds and those bonds would lead to potential favours later. He knew the pattern because that was exactly what *he* hoped to do with his professors.

But what was he to do?

Standing out at the school would be helpful to him as long as it was because of talent. Making friends was great and would help him look normal. If *he* suspected the Fool were hiding somewhere among the students, the first person he'd look for would be a standoffish loner that didn't let anyone get too close.

Telling a random friendly student to 'leave him alone' would be a good way to stand out in the wrong way. And even *if* he would be in the clear suspicion-wise because who *would* want to have anything to do with a known cheater, what he *didn't* need was to start making enemies. Especially noble enemies who were known cheaters. He needed to shake the attention off of himself, in as smooth and quiet a way as possible. He glanced down to a student ahead of him in the front row. A goblin with a massive green head and large ears.

The little goblin was petting a familiar—a brownish-green scaly creature with webbed toes and large teeth. It chirped like a bird.

"Oh, I'm—Oh, hello! What's that little guy's name?" he turned and asked in the same tone Selina would at seeing a pretty bird. He used the Mark to help him craft his facial expression into one of 'distractible curiosity.'

"Eh? Who-wha—Oh, this is Harmless," said the goblin, his head turning around almost 180 degrees like an owl.

Alex kept his expression curious, like he'd actually gotten distracted in mid-conversation by a reptile. "Oh, he looks very cute... um..."

"Kybas," the goblin said. "And he is *now*, but when he grows up, he will be a powerful water hunter. Twenty feet long and able to kill water drakes!"

"I thought his name was Harmless?"

"It is!" Kybas scritched his familiar under the chin. "Funny joke! I am going to feed him lots of body-enhancement potions so he grows up *very* big and strong! And *killy*. Then, when bad guys are running and screaming, I can say: 'No way! He's Harmless!'"

The goblin gave an evil little chuckle.

Alex shuddered, then something Kybas said stirred a memory.

"Wait, body-enhancement potions?" He remembered Thundar's body-strengthening spell. "Are those permanent?"

He hadn't seen anything about that in Dexter's book. The recipe in there said such a potion would only last minutes.

Maybe some of the ones from more advanced books were permanent?

"No, no, they're not permanent," said the goblin. "But if you feed very many to creatures when they are still growing up, then they grow up very *big* and strong. It is an expensive thing to do, but only best for my Harmless!"

Body-enhancement potions helped with growth if fed to young ones, did it? For a mad moment, he imagined brewing such potions and giving them to Selina. He could brew himself a giant sister, a sister the size of Thundar. A giant sister who would find out what he'd done and would have all the potion-boosted size and strength to snap him in half like a twi—Yeah, that was a stupid idea.

He told himself that maybe he *did* have issues.

"Um, excuse me," Derek said.

Oh, right, him. Alex *had* actually gotten distracted.

"Uh, sorry, what'd you say again?" he asked. "Sometimes I get distracted, you know." He glanced to the front of the class.

Derek's smile had faded a lot. "Um, I was introducing—"

"Wait, wait, look." Alex pointed. "The professor is about to start."

He then faced completely forward, suddenly utterly focused.

"Ah, we'll talk after class, I guess," Derek muttered.

Not if I can help it, Alex thought.

"We are about to begin!" Professor Jules called out, drawing the class to complete silence. She glanced around with a pleased look. "Welcome, all of you, to *POTI-1000: The Alchemy of Potions I.* I am Professor Jules, your instructor for this course and head of the potions department. I am so pleased to see so many of you here. Potions is a subject I favour, of course, but it is not one with the best reputation among the wizardly arts. I blame part of that on too many bards' tales. For some reason, so many tend to paint potion masters as dour villains who act against young, plucky wizard boys. Though, I'm certain you have never read a book or attended a play featuring such drivel. As," she coughed uncomfortably, "I certainly have not."

It was clear from her tone that she was lying, inciting a few chuckles from the students.

"But, of course, there are practical reasons as to why potions are not the most popular subject of study among wizards. The art is difficult. It is exacting. It is expensive. It is also a completely different discipline from spellcraft. Studying potions will train your mana manipulation, but it is not a discipline that is involved much in the way with spell casting."

Which makes it perfect for me, Alex thought.

"Spellcraft, of course, involves using mana to make magic circuits. No expensive components are required, and since many potions are similar in effect to certain spells, many view potions as not cost effective. Thus, potion-craft is often one of the orphaned children of the magical sciences. However, the art opens doors to its own great paths of power."

She leaned forward with a dangerously sly smile. "How would you like to live forever, for instance?"

A murmur went through the class.

She turned to the obsidian stone behind her and drew a rough image of a flask. Within it, she drew several symbols from what looked to be different languages. The one Alex recognized was one from the church school that appeared in books that talked about Uldar.

The symbol for Infinity.

"The Elixir of Life is one of the great crown jewels of potion-craft and alchemy, and is one of the safest ways to ensure ever-lasting youth. It is also so difficult to brew, and requires ingredients so rare, that only a handful of confirmed examples have been crafted through history, but—I assure you—if immortality is your goal for practicing wizardry, then you are far better off researching the Elixir than trying to make bargains with demon lords or engaging in the often-dangerous combination of blood magic and Life Enforcement. Those paths generate far more deaths than they do success. With this one? Failures can result in spoiled pocketbooks, but less spoiled lives."

Derek snorted beside Alex.

Kybas' hand shot up.

"Ah, yes," Professor Jules said. "Mr. Kybas, what is your question?"

"Don't explosions happen if there is failure in potions?"

"Of course they do," Professor Jules said. "Wizardry is dangerous, no matter what discipline. You can also cause a mana reversal that destroys your body with spellcraft, be eaten by an otherworldly entity with demonology, or burn out your lifeforce utterly with blood magic. I shall teach you to practice *safely* and *intelligently*. If you do not try to grasp that which is beyond you, the worst catastrophe you will face is a few spoiled ingredients. And in return? You shall open the door to many other disciplines."

She turned and drew a strange apparatus on the obsidian wall.

"Alchemical Magic Item Creation—"

She drew a hulking humanoid that looked awfully similar to the large man-like figure made of clay he'd seen when first entering the city with Theresa, Selina and Brutus.

"—and golem-craft are just two of the advanced disciplines of alchemy that the art of potion-brewing shall help you to be trained for."

She drew a tree and a beast. "The study of monsters and of magical plants is also related to alchemy and potions, and you will learn much of that sort of lore through this course. It is truly a grand, multi-disciplinary approach to magic that will give you a future skillset *beyond* spell arrays. POTI-1000 has a reputation of being difficult, and rightly so, but I encourage you to try your best. Ah, I see we have another question. Ms...."

"London. Carey London," a young woman said from the middle of the class.

Alex's ears perked up. Her accent was Thameish.

"Ah yes, Ms. London, what is your question?" the professor asked.

"You say that one can learn monster lore through potions and alchemy. Has there ever been anyone at the university that's studied the Ravener and its monsters? The Ravener keeps reappearing in my homeland, and I was thinking if it's studied, maybe there could be a way to vanquish it forever. If that's not a stupid question."

Alex nearly jumped from his chair.

"Ah. Yes, this is a year that the Ravener has arisen in Thameland, isn't it?" Professor Jules nodded. "Of course it's not a stupid question. There is no such thing as stupid questions. The answer to that..."

She looked at the student gravely. "...is yes. There have been attempts at Generasi before."

Chapter 48

The Art of Asking Questions

"Almost every year that the Ravener has risen, a student studying at Generasi has sought to investigate the phenomenon to find an answer to your kingdom's plight," Professor Jules said gravely. "Remains of its monsters have been transported here before. As have remains of its..." She paused. "They are called dungeon cores, are they not?"

"Yes," Carey London said.

Alex leaned forward a bit more. So, they *had* been studied here.

"Even some remains of the Ravener itself have been studied, once your champions achieved victory... I shall not tell you the specific results until you have advanced a little more in your studies, but I can say that no solution to ending the Ravener's threat permanently has ever been found through study here at Generasi, as valiant as the attempts have been."

"Could you tell us what they found out about it?" Ms. London asked.

"While avoiding specifics... I *can* tell you that uses have been found for some of the remains, though I am sure not having a more complete answer must be frustrating for you. There is a reason we do not reveal the magical properties or essences of dangerous monsters or their parts before a student is skilled enough to defend themselves against such creatures. Knowledge affords temptation."

She turned to the board and drew an image of a tooth. "If one thought the key to eternal youth lay in the bellies of great white sharks, for example, and research had confirmed this, how many students do you think would purchase a boat or cast an Orb of Air spell over themselves, dive into the sea and try to wrest such a thing from a shark's belly? Oh, and I assure you, what I just said about great white sharks is a complete lie. Don't try it. But, in Generasi's early days, we misguidedly had monster lore freely available to all students so they might gain some familiarity with it.

"What the instructors at the time found was that they suddenly had an entire new generation of eager and unprepared 'monster hunters' racing off in search of precious organs from creatures that had too many teeth. As a consequence, we were left with many, many dead young wizards. A dangerous stretch of wilderness may be left well alone, until you tell someone that gold can be found in the bottom of its rivers."

She smiled gently. "Don't worry, Ms. London, and to all other Thameish students. As your skills advance, you will be granted more freedom. Eventually, you may attempt such projects yourself, if your kingdom and church provide you materials from your Ravener and its monsters. Just because something has been analyzed before, does not mean it's no longer worth analysis from a new perspective and new eyes. Perhaps one of *you* will be the one to end your kingdom's threat forever. The road of discovery has many treasures to find. I think it is safe enough to tell you one revelation, however, as this knowledge does not lend itself to dangerous action. Quite the opposite, actually.

"If I recall the records correctly, *all* attempts to remove a so-called 'living' dungeon core from your homeland have failed. As soon as they reached a certain distance from the shores of your island nation, they crumbled into dust."

Ms. London leaned forward. "Eh? Why is that?"

"I'm afraid no answer has been found. Perhaps getting too far from this Ravener is no good for them. Perhaps you shall find the answer yourself during your academic career."

Alex looked at Ms. London, watching the young woman slouch in disappointment. It was too bad. She was obviously interested in researching the Ravener and probably would have been interested in analyzing the dungeon core with him, or at least finding any research that had already been done in the lower levels of the library.

Unfortunately, that would bring up all sorts of awkward questions. Such as, 'Where did you get the remains of a dungeon core from?' And judging from the prominent symbol of Uldar hanging from her neck, he doubted she would be too understanding of him running away from his 'holy duties' if she found out who he actually was.

Even *if* he told her humans could control dungeon cores and this threw a lot of their history into question, that might only make things worse. If he hadn't received the Mark of the Fool and just simply come to study at the university and some random student had come up to him saying, 'Listen, I controlled a dungeon core. Want to do illicit research with me?' He would have immediately put a good safe distance between himself and them.

Besides, who knew who could be trusted, and with what?

Best to quietly keep an eye on her.

"Well, if those are all the ques—Ah, Mr. Roth."

Alex had raised his hand. One trick he'd learned for getting professors to like him was the art of asking questions. There was a technique to it. Honest, earnest questions about the subject often drew the best responses. A mistake some gifted students tended to make was to ask questions designed to show how smart they were to impress the class and teacher.

In the end, that only served to annoy classmates and the professor who would always know more than the student, no matter how smart they thought they were. Then there were the questions that only showed the student hadn't been paying attention, which tended to also aggravate instructors.

The best questions were ones from true curiosity, that showed an interest in the subject without looking like he was *just* trying to get into the professor's good books.

Luckily, he had just the right sorts of questions.

"I've got two questions, Professor Jules."

"Ah, I'll answer them both," she said neutrally. "Then we will need to move on."

"Thanks, Professor. I heard from someone that feeding body-enhancement potions to growing creatures can make them bigger and stronger. How does that work?"

"Ah, yes, an excellent question," the professor said.

Kybas gave Alex a quick glance, and Alex gave him a friendly nod in return.

"Body-enhancement potions work by pouring mana directly into the body, in order to *temporarily* energize its processes."

She turned to the obsidian stone, drawing a diagram of a person ingesting a potion.

"This can result in increased strength, speed or vitality, or all of the above if higher grade versions of the potions are used. One simply uses particular ingredients and mana manipulation to focus that enhancement on a single physical aspect. For example, increasing strength. The same principle goes for potions of enhanced sight or senses, those that increase virility or fertility—ever popular with wealthy couples or bachelors—"

Several people in the class chuckled, including Alex.

"—or those that increase the efficacy of specific *actions*, such as potions of jumping. In reality, the mana of these potions enhances *all* bodily processes to a certain degree. It is simply that the effect has been tailored to focus *mostly* on increasing the aspect of the body that potion is meant for. In young creatures, one of the most life-defining bodily processes they undergo is that of growth into adulthood. As such, body-enhancement potions—especially high-grade ones that enhance all bodily processes at once—*will* enhance growth while they are in a young creature's system.

"The effects of a few are not noticeable, but repeated doses —a *very* expensive proposition—can boost an animal or plant to unprecedented levels of size, strength, speed and vitality. The Tauzhian Empire used to make a practice of raising a caste of children into a sort of 'enhanced warrior' through a careful regime of training, diet and a constant supply of relatively low-grade body-enhancement potions."

She drew the image of a thin-leafed plant on the obsidian slab. "When those cheaper ingredients for that recipe or potion went extinct, the practice went with it. The ethics of such a practice are a topic for a different course, but such a thing is possible, even though with most recipes, it is prohibitively expensive. There are also potions that can *permanently* alter and enhance the body after simply drinking one, but those require ingredients both incredibly rare and *highly* dangerous; absolutely fatally toxic if mishandled. Now, what is your second question?"

"Um, what's 'golem-craft?'" he asked. "And what does that have to do with potions?"

"Ah, you do like getting ahead of yourself, don't you, Mr. Roth?" She smiled. "A golem is an alchemical construct. An automaton crafted through high-level mana manipulation, specific ingredients and a *lot* of mana. The result is something like an elemental made from clay, wood, bone, flesh, stone, steel or even rarer substances, depending on one's budget, mana reserves and level of skill. They are then controlled by verbal command or—if one is very skilled in the art—direct mana manipulation. A golem can be a powerful servant or soldier to its master, and though the construction process is rigorous, its foundations lie in alchemy. If you have an interest in golem-craft, then I would suggest you pay careful attention in class, Mr. Roth, and develop the skills necessary to produce such marvels."

Alex's imagination went wild at the possibilities.

He thought back to the large, clay humanoid from the city, and how it had carried a burden that must have weighed at least a thousand pounds. What would such a thing be able to do in a combat situation?

His mind flashed back to the Cave of the Traveller.

Back then, he told Theresa to throw the fire-gem at the queen, basically telling another person to engage in an act of combat. The Mark had not bothered him about that. Would it be so neutral with a golem? If so, *that* could be a loophole to exploit, as long as he had the supplies to build such a construct.

"Alright, we will now proceed with the lecture and you may ask any more questions as we go along. First of all, we will cover a general overview of potion-making, followed by introducing you to the Table of Prime Essences—the main reference for categorizing all ingredients that may be provided to you or found in the field. After, we will overview the main apparatuses of potion-craft.

"First of all, let us talk about how potions are categorized. Much like spells, they use a tier system starting from first to ninth. Spellcraft categorizes spells into tiers based on the level of complexity of their spell array, how much space the magic circuit takes up within one's mana pool, the power of the resulting spell, and the amount of mana the spell requires. Potion-craft is similarly categorized based on the amount of mana required to craft a potion, and the power the resulting effect has compared to similar spells. Dexter said—"

As Professor Jules moved on with the lesson, Alex drew a little doodle on one of the top corners of the page. A caricature of himself standing beside a giant figure like the one drawn by the professor.

The lesson went on from there, and much of it—to Alex's delight—was review, thanks to his diligent reading of Dexter's textbook. He still took careful notes on the lecture, though, since the instructor added anecdotes from her own abundant knowledge. His handwriting had greatly improved in neatness, size, and speed in the last month.

As the lecture went on, he filled an entire page with organized notes, including sub-sections indicating new material that differed or expanded on the textbook's. From the corner of his eye, he noticed Derek watching what he was doing closely, but also looking around at other students in the row in front of him or close by.

Good. It seemed like he was expanding his net, meaning he wasn't the cheater's only mark.

The most fun part of the lecture, though, came during the demonstration. Professor Jules indicated the flasks in front of her.

"What you see here only looks like coloured water, but they are actually suspensions of certain ingredients that have been processed into *almost* complete potions," she said. "I will now demonstrate the application of mana manipulation to finish the final catalyzing of the mixture into a complete potion."

She drew a long two-pronged fork from a drawer at the front of the class. "This is a mana conductor, and it is the key to potion-craft. It is the equivalent to a mana pill furnace, a cauldron of witchcraft, or a sangoma healing bowl, but miniaturized, and not as powerful as any of those tools. It is useful for preparing potions up to the third-tier."

She placed the mana conductor into one of the flasks and gave the fluid a stir. The conductor lit up with mana, which poured through the tines and into the potion, causing the liquid to shine with an inner glow.

"And this completes the potion," Professor Jules said, taking it up and drinking it in one gulp. The class gasped as her skin, hair and even her eyes turned a bright shade of blue. "A potion of pigment." She smiled, revealing bright blue teeth. "As are the rest."

She went down the line, placing the mana conductor into each flask, one after the next, finishing the potions. There would be a flash of light, and the potions would glow before returning to their original colour and consistency.

Each time she drank a completed potion, she would turn a different colour: orange, green, grey, purple and red. Then, the final potion washed away the magical effect, returning her to her normal skin tone. She smoothed her white hair.

"Notice how I held the mana fork for a differing amount of time in each? Even similar potions require different amounts of mana and specific techniques in terms of mana manipulation." She placed the mana conductor down. "Other important apparatuses," she brought up a brass tube with a sharp point, "include the mana vacuum and the waste mana container."

She brought up a large glass and metal jar, covered in arcane symbols. "The mana vacuum is always placed as a safety measure in potions you are crafting. If the reaction goes wild, you activate it and it will drain all mana from the reaction and vent it into the mana waste container. The latter will hold the excess mana from the reaction temporarily, so it can be used for further reactions by attaching a portable mana conductor to it. And—this question is asked every year—no, the mana vacuum cannot drain your mana if you cut yourself on it."

She tapped the sharp end lightly with her finger. "To face such a danger, you would need to stab yourself in the core of your body and activate the vacuum for it to even be a threat. And even then, your mana is so safely tucked into you, such a device wouldn't work at all unless you recently had a conduit opened to transfer mana directly in or out of your body. So, unless you were attacked by a mana vampire in the previous hour, donated to one, or *somehow* convinced one to donate its mana to you, then you would be safe. In such an event, though, I think you would have greater problems."

She looked intently at the class. "Now, as we're nearing the end, your assignment is to read chapters one and two of *Dexter's*, and fill out the blank Table of Prime Essences I will hand out at the end of class. You will be expected to memorize this table for the first quiz, so study it thoroughly. Next week, I will ask you to attend class in the Cells. We will be having our introduction to potion lab safety then."

Class ended shortly after, with Alex jumping up from his chair to line up with other students to ask Professor Jules a torrent of questions. They were legitimate, but he kept his eye on the seats to make sure Derek had long gone on without him.

Slipping out of class, he glanced around, making sure Isolde's former partner wasn't hanging around, then stepped out the door, quite pleased with himself.

"Excuse me!" a voice cried.

He froze.

Carey London, the other Thameish student, was hurrying up to him. The symbol of Uldar bounced on the long chain hanging from her neck.

Chapter 49

The First Classes

"Hey, I recognized your accent in class!" Carey said cheerily. "Good to meet someone from home here, especially in these dark times, when Uldar's voice seems so far away. Have you been to a worship service at his church in the city yet?" Her eyes bored into him as she continued. "I've gotten a group together and we go weekly."

Alex resisted the urge to scream.

His mind worked quickly, trying to think.

"Oh, uh, I um, am fairly private in my worship," he said. "My relationship with Uldar is a... a bit personal."

The truth of it was that he wasn't even lying.

"Oh, that's too bad," she said with a shrug. "Well, if you ever change your mind, the invitation stands. Our little group rents a sky-gondola to go to church once a week, even though we wish we could attend every day. You'd be more than welcome to come along with us, if you like. I just wish they would let the priests come onto campus, though. They receive news from home much faster than we do, and even by sky-gondola, it's still really far to get there. Have you taken a sky-gondola yet? It's delightful! An experience you'll never forget."

As she continued talking, he thought back to meeting the gondolier, Lucia, and the explosion in the Cells as they were approaching the school. He definitely wouldn't forget those two events any time soon.

"Yeah, I didn't think flying boats even existed before I came here," he said with false cheer. "And speaking of amazing things, I'd love to keep talking but, I've got to get to my next class. I wouldn't want to show up late on my very first full day of classes"

"What class do you have next? Maybe we're in the same one," Carey said.

Alex considered lying, but decided against it just in case they *were* in the same class.

"I have FORC-1550."

"Oh? Where's that?"

"Room 103 in the second western tower."

"Oh! My class is on your way; it's in the *first* western tower," she said expectantly.

Alex's smile was forced. "Oh..."

Well, there was nothing for it now.

"We could walk together?" he said, uncertainty tingeing his voice.

"That would be marvellous!" She smiled, as if overjoyed. "My friends all have classes across campus, so it'll be nice to have someone to walk with. Come along then; we can talk about home along the way. There are so few of us here!"

The two students from Thameland began their trek to class, with Carey filling the air with her words. Between her bright, cheery tone and rapid-fire way of speaking, she reminded Alex of an overly animated baby bird.

And about three times as curious.

"Which part of Thameland are you from, Alex? I'm from Wrexiff, in the west. Near Crymlyn swamp. Did you know the Sage was selected from the witches of the swamp? It's a shame

I actually never got to meet her... but yes, where are you from?"

"Uh, Alric."

"Alric! Oh my goodness, that's near the Cave of the Traveller! Were you one of the lucky ones who left through the cave right after our priests consecrated it?"

"We got out earlier than that," he said with a friendly tone while being nonspecific. It wasn't a lie, and the less specifics he gave, the less holes that could be poked in anything he told her.

"Ah, that's too bad!" Carey said. The symbol of Uldar—consisting of the familiar rendition of the god's raised hand—bounced around her neck with every movement. "The Cave of the Traveller was dangerous, and there was a dungeon core there! Did you know that?" She continued, not waiting for him to answer. "But the Traveller's power vanquished it. That made it safe for everyone to use. My family was one of the first through. One of my ancestors was an assistant to the magistrate of Alric generations ago, but we still have some connections. We were able to secure one of the first places through a portal. I am so glad we did, because it was incredible! When the war's over, you should see it."

She finally took a breath, then sighed. "I *hope* it's over soon."

His ears perked up. "You mean it might not be?"

"I don't know." She frowned. "The priests say the Ravener has become *very* aggressive compared to historical records. Building dungeons faster and spreading them wider. Its monsters have been moving to attack any and everything, not just the people left in Thameland, but even wildlife! They say that when it's like that, the cycle tends to be much harder than usual. And also, one of the Heroes is still missing."

"Oh? Which one?"

"The Fool... And don't give me that 'so what' look. Uldar says the Fool has a role to play, so we should at least find them. They've been known to disappear before, but that could mean they could be dead or worse! The Fool definitely has a purpose, as we all do."

Alex wondered what could be worse than being dead, but only said, "And you want your role to be researching the Ravener?"

"Well, of course! It's my duty to give back to Uldar in whatever way I can."

"Wouldn't the priests... not like that?"

"Well, all of their records on what the Ravener has done has to come from *somewhere*, doesn't it? And you heard what Professor Jules said, they *have* allowed the university to research remains before, after all."

He frowned, wondering exactly how far that research had been allowed to proceed. He decided to push a little more. "Do you know anything about any of that research?"

She shook her head. "If the church has records, then they do not share it with the people, likely to keep us safe, just as Generasi's policies are *supposed* to do. But *we* are not the general populace. We can blaze our own paths, I say."

She glanced at him. "Are you sure you don't want to join us in our weekly outing to the church. Uldar's hand *does* reach far, but it must be lonely not having a worship to attend."

"It's alright, I feel he's always with me in his own way."

"I see, I see. It's too bad, though. In these times, the church could use all the donations it can come by, and students here tend to be well off. A 'Campus for Uldar' could do a lot of work here."

"A what now?"

"An organization. Like one of the many clubs or the student union on campus, but one devoted to spreading Uldar's glory and finding donations and faith for him. Since the priesthood has no advocates on campus, it falls to us to take their place. We could create donation drives for the church, worship together and do great works in his name. I was even thinking..."

She leaned closer, like she was whispering a grand conspiracy. "If we had enough members, we might be able to petition the school's leadership to allow the priests onto campus. This policy of banning our priests is most harmful to us."

Alex literally could not think of a worse thing that could happen to him, aside from maybe the Ravener lifting up a bunch of monsters and throwing them all the way to Generasi. Or a mana vampire sucking the life out of him. Or blowing himself up while practicing spells. Or something happening to—

Okay, maybe priests on campus weren't the highest thing on the list of 'Worst Things that Could Happen to Alex Roth,' but it would certainly be *on* the list.

"It's early days, but we've already had a few meetings," Carey said. "Just getting things set up, you know, and organized for later. You sure you aren't interested?"

Alex barely resisted the urge to scream, 'No! Thank! You! And please, never, ever, *ever* ask me that again!'

"I wish you luck," he said firmly though politely, letting her know his refusal was final.

She sighed. "Fine, fine. I won't pester you about it."

He could almost hear the 'for now' in her voice.

"But don't be a stranger in potions class. Ah, this is me."

They paused in a hallway that opened up onto the first western tower.

Carey turned and gave him a polite nod. "If you hear anything about home from you and yours, do share. If I hear anything, I'll be sure to as well. Don't be a stranger, Alex! Ta-ta!"

She waved lightly and quickly scurried up the stairs.

Alex sighed.

Derek Warren, known cheater who seemed to be trying to make connections.

Carey London, an Uldar-devotee who wanted the school to let the priests onto campus.

There would be dangers in potions class, as Professor Jules warned, but for Alex, it looked like exploding potions might be the least of his worries.

He turned, making his way to FORC-1550. He took his textbook and notebook from his bag. The notebook was already filled with notations and observations from his pre-course studying.

As his mind turned from Derek and Carey, it went to something far more pleasant and exciting.

Golems.

Luckily, the rest of Alex's classes were a reprieve from cheaters and Uldar-enthusiasts.

Room 103 was a lecture hall filled with students. Judging from how many were seated at desks hovering about a foot off the floor, FORC-1550 seemed to be more popular than potions. He didn't even blink at the sight of the hovering desks.

The first class was about introducing the students to the study of force magic in general. They were given information about their first lab, which was going to involve the hovering desks, and they had also gone over the required spells for the semester.

Alex felt pretty confident, since he'd mostly mastered one spell—forceball—and was working on the next, forcedisk. Wizard's Hand would after, but he would have time to finish mastering forcedisk before having to pick up the more complicated spell. What he was *really* looking forward to was the spell after Wizard's Hand.

Force Shield.

It was a spell that conjured a stronger version of the forcedisk. It was meant to serve as a floating shield that spanned about three feet wide and could be controlled at will. It always floated to protect its caster. With how strong he'd gotten his forceball, he could imagine how powerful a defensive spell like that could be when he mastered it.

After Force Shield would come Force Missile, a combat spell that blasted an object with a bolt of force. He didn't expect that one to be easy to learn, but Lesser Force Armour would be the spell taught after that.

Mastering Force Shield, Lesser Force Armour and then the upgraded versions, which were Force Armour and Greater Force Armour, would increase his durability tremendously. Thinking about it, his likely order of learning would be to finish mastering forcedisk, then learn to cast Wizard's Hand, and then immediately jump ahead to start focusing on Force Shield. After that, he could return to mastering Wizard's Hand.

The ultimate scenario he imagined in combat would be using the footwork of the Spear-and-Oar Dance, while protected by multiple force spells, and using his forceball and Wizard's Hand for distraction, while forcedisk carried his items.

Or even carried *him*, if he got good enough with it.

His next class was magical theory, and it had absolutely fascinated him, though the reaction of the rest of the large class was mixed. Mandatory classes tended to be like that, he'd heard. Even if the subject matter was incredible to him and some others, there were always those who just didn't enjoy them and didn't want to be there.

The first magical theory class had gone over the general theory of mana. If Divinity was the essence of the gods and nature, and lifeforce was the essence of... well, living things, then mana was theorized to be the essence of the universe. Wizards often said mana was the first of the essences to be created, and that—before gods shaped things to their will—the cosmos was likely nothing more than an endless sea of formless mana.

The professor had noted the bias of the theory. Wizards were the ones who researched and proposed this after all, while priests often said that 'the divine' was first before all things. To Alex, that was some of the fun of it. No firm or complete answer meant more questions. He liked questions.

His next class was mana manipulation and it seemed like another class where the professor was half-trying to scare the students away. Professor Val'Rok talked about how it was a very difficult subject, and how the dropout rate for the course was over thirty percent.

"Look to your left and then to your right," he had said. He was a tall beastfolk resembling a massive, sharp-toothed lizard. "One of you will not be here by the end of the term."

Then he'd paused, his expression taking on a humorous note. "No, that's just a bunch of dragon-shit. The truth is that all of you who *want* to be here will be here."

Then he'd given them the reasons why they *should* stay.

Mana manipulation was the foundation to many sustained spells. The more one was able to manipulate mana, the higher precise control one had over these spells. They would also have an easier time modifying how much mana the spell was fed, and be able to control certain magical items, craft potions, and create constructs, like golems.

He had let out a high-pitched laugh as the students became excited and starry-eyed at all the possibilities. But when he'd gotten into the specifics of how mana manipulation worked, most of them had fallen into confused silence. He'd explained the art was a mixture of precise mathematical control, spiritual awareness of one's own mana, and exacting control of its flow.

It required a *lot* of practice and many were never able to master it. Risks of delving too deeply and causing mana reversals were also present. Alex, who had already practiced it for years through his forceball spell, only saw it as a field of infinite possibilities.

He had been really excited about their first homework assignment. Read chapter one from the textbook and use what was listed at the end to operate a magical practice device the professor had handed out. It was a small metal box covered in magical glyphs. When powered through mana manipulation, the glyphs would begin to glow. The better one was at the *art*, the more glyphs would light up.

The first assignment only required they light one of the glyphs in a month.

Alex vowed to complete the assignment much faster than that.

Yet, even though there was so much he'd enjoyed about his first full day, after the first class—potions—one thought stayed in his mind: Golems.

Throughout the day, he'd become more and more fascinated with them like how most young boys in Thameland became fascinated with the idea of knights. At the end of his last class, he'd asked around campus and had gotten some news that made him incredibly eager.

In addition to being made at the university by some of the higher year students, there was a small workshop in the city that specialized in creating the constructs.

Alex knew where he'd be spending his weekend.

It was time for a visit to the city.

Chapter 50

Familiar Encounters

Sometimes, life was generous with its coincidences.

Alex already believed this. There were times where he'd go through months of everything proceeding as normal and uneventful.

Then, for a period of time, there would be instance upon instance of coincidences.

He remembered a particular week in his life when he was sixteen and it had seemed like everything had become interconnected. He'd been wondering about a historical event one morning, only to find that it was the subject being talked about at school. The Lu family had mentioned missing their relatives in the Rhinean Empire and then received a letter from them the very next morning. Individuals who he hadn't thought about or seen for a long time would appear at the bakery. He remembered wondering what the new Thameland gold coins would look like, then finding one on the ground on his way through town. And there were lots of other incidents.

Those occurrences had been so unusual, he'd spent a lot of time half-convinced Uldar was trying to tell him something through his 'mysterious ways.' Of course, Uldar *would* eventually reach for him—in a much less desirable way—while the earlier coincidences were just that.

Coincidences.

Which was why he was surprised, but not completely freaked out when the sky-gondolier he and Theresa had gotten had turned out to be none other than Lucia.

"Welcome to Generasi Sky-Gondolas, I'm Lucia, your gondolier," she said while they were stock-still in surprise to see her. "Please show me your booking tokens and place them in the box at the end of the sky-pier."

He showed her three wooden tokens—for him, Theresa and Brutus—and slipped them into the wooden box.

"Enter the gondola one at a time, please remain seated and don't push on the wind-and-rain shield." She gave them a glance as she rested against the sky-gondola's pole. "Where're you headed?"

"To Shale's Golem Workshop," Alex said, double-checking the city map.

"We, um, we meet again," Theresa said as she climbed into the floating boat and coaxed Brutus in.

"We do?" Lucia seemed to be fighting a yawn. "I've got a lot of customers. Wait... cerberus. I remember you now. Welcome back to Generasi Sky-Gondolas." Her voice still had that deadened quality to it.

She tapped her pole against the side of the gondola and set them off through the city. Silence descended as it left the campus. Lucia did not look back once.

"Hey," Alex cleared his throat. "I, uh, am kind of glad we got you for our sky-gondolier again."

"Please note that it is against Generasi Sky-Gondola policy to engage in fraternization with or attempt to start personal relationships with sky-gondoliers while you are using our service." She rattled off the policy as easily as if she were telling someone her own name.

"What? No! No!" Alex waved his hand. "No, I just wanted to apologize!"

"There's no need. Generasi Sky-Gondolas puts the client's comfort first in all situations that do not involve destruction of Generasi Sky-Gondolas' property, or direct verbal or physical assault of its workers."

"No, I mean... Look, I don't know if you remember, but you told us that you used to be a student at the university and uh..." He scratched the back of his head, struggling for words. "I was kind of rude about that and your decision..."

"To drop out?" She raised an eyebrow. "I remember this now."

"No, uh, I was going to say, ummm, 'decided to leave?'"

"Why? I dropped out. That's what I did and that's what people call it. Playing with words won't change that."

"Uh, right..." He coughed, looking at Theresa for help.

For some reason, the brave young huntress seemed to have become *absolutely* fascinated with the few clouds drifting through the blue, sunny sky. She wasn't even paying attention to the pair of flying ships that were above them.

He was on his own.

"Well, my words were pretty harsh, from the way I look at it. You made a decision that affected your life based on your own experiences. It wasn't right to judge that and throw words at you while you're just trying to do your job. It wasn't my business. So, I just wanted to apologize for that."

The sky-gondolier looked past him. "We're almost there. Look."

He turned and saw a squat building spreading half a block in width. It looked like a fortress, with heavy stone walls and a roof made of slate. It bristled with chimneys like a hedgehog, which belched lines of smoke, filling the air with the scent of hot iron, fire upon stone and what resembled burning soil.

They were all acrid scents that hit all the way to the back of the throat.

Brutus whined and sneezed at the odours. Theresa petted one of his heads while Alex idly reached to pet one of his other ones. The head turned to look at him for a long moment, but didn't pull away or growl when his hand stroked its fur.

Even if things had been rocky at some points, Brutus and he had gotten a lot closer since their trials in the Cave of the Traveller.

Alex kept patience in mind, just as Theresa suggested.

The sky-gondola pulled into a nearby sky-pier down the street from the golem workshop. Luckily, the district was near enough to the university that there was a very low chance of priests lurking around the surrounding area.

Despite what Carey London would have preferred.

"I'll take my fee now." Lucia held out her hand. "And about your apology. If saying that makes you feel better, then good for you. I hope your experience there is better than mine. For what it's worth, thanks, I guess."

Alex, Theresa and Brutus watched the sky-gondola rise above the roofs, bearing a new load of passengers.

"That was so awkward, I just wanted to jump out of the boat," Theresa muttered as she watched it go. "But, I think it was the right thing you did. What made you do it?"

"I dunno," he admitted. "After Baelin's test, what happened at the Cells and what you said happened at Life Enforcement, it kinda hit me that... this isn't for everyone, as excited as *I* am for it. Plus, like, I'm the last person that should be trying to tell someone else how to live their lives."

"Well, good for you." Theresa smiled. "Though I think she's

the kind of person that'd probably prefer good tips to good words."

He sighed. "That'll be after one of us finds some work. Or both."

"Yeah." She frowned in frustration. "I keep looking around, but there's not a lot of need on campus for hunters that kind of know how running an inn works. Especially in this place. The benches move, the ships fly… I wouldn't be surprised if the inns *wander*."

"Hah." He chuckled. "That'd be a neat job. Inn driver."

"I'm pretty sure that would be Selina's dream life…" She paused in thought. "And, heck, even I might be more interested in taking over the family business if our inn could move."

"I think your brothers would have something to say about that. Pretty sure you're far down the list for inheriting the inn."

She shrugged. "Maybe I could duel them for it."

"I don't think that'd work under Thameland's legal system."

"Probably a good thing too, now that I think about it." She glanced toward the sign hanging in front of the golem workshop: a symbol of a hammer above some sort of glowing pyramid-shaped object. The paint used for the object actually shed a low degree of light. Surrounding both it and the hammer were four figures: one grey like stone, one grey and shiny like metal, one brown like clay, and one covered in stitch designs. "So, a golem is like that big clay man-figure we saw when we first came to the city? And they're built here?"

"Yeah. From what I've read, they make custom golems for people with a lot of coin—and I do mean a *lot* of coin. They also rent out space and supplies for wizards to make their own. Apparently, they don't only do tours for small groups like ours, they also do them for school groups, tourists, pretty much anybody who's interested in learning about them."

"It's too bad Selina's class had that outing today," Theresa said. "She'd love it."

"Hey, they went to tour the countryside on one of those flying ships, so—if anything—*I'm* jealous of *her*. Besides, it's not like this is 'The Wandering Workshop.' It'll be here for her another time."

Theresa laughed.

The interior of the workshop was *hot*.

The front desk and waiting area were situated on the corner of the building and farthest away from the working areas, but it was *still* filled with an insane amount of heat. Unlike the rest of the building, this space had a lot of windows on an outer wall, and the breeze they provided was a welcome relief.

Though it didn't seem quite as hot as the Barrens had been.

"What can I do you fo—" A young, shaven-headed man looked up from the front counter, where he was using a strange pen-like device to etch symbols into a clay tablet. "Hey, is that beast house-trained?"

Brutus gave him a hard look with all six eyes.

"He is," Theresa said almost in the same dead tone as Lucia.

She should start charging every time someone asks her that, Alex thought. *She might end up with a tidy sum of coin.*

It was a good thing familiars and tamed beasts were so common in the city, or poor Brutus might have been less than welcome in many places he'd been allowed into.

"Good, then welcome to Shale's. What can I do ya for?"

"I heard there were tours?" Alex asked. "Held around lunch?"

"You heard right. The dog will have to stay in the waiting room here. It's five copper coins for each adult. No food or drinks allowed, and you'll both need to wear a mask."

"Mask?" Theresa asked.

"Fumes from stone, steel, flesh-warping and clay just to name some of the materials," he said. "Not good for the lungs. Trust me, you'll be better off with a mask, even if it does get hot."

The masks were black, full-face coverings with a long beaked nose and two raised eye holes made of metal and glass. They had a strap that wrapped around the back of the head to keep them in place, and they made the wearer look like a strange, leather-beaked raven. Within each mask, a spell had been cast that continually provided freshly cleaned air.

After Alex and Theresa slipped the odd-looking masks on and burst out laughing when they looked at each other, Theresa coaxed Brutus to 'lie down and stay' in a designated area of the waiting room. Alex began making cawing sounds behind her as they made their way to the opposite end of the waiting area and through a set of iron-shod doors. He only stopped when they met up with another group of tourists.

Their guide was a short, grey-skinned man whose mask had been painted to look like a long-snouted dragon's face.

"Welcome to Shale's Guided Tour," he said with a surprisingly deep voice for one so slight. "I'm Sim Shale, son of Toraka Shale—my mother—who owns the shop. Some of you might be coming here to peek out of curiosity, and some of you might be looking forward to starting a business relationship with the shop. Doesn't matter who you are, everyone's welcome, and at any time, you can ask any question you'd like. There's no such thing as a stupid question in Shale's, unless it's 'do you work for free?'"

Some of the crowd chuckled.

"Alright, touring folks, if you'll please follow me up the stairs in the hall, we'll take the catwalk above the main work area."

They followed Sim into a catwalk above an area full of marvels. At this point, even the Barrens' heat seemed calm by comparison and—to Alex—it felt like he'd just walked into a blacksmith's shop during preparations for a rush order.

The area below the catwalk was filled with ovens, vats and kilns all of enormous size. Materials of varying types were fed in as if each of them was a hungry, fire-belching giant.

Shimmering black buckets full of molten metal, lava or other materials were being removed from the oven by way of immense, high-powered forcedisk spells, and transported to smaller, closed workshops built along one of the walls. While much of the work floor was dominated by this fiery process, there was a section where clay was being transported by the barrel-load to other workshops.

"Here on the floor, you can see all the raw matter being made for golem bodies," Sim boomed over the loud ruckus from work and workers below. "They'll be taken into the back workshops, where they'll be shaped through a mix of spellcraft, good hard elbow grease, and old-fashioned skill."

"How many are you currently working on?" an older man near the front asked.

"All this?" Sim gestured below. "That's just ten of them, and each one will be shipped throughout the world. We've got some for distant wizards, princesses, overlords and even a king. Especially the ones that use higher end materials. They're worth more than most folks'll see in a lifetime."

"And what of the cores? Are the cores made here in the workshop?" a woman asked.

"Oh no, no, no, they're not suited for heat like hell, clay dust, and iron fumes," Sim said. "That work's a lot more delicate, and it's where we'll be going next."

The sweating tour swept through the catwalk and made their way to an upper floor of the complex. Within a sweltering hall, though marginally less than the main floor, were three reinforced doors. Sim glanced at each before knocking on the middle one.

A slot at eye level cracked open and a quick conversation passed between the guide and the room's occupant. Sim turned back to the group, his dragon mask bobbing.

"We ain't completely lucky. One of the cores is close to completion and I thought we *miiight* be in time for the final stage, but at least you'll be able to see the shaping process. Only two of you at a time now. The room's not the biggest."

He stood aside.

Two by two, the tour group entered the workshop. As Alex and Theresa's turn drew closer, his excitement grew like a child's on Sigmus Eve. At last, it was time for them to enter.

The workshop was large, and filled with multiple devices—many of which Alex did not recognize. Some he did, though. What was clearly a waste mana container stood at the side of a work table, connected to a large symbol-encrusted cauldron by a mana vacuum.

The artisan over the cauldron stirred the mixture using a mana conductor, and the raw liquid glowed with a soothing teal light.

It was beautiful. Alex couldn't tear his eyes away from the glowing liquid that would soon become a golem core. He watched its light, he felt... its...

...mana.

He froze.

Still in its raw state, the liquid leaked much of its mana into the air, and it permeated the space around him. It felt... familiar.

It didn't emit a squirming feeling.

It didn't feel antagonistic. It actually felt alive in a way that he'd already encountered.

He'd felt such a mana before.

Just once.

When his mana had come in contact with the dungeon core.

Chapter 51

Help Wanted

"Alright, I think it's time for the next folk to have a turn." Sim cleared his throat behind them.

"Alex?" Theresa poked him, her worried eyes watching him through the bulging lenses of her beak mask.

"What? Yeah, sorry, it's just really cool. I lost myself for a moment," he said quickly. That wasn't a complete lie.

"Happens to the best of us. Golem-work is one of the most awesome disciplines in alchemy," Sim said emphatically as he guided Alex and Theresa through the door of the workshop.

Alex was quiet as the rest of the group went through the golem core's workshop in pairs, and he remained quiet for the rest of the tour as his mind worked on what he just sensed.

The golem core's mana gave off a similar feeling as the dungeon core's, but not identical. It was like seeing two similar breeds of dog side by side. They were the same species, with a lot of similarities, but there were still major differences in them. Also, he didn't know whether or not the dungeon core and the golem were actually related. The similarities could've been only superficial.

He'd learned in school that, long ago, whales were considered a kind of fish because they swam and had fins. It wasn't until an explorer found out that whales could actually drown that the difference was noted. Still, this was one of the first leads he'd gained since coming to Generasi. Since he was going through a 'golems are awesome' phase, it would make sense to explore that question.

The rest of the tour was fairly straightforward, with Sim showing the group some of the individual rooms where they forged the golem's bodies. Each room was dedicated to the crafting of one particular kind of golem. The busiest workshop was for the sculpting of clay into clay golems, which Alex had learned were the most common type.

Next, they visited a pair of rooms devoted to the sculpting of stone, and finally, a room devoted to the forging of iron or steel into massive bodies.

"Clay's the easiest to get a golem core to attach to," Sim said as he closed the door to an iron workshop. "It's malleable and has lots of 'earth' in it, making it easy to get a core's mana to flow through and animate it. Stone's a little harder, mostly because... it's harder."

He paused, waiting for laughter, and a few people chuckled.

Theresa leaned close to Alex. "You think he makes that joke every tour?"

Now Alex chuckled.

"But stone's still a more natural substance than iron, which is processed and tempered from the earth. Steel, of course, is damn hard to get a core to take to, and it needs a lot of mana and careful manipulation."

Sim pointed to a room at the end of the warehouse that was sealed with a massive lock. "The final room's for special orders and materials. Though iron, stone and clay're the most common materials for golem bodies, they're not the only ones. We crafted one *entirely* out of gold for an emperor. Heaviest you'd ever see in your life, I swear to all the gods. Some golems can even change on their own if they encounter the right mana, magical effects, or spells. 'Golem Evolution' we call that, but it takes a core made with materials that can generate a lot of mana and that are able to produce a variety of effects naturally. Chaos Essence is a good example, with its ability to mutate monsters. It's all expensive stuff that's tricky to process."

He shrugged. "In the end, Golem Evolution is a neat process, but—if you just want a good golem—it's cheaper to build one out of stone or iron in the first place than it is to get all the rare material you need to make a clay golem that evolves into stone and then into iron and then wherever else it might go. And for a golem to evolve, you've *got* to start with good, solid clay. Can't start with a stone or iron golem."

He glanced around, noting the engagement of his audience. "Right, time for the last spot on our tour."

Sim took them to a large, well-ventilated office with older, sturdy-looking chairs and a table covered in sheets of paper near the top of the building. Several sweating copper pitchers lined a side table, surrounded by cups. The liquid within smelled strongly of mint.

At the end of the room was a massive desk backing a large open window. It was covered in papers weighted down by paper-weights.

"So." Sim closed the door behind them. "This is the part of the tour where I try to convince you to join a cult and donate your life savings to it." He paused, then laughed. "Just joking, folks, just joking... What I'll be proposing next doesn't involve any brainwashing. To any of you who might be interested in having a golem built now or anytime else, now is when I sell you on using Shale's Workshop for all your golem-related needs."

He then launched into a pitch that would have put any travelling peddler rolling through Alric to shame. Alex and Theresa settled into a couple of comfortable chairs in the back, and Alex's thoughts drifted. He had neither the wealth, the resources nor the skill—yet—to rent out the workshop to make a golem of his own, or order one made by the masters here. Sim's pitch wasn't exactly relevant to him. For the time being.

He leaned toward Theresa. "Want something to drink?"

"I'd love it," she said. "We should also think about lunch before we go back to campus. My stomach's starting to rebel."

"Yeah, I think I saw some places across the street." He pulled himself from the chair and went to the side table with the copper pitchers.

Pouring two cups of minty water, he stepped up to the desk and peered through the window behind it. Across the street were a line of eateries—some were food stalls and some full-on restaurants. There were signs advertising grilled meats or vegetables while others displayed pictures of steaming bowls of stew.

It'd been a while since they'd had a good stew, and his belly rumbled as he took in a giant sign featuring steam rising from heaps of vegetables surrounding a browned leg of meat jutting above the rim of a pot. There were also a few bakeries that looked like they'd satisfy his sweet tooth after the stew.

His eyes lingered on one that caught his interest, but for all the wrong reasons.

McHarris might have been a bully and tried to hide rotten eggs in his baked goods, but the man had always made sure his building's facade always *looked* to be in good repair. Presentation was key for any business involving... well, anything, but especially food. The last place someone would want to buy bread from was a place that looked like a cockroach palace lay inside its walls.

At least, that would be the case as long as there were other alternatives to buy bread from.

The bakery that caught his eye looked like it might have seen better times a long, long time ago. The sign, with its flaking paint, had the image of a faded loaf of white bread being drenched in melted butter. Chipped paint peeled from the wood on the front facade, and the stoop looked like pigeons spent a lot of time there. Some of the shutters were cracked or missing slats, and the general appearance of the place seemed to be screaming, 'Eat here if you want to live in the privy for the next three days.'

Huh, he thought. *Well, that place probably won't stay open much longer.*

The second and third floors seemed to be housing, if the clothes on clotheslines hanging from one side of the alley to the next were any indication.

His eyes narrowed in thought as he wondered if the bakery might be going under.

As he turned away from the window, his gaze fell on the desk and spotted the papers strewn across it.

He paused as his eyes caught the words written on a half-finished document lying at the corner of the desk. It was dated for early in the next month, and the largest words on it were:

'Help Wanted. Evenings.'

"It's *perfect.*" Alex nearly vibrated with excitement. "Think about it, I cou—Agh!"

The stew burned his tongue.

"Slow down, slow down." Theresa raised her hand. "It's as hot as a forest fire in mid-summer at noon. I get it, you're excited, but you won't be able to tell me anything if your tongue's burned and swells to the size of a cow's. And if you're worried about Brutus, don't be; the meat platter from the stall will keep him happy 'til we're done."

"Yeah, yeah." He blew on his spoon before scooping the creamy mushroom and beef stew into his mouth. The restaurant was bursting with people having their noonday meal. A mixture of strong-armed folk and scholarly ones from the golem workshop poured down cups and bowls of stew, followed up with cups of weak wine.

"Listen, it doesn't get any better than this. I can learn all about golems *while* getting paid for it."

"Uh, maybe I don't know how skilled jobs work here, but shouldn't you have some kind of knowledge of the thing you're getting a job in?" Theresa asked.

He waved a hand. "All I have to do is get ready for it beforehand. The job said it needs folk who are good with mana manipulation and have experience with crafting using magic. I'm in potions class and mana manipulation, which'll teach me what I need to know. There's a month before it even opens up for application. All I need to do is get good enough to qualify for Crafting Assistant. It's an *assistant*, not an expert."

She frowned in worry. "Is a month enough time?"

"With..." He paused and she nodded, indicating she understood he meant the Mark. "...I could pick up what I need before it's time to apply. It's *just* an assistant, but it pays *two gold coins* a day. Fifteen days and that completely pays for our lodgings, Selina's junior school and your auditing. At the same time..."

He glanced around and whispered what he'd felt from the golem core's mana in the workshop. She gasped. "Really?" she mouthed to him.

Alex nodded. "We could learn something if I get experience with those cores. Even just being *around* the mana could give us lots to look into. It's worth at least a try. Like, a *lot* of problems at once are solved by this, and if it doesn't work out, we don't really lose anything."

Theresa nodded. "And I guess it's less dangerous than Life Enforcement or Art of the Wizard in Combat..." She had audited part of Baelin's class earlier in the week, but they hadn't had time to talk about it much.

Her eyes drifted up to Alex and they held an emotion that was rare for them to display: unease. A strong unease.

"Is..." She slowly stirred her spoon in her soup. "Is he always like... *that*?"

"Who do you mean?"

"The chancellor," she said. "His eyes... they feel like... like they look right through you."

"Oh, by Uldar, I thought I was imagining that," Alex said, slipping his spoon back in the bowl. "It feels like he's peeling you away, doesn't it? Like there's *something else* in there. But like, when he talks, he's just a nice older guy most of the time."

He remembered Baelin's small speech about how 'gods were parasites,' and his unique philosophy on the Art of the Wizard in Combat in general. Almost every other professor he had met talked about avoiding dangers. Professor Jules kept emphasizing the need to learn procedure and study only what one was ready to handle.

But Baelin? Baelin had just thrown everyone into the Barrens as a test and told them to make it through with what they had. In the end, Alex learned a lot from that test, and students who the course might have been especially dangerous for were weeded out. It made sense from a certain stand point. A harsh one.

"It feels like... he's from a different time," Alex said. "Like all that stuff he says about harsh, barbaric times for wizards; that doesn't sound like stuff he's only read or heard about."

"Yeah, it feels like history itself is talking to you," Theresa said. "But, all that stuff about being prepared for anything *does* make a lot of sense. Even judging from what *we've* been through, you never know what dangers might be lurking out there."

She was interrupted by a harsh, mocking laugh from the next table. A rough-looking bearded man had thrown his head back and was clutching the table for support. Alex glanced over and noticed a falchion in a scabbard at his side.

"One hundred gold?" the man said, his accent harsh and chopping through the words of the Common tongue. His eyes were like steel. "You should've said so in the first place. I wouldn't have wasted so much time making you convince me."

"Good coin here; that's a king's ransom elsewhere," an older woman said, leaning over the table. Her leather apron from the golem workshop creaked as she did. "That's why I wrote to you, cousin. A mana vampire would be no problem for you. You fight by sword and crossbow, not spell. The bounty is always open, and recently, there's been some strange happenings outside the city. Even if it's nothing, there are other bounties. Other monsters. You and the boys would make a killing. Literally."

"Fair enough." The man smiled. "How much is your finder's fee?"

"Ten percent. I'm not greedy, and it's just telling you what I hear."

"Deal. I guess I *will* be moving the band to the wizard city for a bit. Easier than whatever nonsense is going on in Thameland."

Alex frowned.

A mana vampire in the countryside. Or maybe more than one.

"Yeah," he said to Theresa, his tone serious. "We really don't know what's out there. But hey, I'd feel a lot safer with a big golem at our side, wouldn't you?"

Chapter 52

Manipulating Mana and Mind

The box Professor Val'Rok assigned in mana manipulation didn't prove to be a very worthy adversary.

Alex concentrated on it, guiding his mana through the specific pathways built into its inner structure. It was a puzzle in a way. A magical object that ran on mana combined with a child's toy maze.

The glyphs on the side required one to guide one's mana through the specific pathways—in the correct order—and 'touch' the underside of each glyph with mana in different ways. Some would require a sort of twist with mana in order to activate, or needed a slight impact or bop, while others had little energy clasps to wrap one's mana around and pull it in order to activate the glyph.

While the first glyph his class was expected to empower had its activator right at the edge of the mana pathway leading into the box, the rest were behind increasingly complex pathways within the maze. To make things worse, if one touched the side of a pathway with their mana, or engaged with an activator incorrectly, the box was designed to eject the student's mana.

Then it would scramble the pathways within the box so the inner maze would change slightly after each failure.

In the end, students would have to weave their mana—contorting it like an acrobat—in increasingly complex patterns to reach subsequent glyphs' activators, all of which would require different motions with one's mana to activate successfully.

It started off easy and became incredibly difficult as the task continued.

To Alex, the entire device proved to be a fun diversion which also happened to train his mana manipulation. He liked puzzles.

His years of experience controlling his forceball with his mana left him very capable of making it flow in different ways according to his wishes. Then, his experience pitting himself against the dungeon core in the Cave of the Traveller had taught him how to manipulate his mana against a weakened but active opponent trying to stop him from performing a task.

The professor had only required the class to activate one glyph.

He'd managed two—almost three—on his first try.

Then the Mark began to work with him.

Images of all the correct choices he'd made during previous runs flooded his mind, with it focusing less on solving the puzzle in particular, and more on *how* he contorted his mana to reach further into the maze. With this, the act of manipulating grew a little easier each time. His mana grew more controlled and 'shook' less the further he pushed and contorted it through the maze. Each time he ran into a dead end, it grew easier to simply pull his mana back along the path without losing focus or the feel of his energy, and avoid touching one of the sides.

It also helped him become more proficient with the particular motions required to activate each glyph. Again and again, he reached into the box, guiding his mana through its different pathways and touching the different activators. As successes piled up, he was soon able to activate the third glyph, then a fourth and a fifth in the space of an afternoon.

As it became easier, he decided to add in extra challenges when he realized he would likely solve the entire box in a day or so. The first challenge he threw in was trying to maintain the forcedisk spell at the same time.

Forcedisk had also shown massive improvements in recent days.

He used the same process as he had to perfect the forceball spell while the Mark, naturally, tried to ruin his concentration with failures. He'd been able to identify his mistakes, repeat the process with modifications, and build the spell array.

It was getting easier, and the forcedisk was growing rapidly in speed and power as both his skill with the spell increased, and his mana manipulation started to spike.

Today, he would try to combine both forcedisk and glyph box mana manipulation exercises.

First, he conjured the forcedisk, then he placed the box on the disk while manipulating his mana through the maze and the spell at the same time. When he found that to be easy, he began drifting the forcedisk back and forth in front of him, which meant he had to push his mana in *two* directions at once: toward the spell and toward the magic box simultaneously.

That proved to be mind-bendingly difficult at first. It was like trying to write two different things with each hand. One needed to split their concentration into two directions *and* keep two separate sets of movements coordinated while trying to reach two different goals.

The Mark was very helpful here and it aided him in a way that took him off guard.

It began by showing him images of itself helping him in unrelated circumstances, and it took him a few tries to figure out what it was trying to show him. He began to see that each time the Mark presented him with images of successes or failures, it had actually been helping him learn how to split his concentration to take in different information, examine it, and build on it while focusing on whatever task he was performing at the time.

It brought up the times when he directed his forceball while performing the Spear-and-Oar Dance. He had been sending his concentration in two different directions then.

It all came together in his mind and something clicked.

He lit up five glyphs in the training box while making his forcedisk circle his body like a vulture circling a corpse in the Barrens.

"Ugh," he said at the thought.

His concentration abruptly slipped, and all the glyphs winked out.

"Ah, shit," he swore. "Oh, sorry! Didn't mean to disturb you, Theresa."

He paused, hearing no response.

"Theresa?" he glanced over his shoulder at the balcony.

While he'd been practicing at the dining room table, Theresa was engaged in her Life Enforcement exercises on the balcony. Sitting cross-legged, her eyes were closed and her hands pressed to her knees while her chest and stomach rose in deep belly-breaths.

The rest of her body was so still, if it weren't for her breathing, Alex could have mistaken her for a lifelike statue. Though her expression had naturally fallen into deathstalker face, there was a serenity coming from her entire body that made Alex's breath catch.

Her bucket lay close by, but she hadn't needed it that afternoon. She was coughing up that foul-smelling stuff a lot less lately, and getting rid of it seemed to be having a pronounced effect on her.

An inner glow shone from her these days—even after fatiguing training—and her movements had become more graceful and fluid than before. On their long morning runs, she,

Alex, Khalik—and now Thundar—used to start off running hard neck and neck until they tired and then, one by one, slow to a jog, then a walk. Alex would normally be the first to slow his pace.

In the weeks since Theresa started her training, her stamina had grown by leaps and bounds. Where before she would keep up with Khalik, now she was regularly outpacing him, leaving the athletic man behind to catch his breath. Even Thundar—the most physically powerful of the group by a wide margin—started to have to push himself to keep up with her.

Alex quietly continued working on the puzzle box distractedly. He also watched his oldest friend while she continued her meditation until, at last, she slowly opened her eyes. She stretched like a she-wolf rising from her den.

"Was it that interesting to watch?" she asked without looking at him.

He jumped. "Huh, wha—? I, uh, wasn't watching."

A sly smile crept across her lips and her eyes had a dreamy look to them. "Your eyes were boring into me like a mole trying to find its home. Was it that interesting?" She cocked her head, her face a mask of innocence while her eyes were downright predatory.

Alex's heartbeat quickened. Something about that look did things to him.

He did not have issues, he assured himself.

...or maybe he did, but he liked *those* issues.

"Alright, guilty as charged, but how did you know?" he said. "It looked like you were deep in your own pleasant little world. I was making noise and stuff and you didn't budge. I could see Brutus was completely in another world, I mean..."

He glanced over to Brutus.

The cerberus had inhaled a massive meal earlier and had immediately gone into a food coma. Even now—lying on his side—his legs scrambled at the air while his three snouts snarled and snapped at nothing in the room. It looked like he was running and dreaming. Well, that or horribly mauling something to death in his dreams.

Alex chose to think that it was the former.

"Yeah, I think Isolde could drop a lightning bolt beside him and he wouldn't wake up, but you? I thought you could hear me and would've asked me to be quieter by now."

"Ah, that is..." Her eyes grew very, very wide. "Uldar's beard! I must be the *dumbest* person who's ever lived!"

She shot to her feet so quickly and smoothly, the movement looked unnatural, then she rushed inside, closing the door silently behind her.

"Theresa? What's wrong?" Alex asked.

"Nothing's wrong, but something might be *really* right." She sat down beside him at the table, looking so excited, she was nearly jumping out of her skin. She glanced around before leaning in close.

"What do you know about meditation?" she asked.

"Uh... It's part of your Life Enforcement course."

"It's *more* than that, Alex. It's a calming exercise and it's one that can help you focus. Remember you told me how... *the Mark*," she whispered, "basically just smashes your mind with all kinds of stuff? Well, here's the thing..."

She pressed her fingers to the side of her head. "Professor Kabbot-Xin taught us meditation to help us focus our life-energy. We don't tune out the world; we learn how to notice outside things without getting pulled into them. We learn how to manage our thoughts. We let them and outside influences pass as we focus on a single thing. Sometimes it's the voice of whoever is guiding us. Sometimes it's our own breath. Sometimes it's life circulation. But its purpose is to help us focus without getting distracted and falling into outside thoughts."

Alex's eyes grew wider and wider with each passing word.

The skill she talked about sounded a lot like what he did to get through the Mark's brutal onslaught of failures. It was something he'd figured out on his own as a way to help himself deal with his grief and sorrow when his parents died. It had helped him learn how to get through it.

But if *this* was a formalized skill for it...

"Theresa, do you know what you're telling me?" he murmured, vibrating in excitement. "If it isn't considered a Divinity and it helps with letting different thoughts pass... I might be able to use the Mark to learn how to *defeat* the Mark."

She held up her hands. "Now it isn't a magic arrow," she said. "It might not work at all, and even if it does, meditation isn't perfect. One of the reasons some cultivation practitioners make temples in remote places is to eliminate as many distractions as possible. If meditation could work against all distractions all the time, they probably wouldn't have to do that. But... I think it could help."

"Like, I'm sure it will. It's already similar to what I've been doing to get through stuff. And—even if it's got limits—finding ways to build my concentration will definitely help with mana manipulation." He paused. "Only thing, though... is it a Divinity or not?"

She frowned. "I don't think so. I think only the parts of qigong that directly affect the lifeforce are the Divinity part. Like, when a bunch of students couldn't do the ten-minute meditation, our professor said that a meditation club might help them, and she didn't talk about it like it was a dangerous thing. I'd *love* to teach it to you, if you think it'd help."

Alex thought about the idea. As long as it wasn't a Divinity, trying it was a no-brainer. It would likely help him in mana manipulation, spellcraft, combat, general concentration... *If* it wasn't a Divinity.

If it was...

Then it was still worth a try. As long as it didn't interfere with his lifeforce, then the worst that could happen would be having the Mark scream at him. And he was getting pretty used to that.

"I want to try it," he said enthusiastically. "I *absolutely* do."

Theresa smiled and made a motion like she was adjusting imaginary spectacles. "Then, my student, I expect you to follow everything I say."

"Yes, Professor Lu."

She giggled, and then her smile faded. "Alright, let's hope this works. I'll be with you every step of the way."

Chapter 53

The World Opening to the Senses

"The key to meditation, according to my professor," Theresa said, sitting cross-legged across from him on a blanket on the balcony floor, "is that failure is your friend. The point of meditation is to keep concentration on a particular thing, but you will get distracted and your mind will wander. Things outside of your thoughts will pull at your attention. That's all perfectly natural."

"Right," Alex said, watching her closely—something he was happy to do for multiple reasons—and making sure he matched her position as best he could: cross-legged with back straight, shoulders set comfortably and his hands on his knees. "So, you then push yourself past those distractions... right?"

"Not quite." Theresa took a deep breath and blew it out. "What you're supposed to do is *notice* those distractions and acknowledge them."

"Acknowledge them? Aren't you supposed to just let them pass, like you said?"

"It's harder when you just try to do that," she said. "By letting them pass without acknowledging them, even briefly, means they're more likely to 'pop back up.' Your mind is going to *want* to look at them. I mean—Okay, remember that year you peeked at your Sigmus presents?"

"Yeah!" He grinned with absolutely no remorse. It was a good memory and his parents had never found out. A dull pain stung his heart, but it was mixed with happy memories of that Sigmus and previous ones. "Took me two years to find Dad's hiding place, but I did it."

"I remember that," she said. "You were *obsessed* with finding that hiding place."

"Yeah, I really was."

"And when you found it, what happened?"

"Well, I didn't really need to look for it anymore, I had already seen what was there—Oh." Recognition flashed in his eyes. "Right... I got obsessed with the hiding place until I looked at it."

"And then you didn't need to look for it anymore," she said. "It's the same thing with thoughts or distractions. If you just try to ignore them or 'let them pass' without acknowledging them, your mind will drift toward them. It's like... Hey, listen to me, whatever you do, do not imagine Brutus with bright pink fur and wearing knight's armour."

Immediately, an image of Brutus with bright pink fur and wearing a knight's full plate came to mind. He choked back a laugh.

"Tell me, what did you imagine?" Theresa asked.

"Brutus with bright pink fur and wearing knight's armour..." Alex admitted.

"Exactly, and if you don't acknowledge Sir Brutus, he's just going to keep staying in your head. According to the professor and the textbook, you have to acknowledge thoughts *in order* to let them pass."

"Okay, okay." He mulled it over. "I got it. So that's how we succeed in getting better at concentration?"

"No, we have to fail first."

"Right, we're back to that. What do you mean?"

"While we're being mindful of our thoughts and acknowledging them, our minds are going to wander," she said. "It's inevitable. Things catch our attention. At least it's that way with me. But *every* time you notice a new thought or distraction, acknowledge it, and bring your attention back to what you're concentrating on, then your mind gets a little better at doing it each time. Each failure and break in concentration—if followed by acknowledgement of the distracting thought and *gently* bringing your attention back, then you—Ah!"

"What?" he startled. "What is it?"

Theresa held up a finger. "I forgot maybe the most important part of this entire kind of meditation, sorry."

He sighed in relief. "Hey, it's okay. You're trying to teach me something you just started learning yourself. Take your time. I'll be a patient student... Unlike how you were back in the church school."

"Ugh, you were doing so well, but you had throw that in, didn't you?"

He shrugged. "Sometimes my mouth rebels."

"Don't I know it." She chuckled. "Alright, stop distracting me."

"No, no." He grinned victoriously. "*Acknowledge* the distraction—in this case, my clever words—and *then* let it pass."

Her eyebrow twitched. "They will never find your body, Alex, I swear to Uldar, they never will."

Despite her words, he saw she was fighting a smile.

"Okay, I'll stop. What's the important thing?"

"It's about focusing on the *present* moment," she said. "The professor talked about how—during Life Enforcement—your mind will be left focusing on the same motion of circulating your life force through your body. That means, as you get better at it, your mind is free to wander to whatever it wants, and that's dangerous. It makes you lose concentration. She said the key is to not get stuck on ruminating over the past *or* thinking about the future. It's to keep the mind focused on the present moment."

She tapped the side of her head. "Let's say you were focusing on spreading butter on a piece of bread, but you kept thinking about eating it later. Your mind wouldn't be on the task at hand, and if it were something more complex than spreading butter, you'd be more inclined to make mistakes and get distracted."

"Holy crap," Alex muttered.

It was like she had just described the moment-to-moment of how the Mark destroyed concentration and any attempts to practice its forbidden areas. The memories of the failures would slam into the mind so hard, that sometimes it became hard to distinguish what was happening in the moment, and what was a failure from the past.

With his forceball, it had been like spreading butter on toast. He'd been so familiar with the motions, even with the Mark screaming at him, he was still able to cast the spell and have enough mental fortitude to alter it. As forcedisk became more familiar, he was able to continue with that pattern.

But it was still a struggle.

When it came to actions of combat, which he had no experience with, the act of learning the motion *while* dealing with the Mark had proven to be too much. He couldn't manage to let the memories pass over him, and he didn't have enough expertise to simply complete the task in spite of the Mark's interference.

Yet, this meditation skill sounded like its very *purpose* was to train the mind in acknowledging memories and thoughts, and then pull you back into the present.

It could be the perfect weapon against the Mark.

He wasn't sure how *far* it could help him in fighting its influence, but it was still worth diving into.

"I think it's going to be great; it sounds *perfect*," he said enthusiastically. "I think it could help with a whole lot of things."

"And the best part is, each time you fail and get distracted, as long as you bring your mind back to the present moment after acknowledging what distracted you, you get better at it. Failure brings success."

Just like how he'd managed to get the Mark to work for him despite its intended purpose.

"Okay." He straightened himself. "Let's get started."

"Alright, first of all, you need to take a deep breath." Theresa paused. "So, like, I'm learning this myself and everything I just told you is pretty much from my professor and the textbook. You might want to find a more knowledgeable teacher after today."

"Hey, you know me. You know our situation. You know this. There's no one I'd take as a teacher over you, Theresa."

The smile that came across her face could have lit up a moonless night. "Alright, my student, follow my lead. I'm going to try to remember step by step. First, listen to the sound of my voice..."

Theresa led him into the meditation as she had described it.

She told him to listen to the sound of her voice and to take deep belly-breaths.

Luckily, since he'd already been practicing breathing with the Mark, that part felt natural and relaxing. Then she guided him through shifting his awareness, focusing on different points on his body, and paying attention to how each section of it felt in that moment.

He was surprised at what he found.

There was a slight tightness in his head and neck he hadn't noticed before.

A lingering soreness in his shoulders, arms and chest from his push-up routine. Yet, he also noticed a feeling of *strength* in his torso he hadn't been aware of. His muscles felt stronger. He noticed the breath entering his chest—especially as he swelled his belly with the movement—and the sensation as he exhaled. Relaxation swept through his body.

There was a slight tightness and burning in his thighs from their daily run, and also a dull ache in his feet. All these things were a part of his body—a part of Alex Roth—that he hadn't paid attention to before.

His mind began to go down that line of thought.

How much of his life had passed him by without him noticing? It was pronounced with the Mark, but things about his *own body* were becoming so obvious just by concentrating on them, how many other things had he miss—

Oh, wait. He noticed he had become distracted. He acknowledged the thoughts and gently pulled his mind back to the present moment, concentrating on the last part of his body.

The meditation continued with Theresa directing his attention to each of his five senses. He noticed the faded aroma of the bread he'd baked that morning, the sound of students talking in the adjacent apartments, and the feel of his own bodyweight on the blanket beneath him. Sensation fed into sensation, and his awareness expanded around him. He wasn't sure if his senses were improving, or if he was just paying more attention to what they were already trying to tell him, but he felt like he knew more about the world around him in those moments than he had in a long, long time.

The clutter in his mind calmed, and soon, there was only himself and what he was focusing on. He noticed strong feelings of excitement and elation rising in his chest, and he acknowledged them, then brought himself back to focus.

He could bask in them later.

As the meditation came to a close, Theresa brought his attention back to his own body and to his breath, and then—right at the end—told him that he could allow his mind to go wherever it wanted.

His thoughts exploded.

Dozens of plans and pathways opened up to him, and his expectations of the future seemed to shine brightly like the sun rising at the end of a long night. In a mere ten minutes, he had quieted his mind and brought himself in touch with his senses. What would he be able to do once he had put a lot of practice into this?

"Alright, and we're back," Theresa said. "Well, look at that expression on your face. Did you enjoy yourself?"

"Theresa... this is huge. Like... I can't even..."

"Sounds like it had to be really good or really *bad* if it left you, of all people, speechless."

"Are you saying I talk too much?" Alex asked with mock anger.

"No, you talk a lot, which is fine by me. I wouldn't have kept hanging around you if I didn't enjoy listening to you," she said with a sort of dreamy, satisfied smile. He wasn't sure if that meant she was thinking positively about the meditation or about him. As they had grown even closer since their journey started—which he hadn't thought was even possible—he was starting to be more confident that it was the latter.

In a moment of clarity, he started to realize there were less and less reasons for him not to take a risk and tell her how he felt about her. He was becoming increasingly convinced that he was getting signals in return, which was supported by Khalik's not-so-subtle encouragement. Alex Roth had always been the kind of person to only take risks when he was sure things would go the way he wanted them to. There was a reason why he had endured McHarris' abuse for years *until* he was one hundred percent sure the baker couldn't hurt him in any way.

But when were matters of love ever guaranteed?

Relationships were between people, and trying to completely control the outcome of someone else's feelings wouldn't lead to anywhere good. He could pretty much guarantee his own feelings and that was it. Besides, he was diving into the dangers of magic, combat and investigating the remains of a dungeon core.

This risk was nothing compared to that.

He decided then. He'd need the right moment. Theresa had talked about hunts and waiting for the right moment, and if that was how she thought about things, he'd just need to notice it when it came.

And, this skill was all about helping him notice things in the present moment.

His eyes narrowed in thought. "Hold on for a second. I want to try a couple of things."

Concentrating on the Mark, he focused on the idea of growing his skill in meditation. Images of the meditation session rose before him, with the Mark pointing out the times he performed what was instructed perfectly. It showed *how* acknowledging the distracting thoughts helped bring him back to focus, and also showed him the times when he brought his mind back to the present *gently*.

Good. It *would* help him improve the skill.

Now for test number two.

He started to construct a spell array for forcedisk.

The Mark threw his failures at him with all its power, and—though he might have imagined it—it seemed to be trying even harder than usual. Maybe he was just noticing its actions more now that he was so aware of everything. Instead of merely trying to guide his way through the memories or noticing and trying to study the failures, he engaged in the meditation process. Acknowledged each one and then gently brought his mind back to the spellcraft.

He noticed an immediate difference.

Memories he acknowledged and then gently pulled his attention away from were less likely to try and force their way back into his mind. Or maybe they had more trouble trying to pull his attention back to them. Either way, he found it easier to get past those memories with this new skill. Of course, it wasn't perfect. There was a major difference between meditating and simply focusing on senses, and trying to do the same thing while actively engaged in spellcraft while having a magical symbol trying to destroy his thought processes.

It was the difference between studying in a quiet meadow and studying with an angry, drunken bard who had spent their whole life mastering the largest, loudest drum ever made, while he gave a full-on drum recital five feet away.

But, the forcedisk formed faster and smoother than it ever had.

Progress. And a path to fight the Mark.

"Theresa, thank you. Seriously. I don't know how to explain what you've done for me." He smiled broadly, fighting back tears of happiness.

Theresa looked at him for a long moment, as though she were about to say something. In the end, she only sighed and smiled. "It's the least I can do... You helped me find this path for my life. I'm glad I got to do some of the same for you."

Her smile warmed her entire face and her eyes seemed to shine. They drifted up to the sun's position in the sky. "Oof, we should go pick up Selina; she'll be out of school soon."

She was on her feet in a breath, and half-jogging inside.

Alex watched her go with tender eyes before getting up.

A whistle from across the insula drew his attention.

He glanced over to see Khalik sprawled in a chair with one of his textbooks in hand. With a wide, knowing grin, he gave Alex a thumbs-up.

Smiling, Alex gave him a thumbs-up right back.

Chapter 54

Safety in The Cells

The Cells loomed before him across the grass.

Though it had been long fixed, the stone was still blackened in parts from previous accidents. There seemed to be a dangerous energy surrounding the building, one he noticed more strongly than before. He wasn't sure if he was becoming more sensitive after a week of solid meditation practice or if it was just his own nerves colouring his perspective.

After all, today—in his second week of POTI-1000—would be the first day he'd be actually entering the building. Taking a long, steadying breath, he started striding toward the structure. It was his first lab in potion-craft, his first step into a new art, and the true beginning of his journey to make a golem.

Also, it would be his first chance to impress Professor Jules.

Earlier in the week, during the lecture portion of POTI-1000, she had told them the day would start with an explanation on lab safety, followed by the simplest of tasks: learning how to use a mana conductor in order to transfer mana to a special potion that would change colour as soon as mana touched it.

Hopefully, it would be easy, but nerves ate at him anyway.

He took another deep breath, acknowledging his emotions

and then gently pulling his mind away from them. To calm himself, he focused on the mana manipulation box, shifting his hand into his bag to grip it.

He exhaled and let his mana run through.

It rushed into the maze like a trained racing stallion, but with the agility of a show jumper. The Mark gave him his previous successes as a guide, and once again, he broke his personal best for going through the mana maze.

In a minute, every single glyph lit up on the box and he grinned. Each time doing it made it a bit easier. After spending so much time on the exercise, his mana felt like it was flowing like water, and between all the practice he was putting into casting spells and this exercise, his mana pool had expanded.

Soon, it would be time to try maintaining two first-tier spells at once.

If he did that, he would know he was ready to start studying a second-tier spell.

But those were plans for later.

For now, he put the box away and marched up to the building, taking out the round wooden card that served as his student identification. On it was inscribed a new symbol drawn on in class by Professor Jules. It allowed him access to the building during certain predetermined time periods—when POTI-1000's labs were held.

The glowing glyphs on the doorway brightened as he approached, flashing in time with the symbol on his card. There was a click and the iron doors parted, revealing a stone hallway that would have been pitch black if it weren't for the glowing forceballs suspended at equal distances.

In some ways, it reminded him of entering the Cave of the Traveller all over again. He stepped inside, wincing as the door swiftly closed behind him with a firm click. His footsteps echoed through the hall and the stones took on a sinister look cast by the deep, green forceball light. Strange odours reached his nose.

Acids. Brimstone. Burning meat. Fire and wood. Even smells like those coming from the golem workshop. He passed a series of iron doors and from one wafted something sickly sweet and alluring. Something about the scent pulled slightly at his mind, not enough to alarm him, but enough to let him know that something was unnatural about it.

His footsteps quickened.

At last, he reached Cell-207 and pulled open the door.

He had never seen a dungeon before.

Well... he'd seen a *Ravener* dungeon but not a *castle's* dungeon. He'd heard about castle dungeons in bard stories about impossibly attractive, good-hearted thieves who broke out of them to save swooning lovers from grim fates.

Whenever he'd imagined one, *this* room was pretty much what came to mind. It was dark, with more green forceballs to give it a sinister appearance. Again, he was one of the first students to arrive—though not *the* first. His plan had been to make sure he could wedge himself between two other students to avoid Derek and Carey. The few others present looked unnervingly like demons in the shadows and green light.

Mana apparatuses hung from the ceiling or were perched on desks like evil, mechanical spiders. The room stank with faded smells of old potions.

Professor Jules was already at the front of the room, writing the agenda for the day on an obsidian slab. She gave him a quick glance and a nod before returning to her work.

"Alex! Alex! Over here! I have a free spot over here!" a familiar, inquisitive, bouncy voice called from across the room.

Speaking of demons, he thought.

His head slowly turned in the direction of the enthusiastic Carey London as she waved at him from across the room. "I have a free spot beside me!"

She patted the seat next to her, one at the end of the long experimentation tables where they would be practicing.

He sighed. On the one hand, talking to her drained him more than running sprints, but on the other, with her beside him on one end and no seats on the other, there was no chance for any known cheaters to slither into a seat nearby.

There were stools open on the other side of the table, but the mana waste containers hanging from the ceiling would be more than enough to block any views and conversation.

He dropped his bag beside his fellow Thameish student. "Hey, Carey, you all ready to horribly blow ourselves up?"

Her smile twitched. "I, uh, not really."

"Oh no, that was a joke."

"Ah! I see," she said. "Well, Uldar will hopefully keep us safe through today's lab and through all the others during the semester."

"Uh... yeah."

He mentally noted not to make morbid jokes around her anymore. Unless, if he kept doing it, she might stop 'subtly' hinting for him to join her Uldar-centric society.

He placed the idea in the back of his mind as an emergency weapon.

It didn't take long for the rest of the seats to fill up, and he noted there were metal shutters on the *inside* of the windows as well as on the outside of them.

"Alright, let's begin," Professor Jules said. "Welcome to the first Lab of POTI-1000, where you will do much of your learning for the semester. Like any art of wizardry, there is only so much that reading a book or listening to lectures can tell you. True learning comes from practical application. Here is where you will engage in that practice. But in order to do so, and survive the rigours of alchemy—Safety. Comes. First."

She waved a hand toward the tables. "Beneath your work stations, you will find aprons, coats, gloves, and masks. They'll make you sweat like you were on the Barrens of Kravernus, but you will be kept quite safe by wearing them. Please put them on.

Choose your correct size as they will be yours after today, and you are expected to keep them laundered and in good repair. Should they become damaged, please report to the desk in the basement of the Cells for replacements."

Alex and Carey glanced at each other before reaching beneath their tables and choosing the right size of equipment. It consisted of a heavy leather coat—reinforced and treated to avoid chemical burns—with an apron for increased protection. The mask was similar to the ones used in the golem workshop, though the 'beak' was shorter. The gloves were heavy as well, and by the time Alex finished slipping on the whole outfit, he felt like a knight who had just strapped on their armour.

He and Carey looked at each other.

"Well, now I know how a bird feels," he said, pointing to the beak of his mask. "Now if we could only get the flying part down."

"Oh, I think I've heard there's a potion of flight we'll eventually have to brew," she said seriously.

Alex made a mental note not to make *any* jokes with Carey London.

The first part of class went by fairly quickly, as Professor Jules explained the most common procedures in the Cell. Much of which was common sense. Don't taste anything without having her examine the potion first, don't rub anything on the skin, and always wear the safety equipment. She absolutely stressed the importance of *always* having the mana vacuum lowered into the mixing flask during the entire process of potion-brewing, and making sure both the vacuum and the waste container were fully operational.

Not doing so would be grounds for immediate ejection from the lab.

Some things were less obvious, though. She taught them to only smell a potion or ingredient by holding it away from the face and wafting the scent toward the nose with their hand. A process when one was trying to identify ingredients in the field. Another was a specific method to remove gloves that involved not touching the outside of the glove with one's bare hand.

She also showed them a station that magically produced clear, neutralizing water to flush their eyes in case anything got through their masks and the location of the emergency kit. After that, she taught them the importance of washing their hands and equipment at that station before every single lab and after it was complete.

From there, she cast an illusion that floated at the front of the class, depicting a series of scenes that looked to have been simulated using actors, stage effects and simple magic. It was a bizarre display. Each scene went through examples of students not participating in proper safety procedures, and then receiving increasingly horrific and gruesome injuries simulated through makeup and *a lot* of bad overacting.

The entire thing was so over the top, he almost burst out laughing several times. Luckily, he had the sense to not appear like a maniac and kept his laughter stifled.

From across the class, he heard Kybas' voice breaking down in strangled chuckles as the illusion went on. Alex was sure he could make out someone sliding their stool away from the little goblin. It seemed he and Kybas shared a similar sense of humour.

When the illusion finished, Professor Jules glanced around at the entire class. "Did you pay attention to the information? I hope you did..."

With a smile like a scheming devil, she drew a large sheath of papers from beneath her table. "Because we'll be having a quiz on it immediately."

Groans echoed through the class.

Well, that was a surprise, but he had been paying attention to the safety procedures anyway.

Just in case, though...

He focused on the Mark, thinking of getting better at 'lab safety.' Instantly, images of himself putting on gloves properly and paying attention to the illusionary scenes rose up, focusing on the most important aspects of the presentation.

A smile crept across his face.

He wondered what university policy was on using a heroic blessing to enhance one's learning during a test. Would it be considered cheating? Probably not a case that came up very often. Besides, the Mark was using his own memories. He was basically consulting *himself*.

Perfectly legitimate.

At least, from *his* perspective, which was completely unbiased, of course.

Between his own diligence and the Mark's support, he tore through the short, multiple-choice quiz like Cedric through a horde of unsuspecting silence-spiders. The questions ranged from simple at the beginning, to twisted in ways to make sure students were *truly* paying attention to the specifics of the safety procedures.

With the Mark having illuminated details, neither proved to be much of a challenge, and he was the first to proceed to Professor Jules and present her with his finished test paper.

She raised an eyebrow at him as she glanced down toward the sheet.

Her eyebrow raised a little higher as she scanned over the answers, then produced a pen and checked off each question.

He smiled as she wrote and underlined "100" at the top.

"For someone so eager to go ahead of themselves, you surprise me with your diligence toward safety," she said quietly, handing him another sheet of paper. "Look over this sheet and once I say the quiz has ended, you may set up your workstation."

"Thanks, Prof," he said, already looking over the piece of paper as he made his way back.

Thanks to his newly trained reading speed and comprehension, he had the entire procedure read over in detail by the time he sat back down. His eyes paused at a line buried in the relatively simple procedure, and he barely resisted a chuckle as he doodled a small, bulging-eyed fish at the top of the sheet, then laid the paper in front of him.

As the other students finished, Professor Jules graded each test with shocking efficiency, and either congratulated successful students or told them they would have to review lab safety procedures found in the textbook. There would be another quiz for them.

"Alright, well done. None of you did so poorly that I'd have to stop you from proceeding with the next part of the lab. You all now have your procedure sheets. Please set up your workstations and raise your hand when you are done."

Alex followed the procedure written on the sheet—similar to one described in the textbook, just without that second to last line—and placed his potion flask in the centre of his workstation, cleaned it, lowered the mana vacuum into the empty flask, flicked the switch on it into the 'ready' position, and then inspected the mana waste container.

He was the first to raise his hand.

Professor Jules looked over his workstation, giving a nod of approval, and then glanced down at the top of his sheet. She quietly gave him a thumbs-up and a nod before examining the rest of the class, correcting a few of their aparatuses' positions.

When she was done, she addressed the entire class. "How many of you saw the second to last instruction: 'Please draw a bulging-eyed fish at the top of your procedure sheet?'"

The class went silent. Many of them looked fairly comfortable, and a glance to his side revealed that Carey London had been one of those who'd caught the instruction. Alex quietly gave her a nod of congratulations.

Other students, however, immediately snatched up their sheets. Their faces became stunned as they found the hidden line. Professor Jules watched them, looking a mixture of stern and amused.

"All alchemy is about *detail*," she said. "The procedure you have in front of you today is a single page, because you are simply using a mana conductor to activate a prepared solution. First-tier potion recipes can range anywhere from two to ten pages. The most demanding potion procedures can literally fill several books. Every step written in one of those books will be important for your success and safety. Read *all* material carefully, and do not assume you have the answer just because you *think* you've skimmed all of it. Detail. Detail. Detail. Now, once you are all done drawing your fish—yes, I *am* going to make you do it—we can begin."

She went through the rows of students, pouring a solution into their flasks using carefully measured glass tubes, and inspected their stations one more time.

As she poured the solution into Alex's test flask, she nodded to him. "You may begin. Raise your hand when you're done."

Eagerly, Alex took up the mana conductor and lowered it into the potion.

Professor Jules made it one step away from him when he raised his hand. "Done," he said.

Her eyebrows rose and she owlishly blinked several times. "That..." Her eyes seemed to be searching him for a long moment. "Mr. Roth, do you have a few minutes after the lab?"

He couldn't contain his smile. "Absolutely."

"Good, please stay behind."

She moved on to other students. As he watched her go, he caught several people looking at him in surprise. Carey was staring down at his potion while holding her mana conductor steady in her flask. "Uh..." she murmured. "Well done."

"Thanks—" he began to say.

Then he caught Derek Warren *staring* at him from one of

the other seats, but the red-haired young man quickly shifted away from Alex's gaze.

Alex frowned, watching as Derek took a surprisingly long time to change the colour of his solution. His speed compared to the rest of the class wasn't bad, but considering that he had taken most of the course already?

It seemed Mr. Warren had surprisingly little idea as to what he was doing.

And in a field of study like this? That could be *very* dangerous.

Chapter 55

Reflecting on Different Paths

"Mr. Roth, have you studied alchemy before you came to Generasi?" Professor Jules asked.

They were alone in Cell-207, and she was looking pointedly at him. Not a hostile look, but simply an appraising one.

"Um, no, Professor," he admitted. "The only magic I knew before coming here was forceball."

Her eyebrows rose. "You got into Generasi knowing one spell? And you've had no other magical training?"

"A little bit of magical theory from some books, but that's it."

"No training in alchemy, then…" Her eyes narrowed. "Are you taking first-year mana manipulation?"

Alex cocked his head a little. "Yeah, actually, how did you know? It didn't look like that course was very popular."

"It is more common for students who are going to venture deep into potion-craft or alchemy. You're a *very* eager student in this class, so I thought that might be a course you'd be interested in taking. Have you received your box yet?"

"Uh, yeah, I have." He dug the box out of his bag, showing it to her. "I take it you know all about this?"

"I do." She smiled at it. "Professor Val'Rok and I helped design each other's courses, since there is so much synthesis in the skill sets involved, and 'The Box' has been the bane of many a first-year since *I* was a student here. ...Would you kindly show me how far you've proceeded with it."

Alex could barely keep a triumphant grin from his face. "I definitely can."

He poured his mana into the box, watching Professor Jules closely as her eyes grew. She outright gasped as the fifth glyph lit up and whistled in surprise as every symbol on the box glowed with the power of mana.

"My goodness!" she said. "I'm not sure if you have any idea how impressive that is. Many students of mana manipulation have trouble lighting up the entire box even partway through their second-year, and most who succeed with it early have a strong history in mana manipulation." She frowned. "You must have practiced a lot with forceball."

"Oh yeah, for years."

"Interesting. Tell me, how much of the potions textbook have you read?"

He paused, nearly telling her he'd gone through all of it already. Thinking back to what she'd said earlier in class, he decided not to say he had finished the entire text yet. To anyone who heard he'd already studied the whole book before the first month of first semester was over, it would just look like he'd skimmed it. Or that he was lying.

He'd lowball it a bit.

"I've skimmed most of it," he said. "But I know about a third of it in detail. I went through the earlier parts a lot before school even started."

She frowned. "And did you *try* any of the recipes in it?"

"No, Professor. I just read about them and took careful notes. Didn't try *anything* yet," he insisted.

"Hmmmm," she mused. "If I were to ask you what on the Table of Prime Essences would have a mana weight of 142, what would your answer be?"

"Essence of Grounding," he said.

She quizzed him on a few more things from the table and then on certain parts from the front of the book. He answered each as though he were reading the passages directly from the book. Professor Jules paused.

"Tell me, what are the three uses for adult dragon's bile when it comes to crafting potions of body strengthening."

He froze. "Uh..."

He called upon the Mark, focusing on learning that potion, but no memories came back to him. Had he missed that part somehow?

"I, uh..." He scratched the back of his head. "I have no idea, Professor."

"Good," she said. "That's a subject you will not be learning about until POTI-3000. I was afraid you might have been receiving extra information from a more advanced student."

"Yeah, no, not me," he said. "The only second-year I know is Isolde Von Anmut."

"I see..." She continued to peer at him as though he were a particularly fascinating potion ingredient. "Mr. Roth, I would like to—with your permission—cast a spell on you."

Alex winced. "What uh... what kind of spell?"

For some reason, a wild image came to mind: her using some sort of magic to shrink him down to the size of a bug so she could put him in a jar to examine later. He shook off the feeling. No way would a professor do that to a student, would they?

"It is a greater dispel. It will rend apart any spells currently upon you... Do you currently have any spells on you?" she said.

How would such a spell react with the Mark? From what he

could tell, it didn't use mana. Though it was definitely supernatural. Was it a Divinity? Probably? Either way, would such a spell erase the Mark from him? It seemed too easy.

But if it did...

That would be a good thing, wouldn't it? Wouldn't it?

Not so long ago, he would have been fine with anything that removed the Mark. Now? It had benefited him in surprising ways. He wouldn't be so advanced with mana manipulation if it weren't for its help, and even its hindrances were driving him to grow in new directions he would have never thought of before.

What did that mean? Did he *want* the Mark now? Had he just learned to cope with it? Before he could sort any of that out, Professor Jules completed her spell. He felt a strange wave wash over him—like the pins and needles feeling of having a leg fall asleep—but this came from the air around him. Mana drained from his surroundings like oil being forced away by a mixture of soap.

Then it was back. Curiously, he focused on breathing with the Mark.

Images came to him immediately, showing that it was still on him.

His thoughts paused. Was... was that *relief* he felt? Along with slight disappointment? What did that even *mean*?

"I see you have no spells upon you," Professor Jules noted. "Forgive me, but an old trick some students used to attempt is to craft an illusion only *they* could see, which displayed their textbooks and notes before them. It isn't a common method of cheating anymore, but we still catch some. But, no, it seems you simply have quite a talent, Mr. Roth."

She tapped the desk a few times in thought. "Do you still have interest in personal projects?"

"Absolutely," he said. "Lots of interest."

"Hm." She frowned. "I look forward to seeing your results from the next few labs and the first quizzes. If you perform as well as you did today, then we might have a little discussion, after all."

She smiled. "It warms my heart to see a student take such an interest in alchemy and potions. I look forward to watching you this semester, Mr. Roth."

"Uh, thank you, Professor."

And just like that, he was one step closer to examining the dungeon core's remains *and* constructing a golem.

"I swear on all my ancestors," Thundar groaned, his hands covering the sides of his face. "If a lightning bolt jumped out of the sky and struck my battle-magic professor, I think I'd laugh about it for three days straight."

He leaned over the table while Khalik and Alex returned with a pitcher of lemon water and some cups.

"Is he that bad?" Khalik asked, sliding back down into his seat and moving his textbook so it'd be out of range of any drink spillage.

"Worse," the minotaur grunted as Alex dropped down at the table, pouring him a large cup. "Some of the war-leaders in my clan were hard-bitten bastards, but he makes them look like kindly children. He barks like a dog, and every time you have to ask him a question—which you *have* to 'cause he talks faster than a chattering bird—he acts like you're the one with the problem."

"Oof, that's rough." Alex winced, thankful he hadn't taken battle-magic.

Of course, he *couldn't*... But he wondered if he might have, if his situation had been different.

It had been a few days since his first potions lab, and he'd been thinking about his reaction to potentially losing the Mark. When he'd first received it, it had been nothing more than a curse attempting to ruin his life. At the time, with it hindering his spellcraft and causing him to have to go die in a battle he wasn't equipped to fight, there was no other way to think about it.

Now, though?

He was safely at Generasi and among friends. He had made certain choices in both his education and his life that he doubted he would have made without the Mark's influence.

A lot of those choices were doing him quite a bit of good.

His arms—formerly gangly and thin—were growing muscular, thanks to his daily exercises. As the push-up routine became easier, he'd gone to Khalik for suggestions on other training methods he could use. It was then that the powerful young man showed Alex a hidden treasure at the school: a weight-training gymnasium often used by the Watchers of Roal.

Although Alex had only used it once, the way the new exercises hit his body had left him with an elated—though exhausted—feeling, similar to what he felt after a good, long run these days. The Mark had helped him with the form of the exercises.

Then there was the meditation.

He'd come to understand why Theresa was so taken with the practice. The more he meditated, the more he wanted to. It calmed him, helped him relax, helped him concentrate, organized his thoughts, and it continued to slowly help him develop defences against the Mark's hindrances.

Then there were his course selections. Would he have gone so deeply into mana manipulation or potions if he could learn *any* spell? Would he have decided to specialize in force spells or go broader?

He knew, without a doubt, he wouldn't have ever bothered with the Art of the Wizard in Combat.

He also doubted he'd be looking to try and build a golem so single-mindedly either. Likely, he'd just be trying to excel in his studies, looking out for his sister and trying to avoid Carey London's little group.

His life would have been completely different, and over the last few days, he'd become unsure if it would have been necessarily better.

"What troubles you, my friend?" Khalik asked. "You look like you are contemplating the nature of the universe."

"Maybe I am," Alex said. "Maybe I'm about to unlock the secrets of creation, inspired by what a jerk Thundar's professor is."

The minotaur snorted. "You wouldn't be joking about it if you had to be in there with me."

"Is he as hard as Baelin?" Alex asked.

Thundar let out a deep, rolling laugh. "If only he was like Baelin." He closed a massive hand into a fist. "Deep, deep down, Baelin is harder, I think, but Professor Hartman wears it like it's a badge. He's louder. Meaner. Good at what he does, but less helpful."

"Ugh, my condolences." Alex put his hands together like he was praying over Thundar's funeral. "What about you, Khalik? I haven't heard you talk about your professors at all."

Khalik shrugged lightly. "There is not much to say, I celebrate those that are good and endure those that are not."

"Oh no, you're not getting away with that." Thundar leaned forward. "Tell us what you've got to deal with."

"It is no problem." Khalik waved them off. "Complaining about them to my friends will not change them, only make them be with us when we are trying to study and relax." He took a sip of water. "It's better to come together over *shared* experiences, I say. Though that is just me and my choice." He glanced up to Thundar. "Your professor sounds like bird droppings, and I will listen to you vent about him all day, if you wish."

"Heh, thanks," Thundar said. "Alright, enough pitying myself and whining. So, back into the Barrens next week, eh?"

"Indeed." Khalik glanced at the textbook on tactics for COMB-1000. "Deeper, this time too. I look forward to it. There is a spell we are learning in EART-1400 I want to try there, if I can."

"What's that one again?" the minotaur asked.

"Earth and Mineral Magic. It has some neat applications. A wizard advanced enough in it can empower crop yield for a season, at least for a certain number of farms. There are other uses too."

"Sounds fun," Alex said. "Wait..." His eyes narrowed. "So, it conjures earth, right?"

"That it does."

"Say... would you be able to get some clay for me? High quality stuff?"

Khalik raised an eyebrow. "I do not know such a spell, but I am sure a classmate or even the professor could provide some. Why?"

He thought of the golem project coming up, the job opening soon, and a little sister who had nothing to build or sculpt with.

Alex tapped the side of his nose slyly. "Let's just say that I'll be killing more than one bird with one ball of clay."

Khalik groaned openly and shook his head.

Thundar chuckled.

Chapter 56

Naming and Sculpting Futures

"What're you trying to make?" Selina peered at Alex's crooked, strange-looking creation. "It looks like a bug that got run over by a wagon."

"Hey!" Alex grabbed the mostly finished clay doll he'd been shaping and held it protectively away from his sister. "It's my second time making one. Take it easy on me! Besides, yours is... not... that..."

He couldn't finish the sentence. The truth was, hers was *much* better than his.

She'd shaped a three-headed dog that looked like Brutus out of her portion of clay, and while it was a bit rough, the proportions were actually pretty accurate. Only the thickness of its legs were a bit disproportionate to its body, but she'd probably done that so that they could support the weight of the massive body and three heads.

She'd even shaped the heads with tough-looking snouts, and carved little lines to represent floppy ears hanging down.

"Okay, yeah, uh, that's really good," he admitted. When had his sister gotten that talented? Then again, it had been a while since he'd gone into her room and *really* examined her little construction and shaping projects.

"Thanks." She grinned. "It's easy when you have the right stuff. But yours isn't very good. You should start again. You squeezed the arms and legs too much, so they're all lopsided."

"Oh, and you're the expert now?"

"I'm better than you," she said.

His eyes narrowed. She was right. Now the only question was if Alex Roth was so petty that he'd use a deity-provided power to rapidly exceed a ten-year-old girl in skill and then rub it in her face.

And the answer to that was *yes*.

"Gimme a few days. Then you'll see who's the expert..." he muttered, using the Mark while he continued to shape the little figure into something that was at least slightly not-hideous.

"What'd you say?" She looked up from Clay Brutus.

Real Brutus was at the beastarium with Theresa and Shishi.

"Oh, nothing, nothing," he said with a sinister note in his voice.

She looked at him appraisingly. "You're weird."

"No *you're* weird."

"Your clay doll is weird!"

"Hey, don't insult Mr. Clay the Second like that!"

Her eyebrow rose. "'Mr. Clay the Second?'"

"Yeah? What of it?" He looked at her with mock defensiveness. "You name your little dolls all the time."

"Yeah, with good names."

"Oh *really*." He gestured to a doll she'd set on the windowsill yesterday; an earlier creation of Selina's. It looked like an oversized turtle with massive spikes coming off its shell. "Lord Emperor Spikeon? Really?"

She looked at him defiantly. "*Good. Names.*"

"I'll have you know—"

Thump. Thump. Thump.

A loud knock came from the door.

"One second!" Alex shouted, jumping up. He stumbled and caught himself. Lately, he was trying to copy Theresa's thing where she just seemed to glide to her feet from any sitting position, though with varied success.

He ignored Selina's giggling as he opened the door.

"Uh… everything alright?" Khalik said, his eyebrow raised. "I heard raised voices halfway down the hall."

Over one shoulder, he carried a pile of books while he held a large picnic basket over the other. A spicy scent drifted from the basket that made Alex's mouth water.

"Oh, everything's fine," Alex said. "Come in, come in, and you can see how cruel my sister is, and how bad she is at naming things."

"Alex!" She glared at him "Mr. Clay the Second is a dumb name and you know it! Stop trying to pretend it isn't!"

"Emperor Lord Spikeon—"

"Lord Emperor Spikeon!" Selina corrected him.

"It's not a good name!" he insisted, trying to hide his growing amusement at the whole thing. "You can't be judging anyone else's names. You know what? Khalik!"

Khalik placed the basket and bag down on a chair at the dining room table and held up his hands. "I do not know what this is, but I do know I don't want any part of—"

"Too bad!" Alex gestured to both Lord Emperor Spikeon and Mr. Clay the Second. "Which name is better?"

"Er… What name is yours called?"

"Mr. Clay the Second!"

Khalik's uncertainty vanished in an instant. "Alex, why do you bother me with this?" he said in a deadpan voice, though his eyes were amused. "Your name is obviously much worse. Apologize to your sister at once for wasting her time."

"I… Fine, you win this one, little goblin," he said grudgingly.

"Hmph." She raised her chin with pride.

Khalik burst out laughing. "Alright, I brought lunch. Let us leave the clay be and eat before it gets cold."

Reaching into the bag, he produced well-seasoned dishes of hot flatbread smothered in cheese, garlic, onions and spiced pieces of cubed meat. "One for each of us."

"That looks amazing. Did you make it?" Alex asked, pulling out Selina's chair for her as she sprang up and rushed to the table.

"Oho, I did not," Khalik admitted, sitting down at the table. "Half-burning meat over an open fire is the best I can do. I wouldn't inflict my cooking on you and Selina."

"You don't cook very much at home?" Selina asked, tying a napkin around her neck. "Does your father cook? Or your mother?"

Khalik burst out laughing so heartily, it filled the room to bursting. Alex was sure some of the conversations in the courtyard below fell silent.

When the young man could finally stop laughing, tears were running from the corners of his eyes. He muttered something in his mother tongue, and Alex picked out the words 'know,' 'say,' and 'not.'

"I apologize, Selina," Khalik said. "I do not laugh at you, but the thought of Mother and Father cooking..." He had to fight back another laughing fit. "In any case, eat! The both of you, enjoy. This food is best when it is hot, not when it has been left to sit out while we go on like a bunch of old parrots."

Selina and Alex glanced at each other before reaching for their flatbreads.

"So... Who does your cooking at home?" Alex asked.

For the first time, Khalik looked uncomfortable. "We have someone to do it," was all he said. "Hmmm, young Selina, how are you enjoying the junior school?"

"Mmph!" Selina mumbled around a large bite. "I—"

"Don't talk with your mouth full," Alex warned her.

"Mmm." She chewed quickly and swallowed. "I like it a lot! It's like school at home, but there's a lot more to learn. The library has sooo many books!"

"Oho, and what's your favourite class?" Khalik asked, smiling through his beard.

"I have two!" She grinned. "Math and art!"

"Ooooh, we have a little architect growing among us," Khalik said. "And what of magic? Do they teach you so soon?"

Selina paused, glancing sidelong at Alex. "Um, no."

She had an odd look on her face.

"Selina?" He peered at her. "Is there something wrong?"

"N-no." She was obviously lying as she turned away from him.

He frowned. "Selina? What's going on?"

She wiggled in her chair. "It's nothing."

"Oh no, it's definitely not nothing. You have the same look as you did when you brought that toad home in your pocket."

"No, it's not like that!"

Alex frowned. Was she starting to keep secrets from him? Was she already old enough to be doing that?

"Come on, Selina, tell me. I just want to make sure that you're okay."

She squirmed a little more, and then seemed to deflate. "It was supposed to be a surprise."

"What surprise?" Alex cocked his head a little. Khalik leaned in closer in interest.

"Well... They're not teaching us magic," she said finally. "Yet! But, uh... they're going to test us soon. To see how much mana we have and see if we can learn magic."

Alex's heart nearly stopped.

"I, uh... huh," he murmured.

She looked down. "It was supposed to be a surprise. I wanted to tell you if I passed the test and surprise you."

An awkward silence fell on the room.

"Er." Khalik gave a small cough. "Sorry for helping to expose you, Selina, but if it's any consolation, they notify a child's closest guardian for permission before they do the test, so your brother would've known anyway."

"Awww," she groaned. "That's too bad!"

Alex, meanwhile, was speechless.

All things considered, he should have thought about the possibility. After all, it was a junior school attached to the greatest university of wizardry in the world. It made sense they would test the junior students to see if they had the knack for magic.

The question was, what would they do after?

"Khalik, how do you know about the test?" Alex asked. "And what do they do if a child has the mana for wizardry?"

"My eldest brother came to Generasi and learned of the practice," he said, his eyes growing distant. "And as for what they do, my understanding is those that can learn the art of wizardry are given some beginning lessons on magical theory. Simple things that can prepare them for casting spells if that is the path they desire, and if their guardians give permission for them to take the lessons. By the end, it is the hope they will be ready to learn some simple spells when they are older."

"Oh..." Alex muttered, looking at Selina. "Do you want to learn to be a wizard? If you could?"

Something passed through her eyes. "You make it look like a lot of fun..." she said, though there was something odd about her tone. "I want to try it. Is that okay?"

Alex had no idea how to answer her.

Selina learning to be a wizard? What was the likelihood of that? Probably high, if he really thought about it.

Would she have the smarts for it? That was an obvious *yes*. Selina was quick-witted, and she liked to learn, especially about things that caught her interests.

And what about the discipline? That was no question either.

She already spent hours focused on building little models out of blocks or clay. Focus was not going to be an issue.

As for if she had enough mana to do it? That really was the key question. A person's base mana was an odd thing to predict. Sometimes someone with the mana for wizardry would come out of a family that had farmed for ten generations. Sometimes there were entire dynasties that had produced wizards for centuries.

Other times, people would seem to have no mana when they were young, and then an accident, strange phenomenon or years of concerted effort at mana manipulation could generate a mana pool large enough to begin studying the wizardly arts.

In the end, in many cases, a person's mana seemed pretty much left to random chance.

So that left one final question... How would he feel if Selina had the potential?

On the one hand, the idea excited him. If she had the talent for wizardry, she would be set for life. Magic was a powerful advantage that could pave the way toward riches, fortune, adventure, safety and comfort.

On the other hand... Magic was a deadly force. How many times had they been told it was dangerous? In his short time at the university, he'd already seen some of its dangers. The importance of caution and finding ways to keep safe were constantly being reinforced.

Letting Selina go down the path of magic training would be to let her go down a path of infinite danger. Then again, would it be worse to stop her from even trying? *He'd* gone down his path with nothing but an old book, after all. Wouldn't it be kind of hypocritical of him not to let her try magic here at Generasi where she'd be safer than he had been doing it on his own in Alric?

There was also the possibility she might try it on her own in secret.

The whole idea made him nervous, but letting her learn safely, if that was what she wanted, would probably be a lot better and safer. She would be taught by people who knew what they were doing.

"Alright, we can talk about it more if you pass," he said.

"Yay!" she cheered. "I'm going to get a big pointy hat with a huuuge brim!"

"Hah." Khalik chuckled. "We can call you 'Big Hat Selina.'"

"That's a terrible name," Alex said. "Your name-judging privileges are revoked."

"Hey, I might be bad, but you are definitely worse." Khalik laughed. He glanced at the door. "Maybe Theresa would be better at it. Will she be back soon?"

"She should be," Alex said.

"Good, I was hoping we could all talk about the next COMB-1000 class together. It will be her first time in the Barrens."

Alex snorted. "And we'll be better off for it, trust me."

"Oh, I know, but I think it would be better to have some discussion beforehand. It's too bad Thundar and Isolde are busy, but it still will be good to share our capabilities with Theresa so we can move better as a team."

"Don't worry about that," Selina said. "Theresa can beat up Alex, so if he can do it, she can do it."

"That's not the way it works," Alex said dryly.

"Well, her help will be necessary, since we are going to the wild mana vents this time," Khalik said.

"What are those?" Selina asked.

Khalik's eyes looked distant. "One of the most dangerous parts of all the Barrens of Kravernus... and the very lifeblood of Generasi."

Chapter 57

Terrain and Entourages

"A wizard will spend much of their life in hazardous surroundings," Baelin said to the class. "Which you will train for today, with your chosen entourages."

It was another hot day, hotter than mid-summer in Thameland, and the students of the Art of the Wizard in Combat were gathered in the stadium. Despite the loss of some classmates during Baelin's test, the number sitting before the chancellor had grown in the following weeks. Those with entourages had brought them, increasing their number by a few new faces.

The student named Malcolm had been joined by Eyvinder: a tall, bald man with pointed ears and a greenish cast to his skin. He looked like some of the elves Alex had met at Generasi, but his features were harder and sharper, like he'd been carved from flesh instead of being born.

Nua-Oge, the selachar wizard, had been joined by a horrifying looking beastfolk that drew everyone's eye. He was by far the most gigantic beastman Alex had ever seen. The towering Thundar—a foot taller than Alex—and Baelin would have only reached the monster's chest. He was so powerfully built, he looked more than capable of tearing through a castle wall. His skin was a steel grey over most of his body, with stark white over his chest, neck and throat. From the slight hunch in his back emerged a dorsal fin that rose into the air like a knife. His head and neck were so thick, they covered most of the area between his shoulders.

The beast he most resembled was a shark, and his eyes were black and lifeless like those of a doll.

Minervus and Rayne—the pair who'd abandoned their companions during the test—filled out their ranks with five warriors who had come to the university with Minervus. Shortbows were slung on their backs. They were an enigmatic-looking bunch with features similar to Minervus himself, implying some kind of familial relationship. They moved in a way that made them seem like they were the same person.

In Alex's group, only two of them had brought entourage members to join the class. Theresa sat between Alex and Khalik, with both her sword and massive hunting knife belted at her waist. She held her bow over her knees and watched Baelin very closely, her eyes only shifting to look at the newcomers Isolde brought with her.

They had met them that morning. Svenia and Hogarth. Hogarth was a short man built like a boulder. Scars marked a face well hidden by a thick, black beard, long and wild, unlike Khalik's well-sculpted one. Svenia, meanwhile, was as tall as Alex and looked like someone had put her together from iron wire and bear meat. Both were armed with heavy crossbows, broad-bladed swords, and spiked halberds.

They looked hard as nails, but if Alex was honest, everyone's vicious-looking guards and attendants seemed like cheerful babes next to the giant shark man. Even the bonedrinker would have seemed tame next to that burly monster.

Alex looked over the group, counting the new additions to their class. Taking into account the entirety of the new entourage, they actually had *more* people than they'd started out with.

Before Baelin's test, the class saw a mere twenty students enrolled, and the Barrens whittled them down to twelve. Now, ten new entourage members—a full half of them coming from Minervus' group—swelled their number to twenty-two.

An odd thought struck Alex.

Many entourage members hadn't started auditing the class right after the test. A few of them, like Theresa, attended the lectures, but for most, today's practical battle class would be their first class. The surprising thing was they were all allowed to enter without being tested.

Alex raised his hand.

"Yes, Alex, what is it?" Baelin paused his lecture.

"Ummm, is there a test for entourage members, before they can go into the Barrens?"

"No. *You* have all passed the test," Baelin said. "And so, all of you are trusted now, and that extends to those who you are responsible for. You made decisions and adapted to the circumstances of the Barrens, and so I trust your judgment. Besides, you are walking down a dangerous path, and one that you are ready for."

He gestured to the class. "Were I to deny your entourage the privilege of auditing COMB-1000, I would be denying you resources for the class, and the opportunity to experience perils with those close to you, training for those who will accompany you outside of the university, and preparations so that all of you might work together as a group. That is why I hope you have brought *every* member of your entourage."

Alex chuckled. "I brought half of them. The other half is my ten-year-old sister. I don't think that would be a good fit."

He continued to laugh, and a few others, including Theresa and Khalik, joined in. They only stopped when they realized the chancellor wasn't laughing.

He wasn't even smiling.

At all.

"I fail to see the humour, I fear." Baelin's eyes bored right into Alex, making the young man squirm in his seat. "Did she refuse to attend? Of course, that is her choice."

"Uh..." Alex said, his eyes shifting back and forth uncomfortably. "Well, I never offered."

"I see." Baelin's words rang with a flat disappointment. "I am surprised, I have to say. You show a lot of sense."

An air of discomfort descended over the class. Students and their entourages exchanged nervous glances. Baelin himself did not change at all. Yet, he suddenly seemed *bigger*.

He hadn't shifted his position, risen up to his full height or done anything intimidating, but it felt like the ancient wizard became much larger. Like there was an aura coming from him that had spread to fill the stadium.

Alex swallowed. "I... well... She's a child, Chancellor."

"I see. A child." Baelin nodded, his body visibly relaxing. "Of course, of course, a child. Alex, would you mind answering a question of *mine*?"

Alex had a bad feeling that he wouldn't want to. "Uh... sure?"

"Can children die?"

Silence swept the stadium. Not even the wind broke it. In that stillness, every student held their breath and Baelin's eyes seemed to dig into Alex's core.

"I... Pardon me?" he asked, unsure if he'd heard right.

"Can children die?" Baelin asked with the same easy tone as though he wanted to know what the market's daily special was. "Can they be killed? Hurt? Harmed? Massacred?"

A horrible image flashed into Alex's mind at that moment. What might have happened if he hadn't seen the silence-spider in Coille forest when it was hidden in that tree, ready to drop down on his sister.

He forced the thought away, unconsciously sliding into the deep belly-breaths of meditation breathing. "Um, they can."

"They can, Alex. They most certainly can." Baelin let out a long breath. It sounded tired in a way Alex couldn't even begin to comprehend. "And it is not only children." He glanced over the class. "Mothers. Fathers. Brothers. Servants. Attendants. Teachers. The more you grow in power, the more people in your lives will be endangered. Power. Attracts. Attention. And wizards must not only safeguard their loved ones, but ensure they have ways to safeguard themselves."

The beastman paused for a moment. "Let me tell you a story, one that is relevant for both our task in the Barrens and to the topic young Alex has brought up. A long time ago, there was a wizard by the name of Hathar-Motkin. He was a powerful sorcerer and demonologist of his day, and he—like all of us—sought power. And he achieved that by way of sacrifice. Demons can have vile ways of feeding themselves, and he provided them with what they wished to eat most. I won't detail what that was, because I'm not going to make some of you *sick* before class even starts."

He began to pace back and forth, his hooves thudding into the stone. "Suffice it to say, many other wizards lost family to Hathar-Motkin's inclinations. And he made a *lot* of enemies. Many wizards think they are safe in their towers," Baelin continued. "Or their sanctums or schools. Almost every other wizard worth remembering at the time wanted his head, and if you had put them all together, they would have filled every single seat in this stadium. And *one* of his enemies was me."

Murmuring spread through the class.

"To avoid his enemies, he thought to build himself an impenetrable fortress." He gestured behind himself as though that fortress was standing right in the stadium. "He forged a wizard tower out of star metal, then warded it with spells that repelled all magic but his own. Spell after spell after spell was linked together like chain mail, and then he placed a massive force sphere over his entire domain. Wizards tried to break through. So did demons and armies, and even one particularly angry dragon."

He shrugged. "And none could get to him. Until one very clever sorceress conceived of a notion, and sought out me and a number of his most powerful enemies to enact it. And what do you think we did? Hmmm, any guesses how we adapted?"

The student named Rhea raised her hand; she was part of the battle-mage group of second-years. "There's a saying among my people," she moved her hair to the side, revealing a pointed elven ear, "that no tree can stand against a strong enough wind. You combined your strength and blasted his defences to nothing."

"Hm, a good thought." Baelin nodded. "But one that failed us. Our enemy had prepared his defences well, and made the field his own. He could repair his defences faster than we could rip them down. And we *really* wanted to rip them down. Who else—Ah, Isolde."

"The terrain was to his advantage... So you used magic to change it so it was to *your* advantage?" she guessed, leaning forward slightly to see if she had answered correctly.

"Very good!" Baelin boomed, making many of them jump. "We did just that. Those of us with the power carved an even *larger* circle of magic around his domain, outside his wards and spells. He'd guarded a large area, but by working together, we could affect an even larger area. Which is precisely what we did. We were able to teleport his *entire* domain into the ocean. The most northern ocean, where the water is so cold, it would be ice if it weren't for the saltiness of the sea. And we waited for him, and we bombarded him with our most powerful spells, again and again."

He laughed then. A hard laugh like stone grinding on stone.

"Not only did Hathar have to combat *our* attacks, but he

also had to cast magic to make the temperature in his domain—which was dropping so very, very quickly—livable, deal with the pressure from the water's mass crushing his force sphere, and adapt to his own bewilderment and fear. He couldn't, so he panicked, teleported away. And we tracked him. *Then* it was all of us, against *one* of him, and none of his stolen power could help him."

Silence followed.

"Um," Caramiyus—one of the Doberman-like beastfolk—raised a hand. "What happened to him?"

Baelin gave another hard laugh. "Again, I would not want to make you sick before our class. In any case." He looked back to Alex. "I'm not insane, Alex. I'm not going to demand you drag a ten-year-old child with no experience into a battlefield, even if I am present to safeguard you all. But attending some of the lectures and discussions might do her some good. She might learn ways to protect herself, ways that might have indeed saved some of Hathar's victims. Give her things to think about, Mr. Roth. Do think on offering her a choice."

"Um, she has class at this time. She's in the junior school."

"Ah! Of course, that makes sense! Well, her general education takes precedence. Minds are sponges at that age. No sense in denying her the chance to fill it. I would suggest, though, discussing some of the topics from this class with her yourself. Such as the other point of my story, the importance of terrain."

He turned to the entire class again. "Today, your task will be to capture ten vent-drinkers. They are common in the western wild mana vents where you will be going. These rifts in the earth concentrate and pour the world's ambient mana up from deep within in its core and into the air. They are the source of Generasi's high ambient mana, and they are also very dangerous."

Baelin waved a hand behind him.

The air rippled and pulled apart like a curtain, revealing a strange chasm glowing with different coloured lights. It was like looking through one of the Traveller's doorways.

"Such pure, wild undiluted mana cannot be utilized unless processed in some way. Further, standing too close to the vents can cause you physical burns or disrupt your mana. The wild mana in the air can warp your spells unless you have a profound control over them, and for wizards and others sensitive to mana, walking near the vents will feel like you're attempting to swim through something akin to hot mud. And your opponents, the vent-drinkers—while harmless to *most* things—are far better adapted to the terrain than you are. Find ways to take away that advantage without wounding them mortally. Utilize your strategies from the test and tactics we have discussed. And work together. Now, without further ado, let us begin."

Chapter 58

Planning Around the Mana Vents

Baelin had not been exaggerating about the impact the mana vents would have.

The moment Alex stepped through the portal, it felt like he'd walked into a wall of thorns that pricked at his mana instead of his skin. It didn't feel as deadly as the mana vampire sapping his mana through his forceball, but there was a pain and invasiveness to it.

He squinted against the blast of light that suddenly hit his eyes.

Baelin had teleported himself and the group a short distance from the mana vent, and being so close was blinding. The light coming off of it burned intensely, and squinting gave little relief from a glare blazing like the noonday sun.

The other students groaned, holding up their hands in attempts to block the blinding radiance, while Najyah shrieked, burying her head under a wing.

"Ugh, that's bright!" Theresa grunted. "I—Alex, are you okay?"

The stinging feeling in his mana was driving him crazy. It was like having an itch deep beneath the skin, somewhere completely impossible to scratch. Khalik, Thundar and Isolde were groaning, cringing against the wild mana, while Svenia and Hogarth rushed to their lady's side to support her.

"Do you feel that?" Baelin's deep voice said from somewhere above. "That is the world's blood and the blood of Generasi, flowing up in all its glory. It's like a tiger raging through the wild. Untamable, unharnessed and deadly."

Through the stinging irritation, Alex couldn't help but wonder what the hell a tiger was.

"We will move back a bit now," Baelin said.

Alex felt the rush of his transportation magic as it pulled them away from the mana vent. He wasn't sure if it was his mana manipulation training or the fact that this was the fourth time Baelin had cast the magic on him, but it was more comfortable, like he was growing used to it. The ground where they set down was uneven, but Alex shifted his body naturally, assuming proper footing and balance. The stinging had faded to a slight itch.

He opened his eyes, noting the light had receded. The chasm was now at least a hundred feet away. From this distance, the light no longer assaulted his eyes; instead, it was quite beautiful in its own way.

He noticed figures walking around the edges of the glowing vent.

They were about as large as medium-sized dogs, but walked upright on two legs, and resembled a cross between a massive lizard and a bird. Back in Alric, he'd seen chickens walking with the same gait as these creatures, with strange head-bobbing motions followed by sudden, quick bursts of speed. Their necks were long, snake-like things, and their tails waved behind them like whips.

From where he stood, he couldn't be sure if they were covered in tiny scales or leathery flesh. Either way, their skin shimmered with colours that shifted to all the hues of a rainbow.

There were several groups herded together, moving in numbers of roughly twenty to thirty. The heads of those closest suddenly rose and turned toward the young wizards. Their eyes flashed with an inner light that matched their shimmering hides.

And then they ran.

Their clawed feet tore across the Barrens, kicking up dust and receding around the vent. Farther away, other groups simply looked up, then dipped their heads into the vents like beasts at a watering hole. Their shifting colours brightened as they drank in the ambient mana.

Baelin stood at the front of the group, looking at the mana vents with his hands clasped behind his back. His beard clasps clinked.

"Take note of your opponents there." He gestured to the vent-drinkers. "While we can only endure this environment, or perhaps even be forced to retreat from it, they are no worse for wear. They are thriving."

He waved a hand over the dust in front of them, which instantly began to shudder and rise into the air. The tiny particles came together, solidifying into long, lean threads that vibrated in the air before coiling around each other in long, fibrous braids.

Once the transformation had ended, twenty coils of rope dropped to the ground before them.

"You will have to discover how to make your captures while your surroundings are hostile to you, yet beneficial to your opponent," he instructed them. "Use what you can, test your limits, beware of dangers, and keep in mind the resourcefulness you exhibited during the test. Potential threats this close to the vents include muupkaras, bonedrinkers and the occasional xyrthak, but I will ensure that nothing beyond what I see as your limits accosts you. And with that, I wish you all good luck."

With a nod, he stepped back into the shimmering air and vanished, reappearing high above them as a distant figure floating in the sky. As Alex looked up, he found himself being very thankful the chancellor wore *pants* beneath his impressive robes. He shook his head at the thought.

Only someone who has issues would be having thoughts like that at a time like this, he told himself.

"We need a perimeter and a plan," Khalik said as soon as they were left alone. "Baelin said he would keep things away that would be beyond our limits, but that does not mean he will drive away every threat."

"If anything, it'll most likely be the opposite," Alex added.

"I'll watch our east flank," Theresa volunteered.

She stepped out of the group and moved to the east of them, nocking an arrow onto her bowstring and eyeing the empty wasteland. Massive rock formations rose far to the east, blocking their lines of sight past a certain point. Alex wasn't sure if he was imagining it, but one part of the formation looked like the open jaws of a beast.

Small, black, winged silhouettes soared over the rocks and fluttered down on the other side. Vultures. Something was dead over there. He hoped if something had killed whatever it was, that it would stay with its meal.

Khalik looked at Minervus, who was still shaking off some of the effects of the mana vent. "Minervus, would you mind having your entourage form a perimeter to the north and west of us? There are many with you and they could cover much of our flanks."

Minervus looked from his entourage to Khalik before nodding at the five he'd brought along. They paused for a moment, blinking as though they'd just woken up, then proceeded to go flank the north and west.

Eyvinder and the massive shark man volunteered to help form the protective circle to the south, leaving only Hogarth and Svenia standing beside Isolde as if they were glued to her sides.

"It's alright," she said, rising to her full height. "Help to protect all here."

"As you command," the two halberdiers said.

They joined the others in forming a protective wall of flesh and metal.

Alex glanced at their surroundings and snorted, slightly amused when he looked north. There—far away—was the escarpment that served as their goal during Baelin's test. From this distance, it might have taken them twice as long if they had to reach it from here, so it was good they weren't heading back there. Hopefully, there wouldn't be any sign of muupkaras or bonedrinkers this time, though the former could be hidden under the dust.

"So, uh," Angelar, one of the two Doberman beast folk, grunted from his canine snout. He sniffed the air toward the chasm. "I don't smell any threats. Does anyone have any ideas on how to do this?"

Alex was surprised when Angelar, as well as most of the rest of the class, looked toward his group as if expecting them to speak first. Then again, it made sense. They had been the only group to pass the test unscathed, despite being made up of more first-years than seconds.

He also noted several students throwing cutting looks at Minervus and Rayne. Some even edged away from Minervus' entourage positioned in the encirclement, even though *they* were supposed to be part of their protection.

His brow furrowed. That shouldn't really be a big surprise, all considered. Even if today's task wasn't a test, and the stakes were lower, no one wanted to chance their safety to the two who'd abandoned their group members. The memory of them flying off to the goal by themselves was still very fresh.

If there was already distrust, what would happen when it came time for cooperation? Or when trouble actually showed up?

"Before we generate ideas, we should go over what we know and make sure all understand the threats around us and the capabilities of our prey." Isolde stepped forward, appearing every inch like some sort of military general. "To review, we have seen muupkaras and a bonedrinker, but does anyone know much about vent-drinkers or what a xyrthak is?"

Alex looked over the other students, watching for certain tell-tale signs. When a teacher would ask, 'Did everyone understand that?' they'd usually get a range of responses.

There would be the blank stares or distracted looks from students who knew and didn't want to respond. Blank looks would also come from students that didn't understand and didn't really care to. They tended to be the ones who complained the loudest about a teacher 'not explaining things properly' when they did poorly on a test.

There'd also be those who'd nod openly, *wanting* the teacher to know they understood. Then there'd be those who wouldn't know what the teacher was talking about, quickly looking away. *They* were usually the ones who hadn't grasped something and were too embarrassed to admit it.

Rayne and Caramiyus, the other Doberman beastfolk, looked away at Isolde's question.

"Isolde, you might want to explain," Alex suggested, stepping beside her like he was some vizier to a ruler. He rose up to his full height and placed his hands behind his back. For some reason, he felt like *looking* impressive.

"We should make sure that we're all working with the same knowledge here." He smiled, using the Mark of the Fool to help mold the smile into something a commander would give. Past smiles from him heading class projects in Alric came back, along with memories of Fan-Dor's, Cedric's and even Khalik's grins. "And, if there's anything anyone wants to add after Isolde, they can feel free to share it."

The raven-haired woman looked at him sidelong for a

moment, and something seemed to pass across her face. Before he could begin to consider what it might have been, she launched into an explanation.

"Xyrthaks are higher predators in the Barrens. Something bonedrinkers and muupkaras avoid," she recited. "They are flying creatures with long beaks that are filled with teeth like those of a giant reptile. They are very large, as well. A full-grown xyrthak can carry off an adult man with ease. Their wings are roughly thirty feet wide and they can race the fastest falcon. Their most dangerous aspect, however, are their cries and their lances."

She made a grasping gesture. "A xyrthak's cry comes from a mana-rich organ deep within its chest between its lungs. This organ laces its voice with magical energy. Their cry can hit a frequency that resonates with the mana inside all creatures within approximately a fifty-foot radius. Depending on what the xyrthak wishes to do, or how vigorous its victims are, the cry can stun, knocking a creature unconscious, or even cause full mana reversals, which can be lethal."

Murmurs swept through the class and a number of nervous faces looked to the sky.

"Vent-drinkers, on the other hand, are, thankfully, relatively harmless," Isolde said. "They might deliver a nasty bite if cornered, but they rely on their speed and ability to tolerate the wild energies of a mana vent longer than almost anything else in the Barrens to keep themselves safe."

"Do they have to move away eventually?" Thundar asked.

"Technically yes, but a vent-drinker is still able to stay near a vent for days at a time. Far longer than we can afford to."

She wiped her forehead, glaring up at the merciless sun. "Other than that, they simply rely on their senses and high speed to flee from enemies. Their endurance, however, is not the best. Packs of muupkaras can chase down a herd if they pursue them long enough."

"So, here's a thought, then," Nua-Oge spoke up, turning to the massive shark man. "Grimloch, did you feel anything near the mana vents?"

"No." The shark man's voice was deep, and sounded like he *gnashed* his words.

So cool, Alex thought.

"I didn't feel anything either," Theresa offered.

"I did. Like a low, burning pain," Eyvinder, the green elf-like man said. "But I have mana."

"Ek-u-Dari be praised, I think I have an idea," Nua-Oge said. "When killer whales hunt narwhals, they herd the creatures toward shallow water where they can't swim away. What if everyone with low mana drive the vent-drinkers toward the wizards, while the spellcasters spread out like a net. The vent-drinkers will either run at us or scatter, and then we can capture them using our spells."

"That's a good plan," Theresa said. "That's how wolf packs work to separate prey from the rest of a deer herd, or how hunters flush out a fox."

"That won't work," Minervus cut them off, drawing annoyed looks from several of the group. "At least, *I'm* not sending my entourage over there while I'm here all by myself," he said flatly.

"Oh boy," Alex muttered. "Heeeere we go."

Chapter 59

Group Dynamics

Except for the death of his parents, Alex's life had been a fairly safe one, generally speaking.

Until their escape from Thameland and his encounter with the mana vampire, he'd never been in any situation where he'd had to struggle for his life. Baelin's test was the latest time where his life had truly been in danger, and in general, those events were all new to him.

But in each of those instances, he'd been fortunate enough to be surrounded by people he could trust, or at least ones that made good decisions and weren't shifty.

He'd also been part of plenty of groups at the church school that had gone down like a flock of dead birds at a wedding ceremony.

He remembered projects where he'd had to do all the work because of procrastinating group members, and ones where the group made a bunch of excuses for not doing their part. There'd also been projects where someone stopped showing up and their part of the work would end up having to be re-distributed. Some projects even devolved into arguments when certain members decided *they* had to be the leader.

Then there were the worst ones.

The worst ones were what he called 'discussion soup.' Things would start off innocent enough. The group would look good and it seemed everyone was engaged with the project and wanted it to succeed. Then the first issue would arise. There wouldn't really be an argument, but someone would want to alter the plan after the work was well on its way, or wanted their part changed.

Even then, things still often ended well enough if that person was either convinced to cooperate or got their way. If not? *Then* the discussion would start. There would be discussions about alternate plans and that would turn into a discussion of the group process. Then into a discussion about the discussion, which would rapidly turn snarky, becoming loaded with thinly disguised personal attacks.

And the entire time all that was going on?

Only one or two people would be doing their part, and Uldar help them since their work required the others' tasks be completed by a deadline.

Thankfully, in those situations, they had only been dealing with trying to get good marks at the church school, not possible life, maiming or death. Like now, in the Barrens.

Alex had a bad feeling the discussion soup had just started boiling.

"Funny for you to say that *you* don't trust us," Malcolm said. "Funny, all things considered."

"What you're saying doesn't make any sense," Rhea added. "There's no competition here, just us working together to capture some vent-drinkers. Why would anyone do anything to you?"

"It doesn't matter if you *do* anything to me or not. You heard what the professor said. You'll be less likely to trust me and Rayne after that test. And worse, you'll be looking forward to seeing me and Rayne fail. And since I don't know who you all know, you could be friends with our previous group members and maybe you're looking to get revenge for them."

"That's illogical." Isolde frowned at him. "Even if that were true, then why would we do anything to you while we all need to work together to accomplish one task?"

"People are illogical," Minervus pushed. "I don't know how you're going to act, and that's only the worst-case scenario. The best-case scenario is similar to what happened with my first team. You all don't trust me and we fall apart as a group. I say we just separate now into the same groups we were in for the test."

And this was what Alex had feared. An argument right out of the gate. One that wasn't even about the important stuff like how to work together to get the vent-drinkers. Instead, it was about breaking into groups.

Nua-Oge shifted her stance, looking as displeased as the rest of the group. "It'll be much harder to herd those creatures anywhere with only five... or even four, if Eyvinder has too much mana to stand being near the vent for too long. You'll also only have six bodies to herd the vent-drinkers."

"My entourage moves as one," Minervus pushed. "We'll be fine as long as you all do your part. We'll come together at the end."

"Oh yeah, that's a real good way to earn your classmates' trust," Malcolm scoffed.

"Were you going to trust me anyway?" Minervus fired back.

"Hey, hey, we don't have to fight like this," the battle-mage student, Shiani, cut in. She wore an elaborate necklace of pearls and seashells. "We could combine strategies as a compromise. We separate and then come at a herd from different directions. We are technically acting on our own, but by flanking the vent-drinkers, we *make* them have to run where we want them to run. Everyone wins!"

Alex frowned, looking carefully at Minvervus' five companions. None of them had said anything during the discussion. They'd moved very little and only watched the perimeter.

They glanced over whenever Minervus' voice grew stressed, but other than that, they didn't seem to be reacting to anyone else. It was as though no one else mattered, or were even there.

Odd people. Probably.

"That won't work." Minervus shook his head. "I don't want my people anywhere near the vent."

Isolde's frown deepened. "You don't want to work with the group because you feel you can't trust us—evaporating *any* good will you might have built with us, I might add—and now, what? You sit back while the rest of us fulfill Baelin's task?"

"I'll do things my own way, with Rayne." Minervus' face hardened.

Rayne glanced at him nervously. "I... I don't know, maybe we should stick with the group."

"Like they're going to trust you either," Minervus said. "They'll be waiting to jump us like a troll under a bridge."

"We're wasting time," Thundar grunted. "You want to take yours and go do whatever? Fine. This isn't even being marked."

The other students looked at each other.

"Come on, Rayne," Minervus said. "Let's go grab some vent-drinkers. We'll pull our own weight."

"Hold on." Isolde stepped forward. "If you're not planning on getting close to the vent, then *how* do you propose to catch your share of vent-drinkers? And please don't do anything that would interfere with *our* handling of the task."

"We've got bows." Minervus pointed to the bows on the backs of his five companions. "We'll use those to flush them."

"We're to capture them *alive*, and you're going to *shoot* them?" she asked incredulously.

"No, we're going to drive them with arrows," he said. "Not that it's any of your business."

"Fine, then," she said. "Know that your selfish decisions hurt all of us."

"Well, I wouldn't be talking if I were you. You're the one who helped that filthy cheater in our year," Minervus snapped, anger rising. "*You're* the top of three classes?" He snorted dismissively. "Who knows what *you've* been doing to help your grades stay high."

Isolde turned bright red.

Suddenly, Hogarth was beside her, his hand on his halberd. "Boy, you've got three heartbeats to apologize to the lady before I leave you lying unconscious here in the dust."

"Oh, really?" Minervus cocked his head. His entourage all turned as one, their hands reaching for their weapons. "You're a little outnumbered."

"Alright, I think that's enough of *that*!" Alex shouted, stepping between them.

All eyes turned to him, but he kept his gaze leveled on Minervus.

"You want to go and act all solo? Sure. Go do that. Take some ropes and go shoot arrows or fly at the vent-drinkers or yell at them, but *go* and do that. Over there." Alex pointed outside of the group. "I don't want to stand around all day, debating who goes where or throwing around personal insults or any other garbage. We'll be as separate as you want, as long as *you* do whatever it is you want to do far away from us."

He looked at the rest of the group. "Let's go that way." He pointed to the east. "And we can act separately. And let's do it fast. Baelin's watching us argue like little kids demanding the same toy."

No one disputed that.

Minervus glared at Alex but didn't say another word. The rest of the students took fifteen of Baelin's ropes and moved away from Minervus and his entourage. Within moments, Rayne looked back and forth between Alex's group as they walked away, leaving Minervus standing alone. He joined Alex's group.

Briefly, Minervus watched them before picking up the five remaining ropes and heading off in the other direction.

"And there goes a quarter of us," Angelar said. "And over half of the folk that can tolerate the mana vent."

"You remember what Baelin said?" Alex asked. "How we shouldn't abandon resources unless we *know* they're not going to help us? He's not going to help us. He hindered his first group and he's making bad decisions again. Better that we're down someone than have someone that makes what we're trying to do harder."

Maybe that was one reason the Fool was so dismissed back home, he thought.

He was trying his best in life. Even if he wasn't helping the Heroes directly, he hoped any research he did on the dungeon core would help against the Ravener in the long run. But what about previous Fools? As much as he sympathized with his predecessors, what if some of them had been... well, kind of shitty?

He knew if he'd been one of the other Heroes and saw that the Fool of the party was someone like Minervus, he'd be hard pressed to have any sympathy for them.

He glanced at Isolde, who stood muttering to herself with her arms crossed over her chest. "You okay?"

She scoffed. "I am angry but fine. It takes more than insults from someone like him to cause me dismay."

"Good," Khalik said. "It's good, channel that anger into our task. But do not hold on to his words, for you have nothing to prove. Not to me, at least." He turned toward the vent-drinkers. "Now, we have to come up with a plan using less than we thought we had."

"This would be much simpler if we were culling part of the herd," Theresa said. "It's a lot more difficult to trap animals alive and unharmed. Ugh, now I almost wish I'd brought Brutus..."

She'd left the cerberus behind so she could see what the Barrens were like before risking bringing him there.

Shiani gave a startled look toward the huntress. "Easier to kill them? That's a little cold, isn't it?"

"I don't mean slaughtering animals for no reason," Theresa said. "Sometimes, the deer population in a forest becomes too big, and if there's not enough predators around to hunt them and reduce their numbers, they'll eat all the food in an area. When there's not enough food, many of them get weak or sickly and starve to death. The ones that survive move away looking for more food. Then it becomes a chain reaction and other animals that feed on the deer starve, and the hunters have nothing to hunt. That's why you need to control herd size to keep a forest healthy. I don't want to kill any vent-drinkers right now, but the fact is catching animals *is* harder than killing them, especially when they don't want to be caught."

"I guess that makes sense," Shiani said. "Never thought about it that way."

"We will manage and make do with our task as it is," Khalik said, gazing at the vent-drinkers. "And we will need to do it fairly quickly. It would not do for predators to arrive and scare off the herd. The longer we wait, the stronger that possibility."

"Right," Thundar said. "I still like the herding plan, but we'll need more bodies to make them go where we want."

A low growl sounded from Grimloch's throat, one that seemed to shake the earth. "I'll be enough."

Alex believed him. "Yeah, big guy, I think you'd be enough to scare a dragon, but I—Oh *Uldar*."

The shark man 'smiled' at his words, but the effect was terrifying. His jaw seemed to shift in place, revealing row upon row of jagged teeth. "Thanks."

"Uh..." Alex tried to regain his train of thought. "Yeah,

you're enough, but..." He looked at Theresa. "What would happen if like, two wolves tried to chase a herd of deer?"

She thought about it. "Probably the biggest buck of the herd would gore them until they got the hint or bled out."

Alex winced. "Let's say the deer just ran."

"Well, the deer would run and scatter, then they'd scent each other to come back together again."

"Right." He turned back to Grimloch. "If it's just you, big guy, then the herd will scatter in all directions, which wouldn't be so bad if we only had to capture one. But ten? That's tough."

"Hmm," Khalik mused. "Perhaps we are thinking of this backwards. We are looking for many hunters to drive the prey in one direction, but we don't have many to drive the vent-drinkers anymore." He gestured around. "But we *do* have twelve wizards. That allows us to cover a *large* area to drive them toward. Even if they scatter, we'll scoop them up like fish in a net."

"That's a solid idea," Alex agreed. "Maybe we spread out in groups of two, make a wide net, and then drive them *back* together when they scatter."

"What do you mean?" Caramiyus asked.

"Okay, so." He pointed toward the vent. "We split the people with low mana up—let's call them chasers—into two groups and give each of them ropes. They spread out and come at a herd along the vent." He pointed at the closest herd. "One pair comes from the left along the chasm and the other pair from the right. That means the vent-drinkers have to run away from the edge and into the Barrens, where we'll be waiting. Then, they either scatter and try to get through us and we catch them, or they turn around and run away from us, *back* toward our chasers. Then we circle them—just like in our tactics book—and trap them."

He glanced around at the wizards. "We should probably stay close to the people we worked with on the test. We'll do better if each of us knows each other's capabilities."

"Ah, yeah, that's good. Let's try that," Caramiyus said. "And if we don't get all ten from one herd, we can try with another one."

"Good, good." Khalik lifted his gauntlet, on which Najyah was perched. "And I'll send Najyah up to scout for us. She is my familiar and has too much mana to be near the vents for long, but if they are driven away from the vents, she can stun any that try to scatter."

"Heeeey, look at us, all planning and strategizing and removing the advantage of terrain from the enemy!" Alex cheered. "Almost as if we're wizards practicing the art of combat or something."

He laughed, and a few other students joined in.

"Right," Khalik said, sending Najyah up into the sky. "She will watch for threats from around us as well."

"And uh," Rayne raised a hand. "I can, uh, fly up and do that too."

"Aaaah, two scouts, perfect." Khalik smiled before anyone could say anything to him. "Excellent. Let's begin, then; the sooner we have these creatures tied up, the faster we can be back on campus with a cool drink of something fun."

Both Najyah and Rayne took to the air simultaneously. As they made their ascent, Alex watched the skies for any sign of broad-winged, predatory reptiles.

The faster they got this done, the safer they'd be.

Chapter 60

Wrangling the Herd

"Watch yourself. Seriously," Alex said to Theresa. "There's all kinds of nasty things that live out here, and we don't know what might be hiding where. The moment you see *anything* funny, you—"

"Kill it?" Theresa asked, raising her great-grandfather's sword.

"I was going to say run away, but if you can kill it, then sure, do it. But be safe, seriously."

"I'll be fine, Alex," Theresa said, patting him on the shoulder. "And I'm not going to be alone."

She glanced toward where Isolde was instructing Hogarth and Svenia in exactly how they were to proceed. Nua-Oge only wished Grimloch good luck. The massive monster looked very confident in what he had to do. While the giant shark man stretched and limbered up, Alex wasn't sure if he was imagining it, but he looked like he was salivating as he readied for the chase.

"Yeah, I guess," Alex admitted. "I think that guy could take on a bonedrinker all by himself. ...I hope one doesn't appear, though."

"Actually, I hope one does."

Alex looked at her sharply. "Are you serious? You remember what I told you about that thing, right? You don't want that anywhere near you, trust me."

She shrugged, pointing up to where Baelin floated high above Rayne and Najyah's circling passes around the group. "This is about getting experience against opponents while we're being watched over by a probably-immortal wizard, right? Hoping *nothing* goes wrong is like hoping for an apprenticeship with a blacksmith that never gets a tough job. Sure you'll get through helping out your master easily enough, but what's going to happen when that tough job comes when you're all by yourself?"

He winced. "Yeah, okay, well, you're right, but I guarantee if a bonedrinker shows up, you're going to hate it and wish you never saw it."

She gave an ironic smile. "You're probably right. Anyway, looks like the others are ready. Wish me luck."

"Good luck."

The chasers split into two groups. One made up of Theresa and Grimloch, and the other of Svenia and Hogarth. As they began to walk toward the mana vent away from the vent-drinkers, the group of wizards turned to each other.

"Right, let's make our net," Khalik said. "Before the vent-drinkers run away and catch us off guard."

The students split up, spreading out and forming a wide line across the Barrens. Alex's group was in the middle, flanked by the battle-mages and the selachar and beastfolk. They had taken five of the fifteen ropes, leaving four to the chasers and three each to the outside groups.

They watched quietly as the chasers made it to the vent.

A herd of around thirty vent-drinkers, lapping mana on the near side of the chasm, raised their heads in the direction of the strange creatures taking up positions by the vent. The chasers were far enough away that the vent-drinkers weren't spooked yet, but they were alert and ready to run.

Alex glanced toward their rear, making sure no predators were stalking them from behind. His eyes swept the terrain, scanning both the rocky rise in the distance and the sky for danger from above.

He was becoming more efficient at visually sweeping his surroundings for threats. Recent experiences helped him become very aware of where his blind spots were, and where attackers tended to approach from.

"Najyah hasn't seen anything yet, Alex," Khalik assured him from his right. Beyond Khalik, Thundar stood with his arms crossed, and on Alex's left, Isolde watched her entourage while muttering to herself.

"I know, but it doesn't hurt to be too careful, y'know," Alex said, conjuring up his forcedisk. Eyeing the field ahead, he slipped the disk onto the ground between himself and Khalik, and scooped dust onto it, covering the spell. Then, he took a deep breath and tried something he'd only been able to start doing a few days before.

Falling into himself, he spoke the incantation for forcedisk again, using his growing meditative skills to observe and let the memories go that the Mark bombarded him with. He carefully formed the spell array and constructed a second first-tier magic circuit within his mana pool.

The magic circuit formed, fitting neatly in his pool alongside the first, and a second forcedisk formed beside him. He smiled at his accomplishment of expanding his mana pool enough to fit *two* magic circuits within it.

As he buried the second forcedisk, Isolde made an impressed sound. "Well, well, you can cast and maintain two first-tier spells at once now. Well done; you'll likely be able to cast a second-tier spell once you practice one."

"Yeah." He chuckled. Of course, that could wait until he'd

laid a better foundation of practice with first-tier spells. With the Mark interfering, he wanted to make sure he was as ready as possible.

He finished burying the second forcedisk in the space between him and her and dusted off his hands, then paused, looking closely at the fine, sunbaked dust.

"Laying traps?" Isolde asked.

"Yep." Alex grinned. "It won't hurt them much, but it should stop a vent-drinker if one tries to get between us."

Khalik shook his head. "Who would have thought about using a forcedisk to make a trap. What a devious thing. You're *really* going to be a terror when you start learning actual combat spells."

Alex shrugged. "Or I might be a terror with any spell I got. I mean, that's kinda the goal of the class, am I right?"

Isolde shook her head. "You have a strange way of doing things, Alex. Not a bad way, just a strange one."

"I get that a lot." He glanced back down at the dust. "Hey, this stuff that's all over the Barrens. It must get baked by mana all the time, right?"

"Indeed." Isolde looked down. "Being bathed both by wild mana and the sun's rays so constantly is what dries out the earth and makes the Barrens so dusty."

"Huh. So, it takes in a lot of mana." His eyes narrowed as he thought back to his textbook for potions. Substances that usually encountered a lot of mana often had multiple uses in alchemy. "Do you know if it can be used for anything in alchemy?"

"Multiple things," she said. "Though I don't know all of them off-hand."

"What about golems?" he pushed.

She glanced at him. "That's an advanced subject that we're only going to touch on part way through the second year of potion-craft."

"But you've already read the textbook for that, right?"

"Yes..." Isolde said warily.

"Yeah, I thought you would. I do the same thing. Did it say if it can be used in golem-craft?"

"Er, yes. It can often be mixed into the clay for a golem body. It makes it so that the body absorbs mana produced in the core more easily, but in turn, it requires more mana *from* the core in order to power the construct."

"Iiinteresting."

"Look." Thundar pointed. "Minervus is making his move."

Alex followed the minotaur's gaze, spotting the lone student ordering his entourage forward. The five individuals advanced and raised their bows, firing near a herd on the opposite side of the chasm. The arrows went wide at first, but the archers kept drawing and firing with practiced, fluid motions, until eventually, the herd bounded away.

Unfortunately for Minervus, the vent-drinkers ran *alongside* the chasm, staying close to it. Oddly, instead of rushing the creatures, the five archers continued trying to fire arrows in front of them from a distance, piercing some at the front of the herd. The animals screeched, sending every vent-drinker around the chasm into high-alert.

The herd Minervus was hunting started scattering from the wild mana vent, and his entourage spread out and gave chase. Minervus flew above the fray, pointing and blasting the ground near the herd with spells to drive them in the directions he wanted them to go.

"Damn him, he's spooked every animal at the chasm and unnecessarily harmed some!" Khalik swore.

The vent-drinkers rushed every which way, with groups breaking off and running into the Barrens. The chasers sprang into action.

Yelling and whooping, they brandished their weapons above their heads, frightening the herd and making them pause in indecision. Running along the chasm would make them go *toward* one of the groups of two, while running away would bring them to the line of young wizards awaiting them.

Then Grimloch snapped his jaws, a sound so loud, it cracked the air like a whip.

That got them moving.

The vent-drinkers rushed from the chasm and toward the waiting line of students.

"Here they come!" Khalik shouted, spitting out an incantation.

The dust shifted, flowing up his body and forming a hardened shell of earth around his torso and limbs. He took a deep breath and waited.

Thundar cast his body strengthening spell on himself and crouched low, like a runner preparing to sprint in a race at a county festival. Isolde simply watched the oncoming vent-drinkers, muttering under her breath.

The creatures scattered, some trying to rush around their encirclement, while others sprinted toward the wide spaces the students had left between them.

As they closed in, Thundar chanted another spell and his illusionary duplicate shimmered into being. With a roar, it rushed the vent-drinkers and sent them scrabbling to the side. One bounded toward the real minotaur.

He sprang at it. Enhanced by his spell, and with it off balance, he grabbed it up in his massive arms like a farmer catching a chicken.

Khalik whistled and spread his hands, stalking toward the vent-drinkers as they tried to dodge around him.

Then Najyah shot down.

Coiling her talons like fists, she slammed into one's side, knocking it to the ground and stunning it. By the time it started to regain its senses, Khalik pounced. He pressed his weight—

now made much heavier by the coating of earth armour—pinning the creature, then started to coil the rope around its legs.

Isolde spoke an incantation and a tiny ball of electricity appeared, crackling in the palm of her hand. She threw it forward like a rock, where it homed in on one of the vent-drinkers, shocking it. It froze as the electricity coursed through it, and then slumped to the ground, alive but stunned.

She chanted another spell while throwing her rope in the air. The coils sprang to life like a flying snake and shot forward, wrapping itself around the vent-drinker's legs.

Another tried to duck between Khalik and Alex.

Alex waited, watching the creature get closer... and closer... and closer.

Until it was nearly on top of his disk.

Then he willed the forcedisk to rise and spin.

The spell shot into the air, whirling and kicking up a massive cloud of dust, temporarily blinding the creature. Alex was already sprinting for it when he shot his forcedisk down in front of it.

At its leg level.

Pop!

It crashed into the utility spell, popping it, but also entangling its legs. The vent-drinker shrieked and fell to the ground. It was trying to get back on its feet when Alex tackled it. The creature squirmed and wiggled, trying to escape, but it was only the size of a medium-sized dog. Meanwhile, Alex had the advantage of size and strength.

The vent-drinker continued to struggle, while he fought to wrap the rope around its legs while trying to keep away from its snapping jaws.

"Ah shit," he cursed. "Could I get some help? From anyone!"

The sound of heavy hooves signalled Thundar approaching,

and soon the minotaur was helping him hold down and bind the struggling creature.

"That was easier than I thought it would be." Thundar chuckled as the two dust-covered young wizards stood to look over their handiwork.

Each of Alex's group had managed to capture a vent-drinker, bringing their total to four. Others had done well too, even though their positions on the edges of the line weren't ideal and allowed the skittish creatures an easier time getting past them.

The group on the left had captured two, using Nua-Oge's ice spells and Angelar's and Caramiyus' magic bolts.

The battle-mages had spread a smoke screen around their prey and used flashes of light to stun them. Then, they'd encased their legs in short columns of ice, quite literally freezing them in place.

Unfortunately, as the smoke cleared, it looked like two had actually died as the ice had reached too far up their bodies and frozen their cores. Nua-Oge had sprinted to them and was bent over the two dead vent-drinkers' bodies, dissipating the ice from them. Shiani looked on with remorse.

Eyvinder charged another vent-drinker as it tried to duck past him. As the creature rushed away, there was a powerful shift of mana that Alex could feel even from his distance.

Crack.

A wall of stone rose up in front of the fleeing creature. It collided with the wall, stunning itself, and then the pointed-eared man was upon it, binding its limbs. In total, the line of wizards had managed to capture eight of the creatures alive.

And they weren't done yet.

Several members of the herd skidded to a halt, trying to run back toward the chasm and away from the line of wizards. And the chasers were looking for just such an opportunity. Hogarth and Svenia spread out, shouting and swinging their halberds in wide arcs to drive the beasts toward the centre where Theresa and Grimloch waited.

Theresa had her rope tied into a short lasso and was swinging it above her head in wide circles. As a vent-drinker passed close by, she tossed the lasso with precision, wrapping the creature's neck and chest, and then she pulled hard. The line went taut and the reptile was pulled from its feet. She leapt on it, coiling the rope around its limbs while tightening it.

That only left one more to catch.

Grimloch lowered himself and rushed at one close to him, his massive strides propelled him with frightening speed. The vent-drinker shrieked as he closed in and grabbed it by the neck with one massive hand.

In his grip, the little creature had no hope of escape and soon it became their tenth.

"We did it!" Alex shouted, but gathered himself before he got too excited. He glanced around at their surroundings, making sure there were no signs of predators around.

He checked the rock-rise again and turned his eyes to the sky. The vultures were gone. There were none anywhere to be seen.

Instead, he spotted a large form flying high in the distance, one with broad wings and a long neck. It looked to be flying toward them.

"So, you've noticed it."

Alex nearly jumped out of his skin as Baelin's voice came from right beside him. The chancellor had either teleported or silently flown down while he and the others were busy wrangling the vent-drinkers.

Baelin gazed over their work. "Well done, well done." His tone was obviously pleased. "I must admit, you all have performed far better than I anticipated. Well, *almost* all of you."

He looked over to the opposite side of the chasm, where Minervus' entourage still chased vent-drinkers.

A stern look crossed his face. "Come, let's be away from here before the xyrthak arrives, and we shall discuss what happened today."

He waved a hand over the captured vent-drinkers, causing their ropes to turn back into dust. As the little creatures sprang up and started to speed off in all directions, Baelin waved his hand over the class and Alex felt the teleportation magic take him once more.

Chapter 61

Trust

They appeared on top of the escarpment they'd gathered on after Baelin's test. This time, the benches were already there, awaiting their arrival.

"Sit down, sit down." The chancellor gestured to their seats. "I'll be back in one moment. Ah, wait, I almost forgot."

He waved a hand and more benches appeared in a semi-circle around the boulder he'd sat on last time. "There are, in fact, more of you this time. At least... for the time being."

The air shimmered around him and he vanished into it.

His students looked at one another as a familiar, uncomfortable silence filled the air. Alex had experienced the same feeling many times before. At the church school, the atmosphere in a class had become exactly the same when one of their number was about to be in a *lot* of trouble.

The class waited, shuffling awkwardly in their seats.

Until Baelin abruptly reappeared with Minervus and his entourage beside him.

"Have a seat, and we'll get started," he said to a beet-red, sweating Minervus who was clearly on edge. Maybe he was angry. Maybe embarrassed. Maybe both. When Alex had last seen him and his entourage, they were still trying to herd the vent-drinkers. From the expression he now wore, it looked like things hadn't gone very well.

"Alright, let's talk about the practicum today," Baelin began. "You faced a challenge where your enemies, such as they were, had a terrain advantage that you did not. What did you learn?"

Alex had gone into the discussion expecting Baelin to ask 'how did you do?' like last time. Not, 'what did you learn?'

"Ah yes, Thundar," Baelin said.

Alex had been so deep in thought, he hadn't realized the minotaur raised his hand.

"Teamwork makes the dream work," Thundar said with a smile.

Alex started to laugh, along with some of the other class members.

Baelin smiled too. "What a delightful expression. Teamwork makes the dream work, hah! I've never heard that before. This is why I so enjoy teaching; you all help keep me young. Well... Young in my own mind, at least. I'll have to introduce that at the next Administrative Meeting. So yes, teamwork makes the dream work. What else?"

Alex raised his hand next, speaking when Baelin called on him. "You've got to take into account the resources you have, and change a plan when those resources change."

"Very good," Baelin said. "Battle, or indeed anything in life, is constantly moving and changing like a river. Advantages turn to disadvantages. Allies fail and help comes from unforeseen directions. A Proper Wizard adjusts to these changes, quickly and decisively. What else?"

Malcolm raised his hand. "You've got to make sure you prepare for different situations. Knowing a lot of different kinds of spells is better than being hyper-focused."

Alex winced. At the moment, by necessity, he himself was hyper-focused on force spells.

"What makes you say that, Malcolm?" Baelin prompted him.

"Well." Malcolm scratched the back of his head. "I mostly know ice spells that, well, *kill*. I accidentally killed two vent-drinkers when I was only trying to capture them. If I had something less lethal, then I'd have gotten all three, probably."

"A fine point," Baelin agreed, spreading his hands. "These days, specialization is very much in vogue in academic wizardry. It is seen as efficient. Specialists in lightning magic could rend the skies in half, while a generalist wizard might have a larger tool box, but far less mastery over any specific kind of magic. That said, one of the greatest strengths of wizardry is versatility. By learning a wide array of spells, you might be better prepared for any situation. There is one point I might add to your observation, Malcolm. Even if you are a specialist, then you can shore up your blind spots with resources *other* than magic."

He gestured to the rest of the class.

"Nua-Oge knew ice spells less lethal than yours, Malcolm, but she also brought a powerful ally with her, one who was unaffected by the rigours of the mana vents. Isolde, Alex and Minervus also brought allies." He then gestured to Khalik, Thundar and Alex. "Your three colleagues used a hunting familiar and physical force to subdue their quarry. You brought an ally as well, Malcolm, which shows your head was in the right place. It was just a simple misfortune that in this situation, Master Eyvinder's high levels of natural mana were not a boon, and so he was unable to be in close proximity to the wild mana vent. But he was still of great aid to you. Even if you don't have the correct spell, you can substitute your magic with an ally, or a carefully chosen weapon or tool."

"Yeah, that makes sense," Malcolm said, glancing over to Eyvinder. "You can expand in ways outside of magic."

"Well said." Baelin nodded. "What else have we learned?"

A hand rose from the end of the class.

Baelin turned to its owner without missing a beat. "Ah, Minervus. What is your question?"

"With all due respect, what was the point of this?" Minervus asked.

Everything went dead silent. One might have heard a fly cough.

Baelin cocked his goat-like head at Minervus, seeming nothing more than a kindly old man listening to the voice of a grandson. His eyes, however, were utterly focused on the young man like a snake eyeing a mouse.

"Do go on," Baelin gestured to him in invitation.

Don't keep talking, Alex thought.

Minervus kept talking.

"I don't really understand the exercise, Baelin. We're supposed to be learning how to engage in combat, right? Adapting and using our resources? Why're we grabbing lizards like chicken wranglers? I get that it was about getting them away from the mana vent, but if they don't fight back, then how is that training us to protect ourselves?"

"Hm, an interesting observation," Baelin said. "How does what we did today play into the wizard in combat? Hmmm, let me ask you this. Should you kill everything you fight?"

"Well, a dead enemy is one that can't come after you later. Killing it or running away from it makes sense. Capturing it just lets them strike you in the back later."

"I see. And let us say for a moment, that you were trying to track down a creature who could provide an excellent source of mana for your alchemy or even bolstering your spellcraft, but the creature is only useful to you alive?"

"Well, uh. Then I'd capture it."

"Precisely *how*, Minervus?" Baelin pressed him. "You have cornered a beast and it is fighting to escape you because it is a *beast* and it believes you have captured it to make it your meal. Thus, it fights for its life with every fatal measure it possesses, while *you* cannot respond in kind lest you lose the resource the living creature can provide. What then?"

"Um..." Minervus muttered.

"Hmmm, you seem to be having some difficulty with that one." Baelin stroked one of the clasped braids of his beard. "Let us try this. You are returning to your sanctum after purchasing some ingredients you need for a ritual. En route, you are attacked by armed rogues. They move quite well, and it is obvious they seek your head. Using your method, you run away, only for them to pursue you. They are determined, of course. And so, you kill them. What have you learned about who sent them or why?"

"Well, vent-drinkers can't fight back, right? So why them?"

"Hmmm, if I may be so bold." Baelin leaned forward. "Could it be that you do not see the benefit of the task because you were only able to capture *one* of the creatures alive? At times, one can be tempted to disparage areas where they do not excel. One blames lack of oversight, administrative structure, or random chance when things do not go so well. Is this it?"

Minervus winced. "My... my companions weren't able to work well near the mana vent. So, it wasn't fair."

Alex sat back some. That was the first he'd heard of this.

"Your companions? Many of them were able to reach the vents just fine." Baelin waved his hand over Hogarth, Svenia, Theresa and Grimloch.

"No, I mean my..."

"Yes?" Baelin pushed.

"Er, *my* companions, my flesh golems... Being so close to the mana vent disrupted my mana connection to them, and they don't function that well with just verbal orders."

Flesh golems?

Alex whirled toward Minervus' companions. A lot of their strange behaviours suddenly started to make sense. How they had moved nearly in time with each other, why they only seemed to react to Minervus, why they all looked like one another, and why they hadn't said a word for the entire class.

Even now, as everyone's attention lay fully on them, they didn't react or move. Even their breathing seemed unnecessary and intermittent, like it was merely a performance and not an actual bodily process.

"Well, I'll be damned," Alex said. They looked utterly lifelike aside from those few tells. He supposed that 'flesh' was one of the more special materials used to make certain golems that Sim Shale had hinted at on their tour of the workshop.

Alex didn't even *want* to know *how* these constructs were made. A shudder ran through him.

"Indeed. Your golems were at a disadvantage. A major disadvantage, at that. But you had ways to adapt. You had your classmates."

"But you said I'd ruined their trust with what happened during the test," Minervus tried to explain himself. "I determined that resource was spent and decided to act on my own."

"Rayne concluded otherwise," Baelin pointed out. "And so, he was part of a group that successfully captured ten vent-drinkers. Instead, you went out on your own and managed to capture *one*, despite bringing the most companions, who were also the most obedient and coordinated. Trust in you has lessened further, and..." he gestured to the sky, "a full-grown xyrthak was approaching us. Had your classmates taken longer to capture the vent-drinkers because you did not provide them aid, then everyone would have had to deal with a flying opponent that is far beyond *any* of you. It would have been necessary for me to step in and the learning opportunity would have been lost."

"This..." Minervus fell into an angry silence. "This..."

Baelin looked at him for a long time, before sighing. "Alright. I can see that you are not ready. I will put in an immediate transfer request so that you might enter another course of your choice. It is still early in the semester and you can still catch up."

"Wait, what?" Minervus flew to his feet. "What—transfer? But it wasn't a test!"

"A Proper Wizard is *always* tested, Minervus," the chancellor said. His voice sounded firm as iron. "They are tested by their magic, by their foes and their own limits. You have found yours, and until you can learn more wisdom in your decisions, your continued presence in the class would endanger your life, the lives of your colleagues, and hinder all learning opportunities. This is a favour, and should you wish to do so, you may continue to audit the lecture portion of the course if you do not fill this time slot."

Minervus stewed, and then grudgingly bowed his head. "As... as you say."

"Good." Baelin nodded. "I encourage you to take this course again, when you are ready."

After they teleported back to the stadium, the class fell into an uncomfortable silence. Minervus organized his things then stomped through the doorways with his entourage of golems. As soon as they left, excited chatter spread through the class.

Several of the students surrounded Theresa, Grimloch, Hogarth and Svenia and bombarded them with questions, congratulations and compliments. Theresa looked to be growing flustered from the attention. Meanwhile, Alex went to stand in line with those who had after-class questions for the chancellor.

Isolde was last in line in front of him, and she gave him a curt nod and warm smile as she stepped out of line.

"Ah, Alex, here again." Baelin beamed. "I swear, every single class, you're staying behind to ask *something*."

"Hey, I'm at a magic university. I think it'd be weird if I

weren't filled with questions literally every waking moment," Alex said, glancing toward the doors to the stadium. Minervus had exited that way minutes earlier.

"Chancellor," he said. "Those wild mana vents, that's an incredible source of power."

"That they are." Baelin chuckled. "And a very tempting one. If you're thinking of harnessing one, I'd advise against that until you've been studying for a few *decades*."

"Decades?" Alex blinked. "Is it that hard to harness?"

"Indeed, while the air and natural processes of the world gradually calms the mana naturally, doing so artificially and on demand is a very difficult process."

"Ah," he said, slightly disappointed. "That's too bad."

"Too bad?" Baelin stroked his beard. "Alex, each vent pours out enough power per day to energize a sky skip for months. That's more power than most archmages need, let alone a first-year. Why are you thinking about this?"

"Well," he said, glancing back at the gates Minervus had gone through. "I've been thinking about golems, for the future, you see..."

He didn't mention how *near* he intended that future to be.

"But I've learned they need a *lot* of mana, among other things. Probably more mana than I'll be able to provide for a very long time, so I was thinking of substitutes."

"Aaaah, and so you thought to use a gaping hole that pours out the most dangerous mana you can find? And I thought you had *good* instincts, Alex." Baelin chuckled. "It takes a creature or apparatus that can process an incredibly disparate selection of mana and convert it into a single source. Creatures or devices that can do that are either rare, dangerous, expensive or all of the above. There are other, safer things that can donate the mana to power a golem."

"Oh?" Alex pressed. "What would you suggest?"

"The sacrifice of sentient beings," Baelin said seriously.

Alex froze.

Baelin burst out laughing. "I jest! That practice hasn't been common in alchemy for some five hundred years! In *most* places anyway. But magical items could be good donators, if you don't mind them being drained. Better they be embedded, though."

For an instant, Alex wondered if Baelin and Hobb were friends.

Then is occurred to him what Baelin said. "Embedded?"

"Indeed. A golem that produces a great deal of mana to power itself can also power and interface with magical items embedded in its body, if one simply attaches them during creation."

Alex's heart nearly stopped beating. "And... then what happens?"

"Well, the golem can utilize the items. Some golem-crafters graft magic swords onto their arms, or magical orbs into their chests to create a variety of spell effects. When you learn more about golems, you'll learn about this."

"Yeah... yeah... okay..." Alex said, only half-listening. "Thanks."

"Any time. Don't do anything that would get you expelled, now. Don't look at Minervus as an example. His golems are bound to him, but not crafted by him. Otherwise, the connection between their mana would be deeper."

"Right, makes sense. Thanks again."

Alex walked away, considering more possibilities.

Mounted magic items?

An image of a colossal figure of clay came to him.

One that fired deadly red beams as it battled his enemies.

If he did this right, he might have just found the perfect use for the fire-gems from the Cave of the Traveller.

Chapter 62

Glyphs and Quicksilver

"It's time to show off your progress with your glyph boxes—Dun, dun, dun!" Professor Val'Rok said with added effect, looking over the entire class of MANA-1900. "This assignment likely won't be your favourite this semester, and rest assured, you won't be unique in feeling that way. You see, glyph box practice enjoys a long tradition of being hated here at Generasi, but, sadly," he grinned, looking pleased with himself, "it still has to be done. The good news is that today's little go-over isn't for marks; we're just doing a brief check-in to see how things are coming along."

He clapped his scaly hands together and rubbed them excitedly. His tongue flicked out and licked one of his eyes. Several students—including Alex—recoiled slightly.

"So, let's have a show of hands. Who here was unable to light up any glyphs on their boxes?" His tongue flicked out again.

There was a reticent silence.

"Oh, don't be shy, there's no shame here, and we're all going to be taking turns revealing our results anyway."

The silence continued.

"Come on, you're not being marked on this. Here, I'll show

you someone who wasn't able to light a single glyph in their first two weeks with that damned box." Val'Rok raised his scaly hand. "Took me three weeks to light *half* of one, so don't be shy. Let's go. Show of hands."

Reluctantly, a little more than half the class raised their hands. A few students were looking at their boxes with such hatred that Alex was sure if they had hammers, their boxes would be flat disks.

"There, that's the way. No need to worry," Val'Rok said. "Now, of the students who couldn't activate the glyph, who among you was able to send your mana in and feel the first applicator in the box?"

Every student kept their hand raised, though some looked shifty as they did. Alex raised his eyebrows in surprise. He wondered if that look was an 'I didn't actually try the homework but am pretending I had trouble with it' look. He remembered it well from the church school.

That surprised him. It was one thing to sit there and not do any work when school was local, free, and even a bookworm like him had to admit, the lessons varied with how practical they were. But Generasi cost a fortune, and the dangers of magic—Lucia, her massive scar, and leaving Generasi came to mind—meant there was a lot more risk for not doing the assigned work. The danger was real.

Then again, looking around the class, he began to wonder how many students actually *wanted* to be here. Derek was a noble, and so was Isolde and quite a few others. Wizardry was prestigious and provided a path to reputation, riches and power, but that didn't mean it was a path for everyone. He remembered students from the church school who'd gone into apprenticeships or professions because that was what their families expected of them.

Some hated it, though they diligently stuck through the training anyway.

Others also hated it and simply coasted through, doing the minimum, or got thrown out for doing unbelievably stupid things. A potter's apprentice who'd nearly burned his hand off came to mind. He was showing off for a girl by trying to see how long he could tolerate the heat inside a kiln. The skin on his hand ended up looking like old leather.

The girl wasn't impressed.

All types went into all sorts of studies for various reasons. He supposed Generasi was no different.

Either way, if Professor Val'Rok noticed the shifty looks, the cheerful lizard wizard gave no sign. "See, that's the ticket, right there. By finding the applicator, you've learned both how to *move* your mana without the aid of a magic circuit, and how to sense and touch things with it. You've taken the first steps, and now all you need to do is put in the practice."

He licked his eye again in something that looked like a hideous parody of a wink. "Now for all those that did manage to light a glyph, show us what you've done. Who wants to go first?"

Alex did not raise his hand.

He wanted to watch the others first and see just how far they had gotten. If he went first, he could proudly show the class his accomplishment, but maybe others had done even better. Maybe someone had lit up *two* boxes. Also, if he did go first and was the only one to light up every glyph, that might discourage those who hadn't done as well as him.

He wanted to stand out, not embarrass others for no reason.

Unless they deserved it, of course. He smiled as McHarris came to mind.

Besides, people who went last tended to stand out more. There was a reason why Robbing Cloak—the legendary archer—always went last at tournaments in all the popular stories about him.

Alex watched, impressed with some of the students. Three of them managed to light up three glyphs at the same time, though they admitted to Professor Val'Rok they had previous experience with mana manipulation by having assisted in shops that dealt in magic items in Generasi.

That was encouraging. If students who had less skill in mana manipulation than he did were helping out in magic item shops, then there was hope for getting the assistant's job in the golem workshop.

Finally, the professor's eyes fell on him. "Looks like you're the last one, Alex. Come on, no need to be shy."

"Looks like I am," Alex said, lifting the box. He concentrated, letting his mana flow through the maze as he'd practiced so many times. With the Mark's assistance, it was so easy now that he could have done it while half-asleep.

A collective gasp went through the room as every glyph lit up at once.

A stunned silence followed.

"Well! Well, well, well, well!" Val'Rok chattered. "My goodness, would you look at that!" The lizardfolk floated toward Alex on one of the school's flying stone disks. "Well... well, well done! Most don't light up the whole box until at least halfway through the second-year course. Do you work at a magic item forge?" he said excitedly.

"No, but I'm hoping to," Alex said.

"Interesting... very interesting. Would you mind staying a few minutes after class?"

"Um, sure." Alex smiled.

Murmurs were spreading through the class.

Good. People were beginning to talk.

"What kind of job are you looking for?" Val'Rok asked.

"I'm looking to get a job at Shale's Workshop," Alex said, concentrating on casting his forceball and then hanging his basket of textbooks beneath it. If Val'Rok noticed it took him longer to cast it than most other students, then he didn't say anything.

"Ah, a good choice, but a hard one. I know Toraka Shale and she's a particular taskmaster. And golem-work is no easy task among the magical disciplines." Val'Rok looked at him apprais-ingly with one of his reptilian eyes. "Hmmm, she also doesn't have any openings at the moment that I'm aware of. But she always posts her openings at Generasi since we have such a good pool of potential candidates to choose from."

"Well, I want to be ready if one does come up."

"Right... right."

The professor looked at one of the boxes sitting on his own desk. "You certainly have an excellent talent for it. Either that or a lot of practice. I wouldn't exactly say you don't have a chance. Have you built magic items before?"

"No," Alex said. "But I've been doing well in POTI-1000 so far, and I've been a baker's... assistant."

Val'Rok paused. "A baker?"

"Well, I know how to follow a recipe." He shrugged.

The lizardfolk burst into his high-pitched laugh. "I guess there is a correlation there! Well, then." He tapped the box on his desk then slid it toward Alex before digging into the desk and pulling out another two. "Here, I want you to try what you did using these three boxes."

"Right." Alex took them up, one after the other.

The first one he struggled with a little. The maze and appli-cators were completely different from his own practice box. Soon, however, he was able to light up every single glyph on each side.

By using the Mark to point out his previous successful movements, he grew faster and faster with solving each one. Then, feeling more confident, he picked up two at the same time. Falling into a meditative mindset, he took deep, paced breaths while he split his concentration into two boxes at once.

That proved a little over-ambitious.

Controlling his spell while solving one box was one thing, but engaging in something as complex as activating all the glyphs on two boxes at once proved to be beyond him. Still, he was proud to be able to activate *two* glyphs on each one at the same time.

"By my scales!" Val'Rok cried. "Would you look at that!"

"Ugh, that's a little embarrassing." Alex smiled ruefully.

"Please, that's something *incredibly* advanced you just tried, and you did better than most. Tell you what, write your report on how the training exercise with the box went, and then I'll give you the next assignment right away; the first of the mana regeneration techniques. Review it and write the report on the theory of it, so you're ready for when I teach it in class. If you do as well with that technique, then I'd suggest Challenging the Exam for Credit."

"What's that mean?" Alex asked.

"It's a practice that makes it so Generasi doesn't waste young wizards' time and potential," Val'Rok said. "People come from all sorts of backgrounds, and for some, the first-year courses can teach them nothing new. With a professor's permission, a student may challenge the course through a special exam, be given the credit, and then move on to the next course if it's early enough in the semester. If it's too late, there's a supervised self-study program that will allow the student more self-directed learning with the subject. Think of it as a minor thesis."

"Oh, that's awesome!" Alex said.

"Yeah, it is pretty awesome, isn't it?" Val'Rok snickered, tapping a clawed finger to the bottom of his jaw. "And you said you were in POTI-1000 too."

"Yep, Professor Jules was the first person I showed that I

could actually light up the whole box. Aside from my friends, that is."

"And *she* didn't tell me?" Val'Rok looked mildly offended. "Ah well, and how is it so far?"

"We're going to have our first quiz soon," Alex said. "And I'm really learning some interesting stuff in the labs."

"Hmmm, good. I'll tell you what, if you successfully challenge this course for credit, I will personally write a letter of reference for you to Shale's. Without some kind of letter of recommendation, you'll struggle."

"What? Really!"

"Yep." Val'Rok bobbed his head in a nod. "You seem to have a true talent for mana manipulation. An exceptional talent, and that should be supported. Do well, and I'll certainly do well by you."

"Thanks." Alex grinned. "Thanks a lot."

"Well, don't thank me yet; all I potentially have to do is write a letter. You, on the other hand, have to be the one to prove yourself to me."

Alex looked at the glyph boxes. "Oh, I'm working on it. I'm working on it."

"This one's done," Alex said as his potion gave off a strong glow and then settled into a deep, murky grey colour.

The controlled flame beneath the flask snuffed out as he capped it, took out the mana conductor, shut down the mana vacuum, and used his tongs to place the hot flask onto a waiting ceramic plate.

"What, already?" Carey blinked, staring at the potion from the work station beside him. "We just started."

"Well, it's kind of simple once you have the procedure memorized," he said, moving the glass titration apparatus to the front of his station and starting to disassemble it. He used the Mark and it pointed out the proper movements for taking apart the delicate device and properly placing it down. He set it with the rest of the apparatuses he had finished using—they would need to be washed after the lab. "And I'm pretty good at mana manipulation, so that helps speed things up."

'Pretty good' was a bit of an understatement at this point.

Alex had borrowed two mana manipulation boxes from Professor Val'Rok to practice with at the same time after his meditations. Operating two at once was much harder than one, but in a short space of time, he'd already managed to raise the number of glyphs he could light on both from two to three. At this point, controlling forceball and even forcedisk through mana manipulation was as easy as breathing.

He'd already started to work hard on learning Wizard's Hand—documenting his failures as usual—and couldn't wait to see how well he could control it once he figured out how to cast it.

The letter of reference was a potential prize waiting for him and had lit a fire under his feet. He'd definitely be trying to Challenge the Exam for Credit for mana manipulation if things worked out.

Now all that was needed was to make sure he actually *had* the skills to perform the job. Also, if he managed to get the job, then that might help convince Professor Jules to let him do more in POTI-1000. He glanced to the far side of the room where various analytical apparatuses were stored.

Once the potion had cooled enough, he lifted it with the tongs and carried it over for analysis. First, he dropped a bit of it into a mana spectrometer, which broke up a substance's composition by its mana essences. He remembered the textbook's instructions as to what dyeing agents he should add to the sample and dropped those on it.

He ran the spectrometer for exactly twenty-one seconds,

which was the recommended length of time for first-tier potions. What came out was a sheet of absorbent paper with bands of colour running along its length. Alex identified what each colour meant in terms of its magical constitution and wrote them down in his lab book. The pattern present matched what the pattern should have been for this potion, as listed in Dexter's textbook.

He then took out a potion-sensitive bed of blue moss that had been planted on a surface the size of a large coin. Carefully, he filled a dropper with another sample and dropped it onto the moss, watching for any sign of colour changes.

His eyes narrowed behind his mask.

Nothing.

Smiling, he raised his hand and called Professor Jules over. His voice was muffled. "All done!"

Heads swivelled toward him from all over the cell as other students paused in disbelief. Derek eyed Alex evenly through his mask. A student cursed as the distraction interfered with the mana running down his conductor.

He scrambled and activated the mana vacuum, which poured the mana away from the reaction, and up into the mana waste container. A couple of students snickered, and then one leaned toward the other and mimed the motion of drinking. The other laughed and gave his lab partner a light push.

"Careful there," Professor Jules warned them as she eyed Alex's potion. "Hmmm. Alright, what can you tell me about it?"

"Its mana has combined to produce the correct potion, according to the spectrometer." He pointed to the moss. "Kamookak's Moss didn't change colour or wilt, so that means all the toxin from the quicksilver's gone."

"Hmmm." She squinted at the notes in his lab book. "I see. And what did the manohmeter say about its magical conductivity?"

He paused for a moment, and then chuckled behind his

mask. "Are you trying to trick me, Prof? Since the mana spectrometer showed it has the correct composition, and since we only used ingredients listed in the procedure, it's not necessary to run it through the manohmeter. We'd only run it if the spectrometer's readout showed its composition had deviated from standard. Plus, uh, we weren't supposed to do that for today's procedure, and we're always supposed to follow procedure."

She snorted. "Well, don't *we* think we're clever. But, you're right. Well done, it appears this is a fine example of a Potion of Running Enhancement. You may keep it."

"Thanks," he said. "Got anything else for me to do?"

"Hmmm," Professor Jules said. "No. Just focus on cleaning up and then finishing your notes. Keeping fresh notes makes writing the lab reports easi—"

"Oh my gods!" someone cried across the room.

Crash.

Glass shattered.

Someone sounded like they were choking.

One of the students—the one that had mimed drinking the potion—fell back against his work station, clawing at his throat. His mask was partially raised.

"Dammit!" Professor Jules swore. "Alex! Quick! Safety kit!"

She rushed toward the fallen student.

Alex ran for the kit.

Chapter 63

Unsafety in the Cells

Quicksilver poisoning was a nasty thing.

There was a fairly extensive section on it in Dexter's textbook.

One of the nastier things it did was *kill* you. If you didn't die, it could leave you with a whole host of unpleasant symptoms. Depending on how much one ingested, it could cause victims to lose feeling in their limbs and skin, cause itching or a sensation like insects crawling through one's flesh, or worse: permanently damage the mind.

Those effects were increased and worsened when mana was present within a quicksilver solution. Tissue would swell, the body would overheat until it actually began to burn itself, and coordination and balance would be forever impaired.

Quicksilver was just one of many substances that Dexter's textbook had cautioned about, especially when infusing it with mana, unless one had the proper stabilization agents already present to negate the toxicity.

It was obvious this poor bastard had negated nothing.

"The kit!" Professor Jules barked, crouching beside the choking student.

Alex rushed up beside her, passing by a sign stating 'no running in the lab.' "Here it is!" He opened it, looking at the contents. "What do you need?"

"The emergency mana-reducing agent and the aerolizer!" she said. "Then the Potion of Neutralizing Toxins! Quickly, ah wait, her—"

She paused, seeing that Alex had already thrust the aerolizer and small bottle of mana-reducing agent into her hand, and was drawing up the potion of neutralizing agents, seeming to follow the specific instructions in the textbook for preparing it. She had no way of knowing the Mark was enhancing his memory of what he'd read in the text.

Professor Jules wasted no time in attaching the bottle of mana-reducing agent to the aerolizer, then tore off the young man's face mask. "Oh no... I feared as much."

A silver liquid stained his lips.

She pressed the leather cup-shaped applicator of the aerolizer over his nose and lips and flicked a glyph-marked switch. The aerolizer hissed, drawing the liquid reducing agent into itself then vaporizing it and passing it through the applicator.

The vapour rushed through the young man's open mouth and nostrils.

He shuddered, and Alex felt the mana shift around the poisoning victim.

It was like the dispelling spell Professor Jules had cast over him, but far more focused in its effect. As the mana infusing the quicksilver was wiped away, the aggravated effects of the poisoning lessened. The young man began to cough, and Professor Jules turned him onto his side so he could cough up anything that had started to form in his lungs.

Alex handed the potion of neutralizing toxins to the professor and held out his hand for the empty bottle of mana-reducing agent. They exchanged bottles and he turned to the closest student. "Here, can you put this in the glass bin?"

The student looked back and forth for a moment before taking the bottle and scurrying off.

As the toxin neutralizing agent was vaporized into the young man's lungs, his laboured breathing lessened, and his profuse sweating and skin flushing started to reduce. He heaved another heavy cough.

Professor Jules sighed, looking somewhat relieved, and adjusted his arms and legs into what she explained was the recovery position. This would let him rest without danger of rolling or choking on his own spit or vomit.

Reaching into a pouch on her belt, she drew out an odd-looking stone disk with a series of glyphs drawn on it, and concentrated on it. Alex looked on as he sensed a complex web of mana shoot from the stone in a line that travelled through the floor and reached outside of the room.

From the whispers he heard around him, some of the other students felt it too.

"Emergency Office? This is Professor Jules!" she barked into the stone. The mana web vibrated with each of her words. "We have someone who ingested quicksilver from an improperly balanced Potion of Running Enhancement."

There was a sound of tinkling glass and the invisible mana web vibrated again. A voice croaked out of the stone.

"What treatment has he received?"

"A mana reducer and a toxin neutralizer," she said.

"Alright. Which cell?"

"207."

"Understood, sending a team up."

The invisible mana web broke apart from the stone, and Professor Jules looked back to the class. Her eyes were like stone.

"Alright, I want all of you to turn off your flames, siphon the mana from your incomplete potions and go to the other side of the classroom. Now."

Her voice didn't leave any room for questions or hesitation.

Most of the students hadn't even finished cleaning up their stations when the emergency team arrived. They were serious-looking folk carrying satchels with a symbol of two snakes curling around a tower.

They bent over the young man and began a quick, efficient examination, then one of them cast a modified version of forcedisk to lift the student into the air.

"H-How does it look?" Professor Jules asked.

One turned to her and spoke in a clipped manner. "He received what he needed early and fast enough. Hopefully, it was enough to neutralize the toxin and there won't be permanent damage. We won't know until we do some tests. We'll have to do a chelation treatment as a precaution. When can you come down to file the incident reports?"

"I will be down shortly."

She watched them take the student from the room, and then whirled on the class, her eyes narrowing on the other young man who was friends with the victim. "What. Happened?"

"I..." The young man's eyes darted behind his mask. "I don't..."

"Before you continue with your answer," she said, "know that they are going to examine your friend. I already saw the potion coating his lips, and they *will* find its traces in him. If you lie about what happened, then know it will be worse for him, *but* also bad for *you* when it comes to disciplinary action."

"He, uh..." The young man swallowed loudly. "He, uh, thought it'd be funny to sip it. Like a dare! H-he... I tried to tell him not to—"

Alex didn't know the young man, but even he could tell that he was lying.

"—but he thought it'd be fine. I didn't think he'd do it! He even thought it might make him work faster because it was a potion that made you faster."

Alex glanced at Carey and she gave him a worried stare. The

story didn't make much sense. It wouldn't be much of a dare if someone dared *themselves*.

Professor Jules didn't look like she bought it either. "You should go see your friend. The infirmary will need to know *what* happened and how. You... witnessed it."

"Well, I—"

"Go."

The young man winced and hurriedly removed his safety gear and scurried out of the lab. As he did, Alex noticed Derek watching him. His eyes shifted, noticing Alex, and he looked away.

"Let this be a lesson to you all," Professor Jules said. "Potions are not wine. They are not ale or spirits or whatever people brew in dorm rooms these days."

She eyed them all steadily. "Incomplete potions can and *have* killed before. That young man will, at the least, be banned from the lab for the rest of the semester, which means he will *fail* the practical portion of POTI-1000. And *that* is a lucky outcome. He might have liver damage—which means no more wine for him—or even other organ damage. His mana pool might have been affected, ruining any aspirations he has for wizardry. Today, you will go back and you will finish your labs. If I see even a *hint* of foolishness, I will not hesitate to have you *removed* for a period of time at my discretion. Now, get back to work."

She glanced at Alex. "Stay behind after class."

Alex froze, slowly looking at Carey.

Carey simply shrugged.

"Are you alright?" Professor Jules pulled off her mask, revealing a wizened face drenched with sweat. Her white hair was limp against her scalp. "That was a fairly rough situation."

"Me?" Alex asked.

He took a deep breath, like he did when practicing meditation, and mentally checked his body. He hadn't noticed at the time, but his heart was pumping pretty hard. The event had shaken him a little. It made sense, he just witnessed someone nearly die in the Cells.

"I, uh… thanks for asking, I guess," he said. "Uh, are you okay?"

"Hm, me?" Professor Jules blinked. "Er, yes. Yes, I am. This has happened before."

"What, really?"

"Oh my yes, at least once every couple of years. Come, walk with me. I have to be at the Emergency Office. And you'll likely have to fill out some paperwork as well, since you were involved in the initial first aid."

"Alrighty." Alex focused, conjuring his forceball and hanging his books from it.

He paused when he noticed her looking at it. "Uh…" He pointed to the basket. "You want some forceball? It's got room in the basket if you want to put some of your things in, Professor."

"Hah, I can carry my own things," she said, shouldering her bag and stepping out through the door.

They walked through the Cells together, quietly at first, and Alex thought he heard the scuffling of feet down the hall. When he looked, he saw no one there. He noted to himself to listen carefully, but the Cells weren't really conducive to picking up a single quiet noise out of so many others.

Today in particular seemed to be a… busy time.

From Cell-210, smoke billowed that sparkled as though it were laced with shining gems too small for the eye to see. Cell-213 exuded a foul stench, and he could swear he heard enormous hooves scraping against the stone floor within.

Bang.

There was a heavy impact somewhere behind the iron door

of Cell-219—like something gigantic was throwing its full weight against an object somewhere behind the door—but Professor Jules paid it no mind.

He supposed she would be well-used to that sort of thing by now. With a bit of a surprise, he realized he was starting to get used to it himself. At roughly two months into his time at Generasi, he found himself still amazed by certain things, but others had started to become commonplace.

One could only see so many benches in a day that crawled and spoke before they just started to blend into the background. It was too bad, in a way. He remembered when he was very young and absolutely everything was new and utterly fascinating. To his young imagination, every darkened shadow beneath a bridge held a troll, fairies dwelled behind every tree in a forest, every rustle in the dead of night was the beat of a dragon's wings.

As he grew, though, the fantastic mystery of everyday things faded away. Maybe that had been why he'd been so attracted to books. In the everyday routine of Alric, they had been some of the few things that offered continued mysteries, learning and wonder.

He hoped magic would never get to a point where it'd become no more fantastical to him than putting on his own shoes, or the health of his neighbour's cow. What still fascinated him though were devices like he'd just seen in the lab. The aerolizer was able to fill the lungs of the young student without needing to pour a potion down his throat. The stone Professor Jules used to communicate with the Emergency Office was even more fascinating. It removed the need for letters, runners and messengers.

Theresa was *still* waiting for a letter back from her parents. How much easier would it have been if she could've simply picked up a fancy rock and used it to speak to them? He glanced at the professor as they neared the stairs.

"Professor, what was that stone? The one you used to speak to the office downstairs?" he asked.

"Oh, that. That is a far-speaker," she said, pulling the stone back out for him to see. "A clever little invention. It transfers one's voice to a sister-stone located elsewhere."

"Does it do it by using that web of mana that comes out of it? It vibrated whenever you or the person you were speaking to said something."

She looked at him in surprise. "You sensed that?"

"Yeah. Why?"

"Well, it's not an easy thing for most first-years to pick up, unless they're rather advanced in mana manipulation... Which, I suppose you are. I spoke with Professor Val'Rok. He told me some of what you've been up to in his class."

"Oh, what did he say?"

"He *said* that you managed to light up *two* glyphs on two boxes at once?"

Alex coughed awkwardly.

At the rate he was going, he'd have four glyphs lit on both boxes soon.

"Y-yeah," he said. "But I only lit two."

"Only ended up lighting two at the same time? Do you know how big of an accomplishment that is? Good lord, that box gave me *actual* nightmares when I was a student! You have a rather rare gift—"

Alex barely kept his jaw from falling open. Cedric's words to him when they'd met had been almost identical.

"—for mana manipulation, and you have skill and diligence when it comes to the careful work required for crafting potions. Considering what you've done with the box? I'd like to make you an offer."

Chapter 64

Benefits of the Talented

"Oh, uh, thank you," Alex said. "The box was pretty fun to work on, actually. Like a puzzle. What's the offe—"

"'Fun,' he says!" Professor Jules burst out laughing, which disintegrated into a coughing fit. She paused on the stairs, nearly bending double as she coughed into her sleeve.

Alex stood in front of her in case she toppled down. "You okay, Professor?"

"Ach, I'm fine, I'm fine, thank you, though." She waved him off. "Years of looking for ingredients and breathing in odd fumes takes their toll."

"Oh? The mask didn't help?"

"The mask didn't always exist for as long as I've been practicing." She straightened up. "Much of our devices—the far-speaker, for example—draw on Generasi's abnormally high ambient mana to function, and even then, Generasi's mana was not always *this* high."

"What do you mean?" he asked.

"Come, let's talk and walk again." She led him down the

stairs. "The ambient mana in the city rises over time, thanks to the wild mana vents. They keep pumping mana into the world, which circulates and gets stronger over time. Fifty years ago, something like the far-speaker just wouldn't have worked, or it would have been so expensive to make that it would have rendered it entirely impractical. Now that the ambient mana in Generasi has risen enough to power it, it's spreading through the university. As more kinks get worked out, it will make its way into the city."

"That's amazing. I know the sky-gondolas only work in Generasi, so it makes sense that other devices would too. Hmmm, over time, do you think the mana will spread to the rest of the world?"

"Very astute," she said. "Though Generasi is on a large pocket of vents, more mana *is* entering the world over time." She chuckled. "It's funny. My grandchildren will grow up in a world far more convenient than the one I learned wizardry in, and it's enough to make one a little jealous. I've had many talks with the chancellor, and according to him, there was a time when wizards *had* to draw their power from demons, elementals and otherworldly things. There just wasn't enough free mana in the world at the time to power spells and devices, as well as to start occurring in mortals."

Alex winced. "That must have been a grim world. No wonder the people need the gods so much, if you think about it. If you look at the Ravener in my homeland, how were regular folk supposed to fight it and its monsters without magic or the Heroes? The people couldn't fight it themselves, so no wonder Uldar had to do it for them."

"Ah, that is true. Many say the gods became so relied upon by mortals because there simply was little alternative for protection and power at one time. Now? Who knows. Generasi has already cast them off, and perhaps more of the world will follow." She sighed. "Very few of us will live long enough to see what untold generations will experience, so we can only imagine."

"Well, I'm just happy to be here," he said honestly. "You know, when I got into university, I was thinking only about spells, but there's *so* much more to wizardry. It's incredible."

"Ah yes, and that brings us back to the mana manipulation. The box is not 'fun' for most people, Alex." They reached the bottom of the stairwell and stepped into the basement of the Cells. This, oddly enough, was one of the brighter places in the Cells. Well-lit offices lay on either side of the hallway.

"The box is one of the most notorious tasks of mana manipulation. That's why Val'Rok decided to put it at the beginning of the course. It helps determine who has the aptitude for it... and you, apparently do."

"Is that what you were talking about?"

"That and him telling me about how you might Challenge the Exam for Credit. Just to let you know, I have *never* allowed that in POTI-1000. As you can see from today's events, it's important or even crucial for students to go through the entire course. The risks are too great otherwise in a subject like this."

"Yeah, I meant to ask you about that." He scratched his head. Toward the end of the hall was an illuminated door with a sign that read 'Emergency Office.' "Does what happened today really happen so often?"

"Oh *yes*," she said emphatically. "No matter how much caution I take or how much I emphasize it, there are *always* students that come into the course not taking it seriously or respecting the potential for serious harm. Someone thinks it'd be interesting to drink a potion too early, or someone thinks they're *more* brilliant than decades of research and decides to stealthily substitute an ingredient, or someone is too zealous with pouring their mana into a potion because they think 'more must mean better.' Some students think because they drink enormous amounts of spirits they'll tolerate untested potions the same way." She shook her head and sighed. "Even more common are the students who take the class because they wish to impress someone or because alchemy work is lucrative; meanwhile, they feel they can get through with the absolute minimum of effort. There's always *something*."

She sighed again, then glanced over to him. "I'll be blunt. When you came to me before the semester started, asking to start your own projects, I thought you'd be one of the first people the emergency team would be taking out on a forcedisk. But you've shown surprising restraint, and you knew your way around the emergency kit well."

"Hey, I'm not going to *not* learn about what might save my life, and heck, the lives of my classmates while we're learning something so dangerous. It was one of the first things I studied," he said emphatically.

"I see... You really enjoy alchemy work, don't you? Val'Rok told me of your ambition to apply to Shale's Workshop, when there's an opening. That's a difficult thing, especially for a first-year. Toraka Shale is a very particular taskmaster."

Alex winced. Val'Rok had said something almost identical. It made sense, though. Unless he really underestimated how much most jobs paid in the city, he'd be surprised if many others didn't also apply for the position. Of course, it seemed that mana manipulation and alchemy were less common skills for most wizards to develop, but there were plenty of students here at Generasi who would likely qualify if they chose to apply. Probably more qualified than him.

"Well," he said. "I still want to try, Professor. Just because something's hard doesn't mean it's not worth trying, if the goal is right."

She gave him a long look. "I see. Well, I might be able to help you. About that offer: I have been taking on a personal project with some of my graduate students. We could use some extra hands. At least, temporarily."

Alex's heart jumped. "Really?"

"Mind you, you'll basically be an assistant's assistant. You'll be helping *my* assistants, observing their work, making sure we have the tools we need at the correct times and learning what you can. It won't be glorious, but it can help give you experience. If you do well, then I might consider writing you a letter of reference."

"Yes!" He grinned. "I'll make sure you don't regret it."

She chuckled. "I warn you, it'll add extra burden onto your current course load."

"It's alright. I'd be a fool not to step up for that kind of opportunity."

Somehow, he was able to keep a straight face at what he'd said.

Then an odd thought occurred to him. A slight rise of bitterness in his belly mixed with his gratitude. Since he'd gotten to Generasi, he'd made friends, and *two* professors were offering to help him get the job he was seeking. Baelin had singled out his performance twice as well.

Back in Alric, he'd had the love of the Lu family and he'd had friends. But never the sheer amount of support he was receiving now. McHarris had been a bully and he'd just had to deal with it. He'd looked around for other work, but no one paid as well as McHarris for his limited skills, and he hadn't needed him often, so he could still attend school.

When he'd *needed* help—a lot more than he needed now, if he was honest—help had only come from close by. The Lu family, mostly. Now, professionals seemed to be lining up to help grow his already growing skill.

"Hm? Something wrong with the offer?" Professor Jules asked.

"Oh? What, no, no!" He shook himself out of his thoughts. "That's not it at all, by Uldar, I'd have to be crazy to not like the offer. It's just... Maybe this isn't the right thing to say, Professor, but it's a little overwhelming. I had to work *really* hard teaching myself magic back in my hometown." He chuckled darkly. "I nearly got myself killed a few times. Yet, when I come here, I do well in some of my classes and I've just been getting so much help."

"Ah." She nodded knowingly. "When you were struggling, no one came along to sweep you away to a better life, yet when you have gotten here on your own and now that you're *excelling*..." she chuckled, "we professors just seem to be lining up to give you help and opportunities, is that it?"

Alex startled. "Are you reading my mind or something, Professor?"

She laughed again, and her voice sounded many years younger. "No, that's *quite* illegal in Generasi, thankfully. Well, except for special circumstances. Not the point, though. It's just that you're touching on something I used to think about myself at your age. It was hard work working with potions, and I was good at it, but I needed to put in *dozens* of extra hours of study and practice. I think I aged out of my twenties before I'd even turned nineteen. I had tutoring for extra help and took advantage of my professor's office hours, but I had to initiate all of it on my own."

She looked wistful, and he wondered what scene from long ago she might have been thinking of. "Then one day, it all just *clicked* for me. I was excellent at it. I shone above my peers, if I do say so myself. Suddenly, my professors were paying attention to me. Extra help. Extra care. Extra opportunities. I wouldn't be where I am today, if it weren't for what they did for me then.

"It's the nature of life where people support those that already have talent or the potential for success. The beggar suffering from leprosy on the street is shunned, while the mighty, conquering hero is lifted up on the shoulders of the cheering populace. A struggling student has to work themselves to the bone just to avoid failing, while the student who stands out gets suggested for research opportunities or new grants. That is why we have programs for students who struggle at Generasi, to make sure all get the help they need. In the end, people like to see others shine, and people only have so much time and resources. There are only so many opportunities, and I only have so many hours in a day to dedicate to student well-being."

She glanced up to the ceiling. "What if the student I spent hour upon hour helping one day decides to drink quicksilver for a stupid dare and ends up being expelled or killed? What if the student I invite into *my* lab ends up being irresponsible and gets themselves kicked out for cheating on an exam a month later? There's a reason people gravitate toward those that have talent and reliability, Mr. Roth. I'd just be thankful that others can see your innate abilities and the time you've put in."

"Yeah, thanks, Professor."

That made him feel a little better.

Alex thought about Lucia. He wondered how much help *she'd* gotten in her last days at Generasi, and even after. In the end, he supposed he should just be thankful he was getting extra help now. Working to stand out was paying off.

Maybe, when he was a second-year, he could take up tutoring and give some help to new first-year students who were struggling. As long as they weren't like Derek or Minervus, of course.

"It is important to remember that force is not indestructible. While it does not have *obvious* counters like the elemental forces, force spells can be countered and blocked by other force magic. It can be torn apart, and since it is so pure, it is more easily dispelled than many other forms of magic. Force is mighty and versatile, but I encourage you to learn other forms of magic as well."

Professor Ram closed the textbook with a decidedly hard snap. The hand that held the book was not made of flesh. Something had taken his right arm at some point, and it had been replaced by a limb of magical force that connected to his shoulder.

Magical force spells tended to glow different colours depending on their caster, the professor's was a deep, dead black —darker even than his well-sculpted beard.

"Any questions?"

He looked through the class, but everyone—even Alex—didn't have one to ask. Professor Ram never discouraged questions, but there was something intimidating about the man's every movement.

"Excellent," he said, raising his hand. "Today, we're going to do something a little different. You'll have about one free hour for practice. But before you start..." His eyes seemed to spark. "I want you to hang on to your desks."

The students glanced at each other and then quickly gripped the sides of their desks.

The professor clenched the hand of his force-constructed arm into a fist.

Alex gasped as his weight suddenly pressed into his seat. His stomach flipped as his desk and chair unexpectedly soared into the air through the auditorium. Throughout the room, the sounds of gasping, yelping and giggling filled the air.

The desks moved apart from each other, giving each student at least ten feet of open space around them.

Professor Ram smiled, snapping the fingers of both hands.

The desks and tables immediately froze, perfectly stable in midair.

"Pretty fantastic, isn't it?" he asked. "Force is not only about the creation of magical constructs. It is also the bending of the very physical forces of nature, such as gravity, or the repulsion and attraction between objects. You'll find that you're not able to pry yourselves from your seats, even if you use a pry bar. No danger of falling. Not while I have control."

He watched them carefully. "And I always do. By the end of the year and the end of Part II of this course, you'll be able to—or perhaps I should say, be *expected* to do the same yourselves. You'll learn to unravel the spell on your desks and chairs, be able to cancel and recast it. For now, make good use of your hour. Remember, your forceball report is due next week, but if you feel you are ahead, you may practice whichever spell you have received my approval to practice." He started to turn toward his desk, then stopped. "Oh, and by the way, don't hesitate to speak up if anyone needs to use the facilities, and I'll bring you right down. We don't want you up there squirming around like earthworms." He laughed at that.

Alex and the rest of the class looked at each other and began wiggling their bodies to see if they could get out of their seats. They found they couldn't and settled down to work.

His desk and attached chair had floated near a window, offering him an awesome view of the campus from high above. He smiled, watching the students below and idly wondering if any of his friends were down there. Khalik should have been getting out of class shortly, if he remembered his schedule right.

He took a deep breath to focus up and turned his attention to force magic. Once class was over, then he could think about meeting up for some food.

Alex stretched his fingers, then took a deep, meditative breath to bring his mind into focus. First, it would be time for warm-ups.

Chapter 65

Arm-wrestling Wizard's Hand

Alex opened his notebook to a new page, and while using meditation techniques to navigate the Mark's interference, he cast forceball, counting his heartbeats to time the completion of the spell. It winked into existence like an old friend and he cut the flow of mana to its magic circuit. Next, it was time to record how long it took before the forceball faded.

Forceball Spell Formation: Five Heartbeats

Dissipation: Ten Heartbeats

Better.

He'd gotten even faster at casting the spell thanks to Theresa's meditation techniques. Yet, as pleased as he was with his progress, he was also getting a little frustrated.

He still hadn't gotten anywhere close to his speed before he'd received the Mark, and—looking around at his classmates—he noticed most of them were casting it faster than he could. Some had only started learning the spell on the first day of class, and seeing their forceballs appear after only two or three heartbeats was a little annoying.

He took a deep breath, acknowledged his feelings and then

let them go. Frustration was narrowing his focus, causing him to only see part of what was really going on. That wasn't helpful, so he decided to mentally step back and examine their forceballs compared to his own.

None of their spells were as large or as strong as his. Some weren't very stable and flickered, and even some cast by students who'd started the class already knowing the spell, were slower and tended to fluctuate at times.

Their forceballs might have been cast quicker, but his won in power and precision, and it was thanks to his constant practice and analyzing the Mark's interference. The Mark did have its downsides, but it also had its benefits.

He turned his focus back to his work, and this time, he cast forcedisk.

The spell took longer than his forceball before it appeared. While he wasn't as fast at casting it as he would've liked, it *was* still appearing faster, and showing major improvements in power, precision and stability.

It'd better be getting better, he mused, flipping through his notebook. There were a huge number of failures that he'd jotted down and analyzed. It almost hurt to look at the pages.

Unfortunately, he was still hitting a wall with how much he could improve the spell at the moment. He wondered if he would have another breakthrough when he learned more force spells and more about force magic in general. Also, when his mana pool increased, he'd have more room for bigger magic circuits. He could try expanding the circuits for forcedisk and forceball and constructing them in new ways. He wondered what improvements he could make then.

He dismissed those thoughts along with forcedisk.

Those were plans for later. For now, warm-ups were complete.

Now, it was time for the *really* painful part.

He opened up the spell-guide for Wizard's Hand and—

taking a deep breath and readying himself for the Mark—began to cast the spell. Previous failures bombarded his mind like a hailstorm.

He considered one in particular using his meditation techniques. An image from yesterday where the Mark's distraction caused another unique misalignment in the magic circuit.

He winced as he cut off the flow of mana and ended the spell.

Flipping open the notebook for Wizard's Hand to his previously recorded failures, he noted the specifics of the misalignment, frowning as his eyes scanned the pages. Despite being a brand-new notebook, it was already half-filled with failures. He'd generated far more mistakes for *this* spell than he had for forceball *or* forcedisk.

Alex sighed. Even though it was also a first-tier spell, it was more complex than the other two. Wizard's Hand wasn't a simple shape like a sphere or flat circle. It was a force construction that mimicked the complex shapes and movements of a human hand. In the same way, its spell array was far more intricate than the others. Its magic circuit had lots of smaller moving parts and details, and lots of places for the Mark to interfere and make things go wrong.

Still, repeatedly practicing it had generated some progress. He'd gotten a little further into constructing the magic circuit each time.

He glanced around at the other students.

In truth, he was still ahead of many of them in some ways; yet in other ways, they were quickly exceeding him.

Some were already casting fairly solid-looking Wizard's Hand spells. One had even progressed to the point of starting to work on casting Force Shield, and Alex noticed Professor Ram's deep-set eyes watching *that* student very carefully. There was an interest there that he'd seen in both Val'Rok and Jules when they interacted with *him*.

He stifled a chuckle and a little twinge of jealousy. Professor Ram had been impressed with Alex's forceball in the early weeks, but while the instructor was still supportive and helpful to all his students, he showed a keener interest in those that were continually excelling in the class.

And right now, that wasn't Alex. He was only doing *well enough*.

Oh well, he thought. *Shouldn't be greedy. You're already getting opportunities.*

He promised himself that even if he had to try until he went cross-eyed, he'd excel in force magic eventually. And not for favouritism, but for his own benefit. All he needed was effort and time. He looked down at his notebook. Well, time, effort and the willpower to not go mad from having all his failures thrown in his face. With resolve, he began to recast Wizard's Hand.

By the time Professor Ram called their floating desks down, Alex had gone from frustrated to pleased with his work for the period. He'd still only made a snail's progress moving forward with the spell, but there was still time left to work on it before its corresponding assignment was due. He also recognized that not everything in life went smoothly.

He understood that better than many.

Conjuring his forceball, he gathered his class materials, placed them in the hanging basket and stepped out of the classroom, only to run into a waiting Theresa.

"Alex!" She was waving at him excitedly from the wall she'd been leaning on. In each hand, she clutched a letter. "My parents wrote back!"

"From what the mail office said, there was a big problem with delivery in the Rhinean Empire, which is why it took so long to get here," Theresa said as they sat down for lunch at a picnic table on campus. "Some kind of monster was prowling one of the highways; black scaled, but humanoid with big claws. There were travellers who first saw it, and then it was seen near a town. Apparently, a group of elemental knights were sent to the area to patrol and they stopped all travel around there while they looked for this thing. Anyway, they never found it, so they finally opened things back up."

She placed a second letter on the table and laughed. "And *this* one's from Captain Fan-Dor. Would you believe he addressed it to all of us, including Brutus? He's *so* funny. Anyway, it seems you're in luck; he says he'll have time to teach you more Mop-and-Oar—"

"*Spear*-and-Oar Dance," Alex insisted as he broke off a piece of olive bread and handed it to her. "And that's great! But first, tell me how your parents are. How *is* everyone?"

"Well, they're fine, though Father was pretty upset when he found one of his Grandfather's swords was missing," she said. "Mother wrote that he calmed down after a bit. She also said I should have asked permission."

"Maybe you should have?" Alex offered. "I don't think your parents would have been mad if you wanted to take it for protection. I mean, it's not like you were running off to go sell it for loose change at the market or something."

"Yeah, maybe you're right. Either way, I'll get a chance to apologize soon. They want to come and visit."

"Oh man, when?" Alex asked. "For Sigmus?"

"No, they didn't say anything specific yet. They asked where they could stay, though."

"Hrm." He tapped his chin. "There's no room at our place in the insula, and we don't know how much the inns in the city charge."

"Yeah," Theresa said. "I'm going to look into that this weekend."

"Good idea," Alex said. "Maybe I can talk to Hobb. He might know of some place on campus... but, with the prices the university charges, maybe the city'll be better. Anyway, we'll find something for them. Now, what'd they say about you following your great-grandfather in qigong?"

"Uh, well... Mother didn't really say much about that. Just a 'he would be happy, I think.' ...I kind of thought they'd react a little more."

"Huh, how do you feel about that?"

"A little disappointed, I guess." She shrugged. "Though it could have been worse. They could have disowned me for stealing Great-grandfather's sword."

"Hey, maybe they're saving that for when they get here. Just a full magistrate-supervised disownment."

"Oh Uldar, don't even joke about that."

"Well, I'm only half-joking. They *could* be waiting to have a discussion with you face to face, instead of trying to send what they're thinking in a letter, you know?"

She thought about it. "That's probably true. Ugh, now I'm going to be excited *and* nervous waiting for their visit."

"I'm sure it'll be fine, in the end."

"I hope so... So! About Fan-Dor. He wants you to name a time to meet him at the docks. They'll be in port for a few weeks. Do you want to do it this weekend? We could make a day of it with Selina."

"Ugh, I'd love to, but this weekend, I'll be helping out Professor Jules for the first time. I can't miss that."

"Ah, that's too bad." She sighed, then looked at him worriedly. "Are you... are you doing okay, Alex?"

"Hm, what do you mean?"

"I mean, 'are you okay.' You've been pushing really, really hard lately. Exercise. Practice. Classes. Studying. You just don't stop. Then you've been cooking too... and if it's this busy now, what's going to happen during exam time?"

"Hey, one of the reasons I'm pushing so hard *now* is so I don't have to push so hard when it's exam time." He smiled. "Pay it now, instead of paying it later. Besides, your meditation's been helping me relax, rest and cope with the schedule. The exercise helps too. I sleep even better than I did back home and I've got more energy these days. I'm doing okay."

"Hm, and what about this job at Shale's?" she asked. "If you get it, it's going to take up even more time in the evenings."

He shrugged. "I'll figure something out. For now, I'm okay."

"You promise you'll tell me if you're not?"

"Yeah, I promise, I promise," he said. "What about you? You work on Life Enforcement stuff all the time, and then it's exercise and learning things from the Watchers of Roal. And you're taking care of Brutus and watching out for Selina as much as I am. You're busy too."

"I guess. It's all just so much fun, though." She giggled. "It doesn't feel like being busy, and besides, I think I might be able to get a job if I keep at it."

"Oh?" Alex cocked his head.

She leaned in. "There's this Watcher I'm starting to get to know, and she's friends with the wardens at the beastarium. When she heard how much experience I have with animals, she said she'd ask if they needed any help. I know it's not anything really... solid yet, but it's something."

"I think it's great." Alex smiled. "You get to earn some coin doing what you like and what you're good at. That's about as good as it gets, isn't it?"

"Yeah, I just hope it works out. It'd be kind of nice to have a job by the time my parents get here."

"Yeah, I know what you mean. But, hey, hopefully this work with Professor Jules is going to help me with Shale's."

"At least you're in school." She gave an uncharacteristically cute pout. "I'm the one that's just auditing courses, meditating and training. I kind of feel like I'm getting lazy."

"I don't know, from what I've seen, all that cultivation stuff is hard," he said.

"Yeah, but it's fun, so it doesn't *feel* hard. Ach, it's like I'm just hanging around."

"Hey, what do you call people that don't work for their coin and just hang around?"

She cocked her head. "What?"

"Nobility, Lady Theresa of Thameland."

She burst out laughing.

The mana within the cell hit Alex like a club.

He hovered at the door, taken aback. Mana-powered apparatuses filled the room ahead, surrounding a cauldron that was bigger than a noble's carriage. A giant mana vacuum hung over it, connected to a mana waste container the size of a farmer's cart, which sat in a corner of the massive room.

Hundreds of complex ingredients had been set out on multiple tables beside tools of alchemy, some he easily recognized, but most were new to him.

A staircase built beside the cauldron led to a catwalk surrounding its broad, glyph-etched lip.

Professor Jules, completely suited up except for her mask, was talking with two others. She smiled when she saw him enter.

"Ah, Mr. Roth, you're early! Good, good." She pointed to a series of hooks on the side of the room. "Hang your things, wash up, and gear up. We'll be doing some good work today, and there's a lot for you to learn."

"Oh? What *are* we doing, Professor?"

Her smile became a little unsettling. "Chaos Essence to craft mutagens and the potions that can animate the inanimate. Today, you'll see how the building blocks of matter can be a harness. And today, we are harnessing the harness."

Chapter 66

The Summoning

"Stage Two of the brewing process is not delicate, but we'll have to be quick today." Professor Jules addressed her squad of graduate students like she was a general. She looked at Alex. "With chaos essence, it's best to make sure the reaction isn't drawn out. It's too hard to predict, otherwise."

He wrote down what she said in his notebook word-for-word.

"Ah yes, where's my mind these days." She shook her head. "Team, this is Mr. Roth, a first-year student. Today, he'll be assisting you with any ingredients you might need during any moment in the brewing process, and providing you with tools you might want at any time. Think of him as one of your assistants and use him as such. In return, if he has any questions, please answer them if time permits, and allow him to observe you as you work."

She glanced at Alex.

"Do as we say, keep out of trouble, and learn well, Mr. Roth. If you don't know something, then don't pretend that you do. If someone asks for a tool or an ingredient you don't understand how to handle, then please say so. Don't bluff."

"Absolutely." He nodded emphatically, the beak on his mask bouncing.

"Right, now let's get started with planning. Alex, have you gone over our safety procedures?"

He nodded, drawing out a booklet listing the safety procedures, ethical guidelines, required materials and tools for the experiment, which she'd handed him before they'd last parted.

Oddly enough, what followed next wasn't similar to being in potions class. It was like being back in McHarris' bakery. Without his yelling and incessant bullying. Professor Jules' team leapt into action, and while they were preparing for today's set up, Alex was given the task of reviewing the ingredients and tools, and remembering where they were located in the lab.

Some were labelled, though many others were not.

When one of the graduate students needed a tool, he would be expected to provide it quickly, but safely, and then return it to its proper place afterward. He was also expected to wash certain tools and provide ingredients when necessary.

For that, he needed to learn the system of organization, and thankfully, the lab booklet had given him a head start on figuring out what was what. He walked past every table, flipping open his notebook and drawing a diagram of the lab's layout as it would look to someone standing above. Essentially, he created a floor plan, marking in every table, as well as denoting the central cauldron and scaffold. On each table—in meticulous script—he wrote the names for each ingredient and piece of equipment present, flipping back to the lab booklet several times to ensure he'd remembered the names of the tools properly.

He made sure to study the system of organization very, very carefully.

One thing he'd learned well from his time at McHarris' bakery was that there were few things more valuable than an efficient organizing system, and one every worker knew well. That was one of the things he had to give the old bully. The baker had developed quite the system for organizing ingredients over the years, and was absolutely *militant* about it never being altered.

When he'd first started working at the bakery, McHarris drilled that system into his head so thoroughly, he dreamt about the different locations for flour, custards and salted meats for weeks. At the time, he'd resented how strict it was. Then, about a year later, another assistant was hired.

He had been a young man with more experience than any of the others, having apprenticed to a baker for many years when he was younger. He had a lot of confidence in himself and got it into his head that the system used in his old bakery was better than McHarris'. One evening, he decided to surprise McHarris and *change* the system instead of just doing what he was supposed to be doing, which was cleaning up.

Maybe the apprentice fantasized about coming into a new environment, seeing that everything was a mess and knowing *exactly* what to do to transform it into a model of order and efficiency.

Alex had even considered what it would be like to walk into Professor Jules' lab today and use the Mark to improve the system they already had in place. In that fantasy, they would fall all over themselves, thanking him for fixing their way of doing things and offer him permanent positions and greater opportunities. At least he knew better than to act on his fantasies.

McHarris hadn't thanked the young man or offered him great opportunities.

He'd lashed him, berated him and summarily fired him. And before he would let him leave, he made him return everything to exactly the way he'd found it. Alex couldn't recall ever seeing McHarris so angry, before or since, and *that* was saying something.

With that memory in mind, Alex let fantasies go and simply focused on learning Professor Jules' system as fast as he could, and finding ways to make *himself* as efficient as possible within it.

Luckily, with the skills he'd gained using the Mark, there were some easy solutions.

Once he'd catalogued every piece of equipment and ingredient he was expected to know, he conjured his forceball and hung his basket beneath it. He considered trying to cast Wizard's Hand. The spell would have made much of what he was about to do easier, but he'd only made a little more progress with it. In another week, he might have it down, but for now, he could only adapt and use what he had.

Casting forcedisk as well, he set them side by side.

One of the students looked down at him from the scaffold around the cauldron. She was busy tracing the glyphs lining the massive cauldron's lip, passing her mana into each glyph as she did, and Alex noticed that each one lit up with a sapphire light as the mana flowed in.

Two other grad students were tracing the glyphs etched into the cauldron as well. One's glyphs glowed a sapphire hue while the other's was a forest-green.

"I wouldn't use those if I were you," the student who was looking at him said. "Those spells tend to be slow. It's easier just to step down and pick things up, trust me."

"Normally, you'd be right," Professor Jules said from across the room. She was cutting up something that looked like fish-meat, though it was a strange blue colour. "But Mr. Roth has shown himself very adept at forceball. I trust you show similar control when it comes to forcedisk, Alex?"

Without looking at the spell, he used mana manipulation and the glowing spell began performing little tricks in the air. It twisted vertically and spun like a top before turning and flipping horizontally. It spun really fast, then slowly, then shot back and forth across the back of the room like an excited dog playing in the beastarium.

Several of the graduate students paused their tasks to watch his display of forceball acrobatics. One even clapped softly when he finished.

"Alright, a simple 'yes' would have sufficed, Mr. Roth," Professor Jules said, but her voice revealed her amusement. She looked at the graduate student that questioned him. "Does that satisfy you?"

"Yeah," she said. "You must have practiced with those spells for a ridiculously long time."

He shrugged. "I'm like a swordsmaster slowly becoming one with their weapon. Except, y'know, it's a couple of utility spells... Eh, you know, that sounded a lot more impressive in my head. Anyway, let me make sure I've got your system down."

The grad student looked at him for a few seconds as Professor Jules shook her head and went back to work.

Alex went over his diagrams a few more times before finally nodding to himself. He wandered over to the students, watching them trace the glyphs into the lip of the cauldron. The booklet said the glyphs must be traced using mana manipulation, but hadn't really gone into the why or how.

He climbed the stairs and stood at the back of the catwalk, watching the closest glyphs light up under a student's attention. He glanced back at Alex and the beak of the young man's mask bounced lightly. "Hello there, curious about something?"

"Uh... about everything, actually," Alex said honestly. "What are those symbols for? Some kind of mana conductor?"

"Noooot quite." The student traced another glyph, getting closer to one of his colleagues activating glyphs on another side of the cauldron. "This is a built-in protection circle."

"Oh, to stop explosions and leaks?"

"No, to stop what we're summoning in the cauldron from getting *out* of the cauldron."

"Uh, summoning?"

"Yeah, it's the only reliable way to get your hands on chaos essence. The stuff's almost unheard of in the material world, but it's as common as water in certain creatures that occur on other planes. The cauldron's built, in part, to serve as a summoning circle for otherworldly beings. And theeen—"

He pointed down to another circle of glyphs inside the bottom of the cauldron. "You see that other circle there? That's similar to a mana vacuum. Instead, it separates certain essences from any creature within the cauldron."

Alex winced. "Sounds painful."

"It can be," the older student said. "But for the kinds of things we summon, they kind of deserve it, trust me. And in the end, they do live through it and then we banish them back to their home plane. It's no worse than having a doctor bleed you a bit, I would say."

Alex looked down at the glyphs inside the cauldron. There was something sinister about them. There was an aura present that felt like they were tinged with pure malice. Or rage. A shiver ran through him.

"Uh... what's being summoned?" he asked, pulling his eyes away from the cauldron's bottom.

"A lesser shoggoth. You ever heard of them? Probably not, eh?" the graduate student asked.

"No, I haven't."

"Well, the easiest way I can describe them, is they're priests, in a way. The least powerful servitors in a divine hierarchy. Think local priest in a village church."

"Uh, priests? What do they worship?"

The student gave a dark laugh. "You don't want to know."

"Um." Alex glanced at the glowing symbols on the side of the cauldron, and began wondering if he needed an exit plan. "Uh, maybe I do."

"Okay, well, I won't go into too much detail, but there are all sorts of... *things*, out there. What lesser shoggoths worship are kind of like gods or demon lords, but they're older. A *lot* older.

Old enough that they already existed when the gods of this world first woke up."

"Oh." Alex swallowed. "From what you said earlier, I take it they're not friendly?"

"The lesser shoggoths? Absolutely not friendly. The things they worship? They're mostly indifferent, actually." The grad student finished up one side of the cauldron and stepped back, turning to Alex. "And that's lucky for us. We'll be able to do what we have to do without the *big* bosses getting mad. Well, probably. Records of them coming into contact with mortals, well... let's just say they tend to be found in ruins of dead civilizations."

"Oh... and uh, we're going to summon one of these priests and drain essence from it? That uh... well, uh..."

"Sounds like the worst idea ever conceived in the history of the world?" The graduate student laughed behind his mask. "You'd think so, wouldn't you? Think about it this way. If a priest of one of our gods gets disrespected or robbed in the street by some villain, does their god immediately descend from the heavens to seek revenge? Do they descend whenever someone says anything blasphemous against them?"

"I guess not," Alex said. If they did, they probably would have gathered at Generasi demanding their priests be let in a long time ago.

He imagined it for a moment. A series of towering, glowing divine beings all lined up in front of the school's gates like disgruntled villagers waiting to register their complaints with the local magistrate.

"Exactly." The grad student pointed up to the ceiling. "If they acted every time a mortal angered them, they probably would have blown up half the world by now. And these older things? Well, they're even *more* indifferent."

"But... what happens if one of these... lesser shoggoths

happens to be a favourite or something? And us summoning and harvesting from it angers whatever it worships?"

"I suppose, a vengeful entity from beyond time will materialize in the cell." The student nodded thoughtfully. "In displaying itself, we'll be shown an existence so far beyond our comprehension that our minds will turn inside out, followed by our bodies. Natural law will fail, and anything we understand about magic will go with it. Our souls will melt away in an instant, only to be reformed *wrong*, and we'll try to scream, but have no mouth with which to—"

Professor Jules cleared her throat. She had brought out a series of sealed metal containers from a storage room in the back of the cell, each of them suspended on floating stone circles. "If you have time to be idly scaring first-years, then you have time to help me prepare the pre-made solution for Stage Two."

"Right, right, sorry, Prof." The student laughed. "I wouldn't sweat it... Alex, was it? There's always risks with magic, and we're taking every precaution to make an unsafe process as safe as possible. And hey, if we wanted something without risk, we'd go work in a vineyard, am I right?"

The graduate student winked from behind his mask and made for the stairs off the catwalk.

Alex watched him go, a part of him wondering if the local vineyards were taking applications.

Chapter 67

Beyond the Material World

As the last of the glyphs were traced and filled with mana, there was a subtle shift in the mana in the air around the cauldron's rim. It was so faint, Alex doubted he would have detected it before he'd started training in mana manipulation at the school.

With a flash, a purple light washed through the glyphs, wiping away the colours left by the students and every glyph on the edge all glowed the same hue. At the same time, the mana shifted. All the subtle differences between each student's mana were brought together and became unified within the cauldron.

At that, Professor Jules began to organize her students like a general moving an army, and Alex went to work.

Standing by the tables, he watched the students while staying at a distance. In quiet moments, he'd ask questions about specific ingredients, procedures and tools they were using. He also asked which processes were similar to golem-craft, and the answers were not only interesting, but helpful for future golem plans.

As it turned out, many of the materials used for the animation of matter were identical to ones used in golem-craft. By asking questions, handing out what the students needed and observing them work, he learned a good deal about how each material was handled, and how that might differ when building a golem compared to the experiment they were conducting.

Many of the mana tools were also used in golem-craft, and Alex examined them as the students or professor described them and their specific uses. His pen flew across the pages of his notebook when he could spare the hands to write things down, and he was left wishing he'd managed to master Wizard's Hand already. An extra hand or two would be pretty helpful to keep up with all the information coming at him.

When things got busy, the time for questions ended and he was put to work, and with a seamlessness that unnerved him, he fell back into the mindset of an assistant baker with a very particular master. His mind stayed focused on making sure he was quick to get whatever was needed for each step of the brewing process. The pages of the procedure scrolled through his mind, helping him anticipate what they would need for the next part of the experiment.

That was where his spells came in handy.

Using forcedisk and the forceball's basket, he was able to use them to create a system where he took a request from one of the students or the professor, and instead of constantly running back and forth between the table and cauldron, he was able to simply ferry what was needed back and forth between them.

When someone was done with a tool, he would send over the forcedisk for them to place it on and then he'd bring it over to the sink for washing and drying. As his system continued, he noticed several of the grad students throwing him curious looks.

He decided to ask another question.

"Uh, Professor." He cleared his throat. "Um, is there a reason you all don't use spells like Wizard's Hand? I know forcedisk and forceball wouldn't usually work well, but Wizard's Hand has the dexterity to handle delicate stuff, right?"

"Right you are, but there are two issues there. One, Wizard's Hand still proceeds very slowly compared to simply walking over and fetching something yourself." She glanced at his crimson spells, zipping about the lab. "Well, at least it does if someone doesn't put a ridiculous amount of practice into it. But, the mana manipulation and spellcraft required for our work still necessitates full attention. Controlling a Wizard's Hand spell *while* engaging in the mana manipulation required for this alchemy would be a good recipe for both failure *and* disaster."

She glanced at the glowing glyphs around the rim. "And when you're dealing with conjuring otherworldly entities, you *want* to have as much of your wits about you as possible."

Professor Jules had led his labs and set up this experiment with the calm collection of a veteran. Now, though? Her voice was strained.

"Okay, I'll just make sure you have everything you need and keep out of the way," he said.

"Yes, you'd better." She frowned, her eyes flicking to him. "What you're about to see, Mr. Roth, is perhaps the earliest form of wizardry. Before the formulae, the ingredients, the safety procedures, the spellcraft and the harvesting of mana, there was this. The old ways." She looked over their work. "All the ingredients are ready to proceed except for one. If I were you, I would stand near the door."

Alex nodded, and took up position near the door to the cell.

Professor Jules and her graduate students ascended the catwalk around the cauldron. Before this moment, the room had been filled with orders, discussion and planning. Now there was only a grim silence.

The air seemed to prickle with intent.

They all nodded to each other, and Professor Jules looked to one of her students. "Ready the bait."

A gloved young woman raised the strange blue meat the professor had been cutting up. It now glistened from a coating of an odd reddish salve that emitted an unnerving mana. Alex wondered what the thing would have smelled like if he didn't have a mask on.

The student spoke an incantation, conjuring a Wizard's Hand, which lifted the blue meat and slowly lowered it below the rim of the cauldron, down into its depths.

As soon as the bait had been deposited, the student cancelled the Wizard's Hand.

Professor Jules drew in a deep breath. "Are we ready?"

In reply, a series of nods met her. To his surprise, she also glanced at Alex standing by the door. His heart began to thud in his chest and he too gave a nod.

"Let us begin then," Professor Jules said.

She spoke an incantation.

Womph.

An unnatural fire sprang up beneath the cauldron, hugging its metal sides but not touching the scaffolding or catwalk around it. As it flared and crackled, the shadows of the wizards on the catwalk rose high over the room's walls and wavered with each pop of the flame.

Professor Jules slowly raised her hands above her head.

And then, she began to cast a spell.

Words of power poured from her mouth with her exacting efficiency. Not a single word could Alex understand. They were sharp. Guttural. Awful to listen to.

And there was a terrible note of longing in them.

A calling that disturbed him to his very bones.

Something shifted in the air.

As her incantation continued, her students joined in, each adding their own words until the room was *filled* with the strange, disconcerting speech.

Spell arrays formed.

Magic circuitry came alive.

The glyphs on the cauldron reacted, glowing brighter.

The hair on Alex's neck began to rise. Never before had he seen anything like it. In his time at Generasi, all the magic he witnessed was a mix of wonder and exacting, mathematical precision.

This was different.

In the shifting light, crackling sound, and awful words slipping through the air, the wizards around the cauldron didn't look like a professor and her graduate students. Their beaked face coverings seemed to change before him, turning into the ancient death masks of some forgotten demon. Their coats and aprons glistening like the skins of slain beasts.

His imagination began to run.

The room filled with apparatuses and safety equipment shifted, turning into an ancient cave, filled with primal power. The friendly academics became ritualists from a time when the world was younger. Darker.

A time before Generasi and before Uldar and all the things he took for granted.

Something disturbed the air.

He gasped.

Something had entered the room.

He couldn't see it. Couldn't smell it. Couldn't hear it.

But, a long-forgotten part of his brain—the part that knew well why mortals feared the dark—sensed it. On the scaffold, the volume of the incantation rose, and the fire began to writhe as though wind battered it.

He shivered, and suddenly, his mask felt stifling.

Alex Roth edged closer to the door.

The air began to shimmer. He *felt* something touch it. His mana vibrated in his body, reacting to it with familiarity, like the touch of the Traveller's mana.

What was happening above the cauldron was similar, though far more twisted. And ugly.

Something poured out of the air, down into the cauldron,

and a massive presence filled the room. A mind so vast and old, his life seemed tiny. Like a mere flickering candle flame before it.

Similar to when he'd reached deep into the dungeon core and *felt* what was behind it. Though this felt far more alien. Colder.

He shuddered.

The entity continued pouring from whatever lay beyond the air, to splash deep into the cauldron.

It gave a final shudder, and then, it was fully in the room.

The cauldron shifted as something heavy moved within. That something slithered against the inner surfaces, like a mass of writhing snakes, and there was a slurping sound, like someone sucking the pulp from soft fruit.

"What... what the hell..." he whispered.

The volume of the incantation rose higher, until every wizard screamed it. It echoed off the walls and the words combined together until all became a gibbering mass of noise.

"*Now*!" Jules cried.

She slammed her gloved palms onto the rim of the cauldron. Her students following. The glyphs flared so brightly, they stung Alex's eyes.

For a second, the thing inside the pot went silent.

And then it screamed.

Alex pressed himself to the door. When the sound hit him, it hit *all* of his senses. He didn't just *hear* its scream. He *felt* and *smelled* it. He even tasted it, and the taste made him gag under his mask.

Tentacles shot up into the air, each of them shifting with all the colours he'd seen on the cauldron, and some he couldn't even put names to. They made his eyes burn, and he squinted like he'd been staring at the sun. Tears ran down his cheeks, but he didn't dare look away.

The tentacles lashed out, slamming into translucent walls

that rose above the rim of the cauldron. Glyphs flared as the thing pushed against the magic.

"This one's strong!" Jules shouted. "Feed the cauldron! Twenty percent more mana. Now!"

Her students gripped the rim and the mana once again shifted in the air.

The creature screamed in a painful pitch, then tried pushing against the barrier again. This time, the glyphs didn't flare and it scratched against its glassy cage in vain. Its tentacles shuddered, pounding against the binding magic while they sprang pointed thorns like a rose.

Still, the wall did not give.

Its flesh shifted again, transforming into hooked claws that scraped against the barrier. Still, its cage did not fail. With another scream, its tentacles shifted once more, forming bony flanges like a mace.

Crack. Crack.

It snapped the tentacles against the barrier, but that too was futile. The barrier held.

The ends of the tentacles shimmered, splitting open to reveal long mouths filled with fangs and bit at the barrier to no effect. The lesser shoggoth howled in frustration.

Alex felt a shift of... something, in the air. It wasn't mana. He didn't even know *how* to describe it.

Bang!

Something impacted the barrier. Glyphs flared.

"Forty percent more mana!" Jules barked.

The students grunted, feeding their mana into the cauldron at whatever unseen attack was slamming into the barrier over and over again.

Until abruptly, it stopped. Like a breath being held. Then silence. Alex felt a strange probing begin to fill the air.

"That's right," Professor Jules said. "You are trapped, Servitor. You cannot strike our bodies. You cannot strike our minds.

And you cannot touch the vessel you are caged within. By these three facts, I declare you bound."

After a moment, the lesser shoggoth *spoke*.

What came from it weren't words as Alex understood them, and their sound crossed his senses again, like the legs of crawling insects against his skin and deep within his ears.

"That is right," Jules said. "We do wish to bargain. You have feasted on the flesh of Pterophyllia." She raised another piece of the coated blue meat. "A delicacy to you."

That horrible voice answered.

"As I thought. In return for this second portion, I ask that you donate a portion of your chaos essence to our cause. We do not require much, and your life will not be harmed by this donation. Once we have harvested what we need, you will have your freedom, as well as this portion. If you comply, the process will not cause you suffering, or whatever passes for it amongst your kind, and you will be freed to return back to your plane without delay." The professor seemed to tighten her grip on the lip of the cauldron before she continued. "Do we have an accord?"

There was silence.

Then a short grunt.

"Good. I will show that you may trust me in future." She glanced at her students. "Now. Activate it."

Chapter 68

The Devil that You Know...

The grad students poured their mana into the cauldron, this time reaching deep into the metal vessel. Alex could sense the mana travelling lower toward the bottom of the pot. Then the glyphs flared again.

Professor Jules called to Alex, still standing by the door. "It's likely safe for you to join us now, Mr. Roth, and I'd recommend that you do if you wish to see the extraction process. I believe you'll find this to be a very valuable experience, and not one that comes around every day."

"Oh, by Uldar, no," Alex muttered, staring up at the catwalk.

He took a deep breath, putting one foot in front of the other and making for the stairs. His skin prickled the closer he got to the lesser shoggoth, and the sensation of an unnaturalness, or even a *wrongness* crossed over his senses. He was approaching something that should *not* exist in this world.

Yet, he pushed himself to keep going.

It's stuck in the pot. It's stuck in the pot. You're surrounded by wizards with experience, and it's stuck in the pot, Alex repeated in his mind. *You're probably in more danger in the Barrens, and this is stuff you'll need to get used to. Just pretend you're Cedric for like... two minutes.*

Alex stepped onto the catwalk, met Professor Jules' eyes from across the cauldron, and looked down.

His heart nearly stopped beating.

The thing in the cauldron defied his senses as they struggled to make sense of it. Its form shifted constantly. A writhing ooze of tentacles, eyes, mouths and organs. The surface of the main part of its body shimmered with images that were familiar, yet maddeningly corrupted. Entire forests of giant tongues instead of trees, oceans filled not with water, but with infinite swarms of insects, and other vistas that made his skin crawl. From below its body, the runes at the bottom of the cauldron glowed as Jules' assistants poured their mana into them.

Then the creature shuddered.

A strange misty substance began to flow from its sides. When it touched the metal of the cauldron, the substance congealed into a liquid. Like vapour coming into contact with cold air. The droplets shimmered and twitched before pouring down and pooling beneath the writhing lesser shoggoth.

The liquid continued to pool until there was enough to coat the bottom of the vessel.

"Aaaand, stop," Professor Jules said.

Her students pulled their hands away from the cauldron, and each took deep breaths as though they'd just finished sprinting. The lesser shoggoth watched all of them with a dozen eyes, before its pupils shifted to the meat held in professor Jules' hand.

"It's yours. A deal is a deal," she said.

She tossed the meat down.

A mouth filled with serrated teeth split open vertically across blank flesh, and snapped up the morsel in a blink.

"And now, you are dismissed." The instructor raised her hands and spoke a word of power that rang through the air.

Her spell struck the lesser shoggoth, and the creature's form began to shudder. Its convulsions increased until it seemed ready to break apart—and then it did. It liquified and whirled in a circle like flood water around a storm drain, flowing out of their reality.

Its physical form faded from Alex's view. In a few heartbeats, he could no longer see it, though he could still feel *something* present. And then, like dissipating mist, the last of it whirled into that singular point in space.

And it was gone.

In its wake, it left a bubbling, shimmering liquid at the bottom of the cauldron. With a wave of her hand, Professor Jules ended the magical flame licking the sides of the metal, but the liquid within still continued to shimmer, shift and bubble. Within its surface were colours that changed from hue to hue, lights that glowed in one heartbeat to dissipate in the next, and shapes that would begin to congeal before abruptly disintegrating.

"Is that..." he murmured. "Chaos essence?"

"It is indeed." Professor Jules nodded. "One of the most transformative substances in all of alchemy. With the right application of mana and other ingredients, it can become nearly anything or change nearly anything. The trouble is getting it to change in a way you *want* it to. Getting it to *stay* in the way you want it to is even harder."

She glanced at him. "It must never be touched with your bare flesh or any living material. ...or any dead material, for that matter... You know what, for your purposes, don't touch it with anything that's not an especially prepared container."

"Uh... what happens if I do?"

"Well, prepare for anything that touched it to start sprouting tentacles and eyes."

He swallowed. "Can force magic touch it?"

"Yes, which is one of the ways to transport it." She cast a spell into the pot, and a massive forceball appear—No. It just looked like a forceball, despite its much larger size. It split open on one end, revealing itself to be hollow. With another spell, Jules caused the chaos essence to flow into the bubble, which then closed around it.

"Back away." She raised the force bubble and slowly moved it to float above a metal container covered in different glyphs. "Those glyphs on the metal are protective," she explained.

Some of the symbols were the same as those on the cauldron. Once the bubble floated over the container, she willed it to float inside, then carefully split again, allowing the chaos essence to flow into place.

"Perfect," she said, willing away her force construct. "Well done, team."

Her graduate students exhaled in relief and began clapping one another on the back and shoulders.

"But," she interrupted their little celebration. "We still have plenty of work to do in Stage Two. Let us get to work."

The rest of the experiment was far less likely to shorten Alex's lifespan.

The feeling that he'd stumbled across an ancient cave of cultists faded as the professor and her students returned to the familiar processes of combining ingredients, adding mana through specialized mana conductors, and testing solutions.

He got to watch them test the chaos essence with half a dozen different specialized devices, each of which generated accurate readouts of its composition. Once it was confirmed this was exactly what they needed, they poured a solution made during an earlier part of the experiment into the cauldron and re-lit it.

They continued combining ingredients, adding in mixtures they'd created before the summoning. As the solutions came to a boil, they steadied the end of the mana vacuum and then poured their mana into the cauldron's bottom.

Several of the glyphs began to glow around the lip of the pot, and the solution started to stir itself.

"Actually, this part is fairly similar to the construction of a golem core," Professor Jules pointed out.

She explained which parts of the animation potion would be used when crafting one. She also talked about which parts of the process would differ when crafting a core, such as an extra step that would involve solidifying the solution as though it were ice.

"Now, the chaos essence," she pointed to the special containers, "can be used in golem cores too. Anything that can cause changing properties, like mutagens or chaos essence, can be used to make an evolving capable golem. For chaos essence, though, it needs to be diluted. One-part chaos essence for every nine-parts stabilizing agent. Note that down. It's key if anyone asks you, since you're interested in working at Shale's in the future."

Alex jotted down every single tip or instruction she gave, though it was hard to tear his mind free from the sight and feeling of the lesser shoggoth. His imagination kept conjuring tentacles in every shadow in the lab and he had to use his meditation techniques to keep his concentration on the task at hand.

When Professor Jules finally called an end to the day, a wave of relief overcame him, knowing he'd soon be leaving that room.

"You did quite well today," she said at the end of the lab. "We'll be continuing the process next week. Will you be available?"

"Yes, Professor, I definitely will be," he said, trying to keep control of his fidgeting. He needed to get out of there.

Frowning, she pulled off her mask—the lab had long been cleaned up—and peered closely at him. "Do you drink, Mr. Roth?"

"Uh, not really?" he said. "Like, during festivals, but never had much time for it."

"I see. Perhaps you should go have a drink with a friend," she said. "You handled yourself well today, but... sometimes magic challenges our minds, conceptions and emotions. Don't be alone. Have a meal or a drink with someone you care about."

"Yeah, maybe... I... thanks, Professor."

He departed soon after that.

Making his way out of the Cells was nerve-racking. Every shadow, every sound and every strange smell became some other-worldly threat, watching him from someplace beyond his sight. He thought he heard shifting above him when he was coming down the stairs. He doubled his pace.

Even when he finally stepped outside and was under the sun, he found himself jumping at every sound.

His world had gotten bigger again.

Each time it grew, some disturbing discovery was involved.

First, *he* was branded as a Hero. Then they were fallen upon by silence-spiders and a hive-queen. Then there was the discovery of the dungeon core and the revelation surrounding it. Then the attack by a mana vampire and the revelation of were monsters out in the world beyond what the Ravener spewed into Thameland.

Now, he'd just learned firsthand that not only were there planes beyond the world he knew, but that there were monsters *beyond the world*.

Things that defied even his basic senses.

If the silence-spiders could block all sound, then could other things—things beyond the rules of the world—avoid other senses? Some force magics were invisible, why not creatures whose sounds could be *tasted* and *felt*.

He paused on the way back to the insula, looking to the castle.

He needed to do something. Something normal.

Alex started toward the registrar's office.

He entered the hall to find it mostly empty. Some students sat on the benches going over documents, and there was only a short line of three between him and the registrar's desk.

The horned, blue-skinned form of Hobb sat at the desk, speaking to the student before him. From Alex's angle, he could see the registrar was writing something down on two different documents simultaneously. Both hands whipped across the pages at a speed that was almost a blur. Though Alex couldn't see precisely what he was writing, it appeared to be different things being written.

Yet, Hobb was still able to keep up the conversation with the student without looking down or pausing once. When he ran out of room on the pages, two blue-glowing Wizard's Hands materialized, removed the documents, and brought fresh paper for him to continue on.

"Next!" Hobb called when the young woman in front of Alex departed after making a late tuition payment. Hobb peered at the young man from Thameland, his eye narrowing behind his massive monocle. "And what can I do for you today, young man?"

"Hello, Hobb," Alex cleared his throat. "Do you remember me?"

Hobb raised an eyebrow. "I meet a lot of students. Many, many, many students every day."

Creak.

Alex whirled to find a student had simply shifted his weight on one of the benches, and the bench—in turn—shifted its weight upon its legs.

He exhaled in relief and turned around again. He found Hobb looking at him with his head cocked to the side. An intensity lay in his eyes. "Something the matter?"

The registrar's lips spread apart in a wide grin. Slightly *too* wide.

Were Hobb's teeth always that sharp? Alex wondered.

"No, it's... everything's okay," he said.

"Goood, goooood," Hobb said, drawing out the words. "It wouldn't do to have your nerve fail whilst winding the foundations of the universe around your fingers. Now, what can I do for you my young, young friend?"

"I..." Alex muttered.

He must have been imagining it.

Something about Hobb reminded him of the lesser shoggoth. He shook the thought away, telling himself his mind was playing tricks on him. Generasi was attended by so many races of mortals that Alex would have trouble naming them all. Hobb was just one of them.

A perfectly normal mortal.

Well, maybe not 'normal.'

"I'm just wondering if there's any accommodations, y'know, on campus? For visiting family, and such. There's... no room in the insula for visitors. I was wondering."

Hobb stared at him for a full five heartbeats.

Then he burst out laughing.

His cackle reminded Alex of an ancient witch from a fairy tale or a demon hunting an unsuspecting priest in an old fable. It filled the hallway with a sinister mirth, and he carried on with it for a terribly long time.

Alex glanced at the other students.

Some were looking at Hobb in shock, while others simply continued on with their paperwork, as though this were a common occurrence.

"Why of couuurse, of couuuuurse we have accommodations." Hobb chuckled, finally regaining control of himself. "What are we, *barbarians*?"

He snapped his fingers, and a new sheet of paper appeared in his hand, which he slid to Alex with a proud smile. "We have on-campus accommodations as well as a list of inns and hostels associated with the school that your visitors can stay in for a… *handsome* discount."

"Oh, good." Alex glanced briefly at the sheet. He winced at some of the prices, but others weren't as bad as he'd feared they'd be. "Thanks. Um, do you know anything about what the inns are like?"

"I do, somewhat, and I can make recommendations if you…" He paused, his eyes narrowing. "Hmmm, are you normally this pale? It's so hard to tell if that's *natural*. You all vary so much in skin tone, and that tone changes so much depending on all the little *whims* of your emotions."

"Uh, no I… well… uh…" Alex had broken out in a cold sweat.

"Hmmmm." Hobb tented his fingers.

Sniff.

His nostrils flared.

"Aaaaaaah, you were part of a summoning, weren't you?" Hobb leaned across the table and sniffed Alex. "Yes, I can smell *some* kind of otherworldly essence on you. I should have known. Most students who've engaged in a proper summoning for the first time have the exact same look as you."

"Well, yeah," Alex said, a little startled that Hobb had been so sharp. "Good guess."

Hobb laughed again. "Well, it's easy to deduce, frankly. Most folk don't react well to learning that you're actually trying to climb your way from the bottom of a very, very *long* ladder in the universal hierarchy."

You're? Alex wondered at Hobb's use of the word.

"Well, fret not!" The registrar adjusted his monocle. "Not all things that go bump in the outer planes are evil or hungry. Sure, some elder things wish this world to be wiped out, but others simply don't care about it. Some demons want to eat every mortal's children, while others simply want to cause some minor mischief and make crop circles."

His eyes seemed to flash.

"And some *devils,*" his mouth drew out that final word, "want to trick mortals out of their immortal souls. Others, though, truly find mortals oooooh so fascinating. Some devils *like* mortals." He leaned a little closer. "Like me. I find you ooooh so *interesting.*"

Alex's nostrils caught the scent of sulfur.

Chapter 69

Expanding Perspectives

"Wait..." Alex started to take a step back. "You're a what?" His words dropped to a whisper.

"A *devil*, boy!" Hobb's voice boomed. "And no need to whisper, it's not a secret. Not one worth keeping, at any rate. You know? Bargains for horrifying power for the price of your immortal soul? Become a king in return for the death of a loved one? Curse a farmer's wife in return for one year of the lifespan of your firstborn? Come now, don't tell me you've never heard of a devil."

"Y-yeah," Alex muttered.

Today had been a *day* and it wasn't even close to over yet.

"Well, glad to see the old ways are still being taught, or at least ways to *avoid* the old ways," the registrar said. "Don't dwell on it. You people live under a monarch your whole life, don't you? They're much more powerful than you. They could have you killed on a whim and stolen all your cows and sheep and coins and other mortal things. Yet, I assume you do not live in constant abject terror that the king will ride down to your town and strip you of all your worldly possessions and loved ones, do you?"

Alex had actually never thought of the King of Thameland being able to annihilate Alric on a whim, and that revelation did *not* make him feel better about cosmic entities.

"You have to live, despite the dangers hanging above your head, do you not?" Hobb said seriously. "After all, your lives are so, so, so *dreadfully* short in terms of your natural lifespan. And that's not taking into account disease, natural disaster, food poisoning and such. Haha, and *that's* just those who live quietly on their little... vegetable-growing patches—Farms, I mean! That's the term."

Hobb placed his chin in his hand and looked despondent for a moment. "It's a shame, really. Times when I could offer you a contract to extend your lifespan ten times over or more... at a bargain, I tell you, a true bargain! But alas, my current contract with the first chancellor prevents me from further deals with mortals until my time of serving here is done. So, you'll have to find some *other* way of seeking immortality, my young friend. Don't go making any deals with devils, though."

He grinned. "Most of my crowd don't find you mortals nearly so *cute* as I do."

Alex simply stared at Hobb, his mouth agape.

"Now, now, I have paperwork to do and you have your list of accommodations to go through. It's time for you to take your leave. Off you go," he said pleasantly.

"Um," Alex muttered. "Uh, right."

He turned away from the desk.

"Oh!" Hobb said. "And do say hello to that little... siiiister, your other companion and cerberus for me, would you?"

Alex startled, looking back over his shoulder. "I, I thought you didn't remember me?"

"Did I say that?" Hobb grinned like he was sharing a very, very old joke. "I do remember that I said, 'I meet a lot of students. Many, many, many students every day.' At no point did I say I didn't remember you." Hobb chuckled. "You should try to pay more attention, Mr. Alex Roth. You *are* a student, after all."

Khalik lowered the glass from his lips. "A *devil*, you say?"

"Yeah." Alex shook his head in amazement. "Not sitting in some summoning circle or on a throne of skulls or anything like that. Just right there. Behind a desk... Convincing students to go for extra perks from the school. Huh."

"A *devil* as the registrar," Khalik mouthed the words, as though he couldn't believe them. "I can't fathom that my brother never told me about this."

"Well, everyone else seemed to know." Alex threw up his hands and slammed them back down on the table. "Ah, sorry, sorry!" he said when others at surrounding tables turned toward him at the noise.

He'd picked up Khalik from the insula right after his interaction with Hobb, and the two of them had made their way to the Brass Grapes, the closest wine bar to the southern insula. Considering the City of Generasi was right in the middle of some of the finest wine country in the world, it was unsurprising that it was not the *only* wine bar on campus.

With it still being afternoon, the bar was not overly filled with students, but some—along with some staff—were passing the afternoon over glasses of wine, books, and light meals of fresh bread served with butter, cured meats and olive paste. Desserts of fresh fruit stood on many of the tables.

A light breeze blew through the open windows to the terrace and a bard sat on a stage on the far end from Alex and Khalik. She strummed her lute, singing an ancient song from a fallen empire, where those with mana enough to practice were enslaved to a long-fallen tyrant.

She sang of spellcasters uniting in bonds of blood. Of

melting chains with flame-magic, and freezing the hearts of their masters still. The song's tone was triumphant and melancholic, but it didn't raise Alex's spirits in the least.

"Jeez, will you listen to that?" He took a long sip of his drink. It was smooth and delicious. "How the hell does someone enslave wizards?"

"Mmm." Khalik cocked his ear toward the song. "I believe it was a time when those with enough mana to *be* wizards were rare in the extreme. They were outnumbered. That meant less teachers and less opportunity to learn. They could be taken advantage of. Also, there are other powers, right? Divinity, for instance, that could be used to threaten wizards."

Alex shuddered, thinking back on Hobb and the lesser shoggoth. There were always other powers. Greater powers.

"Can't believe it. People who could build all *this*." He gestured to their surroundings, meaning the entirety of the university. "Could be made so small. Domesticated like chickens."

He recalled how Hobb described mortals as 'cute.' Almost as if Hobb was a giant looking down on a baby rabbit. Just like with that shoggoth thing, he'd felt small. Tiny, even.

"Hrmph, for you—who barely blinked at a bonedrinker—to be like this? This shoggoth must have been a frightening thing to shake someone as brave as you."

Alex scoffed. "What? Brave? *Me*?" He glanced down at Khalik's glass. "They put funny mushrooms in there?"

"Not in *this* drink." Khalik grinned. "And yes. Brave."

"Pfffft, I'm not brave," Alex snorted.

The idea was ridiculous.

People who knew about his situation... his *true* situation, would probably outright call him a coward. Chosen as a Hero by his god to help save the land, and choosing to run away instead? That played right into the narrative that Galloway had created of previous Fools: Useless. Untrustworthy. Cowardly.

Of course, he didn't really care about that. He had gotten a bad hand and folded. In gambling, that would be called 'reasonable.' But not brave.

Khalik raised an eyebrow. "You are not foolhardy, and I would not say you have the heart of a lion or such, but you are braver than most."

Alex cocked his head. "How?"

"Now you're just fishing for compliments." Khalik chuckled. "But for one, you're here? And you're focused. Wizardry is not the safest path in the world, and yet you are here. As I said, you barely blinked at the bonedrinker and muupkaras—"

"I was *screaming* when the muupkaras opened their jaws," Alex said.

"Oh?" Khalik looked puzzled. "Those were not your battle cries?"

There was silence for a moment, then both young men burst out laughing.

"No, not my battle cries," Alex said, taking another sip of his drink.

"Well, seriously, you screamed, but then you *attacked*." Khalik made a punching gesture. "And even signing up for COMB-1000 speaks of bravery. Oh, and when that frostdrake charged your sister and your love—"

"*Khalik*."

"Your friend. For now." Khalik smiled. "You jumped in their path, despite the fact that Theresa probably could have gutted the thing, if she can use that knife half as well as I think she can. You are braver than most, is my point."

Alex felt his face grow warm. "Uh, thanks." He scratched the back of his head, a little embarrassed. "For what it's worth, you're brave too."

"I know," Khalik said simply, taking another sip of his drink.

"But like... doesn't this stuff freak you out at all? Devils and otherworldly monsters? How are you so calm about it?"

The young man shrugged and adjusted his long plaits. "I have heard of devils before in my homeland. Our stories of them are not always ones of terror, blood, death and evil. And Hobb has not harmed anyone..." He paused. "That I know of. And as for this shoggoth? What Hobb says is true. There are horrifying powers out in the universe."

"No, no, you wouldn't be saying that so flippantly if you'd been near it, Khalik," Alex insisted. "It just felt... *wrong*. When it made noise, you could *feel* its cries. Smell them. Taste them. And Jules and a bunch of her graduate students needed this super-cauldron and themselves all working together to keep it contained. And *that* thing was called *lesser*! I'd hate to ever be anywhere near a greater one!"

"Ah, I see." Khalik nodded. "It got into your head."

Alex gave him a look. "No, no, don't go on with that kind of 'I let it get into my head' bullshit, Khalik—"

"I didn't say you *let* it get into your head." He looked at him pointedly. "I'm saying it *got* into your head." Khalik's eyes turned distant and he tapped the table with a thick finger. "Have you ever seen a dragon before, Alex? I have. When I was a boy."

"No, uh—Wait, what, a *dragon?* You've seen an *actual* dragon?"

"That I have, that I have." Khalik seemed rather proud. "It was from a distance, but I did see it in the Udan Desert, which lies between the Kingdom of Ibesti and my country of Tekezash to the southeast."

He spread his hands.

"It was like a serpent as long as a city wall, with wings that could have shaded an entire forest. As it flew overhead, it swooped low and breathed fire against the sand. Turned it all to glass. A mile distant and I could still feel the heat. But that's not *all* I felt."

He chuckled, as though mocking himself.

"It flew overhead—over our caravan—not more than a

hundred feet above us, and Alex..." He shook his head. "The *fear*, man. As soon as it got close to us, the fear penetrated my heart like a dagger, and I fell off the back of my horse. I hadn't fallen off my horse for *years* and I tumbled to the sand like I had never mounted before."

"What did—"

Khalik held up a hand. "Let me finish. I was not the only one. The warriors, who I *would* say have the hearts of lions, fell off their horses. My elder brother, who studied here and who I *know* has summoned demons to consult with for their knowledge of certain spells, *he* fell off his horse too. My uncle as well. Just everyone, on the sand whimpering like we were frightened babies. I was so humiliated, I did not want to show my face at home again... and then I found out what *dragonfear* is."

He placed his glass on the table and drew a large, imaginary circle around it. "Dragons have an aura around them of supernatural fear, and the older they get, the *stronger* it grows. The fear penetrates the mind and infests the heart. Not fear from within—" He pointed to his own chest. "—but fear from outside." He gestured around. "It is magical, and digs into the mind like a pickaxe. I bet you that when you learn more of these shoggoths, you will find this is true of them as well. I will bet you a *good* sum of coins on that."

"Oh," Alex said. "If that's true... that makes sense, I guess."

Warping of the senses? Reality not working the way it should? Sounded like something that would affect the mind. And didn't one of the grad students say that, if whatever the lesser shoggoths worshipped showed up, that its presence would turn the mind inside out? Maybe lesser shoggoths had that kind of effect on the mind. Maybe he wasn't exaggerating just to scare him.

He should've asked.

If he really thought about it, it was similar to how the Mark affected his mind, or how the mana vampire's magic had put others into an unnatural sleep. They were effects that came from outside power. If his senses weren't being so twisted, then he might have noticed that about the lesser shoggoth.

"I guess it did," he said.

"And think of this," Khalik continued. "Hobb is bound by a contract, and so cannot do us harm. And this lesser shoggoth was bound and brought to heel by your professor and her students, even if they had to use a magic cauldron to do so. Terrifying things are out there, but we are arming ourselves against them. Think of it this way: who is better off? The person wandering through the forest in bliss, while having no idea it is filled with bandits and killers? Or is it the one walking through the forest with fear in their heart, but are cautious because they know of the danger, and they have elected to bring a spear and sword to protect themselves?"

"Yeah, yeah, when you put it that way... knowing about it and being prepared is better," Alex said.

In the end, it was similar to what he experienced in the Cave of the Traveller. The revelation that humans could control a dungeon core had freaked him out, but once he knew about it, it became a problem he could research and plan for. It should be the same with the revelation that horrifying cosmic entities existed.

Better he should know and be able to arm himself with knowledge and magic, instead of being completely vulnerable and ignorant. Besides, just like with the dungeon core and the Ravener, it wasn't something he needed to dwell on all the time.

"Has anyone ever told you you're like, super wise?" Alex said emphatically to Khalik.

"Haha, I try," he said with a smile

"Hey, it doesn't change that part about kings and queens, though." Alex took another drink. He gave a crooked grin, trying to lighten the mood. "About them being able to come down to the people whenever they want and do whatever they want." He rose in his seat and put on a haughty expression like he was a queen. "What is that? I—*the queen*—am not the fairest of the land? Then off with the heads of everyone more beautiful than me! Poison their apples! Make them sleep forever... with the fishes!"

He laughed at his own joke, until he realized he was laughing alone.

Khalik's smile had faded.

His eyes had turned hard.

Chapter 70

Different Paths in Life

"I would *imagine* they have concerns as well." Khalik's tone was sharp. "There are more people than there are kings and queens. More nobles to appease. Generals. Armies. Merchants. Common folk. They all have mouths to feed, children to raise and coffers to fill. And when a drought comes, or floods wash away homes, or locusts eat all the crops—who do they blame? Who is the one who should be fearing, then?"

"I, uh," Alex muttered. "Ah, that was just a joke. Like, there's this old story about a queen asking a mirror if there was anyone more beautiful than her, and then chopping off the head of her niece who was more beautiful than she was... well, it's an old fairy tale. A children's story, where the queen was supposed to be wicked."

Khalik shook his head. "A fool's story. A queen chopping the head off her niece? C'mon! Then what of the girl's parents? Her father and mother? The noble or military house the girl was from? What if the niece is from a dynasty of wizards?"

"Well, uh..." Alex stammered. "It's just an old story, man."

"A ridiculous one." Khalik's frown deepened. "The girl's family would be *enraged* by the act. Brothers and sisters would swear vengeance. House guards and soldiers would be rallied. Civil wars have started over far *less*, Alex."

Anger had entered Khalik's voice. "It is the same in so many places. Evil kings and evil queens sneering and slaughtering in these foolish stories. Any king who rode around murdering their own subjects at his whim and taking their possessions like a common bandit, would likely have a dagger where his heart used to be, and a head separated from his neck."

Alex chuckled nervously. "Ah, come on, Khalik, look at that Derek guy. He's a noble. Completely irresponsible and he gets away with it. Some of them do."

Khalik raised an eyebrow. "And how long will that last, Alex? His cheating already has him in trouble. And Isolde is nobility too, and *she* is responsible."

"Uh, yeah, I guess, but..." He gestured casually to the bard, who had switched to another song. "Think about all the wizards ground under the heels of those rulers of that ancient empire. *They* got away with it."

"Until they *didn't*." Khalik's expression darkened further. "The song does not even mention the *name* of the empire anymore. That is how *dead* it is. And when those with mana got the strength to snap their chains, what do you think happened to their former masters? You've seen what even *we* can do with magic, and we are at the *beginning* of our training."

Alex's mind filled with images of massive fireballs, crackling lightning, ice and summoned demons and elementals tearing apart jeweled cities. "Yeah, I guess... things wouldn't have gone well for those rulers."

"Exactly. Tyrants abound in many realms, but they have the support of their warriors, wizards and priests. Some of their people love them and only *some* hate them. Most might not even notice they are living beneath a tyrant, as long as the taxes are not back-breaking and the harvest plentiful. A ruler has power, but that power can be lost like *this*."

Khalik snapped his fingers.

"Never really thought of it that way," Alex admitted. "Never really thought of it much, to be honest. Like, Thameland has a king, but aside from paying our taxes to our local ruler who then pays *their* taxes to him, the business of rulers really never mattered much in my life. I think this whole... shoggoth and devil thing just got me a little crazy for a bit."

"And that is the way of it, in real life," Khalik said. "A great ruler is sung of by the people, and a terrible one is cursed. A good ruler is hardly mentioned, until the earthquake or drought comes."

Alex looked long and hard at his friend. As the conversation went on, a suspicion—which he'd had for a while—grew. "Khalik, can I ask you something?"

"You can." Khalik nodded like he was giving a general permission to speak. "Whether or not I'll answer is a different matter."

Alex became quite serious. "Who *are* you, really?"

The young, bearded man didn't answer right away, searching Alex's eyes. "What do you mean?"

"I mean, like..." Alex scratched his head, glancing around the wine bar and leaning across the table. He dropped his voice low. "Are you some kind of noble? I mean, you have a whole room to yourself in the insula, and you said you *were* coming to Generasi with other people. You obviously have a *lot* of coin, and that's great, and then you said to Selina that you have people that cook for you at home. You *laughed* when you thought about your parents cooking, and then you changed the subject. Like, I thought maybe you were just rich, but with how offended you got at that stuff about kings and queens... it makes me wonder."

Khalik frowned. "Erm... well, aren't *you* observant."

"You don't have to answer if you don't want to. I just have to admit, I'm getting pretty curious. And don't worry, I'm not going to ask you for money or anything like that, if that's what you're thinking. I got *some* pride."

"I didn't think you would, Alex, and I believe you have a lot more than just *some* pride." Khalik watched Alex very closely. He sighed. "Promise you won't be... weird about this?"

"I'm not going to be any weirder than I already am."

"Oh, well, *that's* comforting." Khalik chuckled. His humour faded and he rose up in his chair. "Alright. Swear to me that you will not tell *anyone* what I'm about to tell you unless I give you permission."

The air around Khalik changed in an instant. He had gone from a friendly, outgoing young man, to a man who was *used* to giving commands.

"I'm not going to tell anybody," Alex said. "Trust me, I *know* how to keep a secret."

Khalik stared for a long moment. "Alright." He took a deep breath. "I am the seventh son of the Crimson Mantis, the king of assassins and the greatest contract killer in all the realms south of the Udan Desert."

Alex gasped. "What... what the... holy shi—"

Khalik's face was twitching, as though he were trying to fight laughter.

"Oh, you are *so* full of shit, Khalik."

Khalik burst out laughing, clapping and doubling over the table. "By Ash-Badar's shining rays, I am! But you should have seen the *look* on your face!" He outright cackled so hard that others across the wine bar turned and stared at them. "If only I had a painter here so I could have immortalized it. Or even a sculptor!"

"I should sculpt your damn beard off your face!" Alex snapped. "You almost gave me a heart attack, you bastard. Lesser shoggoths, registrar's a devil and then my first friend here turns out to be some super dangerous assassin's son? I might have just gone right back to my room, packed my shit up and left for some mountain somewhere."

"No, no, I'm joking, of course." Khalik waved his hand while trying to get his laughter under control. "Okay, okay. No more foolishness. I'll tell you now."

Once the last of his laughter faded, he waited until those in the room had turned away, then leaned toward his tablemate and spoke in tones so low, that Alex could barely hear him. The bard's song and ambient noise of the wine bar covered his words.

"My full name is Prince Khalik Behr-Medr, the Raptor of Tekezash, Lord of the Sapphire Sea and second son of King Aksuma Behr-Medr and Queen Ishtar Behr-Medr."

"Oh, Uldar's Beard. You're a *prince*?" he whispered.

"An accident of birth, I assure you. A happy one, though," Khalik said. "Please don't spread that... Other accidents ensured I came here in relative anonymity... and uh, I have found I like that anonymity. I wish to enjoy it, for at least a little longer."

"Jeez, yeah, you got it. I'll keep your secret. I don't want you to order that my head get cut off or anything like that."

Khalik appeared wounded. "*Alex*, what did we just talk about—"

"Oh, I *know*." Alex leaned back, crossing his arms. "But that's that revenge for 'I am son of the Crimson Mantis, the super ultimate killer of all murder-dom.'"

"Fair enough, I suppose I deserve that." Khalik chuckled, continuing to speak quietly. "They're actually real, though, you know. The Crimson Mantis? They have killed a few generals and some lords of the realms near my own. *That's* the sort of person you must fear when circumstance surrounds your name with titles and dictates that your blood is 'royal.'"

"Yeah, I guess," Alex said. "Huh. No wonder you got mad when I was going on about kings. Uh, sorry about that, man."

"Thank you," Khalik said. "It is past. Think nothing of it anymore."

"And uh, thanks for trusting me enough to tell me," Alex said. "I mean, this is a big deal and you told *me*."

Khalik shrugged. "It felt like the right time, and I believed your words when you said you would not share it with others."

Alex sat back. 'It felt like the right time.'

For a moment, Alex was *dearly* struck by the urge to share exactly why he'd left Thameland, and that he bore the Mark of the Fool. When friends were sharing secrets, it felt right to share one of his own. Then again, how would Khalik react?

This was a man who continued north to Generasi when those who were supposed to travel with him had to turn back. He'd talked with pride about being brave. Would he dismiss Alex as a coward? And even if he didn't, could Alex trust him to keep the secret?

Maybe. He probably could, if he was honest. Khalik was from a place so far from Thameland that the Ravener would have been completely beneath concern compared to dragons that could melt sand into glass by breathing on it, or assassins that could murder loved ones at any time for the right amount of coin. He doubted Khalik would have a reason to go running to the priests of Uldar to inform them of his desertion.

Not yet, Alex finally decided. *Can't be too careful... Later? Maybe. Maybe.*

The revelation of Khalik's background had not changed much for Alex.

To everyone else in their inner circle, the secret prince still acted the same. Joking and laughing with Alex and Thundar, helping each other out during their group study sessions. He was still friendly to Isolde whenever they saw her, and he still treated Theresa and Selina with the same open friendliness.

As for Alex, being sworn to secrecy made it so that he could speak about it with no one, though he was *dying* to tell Theresa.

As such, the truth of Khalik became a background fact in his mind—never forgotten—but never staying in the forefront of his thoughts for long. What *did* stay in his mind was Khalik's talk about the dangers of the cosmos, and simply living with that knowledge and the knowledge he would be better armed against many dangers than most.

The thought made him redouble his efforts with his practice and training.

Though when it came to Wizard's Hand, his efforts were still frustratingly slow. When he compared the speed of his progress with perfecting forceball and learning forcedisk, it was like he'd gone from a sprint during forceball, to a fast run during forcedisk, and to a stumbling walk with rocks tied to his feet with Wizard's Hand.

Every bit of progress with the spell was a constant fight against the Mark. He again considered just how much further behind he would have been if he hadn't learned the meditation techniques from Theresa. His one consolation was that once he mastered Wizard's Hand, he would have mastered one of the most complex spell arrays for first-tier spells in the school of force.

He had hopes that Force Shield would be easier, though he *dreaded* the time when he'd have to try and learn Force Missile. He knew without a shadow of a doubt that learning combat spells was going to make the Mark go into an absolute frenzy. He was not looking forward to that.

Luckily, in other areas, his progress growing his skills was accelerating.

As he continued to gain experience and the Mark had more triumphs to pull from, it grew better and better at guiding him toward greater successes. In a way, it was similar to how students received attention from professors. The better he became, the more the Mark aided him.

In terms of the few steps he knew of the Spear-and-Oar Dance, the Mark was running out of ways to improve them. Now, while performing the steps, his movements were feeling as natural as his own breathing, and during the routine, he didn't have to pause any longer and think about how to change position or balance.

To advance further, he would need Captain Fan-Dor to teach him the other steps, but he wasn't quite ready to focus on that yet.

Aside from Wizard's Hand, his preparations for applying to the golem workshop consumed the majority of his training time. When he wasn't reviewing notes on ingredients and steps that would apply to golem-craft, he was training his mana manipulation.

Though it had been harder to work on two glyph boxes at once, consistently practicing with them had seen him be able to light up every glyph on each box at once. An accomplishment that had him jumping up and down with excitement.

In potions, he was always first to finish each lab, and that was without making mistakes very often. Professor Jules had taken to examining his completed concoctions with incredible care, searching for any flaw. In the end, she'd be satisfied with his work and sign off on each one. The potions themselves were both interesting and practical. Potions that sharpened each of the senses, increased physical strength or endurance, even a potion that made one more resistant to the sun's rays and heat—which Alex promised he'd brew more of for himself for the Barrens the *moment* he had access to a lab and ingredients—and more.

It had quickly become one of his favourite classes. He was good at it, it was fun in the same way baking was, and he liked his instructor. He could have done without Carey London, but he and Kybas had started chatting a little more during class. The half-mad goblin was a little nerve-racking at times, but he was growing on him.

The days he found the most interesting, though, were when he helped with Professor Jules' mutagen project. He learned more about the deeper parts of alchemy, golem-craft and summoning in ten minutes than he did during a half hour of POTI-1000. He'd wanted to hint to Professor Jules that he might benefit from Challenging the Exam for Credit in her course, but he doubted—especially with her emphasis on caution and procedure—that she would allow it.

Not yet, at least.

His sculpting was improving as well, and the Mark helped him catch up to his sister's greater experience and natural skill. He grudgingly had to admire her talent. Despite him being a grown man and having a divine-granted edge, it was still taking time to match her. Still, he was closing the gap.

To his dismay, though, she realized this and appeared to be applying herself to getting even better. Seeing her skill grow made him push himself even harder.

Theresa had asked him whether it was healthy for him to compete so single-mindedly with a ten-year-old. Except words like 'health' and 'pettiness' didn't matter anymore.

All was fair in love, war and trying to one-up one's sibling.

Yet, for all his progress in the dance, potions, mana manipulation, and picking up the skill to craft the golem's body, the most surprising change he'd made recently was not in any of these areas.

It wasn't even in magic.

It was physical.

Chapter 71

Gains in Mass and Mana

Alex Roth stood in front of the small mirror in his room—the windows firmly shuttered and door latched—staring at himself, half in disbelief. His belly grumbled in hunger, as it always seemed to these days, no matter how much he fed it, but the shape of that belly had changed.

The shape of his whole body had changed.

"Hooooly shit," he said, turning and flexing his right arm. A surprising amount of muscle swelled on his bicep and deltoid under the grinning jester's face that was the Mark of the Fool. If he didn't know what it actually was, it could *almost* look like a badass sailor's tattoo.

Almost.

When he'd first arrived in Generasi, he was a tall, thin, gangly eighteen-year-old. His stomach had been soft and his shoulders narrow.

Then he'd gotten to work on changing all that with nearly two months of solid physical training with the Mark correcting his form. He'd also learned how eating habits affected his body. Using the Mark to eat strategically, while getting stronger, built up his stamina and improved his overall health.

He was making regular use of the strengthening equipment in the gym and using meditation during his routine to rest, as well as help himself sleep better and deeper at night. He'd made a plan, and he'd stuck to it.

The result?

Mr. Lu once said—a common phrase his brother used, 'Young people are like steel. If they forge themselves right, they'll harden up in no time.'

He'd evidently been right.

Alex hadn't exactly become a walking marble statue like Khalik, or a hulking bruiser like Thundar, but most of the traces of his gangliness were almost gone. His limbs had some serious muscle on them, and his belly had flattened, despite having thrown in a few sweets to satisfy his sweet tooth now and then. With more muscle on his shoulders, they'd broadened. His energy levels had soared so much, he could run countless laps around the beastarium without collapsing into an exhausted mess like he used to.

When he first started? He had trouble doing five push-ups in a row.

Now?

He flipped open his notebook, checking what he'd done just this morning.

Push-ups: *50, 47, 45 TOTAL=142*

His chest and arms burned, recognizing the soreness as progress.

He glanced at the glowing Mark on his shoulder.

Over time, his feelings toward it had been growing more and more mixed.

On one hand, if it weren't for the Mark hindering him from learning Wizard's Hand, he possibly might have come to love it by now—stupid destiny and history or not. On the other hand, if it hadn't hindered his magic, would he have even bothered to learn so many other skills or develop himself physically?

He doubted he would have. Alex hadn't been interested in exercise his entire life. That wouldn't have changed just because he'd come to the greatest school of wizardry in the world without something *forcing* him to try other paths and ways to grow himself.

Thump. Thump. Thump.

"Alex, are you ready yet?" Theresa asked through the door.

"Just about," he said, turning and appraising his other side before putting on a shirt and getting ready to head down to the baths.

He grabbed the glyph boxes from his dresser, his notebook and pen, and mana manipulation textbook. Taking a deep breath, he stepped toward his door.

Today was a big day.

Today, he would learn a mana regeneration technique in MANA-1900. It was one of the last things he'd need to know before he could Challenge the Exam for Credit.

"Mana Regeneration is one of the most important things that I'm *ever* going to teach you," Val'Rok said from the front of the class. "You'll learn a less complex version of this technique in magic theory since mana regeneration is a key skill for any wizard, but here is where we'll get into the advanced stuff."

He grinned. "Look at it this way. If the mana regeneration technique is an average beer, then this is a fine wine. As we go through later parts of the course, you'll find even *more* advanced techniques." He made a strange hissing sound. "*Those* are like century-aged dwarven moonshine."

Several members of the class laughed. Alex rose up in his seat, leaning forward slightly to pay close attention.

He'd been waiting for this.

"To more advanced wizards, a basic mana regeneration technique is enough. With practice, the average wizard can regenerate fifty percent of their mana pool in a day. But it becomes less important the more powerful you become."

The lizard man paced back and forth. He eyed a spider that had crawled its way from some quiet hiding place and was perched on the wall close to him. His eyes grew intense, then he shook away the distraction.

"Beginning wizards are only going to be able to cast a few spells in a day before they exhaust their mana pool and begin to draw on their life force, so mana regeneration is absolutely *key*. But, the more you advance your skill in spellcraft, the more your mana pool grows naturally. That means more or larger magic circuits can fit within it, and there's more mana to draw from for spells. In other words, more spells per day...

"It will get to the point where most wizards will have difficulty exhausting their mana pool unless they're drawing on their most powerful spells, so most wizards will learn a simple mana regeneration technique and then focus on growing their pool as much as possible. There's a good reason for this, of course."

Val'Rok turned to the obsidian board and began to draw a diagram of a humanoid that was partially coloured in. "Your mana pool will naturally regenerate in twenty-four hours, even if you run it all the way down to dry. That's fairly quick, already. When your mana pool is only big enough to cast one first-tier spell once in a day, that will seem like forever, but let's look at a more experienced wizard."

He turned back to the class. "When you graduate from Generasi, at *minimum,* you will be able to cast fifth-tier spells. That is the *bare* minimum for receiving a degree from Generasi. Let's talk about what that means. This *might* be a review from magic theory, but that's alright. This is important."

He drew a rising line graph on the chalkboard. "At minimum, a wizard who can cast fifth-tier spells will have a mana pool large enough to cast them about seven times before their mana runs dry. Now, that might not seem like much to you, but you have to understand: a fifth-tier spell packs a *lot* of punch."

Val'Rok drew a symbol for a spell on the board. "Teleport—a fifth-tier spell—will let you transport yourself and three others roughly nine hundred miles when you first learn it. *Nine hundred miles*. That's a *four*-day journey by fast ship, sailing constantly with the wind. Done in an instant. And that's without taking *any* time to explore or master the spell at all. And you can do that seven times in a day."

He drew a symbol for another spell. "Crush Mind will let you... well, crush a mind and leave a full-grown person with the intelligence of an average earthworm. And you can do *that* seven times at minimum.

"And guess what? Fourth-tier spells take up half as much room in a mana pool and roughly *half* as much mana. That's fourteen times at minimum."

The fire-gems were the equivalent to a fourth-tier spell; that meant the worst graduates of Generasi would be able to blast those out fourteen times in a day before they ran out of mana. If they used a simple mana regeneration technique, they could do it an additional seven times.

"Third-tier spells take up half as much as that," Val'Rok said. "That's *twenty-eight*! Third-tier spells include the beloved fireball, by the way. You could blow up a small group of adversaries twenty-eight times a day. You could then use a basic mana regeneration technique to do it all over again fourteen times. Then, if you throw in potions that can refill one's mana..."

He chuckled. "Aren't we *disgustingly* unbalanced in the natural order? And that is *literally* the *worst* graduates of our university. We pack a punch, and that's why advanced mana techniques usually aren't practiced by all but the most dedicated wizards until late in their careers. Most prefer to spend their time learning and perfecting more spells or brewing potions or, you know, using their skills to make good, good, good coin."

Val'Rok glanced at that spider on the wall with a hungry gleam before pulling himself back. "However, the most advanced mana techniques let you pretty much *never* run out of mana unless you're constantly pushing yourself to the limit. You'll be regenerating mana while you walk. While you breathe. While you eat. While you're actively casting spells."

He tapped his desk. "The great wizard duelist Ianus Ruby-Eye beat his opponents not by being the fastest spellcaster or the most powerful spellcaster, but by being the most enduring. In the end, once most wizards' mana is used up, they're just a great big hunk of meat ready to be butchered."

He grinned. "Now let's make sure *you're* not the one that's butchered."

With that, Val'Rok began to explain how mana regeneration techniques worked.

The basic fundamental skill involved stimulating one's internal pool with their own mana.

"If you make a cow comfortable and milk her often, from what I understand, she'll produce more milk. It's the same with your mana pathways. Using up your mana stresses your pool, and weakens the barrier between it and your lifeforce. By massaging the edges of your mana pool internally, you'll get them to relax and begin generating mana again before they have rested for the twenty-four-hour period."

He slapped at the air as though there was some unruly youngster that needed disciplining before him. "The basic mana technique created for general consumption by wizards is the same as a massage technique that's like slapping a tight muscle until it loosens up. It'll do the job, but it won't be comfortable or efficient, and you won't be able to do it all the time."

Next, he made a clutching gesture where he mimed precisely grasping and massaging the air with his fingers. "More advanced techniques require more control over your mana—that's why we've been training your level of control using the boxes—they can relax and stimulate your mana pool much more efficiently and safely."

He drew a diagram of the average wizard's mana pool, breaking it up into specific areas that worked together to contain and regenerate mana. Alex had seen such a diagram in his textbook, but hadn't tried the technique on his own yet. The text mentioned something about 'applying too much pressure to the edge of one's mana pool could puncture it like paper.' He'd decided to wait for supervised instruction.

Once Val'Rok had gone over each of the different areas and their purposes, he began to describe how each was stimulated in order to produce mana. Alex nearly burst out laughing when he realized what the professor was instructing. They were the same bopping, twisting and pulling motions they'd practiced through the glyph boxes.

"We'll start off with simply getting the feel of moving one's mana internally." He tapped a stack of reports on top of his desk. "Since all of you have been able to light at least *one* glyph on the box, this shouldn't be too hard for you now."

He described turning one's senses inward to feel the contours and shape of one's own mana, and then directed the class to shift it back and forth across their mana pools.

Alex turned his senses inward toward his own mana pool. Using meditation, he tuned out all outside noise and slipped deep into himself. The warmth of his mana pool full of power and nestled deep in his spirit rose.

He easily took hold of it, passing his mana from side to side in his pool.

Professor Val'Rok watched the class engage in the exercise, moving over to aid anyone who raised their hand to ask a question or request help. Some students didn't raise their hands at all and continued to struggle, judging from their frustrated looks.

Others were clearly distracted or doing things completely unrelated to class. To these, Val'Rok didn't even spare a second glance.

Alex winced. At the church school, such distraction would have been met with a stern lecture or even harsher punishment.

Here? They were left to their own devices, whether they swam or sank.

Come exam time, Alex was sure they'd be regretting it or offering up a host of excuses for being unprepared.

Focusing back on himself, he followed the professor's instruction as he guided them through manipulating their own mana to touch the relevant parts of their mana pool. Alex activated the Mark while doing so and found it was almost unnecessary. After so much practice with mana manipulation and the glyph boxes, he found it was remarkably easy to sense the targeted areas of his mana pool and make contact with them.

He grew more excited.

Finally, Val'Rok held up a hand. "Stop, stop for a moment. I want you all to cast a spell now. Any spell you want. But nothing that would *blow up* the classroom."

Soon the room filled with forceballs, flares of light, illusions of animals dancing through the air, puffs of mist, and bursts of song. One student even summoned a tiny air elemental and sent it shooting around the room.

While everyone watched and clapped, Alex noticed Professor Val'Rok's eyes darting back and forth. He edged nonchalantly toward the wall with the spider on it.

Thwp.

His tongue shot out in a blur, scooping up the eight-legged snack and bringing it back into his mouth before most caught on.

"Excellent," he said with all the dignity that wasn't there a moment before. "Now that you've put a dent in your mana, I want you to reach into—" he tapped the obsidian board with one clawed hand pointing to the top area of the mana pool diagram, "—here, then 'bop' that area. You'll feel the edge protrude inward in response, then you take that protrusion and *lightly* twist it. Just as you did with the box."

Alex followed the direction, gently contacting the top of his mana pool, then seizing the raised area that followed. He made a twisting gesture with his mana and felt a shudder go through his spirit. A sigh escaped his lips as a spiritual tension, one he hadn't even noticed before, left. The same came from his other classmates, and some looked at each other and giggled.

"Relaxing, isn't it?" Val'Rok said. "I'll give you free time to practice now. Welcome to a path I guarantee you will never regret. Of course the... relaxation one feels, when properly massaging one's mana, can be a little, well, *addictive*, I'd say. There are some accounts that say doing it *too* much leaves one mentally unbalanced."

Val'Rok gave a high-pitched, hysterical laugh. "Complete dragon-shit, I tell you! None of that is true."

He licked his lips, and Alex could have sworn he was licking away an errant spider leg. At this distance, he told himself he was imagining it.

Chapter 72

For and Against Pride

Alex paced back and forth in front of the golem workshop.

It was early morning. Crack of dawn, really, and much of the City of Generasi was still waking up from their night's sleep. A light rain hissed against the cobblestones and rooftops, and he pulled his hood higher and his cloak tighter to shield himself.

Shops were opening all around and the scent of baking bread and stewing meat emerged from stalls, eateries and wine houses lining the street. Coming from within the workshop was the sounds of equipment being set up, forges firing and workers calling to each other. He hoped that, at any moment, Shale's would open and—

Click.

His eyes shot toward the door as a key turned in the lock. A young woman opened it and gasped when she saw Alex rapidly advancing.

"Hello, I—Wait, wait, wait, don't close the door!" he cried.

She paused. "If you're planning to rob us, then let me tell you, robbing a golem shop is a *bad* idea."

"No, no, no." He shook his head and waved his hands. "No, I just wanted to get in first."

She raised an eyebrow, looking around the front of the shop.

No one else was waiting to get in.

"Uh, a little keen, aren't ya?" she said. "Need a golem that badly?"

"No, I was wondering," he cleared his throat, "if I could see if you had any new job postings today."

Look like a professional golem maker, Alex, not an excited puppy, he chastised himself.

"Aaaaah, I see." The employee nodded knowingly. "Someone must've told a friend who told a friend. Well, come on in and take a look at the board. If you're here this early, you probably already know what you're looking for."

She welcomed him into the workshop and he stepped forward, spying the board where jobs and other announcements were posted. He fought the urge to frantically run up to it. Instead, he sauntered over as though he were *all* professionalism and confidence.

He peered at the posting, finding it hadn't changed much in the last month he'd seen it on their tour, save for one important detail added to the bottom:

Help Wanted: *Crafter's Assistant.*
Basic Skills/Requirements:

- *Preference given to those with previous experience in magic item craftsmanship.*
- *Preference given to those who have been apprenticed to a smith, potter or stonemason.*
- *Able to cast at least first-tier magic.*
- *Skill in Mana Manipulation Required (Will be Tested).*

- *Must have knowledge in the construction of clay golems or in related alchemical processes.*
- *Able to work three evenings per week from 16th to 21st chime.*
- *Positions Open: Three.*
- *Duties: The Crafter's Assistant will assist golem-crafters in the construction of golem bodies, golem cores and in the binding of golem cores to bodies. They will also catalogue inventory of supplies at the end of each shift, and place orders for more materials with the workshop manager on shift.*
- *Compensation: Two gold coins per shift (opportunity for raises dependent upon performance).*
- *Opportunities for advancement depending on performance, as available.*
- *Applicants will deliver a one-page summary with self-description, qualifications and previous experience to the front desk along with any proof of apprenticeship, letters of character and so on. Posting will remain open for one month after which no further applications will be accepted.*
- *We thank all applicants for their interest; however, only those considered for an interview will be contacted.*

Alex's eyes narrowed.

He thought the application period would only last a few days. In Alric, most job openings didn't last long. Word of mouth spread about a job and it would be filled within days. He supposed things worked differently in such a large city.

Here, in a city of thousands—many of whom were wizards—there'd probably be dozens of applicants or more.

With the posting being up for a month, that was ultimately a good thing. It would give him more time to practice mana regeneration and learn more from Professor Jules. He'd been starting to get nervous about having to make his application too soon. That would have meant having to rush getting his letters of reference, and not having enough time to build the skills he'd need for the job.

Then again, a longer application window meant more time for a lot more applicants to hear about the job and apply. He had no way of knowing how competitive this position would be. Though, like with any job, the more applicants, the harder his chances.

"Well," he muttered beneath his breath. "At least I'm the only one who knows—"

Creak.

The door to the workshop opened and three young people strode in, each gripping sheaths of paper. None of them even glanced at the postings board, moving straight through the waiting area and right up to the front desk as though they knew the place well. It seemed that indeed, 'someone must've told a friend who told a friend.'

The young woman in the lead placed her sheath onto the desk, stated her name, and said, "I'm applying for the Crafter's Assistant position."

Alex watched in horror as the other two also handed in applications for the same position.

"Well, shit," he muttered softly. "Shit, shit, shit."

This *was* going to be competitive.

He took a deep, meditative breath and steadied himself. That was okay. It wasn't like Generasi had been easy to get into. He'd broken his back studying and practicing magic to earn a position and a partial scholarship. This would be the same. He'd just have to prepare.

Straightening his cloak, he gave a nod to the staff nearby and stepped out through the entrance.

As he emerged onto the street, he put his hood up and glanced around at a growing crowd.

A familiar set of faces approached the workshop from down the street.

"Oh, no way..."

The three figures stilled when they spied Alex standing in front of the doorway. The one in the lead practically glared, and almost in sync, the other two did the same.

Minervus' pale, narrow face stared at him from beneath his hood. It flushed red, though whether that was from anger or embarrassment, Alex didn't know. "You..." Minervus muttered, then he seemed to catch himself and the trio approached the workshop with purpose.

He stopped just in front of Alex, looking up at him—he was a few inches shorter. "Excuse me, would you mind *moving* from in front of the door?"

His words were polite, but there was a sharpness to them.

Wordlessly, Alex stepped aside as Minervus entered the workshop with two of his flesh golems. He turned to watch as the second-year student drew a sheath of papers from beneath his cloak and placed them on the desk, declaring his interest in the Crafter's Assistant position.

"Oooh *shit*," Alex swore. "Not *him* too."

Of *all* people to apply, it had to be him. It made sense in a way. He did have *five* golems built of special materials, of *course* he'd be interested in golems. Baelin said Minervus hadn't made them himself, and Alex hoped he didn't have that much skill and experience in golem-craft.

Then again, if Minervus had *any* experience with magic items—even just by being in the second-year potions class—it'd make him look better than Alex. Hell, just being a second-year *period* was an edge he had on Alex.

Cursing inwardly, Alex started to make his way down the street.

"Hey!" he heard a voice call from behind him.

Alex almost turned but made himself keep walking.

"Hey, I'm talking to you!"

Alex stopped, rising to his full height and squaring his now-slightly broader shoulders. He eyed the approaching form of Minervus and his two golems. "Can I help you, man?"

"Did you apply for the assistant position?" the former member of COMB-1000 asked, not waiting for a reply. "You shouldn't. A first-year couldn't perform the duties. Trust me. My family has a long history of crafting magic items. I have the qualifications and you don't. You'll just be wasting your time and Shale's."

Alex raised an eyebrow and crossed his arms. "Oooh, I see what this is."

"Hm?"

"You start throwing around your experience and whatever, hoping that'll stop me from applying. And for your little bit of effort, in your best-case scenario, you get rid of some of the competition. Am I right?"

Minervus' eyes remained calm. "I've no idea what you're talking about. I'm offering advice to a first-year. If you don't want to accept it, that's not my problem."

He stepped away from Alex and started down the street again.

Alex shook his head and went in the other direction.

Before, he wanted the job because it would provide him with an income, give him experience with golem cores that might help when he analyzed the dungeon core, and help him gain skills to build his own golem.

Now?

He *needed* that job.

If he didn't get it and *Minervus* did? There was no way that would *ever* sit well with him.

And considering his manipulative stunt just now and his

self-serving crap in the Barrens, losing out to him was not an option.

Alex grinned at the clay figure he'd just finished shaping. Before, his creations resembled monstrosities with misshapen limbs and bulging heads. Now, they were looking more and more like humans. They were still blocky and simplistic, but he'd gotten to the point where he was able to get the proportions right.

"Hey, take a look at this, Selina. Mr. Clay the Seventeenth is born! Are you despairing, my dear sister?" he gloated like a dark lord from legends.

Selina's back was turned to him, bent over her own clay creation, and had been silently working on it with single-minded focus. When they'd sculpted beside each other before, she'd obviously been playing, but recently, things had changed.

Now it was clear she was *trying*.

"What's 'despair' mean?" she asked with her back still turned.

"Hahaha! A clever retort, pretending not to know what despair means, but now you *will* know it!"

"Alex, you're being weird. What does 'despair' mean?"

"O-oh, you're being serious. It means, uh, being sad and having no hope."

"Okay," she said, continuing to work on the figure. "I'll look at your doll in a second. Juuuuust, there!"

She sprang up and spun around, presenting her figure to him. Her grin was wide, revealing a gap between her teeth: the last of her baby teeth had fallen out a few days earlier.

"Are *you* despairing, dear brother?" she asked.

His jaw fell open as he made choking noises. "Is... is that a bloody *dragon*!"

"Language, Alex!" she checked him.

He gaped at the horror and unfairness that filled the universe. The little creation in her hands was unmistakably a dragon. Crude in some ways, but with distinct bat-like wings, a long neck and curving horns on its head.

Now that she was trying so hard, she was growing in skill *shockingly* fast. Maybe she always had the ability, but simply had no reason to try her absolute hardest.

"You, bu—" he stammered. "How did you..."

She placed the figure down in front of her.

"Des-pair! Des-pair! Des-pair!" she chanted, jumping up and down in glee.

"You!" He pointed at her. "Do *not* make me regret teaching you that word!"

"Re-gret! Re-gret! Re-gret!" she continued to chant, pumping her fists.

Alex's eyebrow twitched.

He glared at his shoulder. 'Hey! Hey you!' he shouted inwardly. 'Yes, you, the one with the jester's face that's living on my shoulder rent-free; you, Mr. God-provided Hero's Mark, I'm talking to you! Do you feel no shame? I'm trying to keep up with a *ten-year-old child* here and you can't make it so I wipe the floor with her? You're supposed to at least *pretend* to be something that helps a person fight the Ravener, right? Come on, get it together!'

Of course, the Mark, hidden beneath his shirt as it was, didn't respond. Though he would have been a little unnerved if it actually had.

Watching Selina bounce around the room, Alex chewed on his pride, his eyes eventually drifting down to the dragon. He tapped his chin in concentration. He couldn't deny it, it actually looked *pretty* good.

She paused her victory dance. "Hmmm." She squinted at his

clay sculpture. "It's pretty good, though. You're getting better, Alex. Maybe you should've done this before, 'cause we could've had fun making things together."

He noticed the note of longing in her voice, recognizing a peace offering when he saw one.

There were times in one's life when one had to swallow their pride.

Times when, for the greater good, one had to make peace with the greatest of enemies. Or, be forced to admit that one's ten-year-old sister was far more naturally talented at something. That, if he was serious about improving his skill, maaaaaybe trying to outdo her wasn't the smartest idea in the world.

"Alright, Selina. Why don't we try the next one together?"

Alex could tell she was excited but trying not to let it show. "Do you really want to?"

"Yeah, why not. Maybe I could learn something from you."

"You're just trying to learn from me so you can beat me!" she accused him.

"No." He raised his hands and lied—partially. "No, I'm not. I just think it'd be fun, and we could learn from each other."

"Hmmm, okay." She stood up straight and went to get more clay. "But if I can do magic, then we have to do *that* together too!" she said seriously. "Promise."

Alex glanced to his room. On his dressing table lay the permission letter from the junior school asking to allow Selina's mana level and affinity to be tested. He'd signed it but hadn't delivered it yet. He'd have to do it soon, though. The test was supposed to be in two weeks.

"Alright," he said. "It's a deal. If you can do magic, we'll do that together. As long as it's safe."

She frowned. "Why only if it's safe?"

"Huh? Because I want you to be safe," he said. "I've always wanted you to be safe."

Something flashed through her eyes. "Hmm... Okay."

Humming to herself, she went to fetch a new ball of clay for them to work on together. Alex wondered what that last bit had meant.

He promised he would keep a closer eye on her.

Chapter 73

A 'Handy' Breakthrough

As it turned out, swallowing one's pride had some serious benefits.

Going from sculpting alone, or in the same area as his little sister, to working *together* with her, vastly improved his sculpting ability. By working as a duo, he not only got a close look at how she worked, but he also got to try some of her techniques with her guidance. This gave him more successes, and in turn, gave the Mark more to use and feed on.

What he hadn't anticipated was how in sync their learning had become. The Mark's power to correct helped him, while Selina's natural skill, experience, and her own quick mind saw her expand her own ability as well as adopt techniques he'd come up with using the Mark. As he refined his methods, she watched him and refined hers.

They were growing together. Alex began to consider that perhaps, when the time came, they could sculpt some of the golem's body together. Being able to shape a piece of clay that big would probably thrill her to bits. For right now, though, there was something that definitely *did* have her thrilled and excited—her upcoming mana testing.

He still wasn't sure how he felt about the whole thing, but he'd gone ahead and submitted the permission form anyway.

In time, they'd find out if it would amount to nothing or if it would amount to a lot.

For now, he'd been putting a lot of focus into mana regeneration. Due to its complexity, the assignment from Professor Val'Rok's class would probably be difficult for students new to mana manipulation, whereas the technique from his compulsory magical theory class was basic, simple, and far better suited to beginners. As Professor Val'Rok had said, the basic mana regeneration technique was easily available to wizards at all levels of their training and practice.

To compare the two, he *had* tried the simpler technique described in the magic theory textbook by simply slapping the edges of his mana pool to encourage it to begin producing mana quicker. It was easy to do, relatively safe and yielded results.

By spreading out his own mana and contacting the edge of his mana pool with a light slap, the force of the contact was dispersed. He could apply a fair amount of force to the edge of his pool while being in no danger of doing any harm to it.

Val'Rok's method showed results far more quickly while producing that wonderful spiritual relaxation, though it was more difficult and riskier. In using the more intricate movements, the force was concentrated to the edge of one's mana pool. With greater risk, one couldn't be clumsy at moving their mana, but they would reap a greater reward.

A sharp twist to the mana pool's edge might tear it like an overstuffed sausage.

Since he already had a high degree of affinity for the skill—with the Mark's help—he'd been able to make progress even faster. He took to adding mana regeneration practice to his meditation routine. He would sit in his room or on the balcony in his favourite position, then split his concentration, focusing both on his breath *and* on shifting his mana around his pool.

The first day he'd tried it, the results weren't exactly what he'd been looking for. The physical relaxation from meditation had combined with the spiritual relaxation from his mana regeneration practice until...

"Alex. Alex, wake up," Theresa's voice had whispered softly from above him.

"Huh, wha?" He'd blinked awake in surprise. The sky had turned from the fiery orange of late evening, to the dead blackness of midnight. "What happened?"

"You fell asleep; it's the middle of the night."

"O-oh," he'd said embarrassedly.

After that, he made sure to keep his thoughts active and *awake* while combining meditation and regeneration practice. The results were considerable.

In a matter of days, he'd mastered the technique as well as he had the glyph boxes. Val'Rok's assignment had been for the class to stimulate *one* of the sections of their mana pool to regenerate mana. Alex was rapidly able to stimulate *all* of his at once, guaranteeing a nice mark on the assignment.

Being able to progress so quickly had other benefits.

A growing mana pool allowed him to cast more spells in a day, and his improving skill in mana regeneration increased the amount of magic he could perform in a day by nearly twice the amount.

And that meant he could practice more.

Which was a good thing.

Because he needed it when it came to Wizard's Hand.

"Oh, come *on*!" Alex growled as the spell array fell apart and he cancelled it. Muttering, he scrawled another failure in his notebook, then flipped to the final blank pages in disgust.

There were about three pages left before he needed a new notebook.

The rest of the pages were completely *filled* with detailed notes of his failures at casting Wizard's Hand. He hadn't gotten *this* frustrated with magic since his early days trying to learn forceball with nothing but an old spell-guide to learn from.

He glanced around his surroundings and took deep breaths to calm himself.

For a change of pace, Alex had decided to spend the afternoon studying on one of the castle's many high balconies. The balcony he was on—more of a floating terrace, really—was broad enough to fit at least half a dozen stone tables where students could study, practice magic or have a meal in peace. When folks finished using them, the tables and seats would skitter out of the way to wait beside the railings. Floating orbs of air would emerge from openings carved into the castle wall—the mouth of each sculpted to resemble an eagle's head with its beak open—and suck up any trash or mess left on the tables. Once they were filled, they would float back through the opened beaks to discard their messy bounty into the trash holders.

Alex let his imagination run free, imagining Minervus stuck in a sopping wet trash container with some sort of monster with long eye-stalks slithering after him. Reluctantly, he shook away both the image and the smile growing from it. Break time was over.

When anyone entered the balcony, the tables and seats would skitter back to the centre of the space, and wait to be used.

For now, Alex was alone. Khalik, Thundar, Theresa—bringing Selina—Isolde and Shishi were supposed to meet him later that afternoon.

In the meantime, he had to keep trying to push through.

He pulled his attention back to his notebook and wrote down a number, something he'd only recently started doing.

87%.

It was the exact percentage of the spell array he'd been able to consistently cast, even with the Mark's interference. Alex had never bothered writing down the exact percentage of his progress with a spell, but Wizard's Hand had become so utterly frustrating, he needed *some* solid number to show himself where he actually was. It was helping to keep him motivated.

The issue though with recording specific numbers, was it made him painfully aware he'd been stuck at eighty-seven percent for about three days.

There was a final part of the spell array that was *really* complex. It was a 'hand problem.' When he'd learned about art from Mrs. Lu, back when they were painting the mural on the inn wall, she'd taught him that colloquial term used by artists for any problem that was common, finicky and made other parts of their task more difficult.

The term came from the *nightmarish* difficulty many artists had when it came to drawing humanoid hands. Mrs. Lu was *very* good at painting realistic faces, and proportions of the human body. She'd painted most of the figures in the Heroes and Ravener mural.

But, one of the rare times he'd *ever* heard her curse in front of her children was when it came time to sketch or paint hands.

The fingers would end up out of proportion to the rest of the hand, or their shape would be slightly off. The position of the hand would be oddly curved or too straight. Sometimes they'd look more like paws than hands. Other times, she just simply couldn't pinpoint exactly what the problem was.

At the time, Alex thought it was just her, until he'd tried outlining a hand himself.

One of the few times he'd *ever* cursed in front of his sister was when he'd had to outline that hand. Even feet were like that for some artists. Mrs. Lu had told him of a painter named Robert Liefell who refused to paint feet. He'd always have his subjects standing behind something.

For Alex, the part of the spell array he was working on was just such a hand problem. Finicky, complicated and definitely not easy to build when one had a magical Mark screaming in their head. Theresa's meditative techniques *were* helping. He would have made less progress if it weren't for those. Only, they weren't helping enough to overcome this final hill.

He was growing more frustrated. He *really* wanted to learn force shield as soon as possible, and all the extra time spent throwing himself against Wizard's Hand took time away from practicing other things.

He sighed, letting those thoughts and worries pass.

If anything, all the extra pressure was only getting in the way.

Taking a deep breath, he relaxed his mind.

It wasn't helpful sitting there frustrated and doing nothing. That wouldn't help him move forward.

Mana regeneration helped him practice more spells in a day. Meditation helped stave off mental fatigue. Now, it was time to use both and keep grinding away.

Drawing deep into himself, he started to cast Wizard's Hand again.

98%.

He wrote that number down, his hand trembling in excitement.

Days had passed. He'd been practicing Wizard's Hand every moment he wasn't practicing something else.

Now, late at night in his room, with crickets chirping outside and candlelight flickering, he'd gotten close. So. Close.

Again, he cast Wizard's Hand.

Again, it failed in the same place.

He took a deep breath. Observed his frustration. Observed and acknowledged his worry. Then let it go.

He fell back into his spell, guiding his mind through all the failures.

He acknowledged the noise and dismissed it. Did the same for the new notebook of failures he'd had to start. He acknowledged that frustrating final two percent of the spell array that he just... couldn't...

Something clicked.

He'd done something right. He could tell. The Mark was getting especially active, which it was very fond of doing when he did something right in spellcraft.

"I've got you now," he whispered.

99%.

Diving into the spell another time, he pushed against the block. Through his shutters, the light changed as the moon rose higher in the sky. The candle burned down. Sleepiness tugged at the edges of his mind, begging him to take a break.

But he couldn't stop. Not now. Not when he was so close.

He closed his eyes.

Again, he tried the spell.

And again.

And then...

Woom.

The magic circuit completed.

A crimson light came alive in his room.

There was an unfamiliar connection within his mana.

Floating in front of him was a hand a little bigger than one of his own, made entirely of the glowing force magic that made up his other spells. His breath caught. There was a reason why the spell array was so complex. Wizard's Hand gave him *far* more control through mana manipulation than forceball *or* forcedisk.

It was designed so a wizard could do precise movements with it without being an expert at mana manipulation. It was very, very well-designed. Like giving two walking sticks to someone with weak legs to aid them with the movements of walking.

Alex suppressed giddiness as he made the hand 'walk' through the air on two fingers, wave at him, give a thumbs-up and make a certain rude gesture. He even high-fived it. He flipped back to the spell array diagram and made some final notes on the different sections.

Complex sections of spell array likely to help control spell. Maybe only for those unskilled in mana manipulation. Should attempt to simplify those sections, since I need less support for manipulating spells through mana.

This was an incredibly interesting revelation.

The sections of the spell array responsible for helping the caster control the spell after it had been cast weren't necessary for him because of his advanced skill with mana manipulation. It was like carrying walking sticks when one was perfectly capable of walking.

Once he isolated those sections of the spell, he could simplify it. That in turn would make the spell easier and faster to cast. He might be able to apply the same logic to other troublesome spells in the future.

That would be his first attempt at starting to master the spell.

Next, though...

He grinned, pulling out the spell-guides for force shield and Orb of Air.

These two spells would be big ones. The first would be his first truly defensive spell, while Orb of Air would be his first attempt at trying a spell outside of the school of force. He'd try them both while he worked to master Wizard's Hand.

An urge to try them tugged at him, but he resisted.

It was late and he was tired.

Besides...

He took a deep breath, looking at a date circled on his scheduler: Selina's mana test.

The date circled was tomorrow.

Chapter 74

Ghosts of the Past I

"Zachariah Khan!" one of the teachers called.

Selina Roth jumped a little in her chair as the name echoed through the auditorium.

Zach, one of her friends, was the first to be brought onto the stage. She and the rest of her class from the junior school were seated in rows in the centre of the auditorium, waiting for the teachers to call them to the stage to test their mana.

She glanced nervously past the other students and toward a line of chairs set up on the side of the audience hall. A long row of parents, older siblings and others watched the junior students. As her eyes found her towering brother, he gave her a crooked grin and a thumbs-up. Theresa—right beside him—gave her a smile of encouragement, while Brutus lay at their feet panting and watching her.

All had come out this morning to support her. Even their friendly neighbour, Khalik, was there, and he grinned through his black beard.

She smiled back at them and turned away, fidgeting in her chair.

"Hey, hey, look," one of her close friends in the class, Abela, whispered from beside her. "I think they're starting."

Selina looked up at the stage again.

While they'd been getting seated, Selina noticed the teachers had gathered there, waving their hands and muttering strange words like her brother and Khalik did when they were casting spells. Alex had said the teachers would be casting spells, but Selina hadn't seen any glowing lights, moving tables or anything else magical going on.

Spells that didn't do anything cool-looking must have been boring spells, she'd thought. Perhaps she just didn't understand them yet.

Maybe she'd find out what the teachers were doing soon.

Mr. Powell, her homeroom teacher, held up his hands to quiet the class, then turned to Zach. "Alright, Zach, please stand in the middle of the stage. And we can begin." He smiled like a kindly uncle. "Are you nervous?"

"N-no," Zach muttered, his eyes nervously darting back and forth.

"It's alright to be nervous," Mr. Powell said. "But, no worries. What we'll be doing today will be safe, painless and fun. You go on and stand in the middle of the stage and you'll see."

Selina wondered how they were going to do the testing as Zach edged toward the middle of the stage. Were they going to use a little box like Alex's glyph boxes? Were they going to use bowls with water in them? Theresa had said they did something like that in one of her classes.

Maybe they'd put a big hat on them, and it'd sort them into those that could use mana and those that couldn't. Maybe they'd give the students wands and ask if they could use them. If they could, then they'd have mana. She hoped it wasn't that last one. Even if she did have mana, she didn't know how to use wands and other magic stuff or cast spells.

She might fail anyway.

And she didn't *want* to fail.

She remembered the horrible bug monsters Theresa, Brutus and Alex had fought in the cave. She'd been terrified but couldn't do anything to help. Alex and Theresa had talked about something bad happening with that dungeon core and that people might come and take Alex away. Maybe they might come after all of them.

And all she'd be able to do is sit there and let Alex and Theresa protect her. She frowned, turning her head slightly away from her brother so he wouldn't see her face.

She wanted to help.

She wanted to be brave and be *able* to help.

If she found out she could use magic...

"We will now begin," Mr. Powell said.

She was drawn from her own thoughts and began paying attention to the stage. Several of the teachers raised their hands and began chanting, and the air around them started to shimmer.

Selina gasped.

Tiny little creatures materialized.

Each was no bigger than a sparrow, but looked like a tiny glowing person with insect wings on their backs. There were dozens of them fluttering around the stage, and they all froze momentarily as they twinkled into being. Most were stark white, but some were light and dark blues, solid greens, yellows, and even sparkling orange.

Mr. Powell said something to the creatures in a funny-sounding language. The tiny things looked at each other, then broke out into giggles that sounded like tinkling bells.

They began to fly all around the stage, leaving little coloured sparkles behind them as they went, watching and pointing at the people seated. Some flew to the edge, appearing to be prepared to fly out among the crowd, but abruptly stopped as if there was an unseen wall separating them from the rest of the room.

Selina remembered the chanting the teachers had been doing.

"Maybe the magic's keeping them on stage," she wondered quietly.

She noticed some of the little creatures flying around Mr. Powell.

"These are sprites," her teacher said. "Small faeries from this world and other planes, such as the elemental planes. They are highly attracted to places and people with strong mana. Today, you'll sit in the middle of the stage, and through them, we'll learn which of you have a strong mana. Since we've summoned these sprites to help us with this, and they've graciously come to us, they've agreed to cooperate and follow my commands."

He looked toward Zach. "I'm going to ask the sprites to inspect each of you. If you have strong mana, then one or more will land on you and use some of your mana along with their own to create a magical effect. If many are attracted to you, then that means your mana is very strong."

He gestured to some of the sprites that glowed different colours. "Those that don't glow white are from one of the elemental planes. If your mana has an affinity for an element, then *those* sprites will land on you while those from another element will not. But, that's very, very rare. We might only see one or two during today's test. Alright, Zach, are you ready?"

Zach nodded, his earlier nervousness giving way to wonder while the sprites flitted all around him, shedding their mystic light over his face.

Mr. Powell spoke another word in their language.

All at once, the fairies stopped, whirling toward Zach and swarming toward him like bees.

He cried out, half-rising in his chair as if preparing to run away, but the sprites weren't coming to attack. Instead, they giggled like naughty children who'd pulled a practical joke. They fluttered around Zach, closely examining the nervous boy. Now and then, one would flit close to him, but then flit away.

Soon they began to lose interest, flitting off to gather around the teachers and chatter to each other.

Mr. Powell gave him a nod. "You can step down now, Zach. It doesn't appear you have a lot of mana."

Zach nodded, his face showing a mixture of disappointment and relief. Then he stepped off the stage.

Selina and Abela looked at each other.

One by one, Mr. Powell called more students to the stage. The sprites would examine each one with curiosity, but then lose interest and flit away. Some students were relieved. Some disappointed. Others began to cry and ran to their family instead of returning to their seats.

With others, though...

A boy from another class was surrounded by the sprites. As they drew closer, they seemed to grow excited, and soon many of them landed on him. He giggled at their touch. Their bodies glowed brighter when they made contact with him, then they spread their hands out and shot tiny sparkles of white light into the air.

"Well," the boy's homeroom teacher said. "Looks like you have the mana necessary for wizardry, Chelios. Congratulations!"

Chelios let out a cheer, which startled the sprites and sent them fluttering around him while chattering and complaining in the language of fairies. He ran down the stairs to the cheers of his classmates, and the clapping of the line of spectators.

A staff member led him and his family to the side of the auditorium where they left through a narrow doorway. Selina wondered where they'd gone off to. She also wondered why the door was so narrow. Lots of little details about buildings fascinated her. They always had.

One of the very first questions she'd asked her teacher when she was very little was how roofs stayed up when walls only held their edges.

As she continued to think about buildings, more gasps and cheers brought her attention back to the stage. The sprites had come to land on another student, spraying sparkles through the air. That was two now.

A little bit of hope grew inside her, and she began to kick her legs in excitement.

Traveller? Uldar? she prayed in her mind. *It's Selina. Please, please, please, please let me have mana. Please, please, please! I promise I'll be good if I do and I won't do anything bad with it. Ever! Please, please, please let me have it.*

She kept hoping and praying as more and more students came and went. Students with mana and those without. Her heart beat faster as the last names got closer and closer to hers.

Then something wonderful happened on stage.

One of the students, a girl from another class, watched the fairies all around her as they examined her. The sprites that glowed white began to drift away, but the fairies that glowed different colours stayed close by. The green and yellow ones floated up to her and she watched them in confusion. Then the green ones abruptly fluttered away and the yellow ones landed on the girl.

The tiny sprites cheered and raised their hands.

Whoosh!

Tiny whirlwinds shot from their hands, crackling with little bolts of electricity. Selina gasped. Alex's friend, Isolde, had shown her electricity magic one day when he hadn't been looking. It took a lot of begging to get her to do it, but eventually, she'd agreed. It was amazing.

Seeing the fairies do it now was just as cool.

"Well, well, what a rare occurrence," Mr. Powell said. "It looks like you have an affinity for wind magic."

The young girl onstage was gawking in amazement. While

Selina and most of the room had gasped at the lightning, the girl looked absolutely enraptured with it. "What... what does this mean?"

"It means that lightning magic will come easily to you. Your spells with lightning will be stronger, and you will learn them more quickly than most. It does mean you will have great difficulty with earth-based spells, though. That is, if you can use them at all."

The young girl seemed to be listening to Mr. Powell, but soon her eyes were drawn back to the little bolts of lightning. Selina stared at them too, and suddenly had a new hope.

She imagined herself with a big wizard's hat and robes, wielding magic that spread water and ice over everything she could see. She could wash away bad monsters or freeze them. She could wet fields and make things grow.

She gasped.

She could make ice sculptures!

Alex had said they didn't get much snow this far south, but a Sigmus holiday with snow on the ground to play in was the most fun. She imagined herself conjuring snow so she and all her friends from school could have snowball fights, make snow forts, and snow people like she had with her friends and family in Alric.

She even imagined...

Fire erupted in her mind.

It was a vague memory, but as she'd seen hundreds of times in her dreams, her mother and father's alehouse burned while everyone screamed. She remembered watching it... and watching it... and watching the fire.

This time, in her mind, she imagined herself spreading water and ice over it to cool down the building. She imagined the fire going away as her water magic hit it, vanishing in a cloud of steam.

She remembered other fires. Like the time a windmill had

burned down in the next town. Her water magic would put that out too. There would be other fires she could wash away. Others she could freeze.

With a single-minded excitement, she knew she *needed* water affinity. She couldn't think of anything she ever wanted more, like she sometimes got when it came time to ask for Sigmus presents.

Selina glanced at Alex and mouthed the word 'water' to him.

He mouthed 'what?' back.

She frowned and mouthed it again.

"Selina Roth!"

Selina yelped as her name was called.

Mr. Powell was looking at her from the stage, his hand extended.

She swallowed and slid from her chair.

"Good luck," Abela whispered.

"T-thanks."

She started toward the stage, trying to ignore the many eyes that watched her as she climbed the stairs. The sprites fluttered about when she entered the centre area and gave her curious stares without approaching. They hadn't been asked to yet.

Sitting down, her eyes drifted all around.

The sprites giggled and danced through the air, and Mr. Powell smiled at her. "Are you ready?"

She nodded.

He spoke the words to the sprites.

They swarmed toward her, but she didn't stiffen or gasp. She'd seen their pranks, and after seeing those horrible bug monsters, she was scared by a lot less things these days.

The glowing little creatures pouted when their prank failed and fell quiet, examining her. She held her breath.

This was it.

As they got closer, she felt something strange. Like something inside of her chest was being tickled. Was that mana? Did it mean she had mana?

She nearly groaned in disappointment when the sprites that glowed white fluttered away from her, but her disappointment ceased when the ones glowing different colours stayed close by.

Mr. Powell looked at her with increased interest.

Excitement bloomed in Selina's chest.

Was this it? Did she have an affinity?

An old memory came back to her all of a sudden.

That frostdrake that charged and scared her at the beastarium. It was an ice monster, wasn't it? Did it sense something? Could that mean she had ice or water affinity?

Please, please, please, Uldar, she inwardly prayed.

The blue-glowing fairies drifted toward her. Her heart jumped. Were they water sprites? Was that what was going—

The sprites' faces twisted and they turned away, fluttering to the side of the stage. Her eyes widened as she watched all the others fly away.

All save for one colour.

Every single orange-glowing fairy on the stage surrounded her like she was their queen. They made awed cooing noises. Selina could only watch as they landed on her.

Mana! she thought. *I have mana!*

But what did orange mean?

Then her mind began to work. An orange light came back to her mind. Her heart wanted to stop.

She could only watch as the fairies raised their hands and tiny streams of flame shot into the air.

Her thoughts stopped. Her eyes widened and she couldn't pull them away. The tiny flames danced in front of her, mixing with the ones she'd seen in her mind.

She began to tremble.

A single thought rose up in her. One she had been trying to

stomp down ever since her parents' alehouse had burned, and one that occurred to her every time she had seen flames.

"Pretty," she mouthed silently. "It's so pretty."

The warmth of it. The light. The dance. All of it was so pret—

Then her mind caught up with her. The sadness. The fear. The *guilt* she felt every time she'd been fascinated by the thing that killed her parents.

Now that thing was a part of her.

No putting out fires. No making snow people.

Just fire, burning and death.

"Congratulations!" Mr. Powell said enthusiastically. "Selina Roth, you have attracted all the summoned fire sprites, you have a *very* strong fire affini—"

Her teacher's words died when Selina started to scream.

Chapter 75

Ghosts of the Past II

The Ravener's hunter had been seeking its quarry for a long time now.

At first, it hunted with its siblings, each staying in close communication as they moved beyond the territory of their master. As they dispersed, they grew too distant from each other to maintain communication.

And now, the hunter was alone.

First, it had explored the sea, seeking its quarry on one of the great boats its master's enemies had left their homeland in. The hunter had been given careful instructions etched into its instincts at the moment of its creation. Attack none, except the quarry.

Do not be seen and move with all stealth.

Do not kill unless for sustenance or to defend its life.

The quarry was its only purpose. If anything stood in the way of destroying the one who usurped one of its master's cores, then it should strive to evade it to avoid attention, and only destroy it as a last resort.

It silently swam the waves, only killing fish to eat, and sending out pings of magic to seek the tell-tale sign that one who'd made contact with the dungeon core was in range. After a long while exploring the sea, it moved toward the land to the east and south, while others spread out to the west and north, and to the lands of the northeast.

It reached land in the dead of night and began its journey inland.

As it travelled, it began to learn.

The voice boxes within the throats of the hunters were unlike any that lay in other creatures its master had ever birthed. They were malleable, almost as soft as mud, and could form any shape. While the hunter could not disguise its form, it *could* mimic any sound it heard.

As it crept deeper into the wilderness, it began to copy the sounds of the beasts of the land and birds of the air, attracting prey within reach of its hiding places. Meals were caught with piercing claws and venomous teeth.

The farther it travelled, the more it learned of its surroundings.

People made different sounds than the beasts, communicating in a range of varied words and tones and pitches. While it could not comprehend their speech, it had the ability to mimic them.

As it stalked its quarry, it would repeat words it had heard over and over again, imitating a range of voices and perfecting its ability to sound like anyone. It thought that would be a good way to deceive and lure its prey when they were finally cornered. The hunt was slowly stretching into weeks without any sign of the one it sought, and each passing day became more and more mundane. While it remained single-minded in purpose, it began to seek ways to alleviate the tedium.

And so, the hunter developed something that could be called a hobby of sorts. Observing people from hiding places in the wilderness and copying them as they spoke to each other. It grew increasingly absorbed with this hobby. At times straying too close to those it observed.

Then one early morning, a ping returned.

A faint sign.

Its quarry, at some point, had passed this way.

At last! It had something to investigate, but its distractedness nearly proved to be its undoing.

The creature had travelled unseen across four mountains—one that burned, one that floated, one that wept and one studded in jewels. Yet it was here in this quiet, rustic countryside that it was spotted.

A human on horseback spotted it and began shouting, wheeling his horse away.

Snarling, the hunter pursued—falling to all fours to match the speed of the mount—and leapt upon the man's back, wrestling the struggling prey to the ground.

It was larger than most humans and far stronger than its size would suggest. It had no problem pinning the man to the ground and biting deep into his shoulder to send its deadly venom in to do its work. For good measure, it used its claws to rip him wide open.

Unfortunately for the hunter, the struggle and screams attracted more people walking along the road. While some fled, others hurled whatever was close at hand and shouted. Some were armed and armoured, and as its instructions returned to its mind, it ran instead of engaging further.

It lost days hiding within forests while cautiously trying to follow the trail of the one it sought.

That trail eventually led to the sea.

Excitement built as increasing pings showed it neared its prey.

Soon, it would be able to fulfill its purpose and eliminate the one who defiled the core. No thought thrilled it more than this. The Ravener's hunter did not know which of its master's enemies had usurped his core. Many of them were dangerous. But it had been created to battle many foes. It would use stealth and cunning as its weapons, and if those did not prove sufficient, it would seek tools, and even monsters to subjugate, for its cause.

What it did *not* expect was *where* its quarry would be found.

No such place existed in the instincts and knowledge granted by its master. The pings led to a place of power.

It was a city, that much it knew from its travels. However, the sheer amount of magic blazing from it threatened to overwhelm the hunter's senses. Worse, the pings revealed the usurper was deep within a part of the city. One protected by wards and powerful mortal magic users. Glaring at the city from the choppy sea, it dove deep beneath the water and howled its frustration.

After its long journey, its quarry lay so close... Infiltrating this place would be a formidable task with many pitfalls. The chance of being discovered was high, which could lead to its end. Its purpose would be unfulfilled. Floating beneath the waves from daylight to darkness and back again repeatedly, it carefully observed its prey through the pings, learning some of its habits.

Most of its quarry's time was spent inside the highly defended sanctum within the city. Sometimes it would emerge and travel to the city, though rarely far from the defended place. And within the city itself, the Ravener's hunter could sense a host of powerful magic users.

Too much risk to strike at the usurper on one of their journeys.

At other times, they would disappear beyond the range of the pings. It considered this. The prey had left the Ravener's territory without leaving a trail, just as they now seemed able to appear and disappear at will. Could they transport themselves freely across distances?

If so, that would increase the likelihood of their escape.

The hunter needed to observe for a longer period of time.

It also needed to discover the defences around its prey, and most importantly, learn when they would be most vulnerable.

For now, it would be patient.

It would wait and observe.

Under cover of darkness, it swam from its hiding place at the bottom of the bay, emerging away from the city onto shore, and journeyed deep into the countryside. It would find a place far away from people and magic users. It would make a lair, and find resources and beasts it might be able to dominate through fear.

And it would wait.

"I ain't never seen tracks like these before," a gruff voice said. "Think it's the mana vampire?"

The hunter's eyes cracked open.

Voices drifted through the trees somewhere far from its hideout. Since carelessness let it be seen in the other land of humans, it was now far more cautious. It constantly listened and constantly watched.

Now, it had been nearly asleep when it heard the low tramping of booted feet and the quiet voices of people on the hunt. Stealthily, it abandoned its lair in a bog and climbed high into the trees, crossing from branch to branch.

At last, it peered down on those entering its domain.

A group of people, perhaps ten or more. All were well-armed and armoured, and each moved with confidence. The one in the lead had eyes that were hard like stone. His large, curved sword was gripped tightly in one hand, and his beard and hair were tied.

"It might or might not be the mana vampire," the man in the lead said quietly. "I don't know these tracks at all. Either way, if it's a monster, there's probably some bounty for it. There's plenty of them for us to make some coin from."

The hunter watched in complete stillness.

Though it heard and could mimic the words they spoke, it still could not understand them. Instincts and their weapons told it these were dangerous people. It knew well it could likely kill them. After all, it was an assassin birthed to slay the Ravener's enemies. But a fight against multiple foes might cause it injury, making it less likely to succeed in its purpose.

There was also the possibility that chance would favour them and it would be slain. Even if it destroyed every last one of them, they might be missed by others who would come seeking them.

Weighing the options, it decided against open conflict and began to move away through the trees.

Whish!

Something cracked against its leg, striking at it like a jellyfish.

An arrow had bounced off its armoured hide.

"There! I think I see it!" one of the people below cried.

The creature snarled, moving to escape through the trees.

"After it! Payday's here! Take it down!" another shouted.

The hunter moved swiftly, wanting to put distance between itself and its pursuers. They moved quickly across the forest floor. Like experienced hunters.

Still, the more they chased, the more it increased the distance between them.

Arrows snapped against branches, and they too were left behind.

When the voices faded, the creature dropped from among the tree tops and sprinted along the forest floor. It ran, crashing through rivers and streams to hide its tracks, and concealed itself in woodland and thicket, keeping well away from open ground.

Once it could no longer hear the threat, it slowed and sought out a new lair.

Its escape had taken it south, close to where the green fields ended and dusty plains began. Strange mana flowed from that direction, and there were few settlements close by. It was a far distance from the waterways it preferred.

Abruptly, a ping sounded from close by—coming from the walled place of heat and dust.

At last.

It dropped to all fours and hurried toward the ping.

The Ravener's command would finally be fulfilled. The ping repeated once, twice, three times. Each time closer and louder than the last. Its claws stretched out, longing to pierce the usurper with them. Suddenly, there was an overwhelming surge of mana, stopping the creature as if it had been struck by a mighty blow. A being who overflowed with mana had appeared adjacent to the pings. The hunter's survival instincts screamed for caution. Its quarry was so close, yet still far from reach while one with such dangerous levels of mana was present.

Backing away, it waited for its prey to leave the dusty plane. Its pings continued steadily, then suddenly disappeared, abruptly reappearing inside the city.

It had been so close!

Close would not fulfill its purpose. Weeks of creeping near the city walls had not revealed an easy way to enter. A way to bypass the powerful magics near the walls, or avoid detection through the city proved fruitless. That did not mean a way did not exist; it just meant it had not found one yet.

And while its quarry might be more vulnerable in the place of dust, the magic wielder it travelled there with would likely be a *very* fatal opponent.

This called for different measures.

It wavered, unsure if stealth should be continued or if calling attention to itself would work better. If it terrorized the countryside, that might flush out its prey like a beast fleeing fire. Such an act could also make them hide deeper within the protected walls. Killing mortals might also bring more of them to pursue it, interfering with its purpose.

No. Stealth was the better choice. But it needed resources.

First, it would leave this area for a time. The quarry had set down roots and would remain, that was clear. So, it was time to go north and seek its siblings.

Then it would return with greater numbers.

Once that was done...

It peered at the wall separating the green lands from the place of mana and dust. Other sources of mana were coming from within. Beasts, not mortals or others that would oppose its master.

With greater numbers, they could dominate and subjugate some of the beasts. They could be used as a distraction while the usurper was slain through stealth.

Yes. That would ensure success.

Snarling, it sprang away, eager to return to the open sea.

It would be back.

And then its purpose could be fulfilled.

THE STORY CONTINUES IN *Mark of the Fool Book Two*.

Thank you for reading Mark of the Fool!

We hope you enjoyed it as much as we enjoyed bringing it to you. We just wanted to take a moment to encourage you to review the book. Follow this link: Mark of the Fool to be directed to the book's Amazon product page to leave your review.

Every review helps further the author's reach and, ultimately, helps them continue writing fantastic books for us all to enjoy.

ALSO IN SERIES

Book One

Book Two

FROM J.M. CLARKE

Hellooooooo everyone!

Thank you all so much for reading about Alex's early adventures in *Mark of the Fool 1* and thanks for your support. Without you, none of this would be possible. It fills me with joy to think that people out there are actually reading this story. My gratitude can't be described, and for an author, that's saying something.

You know, there's a line from Phil Collins' first hit single *In the Air Tonight* that goes: *Well I've been waiting for this moment for all my life.* This is what this time feels like to me; the moment I've been waiting for *most* of my life. For you and people like you to be reading my words.

Seriously, you've changed my life in ways that I cannot possibly communicate even in another seven hundred pages. I hope we continue to walk this path together.

If you enjoyed your journey to and stay in Generasi so far, then you won't have to wait long to return. *Mark of the Fool 2* is slated for release on January 10th, 2023, all edited and shined up for your reading pleasure.

Also, we authors **depend on reviews and ratings to help us and our works** so—if you really liked your time with Alex, Theresa, Selina, Brutus and their companions—**it'd be fantastic if you left a review or rating on this book and any other books you enjoy!** Of course, the choice is yours, naturally.

Now, if you want to support me and get **early access** to the earlier drafts of Mark of the Fool, I do have a patreon, which is found at patreon.com/jmclarke. There you'll find early versions of the next books in the series before they're published to Amazon.

Thank you to r/pathfinder_RPG, r/progressionfantasy and r/fantasy for supporting me on your subreddits. A big shoutout to my fellow authors, my irl friends, Paul, my protector; and the denizens of Whetstone Tavern who shared Mark of the Fool, and to my publisher, editors, talented cover artist and the magnificent Travis Baldree! A huge thanks to my wonderful patrons and readers on royal road, thank you all so much for reading about my characters' trials, growth, loves, jokes...and my terrible references.

And lastly, to you the reader. Yes, you, the person reading these words on your kindle or page at this moment.

Take care of yourself.

After all, there's only one of you.

J.M. Clarke

You can also join our non-spam mailing list by visiting www.subscribepage.com/AethonReadersGroup and never miss out on future releases. You'll also receive three full books completely Free as our thanks to you.

Keep scrolling for recommendations from Aethon Books.

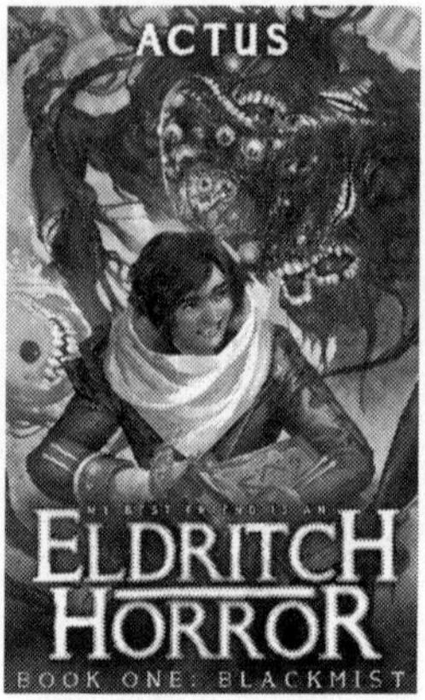

Damien nearly ended the world. Now, his mistake might be the only thing that can save it.

Good things come to those who wait. Damien Vale didn't, and he ended up bound to an Eldritch creature from beyond the reaches of space. It has lived since the dawn of time, seen the world born and destroyed countless times, and wants to be called Henry.

Unusual companion or not, Damien was still determined to go to a mage college and study magic. He wants nothing more than to live normal life as a researcher, but if Henry's true nature is revealed, he'll be killed.

To top it all off, Damien's teacher is a madman from the front lines of war, his alcoholic dean suspects something is awry with his companion, and Blackmist might possibly be the worst school in history. Damien has to prevent the end of the world, but he isn't even sure he's going to make it through Year One at Blackmist.

Read Blackmist now!

Orphaned by Monsters. Matt must power up to save others from the same fate.

Matt plans to delve the rifts responsible for the monsters that destroyed his city and murdered his parents. But his dreams are crushed when his Tier 1 Talent is rated as detrimental and no guild or group will take him.

Working at a nearby inn, he meets a mysterious and powerful couple. They give him a chance to join the Path of Ascension, an empire-wide race to ascend the Tiers and become living legends.

With their recommendation and a stolen Skill, Matt begins his journey to the peak of power. Maybe then, he can get vengeance he seeks...

Read The Path of Ascension now!

The blood of dragons pumps through his veins. Greatness awaits!

Kobolds cower at the bottom of the foodchain, forced to eke out a meager existence in the most wretched of caves.

Most have made peace with their lot in life; one of eating scraps and carrion. They hide and run from predators, delaying the inevitable day when they aren't fast or sneaky enough to make their escape.

But not Samazzar. Sam is different from other Kobold pups.

Traps and caves might keep him and his people alive, but sometimes, just living isn't enough. Dragon blood runs through him, and Sam isn't willing to settle for mere survival. Whether by claw, magic, or cunning, one day he will soar above the plains, predator rather than prey.

And nothing–be it the mockery of his tribe, the hazards of the deep caves, or even the almost insurmountable difficulty of successfully evolving his bloodline–nothing is going to stop him.

Read A Dream of Wings & Flame now!

For all our LitRPG books, visit our website.

Made in the USA
Columbia, SC
13 July 2024

38386557R10416